TOM DALTON—HIS DREAMS WERE BORN OF
SHAME, FIRED BY SHREWD AMBITION.
HIS FUTURE LAY IN THE HANDS OF THOSE
WHO WOULD LOVE AND BETRAY HIM. . . .

Mary Dalton—Tom's mother. The secret guilt of her past would destroy her future—unless she made the most wrenching sacrifice of all.

Billy—New York's most famous madam. It was her love for Tom that made him a threat to all she'd achieved.

Diamond Jim Mulvaney—He'd broken every rule to build a mighty financial and political empire. As a mentor, he was generous and loyal; as an enemy, deadly.

Deirdre—Jim's exquisite, convent-bred daughter. She would defy her father to seize love's ecstasy, but her joy was fated to be tragically brief.

Megan—She was born in the aftermath of heartbreak. For her sake, Tom would seize the ancient Irish legacy that was rightfully his.

"COMPELLING."—*Library Journal*

"FLOWS ALONG WITH AN INEXORABLE NARRATIVE CURRENT THAT PROPELS THE READER FROM ONE INVOLVING EPISODE TO THE NEXT."
—*Booklist*

Also by Cathy Cash Spellman:

NOTES TO MY DAUGHTERS

SO
MANY
PARTINGS

Cathy Cash Spellman

A DELL BOOK

Published by
Dell Publishing Co., Inc.
1 Dag Hammarskjold Plaza
New York, New York 10017

Dell ® TM 681510, Dell Publishing Co., Inc.

ISBN: 0-440-18066-X

Reprinted by arrangement with Delacorte Press
Printed in the United States of America

June 1984

10 9 8 7 6 5 4 3 2

WFH

For my husband,
who taught me that
dreams and love stories
could both come true.

I love you, Joe.

Acknowledgments

There are two people without whose constant encouragement, criticism, proofreading, laughter, and love this book could never have come to be:

Conny Cash, my own dear (and the world's best) sister, who, as always, helped make everything turn out right in the end.

Johanna Lee, my oldest and best friend, who in keeping with twenty years of perfect friendship was as kind to my characters as she always is to me.

"Thank you" seems so inadequate a response for all their help that I can only hope they know the love and gratitude that's in my heart.

I dreamed the first part of this story, and from that moment on a great many wonderful, unselfish friends have helped the dream to reach fruition. And so my grateful and heartfelt appreciation to:

Carole Baron, who not only edited with astounding sensitivity and tenderness—but who *believed*.

Edith Heal Berrien, who took time out from writing her own books to research, critique, and encourage.

Suzanne Bersch, who first researched and typed to help bring the book into being.

Meryl Earl, whose expertise and joyous goodwill made learning about "the world" a delightful experience.

Jackie Farber, who encouraged with warmth, patience, and good cheer, and who helped save Mary from the fate of "the girl on the beach."

Isabel Geffner, whose immense talents and loving help have contributed so very much to *So Many Partings*, and whose friendship I expect to cherish for a great many years to come.

Lenore Hershey, who is unquestionably this book's Fairy Godmother.

Aunt Polly Hodder, whose good wishes cheered me all the way from Ireland.

Robynne Hubert, who kept life organized at the office while all this happened and typed terrifically in the clinches.

Bea Hurwitz, who generously used her expertise to track down permission for all the quotes used in this book.

Mort Janklow, who magically and generously made the dream become a reality.

Patty Kerr, who read and encouraged from near and far.

Harold Krensky, who was kind enough to share his vast knowledge of Boston and retailing, so that Mary would have a place to go in America.

Diane Moriarity, who typed endlessly from hand-scribbled notes without ever losing a single note, her kindness, or her good humor.

Alexandra Penney, who nudged me into imagining it could all really happen.

Fred Purches, whose years of good-hearted urging helped precipitate me into writing books.

Anne Sibbald, who first showed great generosity of spirit toward my story and then became a friend.

Bronwyn Spellman, who helped keep life joyful while I wrote.

Cee Cee Spellman, without whose good-hearted Xerox copying we never could have gotten the book to the publisher.

Charles Spicer, who edited with much-appreciated enthusiasm, a sure hand, a half-Irish eye, and a very kind heart.

Ched Vuckovic, who unselfishly helped at a very important moment.

And very special appreciation to:

Catherine Gibbons Cash, my mother, who taught me from the cradle to love both Ireland's history and books—and who encouraged me at a most critical moment to believe that I could combine both loves in one story.

Harry Cash, my father, who taught me that love is stronger than everything.

Special Note

All places, events, and characters in my book are fictitious with the exception of Andrew Furuseth.

In my research on the men of the sea and longshore, I ran across his story and fell in love, only to find that material about him was almost impossible to locate, and that consequently—despite his remarkable deeds and great courage—he has been all but forgotten.

I have included him in my story, where indeed—as in all stories of the men of the sea—it seems to me, he belongs. However, facts of his life were so difficult to find that I have taken the liberty of re-creating the man as I believe he might have been.

The longshoremen's strike of 1903 that I have described is really an amalgam of events from other strikes (1887, 1907, etc.). I have tried to remain true to the spirit of the labor movement of the time, although, of course, nothing that is in my story actually took place anywhere other than in my imagination.

Prologue

The small boy touched the lips of the man in the rosewood coffin. He knelt reverently beside the waking table and brushed the dead man's auburn hair back from his waxen cheek.

"Don't be dead, Da," he whispered softly. "I don't know what to do without you."

There was no answer in the silent and forbidding room.

"I love you, I'll always love you." Resignedly, the eight-year-old nestled his body in against the mahogany coffin rail, and settled to his vigil with a sigh of resolute devotion.

Thin tapers danced shadows on the paneled walls and flickered leaping shapes upon the Adamesque ceiling twenty-five feet above.

Outside the stately leaded windows the December wind howled angrily, and far above, it shook the chimney pots.

"I heard the Banshee call last night, Da," the boy whispered conspiratorially to the corpse. "She came to my window in the night, you know the way she does. She shrieked and wailed so I'd know someone was to die, but I didn't know you'd be the one to go. You seemed to be forever—so big and strong you were." The child tenderly patted the lifeless hand, three times the size of his own. "You feel terrible cold, Da. I wish you didn't feel so cold." The boy struggled out of his homespun woolen jacket and laid it gently on his father's body, then settled back into his accustomed place, hugging himself to keep warm in the icy dark.

"The house is as much yours as it is theirs, son," his father had said proprietarily in other days, and the child had nodded gracious assent, feeling a curious lump in his throat at the knowledge that because of his illegitimacy he was not even permitted inside his own house.

He looked around him now in the firelit gloom and tried to pick out the particulars his father had described—the plaster rabbit with the curled ear that had chipped off due to the mischievous efforts of a Hartington child a generation past; the satinwood walls made with wood imported from the Continent, the intricate parquetry of the floor beams, polished to a high gleam by generations of servants. Even in the midst of his sorrow he had a visceral sense of belonging.

"What in God's name are you doing here, you disgusting boy!"
An angry patrician voice pierced the silence. "How dare you defile
my home with your unwanted presence?" The boy looked intensely
at the unfamiliar woman, knowing her to be his grandmother,
fascinated by the loathing she exuded toward him.

"I came to stay with me da, Mrs." He knew that she should be
called "Your Ladyship," but under the circumstances he begrudged
her the title.

"Filthy child, how dare you call my son your father! Get out of
here before I have you beaten for your audacity."

The hostile woman wasn't large, but there was power in her
aspect, black with mourning, volcanic in her anger.

"I'll go, mum. But he's me da. Shame to you that you left him
alone and him just dead. Shame to you!"

The pewter-haired woman raised her voice to the tone that had
struck terror into two generations of frightened servants. "If you do
not leave this house immediately, I will be forced to deal with you
myself." As she said it she began a menacing and deliberate walk
toward the small boy. He stood defiantly for a moment, leaned down
to kiss his father's icy cheek, and then scampered for the emptied
doorway.

"I'll be going now, Mrs," he shouted from the safety of the
darkened passage, and his small voice bounced and echoed in the
marble stillness. "But he's my da, and I'll come back to say
good-bye. You'll see! I'll come back to bid him good-bye."

The matron stood astonished beside the coffin; she was unused to
being defied by any in her own home, and she had an instinctive
detestation of the peasantry.

"Fool!" she hissed contemptuously at the dead man. "Romantic,
arrogant fool. We'll all rue the day you bedded that child's slut of a
mother."

Emphatically, she turned her back on the lonely coffin and strode
from the deathroom, footsteps echoing down the long marble corridor.

The stillness in the coffin room remained unchanged by her
hostility. The candles continued their steady burning unabated . . .
the embers of the fireplace continued their slow dying, the wind lost
none of its mournful keen. And Thomas Dalton, small but determined,
crept back silently to the box and resumed his vigil at his father's
side.

Part One

IRELAND
1882 AND BEFORE

The history of a nation is not in parliaments and battlefields, but in what people say to each other on fair days and high days, and in how they farm and quarrel and go on pilgrimage . . .

—W. B. Yeats

1

Drumgillan stood on a gently sloping grassy knoll in County Westmeath, fifty miles from the gray-green bustle of Dublin. Not quite a castle but infinitely more than a manor house, it had stood the assorted tests of time for more than two hundred years, beginning as a fortified dwelling in 1646 and sprouting new wings or decorative façades as the centuries passed and the demands of its aristocratic owners varied.

David Hartington, the distant ancestor of the house's current occupants, had been a bright young officer in the employ of Oliver Cromwell when the general laid siege to Ireland in the name of the English crown in 1649. He had distinguished himself at the siege of Drogheda, and as a reward for his gallantry he had been deeded the vicinity of Drumgillan, which at that point consisted of a small village, fifty thousand acres of prime farmland, another five thousand of peat bog, the remains of an ancient keep, and the charming knoll on which he had built his manor house.

The physical beauty of the Drumgillan landscape was like a watercolor by God's own hand. Green pastures of a distinctly emerald hue, indigenous only to this well-watered corner of the earth, rolled on endlessly from horizon to horizon. Picturesque stone walls crisscrossed the land's gentle slopes at orderly intervals, so that grazing sheep could be pleasantly accommodated. A deep brown bog ran to the west, an ancient geographical monument to a prehistoric time when water and silt had dragged wild beasts to a swampy death so that their moldering bones now helped to provide an endless supply of turf for every generation's hearths.

To the east and directly in front of the manor house, was a crystal blue lake, large enough for little boats to sail lazily upon, small enough to ride around in an hour's time, it added a dreamy dimension and another quiet color to the artful setting. Leading toward the lake on a gentle slope were finely sculptured gardens of topiary, and flowers in such abundance that the fifty rooms of the dwelling could be kept in floral array without straining the gardeners.

The peaceful quietude of the land and the genteel aura of its parklike grounds gave Drumgillan a sense of permanence; as if its great Palladian façade were an act of nature. Like the land and the bog, it seemed a graceful geographic perfection that God had chosen to place there to complete His picture.

Over the centuries since Drogheda, the Hartingtons of Drumgillan had continued to distinguish themselves in the Crown's behalf; first by providing a long line of courtly and courageous officers to the family regiment, the Westmeath Fusiliers, and later by providing an avalanche of much needed merchandise for trade with England. Flax, wool, meat, and produce in abundance left Drumgillan for London and Liverpool, and in return the Hartington family had been amply rewarded by ever increasing rank and privilege.

Sir Jeffrey and Lady Geraldine's marriage was a model of tranquillity.

"I intend to marry Jeffrey Hartington," Geraldine Montrose had told her father, matter-of-factly, when she was nineteen years of age.

"Whatever for?" her father had asked. He had a habit of conversing with his daughter as if she had a well-developed brain instead of the meager and flighty variety expected of women.

"Because, Father," she had replied to his question about her marital intention, as if explaining something rather obvious to a slow child, "he is very rich, very charming, very dependable, and more than handsome enough to produce fine children. He also appears to be sufficiently shy that I shall be able to sweep him quite off his feet, and sufficiently docile so I shall be able to keep him there, for a lifetime."

Since their marriage, which had taken place within a year of her having decided upon it, Geraldine Montrose and Sir Jeffrey Hartington had enjoyed a productive and uneventful life together, just as she had planned it to be. She ran their homes and family affairs brilliantly, although he took her competency so for granted that he barely noticed the flawless performance. This suited her well enough, as her only real requirements of her husband had been his wealth, position, and pleasant, agreeable disposition, all of which he was more than willing to put at her disposal. Geraldine had dutifully produced two sons—Randolph, the heir to the family wealth and title, and Michael, the apple of his father's eye.

Randolph was precisely the son his mother had imagined having— handsome and calculating. He had an innate understanding of power that she greatly approved of, and she felt he would be a worthy bearer of the title she had so assiduously earned for him through her marriage.

Randolph did, she realized, have some perfectly loathsome traits. He was stingy and mean-spirited, hostile toward the tenants, and not inordinately pleasant, even toward his peers. There was evidence of a cruel, conscienceless streak as well, but she reasoned that no one was perfect.

Michael, on the other hand, was her despair. If the truth were known, he didn't even *look* like anyone in her family. He had inherited the giant stature of her husband's stock as well as their fair hair and ruddy complexion, which she considered too close to the look of the Irish natives to suggest good breeding. There was an appalling earthiness about him, and despite his fine performance at his studies, he preferred to be with the grooms and stable hands, the milkmaids and the tinkers, and any other Irish flotsam and jetsam he could find to traffic with. Doubtless he was some dreadful throwback to a dalliance on the part of an earlier Hartington with a peasant, for Geraldine was certain that no fine old Ascendancy family could produce such as he, unless the taint of some inferior breeding was in evidence.

She fervently thanked the Lord that Michael had not been born first.

2

"Let me help with the bellows, Sean," sturdy little Michael pleaded plaintively. The massive Drumgillan blacksmith acceded good-naturedly to his demand. The youngster had been a fixture at the stables since he was old enough to run away from his relentless tutor. He loved Sean and he loved the stables; the smell of the horses and the earthiness of the people who cared for them were in such delightful contrast to his own family.

Through the horse folk—the smithy, the grooms, the stable hands, and their wives and children—Michael learned to know the Irish. He played with their children when time permitted them to play, for the children of the poor had many chores. He even helped them whenever he could, with the milking or the woodcutting, or the thousand chores that the farmers did to keep themselves alive and to fulfill their myriad obligations to the property they tenanted. Because of his warm disposition and his stocky, rapidly growing body, he was accepted by the people of the huge estate, despite the fact that the class from which he had sprung was despised.

Geraldine had been suspicious of this hobnobbing with the tenants from the first. "Rubbing elbows with those grubby little urchins will come to no good, mark my words," she intoned ponderously whenever the opportunity arose. But Sir Jeffrey, having spent a good deal of time around the stable hands himself, without having lost his sense of who was master and who was servant, couldn't take her warnings with real seriousness.

"Do you think I'll be big enough to be a smithy, Sean, when I'm grown?" Michael asked earnestly of the blacksmith one day when he was nine years old. He had been watching with admiration the giant male form at the forge, clad as it was in a dirt-spattered leather apron, with its hands the size of ham hocks, and face in a perpetual weatherbeaten squint from the intensity of the heat given off by the fire. The smith lifted the red-hot horseshoe he had been forging out of the fire with massive iron tongs, and settled it expertly onto the huge anvil in the center of the forge, before answering.

"Well, now, Michael, I have not a doubt in me mind you'll be large enough, for you're sprouting like an arbutus tree these past few months, but I'm afraid that blacksmithing is not likely to be the enterprise for a lad like you."

"Why not, Sean? Just because of my father being who *he* is, do you mean?"

"You'll grow up, lad, to be a fine lordship like your father and brother, and it's little thought you'll be giving to the likes of us."

"That's not true, Sean! My brother, Randolph, is going to inherit everything; my mother told me how the system works. It's called 'primogeniture,' and it means that all the houses and all the money and the horses and everything will go to Randolph when Father dies. Mother says I'll have to get a job of some sort, or a commission in the army, so I can earn a living. I don't get along with Randolph very well, so I don't imagine he'll want to give me anything, do you?"

"No, lad, I don't think that brother of yours will be giving away anything that he isn't forced to. He hasn't the look of a large-hearted man about him, and that, I'm afraid, doesn't change much with age, generally speaking."

"Do you know what he does sometimes, Sean? He takes my toy soldiers and hides them in his room, and if I cause a row about it, he tells Mother that Cook's son stole them, and then Mother gets in a terrible snit and takes the money to pay for them out of Cook's wages, and she won't even listen to me when I tell her about Randolph."

The blacksmith looked up from his hammering on the cooling shoe to regard the young boy sitting contentedly on the ground, legs drawn up and arms around them, all curly red hair and freckles. Were it not for his carefully polished speech and his regal bearing, the lad could be one of his own. It was surely a curiosity.

"What does your mother say when you tell her the truth of it, lad?"

"She says it isn't nice to tell stories about my own brother, and that I always take the side of the servants and that I'm going to come to a bad end, mostly."

"Did you ever try telling your da what goes on about the house?"

"Oh, yes, indeed I have. I'm quite sure that he knows that Randolph is a liar and all, for I've heard him yelling at my brother about his 'inexcusable behavior,' lots of times. But I don't think Father likes to cross Mother about things that have to do with us children, don't you see? He says Mother has charge of everything to do with children and with houses, and it isn't proper for him to interfere with her discipline."

"Aye, lad, most marriages are the same, I expect. Rich or poor, the wanes are the work of the womenfolk, and most men daren't interfere, for fear of provokin' a terrible ruckus." The smithy chuckled to himself at the idea of his illustrious lordship cowed by his wife's wrath.

"It's enough to put the fear of God in a man, Michael, when a woman takes it into her head to favor one wane over another in her brood. There's not one father in ten would mess with a mare that's got a favorite foal."

Michael nodded his head sagely. He could always rely on Sean to understand everything and restate it in such simple, sensible terms. Not at all like his tutor, Mr. Simpson, who could complicate a "hello" into something incomprehensible. Michael thanked his lucky stars that he had no trouble with his schoolwork, for Mr. Simpson, sensing Her Ladyship's preference for her older son, spared no pains in making Michael's lessons the harder and more exacting of the two.

If Michael so much as daydreamed or dawdled, he was severely punished; if Randolph lied or cheated, he was admonished gently and told that he must strive to overcome his little failings. The inequity of this technique helped complete a process that nature had begun; it honed Michael into the intellectual, emotional, and moral superior of his brother, and allowed Randolph to feel quite comfortable with his own peculiarities of character.

3

"Why do you eat so many potatoes?" Michael asked innocently the same year he decided to become a blacksmith when he grew up. The question was precipitated by several mealtime visits to the farm that belonged to the family of Sean the smithy. Eight to twelve pounds of potatoes a day comprised the average menu for the workingman in Ireland, and Michael had been puzzled by witnessing the voluminous consumption of what seemed to him the blandest of vegetables.

"Mother of God!" expostulated the woman of the house, busy doling out the potatoes and stew to her family. She looked as startled by the question as if the boy had inadvertently blasphemed.

"We eat so many praties, lad, because we haven't much of anything else to eat, and because they fill our bellies and give us the strength to do our work." The reply came from a kindly-looking old man who was seated on a chair by the fire. He had an ancient knitted lap robe pulled about him to keep the chill from his old bones, and his withered face was a curious network of fine spiderweb lines.

"There was a time," he said in a voice much younger than his years, "when there was great bounty for the farmers in Ireland, for they were permitted to keep all of what they produced, to feed their own. But that was before the Sassenach enacted his filthy penal laws that made us paupers and took from us what God Almighty Himself had given."

Recognizing the beginnings of a story, the boy happily extricated his young legs from the long wooden bench that flanked the crude table made of bog oak, and went to the rough stone hearth that warmed the room. Seating himself on the floor beside the man's rocker, but at a respectable distance, and looking up, eyes full of readiness and expectation, he prepared to be entertained, for he already knew of the Shanachies like this old man whose business it was to keep poems and stories in their heads, as did the ancient bards, all ready for the telling.

The old man cleared his throat, as if tuning an ancient instrument, and looked the lad full in the eye before continuing. Then he began in the confident voice of one used to commanding the center of the stage:

"In the year of Our Lord 1170, there were four kings in Ireland. Each one was the ruler of a different one of the four provinces: Ulster, Munster, Leinster, and Connaught. Well, now, Michael, what happened was this . . . three of those kings went off to fight in the Crusades—that's what they called wars then—and, as you might expect, they left their wives at home. But one king stayed behind and he took a fancy to the wife of a king who was far off fighting. Well, didn't he run off with the lady to his own castle on the sly, mind you, and there he remained till her husband came home to find out what had transpired! You can just imagine, lad, the ruckshun that followed when the king got home and found he had been made the fool.

"Now, here's where the real trouble begins for Ireland, for instead of going up there to Munster, as any decent man would, to beat the bejaysus out of the rascal, this particular husband sent a message to the king of England, who happened to be a fellow named Henry II, and asked him to come over to Ireland to help get back his runaway wife. Well, now, Henry did just that, and over he came with his troops, and he says to himself, this is the prettiest place God ever made, I think I'd like to own it! So one fine day in the year of our Lord 1171, Henry up and claimed ownership of the whole of Ireland for the English Crown."

"Could he do such a thing, just like that?" asked Michael, wide-eyed.

"Indeed he could, lad, and what's more, he did it! Well, now, that was where all of our troubles began, for Henry divided up the country like a pie, giving some to this one and some to that, and then he went off back to London and his descendants didn't pay very much attention to us for a few hundred years."

"What happened then?" asked Michael, hanging on to the story just as he was supposed to do.

"Well, in 1641 or thereabouts there was nobody much ruling in England, but a cruel man, name of Oliver Cromwell, who was head of the army and a fine man for the dirty work, had got himself a wee bit of power and thought he'd practice the exercise of it in Ireland.

"So Cromwell arrived here, with a large troop of men and horses, and he surveyed the scene and knew just what to do next. He decided he would destroy the whole race of the Irish. Now do you know what that means, Michael?"

Michael shook his head vigorously no.

"It means that one race takes it upon itself to wipe another off the face of the earth, if you don't mind. Like they never existed at all. Think on it, lad. To make a race of people disappear, with all their songs and stories and poetry and history. With all their loves and hates and ins and outs, just like that!" And after sweeping his hand dramatically through the air, pausing for an instant to let the full impact of such a dissolution find its way into the boy's brain, the Shanachie continued:

"Cromwell went about his duties with a vengeance, Michael. He was a hardhearted villain of the Puritan persuasion, with no love at all for beauty, as was made perfectly clear by the fact that he whitewashed over every glorious painting, in every church in Ireland, before he was through! But that's getting ahead of meself. Meanwhile, this dirty heathen marched his troops into the wee villages, and his soldiers had all the town folk line up in the village square, and he told them they must pledge allegiance to the British sovereign. Well, to tell you the truth, very few of the Irish were inclined to do that. So Cromwell says to them, 'Anyone who won't pledge his allegiance to the Crown will be killed.' Now, this allegiance he was so keen on getting them to pledge meant you had to cast off your holy Catholic faith, for that whoremonger Henry VIII had made himself head of his own Church after he got himself excommunicated by the pope. So it was something they mostly didn't want to do, mind you.

"Now comes the terrible part of the tale, for there was a town called Drogheda where the people decided to stand up for their rights. They told old Cromwell they wouldn't knuckle under, and he could go peddle his Protestant papers elsewhere. So Cromwell decided Drogheda would be as good a place as any to make an example for all of Ireland to see. 'Kill them all!' he says to his troops, and they killed the men first. 'The women, too!' says this lovely man with the disposition of a wet fortnight, and they did that, too. But then, soon enough, there wasn't a soul left in Drogheda but the wee children. Now, Michael, it takes a hardhearted man to kill a wee babe, and even Cromwell's battle-hardened men, that had been able to dispatch the mothers and fathers with nary a by-your-leave, balked at the order to slay the little ones. So they went to his highfalutin eminence, General Cromwell, and asked him for mercy for the wanes. And what do you suppose his lordship said to that, lad?''

Michael was too enthralled with the tale to speak, so he shook his head again.

''This fine articulate personage said to them, 'Nits make lice. Kill them all!' And those words, Michael, will live in the hearts of Irishmen forever; for 'tis the perfect description of how the English think of us. They consider us Irish to be pesky vermin they must rid themselves of, before the land can be theirs, entirely.'' He stopped and cleared his throat, staring meaningfully at Michael, then continued:

''Well, now, having dispatched the entire three thousand people of Drogheda to their eternal reward, Mr. Cromwell and his heathen murderers marched into every town they could find, and told everyone they must leave their little cottages and fields, leave their homes and their farmlands, and go to Connaught, the westernmost province of Ireland, and as bleak a place as mortal man ever set eyes on. 'Tis a land so barren, Michael, there's not the wood to hang a man, nor the water to drown him, nor the dirt to bury him in! So, man, woman, and child, he marched the whole lot of them away from the darlin' green hills of their homes and into the craggy fens of the West, where they mostly starved to death for want of edibles the first few winters. The land wouldn't hold so much as a turnip, Michael, till they filled it an inch at a time, with seaweed they carried from the shore, by means of backbreaking labor.''

The old man seemed to have lost interest in the boy who listened so intently now, for his gaze had drifted away as he spoke, almost as if he were watching the story unfold as he told it; so real was the old tale to its teller, he might have seen it all himself.

''Please, sir,'' said Michael, as if to bring the man back to him. ''That's a marvelous story, and I'm thankful to you for telling me about it, but how does it all have to do with everyone eating so many potatoes? If you recall, sir, that's what you said you would tell me.''

The Shanachie raised an eyebrow and continued. ''Well, now, since you are so impatient to get to the potatoes, I must skip ahead a bit in me history of this lovely land. I'm going to skip right over the next one hundred years or so, except to tell you how we got to have an Ascendancy class here in Ireland, for that is important information for you to have, lad, you being one of them and all! You see, Michael, Cromwell divided up the land he had taken from the Irish, and gave it to his favorite officers in the form of land grants from the British Crown. These officers who had received the land then brought their families here to dwell on it, while various titles like earls, and viscounts, and the like were given to the owners of these lands by the king; for by having the Crown's own henchmen strategically placed all over Ireland, the English could be sure to keep an eye on the land they'd stolen from its rightful owners.''

The boy looked thoughtful at the notion that Drumgillan might be pilfered property, but he said nothing, and continued to await further enlightenment from his amazingly knowledgeable source.

"Well, now, as you might imagine, this whole thing didn't set so well with the Irish. For you see, the Ascendancy lords needed people to work their lands for them, so they let the Irish come back from exile in Connaught to farm and blacksmith and tinker and cartwright, and all the other tasks that needed doing on the big estates. But these Irishmen didn't care for the notion of being hardly more than servants on the land they once had owned, so there were a number of skirmishes over these hundred or two years, that I'm skippin' over in deference to your eagerness for news of the potatoes; and there were uprisings and battles and martyrs and many other fine things I'll tell you about one day, if I've a mind to.'' He paused for dramatic emphasis on this extravagant promise, and then continued afresh.

"Which brings me almost to the praties.'' Michael stirred happily in his place.

"You see, lad, these uprisings didn't set well at all with the landlords, who had far too much money invested in Ireland to let any poor peasants take it away again, so they began to invent harsher and harsher laws to keep the Irish in line. Which brings us to the first quarter of this century, and from that point on, my boyo, I can tell you the tale as I saw it with my own eyes, for I was already a man when the troubles came.

"The Sassenach enacted a series of penal laws to keep the Irish in servitude. We were forbidden to own land, we were forbidden to have property worth more than five pounds, we were forbidden our holy religion, we were forbidden our priests and our schools. We were forbidden the freedom of the courts. To use our ancient Irish language was to be sentenced to death. Our songs and our poetry were outlawed, and our manhood was taken from us. For you see, Michael, there was no way a man could protect his family from harm, and that is, I think, the worst hardship of them all. The taxes were impossible to pay—if an Irishman so much as looked crooked at a landlord's overseer, a whole family could find itself out on the high road by suppertime. If a man improved his little cottage that he'd built with his own two hands, by so much as cutting a new window to let in God's free sunlight, his taxes would be raised because the property had become more valuable. Laddie, I'm telling you the conditions were deplorable in those days!

"Well, now, the tenant farmers could keep their little leases as long as they could pay their taxes, but as the taxes went up and up it got harder and harder to pay them, to say nothin' at all about the tithe every family was forced to pay to the Protestant minister, if you can believe that injustice, lad. First they took away our own sweet faith, and then they made us pay for theirs!

"At any rate, pretty soon we had to sell everything we owned, every cow, every bean, every carrot, every turnip, to pay our rents; and finally the only thing we had left to us was the *praties*." The old man looked meaningfully at the boy from under his mighty eyebrows. "That's the potatoes you've been so anxious to hear about. So we boiled them and baked them and roasted them and ate them, and were grateful to God to have them, let me tell you that.

"Then one of the saddest things in the whole long history of the world happened, Michael. For one fine day in 1845, after the potato crop had been taken in on all the farms around, the hand of God reached out and struck us down. Although to tell you the truth, lad, I've not been able to figure out why it should have been so. With all the troubles we already had, it has always seemed to me that God could have saved us the blight. But at any rate He didn't, and the potatoes, which had come from the lazy beds all white and plump and fine, suddenly and for no reason we could think of turned black and rotten right before our eyes. 'Twas just a few years before you came into the world, lad, and there was no food at all for the farmers and their families. No food meant they couldn't work, and no work meant they couldn't make their rents and taxes, and no taxes meant the overseers came and took their houses and turned the families out onto the roads, where they wandered, men, women, and wanes, until they died of starvation. Did you ever hear of the Hungry Grass, Michael? The patches of grass what's dangerous to go near, for fear of dying?"

"I've heard of it, sir, but I don't know what it means."

"It means, Michael, that the people got so hungry that they filled their screaming bellies with the grass from the roadside and they died with the green of it still on their starving faces. And there's those that say if you ever pass over a spot of Hungry Grass, the souls of the dead will pull you down with them and you'll never make it to the other side. But about that part, I don't know the truth of it at all; I only mention it in passing, although strictly speaking, such supernatural things is not part of the history that I'm giving you." He paused as if to be certain that he had mixed no chaff with the wheat of history, and, satisfied, he continued:

"Well, lad, it was so terrible a time that those who lived it through have never forgotten the horror of it, nor the meanness of the landlords who never raised a hand to help us out of it."

A look of horrified enlightenment spread across the boy's serious face. His voice cracked when he spoke almost in a whisper.

"What of my father, sir, surely he wouldn't let people die if he could save them." The question had a pleading belligerence about it, the boy's loyalty to his father raising his ire, his horror at the story making him fearful of the answer to his question.

The storyteller glanced at the other adult faces in the room, as if to gather a consensus of how much to tell the child.

"Let's just say, Michael, your father chose to listen to his overseer, a certain young Mr. O'Leary, who was a hardhcarted liar and a scoundrel, who saw the famine as a means of serving his own cruel ends." The old man looked a little sheepishly at his son Sean, who had pulled up a chair to the hearth and was wordlessly filling his pipe from a worn earthen jar that had been on the mantel. He felt his small concession to the boy's peace of mind had somehow betrayed his own son, whose life had been so fearfully blighted by the famine; but the middle-aged man with the pipe was smiling at his father to show his approval of the small discrepancy; as if to say the boy has had no part in the sins of His Lordship, and there's little need now to force the child to face his father's delinquency, for surely he'll learn of it in his own time.

Michael looked from the old man's face to the younger ones, and somehow knew he mustn't press the questions that were brimming over in his mind any further for the moment. He had the strangest feeling in his stomach, as if something had tightened and hardened there.

"Please, sir, what happened to the people who were hungry?"

"Thousands upon thousands of them died, Michael, by the road-sides and in the bogs, and in the little cottages. When a family knew 'twas utterly hopeless, for there could be no borrowing from your neighbors when they, too, were starving, they would go inside their little cottage and close the door and wait for death together in a dignified fashion. For they had their pride still, don't you see?" The old man cleared his throat self-consciously, and continued. "So many died, indeed, that we couldn't bury them all properly, and many lay where they fell, until the constabulary came and carted them away, to God knows where, with the rats still nibbling at their destitute bodies.

"The able-bodied men were forced to look elsewhere for employment. I meself, and three of me sons, went to England to find work on the docks, and them jobs was scarcer than hen's teeth to find, lad, and a pittance they paid us. But for our family, at least, we was able to send enough back to keep some alive. Not all, mind you. My son Liam's Brigid and his five wanes died when O'Leary repossessed their cottage and turned them out on the road, and two of my son Sean's girls didn't make it through the Hunger, and his wife, Nora, died soon after, of the sorrow at their passing. But the rest of our family survived, one way or another.

"So you see, Michael, the potatoes have a very special meaning to us; we mayn't have much else, when our rents is paid up, but if we have our praties we can make it through.

"And now"—he slapped his knobby knee in a gesture that said his story was ending—"since these days our praties are looking just grand, and we've got a bit of lamb and a carrot or two, and no end of turnips to keep us merry, things are a great deal better than they've been, lad. There's no denying it." He took out a clean but frayed and yellowed rag from his pocket, and blew his nose with a fierce trumpeting sound, and Michael realized, appalled, that the old man had been close to tears at the telling of the story. The boy stood up and looked uncomfortably around him. He felt compelled to speak, although he felt it hard to do so, for the words stuck in his throat.

"I'm very grateful to you, sir, for having told me your story. No one has ever told me such a story before." He hesitated, unsure of what to say next, feeling compelled to say more, a turmoil in his heart and stomach. "I'll never forget what you told me. I'll not let them do anything bad to you anymore!" he blurted out, stood for a moment, and then scrambled from the cottage as if the devil were on his tail.

He ran and ran and ran, until he dropped. Exhausted, he lay on the cool, damp grass looking up at the hazy, cloud-filled Irish sky he'd looked at a thousand times before, and saw that it was changed, and with it everything—for the terrible beauty that was the Irish past and future had been born in him, and there was surely no going back from it.

4

Mary Dalton was daydreaming over the mountain of darning she had piled in the lap of her homespun dress. She had drifted out of her mud-walled cottage and into the drawing room of a mansion in Dublin. She let her imagination admire the glittering crystal chandelier, the gleaming silver tea service on the table, the heavy damask draperies. She sighed at the beauty of it all and let her fingers fondle the rough woolen socks in her lap with an absentminded languor, totally removed from the smoky darkness of the little threadbare cabin and its onerous duties.

Mary was the only daughter of a tenant farmer on the vast Drumgillan estate. The Daltons, Mary's ancestors, like others of the native Irish aristocracy who were dispossessed by the English invasions of the 1600s, had returned after the worst of it to work the fields of their ancestral holdings. As tenant farmers who had once been owners, they continued to live on the periphery of their own exquisite domain, which was by that time the property of David Hartington, first earl of Rathconrath.

Occasionally, Mary, in her woolgathering moments, would imagine herself to be a great lady, as her far-distant ancestors had been. She had worked out an elaborate fantasy life in which she, not the Hartingtons, owned Drumgillan and lived in the huge Georgian manse that was its manor house. The Daltons had worked the Drumgillan land for centuries before Mary's birth—they had also survived the potato famine better than many other family groups in the province of Leinster, for the simple reason that all but the family of Mary's father, Christopher Dalton, had emigrated during the blight.

"Glory be to God, Mary, you are slow as molasses in January with that mending." Siobhan Dalton, forty years of age and looking not a day under sixty, was bent over the huge iron hearth-kettle, tasting the salty broth it contained, nurturing the many potatoes, the few turnips, and the too small piece of lamb that, along with soda bread, would be their evening meal. Mary, bumped from her reverie, hastily put down the overflowing bowl of tattered socks belonging to her father and four brothers, and crossed the dirt floor to her mother's side. The girl was tall and slender, but with a soft, pleasing roundness to her face and body.

"Let me do that, Mama, I can finish the darning after supper. You look like you should lie down for a bit." Mary absentmindedly pushed her hair back from her face as she reached for the spoon in her mother's hand.

"Aye, it's lying down I'll be soon enough, child; and for a long time too, I'm thinking." Mary watched her mother painfully straighten herself from the perpetual hunch of the Irishwoman at the kettle chores, and knew quite well that the older woman might not survive the child she carried, which, with a midwife's accuracy, Mary calculated would be born just six weeks hence. Unlike the other pregnancies she had watched her mother progress through, this one seemed to be sapping every ounce of life-force from the already frail and arthritic woman, and Mary had a nagging sense of finality about the impending delivery.

"You're a good girl, Mary," said Siobhan. "It's a terrible sad thing, to think you might be left with all the responsibilities when the baby comes."

Momentarily, Frank, Paddy, and Dev would burst through the Dutch double door, all full of the smell of earth and sweat, and along with their father, Christopher, would fling themselves at the table with barely a civil word, to consume the gargantuan portions of broth and potatoes that gave them the strength to plow and till. Rory would appear at some point thereafter, hot and grimy, smelling rankly of the forge at the blacksmith shop. Except for Rory, who, Mary knew, had dreams too, she had little use for her brothers.

Christopher patted his wife pleasantly on the rump when he arrived, a proprietary gesture, before seating himself at the head of the table and waiting expectantly to be served.

"I need me supper tonight," he intoned as he tucked the rough muslin into his pants. "With that scourge of an overseer O'Leary out collecting rents in another week's time, there's a heartbreak of work to be done tomorrow." Several grunts of assent greeted the thought. Mary scurried and Siobhan plodded about, ladling out the steaming stew, refilling plates and cups as the bottomless pits began to fill themselves, the women bolting their own food on the fly, between servings to the men.

"Sit down, woman, before you fall down, won't you?" the girl's whisper pleaded with her fragile mother. "I'll clear the table and pour the tea for you."

"You're a good girl, Mary." Her mother's words had the sound of rote in them, although Mary knew she meant them lovingly but was simply too tired to be eloquent.

Siobhan Dalton had been pregnant her entire adult life. The endless sexual cycle of the poor and Catholic, a recurrent nightmare of pregnancies, births, miscarriages, and infant deaths, had been her unquestioning lot from the moment of her marriage. The Church encouraged copulation as a procreative means of bringing more little Catholics into the world, while considering sex in itself a scourge; but the relentless chill of the Irish evenings and the utter lack of other comforts in the stark lives of the peasantry kept pregnancies maximal, and despite the enormity of admonitions against coital pleasure, the people managed.

The village doctor had warned Siobhan to forbear the possibility of any further pregnancies, for he said that the danger to her was considerable, and in her heart she had hoped that Christopher would understand. Sex had been more burdensome than pleasurable to the overworked woman during much of her married life, for her marriage had been one of common sense rather than love; the results of physical union, which she found pleasant enough in her youth, had overwhelmed her as the years wore on. If she could have found a way to avoid sex without offending her husband or the Church, Siobhan would gladly have done so.

Siobhan and Mary cleared the dinner dishes from the table, placing them into a hefty wooden trough that Mary filled half-and-half with scalding water from the kettle at the hearth and cold water from a bucket she had earlier carried with its mate, from the outside well. The two women washed and dried the ugly utilitarian crockery and carried the heavy trough to the cottage door to spill its contents into their tiny flower garden. "As if any Irish plant would ever lack for water!" the mother always said to Mary as they spilled the dishwater on the already sodden ground. Then each took her dutiful place by the fireside, a lapful of sewing and darning for Mary, a lapful of knitting for Siobhan, who could miraculously invent an entire sweater in two or three nights, her fingers flying, needles clicking, stitches counted off in endless intricacies that were the envy of all her peers. If the men wanted tea or tobacco, the women would fetch it for them, otherwise there was little movement within the tiny house.

Rory sat nearest the fire trying to read in the dim, inadequate light; the other three had left shortly after dinner to gather with their friends at one or another of the neighboring houses to talk of heroes and of revolution. Had it not been for Rory's never-sated desire to "better" himself by reading and studying, he, too, would have been long gone.

"I've a new book for you, Mary," he said softly, for his father didn't approve of the time they wasted on reading. "It's by a woman name of Brontë. The lady at the library said it's a fine romance, so I brought it along for you." Mary took it gratefully. She knew her brother's choice of literature ran to revolutionary treatises and stories of the sea. His was a different dream of escape and adventure, but each of them clung desperately to the possibility of a different kind of life: he with a passionate sense of purpose, she with a sort of wistful hope that her time would come and she would be ready for it.

Mary carried her mother's dying with her like an internal rock, a great gray obstacle that couldn't be budged.

The baby, if the pathetic squalling thing that emerged from her mother's loins could be called by so pleasant-sounding a name, was dead within minutes of its birth; the cord, stranglingly wrapped about its neck, had choked its life away. Mary had sat by the hour with her agonized mother, sponging her clay-cold face, dripping water from a wet cloth between her cracked lips, crooning and soothing her in an instinctive reversal of their roles as child and mother.

Now, Mary watched her mother's crude pine coffin, and the tiny one strapped to it, lowered slowly into the ground. A cold, wet wind whipped her shawl painfully about her body and tangled the home-spun skirt around her ankles. She was oblivious to the mud she stood in, and to the wind that bit hard into her tear-stained cheeks—and equally oblivious to the droning noise of the pastor who was end-lessly intoning the prayers for the dead.

"Ashes to ashes and dust to dust. And in the sure and certain knowledge of the resurrection of the body . . . ." and on and on and on. The interminable praying seemed impersonal and grotesquely useless.

"There is a better life than hers was. There is a better life." Mary said it over and over and over in her anguished brain, partially to keep the horror of the death at bay, and partially to wipe away the terror that she, too, might go down into the unfeeling ground, a victim of the inevitable, as her mother had been.

"Come home with us, Mary. You can't stay out here in the wet, lass. You'll catch your death." Rory tugged at his sister's shoulder, the wind blowing the words back harshly into his throat; she stared at him, tear-blind and unseeing.

"I'll not let them bury me, too, Rory. I'll not let them!"

"No, Mary, you don't have to think of that now!" Of all her brothers the stocky little blacksmith was the only one who understood what it was she feared.

5

Michael Harcourt Hartington was the family rebel. For the son of an Ascendancy family to traffic with the Irish peasants on his family estate was more than unheard of, it was appalling. Or so, at least, thought Lady Geraldine and Randolph. Sir Jeffrey, while he found his younger son's habitual involvement with the tenants on the leasehold properties a trifle seedy, paid little serious attention to Michael's curious preoccupation with his inferiors, as he felt certain it was simply the high-spirited behavior of a young man champing at the bit of life.

All Sir Jeffrey's metaphors had to do with horses, for they were his passion and his obsession. He bred them, raised them, raced them, bet on them, made and lost vast fortunes because of them, and showered them with considerably more affection and insight than he lavished on either his wife or his sons.

"Michael is simply sowing his wild oats, Geraldine," he said emphatically whenever Lady Geraldine brought their son's peculiar behavior to his attention. "Can't keep a young man on a short halter, my dear. Don't want to break his spirit now, do we?"

No matter what the opinion of his wife on the subject, Sir Jeffrey thought Michael a splendid specimen. He was strong and manly, intelligent and practical, and he had a way with horses.

Sir Jeffrey spent a good deal of his time in his comfortably paneled library doing his accounting, an occupation that he despised and wished he could avoid. Unfortunately, money was an essential element of his passionate horsebreeding career; for the rent and produce of his farms and leases paid for horses, and for trips to find more horses, and for all the other myriad needs that horses generated—and horses were the center of his universe.

Sir Jeffrey was devoutly grateful that Randolph seemed to have a head for figures. When the lad came down from Oxford, all this nasty business could be safely turned over to him. After all, Randolph would be the next Earl of Rathconrath, and all the lands and peasants and horses and sheep and villages would one day be his. Rather a shame, thought Sir Jeffrey whenever he bothered to think at all on the future of his sons, to leave Randolph the horses. Better to leave them to Michael, for there was a lad who appreciated a fine piece of horseflesh when he saw one.

Sir Jeffrey sometimes mused philosophically that Michael would have made a more sporting earl than his brother, Randolph. He had often thought this over the years, despite the fact that, in principle, he believed wholeheartedly in the English system of inheritance, for there would be no point in chopping up a fine old estate like Drumgillan into little pieces of land to be handed out to younger sons; no telling where such an undisciplined policy would lead. Michael would find his way, Sir Jeffrey would see to that. Pity, though, that the boy hadn't been born first.

Other than his methodical business brain, there wasn't a great deal to like about Randolph, Sir Jeffrey had decided long ago, for the boy had a reprehensible mean streak. He had once seen him purposely tighten a horse's bit till it ate deep into the animal's tender lips, leaving them bleeding and raw, the sadistic smirk on the boy's face sickening his father. He'd whipped Randolph soundly for that misdemeanor, but the incident remained in his mind and he'd never again encouraged his son to involve himself with the horses. You can tell a great deal about a man by the way he handles a horse, Hartington had always maintained—be he generous or stingy, weak or strong, honest or crafty, subtle or blatant—put a man on a horse and you'd know in minutes what his measure was.

The thought filled Sir Jeffrey with a smug contentment; it was comforting to know that the world was fairly easy to understand.

6

Mary swung the little basket of food merrily as she ran across the verdant spring meadow to the stable to deliver to Rory the lunch he had inadvertently left behind. The battered tin pail she carried contained a slice of cold lamb and two thick slices of rough wheaten bread, a hearty if unexciting combination.

Mary loved the long trek across the meadow, bursting as it was with the first glorious bounty of spring; blossoms scattered themselves across the newborn green, and the scent of the arbutus trees and rhododendrons wafted across the rolling fields. There was pleasure in just being alive on such a day, and being free of the cottage where she had felt hemmed in and claustrophobic since her mother's death. She was seventeen years of age, tall, lithe, and full-breasted. She woke up every morning feeling on the brink of some unimaginable surprise, and went to bed each night frustrated with the knowledge that she hadn't touched whatever it was she awaited so expectantly.

Mary called to Rory from outside the superb stables, as was her custom, in a lilting voice that could charm the birds from the bushes, or so her father had often said of it. When her brother did not promptly respond, she thrust herself through the huge wooden doors into the coolness of the stable. She was not prepared, in her exuberance, to find herself bounding headlong into the arms of Michael Hartington, who was striding briskly out of the stable just as she was rushing in. Her embarrassment at nearly running over the younger son of His Lordship, and gracelessly dropping her pail of food into the muddy straw of the stable floor, was nothing compared with her consternation at feeling the strong arms that clasped her firmly to keep her on her unsteady feet. Blushing deeply, Mary looked up into the amused eyes of the most attractive young man she had ever seen. Immobilized by confusion and the inexplicable pounding in her chest, her gaze was held by his eyes. He'll leave the world poorer by those eyes when he goes, she thought, in the instant she looked into them for the first time.

Michael, no neophyte with shy young ladies, held her just a little longer than was necessary, crushing her bosom to his chest playfully, and finally released her with a flourish.

"And who might you be, my beauty?" he asked in a voice that thrilled her for some reason she didn't begin to understand.

"I'm Mary Dalton, sir. The smithy's my brother and I was bringing him lunch, but I'm afraid I've spoiled it now, thoroughly." She looked despairingly at the spilled meal, as if uncertain whether she should pick it up and dust it off, for surely a little dirt did no one any harm, or leave it where it lay, so as not to look the crass peasant.

The stricken look touched Michael, for he knew that food was precious to the tenant farmers.

"See, Mary, it isn't harmed. We all must eat a peck of dirt before we die, and this will contribute hardly a teaspoonful to Rory's quotient."

The girl took the scraggly luncheon remnants from the man's hand gratefully, trying hard not to look again into those periwinkle eyes.

"Thank you, Your Lordship. I'm sorrier than anything that I almost knocked you down. I don't know what's wrong with me today, all ups and downs as I am. My father would never forgive me if he knew I'd been so clumsy."

"No, no, Mary, the fault was mine entirely. I must learn to watch where I'm going. Someone the size of myself must be very careful not to mow down people by sheer dint of mass. You have my humblest apologies. Really."

The smile that accompanied the apology was open and generous. Mary smiled back tentatively and handed the somewhat disheveled lunch to Rory, who had been watching the interchange with increasing discomfort. The ancient custom of droit du seigneur had placed far too many virgin peasant girls in the beds of their local lordships for the brother of a girl so obviously bursting with fertility to be comfortable at the scene he saw unfolding; for if Mary knew nothing of sex, the same could not be said of Rory. He cleared his throat and scowled at his sister in a pointed gesture of dismissal, took the pail roughly from her hand, a most uncharacteristic act for him, and returned to his work.

Sensing that she had somehow managed to anger Rory, Mary gathered her wits and, unsure of what was expected of a girl in the presence of a real gentleman, curtsied in an unschooled but graceful fashion and fled the stable at almost a run.

Michael watched her departure thoughtfully. Noting the smithy's displeasure, he decided not to pursue the questions that seeped unbidden into his brain. There was an unexpected quality about the girl that piqued his curiosity. She hadn't the air of a milkmaid, there was an elegance to her bearing, and her instinctive curtsy was the gesture of the gently reared, not the cottage-born. He would make it his business to see her again.

The thought of the startled girl in the stable played at the edges of Michael's mind. He was therefore delighted to glimpse her walking across the broad meadow one morning, a week or so after their meeting at the forge.

"Mary!" he called to the girl from horseback as she meandered across the broad span of green, trailing her fingers in the tall grass. "That is your name, isn't it, lass?"

She looked up, face full of shyness, but nonetheless she smiled at him.

"Mary Dalton, sir. We met at the stable."

He reined the huge horse in and dismounted, holding the reins casually and falling in beside her, tailoring his long stride to her shorter steps.

"Of course I remember. I'm happy to see you. I was really rather hoping we would meet again," he said enthusiastically.

Mary looked at him quizzically, as if to see if he was mocking, and inadvertently her eyes caught his, as they had at the forge. Why in God's name those eyes should make her feel so uneasy, she couldn't imagine. They unsettled her, so that half her mind wished he would go on about his business, while the other half was thrilled to death that he did not. Michael was very tall, and his moves were full of confidence; Mary wanted to end the awkward silence, but her brain seemed suddenly empty.

Michael, feeling as awkward as the girl, was trying to decide his best opening gambit; instinct warned him that if he said the wrong thing, she might flee again, as she had at the stable.

"Where do you live on Drumgillan, Mary?"

"My father is a farmer. He has the south leasehold and works it with three of my brothers, sir. My brother Rory is the one you met at the forge. He is to be a blacksmith, you see, for our little farm can't support so many sons."

"Your father is a lucky man, Mary, blessed with so many sons to help in the fields." He knew, of course, that to a farmer there was no greater wealth than sons, and no worse burden than daughters.

"Aye. Would that my poor mother had had a daughter or two more to help her, sir. Perhaps she would not be dead these twelve months, had there been more than me to help her in our cottage full of lads.''

Catching the sorrowful undertone in the girl's soft throaty voice, he wondered somewhat, for it seemed to cloak a more complex sorrow than simple mourning for the dead.

"Do you know who I am, Mary?" He asked the question gently. She seemed to him oddly vulnerable.

"Aye, sir. You are His Lordship's younger son. Everyone on Drumgillan knows of you." Her eyes twinkled a little when she looked up at him. "You are the one that has to do with the people of the land. It has come to us that your mother doesn't approve of that.''

Michael laughed. "There isn't much that the 'people of the land' don't know, is there, Mary? What more have you heard of me?" His voice was companionable, and she began to feel more at ease; he was not so different to talk to than Rory after all, provided she didn't look straight into those unsettling eyes.

"We heard you have a way with horses," she said thoughtfully, as if to be sure of the accuracy of the reply, "that you have a better heart than your brother, and that if you were to be your father's heir, there would be less for the leaseholders to fear on Drumgillan." She stopped short, unsure if she should say more.

"And what else?"

She looked at him, amused by his curiosity, warmed by his apparent friendliness.

"We've heard you fancy the ladies, sir.''

He laughed a genuinely merry laugh. "Then you wouldn't be surprised if I stole a kiss from you, lass." He reached for her expertly, but the expression on her face made him stop short before touching her. Mary's eyes had changed in a split second from openness and laughter to deep disappointment. She hadn't been flirting with him, as he had thought, but merely answering a question. He felt oddly embarrassed and angry at his own insensitivity.

"Please, sir," she said directly and with a gentle dignity. "It wouldn't be kind to do that.''

"I'm sorry, Mary. I should not have been so forward with you; you are quite right.''

They began walking again, this time without speaking. It was a damnably funny thing, he thought, that this peasant girl should unsettle him so. He felt as uncomfortable as if he had done something obscene in the presence of a great lady.

7

"What do you dream about, Mary?" Michael asked as they sat together in the meadow beyond the bog one summer afternoon. He couldn't imagine what a girl in Mary's circumstances could dream of that had any hope of coming true.

"Of a better life than my mother's, Michael. Of the love of a fine man, of children." She hesitated before continuing. "Of being a lady."

His eyes softened at her honesty and her guilelessness. She was a continuing revelation to him.

"And what would you do if you were a lady?"

She thought for a moment. "I'd love my husband and my children, just the same as if I were a farmer's wife, I suppose. But"—her eyes looked suddenly full of mischief—"I'd wear silk dresses trimmed with lace, and straw bonnets with flowers. My children would go to a fine school and I'd have a library filled with every book I've ever dreamed of . . . and I'd send my brother Rory to America and buy him a farm of his own." She stopped to think for a moment to make sure the list was complete, then added, "I'd live in a grand big house like Drumgillan with so many rooms everyone would have a private place and a bedroom of his own. I'd have a hairbrush with a silver handle to do up my hair and golden buckles on my shoes!" She ended it all with a flourish and laughed softly as if to say it was all so impossible a dream that even the telling of it was an embarrassment.

Watching the infinite desire with which Mary spoke of things he himself took so for granted, Michael was deeply moved by the girl. It wasn't the first time she had stirred something strange in him . . . a protective instinct.

After their first encounter, Michael had made it his business to find the girl whenever he could do so unobtrusively. He wheedled the schedule of Mary's chores from her reluctant brother, and managed to be where she was when time permitted.

Mary opened a world to him whose fringes he had played at all his life. She was the bone and sinew of Ireland; she was the forbidden peasantry that had always had the capacity to ensnare his

wild imaginings. There was a womanliness about her different from
that of anyone Michael had met before, for it was effortless and,
above all, real. His mother and all the women of his own acquaintance were skillful practitioners of female subtleties, manipulations,
and sexual intrigues that were plotted with the strategic expertise of
a general deploying troops for battle. Such was not the case with
Mary.

Womanliness surrounded her like an unassuming aura. She was
guilelessly feminine, a phenomenon he had never before imagined
possible. Strangest of all, she seemed oddly unaware of her own
female sexuality, strong and insistent though it appeared to him.

They talked, when time permitted, of random things, for without
knowing they were about it, the two were becoming friends.

"What do you dream of, Michael? You who seem to live a dream
already?" She countered his question with her own, for she couldn't
help but wonder what a man possessed of everything might have left
to wish for.

He watched her carefully for a moment before replying, thinking
how glib an answer he might give to that question had it been asked
by a girl of his own class. But he never answered Mary with other
than the unvarnished truth.

"My life has been preordained from the moment of birth, Mary. I
was to grow up a duplicate of my family. To laugh at the same
humor, to admire the same monarchy, to attend the same university,
to despise the Irish, just as they do. But something was different for
me. From as long ago as I can remember, I fit in better with the
tenants than I did with my family and their friends. I'm rougher
than they are, Mary. Fonder of life and nature and the soil. I'm less
refined somehow—I don't mean crude, you understand. I mean I'm
rougher hewn than they; stronger . . . freer . . . wilder!" He grinned,
stuck for how to explain himself further, realizing he had never tried
before today to do so, even to himself.

"I think you are exactly as you should be," Mary said shyly.
"Just exactly perfect as you are, sir." She didn't look at him as she
said it, but down at the grass and the buttercups she had been
fondling with gentle fingers.

He reached across to where she sat, her fiery hair long and loose,
its wisps blown across the skin of her forehead. He reached out with
his hand and brushed the curl back from her face tenderly.

"I am very far from perfect, lass. But when I talk with you, I understand things better. The world . . . the universe . . . me. Especially me. You make everything clearer somehow.''

Mary looked up at his face—he couldn't be more than twenty or twenty-one, she knew, but he seemed older. He represented everything she had ever dreamed there might be in a world better than her own. He opened the doors and windows of her imagination to possibilities; possibilities beyond Drumgillan, beyond her poverty, beyond her social station.

She loved to look at him; his tall, muscular body filled her with indefinable yearnings. That such as he would care for her was an impossible, implausible dream . . . but if Mary had not been a dreamer, she would never have survived at all.

"Have you ever thought of working in the Big House, Mary?" Michael asked it of her to change the subject from that of dreams, for his dreams were curiously beginning to include the strange vital girl at his side, and that was madness.

"How could I do that, Michael, with my father and brothers needing meals and mending done for them?''

"I don't know, lass. It just seems a way for us to see more of each other, perhaps.'' He tried to sound casual, uncertain how she would react, uncertain if it was even fair to ask her. She was so damnably different from the others. Life would be simpler if he could merely seduce the girl and have done with it, but that was out of the question now that she was his friend. Still and all, it would be nice to have her nearer.

Mary looked at the man quizzically, wondering what was in his mind, pretending a calm she didn't feel. It would mean escape, freedom. To exchange the squalid drudgery of the cottage for the splendid drudgery of the Big House would suit her ambitions well enough. And to be nearer Michael . . . just the thought of such intimacy, however tentative, made life seem far more bearable.

Mary dropped the subject of working in the Big House as a servant, after the initial explosion it provoked in her volatile father.

"And what exactly do you think your brothers and I would be doing without a woman in the house to cook and clean? Sure, I never heard the like of it in me life; a girl like you abandoning her own family!'' he said, stomping about the house until the teacups shook in their places, and Mary had to apologize profusely for even mentioning such an unheard-of idea. But in her heart of hearts she was desperate for escape.

More than anything she longed to be near Michael. All her dreaming focused on the man. And, although she never quite allowed this thought articulation in her mind, for it seemed too calculating, there was another reason too. She needed to see firsthand the way in which the wealthy lived. She lusted after the knowledge of grace and style and manners she knew they possessed.

It was entirely happenstance that provided the means of Mary's escape, for she knew from bitter experience there was no moving her father when his mind was set. But to her great amazement, when she was eighteen years of age, deliverance came in an unlikely shape. Her father announced that he was about to take a new wife, Eileen Casey, a widow from the local village. Eileen brought as her dowry two cows, three pigs, much fine embroidery, and the bossiest disposition Mary had ever encountered.

Mary could not help but compare this virago to her gentler mother, and the bile rose in her throat with each new assault on Siobhan's sacred memory. She baited Eileen in insidious ways in response to her stepmother's heavy-handed meanness. The explosive situation raised the tension in the cottage to near fever pitch.

"I've been giving some thought to your notion about taking a job in the Big House, Mary," said her father, not quite unexpectedly, one evening soon after Eileen took dominion over the kitchen. "And I've decided, if it would make you happy, you should do it."

Mary was as elated at the prospect of escape as she was disgusted by her father's hypocrisy.

"I'll go as soon as they'll have me, Da," she said with dignity, trying not to look at the victorious smirk on Eileen's face as she bent over her mending with a smile of her own. She would count the seconds until she could tell the glorious news to Michael.

Working at Drumgillan was an endless chore; one day off a month, and one hour on Sunday, for six o'clock mass. But to Mary there had never been such a time of joyous exhilaration. She was close to Michael, she was learning what she coveted, she was free.

There was a sweetness that flooded over her whenever she could steal moments away from her work in the Big House to be with the man to whom she felt a growing devotion. The look of him standing on the side of the hill where they often met, waiting for her to come to him, rough hair blown awry by the wind, calves slickly booted for riding, slim hips in contrast to his broad shoulders, sent her senses into spins. Whenever she could steal an hour or a day to meet him,

Mary would clutch her shawl about her shoulders, skirt flapping in the whipping wind, and fairly fly to the comfort of his presence. She had let him hold her gently, several times—enough to know the desires it produced in both of them. Mary's heart beat against her ribs, like a bird-wing battering its cage bars, when he so much as touched her hair, something he did with more and more frequency. And those eyes of his still had the power to turn her mind to chaos.

He felt much the same way about her, if the truth were known. Almost from the moment of their meeting, Mary had posed a serious, if pleasurable, problem for Michael. He wanted her, more than he had wanted the other women who had touched his life or entered his bed. She seemed to him an unspeakably winsome anomaly, a woman who could be his friend.

But the question of where the friendship would lead provoked and tantalized him. It would be unthinkable to marry her and equally unthinkable to bed her without doing so. He felt certain he could seduce her; there was no doubt about the intensity of emotion and response he engendered in the inexperienced girl when he touched her. She was too unskilled at flirtation to know how to hide her responsiveness from him, and her very vulnerability made him feel protective and uncomfortable about his overpowering desire for her.

He considered ending the strange relationship entirely, and several times, when aroused by Mary and frustrated by his dilemma, he had sought out local agreeable ladies whose services had entertained and relieved him in the past. The trouble was that he no longer wanted them; he found himself fantasizing too often about Mary's soft white breasts, her unruly auburn hair, her sad eyes, and her laughter. It was a problem that had no solution, and he brooded about it more and more as he pondered his own future.

8

Several months after her acceptance into the domestic duties of Drumgillan, Mary and Michael went riding, as they had contrived to do on one or two occasions before. The sun, never strong enough in Ireland to win out entirely over the slate-gray clouds, had darkened unexpectedly and hidden itself behind one of its cumulus adversaries. Large drops of rain began to splatter themselves on horses and riders, and Mary, who adored the cold and wet of it, reached out to touch Michael as if to share with him the sheer joy of the beginning storm. She had always felt a strange exhilaration during storms; thunder and lightning filled her with an unexpected exuberant energy. Even as a little girl, when all the other children had hidden in their mamas' aprons during thunderstorms, she had been known to run to the yard to drink in their beauty and power.

"Mary," Michael called to her, shouting against the wind that had risen with the impending storm. "There's a small cottage less than a mile from here. It was abandoned in the famine and has been empty since I was a boy. Come, lass, we shouldn't stay out in the rain even if you love the feel of it; 'tis cold to ride in, once your clothes are soaked."

Mary nodded, the wet wind whipping her hair about her cheeks. She rode a horse of her father's, for it was her day off in the month, and she had gone home that morning on the pretext of seeing her family. Her real intention was to borrow the animal so that she could ride with Michael, fearing as she did the gossip that would be aroused if she tried to borrow a horse from the Drumgillan stable.

Mary had ridden since she was a small child, her four brothers had seen to that, and the thrill of it had always warmed her. Today the feel of the damp wind in her hair, the jiggle of her large breasts as she galloped over the heather-strewn fields, the electricity of the gathering storm—all set her senses reeling with an undefined anticipation. There was that curious feeling of power between her thighs; the rough feel of the horse's flesh, and the rhythm of his broad back sending waves of pleasure through her body, waves that were powerful and insistent. They pushed the animals to a gallop and headed them swiftly across the darkening landscape to the safety of the cottage. Dismounting, they tied the horses in a little shed outside and ran hurriedly, hand in hand, indoors. The dark and damp of the small house did not deter the two refugees, for it seemed sweetly private and unencumbered.

"There's a box of turf for the fire, Mary, and a tinderbox for starting one." Michael looked down at the dripping-wet, shivering girl. "I come here sometimes when I want to escape from the world," he said as he set about skillfully laying the fire. "I've even slept here once or twice. It's a fine quiet place to think in. There's a blanket or two in the cupboard. Perhaps you should put one about you, lass, until the fire is laid, so you don't catch a chill."

She watched him hunched over the fire, his huge hands busy at his task, tight buttocks straining against the gabardine of his riding breeches as he squatted, half kneeling, at the hearth. Why was she so painfully aware of the well-defined musculature of his back and legs? Why had she never before noticed the way those auburn hairs at the back of his neck tumbled over the collar of his riding shirt?

Michael rose from the fire, satisfied that it would be ablaze in minutes, and began to peel off his drenched hacking jacket and shirt, both of which had been sticking in folds to his skin. She stood transfixed as he unselfconsciously removed the two garments and warmed his naked body at the fire as naturally as if he were in the habit of undressing in front of young ladies every day. She had never seen anything quite as wonderful as his naked back and chest, and the tension in her mounted precariously. He took the other blanket from the cupboard and wrapped himself in it.

Smiling at her consternation and holding the blanket like a cape, Michael opened his arms to her. "Come, Mary," he said, smiling at her. "Let me hold you in my arms and warm you." She felt herself drawn almost involuntarily into the shelter of his strength and comfort; some things were simply too hard for a mere human being to fight off. The feel of his skin against her rain-soaked breasts and arms was unutterably sweet and sensual.

He bent his head to hers, as she somehow knew he would, and his lips found hers with an inevitable ease. She had never dreamed that a man's lips could be so soft and hard at the same time. His tongue was somehow seeking entry to her mouth, and the velvety intrusion flooded her with primal knowledge of how to kiss back. One of his strong hands tangled itself in her hair, maneuvering her head and mouth to his own rhythm in a dizzying perfection; the other hand seemed everywhere at once, touching her cheeks, her throat, the skin of her shoulder, the swelling of her breasts. She knew she mustn't let him do these things, but how else was she to learn . . . to please him. . . .

He kissed her lips, her eyes, her ears, and the curving hollow of her throat. Her mind was in chaos, and her body no better; she knew she must push him away, but how could she do such a thing? He was driving her mad with his hands and his lips, and it was wonderful. She knew that had always been the way of it, since the very first day at the stables. She pulled away, or tried to, but he held her fast, knowing that she didn't really seek release. Oh, God, how she needed to feel and not to think. There was knowledge in his body, and she wanted it. To abandon herself to feeling was a desperate need. What could she lose but her innocence; a small price in return for what she was feeling. No thoughts of damage, no thoughts at all; she was so lost in the blessed feel of him, it took her a moment to realize he had stopped, abruptly.

Michael's loving mouth buried itself with a long resolute sigh in Mary's tangled hair. His arms went around her body in a protective, not seductive, circle. He squeezed the limp and disappointed girl to him in such a total embrace that she felt with clarity and wonder the huge stiffness that had arisen beneath his breeches. Suspended in his arms, all motion stopped, only their labored breathing sounding in the still cottage, Mary knew she was loved. Nothing but love could have kept him from taking her. She would not have stopped him . . . she would not have denied him anything she had in her power to give. The knowledge that she was loved filled her with a sense of wonder, and she was afraid to move in the shelter of his arms, lest she break the spell.

"Oh, Mary, Mary, my Mary," he whispered finally, into her hair. "What are we to do, lass? We are surely on very dangerous ground."

" 'Tis hard for me to feel danger, in your arms, Michael. I've dreamed so long of feeling them around me."

He looked ruefully at the absolute sincerity of the blossoming girl he still held close. No woman of his class would ever have admitted such a thing to a man who had not declared his intentions. "I would that I could hold you forever, Mary. You feel to me as if you belong in my arms and nowhere else." He was filled with the sweetness of her soft body, its curves and graceful roundness. He longed to feel her breasts in his hands and mouth, to taste her sweet nipples and to lose himself in the fullness of her womanly body. He sighed, for he could see no way for such a thing to be without doing her irreparable harm.

So, he held her and they watched the rain mist away into a foggy dampness, sheltered together in the woolen blanket—and they talked and talked the afternoon away. Each one desperate for the touch of the other's hands and mouth, each one terrified of where such blissful touchings must inevitably lead.

" 'Tis getting late, Mary. We must be going back." Michael hugged her to him as he said it, in the gathering dusk.

"Aye, Michael. 'Twill be hard to be without you this night." He turned her face to him in the dim cottage and looked most deliberately into her eyes.

"I would have you know that I am not trifling with you, Mary. You are no passing fancy with me. I don't know what to do about us, but I must find out."

She said nothing.

"I think I love you." He said it gently, as if afraid to hurt her with the sound of it.

"And I you, Michael," she said without hesitancy. " 'Tis enough for me right now; don't fear."

He smiled tenderly at her attempt to set his mind at ease, and touched her flushed cheek gently in the gathering dusk.

"Nay, Mary. 'Tis not enough for either of us, lass, and there's the trouble. I fear we want it all, my girl. I fear we want it all."

She nodded in hopeless agreement as they stood facing each other in the tiny place, reluctant to leave, wary of staying—each one striving to engrave the other's every detail in memory, to sustain them in the time they would be parted.

He bent his head to hers one last time, and they left the small private place, agonized by the knowledge that now that such a private refuge existed for them, their doom was sealed for better or for worse.

9

Life in service was an exhausting affair at Drumgillan. Mary worked from before daybreak until after the supper dishes had been washed and tucked away gingerly into their individual satin covers. Mary sometimes examined the porcelain with intense interest before consigning it for another night to its plumply quilted resting place. In contrast to the heavy utilitarian crockery she had known all her life, these dishes were as fragile as butterfly wings and as beautiful as a painting in a museum. Delicate blossoms in the palest pastel colors entwined themselves around the center of each plate and saucer and cup, and a filigree of pure gold latticed the delicate rims so that the dinner service glimmered like a king's ransom on the damask of the dinner table, in the aura of candlelight by which the family dined.

Cook had told her the dishes were from the faraway country of Denmark. They were called Flora Danica, the flowers of Denmark, and each was hand-painted by a craftsman who spent his entire life perfecting a single flower. Mary couldn't imagine what the cost of a single cup might be, and had she known that you could buy a cow for the price of a place setting, she would still have thought such perfect beauty worth the cost.

A book she had found in the library when she was dusting there said that the serene Palladian façades of the Irish Georgian manor houses like Drumgillan were superb devices for "shutting Ireland out," and while she was disturbed at the notion that anyone would want to, she felt the author incorrect, for far from shutting out the beauty of the dreamy Irish landscape, the gracious Georgian manor seemed perfectly constructed to take it all in. The immense, nearly ceiling-high windows brought the outdoors in; the house, set as it was on top of a gracious knoll, looked down on perfectly manicured sculptured gardens and finally on the lough, a blue-gray crystal gem set in an emerald landscape, glimmering in the hazy Irish sun. She'd heard it said that Drumgillan had been remodeled by James Gandon, the architect of the fabulous Four Courts in Dublin, and she felt certain it must be so.

The heavy silver that she learned to polish dutifully once a week was another breathtaking enlightenment. She knew the other servants found the task odious, but to Mary, whose only glimpse of silver had been the chalice at the Church of St. Boniface, the rococo scrollwork, the swans and pheasants and enigmatic curlicues that adorned the richly gleaming vessels and flatware, were a fascination. The butler told her she'd polished the ornate tea service better than any of the other servants, and she was certain that was so, for she had spent an entire morning exploring its intricacies and loving it into gleaming perfection.

Michael had laughed at first at her intense devotion to the artifacts of his home, but, he, too, loved the treasures of Drumgillan; later he taught her all he knew of their origins, and together they enjoyed vicariously the treasures they would never share in any other way.

He told her of the famed stuccodores, the Francini brothers, who had come to Ireland to adorn the houses of the rich; to decorate the proper compartmentalized geometry of the ceilings, the Francinis had added human figures, nymphs and satyrs, cherubs with dangling chubby legs, friezes that told intricate tales to any observer subtle enough to understand. Robert Adam, too, had sculpted animals, birds, and garlands in his time, and Robert West, the Irish stuccodore portraitist, had once been asked to do a likeness of Michael's grandfather in the small study off the library.

Aubusson carpets graced the parqueted floors of many rooms, and the Gobelin tapestry in the dining room was worth a fortune. Michael told her how it had been woven, and she was awed by its painstaking intricacy.

The sporting pictures of horses and hounds in endless pursuit that were scattered all around were unappealing to Mary, but Arthur O'Connor's landscapes, and the delicate, graceful pastels by Healey, thrilled her. And when she was shown the engraving of Drumgillan itself in Thomas Milton's book of the Great Houses, she felt a pride as glowing as if the home had been her own.

Michael loved the continuity of the old; he felt a sense of history and pride in the antique artifacts that graced his home. He found that lately, in sharing the visceral connection he felt for Drumgillan with Mary, a certain sense of dynasty had been awakened in him; a proprietary emotion that would have wished to pass on substance to a son.

One day, several weeks later, Michael was on his way back to the house from the stable when his ears caught the sound of his brother's meticulously cultivated voice, arrogant and angry, coming from the vicinity of the kitchen. How odd, he thought to himself. Randy never has anything whatsoever to do with the servants, and I've certainly never known him to frequent the kitchen.

Straining to catch the drift of what was causing the ruckus, he was startled to hear Mary's soft voice, frightened and pleading, following by two harsh slaps resounding in the still air of the June dusk. He saw the girl, face pink with shame, holding her apron to her cheek and running across the kitchen garden toward the pasture. Cook ran after her to the edge of the lettuce rows, shouting incomprehensibly before subsiding into sputtering silence just as Michael, perplexed by the strange scene, reached the kitchen door. Randolph stood, hands on slender hips, a sadistic smirk on his lean face, as Cook ran back in.

"Begging Your Lordship's pardon, I'm sure," groveled the corpulent old woman. "I'll beat the tar out of the young fool meself for it, you can be sure of it." She curtsied ungracefully, nearly falling, and waddled off, muttering, at the sight of Michael.

"What's all the fuss about, Randy?" Michael tried to sound disinterested. "You might have disturbed those resting in the family plot with the noise of it."

Randolph smiled slyly. "Why, I caught that slut of a red-haired kitchen wench stealing a silver spoon from the cabinet, and when I grabbed her wrist and pulled it from her grasp, she had the audacity to fight me. I had to chastise her, of course. She ran to the kitchen and I caught up with her, and with the help of Cook, I gave her a wallop or two for her pains. She'll not be so quick to steal again, I imagine.''

He reached with a studied nonchalance for a pear from the bowl on the table, and began to nibble uninterestedly at its pulp; Michael had to fight his own revulsion at his brother's unmitigated ugliness.

"I see," he said quietly. "And what do you know of this, Cook?"

"We'll have to be getting rid of that one, I think, Mr. Michael, for this is the third or fourth time Mr. Randolph has had to chase her for doing something wrong.''

Michael's head snapped up, awareness dawning. Why in God's name hadn't Mary told him? No, of course, she *couldn't* tell him of his brother's lechery, lest she place him in a position of having to respond to it. Randolph was a rotter where women were concerned; he didn't seem to like them much, but he lusted after them well enough nonetheless. Michael should have realized a girl like Mary wouldn't escape his notice forever. His heart filled with revulsion at the idea of his brother's hands on her sweet body, he turned abruptly and left the kitchen, Randolph's amused laughter following him.

He had no doubt where Mary would go at such a moment, for it was her only possible haven, and he covered the ground swiftly, legs striding angrily over the green field and through the marshy bog to the cottage. He found her lying in a heap on the bed near the hearth, legs folded up in a fetal position, sobbing almost soundlessly. He turned her face to his own and saw that it was swollen and tear-streaked, so that she tried to hide it from him by burrowing into his warm hard chest.

"Mary, why didn't you tell me that Randy has been after you, lass? Did you not know I would protect you?"

She looked up stricken and sobbed afresh into his jacket. He patted her head as if she were a child, until the muffled sobbing began to subside.

"I was afraid if you knew of it," she sniffled into his shirt, "you would fight with him, and they would know of our friendship and send me away from Drumgillan, Michael."

"I'll not let them send you away, Mary. I'll find a way for us, you'll see." His voice was husky with concern. Her heart pounded precipitately, and she wanted to cling to him and not let go. He lay down heavily beside her and cradled her head on his warm shoulder.

"Michael, sometimes it feels so hopeless to me. I think of you endlessly, so I can't think of anything else. I can't even talk to God, don't you see, since the other day with you, for I lusted after you with my whole heart and that's the truth of it! It wasn't me who stopped us, Michael. I'm not the girl I was before I felt your strong arms about me. I'm desperate if it seems I may be taken away from here, and yet there can be no future for us if I stay, and we both know it in our hearts. Sometimes I think I'll die of the longing that I feel for you, Michael, and it's more likely that I'll die of the hopelessness." And she began to cry again, soundless tears overflowing her eyes and making her cheeks glisten in the faint light of the cottage.

He thought of the honest tenderness of her, and of the impossibly precarious position she teetered in; to go home to her father would mean being buried alive, nothing to hope for but marriage to a clodlike farmer from the village. It was unthinkable. To remain on Drumgillan was fraught with danger—some from his brother, but the greater portion from his own love and desire for her. Michael was almost as despondent as she.

He cradled the disconsolate girl in his arms for a long while, rocking gently back and forth—wishing there were an answer to their dilemma. Finally the soft warmth of her body so close to his made thinking superfluous. Almost without caring if it was wise or not, he tipped her face toward his own and kissed her mouth with longing. Mary kissed him too, with so fiery a response that he was lost in its urgency. Michael felt the rising insistence of his own desire. He reached beneath the collar of her dress and pushed it down over her shoulder, kissing the hollow of her throat, struggling to free her breasts from the fabric that entrapped them, needing her beyond all thought of safety. She arched herself to him, all the strength of her young womanhood bursting the seams of her self-control, just as she'd known it would.

"I love you, I love you," she whispered over and over, clutching his hard, strong body to her own, pressing instinctively against the strength she felt rising against her belly, rubbing herself against his protective form, so overcome by the powerful feel of him that thought was useless. Too late for anything but emotion, past caring or wanting to, she opened herself and pulled him to her, filled with a sense of wonderment at the beauty of holding a man within her most private places, of feeling the enormous weight of him on top of her. Never in her life had she experienced anything like the sense of safety the huge male form provided, with its limbs wrapped around her, head bent to her body in an ancient ritual. It was beyond all fathomable beauty, the strength of him between her legs an unbearable perfection.

"Oh, Michael, I never never knew 'twas like this between a man and a woman. . . ." She couldn't help but say it, for the moment was entirely to be savored, devoured, understood. The time would come when the piper must be paid, but not this astonishing, beautiful moment. She opened her eyes almost inadvertently when he was inside her, for the fullness of him had blocked all other senses. She opened her eyes and looked up into his face, which had been transformed by passion into something fierce and primal. The look on his face took her breath away, as much as did the sense of him deep within her, for there was the same primitive power in both. It was all worth it. No matter what would happen to her as a result of this feeling, it would be worth it to her to have lived this one perfect moment. She thought she might die of it; she did not want it ever to end.

Michael lay back on the pillow exhausted and happy after their love. He made a nest for her, tucking her carefully into the crook of his arm, her head resting blissfully on his strong shoulder.

"My darling girl," he said with a soft, sweet smile on his lips, "you are as perfect as I knew you would be and I love you very much."

"Have you done that with many girls, Michael?" Mary asked. She seemed to be drifting placidly, now that the moment had passed, and her voice was small and far away. The young man looked down at her to see if she was teasing him, or vexed, and he was surprised to see her smiling contentedly.

"I've been to bed with my share of women, Mary, I'll not lie to you. But no, lass. What just happened between us has not happened to me with many women. I think, just with you." She was quite ready to believe him, for it was beyond all possibility that such a thing could happen more than once in a single lifetime.

10

"Lusty is precisely the correct adjective, Jeffrey!" Lady Geraldine said emphatically in response to her husband's upturned eyebrow at her use of the word. "I'm afraid that in all probability your son has gotten one of the housemaids with child!" Lady Geraldine delivered the incriminating information with a certain amount of malevolent relish, and waited expectantly for an explosion that never came.

"You don't say so, Geraldine? I hadn't a clue he had his eye on any of the servants. Which one was it, my dear?" Sir Jeffrey's paternal chuckle died aborning, as the disapproving scowl on Lady Geraldine's face made any serious display of mirth dangerous.

"Her name is Mary Dalton, if you must know, and her father is a farmer with one of the thirty-year leases. She is the tall redheaded girl with the strange green eyes who works in the kitchen and sometimes serves table when extra help is needed. Rather pretty for an Irish girl, it seems to me, and unconscionably young."

"Do we know the child is Michael's, Geraldine? What has the lad to say about it?"

"Your son has taken full responsibility for the girl's condition— and says he is in love with her, if you don't mind!" Her voice was frozen with contempt. "He says he wishes to marry her. Jeffrey, you simply must take this seriously! It is utterly deplorable! I have been telling you for years that Michael's perpetual involvement with those disgusting people would lead to some tragedy, and now it is upon us. This problem is simply not going to disappear because we ignore it. Michael is behaving quite impossibly. If we aren't careful, we could be greatly embarrassed."

Sir Jeffrey put both his large hands on his desk and began to drum his fingers impatiently over its brilliantly polished surface.

"I'd better have a talk with the boy myself, my dear. I'm quite in agreement with you that Michael has acted foolishly, but after all, these things do happen. We are not the first, nor the last, family to produce an illegitimate child. Happens every day; matter of fact, my father had several, as I recall. You know how damnably fertile these farm girls are. No great harm in it, if everything is handled discreetly."

Lady Geraldine looked as if she might implode from barely

contained wrath. Her husband had seldom seen her so close to losing control. Women could be so damned unreasonable when it came to a little sporting sex. Sir Jeffrey did not wish to pursue this conversation with his wife any further.

"I shall handle this, Geraldine. Too indelicate for you to soil your pretty hands on it, my dear. Best leave it all to me." And he purposefully put his spectacles onto his nose, to make it clear to her that he was a busy man and the discussion had no need to continue.

"I shall be most delighted to allow you to handle it, Jeffrey," his wife said with an icy malice. "Doubtless you have far more experience in dealing with whores than I."

And before he could respond, she turned on her heel and swept regally from the library.

Michael Hartington lay on the grass, his arm thrown up over his eyes, shielding them from the hazy sunlight, lost in deep, soul-searching thought. He did not intend to leave the spot until he had worked things through. He was sick to death with the uncertainty and the frustration.

When he'd first become aware of the probability of Mary's condition, he had been amazed by his own response to the realization: one almost of relief, as if the reality of this payment for their pleasure might finally precipitate him into taking action in the strange stalemate that was their lives.

One step at a time, he told himself, lying in the damp warmth of the afternoon. One step at a time and we'll work this thing out. He began to organize his disarrayed thoughts into some semblance of order. Most important of all, he loved Mary—enough to brazen out whatever was necessary, he suspected. The idea of having a son or a daughter thrilled him too, although it angered him to think of the burden that illegitimacy would place on the child. His own financial resources were limited. Until Uncle Ned's money came through when he turned thirty, he was beholden to his family for support—a most unpleasant idea in his current predicament. "I love Mary!" He said it emphatically, as if to remind himself that at the end of the dilemma, that fact was all that mattered. Then he laughed aloud at himself, and his elegant chestnut stallion, which had been happily grazing nearby, lifted its muzzle and whinnied as if in reply.

He would find a way.

*   *   *

"Bit of a pickle you've gotten yourself into this time, my boy," said father to son as they walked through the sculptured gardens that occupied the attention of nine full-time gardeners to keep it trim. The morning was nippy and the air redolent with the scent of perfectly tended roses and rhododendrons.

"It isn't the first or last such indiscretion anyone of our class has ever had to deal with, Michael," his father was saying. "Matter of fact, perhaps you should know I got myself into a similar fix when I was about your age. Don't want you to doubt the seriousness of what's been done, my boy, but nonetheless it's quite handleable, as I see it."

The older man cleared his throat uncomfortably and stole a furtive sideways glance at his son. He was unnerved by the boy's curious silence, but, assuming it to be due primarily to embarrassment, he continued.

"There are several ways in which we can deal with this, my boy. The girl will of course have to leave Drumgillan. We can provide her with a sum of money, if you'd like, to tide her over until the baby comes and then we can help her make arrangements with one of those adoption places in Dublin or even London. She won't want to keep the child, of course, or she'll have the devil's own time getting work as a servant, I expect."

The look on Michael's face as he turned to confront his father was a medley of emotions. He must keep control of his volatile temper, he reminded himself. There was no way to make this hideous situation turn out favorably if he antagonized Sir Jeffrey, for he was the only possible ally. Without him, Mary would be at the mercy of his mother and her own family.

"Father. Don't say any more, please. I must tell you how it is for me and hope that you may be able to find it in your heart to understand what, I have no doubt, no one else will."

Sir Jeffrey felt a curious tightening in his throat. He looked appraisingly at Michael and saw a younger but more vulnerable replica of himself. Sir Jeffrey wished suddenly that he had noticed before now that his son had grown to be a man.

"Mary is not, Father, as Mother paints her to be. She is soft and loving, honest and intelligent. I want to marry her, Father."

"How can you even say it aloud, Michael, out of the question as it is! Many of our class have loved Irish girls, son, no one knows their virtues better than I. They have a vigor about them, a vitality, that our women somehow lack. God alone knows why it should be.

Perhaps we breed it out of them. I know what a great joy it is to be loved by a lusty Irish lass. I know, my boy, I know." He paused for a breath. "That doesn't mean we can marry them."

"Does it mean nothing to you that the child is mine, Father? Your first grandchild?"

"Don't go melodramatic on me, young man. Of course I'd be overjoyed to have a grandchild, a son of yours, but it would have been a bit more sensible of you to provide me with one on the proper side of the blanket!"

"I love Mary, Father. I have thought this through carefully, and I do not wish to abandon her."

"Very noble, I'm sure, but not very realistic, Michael. What precisely do you intend to use for money, if we have done with you? You are barely twenty-one years of age, without a university degree and with no profession whatsoever. You will not merely be laughed at by your peers, you will be ostracized, totally. You face precisely the choice that I once faced, and you must choose as I did. There is no alternative for you, whatsoever!" The emphasis he placed on the last word pleased Sir Jeffrey; he thought he was handling this thing quite well.

His face softened, just a little, at the pain in his son's darkening eyes. "Don't torment yourself and the girl by holding out hope where there is none, lad." He said it softly; they walked on in silence for a moment.

"What happened, Father, to the girl in your life? What happened to her child?"

The older man folded his hands behind his back deliberately. He didn't answer immediately, his face averted, as if considering carefully the reply, or perhaps remembering. Sir Jeffrey's voice was strained and husky when he answered his son quietly.

"They died in a workhouse in Dublin, Michael. I had been sent abroad and didn't hear of it till I returned, of course. Damned sad thing it was. I nearly came undone. The boy would be thirty years of age now, if things had not been as they were."

Michael caught up with his father and, standing in front of the older, now quite somber man, forced his gaze to his own. The young man's voice was low and steady when he spoke, but tense with emotion.

"Would you be party to another such injustice, Father?"

"Don't try to manipulate me with my own sorrows, Michael. There is no way for you to do what you propose. I will help you keep the girl from a bad end, but beyond that I can do nothing. If you persist in this madness, you must do so at your own risk. Do I make myself perfectly clear?''

Michael stood quietly for a moment, digesting what his father had said, before replying.

''I understand what you're saying, Father. I cannot expect you to solve this problem for me. That I must do myself.''

Sir Jeffrey looked relieved. He had feared the turn the conversation was taking.

''There's a good lad. Shall I ask Mr. O'Leary to have a word with the girl's family?''

The handsome young man looked sadly at the older one, so like him in appearance.

''I believe you mistake me, Father. I don't expect you to help me; I fully understand the delicacy of your position. But I have no intention of abandoning Mary or my child. I shall have to find a way to deal with this myself.'' The words hung quietly in the air for a moment, then with neither shyness nor seeming self-consciousness, Michael reached out suddenly and clasped his father's large, freckled hands with his own, squeezing them in an oddly moving gesture, as if to say he understood and forgave; then he turned abruptly and walked off alone in the direction of the lough.

''Well, I'll be damned!'' murmured Sir Jeffrey under his breath as he watched his son disappear from sight in the deepening gloom. He remained for a moment lost in a kind of sadness. Having stood very still for what seemed a long while, he spoke aloud to himself in the eerie quiet of the garden. ''I'd give ten years of my life to be able to look back and say I'd done the same as that.''

11

Christopher Dalton's face was red as a cabbage. He hammered his fists on the mantel and stomped about the cottage with such ferocious steps that the crockery shook in its place.

''Thank the Lord your mother isn't alive to see us disgraced as we are!'' Mary stood mortified and white as a Mass card, near the door.

Her brothers, with the exception of Rory, had stormed out of the cottage as she came sheepishly in, contemptuously shouldering past her without so much as a word. She had committed the unpardonable sin of embarrassing them by being the main topic of conversation at O'Shaugnessy's Public House over the past twenty-four hours.

"You're a disgraceful, ungrateful slut of a girl," roared the irate father. "I'll have no part of you or your ill-begotten child! Let your precious Lordship sweep up after himself, I say."

"You don't know what you're saying, Da. You don't mean these things, surely." Mary was struggling not to cry; she was also beginning to be angry. Her father ceased his pacing long enough to confront her already slightly swollen body. "I'll have no bastard son of an Englishman in my household. You've made your own bed, Mary, and you can damned well lie in it too. Didn't I warn you not to go to that house when you wanted to leave your own home?"

"Aye, you did that. And fast enough did you change your mind when you found another woman for your kitchen work, you old hypocrite!"

Rory stood up at that, for he knew the fur would begin to fly in earnest now. Mary had Christopher's own temper, as well as his red hair, and when they were fired up, it wasn't beyond either of them to do something that couldn't easily be undone. Two redheads in a house is the Devil's own invention, thought Rory as he placed himself strategically between the two.

"Get out of my house and bad cess to you, Mary. You're no child of mine," shouted the father, pushing Rory aside.

"Nor are you my father any longer, and good riddance I say!"

Mary's flaming hair bounced, as if electrified, as she threw her woolen cloak about her thin shoulders defiantly and marched toward the door.

"Don't do this, Mary!" Rory cried. "Don't leave like this. He's only riled up because Father McKuen read you out from the pulpit on Sunday, and he's heard nothing else from Eileen's viperous tongue these last twenty-four hours."

Mary stopped with her hand on the door handle and turned to her brother with a stunned look.

"Read me out from the pulpit? What in God's name do you mean by that, Rory?"

"I never heard the like of it, Mary. I wasn't there, of course, but I've heard it word for word from a hundred lips by now. He called you a whore and worse. That squint-hearted young prig said he'd put the ban on any one of the parishioners that helped either you or Michael.''

"The ban, you say. And for what reason?''

"He said you were flaunting your sin by planning to stay on Drumgillan. That he'll have no parishioners of his trafficking with a woman who's living in open sin like there was nothin' to it.''

"Blessed God, Rory. Does he know what he's saying? Even if I could stay, wouldn't I be punished enough by having my baby unwed, and living in sight of the man I love, knowing he can do nothing to change things for us? Has the man no heart at all, do you think?''

"From what I've observed of him, Mary, they can use his heart over again when he dies, he'll have made that little use of it.''

Christopher took a step toward his son, fist raised almost automatically in a menacing arc.

"I'll have no blasphemy in me own home against a priest of God. Do you hear me, boy?''

"I hear you, Father,'' said Rory disdainfully, "but I think you'd be better off if you used your temper on the priest and took the side of your own flesh and blood, instead of that of a shriveled up celibate with a perverted hatred of anything that smacks of love.''

"My children have all gone mad.'' Christopher dropped his fist impotently and thundered out of the dim room, leaving brother and sister staring sadly at each other.

"What will you do, Mary?'' The simple question broke the spell of anger, and with it went Mary's bravado.

She had been trying not to think about the child she carried, for when she did, her spirits either soared or sank. The morning sickness had forced her daily to remember her reality, waking and retching in the morning cold, cloak around nightgown, hair in disarray, sticking to her sweaty cheeks. She was sick to death and scared by the enormity of it. Then she would think of Michael and his sweet arms around her, soothing and comforting, saying it would all be all right, that he'd find a way. His tenderness and strength were a bulwark against the world, if only in her dreams.

"Mary, what does your lad say of it?''

She looked up, wary, to see if Rory, too, was an enemy of Michael's, but it was clear in his honest eyes that he was only concerned about her safety.

"He told His Lordship he wanted to marry me, and a terrible row it caused. Michael has no money of his own because he's the younger son, Rory, so he's trying to work something out with his father, to help us.''

The man, her brother, nodded in a very jaded male way—he had heard of too many other situations like this one to have any illusions.

"Do you trust him to do right by you, Mary?"

"Aye, Rory. I do." It was a simple statement, but it was the truth. Rory sighed and patted his sister on the shoulder, something he had seldom done before. Physical displays of affection were rare in the Dalton cottage.

"I'm going to America, Mary. I've been making plans these three years past, as you know, and I've almost enough saved for the passage and a stake when I get there. But I'll not go if you need me here, girl. So you must let me know how it fares with you and your lad, if he's able to get any concessions from his family and all. For, Mary, if he backs down on you, girl, you are in a fair-sized kettle of fish. Especially since that blight of a pastor has stuck his nose into it.''

"Why do you think he did such a thing, Rory? I've never heard the like of it, have you?"

"No, Mary. He did it because he's out to make a name for himself in his new parish. Don't you see, girl, with this single sermon he has ingratiated himself with the parishioners, for he's shown the old biddies in no uncertain terms what the wages of sin are; and at the same time he's endeared himself to Lady Geraldine and her darlin' Randolph, for neither one of them has a warm spot for your Michael in their tiny hearts, and like as not they'd be happy to see him safely off, in a lovely regiment, somewhere far from here, love. You must face it, Mary. Your future is scragged with pitfalls.''

"So it is, Rory. So it is. But thinking on the bleakness of it all isn't going to help me now, don't you see? I'm nearly five months pregnant and I'm going to have to find a way to live through these other four months no matter what the future holds for me. They want to send me away to some place in Dublin for unwed girls, but Michael has told them no. So I must wait to see if he has a plan he can make them hold to.''

"Mary, Mary, why did you do it, girl? Did you never think on the consequences of such an impossible match?"

She stared at her brother as if considering whether he could bear to hear the truth of it from her. Then she said quietly, "Did you never long to feel the arms of one you love around you, Rory?"

He smiled a crooked little half smile at his sister and shook his dark head sadly. "Aye, girl. That, indeed, I have. 'Tis always easier for a man in these things. We haven't as much to lose in return for a little comfort, have we, lass? Come, Mary, fasten up your cloak and I'll be walking you back to the Big House, for I fear it isn't safe for you in the neighborhood just now, with tempers running so high."

The frightened, heartsick girl took her brother's muscular arm gratefully, and left the home of her childhood for the last time.

"Father." Michael's voice broke the library's paneled stillness.

"Father, may I have a word with you? I've been giving considerable thought to our conversation in the rose garden, and I'd like you to hear me out."

"Certainly, my boy. I, too, have thought of little else these past few days. Come in, lad, and sit with me."

Sir Jeffrey was sitting in front of the huge library fireplace, in the room that was his sanctuary.

"Father, I shall lay all my cards on the table with you. I think I have figured out a way for everyone to win in this, but I shall need your help to make it so."

"I cannot promise you that, Michael."

"Just hear me out, Father, that's all I ask, and then think on it. You're a fair man. I shall abide by your judgment."

Sir Jeffrey nodded.

"Let us be honest with each other, Father. I am a younger son and have limited prospects here. Randolph will inherit, and he is not the one to share willingly, so in a few years' time I shall have to leave Drumgillan, come what may."

The older man cocked his head to listen intently. He liked the lad's candor, it was refreshing.

"When I am thirty, I shall inherit a small sum of money from Uncle Ned's will."

"Hardly enough to live on . . ." interrupted Sir Jeffrey.

"No. Not enough to live on, but enough for a start somewhere else, which is what I propose." Michael took a breath.

"I propose that you let Mary stay on Drumgillan till then. We can surely spare one of the many little cottages on the land to her and the child, and I shall hardly be the first Hartington to have a mistress, if you will, on the estate. I shall make them my responsibility, of course. I know I haven't any money, Father, but I am a hard worker, and perhaps I can earn a place for her by taking on the responsibility of the racers. I know nearly as much about horses as you do. They're in my blood as they are in yours, and added to that I've 'hobnobbed,' as Mother would say, with the grooms and trainers so long that I know more than most any of our class about the beasts. I can help you put together a stable of winners, Father, and you could pay me enough in return to take care of Mary and our child.''

Sir Jeffrey was studying his son with a new fascination—damned inventive of him to have come up with such a scheme. The biggest obstacle, of course, would be Geraldine, but perhaps that could be got around.

"When I'm thirty, we will take the inheritance and leave Drumgillan. Randy will be thrilled to be rid of me, and Mother would hardly mourn my loss. My brother will surely provide you with the requisite legitimate heirs and a suitable daughter-in-law, so I needn't worry that I've left you high and dry from the point of view of dynasty. Father, don't you see, everyone wins! Mary and the child are safe, Randolph gets a future unencumbered by a younger rival, Mother gets her peace of mind, you get your horses, and I get Mary.''

The old man leaned far back in his leather armchair and ruminated for a moment or two on what had been said. Then he laughed aloud and leaned forward toward his son, his large hands on the knees of his riding breeches.

"To be honest with you, Michael, lad, I wouldn't have thought you'd come up with anything so imaginative.'' Sir Jeffrey, whose inclination it had been to help his son, as long as there would be no embarrassment from the situation, felt somewhat relieved. Not an inventive man himself, he was always impressed by inventiveness in others, and this scheme had possibilities. After all, a little harmless sex never hurt any young man. The novelty of it would soon wear off, and there would be plenty of time later for a suitable match to be found for his son.

"Then you'll consider it.''

"Yes, I shall consider it, son, for it has a sporting sound. More or less gives everyone a fighting chance, doesn't it, now?'' He looked directly at the boy hunched forward worriedly on the massive armchair that matched his own. "I haven't said yes, mind you, but I will consider it.'' And he chuckled just a little as he settled back against the comfortable leather. It was a damned inventive solution.

*   *   *

"I will not allow this, Jeffrey! I will simply not allow this to happen." Lady Geraldine was beside herself at the idea of Mary remaining on Drumgillan.

"Now, my dear, you are becoming entirely too wrought up over this incident. I feel strongly that you should leave it in my hands."

"Your hands, indeed. And a fine mess you seem to have made of it already, telling Michael you would consider this utterly ludicrous plan of his."

"You forget yourself, Geraldine. I am, after all, your husband, and while I fully understand your concern over this matter, I have no intention whatsoever of being spoken to as if I were a recalcitrant servant. I simply won't allow it!" Sir Jeffrey mimicked her earlier statement with annoyance. He had really not thought her capable of forgetting her duty to her husband so completely.

Geraldine Montrose Hartington stared at her husband with loathing. She chided herself for having underestimated her adversary.

"You are, of course, quite right, Jeffrey. I apologize for my rudeness. But you must know how distasteful I find this situation."

"Yes, yes, I do, my dear." Sir Jeffrey was somewhat mollified by the apology; even though he was quite aware of its insincerity, he had won the point. It remained to be seen who would win the game.

"You don't seriously mean to allow the boy to contemplate marriage, do you, Jeffrey?"

"Certainly not. Furthest thing from my mind. That's not the point at all. Don't you see, my dear? The boy is all het up at the moment about this little baggage he fancies himself in love with. The safest thing we can do is let him play out the game. I was a young man myself, Geraldine, and I know whereof I speak. To force him to betray the Irish girl will back him into a corner, and he isn't the kind to go down without a fight. Mark my words, if you push him too far, he might do something quite irrational." He paused for dramatic effect. "Might even become a Papist and marry her, or some other such madness. Or he might bolt, Geraldine. Take the girl and what money he can lay hands on and just clear out. I've spoken with him at length. Believe me, I know his temperament."

"I simply cannot believe you are allowing your own son to intimidate you like this, Jeffrey. He has you quite hamstrung."

"Quite the contrary, my dear. I am simply explaining the dangers of forcing a high-spirited racer into the wrong stall. If we let him play it out, he'll tire of the girl soon enough. He's entirely too lusty to be pleased by hanging about waiting for some peasant Madonna to give birth to a bastard. Mark my words, if we give him enough latitude, this whole morbid business will peter out in a few months' time."

"Why can't you simply send him away somewhere and deal with the girl yourself?"

Sir Jeffrey looked at his wife with calculation. She really was being cold-blooded about all this; wouldn't be the same if it were Randolph's indiscretion in question.

"You'd be singing a different tune if it were Randolph who'd gotten himself in this pickle, wouldn't you, Geraldine?"

"Randolph would never have done such a disgusting thing."

"Oh, come now, madam, surely you must be aware that Randolph beds anything he can lay his ruddy hands on, some of whom are none too willing, as I hear it."

"What do you mean by that?"

"I mean, Geraldine, that your precious Randolph is a perfect rotter when it comes to women and a great many other things. I have absolutely no doubt that you are quite right in suggesting we would never be holding this conversation about him, for the simple reason that he would never have the balls to stand up for a girl he'd gotten into trouble."

"If you intend to resort to the use of foul language, I shall be forced to leave the room."

"Geraldine, I have seldom quarreled with you where our sons are concerned, despite the fact that I've seen you ignore Michael for a lifetime and pamper Randolph into a spoiled and conscienceless prig, without so much as a scrap of humanity about him. You have done your job as you see fit, and I have said little enough about it. But they are children no longer, Geraldine. They are men. I am better equipped to deal with what has happened, and by God, I intend to do so."

She stared at him in dumbfounded silence. It was so long since she had thought of him as other than a fool to be manipulated, that she found the current scene utterly incomprehensible; she hadn't thought he had that kind of spunk. She wondered wryly if it were possible to admire someone and despise him simultaneously.

"You will rue this decision, Jeffrey. You will live to see that you are wrong and I am right!"

"That well may be, Geraldine. But it would have been cleverer of you not to have told me so, my dear."

Geraldine Hartington stood facing her husband, bursting with unspoken wrath. She had been bested. But the game wasn't over yet.

12

Mary was six months gone with child when she moved her meager belongings into the small mud-walled cottage that would be her home until the longed-for "better future" dawned.

She stood in the doorway of the little house and thanked God fervently that she wasn't further along in the pregnancy; there was so much work that needed doing. Cobwebs hung from crannies, dust blanketed the atmosphere, and a rheumatic-feeling dampness clung in the thatching, as if there hadn't been a fire's warming grace there for a hundred years. She smiled ruefully to realize how different the cottage seemed to her now, than when she and Michael had made their way to its shelter so many months before. Lord, that seemed lifetimes ago.

"Michael, Michael." She spoke his name diffidently in the eerie stillness of the empty cottage that had once rung with their lust and laughter. "Will we live through this time?" She was suddenly frightened and so alone. Michael had told her he would come to her as soon as he could get away discreetly. Please God, let it be soon, she prayed almost audibly.

She and Michael had won, for the moment; yet the future looked intolerable. Even the simple truth of sleeping alone in this desolate place seemed unutterably scary. Used to a house alive with burly brothers, as she was, or to the comforting presence of the other servants in the Big House, never, until today, had she faced the reality of life alone.

Instead of beginning the work that needed to be done, Mary sat down heavily in the broken, dust-covered rocking chair, and let her mind wander where it would.

At least I haven't been sent away to Dublin, and Michael will soon be here to hold me. She said it comfortingly to herself, but her mind was uneasy. Ah, but I look so awful these days, perhaps he won't want me very much longer. No, no, that's not true, it argued. Don't think such things of him; he's loyal and loving, and if we've come this far, we'll make it through the rest. But what have I to offer him, will you tell me that? Poor and ignorant and without a pretty stick of clothing to beguile a man . . . The monologous debate kept rhythm with her rocking.

After moments that seemed suspended in time, she tied a scrap of scarf about her hair and began to clean. Making things pretty and livable is an act of creation in its own way, she thought; opening wide the door and windows, she swept the hearth. She lit a turf fire in the fireplace and made a list, in her own mind, of what she would need to make the place a home. Curtains first, pots to cook in, spoons and forks for eating, a knife to chop with. There were chairs and a table already in evidence, although in a tragic state of disrepair. Perhaps Rory would see to them, for he was so good with his hands. She would need a cradle for the wee babe; for the first time she thought of it sweetly. Somehow, being mistress of her own home, however bare and poor it was, made motherhood more plausible.

She was feeling better. How odd that simply putting the place to rights had such a calming effect, she thought. She smiled as she pulled a pottery teapot from her bag; blurry figures languished in a Chinese garden, frozen forever beneath its primitive glaze. Rory had given it to her the day before, as a good-luck token for her new life; she knew he had taken the cost of it from his precious passage money, a brave gesture. A splendid beginning, in its own way.

The child had begun to kick furiously this past month or so. She placed her hand on her belly and allowed herself the pleasure of its movements; she had jiggled him into wakefulness with her action. When first she had noticed the life within her, she remembered, it had been no more than a tiny flutter—a movement so small and benign, she'd had to "listen" carefully for the feel of it. Now the kicks and thrusts had become quite constant reminders she was not alone.

She let the sweet remembrance of Michael's arms around her flood her mind. The perfect wonder of his power pouring into her had always calmed her, and she felt revived just thinking of it. She felt womanly standing there in her own little cottage, planning the future. It reminded her, somehow, of the time when the nausea and the imbalance of the first three months of pregnancy had passed, and the more robust strength of the fourth month had suffused her and she had begun to dream again. Yes, that was it—given half a chance, she still knew how to dream. She would hold that thought till Michael came and held her in his arms and made the awesome reality subside into unimportance . . . if only for a little while.

* * *

Michael and Rory sat together on a bale of hay at the back of the forge. One master and one servant, they had developed a grudging camaraderie since Mary's ostracism from the village.

Rory had doggedly taken his sister's side with the family, friends, and neighbors. Not even for the sake of peace and quiet would he allow a word to be said against her in his presence, and Michael, once having witnessed a battle between the burly smithy and the stable hands about his own and Mary's honor, had come to have a warmth of feeling for the taciturn man that he wouldn't have thought possible.

"How goes it with my sister, Michael?" asked the smith, laying aside the book he had been reading prior to Michael's arrival. He always allowed himself fifteen minutes at lunch to "nourish the mind." He had ceased calling Michael "Your Lordship" after they had both engaged in a round of fisticuffs on Mary's behalf at the horse fair, when a neighboring squire had made a derogatory remark about the notorious "whore of Drumgillan" and a fair-sized imbroglio had been the result.

"Well enough, Rory. Worried that the midwife won't attend her when her time comes. I've tried to get her to see Dr. Frank in the village, but she says she'll have none of him."

"Aye," Rory nodded sagely. "Women are a bit strange when they're in the family way. Although I can't say I blame her for wanting a woman to attend her at such a time. She's a mite lonely for the company of women, I'd imagine, Michael."

His ruddy companion nodded affirmatively before continuing the discussion. "We've talked of leaving here, as you're planning to do, Rory. When's your passage booked for?"

"I'll be staying here, I'm thinking, till after the baby comes. I don't like the tone of things in this vicinity since that toothache of a man, Father McKuen, is inciting people to riot over you and Mary."

Michael looked up sharply.

"Do you really think there could be violence, man?"

"I hope not, but I'm not sure. A crowd that thinks it's doing God's own work can be a mighty pain in the ass, as I see it."

Michael laughed and clapped Rory on the shoulder with hearty affection. "Man, you've been a good friend to us in this. I owe you."

"Just take good care of my sister, Michael. She's daft in love with you. I sometimes think she would take on Lucifer and his army to have you and the child that's coming, it's that in love with you she is.''

"And I no less with her, Rory," Michael said with great seriousness, and Rory looked at him with a certain amount of amusement.

"Aye. 'Tis a strange pair you are for sure, Michael. A right strange pair.''

With that he hoisted himself up, wiped his hands on his leather apron, and stretched his short stocky body.

"I may go to see Mrs. O'Flaherty, the midwife, myself before the week is out. She's a fine woman, Michael. I'll see what I can do.''

The taller man nodded, clapped Rory on the shoulder a second time, and left the forge.

Rory silently watched him stride across the stable yard before returning to his work.

13

"How is it with you, Mary?" Michael patted her white, limp arm as she lay on the swaybacked bed they had so often shared, and nervously looked for signs of change.

"You mustn't worry so, Michael," she tried to reassure him. "I can manage for a while longer. Have you spoken with Mrs. O'Flaherty yet? Do you really think that she'll come?''

"I believe she'll come if she can, Mary, but she has the whole of the village against her in this, as well as her husband and the pastor, Father McKuen. It will take great courage for her to oppose them all, lass. I think we'd best rely on Dr. Frank, for he's a fine man and a Protestant, and he has no such compunctions about delivering our child.''

Mary gripped his hand harder as a nauseating pain swept her. She devoutly wished she'd not seen her mother die in childbirth, for the specter of her mother's agony tangled itself into her own pain, and hard as she tried to obliterate the image, it rose in her mind's eye every time her body strained itself toward birth.

"I don't want to die, Michael. 'Tis a terrible way to die.''

Michael bent his body to hers and held her tightly, as if by so doing to absorb the hurt from her terrified body. He cursed his family with every contraction; smug bastards sitting in their manor house, with the safety he longed to provide for Mary.

"I won't let you die, Mary. I'll not leave you except to go for the doctor, when you tell me to do so."

The afternoon seemed endless to Michael, his restlessness mounting with the increasing frequency of Mary's pains. Her body was soaked with sweat, and the bed along with it; she dozed a little between pains and seemed unaware of his presence at least part of the time, as if she were concentrating every ounce of her consciousness on the task at hand.

"I'll not wait any longer, Mary," he said finally late in the afternoon, when he could bear watching no longer. "I must go to fetch the doctor."

"No!" she cried, her voice hard and unlike the mellifluous sound he loved; and half rising from the bed, she reached for him. "It's Mrs. O'Flaherty I need, not the doctor! Don't you see, love, I need a woman, Michael. Please. I need a woman with me now."

Scanlon, Michael's chestnut stallion, felt his master's heels dig deep into his flanks; energized by the emotion he sensed in his rider, the horse flew across the bog and hit the main road just as dusk began to settle over the quiet hillsides. Michael couldn't tell Mary, but he had precious little hope of convincing the woman to assist them, for the collective energies of the entire Catholic community were against it. He knew that when Rory had asked Mrs. O'Flaherty directly if she would come, the midwife had not given him an answer.

He leaped from the saddle, tied Scanlon to a post beside a small pony cart in the yard, and knocked loudly on the cottage door. A dour-looking fifty-five-year-old man opened it, and stood proprietarily in the doorway, blocking entrance.

"My name is Michael Hartington and I'm here to see Mrs. O'Flaherty, if you please, sir."

"Aye. I know who you are," the square-jawed, stocky little man said with some belligerence. "My wife has no desire to see you or your woman."

"Eamon." A stern female voice called from behind the man's back. "Let the man in. I haven't said I wouldn't go to the girl."

Michael seized the man's momentary hesitancy to push past him into the small house.

"Mrs. O'Flaherty, ma'am. My Mary needs you badly. I didn't

know it would be like this for her. She fears the doctor and says she must have a woman to help her with the birth. I understand the pressure being brought to bear on you, ma'am. But if you can find it in your heart to help her, I'd be very grateful. She's in terrible pain.'' The tall, dust-streaked young man with the bearing of a king's son and the terrified face of the first-time father, moved the plump, efficient-looking middle-aged housewife, and she nodded, seeing the worried figure with the practiced eye of one who is seldom fooled by appearances. She said nothing, but began to remove her apron.

''You will not raise a hand to help these sinners!'' a high-pitched male voice trumpeted startlingly from the doorway; none in the room had seen him enter, enmeshed as they were in the dilemma of the moment. Michael turned abruptly to see an ascetic-looking young priest, backed by a crowd of sullen onlookers crowding into the space of the doorway; he wondered how word could have spread so quickly that he was at the midwife's house, then realized that Scanlon was easy to recognize in a land of horse breeders. He remembered, too, that Rory had said the village women had a mathematician's gift for counting on their fingers the delivery date of ''premature'' children.

Mrs. O'Flaherty looked up at the priest and acknowledged his presence, but began to bustle about the kitchen nonetheless, and only when she had finished packing her little carpetbag to her own satisfaction did she speak to him.

''Father, I believe it would be best for you not to interfere in this matter,'' she said steadily. ''Perhaps 'tis not for you to judge them.'' The crowd murmured at her words, and she spoke quickly as if to quiet them. ''I've known the girl since she was a wee babe, Father. She had no mother to help her when she found herself in trouble, and she has need of a woman with her this night. I beg you to leave it alone, Father. Surely a midwife's chore need be no concern of yours.''

''Sin is always a concern of mine, woman,'' hissed the priest with a triumphant ugly smile. ''The girl you speak of has been living in open sin with this man in my parish, and she is under ban of our Holy Mother Church. Go to her now and you risk the wrath of God falling upon your disobedient shoulders.''

Mrs. O'Flaherty cocked her head to the side and paused a moment before answering; when she did, it was in the tone she used to deal with foolish children. ''God has better things to do with His wrath

than that, surely, Father.'' The crowd gasped as with one voice, and
the priest's fanatical face contorted with shock; no one, in his span
as pastor, had ever defied him. There could be no backing down in
front of these people; he must not let this woman flout his authority
with impunity.

"Cross this threshold, woman, to help that whore, and you'll
never again set foot in my church!'' The crowd outside the door,
hanging on every word, murmured at the threat, for it had an
enormity about it that surely no parishioner would risk. The parish
church was the central hub of everything that happened in their small
universe.

Husband and wife looked at each other searchingly as the threat
hung in the night air like a bat. To be ostracized from their little
community could have serious consequences, financial and otherwise.
Mr. O'Flaherty stepped forward.

"Now, Father, don't you be going a little hard on this thing? My
wife has a kind heart and she's not the one to leave a creature,
human or otherwise, in pain if she can help it. Couldn't you find it
in your power to soften to them, just a little, for everyone's sake?''

Ignoring the plea disdainfully, eyes alight with the malignant
fanaticism of the zealot—for this was his first real opportunity to
strike a righteous blow for God—Father McKuen pushed past the
husband and confronted the solid little wife. "You may not leave
this place and go to that sinner,'' he shouted, his shrill voice
reverberating in the stillness of the small house.

Mrs. O'Flaherty closed her eyes for a moment as if in prayer,
crossed herself, and reached out to touch the crucifix held in the
priest's hand, a gentle devout touch. She spoke quietly, but with
deliberation. "It's sad that you're choosing to make such a fuss
about this thing, Father. But after all is said and done, 'tis my own
conscience I must follow . . . and as I see it, I have work to do this
night.''

"You'll do no work of the Devil's, with me here to prevent it.''

"I lost Mary's mother three years ago, Father McKuen. I'll not be
losing Mary too.''

"She can bear her child in her own agony for that is the fruit of
her sin,'' said the priest, pleased with his metaphor even if it was
somewhat convoluted; he spoke triumphantly.

Mrs. O'Flaherty smiled sadly at the young man's callous
righteousness. "Aye, so do we all bear our children, sin or not,

Father. But nonetheless I intend to bring this wane into the world meself.''

"You forget yourself, woman. 'Tis God who brings children into the world.''

The midwife smiled disdainfully at the thought, having seen thirty years' worth of the help that women give Him in the process.

"Aye, and He'll do so with these old hands of mine to help Him this time.'' She looked at him unafraid and, finally, with impatience. "For the love of God, Father, get out of my way!'' Picking up her bag from the floor where she had rested it, she began to move toward the door.

The priest raised his right arm as if to strike the sturdy little woman, and Michael, who had been dumbstruck by the scene unfolding so rapidly before him, reached out to restrain the man; but to his amazement Mr. O'Flaherty's strong arm reached the priest before his.

"I may not agree with what me wife wants to do, Father; but no man, priest or not, will strike me own wife in me own home. I think you had best go.''

Mrs. O'Flaherty signaled with her eyes to her husband, a silent look of gratitude and a thirty-year connection, and Michael saw that there were tears in her eyes. She took Michael by the arm and hurried him out the door and past the angry, surly crowd that was growing rowdy. They could hear the sputtering of Father McKuen behind them. Michael helped her into the little pony cart that stood behind the gate, and turned the cart and Scanlon toward Drumgillan.

Eleven hours and seventeen minutes later, Thomas Michael Dalton pushed his squalling way into being in a tiny mud-walled cottage at the edge of his father's world.

14

Mercifully the pastoral career of Father Francis X. McKuen at Drumgillan was short-lived. His zealous pursuit of sinners, and his fanatical zest in rooting out the sins of the flesh, had brought him quickly to the attention of his superiors, who reasoned that a young man of such incorruptible moral fiber might have invaluable talents to offer to his church. In a larger, richer parish these talents would undoubtedly find their way to the surface, they reasoned, and so nine seemingly long years after Father McKuen's arrival in the sleepy little farm town, he was off to greener parochial fields.

Father McKuen stood in the rectory of St. Boniface Church, carefully brushing the cassock he would wear to the farewell supper the ladies of the parish had planned for him. He had an aversion to dirt and untidiness that rivaled his aversion to sin, and, if the truth were known, he was thrilled that his next assignment promised a fine, newly built rectory, replete with polished wooden floors and all the amenities a man of his station justly required. He had, of course, accepted the dreary little parish of St. Boniface as a mortification God required of him, but nonetheless, having satisfactorily passed that particular trial, he was elated to be moving on. Father McKuen hurried his cassock-brushing just a trifle, for the rickety sound of a jaunting car outside the window told him that the pastor who was to replace him in this backwater parish had arrived on the three o'clock train and been dutifully picked up at the station.

Father Joseph O'Hanlon, the new arrival at Drumgillan, was cut from a different ecclesiastical cloth. He was old and gentle, worn thin by the sorrows of a lifetime of impoverished parishes in other backwaters, all over Ireland. Having long ago reasoned that there was no asceticism as great as that practiced unwittingly by the poor, he had conducted his ministries on the principle that the corporal works of mercy were his own personal mandate. He comforted, visited, cherished, and fed as many of God's children as he could, and tended to take a compassionate view toward sinners that was most unorthodox. In fact he had over the years evolved a lenient and loving brand of theology that was quite the despair of his superiors. Nonetheless, it was apparent to all who knew him that Father O'Hanlon was a holy man, so that not even the bishop had ever questioned his devotion to God or to his Church.

Father O'Hanlon straightened his long, cranelike body as he laboriously left the jaunting car, and rearranged the perpetual wrinkles in his threadbare cassock. When there came a choice between a new cassock and giving a few pennies more to the needy, he had always decided that his current cassock would do quite well a little longer, and the old garment had responded by developing an odd sort of patina and a coat of permanent wrinkling, like a thin black parchment. He walked serenely to the rectory door.

Father McKuen eyed the new pastor with immediate distaste. Any man that old, who was only deemed worthy of being given a parish

the like of St. Boniface, was obviously held in no great esteem by
the bishop. He offered his delicate hand begrudgingly, and was
surprised by the firm grasp of the old, slender fingers that clasped
his own.

"Father Joseph O'Hanlon, at your service, sir," said the old man
in a brogue thick enough to slice with a fork.

"Father McKuen, sir."

" 'Tis a lovely parish you have here, Father; full of soft green
fields and an abundance of God's blessings. I was hoping you might
tell me a bit about your parishioners before you leave. 'Tis always a
mighty help to know a bit about who needs what, before they need
it, if you know what I mean." The old eyes twinkled with merriment,
and the young man's stomach knotted in disgust. If there was one
thing he did *not* intend to do on his last day in Drumgillan, it was to
waste his time talking about the petty problems of his erstwhile
flock.

"Yes, I see what you mean, Father, although there's not a great
deal that is worth taking time to discuss, in truth. It is very similar, I
expect, to all the other Irish parishes you've been in." The old priest
smiled at the barely veiled derision in the younger one's voice and
manner, but said nothing. "There is, however, one rather peculiar
situation that you should be aware of, before you begin your ministry."

"And what might that be, Father?" The old priest lingered a bit
on the priestly title, as if to call attention to it. Father McKuen
looked at him cautiously to see if disrespect had been intended, but
decided the slight was an imagined one.

The younger man cleared his throat before beginning. "His Lordship has a younger son named Michael, who some years ago got one
of our parishioners into trouble. Distressingly enough, instead of
sending the girl off somewhere to have her child discreetly and make
atonement for her sin, this young man somehow convinced his
family to let the woman remain on the estate."

"Did he, now?" said Father O'Hanlon with genuine interest.
"Most unusual, wouldn't you say, Father?"

"Not only unusual, but deplorable. The girl and her bastard son
have been living in open sin with the man—he doesn't actually live
with them, of course, he lives on Drumgillan with his family—but
he is with them much of the time nonetheless."

"And just how have you handled this 'deplorable' situation thus
far, might I inquire?" asked O'Hanlon.

"I have, of course, denounced them repeatedly from the pulpit.

And I have invoked the ban of the Holy Mother Church on them, and any who have to do with them.''

"You did that, did you? Very Christian of you, Father.'' McKuen looked up sharply at the ironic tone in the old man's voice.

"Indeed, I put the ban on them, Father O'Hanlon, and I urge you to do the same, for the good women of this parish take their virtue very seriously, and they will not stand for toleration of a woman who flaunts her whoredom before their vituous eyes.''

Father O'Hanlon smiled ruefully at the unmitigated righteousness of the younger priest.

"It has been my experience, Father McKuen, that the good women of most parishes become more virtuous as they grow older, and that they would generally be better off paying less attention to other people's virtue and more to their own charity.''

"Handle this as you will, Father,'' snapped the young priest. "It is your parish now!'' And he marched, rather prissily, thought Father O'Hanlon, out the door.

Sir Jeffrey had long ago ceased to marvel at his son's dogged persistence in clinging to his peasant mistress and her son. He had done the best he could for Michael, and that was that, but seeing the lad astride a horse, next to his father, sometimes gave him pause. A curious twist of fate it was that made the robust little lad a bastard, and Randolph's son, legitimate though he was, a twit. Not that there was anything that could be done to alter either condition.

Life had settled into a curiously peaceful quietude for the outcasts as the years passed at Drumgillan. Tom, while he was denied the company of other boys his age—for the villagers took their ostracism seriously—had the enormous advantage of being able to spend considerable time with his father. Neither Lady Geraldine nor Randolph ever set foot in the stables, so it was a relatively safe haven for father and son. Tom had even met his grandfather there on one or two occasions, proud of the pride his father had displayed in introducing him to Sir Jeffrey.

Mary kept their tiny cottage immaculate. Except for the nagging pangs of loneliness she felt for the friendship of other women, she was passably contented. She still dreamed always of a better future, and planned their escape with absolute confidence that it would happen; but the future seemed somehow far away and the present had its own blessings. At least her life had not followed the downward path of her mother's, and she had Michael and Tom to love, so that however strange her domestic solitude, she was relatively happy. They had discussed the possibility of leaving before Michael got his inheritance, but while the sum from Uncle Ned seemed a pittance to Sir Jeffrey, it was more than enough to secure a safe future for their little family, and reluctantly they had decided to wait it out.

Michael was curiously devoted to Mary and his son. She marveled at his constancy, for never once in all their time together had she heard him complain of their bizarre predicament; never did he cause her to feel that he had been trapped by their love, and never did he appear to feel burdened by their son. When the three were together, they laughed and comforted each other and were as cozy as a long-married family, in their small world on the edge of the big one, and Michael took it upon himself to instruct the lad in all manly pursuits. He even spent a good deal of time telling him of Drumgillan, just as if the child would some day live there. "He should feel pride in his heritage, not shame, Mary," he would say in explanation, and she would just shake her head at the impracticality of the idea, pleased nonetheless at the love the father obviously bore his son.

Aside from the curious isolation of their lives, the other pall that interjected itself into their happiness was that Mary's fear of another pregnancy strangled their sexual spontaneity into a pattern that denied them the sweetly perfect fulfillment of their early lovemaking. But then, Michael reasoned, it would be the same for them if they were properly wed, for he knew no sure way to limit a family, but with restraint. So they made love at the times that Mary deemed safest, and with the exception of one pregnancy that miscarried early on, they managed.

"My darling girl, how I look forward to being married to you so we needn't be so fearful of our urges."

"Would you keep me pregnant all the time, then, when we're married?" she teased him with her eyes.

"Aye, I would indeed, my love. For then we could hold and touch and love each other endlessly and with no care in the world."

"Don't you ever worry about God, Michael?" she asked earnestly once. "Don't you think he'll punish us severely for our lust for each other? Sometimes when I'm alone, I remember all the terrible things the priest always said of sins of the flesh. I'm certain they're the worst kind of all."

Michael laughingly pushed her down onto the soft bed where she had been primly sitting, and moved his vast, sun-warmed body in beside her. "My adorable Mary. You would have made such a good

Protestant, my darling. For then you could have had a God who was too refined and dignified to care at all what people do with their bodies. Your Catholic God has a voyeur's curiosity about sexual matters, it seems to me." And he had run his large, work-roughened hands over her unresisting body with a joyousness that always thrilled her, and she had forgotten her concerns of conscience for a little while at least.

Mary was seated by the comforting turf fire. Her son, Tom, dozed contentedly at her feet on a little cushion she had made for him long ago. Although he was a brave boy about staying alone and about the dark, which she knew sometimes frightened little children, for some reason she didn't quite fathom, he hated to go to bed without her. Even though the bed was merely twenty steps away, the boy always begged to be allowed to stay at her side while she did the evening chores, and over the years she had grown accustomed to his habit of dozing off beside her, head on the little cushion, feet drawn up in a triangle, face and hair angelic in the glow of the fireplace. She smiled at the sweetness of the husky little boy she loved, and went on mending, thinking of their curious life together.

The knock at the door was so unexpected when it came that Mary fairly leaped from her rocker, heart pounding, nerves alert. She had never really gotten used to living without a man in the house. Michael was in Dublin at a horse fair, Rory long gone to America; there was no one else who had ever visited her home. The young woman instinctively looked about the room for a weapon, and finding none, called out in a small voice, "Who's there?"

"Father O'Hanlon, Mary. I'm the new pastor at St. Boniface Church. Might I come in for a moment, woman of the house, 'tis cold as a Protestant's heart out here."

Opening the door a crack, Mary looked up into a lilting pair of eyes in a wrinkled face. She was too startled to be polite.

"Well, ask me in, girl, or we'll both catch our deaths."

Father O'Hanlon strode confidently into the cottage and looked around appraisingly. "You keep a tidy home, lass; and this, I take it, is the wee lad that all the fuss is about."

Mary nodded and blinked and finally, finding her voice, said, "Would you care for some tea, Father? 'Tis a cold night indeed."

"That I would, Mary. Talk is thirsty and I've come to talk with you, for you are a famous lady in these parts, I'm afraid," the old priest said with humor in his voice. "Yours is the name on everyone's

lips. I haven't been to a single wedding or funeral since I got here
that I haven't been told of your 'scandalous' doings and your life of
sin.'' He chuckled just a little, and she began to relax.

"I don't know precisely why you're here, Father, although I must
tell you 'tis a small miracle to be having tea in my own cottage with
anyone at all, for you're my first visitor in all these years.'' Her
voice was soft and melodious, thought the old priest, and it wavered
a bit with emotion when she spoke. "You will have a cup of tea,
won't you?'' she asked hopefully, and the old man nodded yes. She
bustled about the teapot chores without speaking, although she
looked furtively at the priest several times as his eye wandered
around the little cottage. He seemed a nice old man, she thought,
and decided to speak out to him, for she wanted no misunderstand-
ings with her only guest. "You don't look the scourge that Father
McKuen was, Father, but you are a priest and I'm thinking you're
here to try to win me back to the Church. So it's only fair for me to
tell you how it is with me.''

The wise old face looked interested, and he nodded.

"Many's the night I've lain in my bed and prayed to God for
forgiveness for my great sin. Many's the night I've longed to
confess and be shriven and make my peace with God, for I fear
damnation as much as anyone. But, Father, that's only the half of
the story. For I have no firm purpose of amendment, don't you see.

"Every time I think of my Michael's arms around me, I know in
my heart of hearts that he will always win me over. God help me,
Father, I would do it all again to be with him and to have our son,
it's that much I love them. More now, maybe, than when it all
happened to us; for Protestant he may be, but my Michael is the best
and most honorable man that ever graced God's world.''

The old priest nodded wonderingly at the young woman's
vehemence.

" 'Tis a fine gift you've been given, Mary. To be party to so
great a love.''

The girl looked warily at the old man, to see if there was scorn in
his face, and was startled to see nothing there but kindness and
compassion.

"I've been a priest too long, child, not to know that the good
Lord sometimes moves mysteriously, in his infinite wisdom. I cannot condone your sin in living out of wedlock, but I can perhaps
offer you an acceptable alternative. Would your young man consider
marrying you in the Church, do you suppose?''

Mary's eyes widened in utter disbelief. "You would marry us, Father?"

"Indeed I would, child. And who would ever need to know of it but us and God, if Michael's family would oppose the match, as I suppose they would. I could marry the two of you right in my own little rectory, all nice and proper as pie, and no one any the wiser." His old face wrinkled up in a grin that resembled a leprechaun's. "And then you could go to confession without need of that firm purpose of amendment that worries you so."

Mary clasped the old ascetic-looking hands in her own young firm ones. "I'll tell Michael when he returns from Dublin, Father. I don't know what he will say, but I'll ask him if we can do it."

And so Michael Harcourt Hartington, second heir to the estates of Drumgillan, the title of Earl of Rathconrath, and a great fortune of money and property in England, Ireland, and Wales, was scheduled to be married in the rectory of the tiny church of St. Boniface on January 27, 1883, to Mary Dalton, daughter of an impoverished farmer, on the land that three hundred years before had belonged to her ancestors. Only a small boy was to be in attendance, and nowhere but in the parish register would the wedding be recorded, for Michael feared reprisal on the part of his family were the deed to be known.

The prospective bridegroom began his instructions in the Catholic faith soon after he returned to Drumgillan, and although philosophically he found it a somewhat alien experience, the joy it produced in Mary made his effort seem worthwhile. As the day approached for the tiny ceremony to take place, she talked of nothing else; talked and planned and fairly danced through her chores with the sheer pleasure of the prospect of being his wife.

Michael left the warmth of the Big House feeling robust and exhilarated. The December cold was invigorating, and the clear brisk morning offered the possibility of breaking in the splendid new Arabian his father had purchased at the Dublin Horse Fair. An incredible animal, it was; the most exciting they had ever owned.

Rubbing his hands rapidly together against the chill and turning up the collar of his jacket, Michael headed for the stables thinking of how the fabulous animal had first caught his eye at the show. Haughty head tossing, hooves disdainfully pawing the earth as if he owned it, the horse had been the prize of the show and had cost a bloody fortune. But if he only lived up to *half* his promise . . . with the way luck had been running with them at the track and in the shows lately, this handsome beast would be well worth a king's ransom when properly trained.

Even Mary had been awed by the sure beauty of the animal when she had seen it loosed for exercise in the small enclosure behind the stable, where untamed horses were let run free.

"Have you ever seen such spirit, Michael?" she had asked breathlessly, a certain elation in her voice at the raw power and elegance of the animal.

"Never in a horse, my love," he had answered. "And only once in a woman." And she had blushed at the pretty compliment, and little Tom, watching from the other side of the enclosure, had thought how very handsome his mother and father looked together, and how very happy.

Ever since the priest had said he'd marry them, life in their little cottage had been puffed up with joy, it seemed to Tom. Happiness somehow flowed about like incense, and the child had wondered if perhaps it was the difference between sin and not that had haloed the atmosphere. Not that he'd ever really thought of his mother and father's love as sinful, but he knew that others did. After all, he'd grown up with the taunts of the village children in his ears and the anger he felt at their ugly words rankling his small soul. But he had to admit there was *something* wonderful happening in his home, now that his mother and father were in the good graces of the priest.

Michael had slept at the cottage with his little family through the night, but had returned to the Big House before dawn for a warmer riding jacket. He intended to ride himself this morning and needed something warm enough to keep away the damp chill, for it wouldn't do to catch cold with his wedding just a few weeks away. He chuckled at the consternation such a thought would produce in his mother if she were to know of the impending event. What a contrast her haughty anger would make to Mary's unadulterated joy at the thought of being his wife. *Wife.* He savored the word. He reached the stable, which had grown to twice the size it had been when his odd domestic situation had precipitated him into partnership with his father.

He wished Mary could be there to see him work the Arabian this morning. Although Michael wasn't vain, he knew he looked splendid astride, and he took great pride in his gift for horses. God, it would be grand when he and Mary could share their life right out in front of the whole world. He wondered if other men felt as he did about their longtime spouses. Despite the travail of it, loving Mary was the very best thing that had ever happened in his life.

Michael reached the stable door as the groom led Devil Wind into the ring. He'd have to remind himself to change the horse's name to something a little more Celtic and a little less ominous. The Irish were a superstitious lot about horses' names, and they tended to balk at any reference to Satan or his works.

"Beggin' yer pardon, sir, but he's having a vagary this morning, your honor," said the groom, struggling to control the obstreperous animal, whose nostrils were puffing little clouds of steam into the cold air, and whose prancing hooves seemed to be straining to lift his muscular body completely off the ground by means of some enchantment.

He looks like some Pegasus from the *Arabian Nights*, Michael thought with amusement, watching the patrician animal strain at his lead. Perhaps I'll christen him Caliph in honor of his Arab parentage.

"He's a beauty, isn't he, Diarmid?" he shouted back at the troubled stable hand above the wind.

"Aye," the boy replied, "he is that, sir, and a beauty of a temper he has to go with it. I'm not at all sure you should try to ride him this mornin', your honor—he's had a restless night and he seems not to fancy the company of us humans today. It may be there's a storm comin' up that's spookin' him. Old Derry says his corns have been achin' him somethin' fierce."

Michael looked at the boy with amused tolerance. He respected the lad's knowledge of animals, and Derry's corns were legendary for their ability to forecast weather, but he thought it best not to let the superstitions of the horse folk interfere with his plans for the day. He reached up confidently and patted the velvet nose of the agitated animal with a sure hand.

"There, now, my fine desert beauty," he crooned in the soft, lulling tone he used with horses. "I'm not here to hurt you. Just to teach you a thing or two." The horse snorted but nuzzled the man's hand nonetheless, to the surprise of the groom. "I'll bet you could teach *me* a thing or two, if you wanted to, couldn't you?" Michael continued, pleased by the horse's response. He took the rope from the young man's hand and began to lead the huge snowy animal slowly around the enclosure, talking in the same soft singsong voice that the boy had seen him use to mesmerize other horses.

The groom looked up at the sky with a practiced appraisal. "Old Derry's corns seem to know their business, your honor," he shouted across the ring to Michael. "Them's thunderclouds comin' in off the mountains, sir."

Michael raised his hand to silence the voice, for it seemed to startle the horse and he was already making great progress in calming him. He could feel the animal's confidence toward him growing; he would mount when they reached the back fence. The exhilaration of the thought thrilled Michael; he loved the feel of a wild, unbroken horse beneath him, the heat and the strength and the power. He glanced at the clouds rolling in from the east, and decided the storm would hold off long enough to accomplish his desire.

He signaled to the groom that he would mount, and saw that a handful of other watchers had gathered around the fence. It was considered a fine manly art form, this business of gentling a prize horse; he felt a small glimmer of pride in his own ability as he swung himself onto the horse's back with a practiced expertise.

Tom ran breathlessly up to the enclosure, his small sturdy legs cramped from the long run over the dew-damp grass; he was just in time to see his father mount. The horse's silver-white coat gleamed brilliantly against the lowering purple of the dawn sky, and the little boy thought the beauty of the sight of his huge handsome father astride the magical white beast would be with him always. Tom chided himself for having overslept, but he'd been awakened in the night by an awful, eerie howling that had frightened him, and he'd crawled in between his mother and father on the bed for safety. He still felt a tingling uneasiness because of the ghostly sound—his mother had sought to soothe him by saying it had been the cry of an animal, but it had been too unearthly, too agonized, too full of sorrow to be animal—yet the excitement of seeing his father ride the treasured Arabian banished the worries momentarily from his eight-year-old mind.

Climbing up onto the fence, the boy saw the horse stand absolutely motionless for a moment as Michael's huge body settled comfortably onto its back. Time seemed unnaturally suspended, as if rider and horse were frozen for one split second before the insanity began. Suddenly, deliberately, the mighty horse reared onto its hind legs, pawing the air ferociously with its flying hooves, screaming a wild horse-sound the boy had never, ever heard before. The child saw the suddenly stricken looks on the faces of the grooms as the animal began to fly, all four feet, it seemed, lifted off the cold, packed dirt in a mighty leap, then all four feet down again with a sickening thud. He saw the startled look on his father's wonderful face as the beast somehow managed to *twist* itself under him as the man's body left the horse's back; with the momentum of the improbable leap the horse turned, *somehow*, turned and twisted, as the awful scream, triumphant and filled with rage, tore from the animal's great white throat.

Tom saw his father's face contort with absolute astonishment as he was hurtled through the air like a giant rag doll and flung headlong onto the unrelenting ground. With perfect, horrified clarity the child saw the man look up, his eyes so sad, as if he were utterly uncomprehending of how a horse he admired could be doing this terrible thing to him. Then, glistening hooves flying and hammering, nostrils breathing clouds that looked like dragonsmoke, teeth bared in a hideous predatory snarl, the horse trampled the man viciously, pummeling his face and body with a crazed tattoo. The grooms, the stable hands, were shouting, running, trying to grasp the flying bridle. Then just as suddenly as he'd begun the mayhem, the horse was still—standing over his fallen victim, staring defiantly at the dumbstruck audience, like a gladiator awaiting his reward.

In some suspended animation of the heart Tom heard the lethal crack of the bullet from his grandfather's rifle as it pierced the horse's brain. He hadn't seen the old man arrive, but he was there somehow, standing like a mighty statue with the gun to his shoulder, shooting with a deadly accuracy. The whole scene had surely taken less than a minute, he later calculated when he could bear to think of it at all.

Less than a minute he would remember *always* in agonizing detail. For a lifetime, he would remember running to his fallen father, throwing desperate arms around the crumpled, broken body, begging it not to die. He would remember the blood, so much blood on the ground, on the beautiful jacket, running down his father's wondrous face in rivulets, as the cold, relentless rain began to fall, as he cried out uselessly to God.

He would remember the shouting and the sobbing and the clinging to the dead man, as hands that might have been his grandfather's began to try to drag him away. And the awful finality of what had been done seeping into his mind. That's what he would remember most . . . afterward, when he could bear to think on it . . . the deadly cold of the hateful knowledge trickling into him. That, and his mother's face as she reached the fence. It had taken him a very long time to come out of the darkness, after seeing her face.

Part Two

1882-1900
THOMAS AND MARY

Lord thou art hard on mothers. . . .
We suffer in their coming and in their going.
                    —*Padraic Pearse*

15

"Nothing's ever going to happen to me. . . ." The words rang in the child's head as he prepared to leave his home forever. He'd heard his father say them to his mother, Mary, in their little cottage on the edge of the Drumgillan fen, in a reassurance that had never really reassured him.

Now the *something* of his mother's fears had happened. His da was dead, and the little cottage with their meager belongings would be theirs no longer.

He was trying hard not to think of all that had happened in the last three days, but the awful memory of the morning after the funeral kept pushing its way into his mind.

His father's older brother, Randolph, and the overseer, Mr. O'Leary, had come to the cottage and told them that the little house was to be taken from them.

"But Michael said he'd leave it to us in his will, to keep us safe!" his mother had cried, distraught enough to be indiscreet for once.

"Nonsense," his uncle had brutally replied. "My brother died intestate. Michael always was a fool about money. But even if he had been a financier of note, he would not have left a penny to a housemaid and her bastard son. Surely you can see that, madam."

"See that you're gone by noon tomorrow," Mr. O'Leary had added gratuitously in his deadly rasp of a voice. "He has a heart so small you could strap it to a sparrow's knee and not impede his flight," his father had once said of Mr. O'Leary, and his father had seldom been wrong about such things.

Tom noticed that his mother, too, was looking about her, as if lost in reverie. She had already packed what they could carry in the cardboard box with his father's belt around it, and in the knapsack she had made for each of them. He knew she had tucked in her Sunday Mass dress and his two changes of breeches, and his one good shirt. She had packed, too, the lovely silver-handled hairbrush his father had given him, once on a birthday, long ago. "The brush is engraved only with your first initial, son," his father had said, "so that when your mother and I are properly wed, I'll have your true surname emblazoned on the silver forever.'' Now that would never be.

Tom stood patiently watching his silent mother. He saw that she was fingering nervously her one treasure, a fragile golden locket housing a miniature of his father. It was the only impractical item she had ever owned. ''I'll starve to death, gladly,'' she had told him, ''before I'll ever part with it.''

Resolutely, Mary picked up the cardboard box and Tom did the same with his knapsack. She looked around the cottage a final time, and he saw that there were tears glistening in her eyes as she shut the door quietly behind them.

Mother and son marched with a pride they did not feel, past the picketed gate in the random stone wall that marked the edges of their world. The day was dark and blustery cold, and the fine rain that had been falling since dawn made the mud slippery beneath their feet. The little boy wondered if the woolen shawl his mama had wrapped about her could keep out the dampness any better than his own little coat. He felt cold in an unaccustomed way, but didn't speak of it.

''Where will we go now, Mama?'' he asked instead, trudging resolutely down the bog road, taking care not to look back at the home no longer his.

''To the priest, son, where all lost souls go. To Father O'Hanlon, with hopes he'll know how to help us in this terrible time.''

Nearly seventy years later, when Thomas Dalton was on his deathbed, some fool would ask him what he remembered best in his long life. ''The partings,'' he would reply, and no one in the deathroom but one would know he was recalling with infinite detail the moment they had begun for him in the cold, desolate winter of 1882.

16

Father O'Hanlon was fretfully saying his daily office in the nave of St. Boniface's when Mary and Tom, with all their worldly goods in hand, appeared in the gray light at the back door of the darkened church.

''Sweet Jesus,'' murmured the old priest to himself and to God.

"Help me to help these waifs of Thine," and he painfully rose to his arthritic feet and ushered them into his tiny threadbare rectory, in the kindly, absentminded way of the old and compassionate. He watched the silent mother and son out of the corner of his eyes as he put the tea kettle on to boil, an ancient Irish remedy against all ills of the body or spirit. A thousand memories of the young man and woman he had planned to join together scattered themselves through his mind, like flower petals on a meadow. He sometimes wondered mightily at the mysterious ways of the Lord.

"As you know well, my dear child," he began in the voice he generally reserved for sermons, as he struggled to control his emotions. "Despite the fact that he got you with a child he could not acknowledge, it is my opinion that your Michael was as decent a young man as ever I met. A damned sight better one than that pompous prig of an elder brother of his, that sits in the Big House counting his money, this very minute." He checked the water on the stove, put out three teacups, and walked slowly to his desk, where he motioned them to be seated.

"At any rate, whatever else he has to answer for at God's judgment seat, Mary, Michael always tried to do right by the boy and by you." The old priest pushed the papers on his debris-strewn desk to one side and reached for a small wooden box that was locked with a key he wore around his neck. "You see, Mary, Michael spoke to me of your future when I was instructing him in our holy faith, and he entrusted me with a sum of money to be used for two purposes, so he said—if there should be need."

Father O'Hanlon paused, and Mary raised her eyes to his with a startled look.

"If, God forbid, he was to die, Michael said, he had no doubt that his godforsaken pinch-hearted family would cheat you and the boy out of your winter drawers, if they could. So he says to me, 'Father, take this purse of money and put it under your floor. If anything ever happens to me, take it out and do two things for them I love. Send Mary to America, to find a new life—and give the boy the best education you can buy or beg or steal for him. He's a smart one, Tom is. He's got the gift. He's got the analytical mind, the quick wit, and he's got the poetry. But born on the wrong side of the blanket as he was, his life will go nowhere at all, says he, unless he's got the education to beat them at their own game."

Mary and Tom looked at each other, their eyes full of wonder that they could have been loved as much as that, and terror at the implications of fulfilling the stipulations of the gift.

"America, Father, and what in the name of God would I be doing in America?"

The old priest squinted at the strong young girl before him, weighing the words he would try to find to make her see the way it was. Why did they never tell you in the seminary what real pain was like to deal with? Them with all their highfalutin ritual and pomp and empty words from an old catechism that had no heart. Small solace they were when you looked fear full in the face, or death or pestilence, or a frightened mother and her little son.

"Mary, child, think first of the choices. Think first of your son. His father was right about the lad; you know he's a smart one. He'll make his way if he's got an education. And you . . . you're a fine strapping girl, and once you're in America, there's a priest I know named Father Grogan who helps the Irish girls to get along. He'll get you a job at a fine house with a good family and you'll have a chance for a life, Mary. Don't you see you cannot stay here any longer?"

"But Father, Tom's my son. I could never leave him!" Her stricken face made the old man wince with anger at the world's injustice. He cleared his throat in an effort to sound resolute.

"Nonetheless, child, you must do as I say. I can send Tom to a place in Westmeath that's a teaching monastery. It's your name he'll be using there, and the good fathers will raise him as an orphan and no questions asked." He looked Mary straight in the eye as he told her the unappealing truth. "You haven't any family that'll speak to you since the boy. You cannot raise him alone, and you cannot take him to America. Who'll hire an unwed servant girl with a child? Mary, Mary, you have no choice but to do what Michael has asked of you. No choice at all."

As if to punctuate the finality of his words, Father O'Hanlon reached into the wooden box he'd been toying with and extracted two sealed letters, one addressed to Mary, one to Tom, and handed them to the sorrowful pair before him. With trembling fingers the young woman broke the seal and read the last letter she would ever have from her love, tears brimming over and gliding down her face.

"My dearest girl," the letter began in Michael's strong, elegant hand.

That you are reading this letter means that the worst has happened and I am no longer with you and our son. Forgive me, Mary, for the wrong that I've done you—it is a great burden to carry with me to the Place of Judgment. I can only hope that God in His mercy will understand the love that I bear you, and temper His justice with enough mercy to allow us to find each other once again, beyond this world.

I have loved you with every breath I've taken—neither death nor my wretched family can take that from us. I've left whatever I own to you and Tom. The will, such as it is, can be of no use to you now, for the law will hear my family's side in this; however, should your fortune or Tom's ever make it possible for you to retrieve what was mine, I leave it in your hands. Because of the precariousness of your circumstances, I have taken other steps for your safety.

There is ample money in Father O'Hanlon's possession to take you to America and to establish you there until you can find work and, I pray, a new life. I entreat you to find the strength to leave Tom behind. His will be a hard lot, Mary, and he must be equipped with all that you and I can give him for the good fight. I have arranged for him to be educated, if not quite as a gentleman, at least not as a farmer or a bastard. He will be schooled through university with the help of Father O'Hanlon, whom I have taken into our confidence, so that he will, I trust, have the wherewithal to make his own way in the world, when his education is done. All that I could do for my son, I have done. I pray God it will be enough.

I love you, my beloved girl. Do not forget me.

Michael

Mary laid the letter on the priest's crude desk of bog oak, struggling hard to retain her dignity. It was too much to bear with, the letter, somehow, making the hopelessness real.

Tom watched his mother's gesture with a sorrowful intensity before opening his own letter, for he had a terrible feeling that he held his own doom in his hands. Sensing his trepidation, the mother reached across to her son and clasped his little shoulder, as if to impart the strength that was needed. "You must read it, Tom. 'Tis all we have of him now." Without looking up, the boy broke the envelope's seal, with care lest it be needlessly harmed, and began to read with brimming eyes.

My dearest son,

When you are a man, I pray that you will better understand the circumstances of your birth. If you cannot forgive me the wrong I have done you and your mother, at least you will perhaps understand the infinite love that caused the pain.

No father has ever loved his son as I love you, nor believed in him more. You are my hope for the future and my only immortality. Learn all you can, Tom. Education is your means of escape. With it you can cross the barriers of class and money, of prejudice and privilege. Be smarter than the rest, and stronger and surer, for you must find your own way. Go to another country and begin life again as the gentleman you were born to be.

I have little to leave you but my acknowledgment of your birth and heritage. Had God decreed the circumstances to be different, you would be my lawful child and inherit all that was once to be mine.

Take pride in your heritage, my son. Your mother bequeaths you the beauty and love and mysticism of her Celtic forebears, and I bequeath you the blood, if not the name, of one of the finest families in Ireland.

God be with you, my dearest child. I love you so.

Your Father

17

The bewildered little boy stood in the courtyard of the ancient stone monastery, clutching his woolen cap in his small hands, sweaty despite the bleak cold of an Irish December. Men in dark garments were scurrying noiselessly to the candlelit chapel, for the Angelus had rung and it wouldn't do to be late to one's appointed pew. Instinctively he hugged himself for protection against what was to be his world for the next ten years.

Father O'Hanlon had told him to be polite to the good brothers at the monastery and to do everything they said to do. He had said the Christian Brothers were great scholars who would teach him all the things his father had meant for him to know. The prickly hairs on his neck gave Tom the uneasy feeling that perhaps the good brothers would be teaching him other things besides, for the place had an eerie, indefinable sorrow that hung about it as thick as buttermilk. His wariness escalated chillingly as he stood and waited in the quiet courtyard.

A secretive-looking middle-aged monk appeared from nowhere and spoke to him.

"I am Brother Ambrose," he said in a whiny bronchial voice. "I'll take you to the abbot. You must be Tom, the orphan boy Father O'Hanlon has sent us. If you need any advice while you're here, come to me and I'll help you if I can. The rules are stringent, though, and I may not be able to do much."

He pushed the boy toward a massive carved oaken door that looked too opulent for its severe surroundings. Looking apprehensively to right and left, as if unsure if he should go or stay, he whispered, "This is the abbot's study. Just knock on the door and wait to be called. And God help you, child." Brother Ambrose blessed himself hastily and was gone as mysteriously as he had appeared.

Tom knocked on the door almost soundlessly and waited his turn with a pounding in his chest that wouldn't be quieted.

"Don't just stand there like the ignorant peasant you are," called a disquieting voice from within. "Enter."

The abbot was tall and cadaverous, with cold, deadly eyes. He was fingering a rod of some sort with a fervor that made the boy want to run and hide. Tom struggled to breathe against the constriction of fear in his small chest. The ascetic old man stared with distaste at the disheveled youngster, his aristocratic nose offended by the unsavory smell of child and woolens.

"You are even less than I expected." The voice seemed too large for the bony body.

"While you are here, you will be disciplined in an effort to turn you into a gentleman, impossible though that may be. You will be beaten for the slightest infraction."

What, dear God, might an infraction be, thought the desperate boy—and how will I know if I do one?

"You will obey all rules and orders immediately, you will work for your keep from dawn till dark, you will speak perfect English at all times—not that disgusting peasant dialect you come possessed of—and you will have no unclean thoughts. Do you understand?"

Tom nodded his head vigorously. "Oh, yes, your reverence. I

understand entirely, sir." He lied, hoping the unpleasant interview would end soon.

"Take off your filthy shirt." Tom looked blankly at the strange figure before him to be sure he'd heard correctly. My shirt isn't filthy, he thought, my mother made it, and Father O'Hanlon washed it just yesterday.

"I said remove your disreputable garments!" There was no mistaking the intent in the thunderous voice this time.

Obediently, Tom fumbled with the homemade buttons and removed his best shirt with the awkwardness of fear, wondering if he would be given one of those strange long gowns to wear, like the scurrying monks outside this room.

"I intend to beat you," said the old man with no emotion whatsoever in his deadly voice. "To show you what will happen to you every time you choose to break a rule here in God's house."

The horrid cat-o'-nine-tails whizzed through the cold air, and Tom began his education. On the day he died, it was another thing he remembered with absolute clarity.

Although Tom knew nothing of such history on the day he entered there, St. Ignatius was one of a great many monastic retreats that had figured prominently in Ireland's history. Monasteries and abbeys by the hundreds had been closed and abandoned throughout Ireland during the continuing assaults of the English landlords, but the monastery of St. Ignatius had managed to retain its foothold in an Ascendancy world, primarily because of the strength of will and the powerful family connections of the abbot himself. Francis Plunkett Fitzpatrick was the son of one of the few Irish Catholic landowning families who had maintained power through the English invasions; his lineage, despite its Catholicism, was quite as impeccable as that of any of his Protestant counterparts.

His brilliant educational career on the Continent, and his family's enormous wealth, had early on brought Francis to the scrutiny of the Vatican. As a young man, he had been privileged to walk the religious corridors of power, with every prospect of one day realizing his most ambitious dreams. But young Fitzpatrick was at heart an ascetic; cut from the cloth of flagellants and martyrs, he had found the excessive wealth of the Vatican, and the general decadence of the city of Rome, morally distasteful. So, after considerable soul-searching, fasting, and increasingly austere penances, he had concluded that his vocation was of sterner stuff than that required for a papal politician. Accordingly, he had petitioned his Eminence Cardinal Ponzini, papal nuncio and closest confidant of the pontiff, for permission to return to Ireland, for the express purpose of founding a teaching monastery to be funded from his own personal wealth. It would, he said, provide a bulwark against the assaults of the Ascendancy on the Church, and his Holiness had replied via Cardinal Ponzini that, while he personally regretted the loss of one so promising to Vatican internal affairs, he applauded the young man's courageous decision to espouse the monastic life and the ascetic regime. He had also sent his blessing.

Monsignor Fitzpatrick had promptly returned to Ireland, divested his family of as much money as their consciences would allow, and proceeded to restore to usefulness a fourteenth-century ruin of a once prosperous monastery. Fitzpatrick imported gifted architects from Europe to supervise the restoration, and, drawing from his considerable classical knowledge of art and architecture, he collaborated with them on all plans. Although the artisans were at first disturbed by the austerity of the abbot's vision for his abbey, they were eventually forced to admit reluctantly that this knowledge of native Irish fourteenth-century architecture, and his passion for superb detail, would surely produce a uniquely authoritative and authentic structure. It chilled them, of course, to imagine anyone living there . . . but aside from that, it was considered by all to be a remarkably scholarly restoration, one that would do credit to the holy Catholic faith.

Catholicism in Ireland had had a storm-tossed history. It tended to provoke volatile passions on the part of those who addressed it, whether they applauded or opposed the tenacious faith. The Celts, from whom the modern Irish had sprung, were a mystical race, prone to sacrifice and religiosity, and the advent of Catholicism in the tiny island kingdom in the fifth century A.D. had allowed an already mystery-oriented people to quite comfortably substitute a new mysticism for an old. The sacrificial character of the new religion had delightfully reminiscent overtones of their druidical tradition, and the magical properties of priests were an easily acceptable wrinkle to the mystic Irish, so the transition from old religion to new had gone smoothly.

As a result of this comfortable mélange of theologies, the Irish landscape was soon dotted with abbeys and monasteries housing a class of scholarly priests and brothers that provided both an intellectual elite and a governing body for the little country throughout the Dark Ages. Scholarship under the monastic rule reached an apogee during the sixth, seventh, eighth, and ninth centuries, when learned monks in quiet scriptoria created masterpieces of religious and secular art; proselytizing missionaries like Saint Columba and Saint Aidan, set sail, manuscripts in hand, to spread learning and religion (which in the time were synonymous) to the less civilized nations of Europe.

The English invasions and their subsequent cycles of rebellions and oppressions served to reinforce the stubborn Irish attachment to its Church. Although Catholicism was totally outlawed by the English during large parts of the eighteenth and nineteenth centuries, the people always contrived to hear Mass and to protect their priests, in a gesture as much of rebellion as of religious fervor. Far from dampening the people's Catholic convictions, the continuing oppressions merely fanned the flame of their religious passion and forged an ironclad connection for them to Catholicism.

The Church promised a happier and more prosperous eternity to those enmeshed in a poor and paltry present. As sacrifice and suffering were commonplace everyday realities in Ireland, the notion that such misery was simply a means to a better end had considerable appeal. Grappling an image of eternal bliss to their bosoms, the people offered up their sacrifices with a willing relish, and espoused the myriad rules and regulations of Catholicism, by means of which the priests assured them they would achieve their place in heaven. Religion, like whiskey, was a means for most men and women to make it through the stark reality of their lives. More than an opiate, Catholicism allowed an impoverished and repressed people to experience royal pomp and ceremony, to partake of ennobling sacrifice, and, finally, to believe in miracles.

The reverence felt by the Irish people for their religion was further compounded by the reverence they felt for the education offered by the monastic system. The Irish worshiped words and learning; the smallest villages possessed a library, the poorest fisherman could recite poetry. When the English invasions closed the Irish schools and denied the people access to both their history and their beloved literature, "hedge schools" were organized to teach the young behind fences and in ditches by the roadside, but the longing the people felt for education and the connection they felt with the magic of words, could be neither repressed by the English nor fulfilled by the hedge schools. Monasteries and the priestly teaching elite, with all its centuries of scholarly precedent, became the repositories of the learning the Irish revered and desired. These monasteries provided, for priests, nuns, brothers, and a smattering of children, a breathtaking scholarly curriculum. Such a place was the monastery of St. Ignatius.

18

Mary Dalton stood bewildered on the North River pier with her carpetbag in her hand. She was weak with apprehension, fatigue, and sorrow. The crossing to New York in steerage had been a fearful thing—she had been nauseous and terrified, when she wasn't numb with the grief of all that had befallen her.

Michael was gone. Never again would his strong arms enfold her and keep her safe from the world's assault. Tom was gone. No more would she watch his fiery head on the hearth pillow as she crooned him tenderly to sleep. The future was gone. Never would they be a family, warm and protected by love, off to seek the future in a new land full of promise. She blinked back the tears that seemed now always to hover just behind her lids, and looked around the pier for the priest she had been told to find.

Father Grogan was his name. She knew they called him "The Saint of Hell's Kitchen," this man who met the Irish girls off the boats and saved them from a life of sin or starvation. Seeing a gaggle of women collecting tentatively near the end of the dock, she headed toward the crowd.

A tall, middle-aged man with a careworn face and eyes as alert as a two-year-old's reached out a hand to her as she drew near. "Is it Mary Dalton you are?" he asked her in a kindly voice. "Ah, but you must be, and thanks be to God for it! You're the last of me little flock for today." He sounded immensely pleased to have found all his charges.

Hesitantly, Mary held out the letter of introduction she had been given by Father O'Hanlon, and the priest took it wordlessly, looking her up and down unabashedly as if to appraise her possibilities.

"Father O'Hanlon told me I must remind you that I can read and write, Father," she said suddenly, remembering the old priest's last admonition to her as she'd boarded the boat.

"Praise God, child, but now isn't that the best news you could be givin' me? Sure and haven't I a fine position in Tuxedo Park just waitin' for such a one as your own fine self.'' He beamed benevolence on Mary and then turned to the eight other girls who had been fortunate enough to be entrusted to his care. ''Now, my dear young ladies,'' he said cheerfully. ''You must wait here for me for a wee moment while I seek out the strays from His flock,'' and leaving the young women already in his charge to themselves, the tall, sturdy priest, who looked more like a pugilist, strode off to hail whichever young girls still remained at large on the pier. By the time he returned to the original group, three more girls had been added to his covey.

''You see, ladies,'' he said by way of explanation, ''there are those who arrive here with no place to go at all. They hope for streets paved with gold and are greeted by dirty cobblestones, God help them. Sometimes, the grace of God commends them to my care.''

And with that he bustled them off—eleven young women, bags and baggage—in the direction of the Holy Rosary rectory, two miles south of the pier.

Father Grogan was seated at his desk in the Holy Rosary rectory the morning following Mary's arrival, when she dutifully answered his summons. The balding man looked up from his writing, spectacles perched on the end of his plump little nose. He motioned her enthusiastically into the room that served him as a study.

She walked with a quiet dignity, he noted; graceful and restrained. She was rather a beauty by the world's standards, he thought; most likely it was this very fact that had brought her to a life of sin and sadness. The letter from Father O'Hanlon had told him the curious history of Michael Hartington and Mary Dalton.

''Mary, dear,'' he said quietly. ''I know more than a little of what has befallen you, and it behooves us, I think, to speak of your past before you leave to go to your new position.''

Mary nodded. Her fate was now in this man's hands; she would listen to what he had to say politely, but she felt too listless and numb to care much what was in store for her. Her detachment wasn't lost on the priest, who had seen much of dislocation and suffering in his ministry.

'' 'Tis not my custom, Mary, to counsel people to be less than perfectly honest,'' he began, uncertain of how to explain himself. ''But I am, you see, a practical man as well as a priest at the end of it, and it has fallen to my lot to see much of sorrow and want and injustice meted out to our Irish men and women when they arrive in America. So in your case, child, I am moved to counsel—if not quite a lie—a wee bit of discretion."

Mary looked up warily at the priest. He cleared his throat and continued.

"Were you to tell your prospective employers of Michael and Tom, Mary, I'm afraid they would see no choice but to brand you as a fallen woman. Inasmuch as they have young children who would be in your charge, I don't doubt that they would feel quite justified in rejecting your bid for employment, on moral grounds." He saw her stiffen, but pressed on.

"Therefore, Mary, it appears to me that we must be a trifle inventive in the tale that we weave for them as has so little imagination of their own; wouldn't you agree with me, lass?" He paused a moment to see if she rebelled, and seeing that she did not, went on. "Shall we perhaps tell them that you came from a family of farmers, and that having by the grace of God learned to read and write, you desired to better your station by seeking employment in America? Now, that's not so far from the truth that you couldn't throw a stone at it, is it, Mary?"

"No, Father," she said solemnly, feeling as if she'd left all her words behind in Ireland. He smiled at her, relieved that she was tractable.

"And, Mary, child, you must be a bit freer with your syllables if you are to convince these fine people that you can teach their children to read and write. After all, Mary, articulation and eloquence surely they have a right to expect from an Irishwoman. For didn't the English take everything else from us and leave us only the magic of the words?" He had hoped to make her smile, but he could see there was too much trouble weighing her down for that. He'd try another tack.

"Would you care to tell me of your lad, Mary? I'm told he's a fine strapping boy, like his father."

The large sad eyes came alive in an instant at the mention of Tom. "What will become of him, Father? Without me and Michael? He's but eight years old and he's all alone now!" The sudden anguish and fear in her voice touched the priest, and he reached out to take her hand.

"Mary, Mary! You must not despair so, child! Your son is in God's hands, as are you yourself! Many's the lad has been thrust upon the world with less to protect him than Tom has. He is cared for by the Holy Brothers, he's fed and clothed, and he'll get an education even an Englishman would envy! He's got your blood and Michael's in his veins, girl . . . and a strong, loving, intelligent heritage it is. God will show him the path he is to tread, Mary. Just as he will show it to you. We cannot question his mysterious ways, for you and I know not what he knows." He said it with the ponderous conviction of absolute faith.

"It sounds empty to me, Father!" she snapped back at him, and her voice shook with emotion. "I *do* question Him. For all my great sin, I *question* Him!"

The priest looked at the beautiful, stern face and knew that whatever he might say would sound empty as the wind to a mother who has lost both her child and the love of her heart. He chose not to remind the girl that it was her own sin and pride that had brought her to this fate, for in his infinite faith it seemed to him that all of it must somehow be part of God's great plan.

"Let us pray, then, Mary, for your future and for Tom's, that God keeps you in the hollow of His hand in your separation."

She nodded again, knowing argument useless, and he saw in the somehow eloquent gesture the courage and strength of this silent young woman. He said a small prayer for God's mercy.

She's a smart one, this Mary Dalton, he thought. It would be interesting to see what would become of her.

He hoped he had given her the right advice about reinventing her history. These Irish girls had such an undeservedly bad reputation for loose morals as it was, it had seemed to him her only option.

Father Grogan watched thoughtfully as Mary left his study, her graceful, upright carriage curiously at odds with her station. "Help her, Lord," he prayed. "She has possibilities."

The trap that picked Mary up at the Tuxedo railway station was driven by a small shriveled man with one walleye and the hunched posture of one who has spent his days and nights in a self-protective huddle against the weather that plagues coachmen. She thought absentmindedly that he looked like a man from the land of Faery.

He acknowledged Mary's arrival with a tolerant smile and a grunt and carried her bag to the trap, but made no offer to help her mount to the leather-covered seat.

"Me name's Sean and yer the new gurl, I suppose," he said in a thick, cheery brogue when she had managed to seat herself with some difficulty.

"I am," was the answer.

"They'll treat yer well here if yer don't put on airs and yer know yer place."

"They will."

"Yer don't talk much, is it?"

"No," she said sadly.

Don't put on airs indeed! That was precisely what had been her downfall. She had pictured herself the *wife* in a house like the one she was going to, not the servant; and servant she was born to be.

"Tuxedo Park's a foin private place," the driver continued, watching her with the eye that wandered away from the other one. " 'Twas built fer the rich to hobnob with each other, don't yer know. You'll not believe the size o' the houses, I'm thinkin'."

Mary smiled sadly. She had seen big houses before, to her detriment.

"There's forests there too, in the park, and lakes. Two of them, the Big Wee Wah and the Little Wee Wah, they calls 'em. Not the likes of those as you'd find in Ireland, mind yer. But good enough for Protestants." The little man chuckled at his relegation of his "betters" to an inferior status.

"What happened to the last governess?" Mary asked, warmed by the old man's irreverence.

"Ah, now, lassie, that'd be quite a tale it would."

"I'd like to hear it, I expect." She said the words thinking she'd best try to be a little friendlier toward the man; God alone knew when next she'd find a friend in this new world.

He turned his good eye from the road to his passenger.

"So you've got a tongue in yer head after all," he chuckled. "I was after believing you were a mute." She smiled at him and he nodded, satisfied at her response.

"Well, now, this is the way of it: Eileen Casey was the last governess, and a foiner woman you'd never meet. She and her husband, Frank the gardener, were in service here for thirty years. Until just a month ago." He added the last with an ominous emphasis.

"Now, the Caseys have six children, all lads, you see, and all as decent a lot as you'd find in a day's travel. Hard workers they was, like their mama and da.

"Their youngest son, Tim, was the smartest of them all, and he'd heard tell that if he could do well enough in school, he could win himself what they calls a scholarship, so he could go to college like the lads from the foin families. So Timmy worked himself to a fare-thee-well with his schoolwork, till there wasn't a better student in the whole state, and didn't he win himself a scholarship to Notre Dame University, the place of his dreams. Now, off he goes with his parents' blessing at his back just a few months back.'' Mary looked closely at the little man, wondering what all this might have to do with the departure of the previous governess.

''Well, now, one foin day, Mr. Cooke—the master, that is—asks after the lad. 'I haven't seen that fair-haired youngster of yours around here, Frank, for a while,' says he to the gardener. 'Has he left to find work in New York?' 'No sir,' says old Frank, proud as a peacock. 'Sure he's gone off to Notre Dame College he has, to learn to be a doctor.'

''Well, Mary, now Mr. Cooke gets red in the face, like a ripe tomato, and away he stamps back into the house with never so much as a good-day-to-you for old Frank.'' Sean turned toward Mary to deliver the final announcement in a dramatic whisper. ''They was all dismissed the same week! Eileen and Frank and any of their lads that was old enough to be in service. Yer see, the toffs don't like to think that the likes of us could better our lot.

''On the other hand,'' said the driver implacably when Mary didn't answer him, ''if yer don't get above yerself, you'll be all right.''

Get above myself, thought Mary. What an idea! I don't even know where I begin and end these days, so how could I possibly get above myself? I wonder what this little man would say if he knew how far above myself I was once—and how low I have fallen because of it.

The slow, dull ache under her heart, which was the internal place reserved for Tom, began to throb and grow. Like a mushroom on a wet day, that pain could expand from a tiny hard point of controlled anguish into a huge growth of grief that could overwhelm and destroy, if she wasn't careful.

Mary knew she could force the pain to confine itself to a small space by strictest concentration, but the effort was immense and constant. She'd had a dream in which she was desperately trying to hold closed a door that led to her grief; the force behind the door kept pounding to be let out, and her strength was ebbing.

Sean spoke again, and she felt herself pulled back by the sound into the outside world. ''Them gates is the entrance to Tuxedo Park,

Mary. Inside there is the world of the rich, and of those who serves them. You'll like it well enough.''

They drove past the guard at the security station and on up the winding road into a vast and beautiful park. Huge oak and elm trees vied with giant pines for space and sunlight, and below the road Mary could see the shining waters of the Wee Wah with tiny people in tiny boats gliding over its glittering surface.

This was the place where her world was to begin again. Mary took a deep breath and, with a huge effort of concentration, confined the pain to its tiny space.

19

Tom and Seamus, his dearest friend, along with their seven young compatriots lived in the coldly elemental splendor of the old abbey. They were expected to rise, as did the monks, at four A.M. to hear Mass or to serve it, and then to dine silently together with the brothers in the dimly lit refectory. Each morning, the oatmeal that at home had filled Tom with a delicious sense of sated well-being was transmuted at St. Ignatius into a thin gruel that didn't satisfy his stomach. Like everything at his abbey home, it seemed unwholesome and mean of spirit.

During their silent breakfasts, as at all other meals, one of the monks would read from the New Testament or from Saint Augustine, or Saint Thomas Aquinas. The brothers' sexless voices would drone endlessly; brown-robed orators intoning holy writ and theological verbiage in singsong boredom, while the diners at the long quiet table would nod sagely when an especially edifying religious thought was put forth. The young boys, of course, took the opportunity to allow their thoughts to wander happily out the refectory doors to freedom, but as they were sometimes abruptly brought back to reality by the abbot's autocratic voice asking questions about the text just read, they had to keep at least half an ear on the lusterless soliloquy.

Only one of these ecclesiastical orators ever captured Tom's undivided attention. Brother Damien, an aged, slightly built brother with curious nobs where other people had a nose, knees, and elbows, read like an angel. In his melodic Irish brogue he made even Saint

Paul's dreary epistles live, for not only did he love the material he read from, but he, perhaps alone of all the assembled breathren, understood its essential Christianity.

Brother Damien was the kindest, gentlest man Tom had ever known. He was so quietly unassuming as to be utterly unobtrusive. And yet, once one became privy to the progeny of his generous spirit and brain, it was impossible not to be captivated by the man. He alone, it seemed to Tom and Seamus, who were often the recipients of his largesse, was worthy of the name of "Christian" Brother. He was the kind soul who would mix a cough remedy from honey and horehound and sneak it into Seamus's room under the folds of his scratchy brown robe, so that Seamus's always cough-roughened throat would be soothed into quiet, and so not disturb the decorous refectory table.

He alone would harbor in his pocket an occasional biscuit pilfered from the cloister kitchen, to be produced for the boys' pleasure in the hungry afternoon; he alone would take the two from the relentless boredom of their proscribed lives and walk with them around the grounds of the ancient abbey, talking to them as if they were grown-ups. Kindness flowed from his elderly spirit like balm, and many's the time Tom and Seamus felt they owed their very lives to his gentle understanding.

"Well, now, gentlemen," he would say in his thick Galway brogue, for he always insisted they think of themselves as gentlemen, although they were temporarily at odds with fortune. "What heavenly tale shall I weave for your personal edification today?" And the next hour or so would be filled to the bursting with magnificent oratory. Stories of the Red Branch knights and their lusty ladies, of the sorrows of Deirdre, or the magical journey of Ossian, leaped to life before their very ears, and they were transported to a more poetic age, on the unfettered Pegasus of imagination.

He would hear the boys' tales of beatings and unfairness at the hands of the other brothers, and give them the only advice he could. "Offer up your suffering, lads, for the poor souls in Purgatory. The brothers, God help them, are sometimes unkind, I know 'tis true. But they do the best they can as the light is given them to see it. Their lives are not easy ones, to be sure. They have little softness about them because they strive so hard to reach their God through pain and sacrifice . . . an unfriendly route, to be sure, gentlemen. Why, the gentleness goes right out of them along the way, don't you see? You must forgive them if you can, lads, for by doing so, you strengthen your own souls and make them grand and glorious before God.''

Tom, unconvinced of the logic of the statement, but devoted to Brother Damien because of his gentle heart, decided to change the subject. He thought the old man's faith touching and dear, and he felt no great need to challenge it, for he had already come to his own conclusions about the Catholic Church.

"Will you tell us of Cuchulain?" he asked, knowing the way to Brother Damien's bardic heart.

The old brother's eyes twinkled at the gentle manipulation of the boy, leading him stealthily from theology to more Elysian fields.

"Aye, Thomas, that I will, for no Irishman should call his soul his own if he knows not of his own heroes. Didn't Saint Patrick himself have conversations with Ossian, and he the son of Cuchulain's friend from the olden days?"

"Tell us the part about how he died, would you?" encouraged Seamus. " 'Tis a noble tale."

"It is that, lad. A tale to stir the blood, indeed, and to bring a tear to the eye as well, don't you think?"

He rearranged his brown woolen cassock on his lean old frame, so that the scratchiness redistributed itself on bony shoulders, knees, and elbows; he tipped his head way back in the gesture of an old minstrel set to render his gift before a royal throng, and he began his tale in the rich, mellow voice of the true bard:

"Once upon a time, and a very good time it was . . . 'twas neither in your time, nor in my time, but it was in somebody's time, when there were giants once in Ireland. 'Twas long, long ago, lads, when the world was young and all the roads led home; when heroes were of giant stature, not the paltry sort of men we see about us now; when the High King ruled at Tara and the knights of the Red Branch held their sway. 'Twas in such noble times as that, Cuchulain (whose name, you may recall from previous tales, means 'the mighty hound of Chulain') was the strongest and the bravest and the finest warrior in all the world.

"He had been instructed in the fine arts of warfare by the fierce warrior women of Scotland, and he had as his charioteer a man named Laeg from the magical land of Tir-na-n'Og. Aside from being the finest charioteer the world has ever seen, Laeg was also a sorcerer of sorts, for he could stop the flow of blood or heal a wound where earthly doctors might have failed, and, lads, above all he loved Cuchulain with his whole heart and swore to be his faithful servant to the death.

"Now it came to pass that a surprise attack came when the knights were all away from home and none but Cuchulain there to guard the place. So Cuchulain and Laeg were forced by fate to fight the enemies of the Red Branch at a certain ford. But before they went out, a passing strange thing happened. The Gray of Macha, Cuchulain's mighty horse, that had borne him always into battle, refused to be harnessed to the chariot of war. Not even Laeg, who could talk to the horse in his own tongue, could move the animal to obey. And when Cuchulain came to the stables, the majestic beast knelt at his knee and wept tears of blood at his master's feet. But Cuchulain knew there was no turning back, for the Fates were upon him, and the night before, he had heard the Morigu call his name, and she the banshee of warriors.

"Now, before they left, an old crone cast a spell upon Cuchulain that crippled his left arm and leg. But despite this handicap the mighty hero fought the good fight and felled a thousand of the enemy, ere he took the fatal wound.

"Now, gentlemen, Cuchulain knew that the time of his departure was at hand. So he called to Laeg and he said to him, 'Laeg, my faithful friend, my time has come.' 'No, no,' cried Laeg. 'Master, I will heal you with my magic runes and you will rise and slay them all.' But Cuchulain looked at his faery companion with sorrowful eyes and said, 'Not this time, old friend, for I have heard the banshee call my name. But I beg one last boon from you, who have served me so faithfully and well.'

" 'If it is within my power, master, the boon shall be yours,' said the sorrowful charioteer.

"Cuchulain said to him, 'I would meet death on my feet, not groveling in the dirt like a stag that has been felled and waits the huntsman's ax; I cannot stand alone, old friend. Lash me to the tree that I may die a man.'

" 'It will be as you would have it, master,' said the man from the land of Tir-na-n'Og, 'for no braver mortal man has ever graced this world than thee.' And he struggled to raise the failing giant, and with the help of his magic druidical spells, transported Cuchulain to the trunk of a tree that stood beside the ford . . . and with his own magical girdle he bound him to the tree.

"Cuchulain's body sagged against the thongs as he waited for the sounds of battle to begin anew. Seeing that their foe was dying, his enemies fell upon the giant and pierced him through his heart.

'' 'Twas then that an eerie glow was seen, leading a column of brilliantly clad beings, all robed in light. 'Twas Laeg at the head of a faery host, for surely no mortal army ever wore such raiment.

'' 'Touch him not!' called a thunderous voice. 'He belongs to the people of Tir-na-n'Og. He has been gathered into the bosom of the Great and Mighty. His like will not be seen again.' And right before their astonished eyes a guard of honor cut the body of the fallen hero from the tree, and placed him tenderly on a golden bier. And they vanished with him and all their golden host, gentlemen, never more to be seen outside the land of Faery.''

Brother Damien's voice had the versatility of a harp—he could manipulate the emotions of an audience with his melodious tones, so that when the story had ended, the listener felt he had heard the music of a minstrel.

Tom and Seamus sat transfixed by the sheer loveliness of the heroic story. How marvelous to be a giant hero, a warrior, a poet; to be carried off by an envoy of heavenly host, and, after all was done, to be remembered.

'' 'Twas a glorious talk, Brother Damien. Sure and you have the magic in your voice.'' Tom's compliment carried the weight of absolute sincerity, and it was not lost on the old man.

''Aye, lad, we could all have been bards, we Celts, had we but been born in other times than these. Did you know that in days gone by, 'twas a capital offense to harm a minstrel? And 'twas expected that any landlord would provide the best of room and board for a traveling bard, for 'twas against the very law itself to turn one out into the cold who sought your hospitality. Ah, lads, my father was a great man at the storytelling. The poetry gets stuck inside of you, you know, and it holds in you. He used to say to me when he was old, 'Ach, the only reason I talk anymore is to keep meself warm.' But, you know, lads, that wasn't the truth of it. He talked because he had the gift.''

Brother Damien began to rise in the awkward way of the elderly, having been seated in one spot for a long while.

''We must get back for the evening meal now, gentlemen. Let us decide what we shall tell the abbot, if he should chance to inquire where we have been. Let me see, now, we shall say that I was informing you on the subject of ancient Irish mythology and . . .''

''And theology, too, brother,'' volunteered Seamus with a grin.

Brother Damien smiled contentedly. It would not be his way to lie to the abbot, but neither would he consider it a fabrication to say that he had spent his time with the lads in teaching them theology. In his mind the history of the Church and the myths of Ireland seemed quite interchangeable . . . like a continuous thread that wound its way through parable after parable in an unending tapestry, both heroic and religious.

He loved the lads, these two in particular. Seamus was a gentle soul, not meant for the harsh discipline of St. Ignatius; he could see the toll already taken on the boy. Tom, on the other hand . . . there was a spark of the old heroes in that one. The poetry and the valor were there, as surely as the intellect. 'Twould be a glorious thing to nurture the seed of greatness in him—for other hands had planted it, and other eyes, perhaps, would see it flower—but he himself could do quite a little gardening in the meanwhile. Aye, 'twould be a glorious thing to nurture such a seed as that.

20

Mary took to life in service with bitter resignation. The care and training of the five Cooke children, who ranged in age from four years to eleven, were her responsibility. She was expected to teach them their letters and numbers, to instruct them in all areas of social grace, and to instill in them both a refined Episcopalian connection to God and a robust Republican understanding of their particular social status. The nursery was Mary's domain from six A.M. when she arose, until after all five children were tucked into bed at night. Once they had retired, she was expected to tidy their rooms and the nursery, to care for their clothing, and to prepare their lessons for the following day . . . an all-consuming task because of their varied ages.

At first she had been grateful for the work that occupied her mind and body so endlessly; grateful for the fatigue that helped to keep her fears and sorrows in tired abeyance.

But as Mary's first year in service gave way to the second, and the second began to lumber toward a third, the narcotic of time began to spread soothing forgetfulness through her troubled mind and heart. She found that she could go for days at a time without thinking once of Michael or Tom, a trick she tried to cultivate for the sake of her own sanity. The only trouble was that as her pain lessened she saw that the old longings still lived within her. Bit by bit she began to *want* again; to want to live, to want to have things of her own, to want to be someone other than a servant. In her third year of service a new and more immediate problem was added to her trials.

Mary sat in the pleasant sewing room one Saturday, more than two years after her arrival in Tuxedo Park, mending the tears in Jonathan Cooke's breeches and musing over what strange demons seemed to take possession of nine-year-old boys the instant they were out of your sight.

All five children had been taken on an outing by their mother, so Mary had ventured from her attic room to do her mending in the pretty little second-floor room that was reserved for the family's sewing chores.

It was a small room, but a sunny one, with gaily colored wallpaper, and its opened window faced on a giant apple tree that graced the rear of the house and had just that week burst into riotous bloom. Mary seated herself on a chintz-covered settee that faced the window, humming softly, grateful for the freedom of an afternoon to herself, a rare occurrence in her harried life. She barely heard the footfall behind her and was startled by the sound of a key turned in the lock; she glanced about to find that Mr. Cooke had entered the room and was standing quietly behind her.

"Good afternoon, Mary," he said cheerily and with none of his usual reserve, and before she could reply, he seated himself beside her on the little chintz sofa. He was a portly man, and the small settee groaned as he overburdened it with his unlooked-for weight.

"Good afternoon, Mr. Cooke," she managed to reply, discomfited by his unexpected entry; she started to rise from her place, but he stayed her movement with the pressure of a hand on her arm. She settled back onto the sofa nervously, glancing instinctively at the door behind her. It was now closed and locked, although she had left it open when she'd entered the room moments before. Icicles of fear crystallized along her spine, and she held herself rigid and erect where she sat.

"I've been watching you, Mary," Mr. Cooke said companionably, "and I rather like what I see." The impact of the words was made more consequential by her realization that Mr. Cooke's leg and thigh were somehow pressing tightly against her own. Unsure of what to do, she shifted her legs as far to the left as the confined space of the sofa allowed, and was appalled to feel his limbs follow hers to their new resting place. Not only was he pressing his body against hers, but he was moving his leg up and down her leg in an insistent rhythm.

What should I do? She plumbed her mind as she struggled to calm herself. Pretend that this unasked-for intrusion wasn't happening, that Mr. Cooke's body had somehow *accidentally* followed and caressed her own? Did she dare to anger this man whose home and employment so circumscribed her life? Who would hire her if he refused to give her the reference she would need? The thoughts pushing simultaneously into her consciousness made her feel dizzy and disoriented.

Dear God, couldn't he just go away? She tried to rise again, but this time an iron grip closed on her arm and pulled her pointedly back onto the sofa.

"You know, my wife doesn't like you, Mary," the man said maliciously. "She says you think you're better than you are. Is that so, Mary?" He still gripped her arm as she tried feebly to extricate it.

"Please, Mr. Cooke," she managed, "I only want to do my job . . ."

"Yes, yes, of course you do," he whispered placatingly, and she could hear the excitement in his voice, "and I can be very helpful to you, Mary, while you're doing your job." She saw that Mr. Cooke's face had grown red with excitement and that there were beads of perspiration on his forehead. Some primal knowledge flooded her; she somehow knew that if she ran, he would come after her; if she struggled, he would overpower her, that the struggle itself was part of what he wanted. There was no way for her to steal the key from his grasp and make it to the door without his being upon her.

Where the inspiration came from, she never after could imagine. She only knew that suddenly some instinct gave her the courage to act. The sewing was still where she'd left it at her side; Mary reached beside her with the hand that still was free. She gripped the heavy sewing shears firmly by the handle, and plucking the great scissors from the basket, she held them in her lap angled toward her tormentor. The large blades ominously pointed outward, she said in as calm and firm a voice as she could muster, "You are very kind to want to help me, Mr. Cooke, but I can manage quite well on my own, thank you.''

Something fearless in the young woman's manner broke through Mr. Cooke's impassioned haze; he stared at the scissors. Could it possibly be that the little Irish slut actually meant him to know that she would attack him if he persisted? Surely she wouldn't have such courage! He looked up from the scissors to her eyes, which were fixed on his own; deep within the ice-green circles he glimpsed the soul of one who understood survival no matter what the cost. He was chilled by the desperation he saw so clearly.

Slowly he relaxed his grip on Mary's arm and let her go. He heard her exhale audibly, then, still holding the scissors in her left hand, she gathered her sewing into the tiny basket with her right. ''I must be going now,'' she said quietly as she rose to leave. ''You'd best give me the key, Mr. Cooke.''

Watching her with infinite fascination, he handed Mary the key. She unlocked the door, never letting her eyes leave him for a moment, and in a very dignified manner let herself out of the room. He saw that the knuckles of the hand that clutched the scissors were white as bone.

Mary did not begin to breathe again until she had reached the attic landing. She would not cry or lose control, she told herself; she would remain very, very calm. Her hand trembled as she let herself into her tiny room and locked the door behind her. She sat upon the little bed facing the door, expecting to hear the terrifying sound of footsteps or an insistent knock; then she realized she was still holding the scissors in both her hands. She laid them gingerly on the bed and saw that her hands were shaking uncontrollably. The only sound she heard was the reverberative beating of her heart.

After several minutes, when no other sound disturbed the frightened silence, Mary lay her body down quietly on the bed and tried to think. She was safe for now, but Mr. Cooke would not forget this rebuff. Memories of Randolph Hartington flash-flooded through her like a November storm, and with the torrent of memories came the realization that *this* time she must act to save herself. This time there would be no Michael to protect her, no welcoming arms to run to. No love to hold fate at bay.

This time she would have to find the means to save herself.

21

"Tom." The whispered call in the dark sounded desperate. "Tom. Are you awake?"

"Aye, Seamus. What do you want?" The two boys shared a cell with seven others, all of whom seemed to be sleeping soundly, if the even breathing from seven little bodies of varying ages, was an indication.

Tom felt, more than he saw, his friendly conspirator leave the little cot across the way and stealthily tiptoe to his corner of the long, pitch-black room.

"I'm in for it tomorrow, Tom," the frightened voice said when he had reached his destination. "I cannot seem to get this Latin into my thick skull, and they'll have my hide for it if I fail again tomorrow."

Tom looked sorrowfully at his friend, for he knew the boy had every right to be fearful. Somehow everything came to Seamus the hard way, and the child was so beaten down by the inevitability of punishment that he lived on the quiet edge of desperation at all times. Tom touched his friend's thin hand with his own stronger one, as if to impart strength to the weaker boy, and he felt a strange, unnatural heat rising from the bony fingers.

"You've a fever again, Seamus. You must get back to bed or you'll have another one of those fearful attacks."

In his heart he cursed the monks who had driven the boy to such a pitifully vulnerable state, for his instinct told him that Seamus's constant bouts with illness were somehow brought about by his victimization.

"I can't sleep at all, Tom, it's that nervous I am. Could you help me with my declensions one more time? I think for sure I'll get them right this time." The pleading little voice pierced through Tom's desire to go back to sleep, and he sat up quietly in bed and reached for the Latin grammar he had secreted under his mattress, for this was not the first time Seamus's sleeplessness had made him the nocturnal tutor.

"God blast their unchristian souls," Tom cursed their cassocked jailers in his heart as he began resolutely to drill the younger, frailer boy in his lessons. They would not kill *him* as they were killing Seamus, he vowed to some unknown deity. He would beat them at their own game.

Seamus O'Toole was the closest thing to a friend his own age that Tom had ever had. The almost total isolation caused by his family situation had kept him from his peers when he was younger, and neither friendship nor any other form of human connection was encouraged at the monastery. Beyond that, the other boys who shared his fate at St. Ignatius did not appeal to his spirited nature, for they were so Catholic that they seemed to love their chains; no matter what the unfairness heaped upon them in the name of knowledge or religion, they seemed devoid of a desire to fight back. Only Seamus was cut from a rebel cloth. Before the lung sickness had gotten hold of him, they had conspired together whenever their lessons and endless chores would allow camaraderie, and on more than one occasion they had plotted their escape and planned their adventurous future together. Without the dreams and the friendship, life would have been altogether unbearable.

Yet the incessant misery had gradually broken Seamus's health and spirit. Over the years Tom had watched him decline and wither, instinctively knowing that the child had simply lacked the physical and mental strength to survive the many assaults they had to endure. Tom, on the other hand, had toughened into tempered metal. His sturdy body at eleven seemed destined to emulate his father's stature, for he already towered over the other boys, and his ability to withstand caning and other physical indignities was a marvel. His mind, too, had toughened with the hardships—he expected little from life and was consequently seldom disappointed.

Thaddeus Martin was a merchant. From the time he had been old enough to talk, he had been selling things to people. Slow at school, he was astoundingly good at anything practical. He was the despair of his third-grade teacher at geography and history, yet he could add a column of figures in his head as fast as the eighth graders, and he could calculate anything that had to do with buying or selling as if he were a machine.

More than that, he loved to sell. When he left school in the fifth grade to become a full-time employee of Mr. Jenkins's General Store, he knew precisely what his own future was to be.

He would be a merchant. He would find things that people wanted or needed; if he couldn't find them, he would have them made. If people didn't want things, he would inspire them to want them. And he would get rich doing it. Not comfortable like Mr. Jenkins, or wealthy like Mr. Davitt, the local lawyer, but filthy rich like the people he read about in books. And he'd accomplish it all by buying and selling things to people.

By the time he met Mary Dalton, things were going quite well for Thad, and exactly according to his plan. He had talked Mr. Jenkins into letting him expand his small business by taking it on the road. First he had taken a pushcart through the streets of New York City to get a feel for the people: what they needed, what they wanted, what they dreamed of yet couldn't imagine possessing. But the people he learned about there were mostly the poor, and they were a limitation he didn't wish to cope with.

Thaddeus Martin wanted to deal with the rich, to learn their mysterious ways and their exotic tastes. He had heard of a colony composed of the wealthy and powerful. And it was near enough to New York so that he could travel there with his wares. Having first made a deal with Mr. Jenkins that the new business, which would cater to a higher class of trade, would demand a different inventory, he had loaded up a wagon with what his research had led him to believe would be needed in a wealthy household, and had taken his business directly to his customers.

Much of what he had they'd liked; what he didn't have, he offered to get for them. Within three years of doing business in this manner, Thad had enough money to leave Mr. Jenkins entirely and start out on his own; plans of expansion, of a whole new life, began to foment in his fertile brain. He had decided that a young man with his business acumen and immense potential should seriously consider the acquisition of a wife and family. It was at just that auspicious moment of decision that he encountered Mary Dalton, governess to the Cooke children.

Thaddeus Martin had no illusions about his current status in life—nor did he have any doubt that it would soon be bettered. Thus the question of finding a wife was a somewhat complicated one. What he needed was someone gently bred but somehow enough at odds with fortune so that she would consider his advances. It had seemed a difficult dilemma until he happened onto Mary Dalton in the Cookes' kitchen one autumn afternoon. Her straight back and regal bearing, her lilting ladylike speech, her gracious manner with the children . . . all had convinced him that the Lord had provided him with precisely the mate he sought. Thus, he had patiently and methodically gone about wooing the young woman, with absolute certainty that she was meant for him and for his future.

"The harder you work, Thaddeus, the luckier you get," his father had told him when he was very young. He had lived by the adage every day of his life, and so far it had proved absolutely accurate. He felt certain that if he worked hard enough at courting Mary, the luck he needed would come his way.

Thaddeus looked tall and intense. He seemed thin almost to the point of frailty for one so tall, and he had a nervous disposition.

Mary sat quietly on the little bench in the garden as Mr. Martin told her of his plans for the future. He had a lovely deep voice and his gestures were genteel, she thought, assessing him. His eyes were intelligent and deep-set, and his face, while no one would ever call him handsome, was a nice face. She tried very hard to feel something . . . anything . . . for the man who was being so nice to her, but the heart is an unruly principality. She sighed, hoping she could find enough conversation to last through the afternoon.

Every month on her day off, Mr. Martin would come to take her on an outing. He treated her as if she were a fragile treasure that might shatter if manhandled. He would take her to a quiet place, inside or out of Tuxedo Park, and they would sit for several hours and talk.

In actual point of fact, *he* would talk. Pacing up and down as she sat, waving his scarecrow arms about as he told her his dreams. He would be a great merchant with a fine store, he told her. One day he would have a great house full of cultured children. A wife with all the social graces, enjoying all that the wife of a rich and cultivated man should have.

But he was a shy man and inexperienced with women. In fact, the only time in his life when he wasn't at all shy was when he was selling things to people. *Then* some alchemy turned his speech to silver, and golden nuggets of inspiration rolled off his tongue. *Then* he could charm the birds from the bushes and inspire the most listless to buy at least a little something because of his charm.

But with Mary, he was shy. He thought that she was too, for she was so reticent toward his advances, and yet she always seemed eager to accept his invitations.

However, the time was coming when he must make her understand his intentions. He had nearly enough money for his shop, nearly enough for his new life. He must very carefully find the way to inspire this virginal girl to be his bride. He had assiduously avoided using his salesmanship on her until now, but it was fast approaching the time when he must inspire her to "buy" what he was offering.

"Mary," he said, folding his long body into a seated position next to her, "have you ever been to Boston?"

She turned to him with a soft smile and shook her head no. The beautiful summer sun filtering through the trees overhead shone on her face and her fair red hair. It nearly took his breath away.

"In another month, Mary, I'll have enough money to do as I've planned, and Boston is the city I've decided on." His eyes sparkled with excitement when he spoke of the future. "Oh, Mary, it's a city of great beauty and intellectual wealth; in fact it has no equal in this country. There are great colleges there, even Harvard University for my sons to attend." He smiled proudly at the thought of his sons at Harvard, and Mary's face softened toward him for a moment.

"It's a melting pot like New York, Mary; rich, poor, old money and new immigrants . . . but it is more refined, more dignified. There's a gentility about the place, even in the poorer quarters, that is most appealing." He paused for a moment as if entranced by the remembrance of what he had seen there.

"Mary, in another month I shall make plans to go to Boston . . . permanently. I want you to go with me."

Mary's stomach clenched itself into a hard, painful knot. This was what she had been expecting; indeed, waiting for, hoping for, and fearing. All the Sunday afternoons, all the conversations about the future had been leading toward this moment. All the nights that she'd lain awake making desperate plans to escape her servant's future and Mr. Cooke's attentions, no matter what the cost, had led inexorably to this terrifying moment of decision. She hoped she'd have the courage to live it through.

Mary spoke; her throat, suddenly constricted and dry, produced an odd rasping sound as the words began. She struggled to clear it and went on.

"Mr. Martin, I'm both flattered and overcome by your kindness in wanting me to be your wife." She found she could barely say the word. "This is such an immense decision that I can only beg you to understand that I cannot make it lightly." She searched her mind for the right words.

She looked into his deep-set brown eyes with their low-overhanging growth of dark eyebrows, and tried to be honest.

"I need a little time before I give you my answer."

Thaddeus Martin had the temerity to touch the girl he wanted to marry. He awkwardly placed his hands on her shoulders and kissed her on the forehead.

Mary's stomach lurched inadvertently. She wondered, if she said yes, if she would be able to bear with his sexual needs as she knew she must. Oh, Michael, Michael! How could you have abandoned me! She pushed the awful thought away and tried to be calm.

"You're a wonderful woman, Mary, and everything I've dreamed of in a wife. I understand that a decision like this is a hard one for a woman to make. I'm thankful to God that you wouldn't take such a step lightly. When I come back in a month, do you think you could give me your answer then?"

She nodded quick assent, grateful for the reprieve.

He patted her knee with his big bony hand, satisfied. She was so pure and good.

22

"Sweet the wine, but soon the payment." Mary could hear her mother's voice propounding the proverb. "Oh, my beloved Michael, how sweet you were to me, my own love," her heart would respond to it. Dear God, but the payment was bitter.

Mary sat on the little bed that was hers, on the fourth floor of the elegant old Tudor mansion, trying to still the inner voices. Compared to the lavishness of the three floors below, the servants' quarters in which she lived were austere as a nun's cell.

The iron bedstead, the pine chest and porcelain washbasin, the tiny bookcase she was allowed because she taught the little ones their ABC's—these were the only accumulation of property she was permitted after her three years of residence. And she was better off than most of the servants because of her position as governess.

She had a decision to make today. Finally. The terrible opportunity she had worked toward relentlessly, if unenthusiastically, for more than a year, was upon her.

Mary took a deep breath and tried to think clearly, her pounding heart somehow interfering. If she married Mr. Martin, as she had so assiduously tried to talk herself into doing, there would be other things. Marriage to a man she did not love, God help her, but children to fill up a lonely, loveless life. A house of her own . . . a position in society with some potential for betterment in the future.

But marriage to a man she did not love was a grievous thought; its reality kept pushing its way into her troubled brain. Cold, long, loveless years seemed to stretch before her either way. She could hardly believe she'd had it in her to encourage the man as she had, but the horror of her futureless life had seemed the worse of the two evils.

"Michael, Michael, I'll always love you." She had repeated it like a litany for the first two years of her servitude. But Michael was dead, and it was beyond her to imagine that God would grant her another wild love in this lifetime.

Mr. Martin might be an itinerant merchant, a purveyor of goods to the rich, who went from door to door in wealthy neighborhoods and sold his wares to any who would buy—but he was also smart and ambitious and full of plans for the future. Plans that would include her if she only had the courage to say yes to his proposal this afternoon after church. At the moment, even a loveless marriage looked safer than her immediate prospects in this house.

She fingered the tiny golden locket on her neck. She had worn it night and day since Michael had given it to her so many years before. Dear God, it sometimes seemed a lifetime ago, that she had lain in his comforting arms. She clicked open the locket and looked intently at the handsome miniature of her dead love. For several minutes she stared at the image, until the tears in her eyes made the picture bleary. "Forgive me, Michael, my own love." She said the words aloud as if to give them power. "Forgive me for what I must do . . . life is hard for a woman. . . ."

With resolute fingers Mary unhooked the clasp of the delicate gold chain and took the locket from her neck for the first and last time. She pressed it to her lips, feeling the warmth that the small treasure had absorbed from her bosom where it had always lain.

She wrapped it in a small square of her best handkerchief and laid it in the drawer of her little chest, hot tears running in rivulets down her cheeks.

Then she dressed for her meeting with Mr. Martin. The only thing she had not yet resolved was how to tell him about Tom.

"Mr. Martin." Mary's voice carried in it a question mark as they walked along the banks of the Little Wee Wah. "I've been meaning to ask you something."

"Yes, Mary, ask me anything you wish."

Mary's voice sounded low and concerned, and Thaddeus suspected that she was worried about the marriage decision.

"I heard a story about a girl . . . one of the servants . . . who had a child out of wedlock." She stopped, embarrassed, and Thaddeus thought it charming that such a story would disturb her so deeply.

"This girl . . . she had been very much in love with the man who was the child's father, but he died before they could be married."

Thaddeus looked at Mary closely; she seemed terribly unnerved by the story. He couldn't think where it was leading.

"A most distressing story, Mary," he prompted her. "What did you wish to know?"

She looked up at him suddenly, her deep green eyes seeming fathomless in the flickering shadows of the trees.

"I need to know . . . want to know . . . what you would think of that girl, Mr. Martin, if you knew her." She sounded breathless, as if this were a most significant question.

Thaddeus considered his reply carefully. Mary was an innocent girl who had obviously been deeply disturbed by this unsavory story. He sensed how important his answer would be to her; she was trying to assess his character as part of her effort to decide about marriage. He would answer with care.

"I would feel sorry for this poor unfortunate girl, Mary, I think. If I knew her, I would feel constrained by conscience to remind her that it was sin and folly that had brought her to such pain."

Mary looked crestfallen; it hadn't been the right answer. He would try again.

"I would of course be kind to such a person, Mary." She looked relieved.

"Would you marry such a person, Mr. Martin?" She was watching him very carefully; it was curious that she was so concerned with this unknown girl . . . or perhaps it was the first time she had run across a fallen woman and was rightly disturbed by the sordid business.

"Good heavens, Mary, what a question!" he responded with a laugh. "Of course I wouldn't marry such a person. The kind of woman I wish to marry is a woman like you, Mary. Pure and good and innocent. A woman's innocence is a great gift she brings to a man when she marries. 'A golden diadem,' as it says in the Bible. No, Mary; I would try to help such a person if I could, but I would not want to make her my wife."

He could see the tears gathering in her eyes; what sweetness she must have in her nature to be so concerned over another's trouble.

"There, there, Mary," he tried to comfort her, "I'm sure this girl will be all right. There are places for unwed mothers, you know, places where the child can be put up for adoption and so forth."

She nodded, unable to speak.

"Are you worried about this girl, Mary? Is she a friend of yours who got into trouble?"

" 'Tis her son I'm worried about," she managed to say, truthfully, her voice thick with emotion.

"Yes, I can see how that would disturb you," said Thaddeus thoughtfully, "the life of a bastard child can be a grim one. It's a great pity that young women like your friend don't give thought to that before they bring these children into the world."

Mary looked at the man with a stricken expression on her face.

"This whole business seems to have upset you greatly, Mary," he said in a kindlier voice. "Why don't I take you home now, and I'll come back in a day or two to get your answer about my proposal of marriage. I don't think it would be proper for us to leave such a distasteful subject and talk of our own happiness." He patted her arm and put it through his own.

She's a gentle one, he said to himself. I must be sure to keep her from seeing the seamier part of life. He was elated to have found such a perfect life's companion; he would take very good care of her.

"What else can I do? What else can I do?" The voice in Mary's head fairly screamed the question as she tried to calm herself enough to answer the man's nervous proposal.

She saw him sitting worriedly before her on the little bench, hoping against hope that she would agree to marry him. The silence was palpable as he awaited her reply.

Sweet Jesus, forgive me, she murmured internally as she gathered her resources to respond to this earnest suitor.

"I would be honored to be your wife, Mr. Martin," she finally managed to say, her throat closing over the words. "But I feel I must tell you that I am far from the perfect person you seem to make me out to be . . . but such as I am, I will marry you." She stopped in frustration . . . more than this she didn't know how to say. She would simply pray that the time would come when she could tell him of her son. She had lain in bed last night in the quiet dark, desperate to find a way out of her dilemma. But there was no way! No means of being honest with this honest man and still doing what she must do.

Finally, after hours of uncertainty, it had come to her: Tom would be in Ireland for ten more years at least, and ten years was a long, long time. Long enough to solve her problems, long enough to find a way to tell Mr. Martin, long enough for it all to work out in the end. If she could make him love her, truly love her, perhaps when the time came, he would understand.

What else can I do? The words still echoed in her head as she saw the elation in Thaddeus Martin's homely face and felt his long, gangly arms entwine her in a thankful embrace. *What else can I do?* It echoed as he told her he loved her and would keep her safe.

What else can I do?

23

Mary lay in bed trying not to cry. It was her wedding night. The small, uneventful ceremony had taken place that afternoon. Then Mr. Martin had brought her to his tiny rented flat in Nyack. An official act it had been, without an ounce of romance. Mary allowed herself to think how she had once longed for the blessed peace of marriage, and then the pain of the thought made her fight it back behind the door of her dead dreams.

Mary's stomach had been knotted with apprehension since the sun had gone down. Michael had told her long ago that a man could tell if a woman was a virgin, and the moment of Mr. Martin's learning her secret was at hand. She silently promised God that she would make this man a good wife, if only He helped her make it through the next few hours.

Thaddeus Martin entered the small bedroom tentatively. He was wearing a long nightshirt with carpet slippers, and his tall, bony body looked alien in the small puddle of light. If Mary had been less frightened, she might have been moved by his awkwardness.

He slipped into bed wordlessly, still clothed, and blew out the candle. "Mary . . ." he said, as if about to ask a question. Then suddenly, without warning, he began to fumble uncertainly with her nightdress, tugging it ineptly up around her hips. He was whispering something about not hurting her, but she felt so injured by every-thing that was happening that the ridiculous thought almost made her smile in the dark. He made a strange urgent sound as he mounted her rigid body and pushed himself between her legs, almost apologetically. She struggled and cried out, not having intended to, but instinctively repelled by the invasion. I must be kind to him, she reminded herself, trying not to feel the agony of the wrong man within her. I've made my own bargain in this marriage, and I must see it through. He was holding her, touching, kissing, thrusting himself into her life. She gathered her inner resources to respond to the man's inept lovemaking and wrapped her arms tentatively around his back. He made another sound, and was still. For a panic-stricken instant she wondered if he had somehow learned her dreadful secret.

Thaddeus Martin lay on top of his wife for a minute or so, breathing heavily. Then he rolled over in the bed, pulling down his nightshirt as he went. He leaned close to Mary's tear-streaked face and said in a kindly voice, "You mustn't be so frightened, Mary. These things that are done between man and wife are necessary in a marriage. It won't hurt you so much the next time, I'm sure." He kissed her lightly on the cheek and soon appeared to sleep.

Mary lay awake, waiting desperately for the slow, even breathing of her new husband to tell her he was sleeping. Her heart beat so wildly she couldn't breathe. So she hadn't been found out! She could live her lie after all. Even the relief of it filled her with guilt and anger. Finally she slipped from the bed and fled to the tiny kitchen.

She took a wet cloth and dabbed frantically at the sticky substance that was dripping from her body. She felt unclean. So this was why women spoke of sex with loathing! This disembodied pushing, thrusting, sweating ugliness that was so unlike the tender, wild, and passionate caresses she had known. Dear God, a lifetime of these nights stretched before her. She washed away the awfulness as best she could and cried and cried and cried.

Thaddeus Martin, lying in his bed pretending to sleep, heard his new wife's sobs and was unnerved by them. Only the fact that he had been told to expect such from an inexperienced girl kept him from despair. It was quite normal, he'd been told, for a woman of Mary's innocence to be repelled by the marriage act. She would learn to tolerate his needs, as all women learned to do; he was sure it would simply take a little time and patience. She was so lovely and so reticent. He would give her time and she would learn to be a good wife. Anyone could see she was an honorable and loving woman. He turned over, and slept.

Outside the bedroom, in the small cold kitchen, Mary stood at the sink in an agony of self-recrimination. She had sold herself in return for this awful bargain, but could she keep it? Could she submit to these fumblings and wake up to this stranger every morning of a lifetime? Had she simply traded bondage of one kind for a far worse bondage of another. The disappointment of life seemed incomprehensibly overwhelming, and the grief that tore at her heart was complicated, made worse by the guilt of knowing that to achieve this agony, she had sacrificed her connection to her son. She had chosen what seemed best for her, without his welfare entering in, and she was being punished. Retribution would be exacted from her every day of her married life, she felt certain. Surely it would be easier to simply end the struggle here.

She had betrayed Michael's memory, she had betrayed Tom, she had even betrayed her new husband. And, dear sweet Jesus, she had betrayed herself.

And all had been done with the best intentions. She had meant to do the right thing, the only possible thing. Good intentions! The road to hell was paved with them. What were all the good intentions worth when all she had achieved with them was this ghastly betrayal of everyone and everything she held dear. She had thought to save them all by this sacrifice, and instead she had sealed her doom.

Mary stared at the kitchen knife that hung in its wooden holder over the sink. One slash of it, one plunge of the long steel blade and her agony would end. She lifted the wood and steel instrument.

But what if suicide could keep you from the souls of the just? The chilling thought took hold of her spine and crept insidiously about her body. What if the priests were right and the soul of a suicide was lost forever, doomed to endless fruitless searching for those it would never find? What if she could never reach her mother, or Michael, or anyone she loved, for all eternity?

The chill had settled in her brain, and a terrible fierce pounding had begun there. Unsure now, she replaced the vicious blade into its rack and sat despondently on a chair at the kitchen table. She tried to make herself think clearly. All life seems worse at night, she told herself. She knew that from the sufferings of her nights in Ireland. Many's the long night she had lived through alone in her mud-walled cottage with her infant son, her Catholic guilts, her fears, and her hungers for a better future.

Then, too, the anguish and the helplessness and the despair of it had seemed worst in the long lonely nights. But she had clung to hope and she had survived, some instinct now reminded her. Hang on, it said; if you stay alive, there's still a chance for you and Tom. If you give up now, he will have no one.

Toward morning, Mary returned to bed and fell into an exhausted slumber.

My dearest Tom,

What I have to tell you will not be easy for you to accept, I feel sure. I can only hope that someday you may understand why I have made this choice.

I have married a good man named Thaddeus Martin. You alone in the world know how I loved your father, so perhaps you alone can understand the pain of this decision. I have not married Mr. Martin because I love him as I loved Michael— never again in this life, I fear, will such a glorious emotion be given me. How can I explain to you why I have done so?

Life is hard, my dearest child, and I am frailer than I knew. You are too young to understand the hardships I have faced since leaving you—suffice it to say that I have lived to learn bitter truths and I have lived to find that a woman alone has nowhere to turn for help but to a man's protection.

I have been so alone, dear Tom, without you. Alone and frightened and heartsick and desperate for us both. I miss you so that sometimes the pain of it overwhelms me and I feel unable to continue.

But continuing is all we have, isn't it? Continuing, and trying to believe that the future will be better.

And that, my dearest son, is why I have married. In the hope that I can bring you to me, in a life that will be a better one for both of us. Soon, soon I shall be able to tell Mr. Martin about you, for he is a good man and he will surely understand.

Forgive me, dear Tom, for not knowing better how to fix things for us. I am trying very, very hard. Harder than I can say.

I love you so,

Your Mama

Tom reread the letter for the last time and crumpled it in his fist. *This* letter he would not keep. How could she have married that man? How could she have married anyone? Why couldn't she wait for him to grow up? Why had his father died? Why? Why was anything as it was? He threw the strangling letter into the corner of the room and walked out, slamming the door thunderously behind him.

24

Boston was a city that prided itself on its respectability. Thad and Mary toured it when they first arrived, and Mary could see that everything about the place, especially its respectability, filled her new husband with a sense of his having chosen rightly.

Their flat was small but airy and filled with sunshine; the neighborhood was far from wealthy, but there was that pervasive Bostonian air of respectability that somehow caused Mary's soul to sigh with relief. There was safety in respectability; safety and the promise of better things to come. *Respectable* people were not forcibly torn from those they loved; they were not accosted by lecherous employers or threatened by circumstance. Respectability was the first step toward a better life, and she, no less than Thad, desired that with all her heart.

Too, the people of Boston seemed different from those of Ireland or Tuxedo Park. She noted that they were gentle in their bearing and their ways. They had character. Even the poor seemed to live as decorously as they could. She had smiled at first to see that the landlord of the small house they inhabited dressed every Sunday in his celluloid collar and a suit and tie to sit in his tiny parlor and read the Boston papers . . . just exactly as he would do, she thought, if his home were one of the stately mansions in Beacon Hill.

Thad had been right about the place; from Faneuil Hall—which had been given to the city of Boston by a public-spirited citizen to be used forever as a free place for people to meet to discuss public affairs—to the fabled wharves where ghosts of whalers, clipper ships, and rumrunners seemed to converge, Boston was exactly the right place to have come to.

It was a place for new beginnings and even a new family. Mary's emotions, of course, were mixed. For she still had never told Thad of Tom's existence.

Not that she hadn't tried, exactly; she had come very close to telling him at one point, soon after their move to Boston. He had arrived home despondent about a mistake he'd made at the store, which he said had cost them a good deal of money. Thad had seemed so distraught about his own failing that she had put her arms around his thin shoulders and tried to give comfort. Poor Thad, she'd thought. So hardworking, so sensible, so unutterably upstanding. It was wrong of him to be so hard on himself over a stupid mistake. And then the idea had come to her: Perhaps *now* was the right time to unburden herself of her secret failing.

"Everyone makes mistakes, Thad," she'd begun bravely. "If only you knew how imperfect I am—"

"No!" he had said vehemently. "No, Mary. I'll not hear of any fault of yours, my perfect little wife. If only you knew how I love your perfection. Your clear, shining purity and softness that makes everything worthwhile."

She had looked at her husband helplessly then, wishing she had the courage to tell him all, despite his protest. But it seemed of such great consequence to him that she be unsullied, that she did not persist. His perfect wife, he had said . . . the irony was enormous. Later, she'd consoled herself with the thought that another time would come.

There were four great department stores already doing business in Boston when Thaddeus Martin arrived there with his new wife, his savings, and his dreams. Jordan Marsh, under the proprietorship of the Mitton family of lengthy Bostonian lineage, was known for providing quality to the masses. Its large and prosperous store occupied one of the "Four Corners," the square mecca of retailing to which Boston's women flocked to refurbish their homes, and their wardrobes.

Filene's, the second of the great shopping emporiums on the square, had been opened in 1875 by the Filene family, who had begun their retailing careers in Lynn, Massachusetts, and had in their second generation of merchant talent decided to share their expertise with the larger audience of Boston. The Filene brothers had the foresight to bring fashionable European dresses to Boston so that local ladies would have the latest Paris offerings. They also had the shrewdness to declare on their opening day that they would not take possession of their store unless the builders turned on the heat to be sure it functioned. Inasmuch as their opening day took place in

August, it was one that customers long remembered as one of the
hottest in retailing history.

Gilchrist's was the property of Felix Vahrenberg, a tyrannical
Bavarian who, having created a fine business from the humble
beginnings of a pushcart, ran his empire with an iron hand. He was a
short, heavyset man with a celluloid collar, who struck such terror
into his employees that when he left his office on the eighth floor of
the tall, narrow building that housed Gilchrist's to make his rounds,
word would spread with the surety of jungle drums to warn employees of his impending approach.

Slattery's, which was on Tremont Street, two blocks away from
the other emporiums, was an expensive and fashionable ladies'
specialty store. It was owned by a colorful charmer named P. A.
O'Connell, who every Wednesday night for a lifetime took his
ladylove to sup at Dinty Moore's, proclaiming to the world that
unlike his merchant counterparts, O'Connell would never consider
letting his store stay open late one night a week for the questionable
convenience of the public.

Thaddeus had researched the market as thoroughly as he could
before choosing it for his future. The competition didn't deter him;
there was plenty in Boston for them and for him. The city was filled
with wealthy Brahmins whose lineage led to the *Mayflower*; it
boasted the children of sea captains who had made fortunes in the
China clipper trade or in whaling; it housed the progeny of the
northernmost angle of the triangle trade; it abounded in bankers,
doctors, lawyers, and academicians. In short, Boston provided precisely the wealthy clientele he had always dreamed of finding, and
provided it in abundance.

Thaddeus had spent long years planning his store to meet the very
specific needs of Boston. He would cater to the young men at the
universities, providing them with the clothing they needed at fine
prices, and he would have it sold to them by the most beautiful
young salesgirls he could hire. He would provide only the *best* in
every category of merchandise, and he would greet each customer
by name and send a thank-you note when large purchases were
made. He had hundreds of ideas for how to cater to the elite clientele
he envisaged. It would only be a matter of time until they would
help him make his dream come true.

25

The infant that lay at Mary Martin's breast looked not at all like Tom. In a way, she felt relieved that he did not. Where in God's name might her firstborn be now, she wondered as she looked at the tiny face . . . just as she had wondered nearly every day of her life during the years since she'd left him.

Tom must be a great boy by now, thirteen years old and very nearly a man. She tried to imagine how her son must look. Like Michael, she imagined, only fairer; a little like herself, perhaps. The baby moved at her breast, the tiny mouth hungrily clasped to her nipple like a suction cup. She must love this baby as she loved Tom, she told herself. She must not remember that her son was gone from her and that this little child was to take his place.

She had not written frequently to Tom since her marriage, for fear of the secret of his existence being betrayed to her husband; she could not risk the boy's writing back directly, so letters were all sent care of Father Grogan and then passed on to her local pastor in Boston. But letters were few and far between. Ah well, perhaps it would be best for the boy if the memory of his mother grew dim. Perhaps it would all be for the best if he could forget her entirely.

The agony of her loss, which had begun to dim with time, had seemed somehow worsened again during her pregnancy and the birth of this small son. So many memories had been brought back; so many memories best forgotten. She felt Thaddeus enter the room and tensed slightly as he put his arms around her and the child. It was an involuntary gesture, for he tried very hard to be a good husband and she knew his prim demeanor that depressed her was simply part of the righteous code he demanded of himself.

"Oh, Mary, Mary!" he said as he hugged her decorously. "He's a wonderful present you've given me." She had never seen her husband so animated, so enthralled, as since this little baby's arrival. "We must have many, many children, Mary," he beamed, then looked suddenly concerned. "If you're up to it, of course, my dear."

She smiled at the homely man and let him touch her cheek. He worked so diligently to better their life. He had a little store now, instead of a pushcart, and there were two young boys who worked for him. Mary had come to terms with being his wife; he was a decent man and she intended to make him a good wife.

"He is lovely, isn't he?" she said, trying to think it was true. In actual fact the baby had his father's owlish expression and a nose two sizes too large for its tiny face.

"He's the most beautiful baby in the world," he told her, meaning every word. "Wait and see, Mary. I'll give you and our children all the security in the world to pay you back for this great gift."

The sated baby's mouth came away from his mother's nipple with a milky popping sound, and the father laughed happily as if the child had done something marvelous.

"You are happy now, Mary, aren't you?" asked Thaddeus Martin, suddenly concerned.

"Of course I am, my husband," she said as earnestly as she could manage. The man smiled benevolently on mother and child before he left the room and began to think again of business. His wife's happiness was something he could never quite be sure of.

Thomas Dalton sat by the bedside of his dying friend. Seamus's fever-parched lips were cracked and dry, his sparse hair was matted with sweat, and his breathing was shallow and rattling.

Two days and a night had gone by since the doctor in charge of the infirmary had told Tom he must go to bid his friend good-bye. Tears of rage slid down the fifteen-year-old's cheeks; he was past sorrow, but not past anger. They might say Seamus was dying of the lung fever, and that might be so, as far as it went—but the truth was that, more than anything else, the boy was dying of a broken heart, and only Tom and Brother Damien understood or cared.

Tom smoothed the tangled, dank hair away from the boy's insensible forehead, and wondered why it took so long to die. His outrage at the unfairness of the very act of dying was keeping him awake despite his exhaustion; he was determined that he would not fail Seamus, as everyone else in this life had failed his friend.

The room was dark but for two sputtering candles, and Tom had covered the boy with his own blanket and coat, for Seamus had a horror of the cold, which could sent him into paroxysms of coughing and gasping for breath that was too sparse in coming. Tom could not let himself think of his friend's frail body being consigned forever to the frozen ground.

"Tom." Seamus's voice was barely real. The older, much larger boy bent his head almost to Seamus's lips to catch his small, precarious words. "Tom, I'm afraid to die." Tom put his strong arms around his friend and held him close in a futile gesture of protection, for he knew not what else to do. "You must do the things we planned, Tom. You must do them all, and think of me." The labor of speaking exhausted the boy's resources. Tom felt his heart quiver like a bird's, against bony ribs scrawnier than a girl's. " 'Tis very cold to die. . . ." Tom felt the life go from the frail body, soundlessly. He crushed the lifeless boy to his own strong self and cried out in anguish, clutching his friend as if to give him life again, as the minutes ticked away in the inexorable stillness.

Tom felt a hand touch his shoulder gently, and looking up through tear-blind eyes, he saw the sorrowful face of Brother Damien.

"Will you pray with me, Tom, for the lad? He had the last rites from the priest this evening, and he died in the state of grace."

Tom's eyes flared contemptuously at the inanity of the statement, but Brother Damien said gently, "I loved him, too, lad."

"Then how can you talk of grace when you know they killed him?"

"The reasons for a death like his are in God's hidden place, Tom. We none of us can know the why of it."

"How can you ask me to pray for him, when it was the Church that murdered him?"

"Not so, lad. 'Twas the stupidity of ignorant men, perhaps, but who are we to say he is not better off by far, this night, than any one of us? His trials are over. He has no fears any longer."

"Nor any life, nor hope, brother! I hope the heaven you have promised him makes up for what he has suffered here at St. Ignatius."

"Let us pray for this immortal soul, Tom," said the old brother relentlessly, as he bent painfully to kneel beside the little cot.

"Why should I?"

"Because he is beyond all else that you can do for him. 'Tis the only gift that you have left to give."

"No, brother, it is not. I can do the things we planned and live a life—and I can remember him. I can remember." Silent tears spilled in streams down the cheeks of the defiant boy.

The old brother blessed himself silently, and took his ancient blackthorn rosary from the folds of his robe and began in his beautiful Irish voice the words . . . "I believe in God the Father Almighty, creator of heaven and earth, and. . . ."

After a long silence in which Brother Damien prayed alone, Tom

began the replies . . . ''Holy Mary Mother of God, pray for us
sinners now and at the hour of our death.'' For there was nothing
else that he knew to do. Brother Damien's soft hypnotic voice was
invoking the Trinity.

Trinity! thought Tom with bitter anguish. Seamus is the last link
in the only trinity I've ever known. First my father, dead too soon
and lost forever; then my mother, torn from me, perhaps for all
time, judging from the tone of her letters. Now, Seamus, kind,
gentle, rebellious Seamus, friend of my heart . . . my trinity of
partings.

Yes, that's it . . . I've parted from everyone I've ever loved. My
own Trinity . . . He wiped the tears from his face fiercely.

He looked again at the body of his friend, and at the old Christian
Brother and at the silent room, and it occurred to him that now he
was completely alone.

Tom applied himself to his studies with an added vengeance after
Seamus's death. He would do exactly as his father had instructed
him. He would learn everything he could to beat them at their own
game.

He had an agile mind and a fierce determination to succeed . . .
to take from the brothers what they had to give and to give nothing
to them in return. When they beat him, he responded with an icy
disdain that they couldn't subdue. When they praised his intellectual
prowess, he responded with the same coldness. His only passionate
desire was to teach them that they could not reach his inmost self.
Not with their praise, not with their punishments, not with their
religion. His mother's letters—part apologetic, part belligerent, part
wistful—had grown more sporadic since the ghastly one that had
told him of her marriage.

Christ, he had cried that night that letter came. Cried and pounded
his fists on the walls in fury and pain.

Never until that moment had he believed his mama would betray
his trust. Even when he'd been asked to forward his letters to her
through Father Grogan; even when he had offered repeatedly to
come to America and she had said no; even when he had begun to
fear that she might marry. *Never* would she desert him if she could
help it, he had believed. Until that letter.

Never once had he written to tell her the conditions of his hated
servitude in the monastery, for that was a sorrow he thought a man

must bear alone. He had been brave, he had kept the faith, preserved the trust—but she . . .

She was only a woman . . . alone and frightened and helpless. That's what he had finally decided. She had done what she had to do, for she was too frail to have been left alone.

The generous thought had finally sustained him, and he had survived this new abysmal sorrow just as he had survived all the other ones.

He would fulfill his father's dream. He would get his education. He would grow to be a man and he would go to see her in America. And she would be proud of the man her son had grown to be.

26

Mary brooded over the question of what to do about Tom. Her sin of omission had grown larger over the years she had been married, so that by now it seemed an insurmountable obstacle. Had she only had the courage to tell Thaddeus of Tom's existence in the beginning, the ghastly guilt that plagued her would not exist. She sometimes wished fervently that he had learned her secret in their bed on that first dreadful night, as she had feared he would; but he had not, and now it was too late for revelation.

They had a small house now, and a life with prospects, and he was kind to her in most things. He didn't, of course, treat her as if her opinion valued much in any decision, but that was typical male behavior. Michael had been a rare one, loving her and confiding in her as he had . . . oh, so long ago.

She sighed, thinking of Michael, who at last was becoming a memory, painful and fraught with tragedy, but one that after all this time could be borne. But Tom—he was flesh and blood. Like this newest, newborn baby who was part of her new life of motherhood, Tom would not cease to own a segment of her heart until they laid her in the ground.

What might he look like now? Would his eyes be like his father's, clear and periwinkle as a mountain flower? So unlike the tiny eyes that stared up from her newest son's face.

She had confided in the young priest who gave her Tom's letters, that she kept a terrible secret. She had thought, when she first confessed the story to him, that he would tell her she must clear her conscience with her husband; but instead he had told her that she would injure her husband and family if she did so now'. Pray for God's guidance, he had counseled, and hope that the lad stays in Ireland with the brothers for a good long time.

That, of course, was the key to it all. If Tom stayed in Ireland until he was grown, it would give her time to work the insidious problem through. Perhaps that unexpected moment would present itself, when she could tell Thaddeus the truth. He was a good man . . . perhaps he would understand. But how could she tell him she'd lived a lie every day of her life?

The impossible dilemma always made Mary's head throb wildly. Sometimes she would have to take to her bed for days, lying in a darkened room and struggling not to let Tom into her mind at all. At the end of her pain, the decision was always the same: She must keep him in Ireland just a little longer, and she must try to make him a less painful memory, so that she, too, could live. She had many obligations now that had to be attended to, so that she could not let herself be destroyed by her guilty secret.

She had received a letter from him only yesterday, telling of his intention to leave the monastery and make his way to America. . . . She would have to write back immediately if she would stop him. Dear God, but her head hurt when she had tried to compose in her mind what she would say.

Sweet Jesus, Tom's letters hurt, filled with hope and goodwill for her . . . filled with grief at their separation. Some day she would pay for her great sin of abandonment. Some day she would surely pay.

Dearest Tom,

I was terribly disturbed by your letter saying that you wish to come to America when you leave the monastery. If you only knew how much I love and miss you, perhaps you would better understand the confusion I feel at what I must say to you.

Now is not the time for you to come here, my dear son—for your sake and for mine. Let me try to explain.

I have always hoped with all my heart that you would do precisely what your father asked of you for a very special reason. You know that his most impassioned wish was that you be educated in Ireland and equip yourself with every possible educational tool before embarking on your life. You, more than any, understand the awful agonies the circumstances of your birth have made you heir to. If you are to breach the boundaries of class and legitimacy, my dearest child, you must have every conceivable intellectual skill at your disposal. Believe me, I have lived to see how hard the road is for any who has the slightest taint of scandal to blight his way. Please believe me when I say that you *must* have your education to see you through.

The rest is harder for me to say to you, dear Tom. But due to the circumstances of my life, which I cannot go into here in detail, I cannot ask you to come to me now in Boston . . . much as I would wish you here with all my heart. In fact it is of the utmost importance to me that you do not do so at this moment. Please knew however that I will try with all my heart to make it possible for you to come to me very soon.

For now, I entreat you, my beloved son, to do as your father asked and finish your schooling in Ireland. Become the gentleman fate meant you to be and then come to me. Please God that I shall be better able to receive you then.

All my love, as ever,
Mama

27

Brother Matthew was a surly, muscular brother, at constant battle with the temptations of the flesh. Nightly he dreaded going to his cold stone cell, for there the Devil waited for his visit, sending him vile and unclean thoughts, and viler temptations. Flagellate himself as he would, that evil member of his would rise of its own volition, drawing his hand inexorably to the hot, hard flesh, dragging his screaming mind into the disgusting process as images of naked bodies rose unbidden to his mind's eye and his swollen penis, desperate for release, forced itself into his unwilling hands.

This particular morning Brother Matthew had arisen from a tempestuous sleep in which the Devil's handmaiden had actually taken his offending flesh into her hot wet mouth, to do with it God knew what, when he had been awakened by the morning prayer bell and had been forced to tear himself and his large, hard problem from the coarse pallet on which he slept. He had poured the icy, half-frozen water from his bedstand bowl on the outrageous thing to quiet its urgings, before racing out into the still dark morning on his way to four o'clock mass. Although he had won this morning's battle with the flesh, his never cheerful disposition had not been enhanced by this new trial. Brother Matthew wanted to inflict pain on someone.

Nine-year-old Sean Sullivan was unlucky enough to be the first likely candidate to cross his path. Sean, the son of the seamstress from the village, was a new addition to the sad-eyed group of youngsters whose misfortune it had been to be sent to the monastery of St. Ignatius for their education. His dull-eyed mother sewed cassocks for the holy brothers free of charge, in return for the book learning they had promised to impart to her darling Sean.

This particular morning the towheaded altar boy, sleepy as a nine-year-old would be at four A.M. on a cold winter morning, had forgotten to remove the wine from the little side table in time for the service of offertory events, and now that Mass was ended, Brother Matthew swooped in quickly on his helpless prey.

"You wretched ignoramus," he shouted at the startled boy. "How often do you have to be told when to get the wine in the holy Mass?"

"I'm sorry, Brother Matthew, I was awful tired and me head just clean forgot. I won't do it wrong again." The child instinctively glanced left and right to see if escape was possible or help near.

"Indeed you won't, you worthless child, because I intend to leave sufficient welts on your back to make sure you remember well enough the next time. Take off your clothes this instant and take your punishment like a man."

"No, brother, please, not the cat! 'Tis cold as a coffin out here. I'll catch me death if I take off me clothes, and you could break me back with that thing, you being the size you are, sir." The child backed away as he talked, but Matthew caught the boy by the collar of his homemade coat and ripped it from top to hem, throwing the child to the ground with the same rude gesture.

The helpless boy started to cry silently, knowing better than to cry aloud for help that would not come. His frightened stare caught a curious lump at the front of Brother Matthew's cassock.

The towering brother brought the leather thong down with a sickening thud across the child's tiny shoulders. Raising his arms high above his head for the second blow, Brother Matthew was startled to feel a muscular arm tighten around his throat, gripping his large straining body from behind. Stunned by the unexpected assault, Matthew struggled to break the grip that had caught him unawares.

"Who are you," he rasped, "that you would assault a holy brother in this way?"

"Holy brother, my ass," came the reply. "You're a filthy, sadistic bastard, Brother Matthew, and I've had my fill of the likes of you. 'Tis just such holiness as this that killed my friend Seamus these three years past. I'll let you go when the child is gone." He gestured to the terrified boy to leave. "Off with you, boy, run for your life, now."

The tall, sturdy young man carefully loosed his hold on the astonished brother, who tore himself free and turned to face his opponent.

"So 'tis you, Thomas Dalton. I should have known your heathen soul. I'll flay you alive for this."

Tom's cold blue eyes met the older man's furious stare disdainfully.

"I think not today, Brother Matthew," he said quietly, "nor any day after this. I have finished with your sadism and your stinking hypocrisy—you and the rest of your holy brethren that get joy from tormenting children in God's holy name."

Matthew eyed the massive boy with the appraising stare he usually reserved for horses. Six foot three or four he must be, and broad as a barn door at eighteen. Young and untried, yes, but strong as a bull, judging from the feel of his arm around his neck, and obviously unafraid.

"You'll fry in hell's fire for this desecration, Tom Dalton," spat the deflated bully.

"I'll see you there first," said the boy. "And if you hurt the child again, Matthew, I'll send you there myself . . . today, before I leave this godforsaken asylum."

The handsome young man, who looked older than his years, turned abruptly and strode from the monk with deliberate steps. He was eighteen years of age and it was over for him now. The fear and the horror were done. Only the anger remained. Never after today would he set foot in this place of sorrow—this dark place of terror and cruelty where Seamus had died and his own heart had nearly perished too.

Thomas Dalton had only two possessions that amounted to anything when he packed to leave the monastery of St. Ignatius—a silver-handled hairbrush and a letter, old and a little faded but inordinately precious to him. He had, too, the letters from his mother in America—but they were somehow not the same to him as his dog-eared legacy, for she had lived long enough to be a fierce disappointment, while his father's memory had been burnished into hallowed perfection.

He looked ruefully at his small mound of possessions and felt the desolation of commitment to an unknown future—but just for a moment. At heart, there was always a vestige of his father's relentless optimism about him.

He was a fine scholar. In Latin and Greek he had led the others easily, and he had a gift for numbers. Sums seemed to come to his mind in a magical fashion, as if he could think in numbers with the same facility he experienced with words. He was handsome and strong, but perhaps more important, he was determined; and taking stock of his inventory of talents and attributes, he decided he was no worse equipped for life than any other man, if a little poorer than most.

Tom was above all then, as at all other times in his life, practical. He knew he had only whatever money was left with Father O'Hanlon, which he imagined would be precious little after ten years' time. He was equipped only to be a scholar or a schoolmaster, or to work with his brawny hands and body. He would need a profession or at least employment, and quickly. But before he could begin the future, he felt he must go to Drumgillan. He had unfinished business with his past that must be handled before the future could begin. He would see his father's grave before proceeding with his life.

Well, Da, I've got my education and a high price I paid for it, he thought as he closed the cold iron gate after him and swung out onto the road to Mullingar. But you know I'm strong. Did you count on them to make me that way or did you think that the Christian Brothers were kindly, learned men? What matter, now, Da? They've done their work well. And we've all got more than we bargained for from them, haven't we? We've all got more than we bargained for.

The route from the village road through the peat bog was sweetly familiar to the young man as he made his way, past the overgrown stone stiles and across the turf-cutting grounds, to the verdant meadow that swooped its impeccably manicured way from the great house to the beautiful blue lake at the bottom of the hill. The house was a monument to Georgian grace and elegance, with its dignified leaded windows and great French doors that faced the world like heavy-lidded eyes at every exposure. Huge chimneys dotted the rooftop. It nearly took the boy's breath away, that beautiful morning in 1892, as he stood by the lough, looking up toward the splendor of the big house, once his father's dwelling and, in an odd way, his own patrimony.

He resolutely climbed the hill, and straightening his travel-weary suit of clothes, having run his fingers through his thick wavy hair in a useless effort at tidiness, he raised the splendid gleaming brass knocker and waited for the specter of his past to open the paneled door. Not since he had spent the night by his father's coffin had he been inside the grand old house. An aged manservant opened the door.

"My name is Thomas Dalton, sir, and I'm here to see His Lordship, if you please."

"Yes, of course you are," said the man incredulously before recovering himself. Tom's resemblance to his dead father was astounding.

"His Lordship is in the morning room . . . young man, doing his accounts. I don't know if he can be disturbed. Wait here until I find out if he'll wish to see you." The old man pattered off on oddly soundless feet, along the corridor of white and black checkerboard marble, and disappeared muttering to himself about people risen from the dead; anxious to see His Lordship's face when he would lay eyes on his brother's son, for that without a question was the identity of the boy who stood so resolutely in the sunlit foyer. Tom marveled at his own curious calm.

"The master says he will see you in the morning room." The curious look on the ancient servant's wrinkled face suggested he would have given a week's wages to be party to the scene about to unfold.

"I know the way," said Tom, his mighty strides making the old man scurry in an attempt to reach the ornately paneled door to the morning room before the boy did.

A man stood silhouetted before the fifteen-foot windows that flanked the east side of the most beautiful room Tom had ever seen . . . although it did appear to him curiously smaller than it had when last he'd viewed it. The windows faced the lake, and the peaceful green lawn that ran to it. The house and gardens seemed to shimmer in the misty-pallid sunlight of the Irish afternoon. The man was tall, and his back was to the newcomer when the boy entered the room. His manner was imperious.

"Who are you, and why have you arrived to see me without a proper appointment?" The voice was much as Tom remembered it from the time this man, his uncle, had come to take away their cottage.

"My name is Thomas Dalton, sir, and I'm the son of a former servant of this family, Mary Dalton."

"Oh, yes, I seem to remember her." Randolph's voice was disdainfully arch. "A rather ordinary girl, if I recall, who got herself pregnant and had to leave our service. Is that the one of whom you speak?"

Tom's fists tightened as he replied.

"I never found my mother to be at all ordinary, sir. And as to her leaving your service, it had indeed to do with her having a child, but I thought that perhaps you would prefer not to discuss that with me." The man now turned from the window to confront him.

"Your mother was a beggar and a whore," said the man in flawless Latin.

"And yours, sir," replied the boy quietly in the same tongue.

Randolph's eyes indicated his surprise and anger. "Where did you learn to speak Latin?"

"With the Brothers of St. Ignatius."

"And what else did you learn there, young man?"

"That the son of a servant girl is as much in need of an education as the son of an aristocrat, My Lord. Which is why I have come to you. I have need of a letter of introduction to the university where I shall go seeking both an education and employment. My father made mention, in a letter I've kept, of having made arrangements for my education. I've come to seek the means he spoke of." Tom said it in a quiet and straightforward way.

Randolph Hartington's eyes narrowed slowly, and his expression became disdainful. He had sometimes wondered what had become of his brother's child and his slut of a mother.

"You arrogant lout, because you speak a smattering of Latin, you think that you should hobnob with your betters, do you? How dare you come to me? Do you think I would have anything to do with the likes of you? You are my brother's bastard and you overstep yourself mightily. Get out of this house before I set the servants on you!"

"I shall leave your house, sir, where my father's memory is

spoken of so lightly. I thought to see if you were as cold-blooded
and small-hearted as my mother thought you, and I see she had a
more than *ordinary* insight where you are concerned." Tom paused
deliberately and moved a step closer to his uncle. "Set the servants
on me if you will, Your Lordship, but remember, I could break you
in half before they came to your aid." Again the words were quiet
and unafraid.

"Get out of here, you ignorant bastard," Randolph sputtered furiously at the boy's audacity. "I'll see you dead before I'll see you at
Oxford!"

"I haven't an inclination toward Oxford, My Lord, despite my
father's having gone there, for I've no great love for the English, of
which you seem such a shining example. I have more a mind for
Trinity or Queens, and you mark my words, I shall get there without
any help from the likes of you." He turned his back on the infuriated Hartington, and strode from the house with a firm conviction
that he would never allow anyone to be in a position to deny him
anything that he truly wanted, the longest day he ever lived.

28

"Young man, slow down if you please. Young man!" an exasperated but kindly voice called breathlessly after Tom as he strode from
the house at a brisk clip toward the wood that fringed the lake.
"Young man, how do you expect me to catch you, with your legs
three times the length of mine? Will you not give me a chance to
catch you?"

Lost in his own anger at the deplorable conduct of his uncle, Tom
did not at first realize that the cultivated and elderly female voice
was directed at him. When he did, he turned to see a tiny, elegantly
dressed old woman tottering down the hill in hot pursuit of him,
undeterred by the swishing taffeta skirts that rustled around her
ancient ankles. The tiny determined shape kept coming toward him
across the damp green grass.

"Well, now. That's considerably better!" The woman, who was
small and delicate with snowy hair and jewels at her ears and throat,
sounded triumphant as she arrived at his side and stared intently up
at his troubled face. "You are the absolute image of your father,

child. I've never seen such a delicious likeness. You have your mother's eyes, I think, but the rest of you is Hartington, to the marrow!'' She chuckled, and her own eyes seemed to glitter with vindictive merriment. Tom thought she had quite the most interesting face he had ever seen. Not beautiful at all, and as wrinkled all over as parchment, but alive with wit and mischief.

"My name is Thomas Dalton, ma'am,'' he said wonderingly. "How do you know about my father, might I ask?''

"I know about him because he was my nephew, of course, dear boy. My *favorite* nephew, by the way, his brother never provided much contest when it came to affection, I'm afraid. But come with me, we mustn't stay here or we'll be seen and they'll come for me and I'll not be able to talk with you. I heard the whole thing, you know. I was eavesdropping on my nasty nephew while you were with him. Kevin, the butler, tipped me that you were with Randolph. Oh, you gave him quite a start, you did. He is a loathsome lout, isn't he, my dear? But I thought you handled him just splendidly. He's a perfect bully, you know.''

Tom marveled at the torrent of words that flowed from this perfect stranger, who apparently wanted to be his friend.

"I may have handled it splendidly, ma'am, but I'm afraid I'm still without my introduction to the university, and I'm angry that I allowed myself to be placed in such a demeaning position. I don't know why I should have had such an absurd desire to come back here at all. I must have been daft to put myself in the same room with one who treated my mother and me with such contempt.'' He smiled a little ruefully, and the twinkly little lady smiled back.

"You mustn't let that worry you one whit, my dear boy. It was only human to want to confront your uncle with the inhumanity he excels at. I cannot assure you a place in the university, Tom, as your father once asked me to do, for I fear that none of the Irish are welcome there. Yet there may be a way for you to gain the education you seek, if your plight can be brought to the attention of the proper persons in Dublin. My brother Edmond lives there, you see, and he has three grandsons in school, and I believe you could secure a position as their tutor to earn your way. I must believe there are those who can be found to teach you, if you seek them diligently, and with my help. If you are the lad I think you are, you shall grasp the opportunity I shall try to give you with both hands, and swallow your pride if need be, in order to get an education. There's always work for the young and strong, if you are courageous enough to survive it."

She stopped for the briefest of pauses to catch her breath. "You are good at your studies, aren't you, Tom? Yes, yes, of course you would be," she answered her own query instantly. "You are Michael's son," as if that settled it. "Oh, we shall triumph over this scoundrel family, Tom, you and I; just you wait and see. Your father was a better man on his poorest day than any of the rest of them on their best, and we shall give them their comeuppance!"

Tom and Eleanor Catherine Hartington Deveraux spent the better part of the afternoon in a tiny abandoned cottage on the grounds of the huge estate. They reminisced and laughed and pretended they were sharing a lovely pot of tea and hot buttered scones with blackberry jam.

"You must tell me where you have been all these years, young man. I've thought of you often since your father's untimely death—wondered where you were and all that. As a matter of fact, when my husband and I returned from his post in the East, I went looking for you and your mother—you know, Michael had written me about you. But I'm afraid I was told that your mother had emigrated to America, so it didn't occur to me that you might still be in Ireland."

Tom told her of the hairbrush his father had left him and how very much it meant to him. He told her, in fact, everything he could remember of his father, which was a considerable amount, and she marveled at the devotion the lad had kept alive in his heart for so many years.

He told her of his odyssey since his father's passing, of O'Leary and the cottage, of his mother long gone to America, of Father O'Hanlon and the Christian Brothers, and finally of his ambitions for the future. She was easy to talk to and interested—and it had been so very long since he'd had a friend to confide in.

"My dear young man," she said when she'd heard the rest of the story. "I have a little maid who can be trusted. Tomorrow at noon I shall send her to the fork in the road, beyond the stand of hazel trees past the lough, to meet you. She shall have a letter for you to take to my brother, and another for the bishop of St. Bartholomew's in Dublin. If one fails you, I'm certain the other will honor my request. My brother will not be sympathetic to your plight, I'm afraid, but he is quite fond of me and perhaps he will do as I ask for my sake, if not for yours.

"There will also be a small sum of money, whatever I am able to gather overnight. It won't be a great deal, mind you, as I don't keep very much at hand generally, but at least it will be enough to get you to Dublin, and to buy you a decent suit of clothes."

Eleanor Devereaux paused for a moment, as if gathering her thoughts, then said, "I loved your father very dearly, Thomas. Had I not been living in the East when all that awful scandal happened, I might have been able to help you and your poor mother. If it is in my power to be of assistance to you, you may rest assured that I shall do so. I do wish my dear husband were alive, for David would help me in this, I'm certain." She seemed suddenly frail and vulnerable to the boy. She looked at him earnestly, as if engraving his face in her memory or perhaps remembering another face she had held dear, in the long ago.

Tom had a sudden desperate desire to hold the tiny woman in his strong arms, but thinking it would hardly be an acceptable thing for a man to do, he simply took her little jeweled hands in his own and bent his head to kiss them. Eleanor Devereaux leaned forward and kissed the bent head lovingly on its wavy crown, rose from her chair, and walked with the greatest dignity out of the little quiet cottage, leaving Tom still stunned by the curious turn of events and thrilled by the warmth of emotion he had felt for the first time in all the many years since he had been abandoned.

Unfortunately, it was to be one of the only pleasant afternoons he would experience over the next few years, for although she was true to her word, Lady Devereaux had it in her power only to open the door for Tom into the world of his "betters"—she was not able to protect him from their prejudice. That, he had to learn to do for himself.

Eleanor Devereaux was a curious mélange of proper lady and mischievous rabble-rouser. Born a Hartington, younger sister of Sir Jeffrey, she had made a point of kicking over the traces all through her youth—a habit that did not endear her to her sister-in-law, Lady Geraldine, but that tended to amuse her brother, who thought her "spunky." "Wouldn't want to be married to you myself, Elly," he had told her on a number of occasions, "but aside from that, I think you've got a lot more spunk than most any woman I know."

Elly tended to quiet down somewhere in her mid-thirties when, having repaired to Paris to be an artist and having stayed on to be a patron of the arts, she married David Devereaux, a handsome, wealthy intellectual expatriate, part of the British diplomatic corps in France.

David's diplomacy carried them from continent to continent as he rose inexorably in the ranks, and Elly had the opportunity to conduct her witty salons in corners of the far-flung empire from Moscow to Zanzibar, an upper-class nomadic life that suited her adventurous nature to a T.

Indeed, even after her husband's death she had remained abroad, until news of her brother's terminal illness reached her and she decided to take upon herself the duty of entertaining him at the end.

Inasmuch as her brother Jeffrey stipulated in his will that she was to remain at Drumgillan, with care and a generous allowance until her death, Geraldine was forced to permit her sister-in-law's residence, despite their antipathy.

For the most part Eleanor Devereaux led as enjoyable a life in her old age as she had in her youth, a characteristic that her remaining older brother, Edmond, found unseemly but interesting in its own way.

Edmond lived in Dublin in a magnificent Palladian structure not far from the Four Courts. With him lived three of his grandsons who were currently quartered in Dublin to receive their education.

Eleanor ferried herself and whatever she needed for comfort— generally no more than Marie, her little French maid—back and forth to Edmond's or to the Continent when the spirit prodded her. Thus it was that she felt certain that while Edmond would cluck his tongue as usual in disapproval of her involvement with their illegitimate grandnephew, he would most likely acquiesce to her entreaty, as he had to most of her other ideas over the years.

As long as Tom lived up to his promise, of course. If he didn't, not even her plea would secure him a place as tutor. She thought she'd cross that bridge when she came to it.

"God damn it, Eleanor, why do you never come to me with a request I thoroughly approve of?" Edmond's chubby chin wobbled like that of a turkey when he was overwrought.

"To be consistent, my darling Edmond. To be consistent. You know very well that at your age a shock is the last thing you need!" Her old eyes twinkled merrily, as they always had, thought her brother; from the time she'd been born, she'd been an adorable minx.

"Well, Elly, as you very well know, I've never been able to say no to you in a proper fashion, and if this young man is as sterling a character as you say, I'm sure I can get him plenty of tutorial work by having a word with the dean. However, I shall go no further than that. Absolutely no further! Michael's indiscretions are not my responsibility, no matter how fond we all were of the lad. He did a headstrong, nonsensical thing in keeping that woman and her boy about, and I'll not perpetuate such silly business."

He looked up over the rim of his glasses to see if she intended to permit him such an arbitrary stand, and was relieved to see her smiling at him benevolently.

"You are a very dear boy, Eddy," she said affectionately to the seventy-six-year-old man. "Always were. I was sure I could count on you to indulge me in this. Just see that the boy is paid a living wage and accepted into Trinity—provided, of course, that he measures up to your standards academically—and leave the rest to him so we both may see what he's made of. Agreed?"

"Agreed. Although I must tell you, Elly, I don't much care what he's made of," said her brother, and they rang for tea.

29

Mary, seated in the rocker, hugged the new baby to her breast and rocked the cradle of her twelve-month-old with her toe. Keeping both vehicles in simultaneous motion was a trick she felt certain only a mother could accomplish.

This new baby, so close on the heels of the last one, had really sapped her strength. It frightened her to think that she might be turning into a brood mare, as her mother had before her.

The twelve-month-old in the cradle started to hiccup, and she pulled herself and her tiny infant burden up gingerly, trying not to wake the baby as she headed for the kitchen for sugar and water to cure her older brother.

Surely four children in six years was repayment enough for her Church and her husband. She laid the sleeping infant in its bassinet and picking up the hiccuping child, fed it the sugar and water and put it up over her shoulder in a well-practiced gesture. Then she walked to the little table, in whose drawer she had begun to collect literature from the suffragettes. Still holding her second-youngest child, she settled down into the rocker again to leaf through, with her one free hand, the brochures she had picked up on the street from the ladies who had chained themselves to the city hall gates. She mused as she did so on the amazing one-handed dexterity that a mother develops during the years when there is always one child at the breast and another on the shoulder.

"I really wish you wouldn't fill their heads with fairy tales, my dear." Thaddeus's voice had an edge to it that startled Mary in the midst of her story to the two little boys. "I realize you mean no harm by it, but I feel strongly they'd be better off dealing with reality from the earliest age."

"But surely every child needs some stories of princes and princesses and evil dragons and such, Thad. There really are fine lessons to be learned from them." Mary felt singularly embarrassed by the interchange, as if she were suddenly forced to defend her motherhood.

"Nonetheless, my dear, I would prefer that they learn their lessons from Scripture or from moral tales that you create for them. This is a hard world, Mary; no good can come to them from thinking a fairy godmother can make everything turn out right. Hard work is the ticket. Hard work and stern moral fiber, and the sooner they know that, the better."

"But, Thaddeus, surely I can be the judge of what stories they may hear." She could hear the indignation in her voice.

"No, my dear. I'm afraid I feel very strongly that I must be the judge. You are well intentioned, Mary, but not very worldly, my dear, and you can have little idea of what a young man must go through in order to make his way. I must ask you to accept my authority in this." He smiled benevolently and went back to his eternal newspaper.

The iron hand in the velvet glove, thought Mary. I'm good enough to give birth to them and do the work of them, change their diapers, clean their eternal messes, soothe their hurts. But not good enough to make decisions. At least in Ireland a mother's voice was heard where her children were concerned; her knowledge taken into account.

Her husband noticed the sullen acquiescence and raised his spectacled gaze from the page. "Soon, Mary, if business continues to prosper as it's doing, we shall be able to hire a woman to help you with the children. I know what a burden the little ones can be. Especially as our brood seems to be increasing with alarming regularity.'' He chuckled in a very male proprietary way that made Mary bristle.

Proud of his manhood for fathering a new child every year, is he? she thought with a subdued resentment. And what am I proud of myself for, do you suppose? For raising a gaggle of children to someone else's specifications. God-fearing, proper, poetryless Bostonian children who were just what Thaddeus desired most, after his store, of course.

But surely there has to be something else for me, she thought. Something that would give me the pleasure and fulfillment that Tom once did. She sat back thoughtfully as the two little boys turned their attention from her aborted story to a box of toy soldiers their father had given them.

Perhaps Thad had inadvertently given her part of the answer. Perhaps having someone to help with the children could change everything. Thad's business was prospering; he had mentioned to her several times that there were people it would be advantageous to entertain if they had the means to do so. Perhaps if she could be rescued from the endless drudgery of little ones, she could even be a help with the business. It would be so good to talk to someone over five years of age for a change!

But she would have to be subtle in the way she went about it. Somehow she must make it appear to be Thad's idea; she must help him to feel that she was not abandoning her duties to her children, but rather turning them over to someone more competent at child-rearing than she. Mary knew that although her husband loved her, he deemed her too softhearted where the children were concerned, and not nearly the disciplinarian he would have wished.

She would have to find someone who could fulfill Thad's stringent requirements, but who was kindly and would treat her children with the affection they needed. Perhaps an older, grandmotherly sort would be best. If she could enlist the aid of Thad's Presbyterian minister in the recruitment program, she was sure her husband would approve.

Then she would find a way to become a more integral part of his ambitions. If she couldn't be part of the business, she would find a way to become the hostess he desired. Suddenly everything looked plausible again. Just one simple sentence tossed out as a benevolent reprimand, not a boon, and there was a future again. Mary felt relieved and secretly content for having found a way to turn the rebuke to her own advantage. Sitting back comfortably, watching her children playing on the floor contentedly, she smiled to herself.

"Now what precisely has made you look like the cat that swallowed the canary, my dear?" asked her husband, somehow aware of the change.

"I was just thinking what a dear husband you are to have thought of finding me help with the children, Thaddeus. You really are very good to me, you know."

"I certainly mean to be, Mary," he said, obviously warmed by the unexpected turn of events. It really was quite fascinating to see how women responded to a bit of discipline and a firm hand. How very like children they were after all.

30

The cold and squalor of Tom's Dublin boardinghouse made it a fitting sequel to the cell he and the other boys at the monastery had so cheerlessly inhabited.

The only room he could afford was on the uppermost floor of an old frame dwelling, eaves so slanty he could straighten his tall body to its full height only in the center of the room. A swaybacked cot was tucked unceremoniously into the lowest corner of the dingy interior, and Tom had learned, ruefully, that he must move the bed away from the low-hung ceiling to avoid the surprise of sitting up when half-asleep and crashing his head painfully into the angular eave. Curiously, the room suited Tom quite well, for it was his own, bought and paid for with his meager wages from tutoring dull-witted, spoiled aristocrats and from doing what day labor he could. Airless as it was, it spelled freedom to his restless spirit.

To Thomas Dalton the only thing that could be allowed to matter now was to follow his father's advice and learn all he could. Books were his mistresses, his teachers, his companions, his friends. He lived for the time he could spend in the Dublin library, and contrived to read nightly in his tiny room as long as the light from his one small candle sputtered in its cracked white dish.

Life at the university was a boon to his mind and an affront to his heart. True to her word, Eleanor Devereaux had secured him a place tutoring her three nephews, a relatively easy task, and through them he had had the opportunity to find similar work with many of their peers.

His experience of the university—at which his presence was suffered at first only because he was under the patronage of Edmond Hartington, and later because of his own gifts—was a grueling time. Only his intellect, which frequently left both his peers and his teachers awestruck by its virtuosity, allowed him to survive. The brothers had taught him many things besides a loathing for their order and a stern, hard discipline.

"Thomas Dalton," intoned one of his professors at Trinity when he met him in the college courtyard, having just learned that he had again placed ahead of his betters in the Greek and Latin forms, "it is pity God saw fit to waste a brain such as yours on a poor Irishman. Imagine what heights you might have risen to, if you were but a gentleman."

"Indeed, sir," Tom had replied to the man with a cool and disarming smile. "I would perhaps have risen to the heights of tact and charity you have attained." And he had proceeded, hands in undersized overcoat pockets, for he could afford no gloves, down the cobblestone path past the churlish professor, without a backward glance. Never in his life had he much of either fear or respect for authority.

"Learn all you can, son—beat them at their own game." So his father's letter had admonished, and so he would do.

Tom's creaky cot was unfortunately a size too small for his lengthy frame, so he was forced to sleep in a sort of fetal position, legs drawn up to his stomach, covered with his small coat and the thin ragged blanket that came with the room.

When I am rich, thought Tom, for it never occurred to him that he would not someday be rich, I shall build the largest bed in the whole of Ireland and spread myself from corner to corner. The thought consoled him when his back ached for the freedom to stretch and unfold itself.

He felt less tolerant toward the bugs and rats. They scurried through the ancient walls and crept out beady-eyed at night to examine their fellow dweller and to pursue their nocturnal quest for mislaid morsels of food, which Tom had no trouble in denying them, as there was seldom enough to fill his own stomach, much less those of his many-footed companions. He was scrupulously clean in his person and his belongings, and pursued his nasty roommates with a relentlessness that, while it did not deter them entirely, at least held them at bay for most of his tenancy.

Poor he might be—a laborer for his bread, momentarily at odds with destiny—but never, never for an instant would he feel himself to be of the lower classes, for neither his breeding nor his dreams could allow that to be.

Dublin in the late 1800s was a remarkable city. It contained both the worst slums in Europe and a glittering social life reputed to be more dazzling than that of any colonial post but the courts of the maharajas.

The Castle Season called out both the native Anglo-Irish aristocracy and the Garrison stock, the socially elite regimental class with their fancy uniforms and manners and their tales of exotic duty in the empire's many colonies.

The juxtaposition of extreme poverty and absurd wealth was beginning to cause foment in Dublin by the time Tom Dalton arrived in the city in 1892. There was talk of Home Rule for the Irish, after seven hundred years of English domination. There was even a revival of interest in Irish myths and the old Irish language, and a strong sense of Irish nationalism was beginning to emerge. There was talk of a labor union to protect the workers, and there was an extraordinary literary renaissance being fostered by writers and poets of stature. In short, the Dublin in which Tom's odyssey began was a city full of fascinating possibilities.

Tom's relatives in Dublin, and the others of their class, took little notice of the implications of such a nationalist rekindling. But the young men of the university debated everything hotly, the upperclass students speaking derisively of the peasant agitation, the lowerclass boys excited to a frenzy by the sudden possibility of freedom.

Tom was in a curiously fortuitous situation for hearing both sides of the explosive debate. He tutored the rich, whose views were predictable: Home Rule was insane, a bunch of stupid peasants couldn't govern themselves . . . the Irish should be grateful for Mother England's supervisory control of Ireland's destiny . . . this business of reviving an antique peasant language full of ugly gutturals and glottals was ludicrous when English had been spoken in Ireland for hundreds of years. And as to their literary pretensions . . . Ireland never had produced a great poet or playwright and she never would! He heard all their self-satisfied views with an amused tolerance.

For the story told in the pubs he frequented, when money permitted, was a vastly different one.

"Have you heard of the Gonne woman traipsing around the country helping the farmers?" The young man named Richard stood with a mug of beer in his hand and asked the question of all at the bar of the small, pleasant pub.

"I have, that," said his companion, "and Godspeed to her, I say."

"Who is she and what's she up to?" asked Tom from two places farther down the bar. The first man turned to him and raised his glass by way of introduction. They'd spoken before in the pub's informal cordiality.

"Daughter of some garrison colonel, she is. And the most magnificent woman in Europe, according to the newspaper accounts of her socializing," said the second young man by way of corroboration. He was a pudgy lad of twenty-two or so, and another familiar face at his particular pub.

"I've not a doubt in the world she's gorgeous," said Tom with a laugh at the enthusiastic description, "but what the hell is she up to?"

"She goes from cottage to cottage, near as I can tell, and organizes the farmers against the landlords up in Sligo. You know times are hard there and the rents on the wee farms are outrageous, for the landowners are trying to drive out the Catholics from their land so they can pass it out to the Prods who are more to their liking.

"Then along comes Miss Maud Gonne with all her six-foot frame of proud beauty and she tells them to stand up on their hind legs and fight like men! What's more, she gives them money collected by her and her Ascendancy friends and she gets them legal advice and tells them to vote on the Sinn Fein candidate when the time comes. And by God they do it!"

"She must be quite a lass," chuckled Tom admiringly, imagining the consternation those of his father's class must feel that one of their own was so vocally on the side of the Irish.

"Are you going to hear Mr. Yeats, Tom?" asked the round-faced boy. "He's to be reciting some of his poetry on Tuesday night at the hall."

"Aye, George. I'd not miss Mr. Yeats if I could help it. He's got the power to stir a man with his quiet words, hasn't he?"

"Right enough," said the young man who had spoken first.

"He's the best of the lot in my opinion, although I do get a big bang out of Dr. Gogarty at times, too. They say Mr. Yeats is wild for Miss Gonne, you know."

"It sounds as if he'd have his hands full with that lass," laughed Tom as he drained the last of his beer and felt in his pocket for a coin to pay for it.

There is life in Dublin these days, he thought as he bade good-bye to the two at the bar and turned up his collar against the cold of the night air. There'd be much to hold me here if I didn't have other plans. Revolution and politics and poetry are a heady mix for a man, he thought, and smiled to himself on the cold street. But he had unfinished business to attend to. .

He must go to America and see his mother . . . find out how she was faring and see that she was safe. Then he could go his own way with a clear conscience and a settled heart.

He had written her of his intention and would await her reply before leaving.

"Aunt Elly?" Tom stood in the doorway of the drawing room in Edmond Hartington's house, his bearing full of agitation and distress.

Eleanor had made it clear to her brother and his family that she intended to receive her grandnephew whenever she was in Dublin, no matter that he was considered a servant in the Hartington house. If Edmond did not wish her to do so, she would stay at the Shelbourne Hotel and receive him there.

Eleanor Catherine Hartington Devereaux looked up from the escritoire at which she was seated and saw a very sad young man. He was also very handsome, a fact that struck her each time she saw him. He was tall and broad, his red-brown hair was abundant if a trifle unruly, but there was an uncommon virility to his appearance. And his eyes were a special blue, a curious deep color that somehow hinted at mysteries within.

"You look a bit downcast, my dear boy," she said, motioning him to enter and seat himself near her. She had no illusions about the hardships of Tom's life, although he refrained from discussing them with her, a gesture she attributed to his good breeding.

"I'm in need of advice, Aunt Elly . . . and in need of a friend." He smiled ruefully at her, and she smiled back with satisfaction that he thought her such.

"Then it would seem you have come to the right place," she said quietly. "What is the trouble, my boy?"

"My mother, Aunt Elly . . . I've had an unsettling letter from her. You know that I've been planning to go to Boston as long as I can remember, and I'd written her to say that I was saving money and that by next year I could leave my studies and come." He stopped, seemingly embarrassed, then cleared his throat and went on. "She's asked me not to."

The old woman looked into her nephew's eyes and saw there the great hurt of an orphaned child. What an old sorrow this must be for him, she thought, and chose her words carefully.

"Does she say why?"

"She says her husband is involved in community work as well as in his store and that it would be awkward for me to suddenly appear out of nowhere at the precise moment he is getting into the public eye."

She nodded, digesting the story.

"Has it occurred to you that her husband may not wish you to be with them at all, Tom? Few men are openhearted enough to accept a child not their own, even if the circumstances surrounding that child's birth were less *special* than yours." He looked at her closely, and she continued.

"I've given this a great deal of thought, you know, my dear. I fancy that because I am a woman, of however ancient vintage, I can place myself more easily in your mother's mind than you can.

"Let us imagine, for just a moment, the impossible indignities of the life she faced because of your birth and your father's death. Mind you, dear boy, I place no blame at your father's doorstep in this, for I believe he must have loved your mother extraordinarily much to have braved all that he did for her. Nonetheless, the sad facts of the story remain the same, despite the good intentions."

Tom rose from his chair, as if too agitated to remain still, and walked to the window, where he stood looking out so that she could not see his face. Eleanor felt deeply touched by the boy's heartache, but she also knew that he must face the truth before he faced his mother, so she continued.

"My dear Thomas, you have no way of knowing the hardships of your mother's life. For a woman to be branded an adulteress, the mother of an illegitimate child, is a ghastly thing—and the life of a servant can have few rewards, it seems to me. Particularly for one such as your mother, who fully expected to live her life as Michael's wife. It must be hard indeed to have been plunged back into the abyss of servanthood.

"In truth, my dear, I think she most likely did the only thing at her disposal in marrying this man. And who is to say that he wishes to have her son from her other life in his home? The odds are your mother has no choice in this at all!"

She could see the emotion in his tensed shoulders; the veins in his strong neck stood out from the skin with the effort he was making to digest her words. Eleanor softened her voice.

"Thomas, look at me, please. I have something very important to say to you."

With an effort of will he finally turned from the window and looked at his aunt; the infinite unhappiness in his face made her more firmly resolve to say what she had in mind.

The dignified little woman stood up with some effort; she had not been feeling herself of late. She took the young man's hand, marveling at the immensity of it next to her own small one, and led him to one of the brocaded sofas that flanked the drawing room fireplace. She sat down very close to him.

"You must believe that I do not say these painful things to you to be unkind, my dear. I have watched you learn and grow and develop now for several years, Thomas. You are a most remarkable young man. Gifted in so very many ways. Intellectually, you can run rings around my overbred nephews and their pompous friends. Physically . . . why I believe you are quite the most dashing young man I've ever laid eyes on, and you must believe me when I say I've laid eyes on quite a few!" She chuckled softly, having hoped to make him laugh, but seeing that he did not, she went on.

"But emotionally, my dear boy . . . oh, there's where we run a cropper! You have been bruised by fate without a doubt. But you have also been given great gifts and opportunities. After the next few months you will have fulfilled your father's last wish and you will have gotten your education, and a damned good job you've made of it.

"But always in the back of your brain there is this emotional tie to your mother. I see it sometimes in the haunted way you look at other mothers with their children. I see it in the pain behind your eyes for days after you've received a letter from her."

"But she's my reason for doing all this, for trying so hard. . . ."

"She is not!" She snapped the words at him emphatically. "She is most assuredly not the reason anymore! Perhaps when you were a child and you needed a lodestar in your interminable loneliness, she was the reason. But not now, Tom. Now *you* are the reason!

"You deserve to have a life. You deserve to make your fortune, to find someone to love as your father loved Mary, to have fine children, to see your own dreams come true.

"If, in the course of all that, you can find a place for your mother in your heart, then do so, my boy, by all means. But you are a man now. A wonderful, intelligent, strong and decent young man, and you must have your own life—the best one you can wrest from fate. Just as she must have hers!"

Tom held the old woman's hand in both his own for a moment. He somehow, until that instant, hadn't realized how tightly he had gripped it until he saw that her rings had bitten into the back of her hands.

"Then you think I shouldn't go to her?" he asked tentatively.

"Not until she asks you to, or until you can do so with such independence of spirit that it doesn't matter what happens when you meet." Her voice was warm but firm, and he again wondered at the good fortune of her having entered his life when he had been most in need.

"It may not be in her power, Tom, ever to ask you to come. Her husband may oppose it, her children might be harmed by it, her husband's career might be jeopardized, or a host of other possibilities. Surely you know in your heart that some powerful constraint must have been placed upon your mother so that she cannot in conscience offer you welcome."

He nodded. She was right, of course. It was a child's dream that he must abandon. His mother belonged to others more than she did to him now. He must make his own way—must not burden her more than she was already burdened. When he was rich and famous, he would go to her and she would be proud to have him.

"I love you, Aunt Elly," he said with some embarrassment at the catch in his voice as he did so. "I love you very dearly."

"And I love you," said the genteel little lady with absolute surety. She had said what she intended to say, and he had accepted it in the manner she had expected of him. He was a very special young man and he would make his way. She was only sorry that she probably wouldn't live long enough to see his destiny unfold.

Three days after their conversation, which he had taken greatly to heart, Tom arrived to visit his aunt, with flowers he had saved to purchase as a thank you. He found that she had been taken ill and that the doctor had persuaded her to return to Drumgillan. It was a terrible disappointment.

Aunt Eleanor wrote to him often and encouragingly during his last year in Dublin, from Westmeath. He missed her sorely, his one connection to the past, his benefactress and his sensible friend. When he received word of her death, it seemed clear to him that his last link with Ireland had been severed and it was time to move on.

He would go to America, but not to Boston, he decided. It would be painful to be in the same city with his mother without seeing her, and he would not see her until she invited him. New York was the ideal alternative.

Eleanor Devereaux had told him of the time she'd spent there; it sounded as if possibilities abounded in New York, and it was easy enough to find a ship bound for the port. It was near enough to Boston for a visit if the opportunity came, far enough away for him to build a life of his own.

31

"You're looking glum, I must say." The voice at Tom's shoulder was that of the barmaid at the Mews Tavern. It was the public house closest to his lodging and the one in which he felt most at home. The news of Eleanor Devereaux's death had sent him there seeking solace.

He looked up at the bosomy dark-haired girl and smiled. He had found, since living in Dublin, that women gravitated toward him.

After leaving the monastery Tom had discovered girls—and they had discovered him. His large stature and comely face that somehow reminded them of the ancient Red Branch heroes weren't likely to pass unnoticed by the society of the servant girls and barmaids whose acquaintance was permitted a fellow of Tom's low station.

"Aye, lass, it's glum I am indeed. Will you have a Guinness with me while I tell you my troubles?" He moved over on the wooden bench to make room for her, smiling at the way her full bosom bounced when she bent to fill his glass.

"You know old Molly'd let you cry on her shoulder any time at all!" She laughed as she said it, and reached over to tousle his shaggy hair affectionately. "What's on your mind tonight, Tom?

I've seen potatoes in the famine with better-looking faces on them than you've got.''

"There was a great lady, Molly, who took a fancy to me and did me more than a few kind turns. I've just found out she's dead, and it's got me down to know she's gone.''

"A great lady, was she? And here I thought I was your only love!'' She laughed aloud at her joke, and then seeing that he was seriously troubled, changed her tack.

"I'll be off duty at twelve, lad. That's only half an hour from now. What say I try to cheer you up as best I can? It'll be on the house, so to speak, because you're my friend and you're feeling peaky.''

She smiled benevolently at the man. Molly wasn't a beauty by any man's standard, but there was a womanly largesse about her that men were attracted to. Tom had shared her bed on more than one occasion in the past and had had a good time of it.

The whole business of women had been an intriguing revelation to him since he'd arrived in Dublin. The monastery of St. Ignatius had severely neglected the side of his education that pertained to women, although nature tended to provide ample opportunity for him to make up for lost time.

Women came, it seemed to him, in an infinite variety of categories. The barmaids were jolly, good-natured girls of easy virtue and comfortably cushioned form, who knew what they were about in bed and were happy to teach him whatever he wished to learn. Servant girls were sometimes no less willing to be bedded, but he had a horror of them, for they were too innocent to be taken advantage of, and he was told (by the barmaids who didn't wish to share him) that such country girls didn't know how *not* to get with child; thus visions of his mother's plight made sex with any of them an unconscionable act.

Wives of other men he found to be curiously available to his explorations too. It never ceased to amaze him how many sad, lonely women inhabited houses from cottage to mansion. Women to whom husbands had been unkind, or lacking in sensitivity, or simply slow of understanding. There seemed an endless stream of women who longed for someone merely to love them, even a little, and make them forget for a brief moment their methodical, loveless lives.

Not that he really loved any of the many ladies he bedded during this time, for although they stirred his heart or body, they were merely explorations of a whole new world that the monastery of St.

Ignatius hadn't prepared him for; and he always tried to be scrupulously honest with them about his intentions.

Tom never went to bed with virgins if it could be avoided, for he felt that obligations were thereby incurred. He never even flirted with a servant girl if he could help doing so, and he went to bed with the wives of other men only if he felt they didn't love their husbands. He always did his best to make the woman whose body he shared glad that he had done so, and he never, ever, talked of his exploits with other men. Such was the code he evolved for himself out of equal parts of ignorance of how these things worked, a very robust constitution, and a genuine tender love for women.

But tonight he was in need of companionship and comfort. His great-aunt's death and the hurt caused by his mother's letter had left him feeling alone and curiously vulnerable.

Aunt Elly's advice had been just the right ticket, of course. Live! she had said. Enjoy life. Do all the things you've dreamed of.

"Molly, my girl," he said suddenly, realizing the barmaid still awaited a reply to her generous offer. "I can think of nothing in this world I'd rather do than spend a wild night with you, lass." He patted her fondly on the bottom as she turned happily to finish the last of her chores for the evening.

She laughed merrily and threw him a kiss and a wink as she resumed her place behind the bar.

Edmond Hartington sat behind his study desk as Tom entered the walnut paneled room to which he had been summoned and stood quiety waiting for the older man to acknowledge his presence.

Aunt Eleanor's brother had done him a number of good turns since his arrival in Dublin. Introductions, tutoring jobs, even his place in the university, could be traced to this rotund old gentleman's intervention, however under duress from Aunt Elly it might have been.

The old man looked up over his spectacles, cleared his throat, and motioned to Tom to be seated.

"My sister was very fond of you, young man. I suppose you know that. And I was very fond of her.

"She asked me to see that you got this letter . . . before she died, she made that very specific request." He stopped speaking, and extricating a linen handkerchief from his pocket, he blew his nose and wiped his eyes.

"Damned good woman she was," he said by way of explanation. Then put the hankie away.

"Can't say I've fully approved of this business of getting you educated. Not that you haven't acquitted yourself like a man; you have. Just that I don't hold with people getting above their station, and education, strictly speaking, is best left to the class that can make use of it, if you ask me." He looked up at Tom's steady gaze.

"Of course, you didn't ask me, did you? . . . well, neither did Elly, and that's all over the dam or under the bridge or wherever it goes.

"At any rate, here's the letter she asked me to deliver and a package. Don't know what's in it, but here it is."

Edmond Hartington raised his bulk from the chair and made a gesture of dismissal.

"Good luck to you, lad," he said, suddenly holding out his hand. Then, peering over his spectacles again he looked directly into Tom's face, as if studying it.

"Damned strange thing, but you certainly look like a Hartington!" he said with finality. "Damned funny thing, that." And he left Tom standing alone at the desk with the letter and the package.

He opened the letter first:

My very dear nephew Tom,

What can I say to you now that the end is near, and I shall vanish without seeing you again, I'm certain.

Don't grieve for me. I've had a lovely, long life, filled to the brim with adventures. Perhaps death will be simply another of these. I'm not in the least afraid, as I've always loved journeys to foreign lands and they've always been kind to me.

I have adored knowing you. Sharing your life in even a small way has given me inordinate pleasure. And I believe that in my own way I've been able to help you a bit and to fill a void in your life, just as you've filled one in mine.

I've left you a bit of money. Not a lot, as you were always so stoical about refusing my offers that I do not want to take advantage of overcoming your scruples at the end. Besides, if the truth be known, I haven't much money of my own—most all is a trust from Sir Jeffrey that reverts to ghastly Geraldine when I go.

Not that it matters, I think, for I have no doubt you will make your own fortune when you get to America.

And I do urge you to go there, Tom! Escape the class system of Ireland. Go to a land where the only aristocracy is one of achievement.

More important than the money, I've left you a small gift to show you I remember the story you told me that moved me deeply when first we met.

Bonne chance, dear boy! If there is anyone waiting on the Other Side when I get there who can be of use to you, rest assured I shall badger Him as mercilessly on your behalf as I have badgered poor Edmond.

With love and confidence,
Your Aunt Eleanor

The box held, besides a small sum of money, a silver-handled hairbrush, the mate to the one his father had given him so many years before. Engraved in its glittering surface were the initials TH and the Hartington coat of arms.

32

Mary Martin looked at her husband across the dinner table and sighed. Only on Sunday afternoons was there any assurance of his dining with her and their brood of four. The more successful he became, the more time he spent away from them, it seemed.

He would arise at five to be at the store by six. There he would wander the aisles waiting for mercantile inspiration; often it came to him. Like the bargain tables at the front of the store where obsolete inventory could be sold for little more than cost. Anything from lace jabots to ladies' shoes might find their way there, and Martin's was gaining a reputation for having the customer's welfare at heart despite the fact that the bulk of the store was filled with very costly merchandise.

Thad had discovered that there were always people with money who would pay for quality; the lesson of Tuxedo Park. Mary was his other Tuxedo Park acquisition, of course, and she knew she was as much part of his ambitious plan for the future as was the merchandising experience he gained daily.

He had big plans, increasing month to month, it seemed. She

looked at him across the table with a certain amount of pride now. Yes, and if the truth were known, fondness. Not the wild, passionate love she had felt for Michael, and not the bright-burning-coal-in-the-breast love that had nearly killed her when he was gone. But a secure warmth that was steady and reliable. Thad would make something of their life, and she would always be safe with him.

Poor Thad, she thought without meaning to. He did the best he could. It was not his fault that she had known so much better.

She wished he had a few more frills where the children were concerned, too. Proper Mrs. Anderson minded the children during the day, and there was no nonsense at their house at dinnertime, either. Each child was expected to have a story to tell about his day. Preferably a moral lesson to report, but a piece of news gleaned from the Boston papers was acceptable too. No hushed lullabies or Irish rebel songs were sung to them; no fairy tales of the wee folk or the fairy cairns that contained them. Just safe, commonsensible lessons and as much knowledge of the world around them as they could tolerate.

She suspected that she and Thad would raise no poets together, as she and Michael had once imagined doing. Ah well, she couldn't see that Thad's child-rearing theories were doing them much harm at all. The three little boys and one girl seemed to adore their somber father, and it suited his ambitions very well to have three sons.

"Anna," called Thad to his youngest child, "do you have a story to tell us today?" Mary watched the small face compose itself for recitation, thinking it was a strange thing indeed for a mother to have children who didn't look or behave like her at all. It was as if she were simply a conduit for Thad's progeny, a means for their entry into the world, not a part of their blood and bone.

"Oh, yes, Papa," lisped the five-year-old. "Today I learned about a little girl like me who was on a big boat with her papa and he was the captain and there was a big storm and everybody said the boat would sink but the little girl said no it wouldn't!" The entire story was one long sentence without pause for breath. Thad looked at Mary, an amused twinkle in his eyes behind his rimless spectacles.

"And why was that, Anna?"

"Because the little girl said, 'Isn't God upon the ocean just the same as on the land?' 'Cause everybody else forgot God could take care of them except the little girl."

"And did they get saved?"

"Oh, yes, Papa, 'cause God saved them."

"*Be*cause, dear," said her proud father.

"*Be*cause He did," she repeated pleasantly, and then it was Ted's turn. After that it would be Robbie and finally Andrew. All fine Anglicized names her children had been given by their father. No Desmonds or Seans or Siobhans would she hold at her overflowing breasts.

She sighed again. It was after all a perfectly good life, and there were prospects that it would get better.

She hadn't heard from her *other* son in a very long while now. Mary wasn't sure if not hearing made the guilt more or less bearable. He was a man now, this long-lost son of hers, and he had most likely forgotten her entirely. God knows, he'd had every reason to do so. But she never could forget.

Mary laid down her pen and reread the letter she had written to her brother Rory in California. His letters to her always sounded so cheerful and optimistic; she wanted hers to him to be no less newsy and full of enthusiasm.

Rory had prospered in his new life in America, almost from the first. All the books he had read about America had finally paid off, for he had headed west as soon as he'd landed on United States soil; west toward the farmland he had always dreamed of. "California, Mary!" he had written to her. "A golden land where the sun shines all year long and the ground is so fertile you barely need to scratch its surface for young seeds to take root!"

He had a farm in a lovely green valley where fruit and vegetables fairly grew themselves, if you could believe his stories—and the horses he now shod were his own. He also had a wife and two sons whom he adored; Rory's letters were always brimming with news of those he loved.

Mary hoped her own letters gave her brother as much joy as his gave her; he was the only connection she had with the old days of her family. He and Tom, of course. She sighed as the thought of her son flitted through her mind, then pushed the thought away and began to reread what she had written.

Dear Rory,

Life in the Martin household is much as usual. I am once again expecting, much to my surprise. Anna, Ted, Andrew, and Robbie are well and sprouting like good Boston elms, and Thad's store seems to be growing by the day.

I now have a maid to help me in the house as well as a governess—little do the servants suspect, I imagine, that Mrs. Martin was once in their position!

Thad is anxious that the boys be sent away to school, although I am resisting the idea. He says my reticence harks back to my heritage from a country in which entire families live together for a lifetime. Obviously, he hasn't a clue about how lacking in familial connection our Daltons are!

Have you heard from any of them, Rory? Needless to say I've heard not a word since the day I left to go to Michael—I expect I shall hear no more of any of them till I die. Ah well, my life has prospered without them.

And yours! My dear brother . . . your last letter makes California sound like the Garden of Eden! I'm so very glad for all your good fortune and happiness. Be certain to give my love to Eileen and the boys.

                                          Your loving sister,
                                          Mary

It all sounded so gay; so happy and prosperous, just as she'd intended it to. Why, oh why was it that with so much to be thankful for, she never felt truly happy?

Why was it that her children gave her so little pleasure? Why, that her husband's love was never a match for Michael's? Why had she never had the courage to own up to Tom's existence? Why could she go for months without giving him a thought and then suddenly be riveted with pain at the remembrance of his face? She pushed the question marks of life aside, a tactic she had become adept at.

She had so much on her mind these days, after all, with the new child on the way. And so much to be grateful for. She would try to feel about it all as she had sounded in the letter to Rory. She would try to do better.

Besides, she had a growing conviction that the child she carried within her would be a happy addition to her life. It was a full five years since she'd last been pregnant and she would have sworn that another pregnancy at this late date would have filled her with anger and a sense of entrapment, as the earlier ones had done. But somehow that was simply not the case.

From the first moment, for some inexplicable reason, she felt wonderful about this new life within her. Not since she had carried Tom had she felt such a robust strength and vitality while pregnant.

Even her relationship with Thad had settled into a comfortable continuity in the past months, and there were other comforts, too. The comforts of growing financial security and a place in the social life of Boston.

Mary picked up the pen again on impulse and added a postscript to the letter.

> P.S. I'm really so very happy about the new baby, Rory—I'll send you a picture of us all when he arrives.

33

Tom sat in the pub thinking it would be the last time he'd ever sit there. He winked at Molly over his glass of beer and saw that she looked sad behind her cherubic smile. The hour had grown late and few were left in the public house; most, having consumed what they could afford, had trundled off to their varied homes or boardinghouses. But Tom had no great desire to hurry back to his, on this his last night in Dublin.

Tomorrow the *Lady May* would sail and he would be one of her crew. Tomorrow his life would begin for a second time.

He smiled at Molly, busy drying glasses behind the bar. "Would you sing me 'The Parting Glass,' girl?" he said questioningly, raising the huge mug to her. "You know how I love your voice."

She nodded acquiescence, pleased by the compliment, but he saw there were tears coming into her big eyes. She knew it was his favorite of all the songs she was accustomed to singing in the pub when one of the lads would accompany her on the penny whistle or the mouth organ . . . and tonight it had a special significance.

She swallowed her sadness and smiled at this nicest of all the men she knew who came and went at the pub. Unlike the others, he was gentle and intriguing. She cleared her throat, and coming to sit beside him, she sang in a lilting low voice that was disproportionately childlike and pure:

> *The fire is out,*
> *The moon is down,*
> *The Parting Glass*

Is dry and done.
And I must go and leave this town
Before the rising of the sun.

And long the road,
And far the mile
Before I'll rest
My soul again.
With girls that weep and girls that smile,
And know the words and ways of men.

For some there are
That may not bide,
But wander to
The journey's end.
Nor take a girl to be their bride,
Nor take a man to be their friend.

And when I'm done
With wandering,
I'll sit beside the road
And grieve
For all the songs I did not sing
And promises I did not keep.

The haunting melody and lyric lingered in the nearly empty pub when she had finished singing, its Celtic strains calculated to induce emotion. She dried her eyes on her apron and took a long swallow from Tom's glass.

"You'll sing all the songs and keep all the promises, I'm thinking," she said bravely when the moment had passed.

"Aye, lass. I'll surely try," he said, and leaning over, he kissed her one last sweet time and then left the little smoky room to pursue the long road and the far mile that the song had alluded to.

Part Three

NEW YORK
1900

To America, my new found land.
The man that hates you, hates the human race.
                    —*Brendan Behan*

34

New York was an astounding mélange of sights and sounds. Teeming life, and rich, beyond Tom's wildest dreams, on the fabulous avenues with their lining of huge elegant houses; and poor, beyond even his childhood's conception of poor, in the squalid streets reserved for the immigrants and their rapidly increasing families.

Thankful that he had been able to work off his passage—fortunately the ship's captain in Cork had not failed to recognize a body perfectly designed by the Almighty for stoking a ship's needy furnace—he had his meager savings in his money belt and his father's letter safe in its oilcloth bag, close to his body.

It hadn't been hard to secure passage on the *Lady May*, an old steamship that ferried goods from the United States to the British Isles on a regular schedule. His brawn had made getting hired easy, although the revelation of what it was like to live aboard ship with thirty-six other men, most of them illiterate, had been a less than pleasant experience. The life of a seaman was woefully unfit for the needs of most men's bodies or spirits, he'd found. It was dangerous work, combined with excessive monotony and boredom, and the unnatural restrictions in living conditions made life at sea appallingly unlivable.

Tom learned on shipboard that only twelve square feet of space per man needed legally be provided by a shipowner for the members of the crew. Recreation was unknown, and both overcrowding and undersanitation made life belowdecks a study in physical endurance. There were thirty-six men jammed into a "glory hole" with bunks three-deep and barely the room between them to stand upright. And the crew quarters were belowdecks on the waterline, so there could be little ventilation because the portholes had to remain closed except in the finest weather.

A single water tap had provided bathing and laundering for all thirty-six men on the *Lady May*, and Tom had learned early that it behooved a sailor to befriend the cook on any long voyage, for heat was provided only by the cookstove in the galley, and any man unlucky enough *not* to befriend the man who controlled the stove might be hard-pressed to find a spot to dry his freezing wet garments after a watch on deck in a downpour.

"Listen, lad," one of the able-bodied seamen had told him before he'd left the *Lady May*, "there's work to be had on the docks of New York, if you're determined to stay in this godforsaken city, with its immigrant stink and its whores and its filthy rich that you'll never meet." He had eyed Tom, as if to calculate his ability to withstand the vicissitudes he had just recounted. "Give me the wide-open seas with their clean air any time, mind you," he'd added gratuitously. "But if you be determined to stay ashore, there's work on the waterfront. Go to Slaney's Saloon or O'Rourke's near the Battery; any man there'll tell you how to get work. Of course, they may break a few of those pretty, even teeth of yours before they do it, mate, but they'll show you the ropes." The seaman had cackled in toothless delight at his own humor, and Tom had once again decided that his dreams had a long way to go before fulfillment.

Starting at Pier 46 in the North River, where the *Lady May* had docked, he began to walk, with no direction in mind but with a need to see and absorb as much as possible before nightfall. The immigrants' hovels he passed by defied description. Ramshackle buildings with sad-eyed scrawny women and children staring lifelessly at the streets; streets where rats gathered in fearless coveys of chattering, squealing ugliness. Ragged children, in garments made of flour sacks or the coarsest muslin, played with homemade balls of rubber bands, and the general air of desolation was as strong as the smell of garlic and of unwashed bodies.

He walked to Fifth Avenue, where handsome horse-drawn carriages pranced along the cold autumn streets, with laughing women in velvets and brocades being transported to shops or proper teas. Women in skirts so billowing they looked as if they might take flight if caught by an errant breeze, minced their dignified way down the grand avenue, accompanied by men in subtle gray wool suits with ruffled silk shirts and gleaming boots, to mark them as gentlemen.

Tom stood for a long time just outside the gate of an exquisite stone mansion at Thirty-fifth Street, engraving each portico, window, and lintel in his memory. To fulfill his dream, he believed, he must keep a clear picture of all the details of it in his mind. This was a fine house . . . the kind that would be his in the not too distant future. There was a poignant but powerful sense of urgency he felt when he ventured near dwellings of the kind he needed to possess.

He walked until his feet ached and his head pounded with the

immensity of contradictions in this city. Knowing he must find a
meal and a bed before dark, and remembering the names O'Rourke's
and Slaney's, he headed back toward the river, munching on the last
of the dried biscuits he had pinched from the ship's galley before
leaving. Thinking about finding a job in New York had seemed an
easier task while still on board the *Lady May*. Something about the
reality of the crushing city made the possibilities seem less plentiful
and the opportunities less golden.

O'Rourke's Saloon, at Pearl Street and Park Row, was a place for
seamen and dockworkers to drink themselves into a blissful stupor,
or brawl, or find a man to talk to or a woman to relieve themselves
with. A perpetual smell of salt air, beer, and sawdust hung about the
old place, to say nothing of the stench of urine and sweat from
unwashed bodies crowding each other at the bar, over which was
hung the portrait of a robust naked lady of Rubenesque proportion,
who looked provocatively at the room, as if to remind the seamen of
what they were leaving behind each time they boarded ship.

An angular, blind piano player was seated with an incongruous
elegance on a broken-down three-legged stool in front of a piano
whose keys were battered and yellowed like an old man's teeth.
Ignoring the condition of his instrument, and the condition of his
audience, the slender blind man, whose arms and legs seemed like
those of a matchstick doll, played unceasingly to the raucous accom-
paniment of drunken singing and frequent fistfights.

What a remarkable place, thought Tom, who—having stood for a
moment just inside the swinging doors to absorb the raw essence of
the room and allow his eyes to become accustomed to the smoky
yellow gloom—went to the long, scarred mahogany bar and ordered
a beer. While the price of the beer was extravagant in his current
financial condition, he knew the accompanying free food would
keep his large body functional. On the bar, sausages and sauerkraut,
roughhewn sandwiches and potato salad, a stick-to-the-ribs delicacy
he had never before seen, were set out for the hungry drinkers. He
helped himself to a large portion, not knowing when next he would
eat, and the bartender eyed him with the same hostile suspicion he
reserved for all newcomers. The man had a jagged scar that stretched
ominously from his eyebrow to just under his ear, and his perpetual
scowl had etched deep valleys into his leathery face.

"You a stranger here?" the bartender grunted with obvious hostility as Tom paid for the beer. "Folks don't think much of strangers
here." He added it gratuitously as the beer was paid for.

"I'm looking for work," said Tom, looking at him steadily and straining to keep belligerence to a minimum. "I need a job badly."

"Who don't?" said a man at his left, and fell to laughing, as if he had said a most humorous thing.

"It doesn't have to be on a boat," Tom added quickly, sensing that the entire line of men at the bar had stiffened at his mention of employment. He guessed they didn't need another competitor for the job of any mate of theirs.

"I'll work the docks, anything I can get. I'm strong and willing, and I don't care what I do. I'll need a place to stay, too, while I'm here."

"Going somewhere else, Irish?" The bartender treated Tom to a surly sneer, and the young man noted several missing teeth in the square, ugly jaw. The bartender was clearly no stranger to violence.

"Maybe to Boston, when I have the money for it," he answered evenly, thinking as he said it what a dim memory his mother was becoming. He would see her one more time to learn how she fared and what she'd been able to make of her life.

"There's no work here for strangers!" snapped the bartender with finality. "Not enough for our own."

Tom gathered his beer and sandwiches and turned away from the bar, taking the provisions to a small broken table at the far end of the crowded room. He needed to think and to let the homely meal replenish his strength.

"There's always work for a man who's willing to break his back, lad." The unexpected voice behind him was strong and deep; a man had followed him from the bar to the table. "What yer do is go to the docks at six in the morning and stand muster. It's called a 'shape-up.' The foreman comes out and looks yer over and picks a bunch of brawny boys to work for the day. If yer lucky, yer get picked to be a 'casual.' If not . . . well, yer try again tomorrow. It's backbreaking work, though, sonny. Makes a man old afore his time." The big man stopped long enough to take a swig of beer from the huge mug he held in gargantuan hands, then, wiping his hand on his pants, he offered it to Tom.

"The name's Donaher, mate, able-bodied seaman all these many years. Yer an Irisher like me, ain't you, lad? Thought I recognized the brogue on you, although it's fancied up some from what you'll hear in these parts." Donaher was a huge man, nearly as tall as Tom and far broader. His muscular frame seemed to have no neck at all, so his craggy head appeared to spring directly from massive shoulders. The kindly expression on his homely face was at odds with his size.

"Tom Dalton, Donaher, and happy to make your acquaintance. You're right about my being Irish; from County Westmeath I am, but a very long time ago it seems to me. Been living in Dublin for the past few years till I took a job on the *Lady May* in return for passage, and here it deposited me, for better or for worse, just this morning." He smiled as he finished his small history.

Donaher looked him frankly up and down. "So Ireland it is, then. I been to Madagascar and around the Cape on the Asia run, but never spent no time in Ireland since I left there with me mum and dad as a lad of fourteen years."

Donaher's face was like a worn piece of India rubber, and his nose had been broken often enough to have no real shape of its own. His eyebrows were bushy, and his eyes were blue and bright as a baby's. The face was old, but the eyes were young and, in an odd way, kindly. Tom hadn't intended to tell his story to anyone, much less a stranger in a bar, but it was hard not to warm to Donaher.

"Do yer have people here, lad, or are yer planning to ship out at the first tide?"

"If I never set foot on another ship, there'd be no complaints from me." Tom laughed good-naturedly and his companion smiled in turn, his smile lighting up his craggy face.

"Aye, yer look fit fer other things, to tell the truth of it, laddie. Yer haven't the hands of a seaman born and bred. Well, what's it to be, then? Have yer anyone to show yer around this here city?"

"I know not a single soul here, Donaher. And to tell you the truth, man, I'm too bone weary to care at all. It's been a long lean day with a long lean month at sea behind it, and right now my only plan in the world is to find a place to sleep tonight so I can look for work tomorrow."

The rubbery face came alive with good humor as Tom finished his statement.

"Tell yer what, then, lad. Yer can stay with me at Barnacle Billy's tonight if you like, and I'll take yer with me to the docks in the morning. Billy'll find yer a place to sleep and a fine buxom girl to sleep on if you'd like it, and I can introduce yer to the fellers what runs this whole part of the world. How's that sound to yer?"

"I haven't enough money for anything fancy, Donaher. Truth is, I may have to sleep in one of those parks I passed today when I was out walking the streets."

"Can't let yer do that, Tom," grunted his craggy companion. "There's too many elements out there'd pinch yer poke and cut yer throat whilst yer sleep, yer being a stranger and all. No, yer come along to Billy's with me and we'll see what we can do with yer, till yer gets work. I been a stranger, too, in this town a while ago. It's a hellhole, lessen somebody takes it into his head to show yer the ropes. Us Irishers got to stick together as I sees it, lad. Come along with yer."

With that he rose and lumbered from the saloon, and Tom, seeing no reason not to, followed him.

35

Barnacle Billy was unlike any woman Tom had ever seen. She had yellow hair of no known natural hue, piled up in ringlets that made her seem a full six inches taller than her already awesome height. She had a pouter pigeon bosom that stood out before her like a ship's prow, as if it had a life of its own. She had the handshake of a strong man and a voice so throaty and full of laughter, Tom felt engulfed by it, overwhelmed by its raw sensuality.

"My, my, my! Donaher," she said, eyeing Tom up and down, like a man about to buy a horse. "This one's a rare beauty, now. Where did you find him? In some fancy drawing room on Fifth Avenue? He looks like he'd make right fine breeding stock, he does."

Tom smiled at the blatancy of the surprising young madam. A peasant's courtesan, he thought, looking her over as frankly as she had him, liking her unabashed womanliness, her obvious good humor, and her undisguised sexuality. He reached out in a courtly gesture, and lifting her ring-clad hand to his lips, he kissed it gently. Much to Donaher's amazement Billy blushed, and for the barest moment looked almost girlish in her embarrassment. "You're a rare beauty yourself, ma'am," said Tom, who, letting go of her hand, stood at a sort of quiet attention as if waiting for the lady to make the next move. She thought she had never seen a man move with such unstudied grace.

"Well, I'll be damned," said Billy, recovering her composure. "Did you ever see the like of it?" Then, smiling good-humoredly, she winked at Tom. "I expect you two gentlemen are in need of a drink and perhaps a wee bit of entertainment? And I suppose it wouldn't be too much trouble for you to introduce me to your friend, Donaher, seeing as how you've brought him to visit?"

Donaher looked chagrined at his breach of etiquette, and Tom thought amusedly that the old seaman obviously adored the young woman.

"This here's me friend Tom, Billy, and he's poor as a church mouse. An Irisher fresh off the *Lady May* looking for gainful employment and such. I told him Billy Henderson was just the girl to talk to."

"I am that," she said with finality, and without further conversation turned to lead them into her parlor, where a great many others were already gathered. There was a garish splendor about Billy's house that was a great surprise, considering the shoddy clapboard exterior of the waterfront edifice. There was shabby gilt and down-at-heel velvet, but it was somehow robust and full of life, like the woman herself. Tom had taken an instant liking to Billy; she seemed to be like him, flotsam and jetsam in life's peculiar sea; one who had managed somehow to make her way in a hard world by the means at her disposal. So he looked around with rapt attention, drinking in sight and sound and scent of the amazonian woman's place of business, listening absentmindedly to the conversation Billy had with each of the guests of her house as she passed them by.

There was a battered grand piano in the front parlor, draped with a fringed, embroidered scarf that had seen better days, as indeed had some of the girls who boisterously entertained a wide variety of men who wandered in and out in a continuing stream. Most of the happy couples meandered up the ornately banistered stairway to the floor above, after suitable negotiations with Billy. Tom noted as the evening ebbed and flowed that she ordered the business of her establishment with the precision of a banker and the efficiency of a titan of industry. To his amusement, her good humor never flagged, and he realized that the men who frequented the place seemed well-heeled and prosperous, with the exception of the seamen who had a separate parlor to themselves.

With Billy the organizer, administrator, bouncer, and general factotum, the evening passed swiftly. Donaher had long since retired with a young lady of his choosing, and Tom had instead immersed himself in the vitality of the establishment; watching Billy ply her trade, admiring her spirit and warmed by her abundant womanliness.

It seemed incredible to her visitor that the young madam managed to keep order as she did among the burly men and women who laughed and played piano, sang, pinched, and drank their way enthusiastically through the night.

"It looks to be a prosperous business you have here, lass," Tom said when Billy, enjoying a slight lull, came and seated herself next to him on the red plush divan near the crackling fireplace.

"It is that for me, Tom," she smiled, her white even teeth and poutily shaped lips making the smile sensuous in the fireglow. "I run an honest house. No panel thieves, no badger games, no chloral hydrate in your drink. Just a fair price for a good time and a discreet forgetfulness that you were ever here." Tom knew what she alluded to; how a man might be taking his pleasure with a woman in a bordello and find a panel thief sneaking out of the woodwork to rifle his wallet while his attention was distracted. Chloral hydrate, used as knockout drops by many of the city's madams, unfortunately often ended in a permanent knockout if the critical dosage happened to be less than accurate.

"Aren't you a bit close to the waterfront for comfort?" he asked, and saw her stiffen, as at an attack. "I mean no offense, lass," he offered quickly, startled by her sensitivity, sorry to have offended this rare creature. "I simply have been noticing the caliber of men here tonight. They seem educated, well-heeled—surprisingly affluent. The waterfront doesn't seem their natural habitat."

"All the better for my clients, that they be far from home, don't you suppose?" she said testily. "Besides, the uptown trade is covered by the Seven Sisters on Forty-fifth Street."

"The Seven Sisters?"

"Seven ladies from Massachusetts—sisters who opened up houses next door to each other in Hell's Kitchen. They cater to the rich and make them really toe the mark, I hear. They make the gents wear tuxedos and bring flowers to the ladies, one night a week. They've made a bloody fortune up there, but they really own the trade from the Tenderloin north." She stopped, seemingly mollified because she sensed that he genuinely sought information and didn't mean to denigrate her "house." "I'm not as ritzy as the Sisters, but I have two nice businesses here. One for the businessmen—that's where I make my money. And one for the sailors, 'cause I've a warm spot in my heart for them, and"—her eyes twinkled with conspiratorial pride—"they protect me. There's not a tough on the waterfront would mess with Billy. It's a kind of code. My father and all eight of my brothers were sailors; poor as it's possible to be, but sailors nonetheless. So I take care of them, and they take care of me.''

He watched the bountiful young madam with increasing interest as the evening became night and the night began its ascent into morning. She was wearing a pearl-gray moiré gown with black lace panels at the low scooped neck that showed off her beautiful high white breasts to perfection. Her corseted waist seemed tiny by comparison with her bouncing bosom, and the flowing skirt of her dress swayed in the rhythm of her sensuous movements, so that he found himself forgetting her great height. Even her hands were slender and graceful. He couldn't help but wonder how such a woman had come to be born to a family of poverty-stricken sailors on the tawdry New York waterfront.

''Well, now, my friend,'' she said to him when the room had finally quieted to a murmur of leftover tipsy customers, snoring complacently where they had passed out, accompanied by a symphony of comfortable giggles and thumps from the floor above. ''We must decide what to do with you, mustn't we? Your friend says you haven't money enough for a bed and breakfast, and I can't turn you out into the streets or my pal Donaher would never forgive me. There seems only one solution that will save face for us both.''

''And what might that be?'' inquired Tom with the amused smile of one who suspects the answer to his own question.

''That you share my bed, my fine boyo, for I can't be giving free bed and board to no one, it would be bad for my reputation. But as everyone hereabouts knows well, no one pays for a place under my covers; I invite who I choose. And if tonight I choose you, who's to say a word about it in the morning?''

Tom smiled broadly at the mighty figure seated across from him, and standing up, he bowed from the waist on impulse, with the same strange grace she had noted in him earlier in the evening.

''I should be most honored to share your bed, Miss Billy. I trust you won't be disappointed in your choice.''

She eyed him with the cool and calculating directness of a woman who knows men to their marrow. ''I'll take my chances, mate, if you will,'' she said. And gliding off, like an Amazon warrior on her way to well-loved battle, she led him to her room on the third floor of the old house—a floor entirely her own, with a prettily appointed bedroom in robin's egg blue, a little sitting room with a rococo marble-manteled fireplace, and a room with nothing in it but a great white porcelain tub with glittering trims and the feet of some mythical gilded beast.

"If you lay the fire, Tom, I'll get out of my work duds and make myself a bit more comfortable. These stays and laces do terrible things to my ribs by two A.M." She said it good-humoredly as she walked behind an ornate screen, and humming softly to herself as she did so, she began to toss her clothes over the top of it with a casual and provocative unconcern.

The lovely cream-colored dressing gown in which Billy emerged enhanced more than covered her vast body, and sitting at the little kidney-shaped dressing table with its triple-paneled mirror, she began to tug at the thousand hairpins that held her elaborate coiffure in place, while Tom watched in pleasant fascination. He had never seen a woman so utterly unselfconscious in the presence of a man, and her very confidence was enticing. In less than a minute the strangely colored blond hair hung about the shoulders of her dressing gown and he saw her studying him in the mirror, as if deciding what the next move must be. He saw her hesitate for a moment or so, watching his reflection thoughtfully, then she quietly turned, and rising from the little chair to her full height she quite delicately opened her robe and dropped it where she stood, standing absolutely motionless, as if waiting to see what Tom's response would be. He had been sitting on the small blue divan angled cozily in front of the fire, watching her appreciatively, and with rising enthusiasm for the task at hand.

"You're a beautiful woman, lass," he said softly and with absolute sincerity in response to her gesture. He had never seen a body quite so lush. "Like a great statue of Venus you are, my girl; you should be in a museum." Leaving her standing where she was, he very deliberately began to undo his clothes and dropped them slowly, one by one, into a little pile on the floor by the fire, never taking his eyes from the woman. The lack of urgency in his manner tantalized and excited her.

Billy's body was younger than her face. 'Twas the whore's paint that fooled me, thought Tom. She's no more than twenty-two, for all her worldly wisdom and bravado. He led her naked to the bed, where she seemed as anxious as he to be. He sensed that there they were on familiar ground for her. Billy smiled knowingly, appraisingly, at Tom's body; when it came to what went on between a man and woman in bed or out, she had paid her dues and knew it all. She flipped down the feather coverlet on the huge bed and turned for a moment to regard them both in the mirror on the wall beside it; she was nearly Tom's size, and they both smiled at the pair of reflected giants. Turning her eyes to what had risen between his legs, she smiled again, utterly sure of her place in the drama about to unfold, and reaching out, she touched him delicately and with talented fingers. "Let me show you what I know of pleasing a man," she said in her throaty, wonderful voice, and she bent her head to the handsome male flesh.

For a while Tom struggled to gain control of the act, but sensing the woman's great desire to show her own prowess, he finally lay back contentedly and allowed himself to feel the exquisite knowledge of her hands and mouth. She sucked and licked and touched him in places no woman, lady, or barmaid had ever touched in quite the same way. She pressed her copious breasts against him, cradling him, teasing him with their rosy tips and seeming to be everywhere his body ached for her, at once. Then, when he thought he would burst from her teasing and probing and playing, she raised her great form up and mounted him so skillfully he moaned in the delight of it. When a virtuoso is at work, it makes most sense to simply enjoy the gift, he thought contentedly, watching her, back straight, hands above her head, in some primitive ritual of mating that brought them both to an explosive climax . . . two handsome giant forms, like lovers in some mythic story, tangled and pleasured in each other's arms.

They lay in the absolute quiet of exhaustion for several minutes, their heavy breathing and the crackling of the fire the only sounds in the old house. "Well, what do you think of me?" she said finally, the madam at the last, in need of praise as payment.

"I think you are so wondrous, girl, that now I'd like to show you what I know about pleasing," he said softly, smiling at her smile, and turned his mouth to hers, his tongue and lips wanting her, seeking knowledge, giving it. He stroked her hot, white skin with hands so large and strong it seemed impossible to her that they could be so sensitive to her wants. He played with her hard pink nipples and took them in his mouth to suckle and nip, until she began to cry out in wonder at his mouth. He kissed her belly and her thighs and parted them gently, roughly, knowingly, playing with the pale hair between them and all that lay beneath it. By the time he was inside her, driving into her in a relentless motion, he had brought her to a place she had seldom been before, for it isn't the act of a whore to be out of control in her own bed very often.

She arched her back in an expert gesture and met his thrusts with a wildness all her own, and they fell asleep a little later in each other's arms, in the sure knowledge that each had found a friend. It was as if two strangers from some other, larger than life-size race had met and matched their strengths in an ancient ritual of combat, and had left the field as comrades.

When Tom awoke, Billy was already dressed and seated on a chair by the bedside, watching him. Her face was soft and dear, and he felt himself quickening with remembrance of her body; as his sleepy eyes focused, he reached out his hand to her.

"Come to me, Billy my girl . . ." he said, smiling lazily to her in invitation.

"No, my fine friend. Not now, nor ever again, I'm afraid, and to tell you the God's honest truth, it makes me sorrowful to say it."

He was up on his elbow, wide awake in a moment, puzzled by the rebuff, disturbed by her serious face and sad voice. "What's on your mind, Billy? What's different from last night? Have I hurt you somehow?"

"I have a tidy little life here, Tom," she said carefully, as if composing the sentence as she went along. "I pay my bills, I keep my girls off the streets, I provide a little happiness in my house for a lot of gentlemen, some of them my friends. There's a man who made that possible for me, when I was a kid from the gutter with no hope and fewer prospects. He took me in and he taught me." She smiled self-deprecatingly. "Not about men, of course, I'd had time enough to learn what I needed to know about them on my own. But he gave me fancy clothes and he fed me and he let me live the life of a human being. Until now, there's been nothin' to come between us, ever."

"I thought you told me you always choose who shares your bed."

"And so I do." Her eyes were challenging his stare, as frank, as in control. "Jim makes no never mind if I take an occasional lover, just so's it's never serious, and never when he's around. Anyway, nothing ever happened to me with a man like it did last night with you, and that's a danger to me I just can't afford. Understand what I'm saying?"

He frowned at her obvious discomfiture. "I think so, Billy. I wouldn't want you hurt, because you took me in."

A little of her usual effervescence crept back behind her eyes, as if she had feared what his response would be and felt relieved.

"Hell's bells, man! What are we hanging crepe for? I can't go back on my word to Diamond Jim Mulvaney, and I can't get myself all in a stew over no stranger." She stopped for a minute. "But I sure as hell can like you a lot, and give you a helping hand, provided, of course, you don't go touching me like you did no more. Deal?" She looked almost innocent, eyes pleading. Tom liked her enormously.

"It's a deal, lassie. You're a rare beauty, you are, on more counts than one, and I'm pleased as punch to have made your acquaintance." Tom raised himself, throwing back the covers, and stretched. He pulled on his trousers as she continued to sit and watch, biting her lip a little in consternation and desire.

"You go with Donaher and try to get work on the docks, Tom, and I'll put in a word with Diamond Jim when he gets back. Mind you, I'll have to be careful to make it seem real casual, so's I may have to bide my time with it. But I've a couple of extra dollars I can give you, to tide you over till you get work."

He looked up, startled at the generosity of the offer. "Why should you do that, Billy? You don't know me from Adam's housecat. You might never see the money again."

She laughed aloud, her good humor restored, having unburdened herself of her problem. "I didn't survive this long by not being a good judge of men, Tom Dalton. It's a gift I have. I can tell the good and the bad and the smart and the cunning, and the honest and the crooks, at a mile's distance. A gift. You'll not ever take anything you can't give back, that's my bet."

She stood up to her imposing six-foot height, took him by the hand, and led him from the room. "There's no law says I can't at least feed you breakfast before you go. Fucking makes me hungry as a bear. How's about you?"

She was halfway down the stairs when she turned to him, her eyes soft and, he thought, very nearly innocent. "Tom, I want you to know it was grand for me last night. You're a lovely man, and it was simply grand." And with that she marched briskly down the stairs and set about the business of making her house run like a finely tuned machine, through another day in anticipation of another night.

36

Dalton and Donaher made it to the docks the following morning at twenty minutes to six, and already a throng of men waited in ragged clothes outside the iron gate. The weather had turned chilly, and you could see their breath in little misted clouds as they moved about in small clusters, stamping their feet and beating their hands in a primitive ritual designed to outwit the cold.

Old men and young men, big and small; hungry-looking men in varying stages, it appeared to Tom, of desperation.

"How many will they choose?" he asked the experienced Donaher.

"No more than a dozen" was the reply. Tom looked around. There were more than forty men already assembled.

"There's a crew of regulars what works here all the time, lad." Donaher spoke softly to keep the conversation between themselves. "Mostly political ass-kissers or brother-in-laws of somebody with pull. They work here pretty steady. Then, whenever a ship comes in, they takes on extra hands. 'Casuals,' they calls 'em. That's a day or a night at a time. It's pretty dicey work, but it's a dollar most can't do without."

"How do they choose?" Tom asked with an almost clinical interest in this new means of demeaning human dignity.

"They pick the biggest and the toughest-looking first, or the ones they think they can push around easiest, or the ones with the right color eyes. Who knows what they choose by? They just has the right to do what they pleases, and so they does it."

A mournful bell sounded somewhere inside the old pier building and reverberated in the cold darkness, echoing out across the river.

A burly-looking man appeared at the huge doorway to the pier warehouse and walked with the arrogant swagger of power to the gate. He looked over the quiet mass of humanity, by now numbering fifty or sixty, Tom guessed, and pointed to a man in the front row.

"You'll do, Farley, and you O'Shaunnessy. That you, Donaher, back there? You're on too."

"How about me friend here, gov'ner?" shouted Donaher. "He's got hands on him like melons he has, an' he's bigger than me, even."

The foreman eyed them both disdainfully but with an astute appraising motion; he nodded his head in assent and the two huge men were spirited through the gate along with the other chosen few.

"Have yer ever worked coastwise, lad?" Donaher said under his breath as they filed in.

"Never even worked as a sailor until I had to find passage to this paradise of a city," said Tom grimly.

"Then keep yer mouth shut and do what I do. It takes more brawn than brains once you've the hang of it. Just watch yer step. It's dangerous work on the dock and worse in the hold. So stay close."

"What are we loading?"

"Barrels mostly. The heaviest stuff gets stowed first. This is a big load. They'll pump out the water ballast and fill 'er with freight."

"Bilge and contline!" shouted the foreman and the men all nodded sagely.

"It means yer load the second tier of barrels into the space between the bulges of the first layer of barrels," whispered Donaher. "That way yer wastes no space."

"Cut out the jabber over there!" The foreman shouted above the noise of the hydraulic hoist. Donaher winked at Tom and they began to lift and stow the heavy barrels. Tom had the strength of size and youth, and could hold his own with most men, but the agility with which Donaher lifted and carried the two-hundred-pound barrels astounded him. When the foreman was out of sight, he told the older man of his admiration.

"Yer gets used to it," said Donaher modestly, but Tom could see he was pleased by the compliment. "After a while yer know how to do it all. Like yer don't put hops near butter, nor dried apples nor tobacco near breakfast cereals. Tea won't set well in the neighborhood of flour nor sugar, and yer never put oil near cotton. That kind o' thing, yer know." He stopped for a moment to hoist another massive barrel.

"A lot depends on how good yer winch man and yer hooker-on man is, too, lad. Yer see how it works, Tom, as the cargo clears the hatch coamings the hooker-on must reach out and fling his hook and rope around the thing. It takes a bit of talent, lad, not to kill yerself or somebody else. You'll learn it all, if it's yer misfortune to stay around here long enough."

"Enough blather over there, Donaher!" shouted the foreman. "This ain't a tea party at the Ladies Aid."

"Much obliged to yer for setting me straight on that point,

gov'ner!'' the big Irishman shouted back, and they continued their backbreaking loading of the barrels in silence.

Tom learned that, in theory, the hours of employment on the docks were from seven A.M. to twelve noon and from one to six P.M.—a ten-hour day if you were lucky enough to be called back after lunch. As a matter of reality, however, the men were most often required to work through the meal hours, during the nights, and on Sundays and holidays, if the foreman demanded it. Two days and a night, he learned, were the usual limit of a man's endurance, and many testified to having worked thirty-five to forty hours at a stretch without complaint. In such cases half hour off at midnight was supposed to be given, although it was allowed only at the discretion of the foreman. Tom found that the men covered for each other in the hold on long stretches—one man resting while the others did his job and theirs.

Hazardous as the long hours were, they were not as dangerous as the problems of working shorthanded. An unscrupulous foreman could pocket an extra salary by working a five-man load with a four-man crew, forcing one man to manage the steam winch as well as the rope fall—an almost foolproof way to cause injury by steam-scalding to some one of the workers. As there was no compensation for the injured, a collection of quarters would be taken up for the man's family during his recovery—if indeed a recovery was in order.

Life on the docks was a study in hardship. Giant bales broke loose from moorings more often than not; the cold salt water bit into a man's flesh until it was tanned like animal hide and creased with the permanence of tooled leather; the heat and the cold made life a year-long misery. Tom soon learned that the only thing worse than the work was not working.

The waterfront area was squalid and decaying. The aura of poverty was everywhere evident, and alleys like the infamous cul-de-sac named Little Water, in the Cow Bay district near the Battery, were the norm. In such places filth littered the streets to above the tops of a man's shoes and pathetic tenements with colorful names like Gates of Hell and Brick-Bat Mansion lined miserable streets where it was worth a man's life to wander into the area for any reason. Visitors were admonished to soak a handkerchief in camphor before entering the region in order to endure the horrid stench. Long, narrow

passages wound into alleys in which a visitor had to be careful
where he placed his foot amid the steaming filth.

Seething pots of butcher's offal soup could be seen cooking upon
little fires in the streets, with hungry derelicts surrounding them,
waiting longingly for a taste of the ghastly contents.

It was an area that had engendered notorious landmarks like the
Old Brewery, which had been transformed into a dwelling in 1837.
The monstrous edifice had housed quaintly named rooms and pas-
sageways like Den of Thieves and Murderer's Alley, and its cellars
billeted hundreds of Negroes and Irish, some of whom never saw the
light of day after being born there, for to leave your tiny cramped
space on the dirt floor might mean that it was usurped by a rival; in
general, the only reason to go abroad at all was to knock a passerby
on the head and steal his provisions, and various members of a
family would take turns at the task.

Fights, prostitution, perversion, murder, death of natural causes—
all these were the daily fare in the Old Brewery and other reeking
tenements in a district that spawned the most illustrious street gangs
ever to grace the city; gangs with quaint names like the Bowery
Boys, the Little Plug Uglies and the Little Dead Rabbits were really
a communal means of survival for the vast numbers of orphaned
children who provided for themselves through thieving learned at
"Fagin schools" throughout the more squalid areas of lower New
York.

Waterfront saloons specialized in unconscious recruitment of sailors,
via the age-old device of shanghaiing. A man might be drugged or
hit on the head, his body lowered through a trapdoor to a waiting
gang in the sewers below the street, thence to be spirited to a ready
ship about to set sail. Many's the man who awoke to find himself
outside the harbor limit and on his way to a three-year voyage, with
no recourse but to make the best of it.

The police tended to overlook most of the less savory activities of
the waterfront, on the theory that it was likely to take care of itself
without intrusion. They were encouraged in this theory by the
handsome stipend they received from both the resident businessmen,
and the uptown ship owners, to make it worth their while to turn a
benevolently blind eye toward the longshore.

Such was the rat-infested, grimy district into which Donaher
introduced Tom, and the juxtaposition of splendor and squalor in his
life almost amused him. The splendor of Drumgillan, beside the
poverty of his own small servant's cottage there; the elegance of the

Dublin homes of the rich, beside the poverty of his garret; the magnificence of the New York City mansions he had observed, compared with the fate he currently inherited. It was all some strange baroque nightmare of darks and lights that he couldn't quite comprehend; as if his life were doomed always to extremes, never providing the blissful quietude of moderation.

Nonetheless, he was grateful for the friendship of Donaher. Without him, it would have seemed a hopeless city indeed.

Tom and Donaher, under the affectionate aegis of Barnacle Billy, who knew all the tricks of surviving waterfront life, had settled themselves into Timothy Sheehan's boardinghouse for seamen and longshoremen. It was an ugly clapboard building near the North River, weathered and down-at-heel but nonetheless the prime place to stay if you were an able-bodied seaman or a stevedore looking for work. It was near enough to the waterfront to be convenient for the rat population, and had a perpetual smell of dampness and poverty that made Tom's Dublin attic look like comparative paradise, but it was considered prime real estate to those who understood the politics of waterfront life.

"He runs the place for the shipowners, lads," Billy had told them earnestly. "But you've a better chance of landing a job if you stay there. The owners and Timothy are in cahoots, so his boarders get first shot at whatever work's available. Of course, you may find yourself in debt up to your ears to Timmy-the-Crimp's company store, but that's the simple facts of life on the waterfront, as Donaher well knows. At least it's safe and relatively clean, and I'll know where to find you when Jim gets back into town and I can try to negotiate a decent job for Tom here."

Billy had turned out to be a remarkably conscientious friend. Learning that Donaher had been her brother's closest pal explained only part of it to Tom; she had a compassionate connection to men of the sea and an inordinate understanding of, and affection for, men in general. They were her doctoral study, her livelihood, her protectorate, her children, her friends—and she added Tom to her list of strays with an air of pleasant inevitability, as if she had always expected to find him on her doorstep.

The room the two friends occupied at Timothy Sheehan's was sparsely furnished and had a brown barrenness about it; low-slung cots with string-bottomed mattresses, a wobbly pine chest and a battered washstand were strategically placed on the carpetless warping floor. The curtainless window looked out on an alleyway where the sound of scurrying vermin accompanied the foghorns on the river and the slap, slap sound of the water meeting the piers, in a shabby symphony of poverty. How many such homeless rooms have I inhabited since boyhood? thought Tom whenever he walked into it. A man shouldn't spend his life in rooms like these.

With the punctuality of a ship's crew changing watch, fourteen massive sailors crowded Timothy's dinner table at six each evening. The gaslit room in which they ate their hearty, unimaginative fare had a curious stale odor of bodies and cleaning fluid that had a tendency to settle into the food on the sturdy oaken table. Conversation during meals was always sparse and guarded at Timmy's, the men tending to eat in silence, grunting occasional information to each other or to the Chinaman who served them. Thus it was the cause of some consternation, one evening about a week after Tom's arrival at Sheehan's, when Donaher inquired of the men at the table if there was any news of the union. Several of the men looked at each other but said nothing, so the big Irishman persisted in his query. "I heard there's a big Norwegian been trying to organize the seamen into a brotherhood against the owners."

A series of sullen grunts greeted the uninvited information.

"Shut up, man!" hissed a nearly toothless sailor with no neck, seated at the far end of the table. "Sheehan's the eyes and ears of the owners. You'll find yourself in an alley with your throat slit if you talk union in this house."

"Sheehan's out for the evening with his ladylove," offered a round-faced man with a sallow complexion. "I saw him sprucin' up for the occasion meself."

"There's no way I can see anybody forcin' the owners to make any changes," said another of the men, begrudgingly. "It's too easy to pay a captain to do away with any man what starts trouble, once they get 'em back out at sea."

"Come on now, men." Donaher's deep, fluid voice sounded encouraging. "Change is bound to come. Conditions on the ships is so god-awful, they've got to change eventually. Besides, other businesses is startin' to pay attention to the unions. It's only a matter of time till the sailors and the dockworkers starts to fight back. The ironworkers has done it, the steelworkers has gotten better wages and treatment, even the women in the mills is getting together in a union to demand better conditions. Why should we be different?"

"Because there's no way we can protect ourselves, Donaher. You know the ropes as well as we do. Once out to sea, we got no rights at all. A captain wants us keelhauled, hanged from the yardarm, dumped overboard—he's got the power to do it. Man, they don't even have to pay us the salary we signed on for, if they don't want to, as you well know. And if we don't like it, there's a hundred more men out there waiting to take our place in line."

Murmurs of assent around the table.

"Much as I like the sound of what you're saying, Donaher," ventured Tom, "I'm afraid he's right. We're all just damned glad to have a job. Any job."

"Aye, Tom," said Donaher sadly. "And that's the reason the owners has us by the balls, I'm afraid." He pushed his chair back from the table in an expansive gesture. "But not forever. Mark my word, lad. Not forever."

"Who's the Norwegian you mentioned? What's he trying to do?"

"His name's Furuseth. Andrew Furuseth. He's a big bloke. Bigger'n you and me both. Six foot six, maybe. Hands like a whole ham." Several eyes looked up from the food they'd been studiously concentrating on, in order to avoid the dangerous conversation.

"He was one of us, from what I hear, lad. Signed up on a freighter as a kid in Norway. Ran afoul of the mate and damned near got hisself keelhauled, I been told. Anyways, he jumped ship in Seattle and they never got him back."

Inasmuch as leaving a ship anywhere other than where your voyage had originated was not only a way to be cheated of your wages but also a capital offense, this new piece of information held interest for the experienced seamen around the table. The sea may have had no laws to protect its sailors, but it had very stringent ones of reprisal for offense against the owners.

"Anyways," continued Donaher, sensing he had their attention, "this big kid, now he was maybe nineteen or twenty years of age, he decides the only way to even up the score is to find a means to make life at sea a decent way to earn a living, and the only way to do that is to learn how to read and write."

"What'd he want to do that for?" asked the man with the lisp, as if learning to read and write was evidence of some kind of perversion.

"So's he could tell his story to the newspapers and the politicians, my darlin' boyo. So's he could start a brotherhood."

"Did he learn to read and write?" asked Tom.

"Aye, that he did, lad, and taught hisself English, too, while he was at it, by takin' lessons at his letters in return for workin' people's fields and such. He got him a book or two from some schoolmarm in Seattle, and he carried them with him to learn from; Shakespeare, it was, and a Bible. Once he knew his letters, he started walkin' all up and down the West Coast, talkin' to newspaper editors, tellin' them the truth of what it's like before the mast; findin' out the names of local sailors and askin' them to sign on for his Brotherhood of Seamen. A lot of 'em did, too. That's how I heared the story, from some sailor what was on me last boat; he's signed up with Furuseth out of Portland. He was right taken with the Big Man. Said he was the strongest man he ever met. Reminded him of President Lincoln, he said.''

The Chinaman from the kitchen had started clearing away the dishes, his pigtail bobbing as he sped around the table, weaving and dipping between the men who, even seated, towered over him. Tom caught his eyes slowly calculating; he was certain the man spoke English although he pretended only the crudest pidgin American. He decided to pursue this conversation out of the man's earshot.

Tom and Donaher left the seedy dining room when the meal had been cleared away, and walked slowly out into the deserted riverfront street. The air was frosty and fresh after the fetid house, and the raw scent of snow was heavy in the air. Tom squared his broad shoulders against the cold and stuck his hands deep into his pockets, wondering regretfully how long it would be till he had the money to buy a warmer coat. He walked silently at Donaher's large side for a moment before saying what was on his mind.

"You're really keen on this brotherhood business, aren't you, Donaher?"

"Aye, mate. That I am. Yer see, what I didn't tell them in there is that I joined up mesself. Met this Furuseth feller out on the coastal run. A great man, that one, lad. I never met a great man before, and he made me believe things could be different if we stick together."

"Is it worth the risk, man? The owners can't afford to let a union get started here. They'll go for the throat of any sailor they know is an organizer."

"Well, Tom, I guess we'll get a chance to see what happens one of these days, when he gets here. Old Andy told me he was headin' for New York this winter, and one of these days he'll make it. Takes a man a long while to walk from San Diego to New York, but there ain't nothin' but a bullet in the heart that'll stop Furuseth. When he gets here, every able-bodied seaman is gonna have a chance to show his true colors."

"Aren't you afraid of reprisals?"

Donaher stopped and stood quietly on the darkened street for a moment, looking out over the inky river before replying. They were directly in front of Pier 46, where a huge four-masted barkentine stood half loaded with cargo, its rigging eerie in the icy moonlight.

"This life ain't treated me so good that I'd be scared of leavin' it for a good cause, Tom. Sailorin' is all I know how to do, all I'm good for. Been at it since I was a lad of fifteen or so, and I'm damned good at it by now. But we got no rights, Tom. They can kill us and they can maim us and they can shanghai us and they can keep from payin' us our just wages after we've worked our asses off on a five-year run, and we got nowhere to go with our grievances. Nowhere at all."

Tom said nothing, but was disturbed by the pained vehemence of his friend's voice.

"I had a wife and a kid once, Tom. Long ago it was, and me a young man. I shipped off on the Asia run for a three-year duty, 'cause the pay was the highest and I wanted to take good care of me own. They was the apples of me eye, Tom. Marie and Daniel was their names, God rest their souls.

"Well, I made me a deal with the shipowner's man that the company would give me salary to me wife whilst I was gone. Oh, lad, I had great plans of what we would do when I got back from that run. How we'd take our money, whatever was left of it, and go west. But a little farm maybe and raise the boy in a pretty place."

Donaher's voice had become ragged as he talked; Tom listened to his friend with a growing apprehension, sensing a sorrowful ending that had to come, for Donaher had never before spoken of a wife or son.

"Well, when I got back from the voyage, lad, I went to our little place all full of excitement to be home . . . and they wasn't there. An old lady was livin' in our flat and she told me they was both dead. Just like that she said it." The man stopped speaking for a moment to regain his composure. "Daniel dead of the influenza and Marie dead in the poorhouse. Can yer even imagine what a shock it was to hear it? After all these years the shock of it is still in me gut. Yer see, lad, the shipowner's man never gave her the money at all. Not a penny of my wages did she ever see, and she a poor immigrant girl off the boat with nowheres to turn, and me long gone to sea. No money for the doctor for the wee lad. No money to just stay alive.

"I near went off my rocker, Tom. I cried for a week and I ain't ashamed to say it. I went to the owner's office, but they wouldn't let me in. They offered me half me wages for the voyage, for they said it hadn't been a profitable one. And, of course, they said they'd never heard of no Marie Donaher.

"So's I waited me chance for revenge and one night it came. The coldhearted son of a bitch who had promised to see that Marie got me wages had his neck broke in an alley, by yours truly, when he was least expectin' it. But of course it didn't help at all. Not at all.

"But making a union, Tom. That could help a mite, I'm thinkin'. The way I looks at it is this, lad. If I live, I help them start a union so nothin' like what happened to me and Marie and little Daniel will ever happen to no one else. If I die, I leave a life that ain't meant much to me since my family's gone. And who knows, maybe there really is a hereafter where they're waitin' for me." The big Irishman's eyes were wet, and he wiped them self-consciously. Tom, moved beyond speech by the story, put his hands on the older man's bowed shoulders and squeezed them hard.

37

Andrew Furuseth, barred from the New York waterfront by the powerful shipowners, stood in the stern of the small boat anchored just beyond the huge tanker docked at Pier 47 in the North River.

His powerful voice carried easily over the waterfront sounds, as he addressed the sailors and longshoremen in the cold gray afternoon sun. Tom and Donaher stood in the freezing November wind and listened to the man's first speech since his arrival in New York.

"Men of the sea, I come to speak to you of our mutual fate, as brethren." His voice was deep and resonant, his cadence almost biblical, his accent sweetly Nordic.

"I say to you, *a seaman has no rights* once he leaves his port. His captain can flog him till his bones are bared, he may incarcerate him in the filthy hold until he be near death; he may keelhaul him, throw him overboard to the great fishes, or have him cast into irons for a minor offense. Who among you has not witnessed some poor wretch went to Davy Jones's locker for a crime that on land would go unnoticed?"

A murmur of indignant assent from the assembled workers met

this sally, and while the foreman walked among them and sought to get them back to their labor, none would move from the hold of the strong Norse voice that had thundered with emotion through the last of it; the crowd was hushed and attentive as he went on.

"*Alone* we are powerless. *Alone* we are disposable. *Alone* we are slaves. All this is true. But what if we are *not alone*? What if we band together as brothers; *men*, standing shoulder to shoulder. Strength beside strength. What if we face the owners with their wrongs and demand our rights? What will happen to us then? you may well ask.

"And I must say to you, in honesty, I do not know, exactly. But *I do* know certain things.

"I know that the Brotherhood of Steelworkers stood shoulder to shoulder and won their rights; I know that the Brotherhood of Ironworkers stood together and won a fairer justice; I do know that the millworkers in Massachusetts have raised their pay and bettered their working conditions by standing together, and they overcame owners no less arrogant and powerful and corrupt than the ones we face. So I know, men, that *it can be done*!

"Do you hear me, men, it is *possible*! Do you know what that one thought can mean to you and to yours? It can mean *freedom*."

The homely, granite-faced Norwegian paused dramatically before continuing. And then, in a softer voice that carried with curious resonance across the dull gray-green water, he said, "If there is a chance . . . just a *chance* that we can live and die as free men, with rights and protections under the law, must we not seize that chance? And asking God for the protection of His divine Fatherhood, must we not stand as brothers, and fight the good fight?

"For if we do not . . . the crimps *win*, and the owners *win*, and for all time and eternity we seamen *lose*! Think on it, men of the sea. That's what I ask of you today. Only that you *think on it*."

Tom looked at Donaher and saw his sparkly little eyes alive with energetic fire. "The man's an evangelist, Donaher. A bloody evangelist. I can see how he captures them."

Donaher nodded quick assent. "We're to meet him at the Longshoremen's Rest on Fourteenth Street tonight at eight," he whispered hoarsely. "I've arranged it so's you can talk with him. A great man he is, Tom. One in a million."

That had been the beginning of it, Tom remembered. Furuseth's face, chiseled from rough stone, weatherworn; the face of a peasant saint, he had thought that night, watching him in the shabby

Longshoremen's Rest. Sitting in his ragged woolen peacoat, a shredding knitted muffler around his neck, hands like gnarled tree trunks, he was committed to the cause of the seaman and the longshoreman, he said, for they were often one and the same man. Beyond his passionate commitment to his cause, Tom also saw he was a strangely gentle soul.

They had become friends, Tom, Donaher, and the Great Man. Talking long into the cold nights, imagining, planning a better world than the one they lived by day. Through Furuseth he met the other union organizers; the visionaries and the fanatics, the honorable ones and the ones who saw a union as yet another opportunity for exploitation. Through them all he learned that the connection between the men of the maritime trades was a curious spiritual bond; almost as if the men who lived by the commerce of the seas, whether they plied their trade on land or water, were a breed apart from others.

He learned how some of the organizers dreamed of overthrowing the powerful owners and establishing power bases of their own. And how others, like Furuseth and Donaher, sought simple justice.

"How did it start for you, Andy?" Tom asked the question as he and Donaher and Furuseth sat in O'Rourke's Saloon one night, nursing their beers as a means of staying off the cold street a while longer.

"I was the son of a farmer in Norway, Thomas. Poor we were and with too many mouths to feed and too few prospects." Furuseth spoke with a strong Norwegian cadence that Tom found winsome and melodic.

"So when I was fourteen years of age, I ran away to sea and joined a ship to Oslo as the cabin boy. We were on our way 'round the Horn and it seemed to me the greatest adventure a man could have, to be a sailor seeing the farthest places of the world, places that I had only dreamed about before.

"Well, lads, like most dreams, it wasn't quite what I had hoped. My last voyage—I was a seaman seven years then—I drew a captain who ran his ship like a tyrant. When I spoke up fer the rights of the men, he had me hung by my wrists from the yardarm." He pushed up the sleeves of his peacoat to expose the scars that ran from wristbone to mid-forearm; more than thirty years old, they were still an angry and ugly disfigurement.

"One night and one day I hung there, delirious I was from the pain. Not knowing if the captain would have me killed when he cut me down as an example to the other men, or if I would ever be able to use my hands again, for the fingers were black and so swollen that they started to split apart. All the time that I swung there in the cold wind, I swore an oath to God that if He save my life and my hands, I change things. Strange it seems to think of it now, but I make a plan half in my right mind and half, I think, in a vision; I saw how it must be done. How I must learn to read and to write, how I must learn the law, how I must show the men how to have the courage to be free.'' The homely, leonine face took on a sheepish grin. ''It was a strange vision for an illiterate farm boy, ya? But I knew from that day, God would show me the way if I be willing to make the sacrifices the job would demand.''

''Have you never wanted a wife and family, Andy?'' Tom asked gently, wondering if it was too personal a question, yet wanting to know. A wife and family seemed so essential a part of his own dream, he was hard pressed to imagine that the big Norseman didn't need them too.

Furuseth looked at the younger man for a long time before replying; his eyes were soft in that moment, almost like a boy's or a woman's. When he spoke, his voice was sad and less vehement than usual.

''Ya, Thomas. I wanted to love like any man. But what kind of a life could I offer a woman or kids—me traveling the country from end to end, getting thrown in jail in half the places I stop at. I guess I just made up my mind that the union would be my life and I would do the best I could for it. If I be married, I always be torn between my two loves, I'm thinking.''

Donaher, who had been silent throughout the questions and answers, laid his glasses on the table with a resounding thud.

''One day, no man will have to sacrifice a decent life because he works on the sea. When that day comes, it will be because of Andy Furuseth!''

''I'll drink to that,'' said Tom, and glancing at Andy, saw that his eyes were shining. He thought his two friends were very special men.

38

"Does it trouble you, lass, if I come here with Donaher?" Billy smiled at the question and at Tom. By God, he's a beauty, she thought. Her house was full and, with a prosperous evening ahead, she was in a jolly mood. She was glad that Tom had taken to stopping by with Donaher at least one night a week, but the fact that he tended to hang around in her vicinity rather than to look for a willing young lady made her nervous.

"I welcome your friendship, Tom, to tell the truth of it." She half shouted it above the babble of voices and music and singing and dancing around them. "But much as I hate the thought of sharing your own fine self, it'll look a bit odd to the girls if you keep coming here with Donaher, and he takes his pleasure whilst you and I just chat. It won't take long for that to get back to the wrong ears, I'm thinking."

"All right, then, my girl. When I come to see you, I'll fulfill my obligations with one of your lovelies and *then* I'll come back to chat with you. How does that sound to you?"

Billy laughed good-heartedly.

"You're a rare piece of work, lass," he said, his own laughter mingling with hers.

"And you, my friend, may end up thanking me for being so charitable, despite the fact that I intend to see you get the homeliest, least talented girl I've got whenever you stop by." The laughter in her eyes was provocative, and he felt himself harden at the thought of her.

Never one to miss any nuance where a man was concerned, Billy casually brushed her hand, as if by accident, across the front of his trousers where a swelling had become visible, and winking at him, she said, "As there seems not a moment to lose, I'll be introducing you to Gloria this very minute." And signaling to a girl in a yellow dress across the room, she kissed him lightly on the cheek and was gone, leaving him shaking his head in amusement.

Billy had thought about Thomas Dalton a great deal more than she wanted to since the memorable evening when Donaher had brought him to meet her. He had the damnable ability to make her wish for things she mustn't wish for, dream of things that were best left undreamed.

Diamond Jim Mulvaney was her future, as he was her past. His money had set up her house, bought her clothes, paid her girls. His pull had brought in the first patrons, his strength had supported her when her seagoing brothers had died, one by one. Three of them, plus her mother and father, had died together before she'd even met Mulvaney, of course, when the cholera had swept the poorest parts of the city. The sea had claimed the others inexorably as the years went on; only Donaher, her eldest brother's friend, was left of the past. Only Donaher, who worshiped her, and Mulvaney, who owned her in a nice, friendly kind of way.

She tried not to remember what it had been like on the streets after her family's death. Her older brothers far away on ships and she a child alone and homeless. She had nursed them all when the cholera struck her mother, father, and three brothers; five ghastly dying bodies in their tiny, airless flat. No money for a doctor, no cool fresh water to soothe their hideous fevers or swollen tongues. She had begged ice chips from the ice-truck drivers to cool the fetid water from the backyard sink outside their tenement—terrified of taking too long at her task of scavenging, lest the unthinkable happen while she was gone from her charges. At first she had sought to cure her patients somehow, then simply to lessen their suffering; finally, heartbroken, terrified, beaten, she had prayed for their release from the wracking agony of the filthy disease.

When they were gone, she had sat in the dark flat waiting for the telltale signs of the ailment to begin in her own frail body—the violent spasms of nausea, the vicious diarrhea that seemed to turn your very bones into water. She had waited two days and a night after the body cart had picked up the five dead members of her family and the men had told her to burn everything they owned. But the illness hadn't come.

Finally, with nothing left, she had taken to the streets and thence to a brothel, from which Jim Mulvaney had somehow miraculously delivered her. At eleven years of age, work is hard to find, and in the five years between the time her life began alone and the moment when Diamond Jim Mulvaney walked into the whorehouse where she worked and saw the most gorgeous sixteen-year-old girl he had ever laid eyes on, she had learned much about life, but very little about dreams. Home, husband, children, respectability, they had never even been deemed possibilities. Until Tom Dalton, it hadn't mattered much.

Billy watched him climb the stairs with Gloria's small hand in his large one; she took a deep breath and a sip of wine, forced herself to remember Jim Mulvaney with gratitude, exhaled audibly, and walked back into the gaggle of happy men and women with the mask of a smile on her marvelous face.

Tom Dalton lay in the little bunk bed—as usual, several sizes too small for his large bulk—and thought about the future. The sputtering candle had been blown out only moments before by his roommate, Donaher, and already the man's comfortable snoring filled the small, dingy room with its noisy rattle.

Tom smiled at the sound; never an easy sleeper himself, he was pleased that his friend had the capacity to drift off like an untroubled baby, as soon as his large frame settled into a supine position. " 'Tis the sleep of the just," Donaher had said with a hearty chuckle when Tom had mentioned it to him. He was probably right about that.

Tom had been on the docks now for nearly two months. His hands had hardened and callused with the heavy work, and already he felt only half dressed without his longshoreman's hook at his belt. He grimaced in the cold dark at the sound of scurrying creatures in the alleyway below. A fact of life on the filthy waterfront, rats made his stomach muscles tighten in loathing.

What am I doing here? he had asked himself a thousand times in the last month. Surely he was not meant to spend his life on the longshore or out at sea. Surely this was just a time of passage . . . but to where, and with whom?

He pressed his hand over his aching eyes and head. Even the cold seemed oppressive, sorrowful. Or perhaps it was just the hiatus in his dreams that had once seemed so clearly defined, so reachable despite the detours. That was it. Somehow he seemed to be lost in this detour; swallowed up by a course not of his own choosing. But soon it would be time to move on.

Barnacle Billy lay in her bed as corpulent Diamond Jim dozed at her side. She ran her fingers idly over his pink belly and remembered all that she owed him. Diamond Jim was not a superb lover, his massive size made movement of a sexual nature a considerable strain, and, in truth, he preferred to leave most of the effort of lovemaking in Billy's expert hands.

But, she thought as she traced a playful pattern on his ponderous belly, without Mulvaney she would still be a pretty, penniless waif with no hopes and fewer prospects. Nonetheless, she had not forgotten Tom Dalton. But she would let it be no more than a pleasurable memory. Billy had a long memory and a profound sense of loyalty to her friends.

"Jim," she said softly, to see if he was really sleeping.

"Um." He opened one eye and looked her way.

"I've got someone I think you should meet. A young man Donaher brought in here a while ago. Said he was a sailor, but there's something about him that's real different."

"And what was that, little lady?"

"I don't know, darlin', just that he seemed like a gentleman, down on his luck. You know, he talked real pretty and he didn't have rough ways like the rest of them. I thought you should meet him. I have a hunch you could use him for something."

"It couldn't be you got *your* eye on him to use for something, could it now?"

"Jim Mulvaney, I can give you my word right this minute that he'll never find his way under my covers! But I'm telling you, darlin', you should take a look at this one. He's something special."

And to reassure her rotund lover of where her affections lay, she dropped her hand a bit lower and began to fondle him in earnest.

"I love you, Jim," she said, and meant it in her own way, as she bent her head to her labors. "You made everything in my life turn out okay and I'll always love you for it."

Jim Mulvaney put his plump hand on Billy's blond head and patted it in a proprietary fashion. He understood her loyalty and accepted it as his due. She had proved a useful friend to him since he'd rescued her from the streets. She'd grown up to be a woman of uncommon common sense, good judgment, and, of course, her sexual ability was a rare gift in any woman. He was well content with their bargain and had every intention of fulfilling his part of it. As long as she played it straight with him.

If Billy said she would not take the young man to her bed, she would not. If she said Diamond Jim should see him, he would do so.

"Billy wants to see you, lad," said Donaher out of the corner of his mouth one morning as they both worked at unloading a vessel from the Indies. "She's fixed it up for you to meet Mulvaney. She says you're to spruce up as best you can and present yourself at Diamond Jim's house on Fifth Avenue, if you don't mind, at seven tonight. But you should go see her first to find out what's up." Donaher winked at Tom as he straightened his huge bulk from hoisting a two hundred and eighty-pound sack of sugar into place on the deck.

"Be sure to save me a piece of those dainty little cakes they'll be serving yer, lad, at Mulvaney's. I loves me tea and crumpets at bedtime, don't yer know." He made a fancy gesture with the pinky finger of his hand, as if he were drinking from a teacup.

Tom bent double under a load of sugar sacking and laughed aloud at his friend.

"Aye, I'd best get my velvet tuxedo and my satin shirt out of storage for the occasion." And they both chuckled as they returned to the backbreaking task of loading sugar into the dark hold of the creaky old ship.

39

Mary sat on the floor of the nursery playing with her eighteen-month-old son. The crisp Boston sunlight streaming in the nursery window glinted on his red-gold hair, and his laughter seemed to her like the clear, clean babble of a country brook in summer.

What joy this little child had brought her! What consummate maternal bliss there was in just looking at his robust Irish face. She had known from the moment he was born that this child was hers.

He had been big and strong at birth, a peaches-and-cream baby with a reddish-gold halo of silken hair just barely visible on his beautiful head.

The doctor had handed the baby to her moments after his birth, and she had gasped aloud when she saw him . . . he was the image of Tom! She had reached for him with tears of joy in her eyes, and the doctor had wondered that a woman of nearly forty years could be so overjoyed by the birth of a fifth child. Of course, you could never tell about women and babies, he'd told himself . . . if there was one thing he'd learned in thirty years of doctoring, it was that you could

never second-guess what made women tick when it came to
motherhood.

"Sean, my darling," Mary crooned to her son as she reached out
to touch his silken cheek, "show mommy how you can pile up the
blocks." She knew it irritated both the nanny and Thaddeus when
she called her son Sean instead of John. But with this child she
simply didn't care what anyone thought. The other four children
would have to be enough for Thad. This little lad was hers. Her
Sean, her son.

Part Four

DIAMOND JIM MULVANEY

"Stand together," Chief Tamanend told his tribe. *"Support each other and you will be a mountain nobody can move."*
                    —The motto of Tammany Hall

40

Never in his whole life had Tom Dalton met a girl who so unnerved him.

He stared at Deirdre Mulvaney as if he had never before seen a woman, and indeed he had never before seen one who filled him with such an implausible sense of destiny. He stood riveted, his gaze holding hers, as if waiting to see if she had felt it too; if she would give him a sign that she had been touched by the same power.

Deirdre was tall and slender, without being frail. Shy and bookish, thought her father. Sensual and intelligent, thought Tom. The girl seemed immobilized for a moment by the curious expression in Tom's eyes.

How strange, she thought. He has the eyes of a poet, not a longshoreman.

Tom had arrived at the Fifth Avenue mansion of Diamond Jim Mulvaney, as he had been instructed by Billy to do. It had not occurred to him that anything more urgent than securing employment with the powerful man could seem important to him on this night of awesome opportunity. But the sight of Deirdre Mulvaney with her golden-brown waist-length hair and her haunting gray eyes took his breath away.

"Deirdre, girl, don't stand there like a milkmaid; ask Mr. Dalton if he would care for a drink, or he'll be thinking you've no manners at all."

"Of course, Father, I'm so sorry," she stammered, trying to regain her composure. "Would you care to take tea with us, Mr. Dalton, or would you perhaps have something a bit stronger, as my father sometimes does at this time of day?"

"Tea would be just fine, thank you, Miss Mulvaney. It always reminds me of my home in Ireland long, long ago." He smiled at her, a warm, open smile, more open, softer, than Jim Mulvaney would have expected from so serious a young man. He was instantly alert to the electricity in the room. Deirdre is meant for a fine rich husband and the place in society I've so hard won for her, he reassured himself. I'll not be having this handsome spalpeen interfering with my plans.

I'm going to have to make myself very valuable to Mulvaney before he'll let me near his daughter, Tom thought with calculation as he sat quietly sipping tea. Tom had been well coached by Billy as to Mulvaney's businesses. She had sketched for him, in succinct terms, the vast scope of Mulvaney's business and political empire.

If it had been obvious in her tone that she was awed by her powerful protector, it was also obvious that she cared for him, so that she was careful not to betray his confidences in what she told Tom. Mulvaney's power was well known in New York, she assured him; had he been living here longer, he would have heard from other sources all of what she was telling him.

All day in the hold of the cargo ship, Tom had mulled over how to handle the evening, how to present himself to Mulvaney as an indispensable acquisition. Now, sitting in the ornate living room, he decided that an honest forthrightness was the only tack to take with the astute Mulvaney, who he was certain would disdain sham and see through invention. He felt relieved by the thought, for he was uncomfortable with subterfuge.

"Miss Billy told me, Mr. Mulvaney," said Tom when Deirdre had quietly slipped from the room, "that a man in your position might have need of an assistant. Someone to be your eyes and ears when you are in the crush of your many businesses. I realize the thought is a presumptuous one, since I have no credentials in business, but I would hope that you might consider me for such a job."

Mulvaney's black eyes narrowed as he appraised the boy. No arrogance there, he noted shrewdly, just pride and a certain innate dignity. "No one is my eyes and ears but me, young man." He said it more harshly than need be, to make the point he was not to be trifled with. "I could, on the other hand, profit from some extra legs and hands, perhaps. My many enterprises would kill a lesser man than me, mind you, and it wouldn't hurt to have a helper." He settled back in the chair expansively. "I always like to think I owe my stamina and my endurance to my Irish forebears. Farmers they were, the lot of them. Poor and beaten down by the English, but scrappy and hardworking and resourceful, and, above all, enduring. Great legacy that, my boy."

Leaning forward, he looked Tom straight in the eye, a lawyer's gesture, a gesture of domination. "Much like your own story, I'd wager?" It was a question, an invitation to a life story, not a statement.

"My mother's family were farmers. I never knew them," said Tom quietly.

"And your father's family, lad, what of them?"

"They had other interests, besides the land."

"And they were?" Mulvaney hadn't made his millions by being reticent.

"I will tell you what you will of *my* life, sir. Of my father, I will not speak." Finality.

"Are you ashamed of him, Tom? You can tell me, surely."

"I feel many things for my father, although he is long dead, Mr. Mulvaney. None of them is shame."

Mulvaney's pudgy face relaxed from its inquisitor's stare. He leaned back, so his round belly seemed to rise up from the chair as the rest of him tipped comfortably to the rear.

"Not easy to intimidate you, boy. You're not the kind that budges easy, and I'm an old hand at budging. I like that. You can trust a man that keeps his own counsel. Mostly, anyways." He extracted a massive Havana cigar from an elaborate leather case, and went about the concentrated effort of snipping, savoring, and lighting it.

"Tell you what I'll do. I'll give you a chance to make something of yourself if you've got the guts for it. Give you a chance to learn the business of business and see if you have any aptitude. You know, just because a man's got a brain and is articulate doesn't mean a tinker's damn when it comes to business. Gotta be shrewd and ruthless and fast. Gotta be able to outthink and outdeal and outrun every man you meet. Some's got it, some's not. Which kind you are, we don't know yet, do we?" He continued the soliloquy, enjoying himself immensely.

"I got where I am by following hunches, not by lallygagging around and waiting for streetcars. I'll give you a chance to learn and I'll give you an even break. But don't ever cross me, lad, for I'm a deadly enemy and I never forget a wrong. My code of honor might not be what my old mother or her parish priest would have chosen, but it's my morality and I live it to the letter. Let no man misuse my goodwill, or he'll live to regret it."

Tom said nothing but sat studying Mulvaney. He was a man of about fifty-five, solid as a rock, with disproportionately large shoulders (from working eighteen hours a day swinging a hammer as a navvy on a railroad gang when he was a boy, Tom later learned) and short, stockily bowed legs. His body, despite its overweight, emanated an aura of power, and his tiny, porcine eyes had the capacity to be cherubic and merry, cold and deadly, or fiery as those of an enraged evangelist in the company of sinners. He had the Irish gift of blarney and could talk the birds from the bushes; he came possessed of a fiercely competitive nature and an incisive mind. "Jim could mind rats at a crossroad," his distraught but loving mother had said of him. Until the day she died and was buried with all the other poor in potter's field, he had loved the ground she walked on. She was, he believed, the only true saint he would ever run across, and he cherished her memory with fitting reverence.

The utter pragmatism of Jim's spirit had made the profession of law a natural one, but the opportunity to learn it had been hard won. Having worked his way across country by the backbreaking means of laboring on the railways, where Irishers were welcomed for their strength and their low cost, he had offered his services, as apprentice and clerk, to a lawyer he met in a Denver saloon. Since he was a bold and brawny kid, the lawyer had agreed to his apprenticeship, provided he also act as bodyguard and servant; so Jim's career as a lawyer had begun by his ignominiously waiting on his benefactor hand and foot, breaking heads for him when the occasion required it, and working as many hours a day and night as he could keep his brain and body awake and alert.

Mulvaney's rise in the world of commerce had by no means been whirlwind, but it had been steady. He had absolutely no morality of the ordinary sort—he could cheat an opponent without a twinge of conscience, and he considered it weakness in a man to be confined by conventional morality. Yet he had a queer compassion for the poor, saw all impoverished old women in the aura of his sainted mother, loved and lusted after younger ones, whom he treated with surprising tenderness. He did not, of course, take women at all seriously, but in this he was no different from the rest of his generation.

He loathed the clergy, for he thought them hypocrites, and secret sinners, and could not forgive them for having denied to the poor their one intrinsic comfort, that of sex. "Scratch a priest and you find a pervert or an inquisitor," he would say often, to the discomfiture of his daughter, who was being bred by the nuns to be somber, God-fearing, and thoroughly Irish Catholic.

Jim acquired the knowledge of the law with an impassioned relentlessness, for in its complexities he recognized the keys to the kingdom. The law was to be his escape from the hazards of poverty, for his pragmatic mind grasped its subtleties with an innate cynicism that astonished his mentor and struck fear into the hearts of the other law clerks. In Jim they recognized the consummate lawyer, one to whom right and wrong had no meaning whatsoever, but to whom clever and devious manipulation was as second nature.

Far into the night Tom and Mulvaney talked by the open fire, Mulvaney savoring his brandy and cigars, Tom drinking Irish whiskey sparingly and speaking with a disarming clarity that moved Mulvaney, for he had a faultless intuition about character. Here was one, he said to himself, who has been deeply wounded by life but who has healed himself without too much bitterness. Here is a gifted intellect and a poetic soul (Mulvaney could forgive him that, for he considered it an Irish legacy). He could, if Jim judged correctly, be ruthless, too, if need be. He was strong without being ferocious, handsome without being soft. Jim liked the quiet, confident way in which he voiced his thoughts. Yet he has been poor as a church mouse, thought the intuitive observer. Hungry and lonely and desperate. An interesting combination, if I can manipulate the ingredients.

The young man's observations, while unschooled in the intricacies of business, were not naïve, and his questions were incisive. His flaw is in his gentleness, thought Jim with satisfaction, for it always gratified him to ferret out the fatal flaw in each man's character.

Gentle people, no matter how strong they be, are reachable by circumstance or by compassion, and gentleness is a trait it's difficult to root out thoroughly, said Mulvaney to himself with a chuckle. But on the other hand, if he were tougher, he would be infinitely more dangerous.

Thoroughly satisfied with the young man he had just measured, the older one hoisted himself from his great armchair in a signal that the evening had come to an end.

"Come to my office early in the morning, my boy," he said genially as he showed Tom to the door. "You have much to learn if you mean to be useful to me."

"I mean to be very useful to you, sir," answered Tom seriously. "I'm grateful for the opportunity you're giving me, and I'll not disappoint you." He hesitated for a moment, as if weighing the wisdom of what he wished to say, then continued. "You see, Mr. Mulvaney, I intend to make a great deal of money, for I would like to call upon your daughter, and she must not be wasted on a poor man who has nothing to offer her."

"You set your sights a mite high, Tom," answered Jim, raising his furry eyebrows in dismissal of the notion. "My daughter is meant for the kind of match that will provide her with a secure position in society and a life of ease. It might be a lifetime before you could offer her that, if indeed you ever could."

"Then I must work all the harder, sir," was the straightforward reply.

Jim shut the door thoughtfully, musing on the instinctive honor that had forced Tom to repay his hospitality with honesty about his intentions, even at the risk of losing favor. He was fascinated by honor in other men, although he saw no need for it in himself. An interesting combination, he mused with a sigh. There was no need to fear the threat of Tom's courting Deirdre, of course, for Jim would have her safely wedded long before this intriguing young man could afford to call on her. Under different financial circumstances it might have made an interesting match, but Jim was a practical man and dismissed the possibility.

As usual, Jim Mulvaney went to bed a well-contented man.

"I've got a problem. I need to talk to you." Tom was shaking his slumbering friend into a grudging wakefulness.

Dazed, Donaher sat up in the bed. "Great God, lad! What time is it that yer wakin' me out of a fine deep sleep to start jabbering? Have you gone daft?" Then, seeing the troubled frown on the younger man's face, cursing at the cold, he slipped his giant body out from under the warm blankets and sat himself squarely on the side of the bed.

"Mulvaney's offered me a job."

"What kind?"

"Apprentice, of sorts."

"God Almighty, lad. You've struck it rich, you have." He slapped his knee for punctuation, but Tom heard the hollow, lonely sound in his friend's voice.

"I don't want to leave you, Donaher. Nor Andy."

"Aye, Tom. I expect you don't."

"It's a good opportunity. I'm good at numbers, and there's a girl there, too. I met her tonight. She was different, somehow . . ." He didn't finish the thought, unsure of what he meant to say.

"What'll I do, man? I'm dying to get on to a better life, to learn a trade, to build a future away from the rats and the hopelessness. This is a chance at my dreams, Donaher. But my heart isn't in it at all."

"So yer want my permission to go and get rich, lad? My by-yer-leave to get the hell out of the squalor and misery and make something of yerself?''

Tom's face looked bleak in the flicker of the gas lamp from outside the window as Donaher studied him.

"Well, you've got it, by God! A full-fledged A-number-1-type dispensation from his holiness H. P. Donaher." He slapped his knee with his gnarled hand for emphasis and smiled broadly, his crooked teeth gustily displayed. "We knowed, Furuseth and me, that you was just passing through, laddie. We love you, sure enough. But we knowed you wasn't to be part of this forever. Yer meant for a bigger life than us, Tom. A life with yer books and fancy houses and a grand wife and kids and a fine cozy future. Old Andy and me knowed it when we first laid eyes on yer. But we was happy to have yer fer as long as the good Lord planned it to be.''

Tom looked at his craggy-faced friend, an immense hulk in the shadowy darkness, and thought there were tears in his shiny eyes.

"You're as good a friend as a man ever had in this sorry life, Donaher.''

"Aye, lad. I'm not a bad sort for an old sailor down on his luck. But you've got a fine life to lead yet. And I'd be much obliged to yer if you'd remember yer old friend from time to time while yer living it.''

They talked long into the night and finally drifted off to sleep in the early hours of morning, Tom electrified with the sudden possibilities, Donaher feeling lonelier than he had in a very long while.

41

Diamond Jim Mulvaney's office was a peculiar mélange of rich furnishings and poor taste. Baroque furniture stood in a massive paneled room that had probably once been grand. A tawdry crystal chandelier overwhelmed the area, and a rococo marble fireplace with gleaming brass implements and a fancy screen dominated a wall on which a huge portrait of Deirdre was hung.

The desk behind which Mulvaney's heavy form was visible was in dramatic contrast to the inelegance of the rest of the furnishings. It was a monument to exquisite carpentry. Huge and masculine, with rich, simple lines, it was somehow sensitive and free. The surface gleamed with a deep, almost mystical glow that seemed to emanate from the wood beneath, as if a life-force had been contained there by the skill of a craftsman capable of designing so beautiful an artifact.

"You like my desk, eh, sonny?" Mulvaney's rich voice boomed at Tom from behind it, and the young man realized with embarrassment that he had been staring at the lovely piece of furniture rather than at its owner.

"I've never seen anything quite like it," said Tom truthfully. "But I think I've dreamed that such as that might exist in the world."

Mulvaney's cherubic face transformed itself into a self-satisfied smile. "Got it from a bankrupt man. Foreclosed on a mortgage a while back, and salvaged this from the spoils before they went to the auction block. Old family, he was. Used to be rich as Croesus, but he had a yen for the gambling tables and wild women that wiped him out. Shot himself in the head, I seem to remember. . . ." He chuckled broadly. "You know what they say, lad, it's an ill wind that blows no good. I'm right fond of this piece of furniture."

Tom wondered if he would ever learn to measure the acquisition of a desk against the loss of a man's life and fortune, but he said nothing.

"Been thinking about what to do with you, Dalton, now that I've got you. You're fit for naught but to use that hereditary brawn of yours, at the moment; and brawn is not the way to make money. Brains is. I worked eighteen hours a day on the railroad gangs and was lucky to get my fifty cents for it. From the time I started using my brains, I been rich as any man needs be.

"I'm what you might call a man of many enterprises; some of them legal, some of them requiring the services of a lawyer or two to make them appear so. How are you with numbers, lad?"

Tom smiled easily. "They come to me with little trouble, Mr. Mulvaney."

"Good enough. Here's what I have in mind for you, Dalton. I could use a lieutenant—someone who knows my business real good and can do my bidding in the places I ain't in, and you got possibilities for that job. But you got an almighty lot to learn, boy. So I'm thinking of making you an apprentice of sorts, to two men. O'Reilly's my accountant; oversees the financial interests of my little businesses. Tierney's my lawyer. I pay them both unconscionable sums of money to keep me on the right side of the law. Not an honest bone in either of their bodies, mind you, but they know the right tricks.''

"What kinds of businesses are you in, Mr. Mulvaney?'' Tom already knew the roster from Billy, but it seemed a sensible question.

"Started with lumber, lad, in Denver and farther west. Thousands of acres of prime timberland out there for the taking, and nobody gave a damn about it in them days, when the railroad was just going through. Owe my successful lumbering career to the lawyer that trained me, mean-hearted son of a bitch though he was. Made a killing in lumber and by making deals with the railroad to haul it, even before there was a railroad.

"Then there's construction right here in New York, and all along the train route. Construction is a grand trade, lad, the whole country has building fever, and everybody needs lumber for it. I've a philosophy that says you tie up all the ends of a business package. If you own the lumber, and the rails that move it, and the construction companies that use it, and the real estate interests that sell the land to build on—then you got something with a certain continuity to it.'' He smiled contentedly at the thought of his conglomerate interests.

"My real business now is politics, however. Can't get anything done in New York without politics; so that's where I concentrate my efforts these days. We Irish have a gift for it, Dalton—the blather and the compassion of politics.''

Tom looked alert at the surprising word. "Why compassion, sir?'' he said, then realized, chagrined, that Mulvaney had maneuvered him into asking just that.

"Don't you ever mistake it, Tom Dalton, the heart of all politics is helping keep those poor bastards out there alive. Have you seen how they live, these shivering hunks of humanity that get off the boats at Ellis Island? They live two or three families to a room, sometimes, with no water and no toilets and no privacy and not a shred of human dignity. They look for work there isn't enough of, and they feed their children on the garbage left over by the rich.

"There's women in my wards stitching seventy dresses a day for thirty-five cents, if they're lucky enough to get work. Do you know what thirty-five cents buys, lad? Not enough to keep one small soul from starvation, never mind a family. J. P. Morgan's dog eats better than ninety-five percent of my constituents.''

"You don't need to explain poverty or hunger to me, Mr. Mulvaney," Tom said in a stony voice, and Mulvaney leaned far forward over the desk to stare him in the eye.

"You may think you know poverty inside and out, my bucko, but until you've seen the Irish in New York and Boston, you don't know a fucking thing about it. And until you know what it means to see a woman's children starve to death in a cellar, because a factory owner fired her husband when he heard she had a seven-year-old boy he could get to work for him for half as much as the father, you'll not understand the business of politics in this city.

"We feed 'em, Dalton. We get 'em jobs when there is none. We give 'em someone to talk to when the law gives 'em short shrift. And then they vote the way we tell 'em to vote, and grateful they are for the opportunity to do it, lad. Grateful they are!"

Tom watched his employer with new interest. The vehemence of the speech left him in no doubt about Mulvaney's rise in politics. The man had the Irish gift for rhetoric, and the Irish sentimentality that made it believable. Tom hadn't a doubt that Mulvaney meant what he said, provided, of course, his compassion didn't interfere with his enterprises. A fascinating combination, thought the astute young man. He is compassionate because it makes him feel good about himself, and ruthless, when it serves his ends, because that, too, makes him feel pleased with his own cleverness.

"The first thing I want you to do, Tom, is to see what life is like for my constituents. See Ellis Island. See the Irish tenements, and don't pass up the orphanages and the workhouse. When you've seen enough of it to understand politics, come back and I'll start your education with O'Reilly and Tierney. Take Duffy with you on your tour. He's the tough little kid you'll find in the outer office. He already knows what it's all about, and can get you in and out of places."

Tom rose to leave, uncertain if the interview was finished. Mulvaney turned his attention to the pile of papers under his pudgy hand. As Tom reached the door Diamond Jim looked up, a benevolent smile on his lips.

"Have you enough money to see you through till your first payday, lad?" His voice was almost soft.

"Aye, Mr. Mulvaney. I have my wages from the docks."

"I have a mind for you to come and stay with me for a bit, while you're under my educational guidance, so to speak. Get your things packed up this afternoon and see my housekeeper about accommodations. We dine at seven thirty, no later. See that you're prompt.''

It had occurred to Mulvaney that having Tom near at hand where he could be kept under close scrutiny would be a sensible move during his apprenticeship.

Tom opened his mouth to speak, but didn't know what he meant to say and closed it again. He put his large hand on the gilded doorknob, and then turned back.

"I want to thank you, Mr. Mulvaney, for your help. I'll see that you won't regret it, sir.''

"That you will, lad, that you will. I never give something for nothing, as you'll soon find out. You'll work your ass off or be out on your ear. There's a lot to be had from this life if you take the chance I'm giving you, and almost nothing if you don't. I'm banking on your being smart enough to see the wisdom in working your ass off.'' He turned back to the papers in a deliberate gesture of dismissal, and Tom left the room utterly fascinated by this anomaly who had chosen to take him under his wing.

Francis Duffy was one of the homeliest Irishmen Tom had ever seen. He was short and square as an icebox. His face was the sickly white of the true carrot-topped Irish, covered with a blanket of freckles, blessedly thick enough to disguise the worst of the pockmarks that marred it. His hair was orange and curly. It seemed to grow in uneven clumps instead of in an orderly progression over his head. His eyes were bright blue and intelligent, but the face that surrounded them seemed to have been put together from spare parts, none of which matched up precisely with the others.

The young boy stood up as Tom left Mulvaney's sanctuary, and approaching the man who was nearly twice his size with a grin, he stuck out his hand for Tom to shake.

"I'm elected to take you on the poor-tour,'' he said with a lilting brogue that reminded Tom of Brother Damien. "Better not eat much breakfast before you go, it's hell on your stomach and worse on your heartstrings.'' He pumped Tom's hand up and down with a vigorous grip and led the way to the street. "Might as well start at Ellis Island, Tom, that's where it all begins for most of us Micks. How'd you get in without being processed, as they call it?''

"I came in as a seaman on the *Lady May*. I guess no one bothers with sailors on the assumption that one day they'll just ship out again.'' He felt a glimmer of warmth toward Duffy, who seemed so ingenuously lovable.

"Diamond Jim said we can take the horse and carriage. It's funny, you know, traveling in style to see the dregs of humanity.'' The boy shook his head, as if it were all too much to contemplate, and they climbed into the sleek black carriage and were off.

"Have you worked for Mulvaney long?'' Tom asked, to start a conversation.

"All my life, more or less. Some think I'm his bastard son, 'cause he's good to me, but that's not so. I don't look nothin' like him. He just drug me out of an orphanage when I was a kid, 'cause he needed an errand boy and such, I guess. Or maybe he just took a liking to me. He was walking through St. Mary's Home and Orphan Asylum one day, doin' his rounds for the benefit of his constituents, as he'd say, and he saw me there. Well, he just stops by the bed, and me eight years old and feeling pretty glum on it, and he says to me, 'Well young man, and what's your name?' And I says, 'Frank Duffy, right as rain, your honor.' I always had a bit of a mouth on me, you see. And he says to the Sister Superior who was with him, 'I'll take that lad with me, sister, for any boy that homely must have been given some other gift by the Almighty, to compensate.' Just like that, it was. I've lived right here in his office ever since. I eat regular, I have a fine little room behind the outer office, and now that Diamond Jim trusts me to do things for him, I got enough money for most all me wants. He's been real good to me, Tom. There's those that says he's just another ward heeler what's feathering his own nest and be that as it may—but he's been real good to me.''

So that's the way of it, Tom thought, amused by the simplicity of Jim's tactic. Most likely every man on Mulvaney's payroll is equally in his debt. He's built himself a palace guard of men whose loyalty is based on devotion.

"What kinds of things do you do for him, Frank?'' he asked, imagining the reply.

"Oh, lots of different kinds. I runs packets back and forth to Tammany, and I shows visitors like yourself around. I see to keeping the office clean and to ordering supplies, and I fix what gets broke. All kinds of things. Whatever he asks of me. Killed a man a few times when he asked me. I guess I'm sort of his bodyguard, you might say. There ain't nothing at all I wouldn't do for Diamond Jim.'' The boy said it earnestly, and Tom was absolutely certain it was true.

Ellis Island was a bleak gray place. One long, austere building dominated the landscape, and a host of small ugly shacks surrounded it. Inside, the noise that greeted Tom was a curious muffled cacophony. People chattered in a Babel of tongues, but somehow quietly, as if they were fearful of raising their voices in the presence of uniformed authority. There was a constant drone of sobbing sounds, like an onerous singsong—little babies, young women, old men, people crying on relatives' shoulders as they embraced securely, others sobbing silently alone and abandoned, in fear for their very lives lest they be sent back whence they had come.

Tom's stomach inadvertently clutched at the sea of rank-smelling humanity that undulated in a disorderly line snaking its way toward gates at which bored, cranky-looking officials guarded the portals of America.

''See those pens over there?'' Frank pointed to a penlike enclosure in which several hundred bodies were pressed up against each other, the expressions on their haunted faces like specters from a nightmare.

''They're in quarantine. That means the officials think there's something wrong with them. Might be ship's fever, or cholera or bronchitis, or dysentery. Might be almost anything, for these poor beggars never get enough to eat on the boats where there's little air or light, and the water's almost always putrid. I come over on one of those boats—I was just a spalpeen meself, but I'll never forget it, I won't. The smell of vomit in the hold of that boat'll be with me till the day I die.

''See that bunch over there, crying and tearing their hair or just sittin' staring off into space like they was dead already? That's the group that's been told it's gotta go back, 'cause of disease, or no money or somethin'. Mostly they won't go back, though. Mostly they'll kill themselves right here at Ellis Island.'' The boy pointed to a spot at the farthest end of the room, where a small doorway opened to the water. ''That's why they calls that 'suicide corner,' 'cause they're mostly penniless and got nothin' to go back to. Only thing keeps most of them poor bastards alive is the hope that once they're here, things'll be better.''

A small child had run from her mother and smashed into Tom's knee, upending herself. He bent down and tenderly picked up the little girl, brushing away her tears.

"There now, lass, there's no need to cry. Your mama will come get you." He spoke gently to the girl, and Frank looked surprised and suspicious at his tenderness. A young woman hurried up to take the girl from Tom's arms. She was at least eight months pregnant, and there were blackish circles around eyes that stared out, frightened, from a thin face. Tom handed the scrawny child over wordlessly, feeling a knot in his stomach as he assessed the chances for survival of these two in their new world.

"What's going on over there?" He asked the question hoarsely, to push the picture of the woman and child from his mind. A throng of ragged men surrounded a more prosperous-looking one who stood on a soapbox shouting above the riot of sound.

"That's the Judas goat from the Railroad," said Frank with obvious distaste. "He gathers together the Irishers fresh off the boats and tells them great tales of the fortunes to be made on the railways. He'll promise them three dollars a day, room and board, and a trip to the Wild West thrown in for good measure! Once he signs them up, and the railroad takes them out to Kansas or Nebraska or wherever the work is, those poor bastards will find out their wages is fifty cents a day, not three dollars, and they'll have to pay seventy-five cents a day to the company store just to eat. There'll be no way to get back to New York, and nothing to do but work themselves to death, eighteen hours a day, seven days a week, till their contracts is done. The railroad hires Irishers to sign up their own, the bloodsuckers!"

"Why doesn't anyone tell these men what they're getting into?" asked Tom, repelled by the ugliness of it.

Frank looked at him with infinite patience.

"If I was the one what told them, Tom, I'd be dead before mornin' in some railroad yard in Jersey. Besides, what else have they got in front of them? There's not enough work here for 'em, nor housin', nor nothin'. At least out there in the West, when their indentures is up, they can homestead or prospect or maybe find some kind of work to keep body and soul together. It's the unmarried men the railroads take anyways, so that leaves more jobs here for the married ones with the wee children to care for. It's better that way, it seems to me."

Tom marveled at the simple wisdom of the boy, his anger boundless at the plight of the poor and unwanted. It was the same here as in Ireland, then. No streets paved with gold, no easy riches, nor assured survival. He thought of Mulvaney's admonition to see the poor in order to understand politics. He was beginning to understand a great many things.

Tom was intensely grateful to be back out in the cold, crisp air—the squalid damp of Ellis Island seemed to have settled in his bones, and he knew it was a spiritual, not physical, chill.

"What happens to the poor wretches when they leave there?" he asked Frank when they were back in the brougham.

"If they have relatives in New York, they generally move in with them for a while, till they can find work and a roof of their own. 'Course, that means they live two or more families to a railroad flat, but that's a heap better off than the ones what's got nobody." He was silent for a minute or two, and seemed disturbed by what he was about to say. "That's what killed my folks, you see. They got here and found out me mother's brother who sent for them had got hisself killed in an accident, so they didn't have nobody to show them the ropes. They got rooked by a slum landlord, too, poor devils. Put them in a cellar and charged them dear for it. Didn't tell them the last man in the place had died of the fever. So they took sick and died, both of 'em, just like that. I was only a lad of six at the time, but I remember sittin' there in the dark with 'em, cryin' for 'em to talk to me, and not knowing what to do. I fell asleep in between 'em, the last night. God help me, I was grateful they was feeling so hot, 'cause we didn't have no blankets and their bodies kept me warm. In the morning they was dead and cold, and I was delirious with the fever, so they say. Got these pretty marks on me old mug to show for it. So they brought me to St. Mary's, and the good sisters nursed me back to health and all. And then Jim found me, like I said." He paused for a moment, as if remembering.

"About the only part what pains me now, is that I never got to say good-bye to Ma and Pa. They was real gentle souls, you know, and it's often enough I wish I'd been able to say fare-thee-well or something to them at the end." He wiped the moisture from his eyes surreptitiously. "Not that it matters much, I guess. When you're dead, you're dead, and that's all there is to that!"

The boy stared out the window for a long time after, and Tom, who knew a considerable amount about death and loneliness, thought it best to leave him alone with his sorrows.

Mulvaney's slum wards made even Ellis Island seem a human place. At least at the immigration center an itinerant breeze might

cool a poor man or a gust of sea-fresh air reward his efforts to
breathe. In the slum, the air itself was stagnant, like the puddles of
water from the ice-truck droppings along Hester Street, or the fetid
sinks Tom saw in the courtyards or hallways of the tenements.

Frank Duffy led Tom through squalid, ugly streets with the unquestioning acceptance of one to whom such places are the only
reality. The faces staring out of windows along the route were Irish,
but Frank assured Tom that he would take him to see Italian, Jewish,
Chinese, and Negro slums of equal ugliness before the day was out.

They climbed a rickety staircase, in a building that smelled of
decay and lye soap. Even Tom's healthy long legs were strained by
the effort to reach the top floor, and on the way he noted bare
windowless hallways, with incongruous white and black tile floors
that already looked ancient, although they couldn't have been more
than thirty years old.

"When were these places built, Frank?" Tom asked as they
passed the fourth-floor landing, simply as an excuse to stop for
breath. The oxygen seemed somehow to have been drawn out of this
enclosed hallway; there did not appear to be a breath of it available
to his laboring lungs.

"Mostly, the Irish started coming in during the famine in the
forties, Tom," Duffy replied, not even winded by the ascent. "The
famine boats started coming in faster than you could believe, so's
they didn't know what in God's name to do with the people coming
off of them. Then some smart speculators started puttin' up these
tenement places, lickety-split. They're mostly all the same, you see.
Railroad flats with no windows except at the front and back. Gets
pretty dicey in them middle rooms in the summer, let me tell you.
Anyways, the rooms with the windows are dearer than the ones with
only an air shaft or nothing at all, so lots of people are grateful for
them middle ones."

They resumed the climb and reached the highest floor. Duffy
knocked on a darkly painted door that was seriously warped and
paint-chipped. "It's me! Duffy!" he called out, with his knock.
"I'm here to bring little Mary a surprise from Mr. Mulvaney." The
door opened immediately.

A haggard old woman in a ragged but clean muslin dress, with an
equally dilapidated woolen shawl wrapped around her shoulders, let
them in. There was no window; rather, a window-like structure
looked out at a dirty brick wall, not two feet away. This must be an
air-shaft flat, Tom realized with a feeling of claustrophobia. A little

dark-haired girl was seated at a crude table near the air-shaft window, with a shabby blanket around her knees. She looked up at the visitors interestedly, and Tom guessed she must be six or seven years of age. She waved to Duffy.

"This here's me friend Tom Dalton, Mrs. Cochran. He's to be working for Diamond Jim from now on, so's you'll be seeing him around here from time to time." The child waved again and the woman smiled self-consciously, for she didn't have all of her teeth and she was obviously shy of strangers.

Duffy put his hand in his pocket and pulled out a bag of penny candy; Tom couldn't imagine where he had gotten it, but the sheer joy on the child's face lit up the tiny, airless room with its pleasure. She fairly danced out from under her blanket and ran to Duffy, hugging him about the knees. Meanwhile he took some coins—Tom couldn't tell how many—from his other pocket and pressed them conspiratorially into the woman's hand. "It's from Mr. Mulvaney, dear," he said quietly. "Just to help out a bit till things is better."

"God bless you and Mr. Mulvaney, Frank," the woman said with absolute sincerity.

Tom walked to the child's side. "What are you doing, sweetheart?" he asked, bending down from his great height to be closer to hers.

"I sew trims for ladies' hats," she replied with the lisp of one whose front teeth were missing for the moment. "I'm getting really good at it, too. See, I can do flowers and beads now, as well as veiling. Mama says I'm a big help to her now that Papa's gone."

Tom swallowed hard, realizing for the first time that the old woman was the child's *mother* and not her grandmother. Despite her aged appearance she was probably not more than thirty. He patted the little girl on the shoulder and turned to Duffy and Mrs. Cochran. "Your husband . . . ?"

She was clutching her shawl around bony shoulders, and Tom apprehended suddenly how very cold it was in the almost furnitureless flat.

"He was killed in the dock riot last year, Mr. Dalton," she said with a wistful sadness. "Mr. Mulvaney's been helping us ever since, God bless his kind soul. Mary here works at the hat trims, and I do piecework for men's overalls, but it's hard to make ends meet in the winter, don't you see, for there's coal to buy and such as that." She moved her hand listlessly, indicating the dreary flat. There was a sad fatigue about her that Tom recognized as hopelessness.

He reached into his pocket, wishing he had something to leave behind as Duffy had, but finding nothing, he just mumbled some good wishes, feeling the inadequacy of it all, and soon after, he and Duffy left the little flat.

"How much money can they make, Frank, doing what they do?"

"The woman sews sixty or seventy pairs of pants a day I'd guess. She probably gets about two dollars a week for it. The child may make another fifty cents or a dollar for her week's wages. You see, the trouble is the employers know these pieceworkers have nowhere to turn for help, so they abuse them, shameful. Those two poor souls may deliver their pieces on Friday, and be told only half of them are any good, so's they'll only get seventy-five cents for the lot. That's where Mr. Mulvaney steps in, you see. Part of his job is to see that the people in his wards gets a fair shake."

"What about the money you gave her—where does that come from?"

"From Tammany mostly, some from Diamond Jim hisself. Even a few coppers can make the difference between living and dying." It was all said in Duffy's curiously detached monotone, as if he were discussing the weather. Tom wondered if perhaps the tragedy of it all came too close to Frank's own history for him to allow himself to care—or perhaps he was simply inured to it, having seen too much too soon.

They spent the balance of the day going from one end to the other of the Tammany-controlled districts. Tom saw the poor in every conceivable stage of desolation. He saw the pushcarts lining the streets in profusion, saw the children scrambling after the ice trucks, hoping to take home errant ice chips for melting into drinking water; he saw the listless faces of the hungry, and the angry faces of men pushed beyond endurance. He also saw the quiet dignity of families who, through Herculean effort and good luck, had found ways to makes ends meet. He saw little girls, in dresses made of flour sacks, sewing beads on the dresses of the rich, and little boys with missing fingers who had lost them in the factories.

"Factory owners likes to hire children, Tom," said Frank in his usual informative banter. "They cost less per day than the grown-ups, and it's easier to cheat 'em. The only problem is the kids get fagged out in the afternoons, and there's lots of accidents that makes the owners mad."

Before the end of the day, the complicated business of New York

politics had become painfully simple and clear to Tom. If the
Democrats cared about you and fed your family when no one else
would, Democrat was the way you would vote, early and often, glad
of the opportunity to do so.

42

Timothy O'Reilly, Mulvaney's accountant, was a wizened man with
a bald head around which a tonsured fringe of hair hung in lackluster
strings. His eyeglasses tended to slip to the end of his nose, and he
had a habit of pushing them back to the bridge of his nose with a
flick of the finger and a simultaneous nod, a gesture that kept his
head in almost constant motion. The man had such a comic look that
Tom was startled by the deadly accuracy of his intellect and the
staccato tattoo of information that he fired at his apprentice whenever possible.

Mulvaney had given the accountant to know that Tom was to be
trained at whatever pace he could maintain, at as accelerated a speed
as was possible. O'Reilly took his employer at his word, and Tom
had to concentrate mightily to keep up at all.

Daniel Tierney, the corporate attorney, was cut from another
cloth. He attacked problems with the quiet yet dogged persistence of
a bounty hunter. "The law is a harlot, Mr. Dalton," he intoned in
his quiet New England articulation. "Use her as best you are able
and be certain you know the exact price of her services before you
indulge."

He trained Tom Tuesdays and Thursdays and three evenings a
week. One of the evenings they played chess, for Daniel Tierney
considered it an essential means for a gentleman to exercise his
intellect and keep it agile.

Tom worked through the days, studied through the nights and
weekends, at long last in his intellectual element. Accountancy came
easily to him, and O'Reilly's high-pressure teaching technique excited him and filled him with a torrent of desirable knowledge.

The law, on the other hand, caused him no end of problems. He
enjoyed his time with Tierney, liking him personally better than
O'Reilly; he admired his quiet, comfortable life and, above all, his
extraordinary library. But the law itself he found alien: a pragmatic

system in which justice had little place and honesty none at all. His exceptional memory made him an apt pupil, but his intrinsic disdain for the subject was a detriment.

"You would never make a great lawyer, Dalton, despite your many gifts," said Tierney thoughtfully, one night during their chess game. "You are forever looking for a *just* solution rather than an expedient one. A serious drawback in the successful practice of the law." It was a good-natured chiding, and Tom smiled wryly at his teacher.

"It makes me a bit unpredictable, I expect."

"On the contrary, my dear boy. It makes you far too predictable. A sufficiently ruthless attorney would sniff out your sensibilities early on and decimate you with your own emotions."

"How so?"

"It is the right of a practitioner of the law to expect in others of his profession the requisite pragmatism that the law requires in order to run smoothly. One who lacks the ability to act entirely from expediency, lacks a singularly necessary weapon in his professional arsenal. Another lawyer sensing such a lack would have every right to exploit your weakness."

Tom bristled at the criticism, but knew it to be true.

"You may find this weakness of yours to be less a liability in business than it would be in criminal law. It is easier to be ruthlessly practical, I find, in matters of money than in matters of life and death."

"Were you never troubled by the compunction I feel about the law, Mr. Tierney? Perhaps as a young man?"

Tierney moved his bishop to Tom's king four, with immense delicacy of motion.

"Not once in my life, my boy, not once. The law and I are one mind on the question of right and wrong. Right is the side that wins."

O'Reilly was an unsettling man to deal with, and Mulvaney was banking on his ability to unnerve even the stout of heart, in having him contribute to Tom's education. The boy needed to be taxed to the limit; Mulvaney enjoyed knowing a man's limits; it was a useful piece of knowledge if ever the need arose to break him.

O'Reilly disliked Tom, not with any personal sense of animosity but simply because he was young and untrained in the ways of the world of numbers. Young, untrained people made mistakes, and mistakes were something that Timothy O'Reilly could not abide. Even a small error in a ledger could enrage him, and he had been known to fire bookkeepers if a blot could be found on their otherwise tidy green pages, or if their tiny rows of numbers did not meet his exacting standards of neatness.

He also found Tom's good looks an indecency, a disturbance. "He has more the look of a matinee idol than an accountant," he told his wife with disdain. "God alone knows what Mulvaney is thinking of, subjecting him to so rigorous a training program. I'll not have him on my accounting staff, and Tierney says he's got no great aptitude for the law."

"Mr. Mulvaney's a smart man, Mr. O'Reilly," his round little wife had replied tentatively and with her usual respectful use of his title, a courtesy he saw no need to rescind after only thirty-three years of marriage. "Perhaps he has some special job in mind for the boy, you don't know about yet?" Viewing the little woman with considerable annoyance, her husband simply made a harrumphing noise and returned to his newspaper.

Tom was an enigma wrapped in a mystery where O'Reilly was concerned. It was not like Mulvaney to trust an untried man with private information. It was most unseemly to make this boy privy to both the financial and legal areas of the business that he and Tierney so scrupulously kept hidden from public view.

Mulvaney was a shrewd old scoundrel, of course. It would be unlikely that he'd let the boy know where the real skeletons lay, but still . . . it was damned unnerving to have to play the tutor to a stripling guttersnipe who carried himself like the king of England.

The only way to deal with it was with caution and discipline. By God, that boy would sweat for whatever he got, if Timothy O'Reilly had anything to say about it. He snapped shut the newspaper; it was apparent he'd not be able to concentrate on it this evening. He pulled a foolscap pad from his tidy desk and began to make fastidious notes to himself about what academic disciplines he would visit upon Dalton come Monday morning. Just the thought of all those lovely numbers eased his mind and began to settle his obstreperous stomach.

"Would you care for a bit of entertainment this evening?" Duffy asked, standing in Tom's office doorway. "You look a bit under the weather from all this studying you're forever doing."

"Aye, Duff. I'm beginning to feel like a bloody bookworm with indigestion, but O'Reilly'll have my hide if I'm not up on these acquisitions by Monday.''

"Monday, man! 'Tis Friday night and me with some teachin' of me own for you. Of a slightly different sort, of course, than the pinch-hearted Mr. O'Reilly can provide.''

Tom pushed back his chair and ran his hands over his aching temples, as if to banish all thought. He had grown fond of Duffy, strange little man that he was, and a couple of beers in one of the many saloons that the small redhead was on intimate terms with would be a welcome relief.

"You're on, man, and glad I am of the interruption. Where are we off to?''

"It just so happens that I am the owner of two fine tickets to the Hippodrome, where a pal of mine is on a double bill with some bloke name of Barrymore.''

"A music hall? I had no idea you frequented music halls in your spare time, Frank.''

"I'm a man of many surprises" was the reply, the tone playful and happy, although as usual Duffy's face gave nothing away.

They walked out onto the broad, tree-covered avenue, and the fragrant scent of the street vendor's cooking greeted them.

"Could I see you to a pretzel, Mr. Duffy?''

"You could that, Mr. Dalton. I've a mind to treat you to a beer before the show.'' They walked down the street, the balmy early summer weather making life seem somehow simpler.

"You've been hard at it these last months, haven't you, Tom?'' asked Duffy, after a block or so. "I was wonderin' if you've figured out why O'Reilly works you so hard, by any chance.''

"Because he's got a toothache of a disposition, I imagine.''

"Aye. He has that, God knows. But 'tis only part of the reason.''

"And what's the other part?''

"He had a son. A no-good bum he was, too; always in trouble, always needing to be bailed out one more time.''

"What's it to do with me?''

"I think he's jealous of you. You've got the brains and the will to succeed his Willy never had. And Mulvaney likes you, to boot, and he's giving you opportunities to make something of yourself. I think O'Reilly figures it's all coming too easy to you, so he tries to make you sweat for it.''

Tom looked at his companion, complacently munching on the thick salted pretzel as he walked.

"And what of you, Frank? Do you think I have it too easy too?"

"Me?" The young man looked genuinely surprised by the question. "Not on your life! All that book learning and numbers and highfalutin business talk would put me in an early grave. You're welcome to it, and that's a fact!" He paused for a moment, as if pondering something. "Besides, I like my job better than anybody's. I'm real important to Mr. Mulvaney. I'm not sure he could do without me takin' care of him like I do."

"You're probably right about that, Duff," said Tom, marveling at the simple satisfaction of the young man, who seemed to be utterly unburdened by ambition.

Tom had developed a certain fondness for Duffy, the clever orphan who had become as mindlessly loyal to his benefactor as if he were a machine or weapon to be used by the man at will. There was something pathetic in his unquestioning loyalty, and yet he had fine traits too. Loyalty and fortitude, kindliness, and even a kind of honor. Mulvaney meant for his protégé to know what made his constituents tick, and Duffy was just the one to supervise such an education. Through slum after slum, tenement after tenement, bordello after bordello, Duffy had wended his astute way with Tom at his side: introducing, explaining, protecting, enlightening.

Duffy had been his guide and instructor in all the more sordid areas of his New York education. The ins and outs of the Tenderloin—the worst of Hell's Kitchen—were his main area of expertise. Duffy knew better how to operate in the slums than any man alive, Jim had said of him proudly, and Tom had been grateful to the young man for sharing his peculiar knowledge.

Duffy was Mulvaney's man: eyes, ears, information-gathering apparatus, carbon paper. There was no experience he hadn't had and reported on, no needy family he didn't know by first names, no out-of-work son or father whose plight he wouldn't bring to his benefactor's attention for use as political fodder.

He was also ruthless in an almost childlike fashion. When he killed a man who had attempted to break into his employer's office, he'd brought the news to Diamond Jim with an innocent smiling enthusiasm, like a child bringing home a fine report card and expecting a reward from his parents for his accomplishment. Tom, expecting Duffy to be upset by the experience of killing, had offered him condolence, and had been startled by the young man's incomprehension of why it should be offered.

"He was trying to steal Mr. Mulvaney's property," he had replied to Tom's offer of support, pride shining in his homely, pock-marked face. "I was *supposed* to kill him."

The Hippodrome Music Hall was a gilded wonder that had wel-comed the likes of Jenny Lind and Lillie Langtry in its day. Tier upon tier of plush balconies faced a proscenium of epic proportion, and Tom and Duffy settled into their seats with the anticipation of pleasure. There'd been little time or money for Tom to spend away from his tutoring and work; what little could be spared went to Donaher and the union men. The Hippodrome was a glorious surprise, a place full of life, and people of privilege. From where they sat, they could see elegantly clad men and women chattering gaily as they arranged their silk and satin garments and prepared for an evening of varied entertainments.

That's where I'll be soon enough, Tom thought as he drank in the look and feel of the glamorous audience in the most expensive center seats as avidly as that of the performers.

"One of these days we'll be sitting down there with two of those fine ladies on our arms, eh, Duff?"

"Down with the swells, you mean?" asked his friend with defi-nite astonishment. "Not me, sir. I'm not one to rise above me station." It was said with pride. Duffy's life was circumscribed by Mulvaney's wards and the constituents thereof; his intimates were the bookies and prostitutes and the abundant poor. It was suddenly clear to Tom that the life of the rich seemed to Duffy so far beyond his frame of reference that it never even occurred to the boy to hope for more than he had. Watching him thrill to the activity onstage, Tom thought that in Duffy he had come to know that social curiosity—a man totally content with the lot God had seen fit to give him.

43

Thomas Dalton made a point of being near Deirdre Mulvaney when-ever it was possible. They dined together, of course, with her father in attendance, in the huge rococo dining room with its gaudy gilded trappings and its oversize mahogany furniture and the quasi-ancestral portraits that had been purchased from a local auction gallery, along with the house, some years before. He'd learned that the girl's mother had died when she was an infant and Mulvaney not yet a rich man, so that no portrait of Mrs. Mulvaney graced their walls.

He found that Deirdre was an early riser, a fact that pleased him immensely, since early morning had always been his best-loved time of day. Even as a child he had loved to watch the fragile tint of morning suffuse the dark sky with eagerly awaited light. The scents and sights and sounds of the daybreak were mystical, to his mind, and he secretly cherished the fact that Deirdre, too, rose every morning before daybreak, for it was one more shared joy that he could add to the meager store he was collecting.

It was not easy, within the boundaries of propriety, to try to engage her in conversation unless the circumstances of the moment provided some excuse. So Tom bided his time, cataloging every nuance of the girl he prized; he noted the way her shining light-brown hair caught the candlelight at dinner in a thousand tiny highlights, how the soft music of her laughter greeted a humorous anecdote of his or her father's, how tenderly she cared for the neighborhood children, who seemed attracted to her sunshine aura as if she were the Pied Piper of Mr. Browning's poem. He knew that the time she spent in the library was not with frivolous girlish romances but with the works of a wide variety of authors that he himself admired. He knew with intimate attention to detail the graceful angle of her long, slender neck when she sat at peace, unknowing of his intense concentration. He knew, with an intimacy that would have made her blush had she been aware of it, the fulsome slope of her firm young breasts, pressing as they always did against the constraints of her dresses or shirtwaists, just as he knew the delicate span of her tiny waist, which he was sure his two hands could easily encompass.

She seemed to like him, too. She smiled so readily when they passed each other on the stair. She watched him surreptitiously from under her dark lashes when she thought he wasn't looking, and she walked with just a hint more femininity to her gait when he was near. He was usually very clever at discerning whether or not a woman wanted him, but in this case the answer to the question was so terribly important that he dared not let himself guess for fear of misinterpretation.

"Why do you always look so sad and serious, Mr. Dalton?" Deirdre Mulvaney asked the question as they walked together in the garden that was her pride, one very early morning while the dew was still wet upon the roses and peonies. The girl had noticed that her father's protégé walked in her little garden whenever he had free time—a giant incongruous shape in the tiny patch of color. She had contrived what she hoped would seem a casual meeting, this morning before breakfast. It wouldn't do to seem too bold.

"I didn't know I was so obvious, lass." Tom replied to her question, smiling at her, and Deirdre's heart responded by beating more quickly.

"I've wanted to talk to you alone ever since that first night with my father. . . ." She knew she was being forward, but she had waited endlessly for him to take the initiative, and he hadn't made a single move in her direction. "I mean, we always talk at dinner and in the library and such, but I've been hoping you would speak with me sometimes . . . without Father."

Tom looked at her questioningly.

"Miss Mulvaney, the only reason I haven't been bolder with you is because I have absolutely nothing to offer you as yet. It was my intention to try to get a stake together so that I'd have the right to . . ."

"Mr. Dalton, surely you don't need to be rich just to be my friend. I'd be much obliged to you if you'd simply talk with me now and then. I've noticed that you are always reading, and I, too, love to read. I thought perhaps we might speak of the books, at least."

So he hadn't been mistaken in divining that she liked him. He felt the warm elation of it fill his being with profound relief.

"Do you think your father would approve of our friendship, Miss Mulvaney?"

"If you aren't a suitor, I don't think he could have any objections."

"Ah, but I want to be a suitor, lass. I want that very much." He also wanted to touch her, but he restrained himself.

"I . . . I think I would like that, too, Mr. Dalton. But since it isn't possible just now, perhaps friendship is the place to begin?"

Tom turned and looked at the lovely young girl with great intensity before replying, deliberately.

"Aye, Miss Mulvaney, I would like to be your friend, and much more than that as well. But I must earn the right to court you. Till such time as I do so, we can talk of books and life and anything else that pleases you, for I would like to know more about you than any man ever knew about a woman."

Deirdre stared at her earnest suitor, her eyes widening with surprise. She had an overwhelming desire to touch him. She had never felt this way about any of the young men who had come to call on her.

The strangest things happened to her mind and body when Tom was near; puzzling, urgent things. She wondered if he felt them too.

"Mr. Dalton . . . I want to know you that way too!" She blurted it, and then, realizing what she had just said, she gave him a startled look and ran up the garden path into the house without looking back.

Tom smiled to himself with the elation of knowing she felt the pull as he did—that strange sense of destiny that nearly overwhelmed him whenever she was near. He would have to work very hard before Diamond Jim would ever consider his courting her, but things were going well with his apprenticeship; he had a gift for business, Tierney and O'Reilly both begrudgingly agreed. He would make his way first and then see Mulvaney about his daughter's future.

It was the following week that Tom was summoned to Mulvaney's sanctum; what was most curious was not the request but that it came on a Sunday morning and that Tierney and O'Reilly were already there.

The accountant's face was, as always, the gray color of the cardboard on the back of legal pads, and as usual his general demeanor filled Tom with distaste, despite the respect he felt for the older man's keen intellect. Jim was seated behind his handsome mahogany desk; Tierney, impeccable as always, was standing, watchfully, by the fireplace. There was an electric energy in the atmosphere; each of the three men seemed alert, like bird dogs on a fresh scent.

Tom nodded to each of the lieutenants in turn, and looking questioningly at Mulvaney, offered him a good morning. It was seldom that he was in the presence of all three men at the same time, and it was apparent something of importance was afoot.

"Sit down, lad," said Mulvaney genially. "We've an opportunity to present to you, Dalton. A means of proving yourself, so to speak, to these two fine tutors of yours. You've been in my employ now for two full years. You've done well in your duties, I might add, but you've never really had to operate on your own without benefit of the wisdom of these two fine gentlemen. The opportunity I'm speaking of will give you a chance to prove yourself to them, and to me . . . maybe even to your own self."

He smiled his politician's smile, and Tom decided to tread carefully over this unlooked-for opportunity.

"I'd welcome the chance to prove that your faith in me hasn't been entirely misplaced, Mr. Mulvaney." He said it cautiously, a fact not lost on the three subtle men in the room.

"There's a small shipping concern out of Boston that it would be advantageous to own, lad. I've had my eye on it for a while now. Just the right size for the transportation of our own, shall we say, produce, in case a war comes." He puffed on his plump cigar before continuing, and shot a glance at each of his lieutenants. "The line's not for sale, of course. Owned by a brother and sister, feisty New England stock, they are. They've been having a hard time of late making ends meet, and if they're squeezed just right, my bet is they've no choice but to sell. Particularly since Mr. Tierney here has enlisted the aid of a few of our banker friends in Boston to cut off their credit."

Mulvaney put down the cigar and leaned forward over the desk to fix his lawyer's gaze on Tom's impassive face. "I want that company, lad. What's more, I want to see if you've the balls to get it for me. If you do, I'm prepared to sweeten the deal with a healthy bonus to be placed in a bank of your choosing. I'm aware of the fact that you squirrel away nearly every penny you make"—he smiled broadly— "aside from what you give away to your friends in the union, of course."

Tom let out the breath he had been holding during the last speech. So this was to be the test; was he cold-blooded enough to bamboozle a man and woman out of their livelihood? He glanced at O'Reilly, who was watching him with disdain, and Tierney, who seemed genuinely interested in observing what his student's response would be to the proposition.

"I'll need a considerable amount of information before I can undertake such a commission, Mr. Mulvaney. I assume Mr. O'Reilly and Mr. Tierney are here to give me their briefs?"

Mulvaney nodded to his two henchmen, and each reached into his briefcase, as if on cue, for sealed folders.

"All financial data you'll need is enclosed here, Mr. Dalton," said O'Reilly in his high-pitched voice. "I suggest you study it before we waste each other's time in discussion. It is a fairly straightforward business, if you've got the stomach for it." He handed over the file with his usual solemnity.

Tom saw Tierney raise his eyebrows as if in amusement at the accountant's assessment. He handed Tom two sealed folders with a smile. "As usual, the intricacies of the law are a bit subtler than those of finance, Mr. Dalton. I've gathered a considerable amount of data about the two principals in the firm, and about the legal climate in the Boston shipping community. When you have perused what I've gathered, and had a chance to ponder the implications of what Mr. Mulvaney proposes, I would suggest that you and I bandy about some of the possible courses of action open to you. Perhaps our Thursday-night chess game may be foregone this week, in favor of a chess game on a larger scale?'' It was apparent that he was making a point of offering help, which O'Reilly was not.

Tom held the folders in his hands, feeling like a butterfly on the end of a pin. He had every desire to succeed in the business of business, every wish to repay Mulvaney's kindness and support with an appropriate return on his investment. More importantly, a substantial bonus might bring his dream of courting Deirdre closer to reality. He'd been expecting a test, but hadn't known what form it would take. There was a knot in his stomach. Could he really oust a man and woman from their livelihood by the exercise of power? And if he could not, what business had he being in the company of powerful men? He had some serious personal contradictions to consider; he couldn't be sure if he felt repelled or exhilarated by the prospects of testing his own mettle.

"I'll do my best for you, Mr. Mulvaney," he said carefully. ·

Well, now, I knew it was coming, Tom thought the words as he walked resolutely out of Mulvaney's office and down the back stairs that led to the street. He should have returned to his desk in the outer office, but he felt a need for air.

It was easy to feel hemmed in by the Mulvaney-O'Reilly-Tierney triumvirate, pragmatic practitioners of the craft of business. Not that Mulvaney hadn't the right to ask for proof of his protégé's worth. The opportunity for apprenticeship had been manna from heaven; it was only fair to expect to pay dearly for the transition to journeyman.

The file folders he had been given weighed heavily in his hand. Weighty matters, these, that would radically affect three lives: a Boston brother and sister he didn't yet know, and his own. Perhaps even a fourth person should be considered in the drama, if you counted Deirdre, whose courtship depended entirely on his getting a large enough stake together to influence her father. Weighty matters indeed.

Without consciously choosing the route, he headed for the waterfront's openness. Endless space was what he needed. No boundaries and the time to think things through.

*   *   *

Tom closed the last of Tierney's folders and pushed it into the pile of paper already accumulated on his desk. The dark outside the windows and the dull aching in his temples from reading by the inadequate glow of green-shaded lamplight, attested to the lateness of the hour. He stood a little .unsteadily, his body cramped from having been seated in the same position for so many hours; he stretched wearily.

The proposition his mentor had laid before him was almost a textbook foreclosure. The owners had been covertly squeezed into a financial corner from which there was little hope of rescue. Had O'Reilly or Tierney been given the task of completing a coup that had already proceeded so far, they would unquestionably have done so with little fuss. But they hadn't been asked to do so, and it was transparently obvious that the reason *he* had been told to perform the function was to see how he would cope with such dirty work.

Henry and Abigail Marshall, the owners of Marshall Shipping, had inherited a small shipping concern from their seafaring father. The hearty old man had shipped before the mast from adolescence on, and, having won his first small craft in a poker game in Macao when he was thirty years of age, he had plied the intercoastal trade of the Orient for nearly ten years. It had been a profitable business for John Marshall, until an attack of dysentery had nearly killed him and he had been forced to return to New England to be nursed back to health by his patient and long-suffering wife, whom he had visited but twice during his decade of Oriental adventuring.

One of the two conjugal visits had produced a son named Henry, an intelligent, bookish child so unlike his father in thought and aspect that if Mrs. Marshall had not been known in the Congregationalist parish as a pillar of both church and community, there might have been rumors about Henry's parentage. On the second seafaring sabbatical John's lusty nature had provided Mrs. Marshall with a daughter, Abigail, a wiry, intelligent little girl with a sharp tongue and a sharper eye who soon became the marvel of the neighborhood. Abby might be several years younger than her brother, but it was apparent that she could, and would, run rings around him when it came to school or life.

Inasmuch as the small shipping company he'd founded upon his return with his China-trade money needed trustworthy employees, Mr. Marshall trained both his children, from their earliest moments, to be his right and left hands. The fact that the ravages of the

dysentery epidemic had left him unable to return to sailing did not
deter him from a happy and prosperous life. The fact that he was not
a brilliant businessman was a bit of a hamper, but he had an
optimistic and endearing nature, and what he didn't know about the
business was compensated for by his talent in dealing with customers.
Regaling them with tales of life at sea, or his flamboyant adventures
in the Orient, John Marshall was able to win contracts and commis-
sions with charm and wit; meanwhile he went about learning the rest
of the business he had chosen simply because it kept him near the
sea.

His son, Henry, was the kindest, gentlest young man John had
ever encountered. He was a pleasant, unaggressive boy who for the
most part did as he was told, whether the directives came from his
mother and father, or from his sister, whom he recognized from the
first as a superior intellect. Thus, John gave to his daughter the kind
of attention most men give their sons, and to his son, the passive
indulgence most men reserve for their daughters.

When Mr. Marshall died and left his little business to his children—
Mrs. Marshall having already passed to her eternal reward—he did
so in equal parts, content that Abby would make the tough decisions
and Henry would help her as best he could.

The fact that the business had grown prosperous under their aegis
had, unfortunately, brought the little company to the attention of
Diamond Jim Mulvaney, who sensed their firm to be small enough
for an easy takeover and competently enough run to be easily
expanded into the perfect little business to give him a foothold in the
New England shipping trade.

Folding up the papers and returning them to their folders, it
occurred to Tom that this trip to Boston might provide the opportunity
of laying to rest the one piece of unfinished personal business that
dogged his memory.

He slid a piece of stationery into place in front of him on the desk,
and picking up his pen, dipped it in the little inkwell and began to
write.

"Dear Mother . . ."

Mary Dalton Martin had sat transfixed at her little writing desk for
over an hour. The letter from Tom was a terrible shock, made worse
by the very fact of its inevitability. All her life, it seemed, she had

known that this day must be faced, this personal sword of Damocles must fall.

Sweet Jesus, how could it be possible that she still didn't know what to do about him! Why had she not told Thad when it was still possible? Why had she waited until their life was settled and happy and above reproach?

Now, of all times, with Thad opening the new department store that all Boston seemed aware of. Now with the business providing the comforts they dreamed of and the position in society they'd both coveted. Now with her second family all ensconced in the right schools with the right connections. Now that she had Sean to love . . .

She would simply have to write and explain it all to him, tell him not to come.

But what if this were to be the only chance she'd have to see her son? The only chance to see what he'd made of his life? How could she *not* see him? Blessed God, how she wanted to see him! If there were no Thaddeus, and no Anna or Robert or Andrew or Ted or Sean. If there were no years of lying and carefully constructed history to intervene. How different it would be then. How she would *long* to see him!

But all the barriers were real. There was no way she could destroy all that she had built. Mary closed the ink bottle and put her head down on her hands and let the long-pent-up grief flow out of her in wracking sobs. She had not felt despair like this in more years than she could count.

Finally, exhausted by the crying and the futility, she raised her tear-streaked face and wiped her eyes with her hankie; she had decided what she must do.

44

Tom left the noisy rattle of the prosperous Boston train in a turmoil of unsettling emotions, and loose ends. He had always intended to find his mother *some day*, ever since the heartbreaking moment when he'd waved good-bye to her as she rode away on the jaunting car that took her to the boat for America. So very long ago that had been, it was strange to think there could still be pain in it. The sorrow of the separation, which he had hidden away so deliberately for so long, seemed somehow almost overwhelming now that the quest was at an end.

He had cajoled his mother's address from Father Grogan, the priest to whom Father O'Hanlon in Ireland had sent her so many years before when he'd first arrived in New York; but true to Aunt Elly's advice he had waited for an invitation that never came. Now the job to be done in Boston had made up his mind for him. *I've two crises to face in Boston,* he'd told himself on the train. *When they're both done, I'll know a lot more about myself than I do now.*

He had ceased to miss his mother a very long time ago; ceased to feel the visceral wrench that had wracked him at every thought of her during his years at St. Ignatius. Then for a long while he had harbored an ache where there had been pain. And there was anger, too. He shook his head in the cold, sharp air, as if to remind himself he must be resolute. This was a damned hard business, after all.

Perhaps that was why he had sent her the letter without allowing enough time for her to reply.

Clutching his mother's address in his suede-gloved hand, dressed in a handsome new suit of dove-gray wool purchased specifically for the occasion, Tom made his way through Boston's bustling cobblestone streets; now that he was so near his destination, he wavered in his purpose as he walked the crowded, twisting Boston lanes. The city was much like New York, bustlingly alive with commerce; Tom knew it to be the richest port on the Eastern seaboard. Generations of New England shipbuilding, whaling, and rumrunning had assured the Boston rich the opportunity to become very rich indeed.

It was so many years since Tom had seen his mother, he couldn't even imagine any longer how time might have treated her. It was damnably hard to try to sort through the tangled emotions, he thought as he strode along briskly. Damnably hard. But he was determined to fulfill his mission.

The house on Beacon Hill was large and important-looking. A brownstone in the Federal manner, the façade covered with red brick, and the shutters sporting a fresh coat of shiny black paint. A gleaming brass oval on the paneled door announced the Martin residence; Tom knocked with a courage he did not feel, his heart pounding. The last time he had knocked on the door of his lost childhood, he had been rebuffed by his Uncle Randolph; he wondered if he would fare better today.

A downstairs maid in a stiffly starched black uniform answered the door. It was obvious that Mr. Martin had prospered with his mercantile establishment; an air of solid comfort pervaded the visible parts of the house. Beautifully etched glass panels separated the foyer from the inner reaches of the first floor, and the soft yellow glow of lamps within gave the atmosphere a cozy glow. He felt a curious mélange of emotions at the obvious prosperity. Was it anger or relief that was foremost, he couldn't be sure.

"Thomas Dalton to see Mrs. Martin," he replied to the girl's inquiring stare.

"Is the missus expecting you, sir?"

"I really couldn't say," replied Tom, somewhat amused at the thought. "I wrote her to say I would be coming today, but I didn't have time to receive a reply." He handed the girl his calling card and she scurried away, leaving him standing in the entrance foyer next to an ornately mirrored coatrack. He glanced at his reflection in the mirror, trying to see there the vestiges of the child his mother might remember; there seemed not to be any.

A man's deep voice interrupted his reverie.

"Mr. Dalton, I am Thaddeus Martin, your aunt's husband. I am delighted to make the acquaintance of the son of my wife's dear brother."

He stuck out his hand and shook Tom's far larger one with seeming enthusiasm.

"I am sorry that I won't be able to join you in your visit this morning, but you see, I'm just on my way to the store. However, my wife will be along shortly to entertain you. I'm sure you'll have a great deal to talk about." Mr. Martin eyed the young giant with a perspicacious stare. "How long is it, young man, since you've seen your Aunt Mary?"

Tom's equilibrium was unsettled by the dawning realization that he was being passed off as his mother's nephew, but uncertain of the game, he decided to play cautiously.

" 'Tis twenty years since I've seen Mary Dalton, Mr. Martin. I was but a lad when we last met."

"I see," said the austere-looking man, watching him appraisingly. "Well, I daresay you will both have a good deal to talk about, then. Your aunt's life has come a long way since we married, my boy. A long way indeed."

"I can see that is so, Mr. Martin," said Tom noncommittally.

"Yes, of course, you can. Well, now, I must be on my way, young man. Perhaps you'll join us for dinner so that I can hear more of you?'' He didn't wait for a reply. "Why don't you just make yourself comfortable in the drawing room for a moment until Mrs. Martin has finished dressing. Did you know you bear a slight family resemblance to my wife, Mr. Dalton?''

"I am more like my father, I'm told,'' said Tom quietly.

"Yes, yes, of course,'' replied the tall, bony man with considerable disinterest. His mind was already at the store.

"Good day to you, Mr. Dalton, then,'' he murmured as he patted his fine beaver hat onto a balding head and adjusted the fur collar of his expensive-looking greatcoat against the Boston cold. "Perhaps we shall see each other again.''

"Perhaps,'' said Tom, doubting it sincerely, and the man was gone.

"Do you hate me, my son?'' A soft, mellifluous voice broke the stillness of the drawing room where Thomas Dalton stood, staring out through pleasantly crisscrossed windowpanes and struggling to control his anger and frustration.

The woman, who had quietly closed the door behind her, was in her middle forties. Her once flame-colored hair was now more gray than red; her long, lithe body had filled out prettily with the years, and the wondrous bosom Tom remembered with affection seemed quite as firm and fair as it had been in his childhood. Her hair was piled high on her head in a fashionable style, and her Gibson Girl clothes were expensive and well-fitting.

"I feel so many emotions about you, Mother, it's very hard to sort them out. I hope none of them is hatred.'' He spoke quietly, his voice choked with feelings he had thought long subdued. He saw that her soft pale cheeks were damp and her eyes puffy, as if she might have been crying.

"Thomas. Little Thomas. How could God have done this to us?'' There was genuine anguish in the question. The woman advanced toward him, arms outstretched and pleading; much as he wished to resist the pull, he found himself holding the strange sobbing woman who was his mother, her fair head cradled on his vast chest in a strange reversal of what their roles had been when they last held each other.

"Mother, what has happened to you?'' He asked the question urgently, his voice muffled by sorrow and anger. "Why does your husband not know who I am? Did you not miss me as I missed you through all these years? How could you have so betrayed my trust?''

She pulled back at the vehemence of reproach in his voice and straightened herself to her full height with some dignity, as if to gather her resources before attempting to reply.

"I've lived this day in imagination a thousand times, son." Her voice was reminiscent of the one he remembered, but not quite the same. "What would I say to you? How could I explain what I've done? Now that you're here, I can see I can but ask you to hear me out, before you judge your mother. You have a right to hate me, without question, Tom. But 'twould be better if you were first to hear how it was for me, before you judge me."

The stare that met the woman's gaze was cold, yet Tom was flushed with emotions he couldn't sort out and didn't wish to show.

"All right, Mother. But not here, not in that man's house."

" 'Tis my house, too, Tom—and my children's."

"Aye, Mother. And that's why I cannot stay."

Mary straightened the hairs that had fallen across her face, dried her eyes on an embroidered hankie she had pulled from her elegant leg-of-mutton sleeve, and stood facing the full-grown man who was her son.

"You are the image of Michael, Tom. Your father will never die while you live." She turned her face away, as if the sight of him were physically hurtful; her voice was almost a whisper. "You cannot imagine the pain of the memories you bring back to me. I thought I would die of them, all those years ago."

"But it seems that you did not . . . Mother." The irony in his voice and the emphasis he placed on the name were not lost on the woman.

Mary Dalton Martin lifted her head with dignity—a gesture Tom remembered she had always called forth when walking past the stinging ridicule of neighbors. She looked her son squarely in the eye and spoke quietly but with immense conviction.

"I have paid my dues, Thomas Dalton, blood of my blood and bone of my bone. Life dealt me naught but pain and ridicule and poverty, and I've turned it, by the grace of God, into a good life for myself and for my children. If you do not think that I have suffered in leaving you and in losing Michael, you are wrong! There has not been a single night of my life when Mr. Martin took me to his bed that I have not thought of my dead love and all that might have been. Had there been a way for me to keep you with me and survive, surely you must know I would have done so. There would have been *nothing* for us in this country, Tom, had I kept you with me against your father's wishes, you may be sure of that." He was sullen and said nothing in response to the torrent of words.

"Do you know what the life of a servant is, Tom?" Her voice sounded harsh and bitter. "Working yourself to death and grateful for the opportunity it gives you to eat and to survive. Waiting on the privileged and longing to be one of them. Scheming and saving and learning and hoping, all lost and alone in a strange new country with your very heart cut out of you, from the losses you've suffered. Do you have any idea what the world thinks of a woman with a child, who has no husband? Surely you know the names they reserve for a woman like me?" Her words were tense and barely audible.

"I was a servant in Ireland and a servant in New York, and if you think for one minute that I shouldn't have taken the one chance God gave me to become a lady and start my life over again, you're as heartless as the rest of them!" Tom started to speak, but she stopped him with a gesture of her hand.

"If Mr. Martin had known I was not a virgin, do you think my chance would have existed? It would not! So I, who had few hopes of ever seeing you again, gave you up for a chance to have a life. And if you choose to hate me for it, you've every right to do so, and I'll be the last to blame. But as God is my witness, I am not ashamed of what I did, Thomas. Sorrowful I am that I lost you. But I would have you know that I am not ashamed!"

Tom stood, fists clenched, tears of rage and sorrow stinging his eyes; fury at a fate that could have toyed so with their lives. He pounded one fist into the other in impotent fury and turned away from the woman, as if that would make it easier to speak. He understood her grief, but it didn't assuage his own.

"I waited for you, Mother. I waited, always. Through all the long years I thought of you with a desperate need. I loved you and I hated you . . . but always, always you were in my mind and heart." He stopped for a moment, as if to gather strength. "But until today, I must confess, I thought of you only with a child's yearnings, never with a man's understanding of a woman's sorrows." He turned to face her. "I don't hate you. You are simply not the mother I remembered. It isn't your fault that you are not. 'Tis the fault of my memory and of fate."

They stood looking into each other's eyes, absorbing what had been said, wishing there were more than words to bridge the fearful chasm. How could this man know her anguish, she thought bitterly; how could any man know what her struggle to live had cost her.

Mary broke the long silence, her voice hoarse and full of pain. "I would tell you my life, Thomas, if you wish to know; and I long to hear what has befallen you since we parted." Something infinitely plaintive in the simple words touched Tom's heart; something that spoke of loneliness and sorrow, feelings he could understand too well.

She watched anger struggle with sadness in her son's handsome face, and finally saw the anger slowly drain away. She knew it had cost him an immense effort of will to let it go.

"So many years. So many sorrows. How can we even find a place to begin?" The tone of his voice was strained but kinder than before, and his mother felt the trickling balm of relief begin to wash her soul.

"Let's go for a ride in the carriage, Tom. I'll show you Boston, and perhaps we may learn of each other in a different way from before, away from this house if it pains you to be here. I would speak to you of your father, for I have something of his that should be yours." She picked up a lavish, fur-trimmed velvet shawl from a table near the door and tossed it grandly about her elegant shoulders, and her son wondered again where his frightened, peasant mother had gone.

The brougham, brought round from the stable by a liveried driver, was a grand shiny black coach with an insignia Tom didn't recognize on the side panel. The matching dappled horses pranced spiritedly in the cold Boston damp; Tom patted them on their velvet noses and they quieted, nuzzling his shoulder. He saw his mother watching the gesture with moisture in her eyes, and he knew she was seeing his father and not himself. If he was indeed as like his father as was said, it must be a doubly sad day for his mother, he thought as he helped her into the lovely carriage, marveling at how small and delicate she now seemed to him, when once she had filled his world with strength and a protective presence.

They rode through the busy streets, and Mary showed him Mr. Martin's new department store; it was the fastest growing mercantile establishment in Boston, she told him with pride in her manner. They passed the immigrant slums and the splendid houses of the Brahmins, the busy harbor and the bustling commercial avenues. His mother was a quick-witted, articulate woman, no longer the peasant girl of Drumgillan who had longed to be a lady.

She told him of the politics of Boston, of power brokers invited to their home for dinner, of the prosperity of the Catholic Church and its clergy, of her conviction that her second family would never know want or sorrow. They told each other stories of what the years had held for each. It was a comfort to be thus unburdened of stored-up information, but the reawakening of hurtful memories battered them both and made them feel frail and vulnerable.

Tom found himself disarmed by his mother's candor and self-assurance, by her easy laughter and her common sense. By the time the morning had passed, he had come to like her and could almost bring himself to listen to her recital of her children's accomplishments and her husband's successes, without anger and a contained agitation. He had come to find his mother, but she no longer lived in this pleasant middle-aged woman whose life he would never share.

"I have a gift for you, Tom," she said gently when they pulled back to the house on Beacon Hill and they both knew their visit had run its course. She reached inside her dress collar and extracted a heart-shaped golden pendant on a thin gold chain. Unlatching the clasp, she pressed it into his hand, marveling as she did so at the contrast of the huge hand and the tiny golden treasure. "This locket has a miniature of your father in it. It should be yours."

"You said you'd never part with it. . . ."

"Indeed," she smiled regretfully. "I said many things in those days, before I learned what life had in store for me. It is your face, too, in the locket, Tom. I've kept it hidden for twenty years, tucked away in a dresser drawer. It was a need to keep Michael's memory alive in the world. But now that I've seen you, son, I know he lives in you and my vigil is, somehow, ended. 'Tis too beautiful to be hidden from view for a lifetime. Someday there will be a girl you love who should have it."

"Are you happy, Mother?" The young man asked the question earnestly, and Mary reached her hand to his forehead to brush his hair back from his face before replying. It was a gesture he remembered, and it made him sad.

"What true happiness I've ever known, my dear, was left behind in a tiny thatched cottage with the two I loved best. 'Twas in another lifetime, I sometimes think." She sighed and paused a moment before continuing. "I'm content with Mr. Martin and my children and my beautiful home; you've no need to fear for me or mine.

"One of my children, in particular, is a great joy to me. His name is John, although I think of him as Sean. He's my youngest and he reminds me so much of you, Tom, when you were a boy, it's almost as if I'm with you again. He brings me great happiness." But she looked so wistful when she said it that his question was answered for him.

She patted his hand, and he noticed that the hands of the peasant girl had become patrician. "And what of you, Tom? Are you happy?"

"There's a girl I love. I haven't money enough to court her yet, but I have reason to believe I've found favor with her. She's to be my happiness, Mother; I can feel it."

"Then you must take good care of her, Tom, and never let anything part you from her. God could not be so cruel as to cause you another parting in this lifetime."

"I love you, Mother," he said, wondering what he really meant by the words after all the years.

"And I love you, son."

He held her for a long time, feeling her frailty and sorrow, and then left the carriage, wondering if they would ever see each other again, aware that each had left the question of another meeting unspoken.

Thomas Dalton walked slowly down Beacon Hill, hands in his pockets, eyes unseeing. She had been so curiously unlike his mother, this lovely middle-aged woman who reminded him strangely of the sad-eyed wives he'd known in Dublin. It was impossible to connect this quietly aristocratic presence with the robust peasant life-force of his mama of the long ago. He tried to guess at the suffering behind the metamorphosis, but there was somehow little room for her sorrow beside his own.

By the bottom of the long hill, he had felt a battering of emotions, among them anger, confusion, and hurt. But there was a certain compassionate understanding mixed in with it.

So there it was. The truth he had never wanted to face. The reason she had never summoned him, never begged him to come to her was the very fact of her own life. *He* was the coin that had purchased her survival—no, that wasn't quite right. Her sacrifice had purchased it, but he had been the substance of the sacrifice. And she had made it, as he would never have done had the situation been reversed.

So, after all, Aunt Elly had known the score. Wise Aunt Elly. "She is *not* the reason for anything," she had said, "*you* are the reason. *Your* life is the reason. You must find your way, as she will find hers."

And his mother had found her way indeed. So she wasn't as he'd hoped, but how could she have been, after twenty years? Had she been the same gentle girl he remembered, she would be long dead. Only the connection between them was dead, and perhaps that was best for all concerned; he would go on with living. He would try to remember her with kindness.

Mary stood at the window and watched her son square his shoulders and start the long walk down the hill. It was all she could do to keep from running after him. But to what possible end?

Lord, he was a fine young man! Strong and gentle like his father, solid and deep. What astounding emotions she was feeling. Anger that she had lost such a treasure, relief that he was safe, happiness at his fine prospects, sorrow that she could not share them.

She had a sudden wild desire to go to church to say ''thank you'' to God; and she wasn't even sure what she was thankful about. For this beautiful boy who was her son and Michael's immortality? For the reprieve of knowing her abandonment hadn't led to his destruction? For the fact that her guilty secret was still safe after all the years? For the simple joy of motherhood that she had somehow never felt with her second family, except with Sean? For Tom was *exactly* as she had hoped . . . *exactly* as she and Michael had dreamed he would be. How absolutely extraordinary a gift from God that knowledge was!

She threw her shawl impulsively about her shoulders and headed for the door. She hadn't been to a Catholic church in all the years since she'd made the decision to stop having children, despite the Church's admonition to the contrary. Thaddeus had been so delighted when she'd announced her conversion to his Presbyterian faith that she'd never even considered telling him the real reason for it.

But Catholicism was the only religion that held any magic for her, however much she railed against it and however often in her life it had failed her. The place she needed to go today was to a Catholic church. She couldn't have named what it was she needed to find there, but she knew beyond doubt that she would find it.

45

Abigail Marshall was a maiden lady; Tom had no doubt that she would remain one till death, for she had inherited the long, horsy bones of her father and the forthright tongue of her New England forebears.

She greeted him with a directness that was likable in its own way, and she introduced him to her brother, Henry, whom she quite obviously adored.

Henry was quiet, unassuming, and bald as an egg. He had the professional squint of one who has spent all his leisure hours in the happy company of books, and he treated his sister with an affectionate respect that Tom found amusing.

"You've come to buy our business." Abigail stated it matter-of-factly. "We do not wish to sell it to you, Mr. Dalton. This company is our legacy from our dear father, and our livelihood as well." Tom had not expected so direct a confrontation.

"You and your brother are in difficult financial straits, Miss Marshall. Would it not make sense to sell the business and invest in another enterprise with the proceeds? I feel, in fairness, I must tell you that my employer generally gets what he sets his sights on."

"It might make *sense* to do so, Mr. Dalton, if our whole lives, and that of our father before us, had not been tied up in Marshall Shipping. It's more than a tidy business to us, it is our heritage, our place in the community and all our fondest memories."

He watched the woman as she spoke. Her hair was chestnut, liberally laced with gray and pulled up on top of her head in a tiny bun. She was not the kind of woman to be vain about her appearance, but rather the sort who thought scrupulous cleanliness and neatness necessary female accoutrements, assets far superior to vanity. She had a strong jaw, alert eyes, a quick wit, and an honesty that he found appealing. He wondered how she had allowed Mulvaney the upper hand, for she seemed no dullard where matters of business were concerned.

"Would you consider inviting me to dinner, Miss Marshall?" He asked it on the spur of the moment, after having talked with her about the business for nearly an hour.

"And why precisely would I wish to cook dinner for the man who intends to force me out of my own business, Mr. Dalton, might I ask?" She said it with an amused glint in her eye, and he liked the pride that prompted such a feisty response.

"Because you pose a great problem for me, Miss Marshall, and my own future is no less in danger from it than yours is. So, to be honest, I think if we get to know each other better, we may have a chance of solving the question together, quicker than if we struggle with it separately."

She smiled quizzically at this odd revelation, and nodded her head.

"Seven o'clock, then, Mr. Dalton, at our house. My brother and I tend toward Spartan New England cooking, so don't expect anything fancy."

"I'll be there, Miss Marshall," he said, and left the small office with the beginnings of a plan forming in his mind. In some unfathomable way, his confrontation with his mother had left him stronger, more independent of mind, than he had ever felt before. Nothing was going to beat him down. Not Tierney or O'Reilly or Mulvaney or God Almighty. He was twenty-nine years of age, and by God it was about time he became his own man.

The wharves in Boston had a singularly different character than those of New York. Walking along the waterfront, pondering his dilemma, Tom began to sense a different flavor to the Boston harbor than that of the one he knew so well.

For one thing, it was cleaner and less ugly, although he couldn't think why that should be. The ships looked the same, the labor to load and unload them the same, but there seemed a crisper, less sullen attitude about the men as they worked, and there was surely less squalor around the waterfront.

He made inquiries about the Marshalls, and everywhere the response was the same: "Henry Marshall, God bless him, is the finest, kindest man you'll ever meet. Honest as the day is long; give you the shirt off his back, he would. And Abigail? Smart as a whip, that one. Calculates numbers at the speed of an adding machine; shrewd and strong, a tough negotiator, too. Teaches Sunday school at the Congregational church. Does work for the poor and the missions in her spare time."

"Will you have more Indian pudding, Mr. Daltan?" Abigail's face was flushed pink from the heat in the kitchen. She had donned a serious dinner dress of dark green gabardine with white collar and cuffs, and for the first time since meeting her, Tom thought she might have been considered pretty in her youth, if she had ever taken the pains to think of herself that way.

"Miss Marshall, another bite of anything could cause my vest to pop its buttons." She smiled at the reference to the amount he had eaten, pleased that her plain dinner had been such a success.

"Don't they feed you in New York at all, Mr. Dalton?"

"Yes, ma'am, they do," he replied with a wink at Henry, "but not nearly as well as in Boston, I'm afraid."

Abigail Marshall untied her apron and folded it carefully onto the walnut sideboard.

Soft words butter no parsnips, Mr. Dalton," she said. "Or do you perhaps expect to *flatter* me out of my business?"

"Abigail!" said her brother, aghast at the social breach. "Mr. Dalton has done nothing to merit being insulted in our home, dear."

Abigail took a deep breath and then nodded her head in agreement. "You are quite right, as usual, Henry, dear. You have an apology, Mr. Dalton. It is simply the strain of struggling to keep our little company together that has tired me to the point of rudeness. And, of course, the knowledge that it was my own stupidity that allowed Mr. Mulvaney the upper hand."

Tom watched the strong but gently bred woman and was moved by her candor. For the twentieth time that day he went over his options in his own mind. He could simply do as he had been instructed to; no one could fault him for doing the job he was paid to do. And Abigail Marshall had indeed committed the unpardonable business sin: She had been outsmarted. But on the other hand she was playing outside of her league; O'Reilly and Tierney were uncommonly ruthless and smart, and they had the enormity of Mulvaney's resources to back their hand. It is surely no blot on one's war record to be routed by superior numbers and artillery.

He could walk away from the whole entanglement, go back with his tail between his legs, and admit he hadn't the balls to do the deed. Not an attractive alternative. Certainly not even an option, if he expected ever to ask for Deirdre's hand.

Or he could find a way out of the maze, a compromise that would keep him from having to be party to an injustice he'd prefer not to live with, while allowing Mulvaney an out from having to fire him for failure. After all, he was not so simple an idealist to save someone else's livelihood at the cost of his own. The glimmer of a possible plan had been niggling at him through dinner. He decided to proceed cautiously, but to proceed with it nonetheless.

"Miss Marshall," he said at length. "I would like to get to know you better, and perhaps to tell you a bit about the man I work for."

Henry Marshall smiled at the serious young fellow. "If it's to be a long story, Mr. Dalton, I suggest we hear it in the study so that we may have a bit of my sister's blackberry brandy along with it, if you don't mind. I have the feeling you might like that even better than you like her cooking. This way, if the story is a pleasant one, we shall already be happily relaxed to enjoy it, and if it is an unpleasant one, perhaps we will not care so much, one way or the other." He chuckled as he led his guest from the dining room.

Tom accompanied the man and woman into the small study; it was his intention to use the next few hours to plumb the depths of their knowledge of business and to assess their characters. It was not his intention to tell them the story of what he owed Mulvaney and how much he wished to court Deirdre, or to tell them of life on the waterfront with Donaher and Furuseth. Yet before he took his leave of them, he had done both. He had also shaken hands with them on a deal that might mean the end of his employment at Mulvaney's. It was a gamble he had decided to take after careful consideration; a gamble he felt he needed to take, for his own sake as much as for the Marshalls'.

Deirdre sat on the side of her four-poster canopied bed and thought about the man she loved. He was so strangely reticent around her, and yet she had no doubt that he felt as she did.

The thought sent shivers of pleasure through her young body. He was so handsome, in a brooding kind of way; she suspected him of melancholia, an Irish turn of mind. She had seen glimpses of joy in him too, and a great deal of good-natured humor at the dinner table. She felt such a palpitation of the heart and mind when he was near; his huge, quiet presence dominating a room, his strong male voice and laughter a joy in themselves.

She wondered which frock to wear today to catch his eye, when he returned from his trip to Boston. She thought he fancied the pale yellow one with the tiny white rosebuds jacquard-woven into the fabric, for she had caught him watching her one day when she wore it on the garden swing. She rose languidly from the bed, and loosing her long silky curls from the ribbon that subdued them, she stood before the oval mirror and examined her reflection with a critical eye. Nineteen years old, slender and tall, but with a full round bosom. She squeezed her breasts in a proprietary gesture; for some reason she felt voluptuous and beautiful today. She felt the nipples tighten and wondered what it would be like if Tom were to touch them, not a little shocked at her own audacity in thinking such a thing. The dizzying thrill of remembering her feelings the day he had touched her, inadvertent though it had been, tingled through her body. She had tripped on the stair and he had caught and held her to him for a small breathtaking moment and she had nearly died from the sheer pleasure of his strong hands and hard body. She smiled at the smiling reflection in the mirror and, humming a sweet, happy tune as she did so, dressed for dinner.

"I'd like to see Mr. Mulvaney, please." Tom wondered how his employer would greet his maverick solution to the thorny Marshall problem.

"Mr. Mulvaney will see you now, Mr. Dalton." The middle-aged woman who guarded Mulvaney's threshold held open the heavy door and stood aside as she did so. Diamond Jim's large body was visible within, standing at the window, looking out over the city. Tom cleared his throat to let the other man know he was there.

"Sit down, Dalton," said the employer as he turned. His pudgy face looked tranquil, but his eyes were alive with energy and power.

"So you've come to tell me what you've wrought in Boston."

"That and a little more, sir."

Mulvaney's bristly eyebrows shot up intimidatingly. "Well," he said, as if expecting the worst. "Out with it, then."

Taking a deep breath, Tom began. "I bought the Marshall Shipping Company for you, Mr. Mulvaney. It's a tidy little package, potentially quite profitable, as you know."

"I expected you would."

"Did you also expect me to hire the Marshalls to run it, sir?"

"You hired them?"

"I did, sir. For life, provided they perform for you."

"Might I ask why?"

"They're good people. The woman has a lightning-fast brain, the man is loved by everyone. They're honorable, smart, hardworking, and respected in the community. They'll do a good job for you."

"They were stupid enough to get trapped by Tierney and O'Reilly."

"Few people go a lifetime in business without a mistake, and few people are sharper than Tierney and O'Reilly."

Mulvaney smiled inscrutably.

"The truth of it is you didn't have the stomach for the dirty work, isn't that it?"

Tom returned the hard lawyer's stare and replied. "It's true that I had no stomach for harming the Marshalls after I'd met them." He paused. "But it's equally true I wouldn't have hired them to run the business if I didn't think they'd be the best people for the job. They're a prideful family, Mr. Mulvaney. They'll do their best for you, and with Tierney and O'Reilly on their side, instead of against it, Marshall Shipping should do quite well for you."

"And what would you, in your almighty wisdom, have done if they'd turned out to be derelict in their duties, might I ask?" Mulvaney seemed more amused than annoyed, but Tom couldn't be sure.

"I would have paid them for their business and seen them on their way, I believe."

"You believe!" Mulvaney's voice suddenly thundered the word. "In business you must *know* absolutely what you would do, not merely believe what you might! I pay you to do what I order you to, not to make moral judgments on the matter, and don't you ever forget it!"

"Then you need Duffy for the job, and not Tom Dalton." The young man's voice was quiet and tense. He didn't want to lose his position; Mulvaney's business was a once-in-a-lifetime opportunity. But neither could he allow Mulvaney to think him a mindless tool. He watched the older man watching him with unrestrained calculation. He saw himself weighed in the balance before Mulvaney spoke again. He couldn't be sure if he had been found wanting.

"Go tell the news to your two teachers and let's be done with it, then." The voice was neutral this time. Tom rose to go.

"And by the way, lad, there'll be no bonus for you from this affair. A kind heart in business tends to cost money. It's a good lesson to learn, you may as well learn it now!"

Tom left the office, not sure if he should be pleased to have escaped being fired, angry that he hadn't gotten the bonus he'd sought, or simply relieved that this particular test was over. He decided to feel relieved.

46

To Tom it seemed that everything changed for the better after Boston. He had not gotten his bonus, but he had been given a small raise in wages. Although O'Reilly had made a point of voicing his disgust at Tom's sentimentality in hiring the Marshalls, and Tierney had chuckled in amusement at the way in which he'd handled the dilemma, the Boston episode had somehow changed his status from apprentice to journeyman in the Mulvaney enterprises.

All three men treated him with more camaraderie, and Duffy, quick to sense any change in his idol's attitude toward anyone, began to treat Tom more with respect than friendship.

" 'Tis the strangest state of affairs, Donaher," he told his friend as they sat in the Longshoremen's Rest one night after his return. "They treat me better now, despite the fact that I failed to do as they wanted me to. Can you beat that?"

He tried to see his friends on the waterfront as often as possible, although his free time was scarce and what was left of it he contrived to spend with Deirdre.

"There's no really big man who wants only yes-men around him, lad. I expect old Mulvaney knows now he got more in yer than he bargained for, and is glad of it. Yer know, havin' a yes-man around can be mighty comfortable, but havin' a man with a mind of his own and the courage of his convictions is a damned sight better, it seems to me." Tom knew his old friend was proud of his rise in Mulvaney's organization, proud of what he was learning and of its potential to build a secure future.

"Maybe you're right, Donaher," Tom said, unconvinced. "But one way or the other, I feel stronger about myself since Boston. I don't know if it's because of finding a way around Mulvaney, or because of finally facing up to meeting my past after all those years, but I feel as if I could handle anything." He laughed almost shyly at his own enthusiastic appraisal of himself. "I've decided to ask Jim for permission to court Deirdre."

Donaher looked up sharply, hoping his young friend hadn't misread the cues. Having a man like Mulvaney give you a chance to prove yourself in business was one thing, getting him to let you marry his daughter . . . well, that was another thing entirely.

"I'll keep me old fingers crossed fer yer, lad. From what yer tell me she sounds like just the lassie fer yer own fine self." No need to worry Tom with his own wariness, thought Donaher. It was just that experience had shown him that the things you want most in life are usually the hardest to get. He looked at his young friend with deep affection, hoping with all his old heart that, unlike those of the rest of humanity, the lad's dreams really would come true.

Mulvaney settled back into his brown leather armchair and made a ritual of lighting his big Havana cigar. Beside him on the table was a snifter of brandy, and all around the library were the artifacts of his wealth and position. Photographs of himself with the greats and near greats; rare leatherbound volumes; costly, if not necessarily tasty, furnishings. Contentment enveloped him, like an aura of sunshine.

"Did I ever tell you about my brief exposure to the cattle business?" He looked expansively at his protégé. The lad was too serious by a long shot; he liked having the young man in his home, liked his common sense and quick wit and probity, but, by God, he was going to loosen him up if it killed the lad.

"That's one phase of your checkered career I believe I've missed." Tom's voice sounded interested and a bit amused—each new chapter in Mulvaney's career was a revelation. The old man was a ruthless son of a bitch, but somehow there was also a softness in him—or why else would he have taken in a young man from the streets and given him such glittering opportunities. And then of course there was the merriment, seemingly so at odds with the pragmatism, and yet, in Diamond Jim Mulvaney all the jumbled components somehow fit together to form a remarkable whole. Tom had come to look forward to the nights when Mulvaney would invite him to share cigars and brandy after dinner; there was so much to learn from the man and he was so willing to expound.

"Well, there I was, my bucko, about to make my way east again after leaving my apprenticeship with my bastard benefactor, the lawyer-timber baron." Mulvaney puffed his Havana expansively and blew a languid, perfect smoke ring into the air between them for punctuation.

"Now, it comes to my attention that there's a herd of cattle to be driven to Chicago for the slaughtering, and Chicago is right in the direction I am headed in. I knew about as much about cows as you do, laddie, but I always had a nose for money and I'd heard once in a saloon about an old Mexican trick that they used to get top dollar on their beef from the gringos down Texas way. So's I decided to take this herd of cows with me on my journey home, after winning the money to buy them in a poker game, I might add. I was pretty good with a marked deck in those days." He looked at Tom from under his expressive eyebrows, as if for signs of disapproval, and then, finding none, proceeded.

"Well, sir, I hired me a bunch of drivers and a one-eared cook with a chuck wagon, and before I went I loaded up three extra wagons with salt." He lowered the punctuating eyebrows into their inquisitor position and peeked out under them at his young listener to see if the sense of it had dawned. Pleased that the man looked suitably puzzled, he continued.

"Well, now, off we went, and unless you've ever traveled in the company of cows and cowboys, you cannot fully appreciate either hardship or your sense of smell. For two thousand miles I held my nose by day and played poker by night with as seedy a bunch of men as God ever made. But that's another story.

"At any rate, we got about a hundred miles west of Chicago and I told the drivers to break out the salt and feed it to the cattle. Now, some of them knew the trick and my stock went up with them over it instantaneous, and the others just thought I was a loco tenderfoot. Now, my Mexican friend had told me cows love salt, and, by God, he was right as rain about that. Those gluttonous bovines just lit into that salt and the more we shoveled out, the more they ate."

Recognition of where the story was headed began to dawn on Tom.

"And those cows didn't happen to get thirsty, now, did they, Mr. Mulvaney?"

"By God, they did, lad!" The older man slapped his own round knee with enthusiasm. "They drank themselves into a bloat the like of which had never been seen in Chicago and we sold those fat old cows for half again what they were worth!"

Tom shook his head in wonder at the canny old man's sheer exuberance. There was nothing Diamond Jim Mulvaney liked better than to beat the odds by means of wiliness.

"I've had many a belly laugh over the years imagining those cows pissing themselves into the stockyards and the Great Beyond, let me tell you!" He laughed so hard his rosy little round cheeks jiggled merrily and his cigar bobbed up and down in the corner of his mouth.

"You never stop amazing me, Mr. Mulvaney," said Tom with sincerity. "Every tale you tell me is a wonder."

Mulvaney stopped laughing, but a benevolent expression suffused his face as he studied his student.

"I've given up on trying to make you devious, Dalton, but I still like to amuse myself showing you how it's done."

Tom looked up to see if he was being rebuked, but Mulvaney waved his hand as if to dismiss the unspoken question.

"I'm not chiding you, lad. You've got other qualities that are quite as useful to me. Besides which, I'm devious enough for the two of us, so never you mind."

He looked at the handsome young man with a benevolent appraisal; his own motives where Dalton was concerned were a constant fascination to him. Tom was too honorable by half and too serious; too good looking and too willing to listen to what an opponent had to say. But he was quality, and Jim had always admired quality. He was first-class merchandise, smart and articulate and fast and hardworking. And he had that special aristocracy that the Irish occasionally produced and that Jim admired. He was a smart, productive worker, too. He'd done just the right thing in Boston, of course. Jim had had some good laughs at O'Reilly and Tierney's expense over that one. The old reprobates had set the lad up for a fall and he'd come out smelling like a rose. The Marshalls were the perfect people to run the business, keep it legitimate until such time as he needed it otherwise. Pillars of the community, they were; Jim liked having pillars of the community on the payroll.

But there was more to it than that, of course; Tom had shown himself to be his own man in Boston. He'd made his own decisions and been prepared to live with the consequences. Diamond Jim Mulvaney had plenty of yesmen on the payroll already. It was invigorating to have one around who had the courage of his own convictions.

Tom, uncomfortable in the long silence, had taken it as a sign he was to go and had risen from his chair, putting his brandy snifter down on the table as he did so.

"Tom." His employer's voice was unreadable.

"Yes, Mr. Mulvaney?"

"I've been thinking it's about time you stopped calling me 'Mr Mulvaney.' The name's Jim or Diamond Jim, understand?"

Tom was startled by the obvious largesse gesture; it was clearly calculated to accept him into the club, if not of equals, at least of confreres.

"I'd like that very much, Jim," he replied deliberately. "Thank you. I'd like that very much indeed."

Tom wondered as he walked back to his room, elated by the evening's turn, what had caused Jim to make the offer of goodwill. No matter how long he worked for him, the man would remain an enigma.

Part Five

DEIRDRE

The Six Gifts of Women according to the ancient Celtic bards:

The gift of beauty
The gift of voice
The gift of sweet speech
The gift of needlework
The gift of wisdom
The gift of chastity

47

"I want to marry your daughter, Jim." Tom said it aloud, just as he'd said it in his head ten thousand times over in the two and a half years that he had worked for Mulvaney.

"I know that, lad. But I can't allow it."

"I've worked hard. You know I'm trustworthy, and you know I'll take good care of her."

"That's all true, as far as it goes, Tom. But it's not enough. I've come a long, long way in this life, and I intend to go a lot farther before I cash in. I've the intentions of marrying Deirdre into society. She's got the beauty for it, and I've got the money and the power. Her children will never need to know that the Irish were once outcasts. They can have the security of old money behind them, as well as new. She's always known what I intend for her, and she's a good, obedient lass. She'll not deny her old father the one thing he's ever asked of her." He said it coldly and assuredly, and the very confidence of it filled Tom with a chilling apprehension.

"Jim Mulvaney, you've been very good to me. You took me off the streets, taught me business and the law, introduced me to the men who make this part of the world work. I'm more than grateful to you, sir, and I think you're fully aware of the fact that I've done my best to pay you back by working night and day to further your enterprises.

"But this is different from all that, sir. I'm in love with your daughter, and I've every reason to believe that I've found favor with her. I ask no more nor less than any other man, Jim. I ask the chance to court her. Beyond that the choice is hers."

"It is not hers!" Jim exploded. "The choice is not hers at all, nor should it be! Do you think I'm soft in the brain, that I haven't seen the looks pass between the two of you? Do you think I'm so old I don't recognize the quickening of the blood between you whenever you're in the same room? Understand me well, lad. You're barking up the wrong tree here. I took you in and I've trained you and I've given you bed and board, but I'll turn my back on you in the blink of an eye, if you persist in this madness. *I'll* choose Deirdre's husband, and by God it won't be an Irishman that I picked off the streets!'' His face had turned a dark red with emotion. He sputtered again, before Tom could respond.

"Oh, I could see to it that you got rich, and I could see to it that her comforts were seen to, and yours in the bargain; but all my money can't buy a place in society like putting her into the bed of a Boston Brahmin can. And I intend to have that, lad, by God I do! Not for myself, mind you, but for my grandchildren and their grandchildren after them. I'll have my seed so grand and proper, they can dine with the queen of England if they choose to, and no one to hold them back. My mother lies in potter's field, Dalton, but her great-grandchildren will dine with kings; you mark my words, they will!''

The anguish of the countless rejections and embarrassments that must have seared this dream into Mulvaney's soul, flooded over the younger, more genuinely compassionate man. He could envision Jim marching behind his much loved mother's coffin to the burial ground for beggars, could see the small, intelligent child vow to some unknown God that never would such horror touch him or his again. The poignancy of it touched Tom deeply, for its pain was not so very different from his own. He decided to be reasonable and try to keep his own temper in check.

"Jim. Listen to me. I'll make a place for us in society, if that's what I must do to have Deirdre. Give me the chance, man, I love her too much to give her up.''

"Do you love her enough to give up my empire for her?'' Mulvaney's beady eyes were cold as death.

"What do you mean by that?''

"Swear to me that you'll never see her again, and I'll make you my heir apparent. Timber, construction, graft, you name it. The whole bloody kit and caboodle, yours for the taking.'' He paused to let the enormity of the offer sink in. "Think how many other pretty women there are in the world, for a man with all that at his disposal. I'm fifty-seven years of age, Dalton. All I have left is to see my dream for Deirdre fulfilled. My daughter as the wife of the likes of them that snubbed me is all I want for myself in this godforsaken world—assure me of that, and I have no compunction whatsoever about letting you follow in my filthy rich footsteps.'' The silence in the overheated room was stifling. "Unless you give me your word today that you'll never again see her, nor talk to her of love nor marriage, you can clear out of this house by suppertime. I wash my hands of your ignorant carcass. You can go back to the gutter I found you in, and believe me, man, I'm a bad enemy.''

Tom stood up, unable to sit listening to Mulvaney. His mind was racing. How in God's name could he ask Deirdre to marry him if he didn't have a job? What job would there be for him, with Mulvaney on his trail? Would she even want him, if he were a common laborer? Would she be willing to move away from New York to escape his influence, and if she would, where would they go? Would she grow to hate him, if he were the cause of an estrangement from her father? If he walked away from this room with Mulvaney his enemy, what guarantee did he have that Deirdre even felt as he did? He had had such dreams of glory, of stature, of building a life, a family, a secure future. . . .

"I can't do it, Jim." He said it quietly and hoarsely.

"Can't do what?" Mulvaney's voice was cynical, for he knew that all men had their price.

"I can't give you my word about Deirdre. I must have the chance to know her mind in this."

"You're not only an ingrate, lad, but an imbecile. To throw away a fortune for a woman you don't even know will have you? My businesses are well rid of you." He pulled his heavy form cumbrously from the leather chair. "You've made a loser's choice, boy. I wouldn't have thought you such a sentimental fool. Don't you think I'll have her out of New York, and into some fine convent where you'll never find her, before the week is out?" And he turned his back contemptuously on his former protégé and lumbered from the room.

Tom walked in a daze, up the banistered stairway, looking at the Oriental treads beneath his feet without seeing them. The disappointment was overwhelming. He felt heartsick. He would pack quickly, and clear out before Jim returned. He must find a way to leave a message for Deirdre, so she would at least know where to reach him if she chose to. His heart cringed at his own stupidity. Why had he asked so blatantly? Why had he imagined Jim would ever sanction the match? If he had kept his own counsel just a while longer, he could have made plans for them. Only a fool doesn't protect his flanks. He should at least have ascertained for sure where Deirdre stood in all of it; a few stolen kisses and a secret friendship were, when all was said and done, all he'd had of her, and women were notoriously fickle.

He closed the door to his room and sat down heavily on the side of the chenille-covered bed, and put his head in his hands, unseeing.

"Tom—?" Deirdre's voice outside the door was soft. "Let me in, please." She was standing in the hallway, her pale lavender dotted-swiss skirt billowing out over small brocade-slippered feet, just visible, peeking out from under the great flounce of hem.

He looked at her uncomprehendingly.

"I heard everything, dear Tom. I was in the flower garden, under the window. I ran up the servants' stair to come to you." She smiled at him tenderly, and crossed the parqueted floor, leading him from the doorway back into the room. "It took great courage to do what you did. I've never before seen anyone face my father down." She reached out to touch his troubled face, brushing the hair back from his forehead with her long, slender fingers.

"Deirdre," he said despairingly, closing her small hand in his larger one. "I've made a fearful mess of things; he'll send you away for sure, now. I'm without work and that changes everything. How will you ever have the chance now to find out your own mind about me?"

The girl looked incredulously at the sorrowful man she loved; men were so slow in understanding some things. Taking his face in both her hands, she leaned her own close to it.

"There is nothing more I need to know of you, Thomas Dalton. I've loved you since the first night we met. I'll go with you anywhere you'll take me, for there isn't a life for me anymore without you." She said it so directly, so sweetly, that he looked wonderingly into her eyes; the soft, strong expression in them held infinite love and tenderness.

"There's precious little money, Deirdre. There's my savings, of course, but how long can that last? Your father is a powerful man and he'll not take this lightly. The only job I'll be able to get may be back on the docks, girl. It's hard to picture you in a hovel."

"Hovel or no, I'm going with you if you'll have me. I haven't any money, but I have my jewelry and my mother's; we'll use that till you get work."

There was no mistaking the determination in the girl's face, but Tom felt conscience-bound to ask the question anyway.

"Are you certain you want to do this, Deirdre?" He asked it hesitantly. "God only knows what I can ever give you to equal this." He swept his hand eloquently around the ornate gilded room.

"What would any of it matter without you now, my love? Would I give up less for you than you've given up for me?"

He took her in his arms so lovingly, she thought her heart would break with the sweetness of it. The feel of his strong, loving embrace set her mind reeling with joy. She sat beside him on the bed, grateful that her father had thundered from the house, knowing that the servants would not tell him she was with Tom, for fear of inciting him to murder.

They planned their departure from the Mulvaney household carefully and parted from each other with infinite difficulty, so that Tom could try to arrange for someone to marry them and a place to stay until he could get work. "We must be married immediately, Tom," Deirdre told him confidently. "Once the deed is done, even if he finds us, there's little action my father can take to separate us." Tom wondered if she had any idea about what she was suggesting, or any comprehension of the power of her father's wrath. A man of Jim's sort did not take lightly to being defied. He thought of asking Billy's help. There would be few friends left, once the word was out that he was Mulvaney's enemy, and Jim was sure to have Donaher and Furuseth watched, for he would assume they would be the people Tom would turn to in time of trouble. Of his three closest friends, only Billy's house would not be considered by Mulvaney as a possible place of refuge.

Deirdre closed the door noiselessly, and lifting the two tightly packed carpetbags with an effort, she moved stealthily across the back porch and through the garden to the hedge where Tom waited anxiously.

"Are you absolutely certain you want to go through with this, lass?" Tom whispered urgently to her as she reached him.

Deirdre smiled at the concern in the face she had grown to love. She wondered affectionately how he could doubt the strength of her commitment, after all that had been said.

"I'm certain of everything that has to do with you," she whispered back in the quiet darkness.

"You've no idea what poverty is like, Deirdre," he said, touching her face gently in his hand. "You may be giving up a great deal for a very long time. I can promise you absolutely nothing about my prospects, with your father as an enemy."

"Can you promise to love me, Tom?"

"Aye, lass. That one thing I can promise you." He looked so

distressed and serious that the young girl wanted to hold him and comfort him.

"You seem to forget, my love, that I am *choosing* to go with you. You needn't fear so for me. I'm as strong as I need to be. And whatever happens, I couldn't live without you now, knowing you love me as I love you."

Tom took her in his arms, not knowing what else to say; he held her soft, pliant body to his own, her brown-gold head clasped hard against his chest, and then, lifting her face to his own, he kissed her once with inordinate tenderness before reluctantly letting her go. Lifting the two bags she had packed, they moved carefully, in the shadow of the huge hedges, to the corner of the street where the carriage waited.

"Where will we go, Tom?" Deirdre asked as she settled herself into the cab's interior.

"There is only one place I know of where we can be safe for a day or two, where no one will expect us to be, least of all your father." Tom hesitated for a moment before continuing, then said quickly, "It's a 'house,' Deirdre, a bordello, but it's run by a good woman named Billy, who I think will help us till we get married and can find a place to stay."

Deirdre's eyes widened; how in heaven's name did her beloved Tom come to be on intimate terms with a madam? She knew that men sought knowledge of such creatures, but to think of one as a friend . . .

"She's an old pal of Donaher's, lass, and she's the one who first introduced me to your father," he said by the way of explanation, sensing her confusion.

"My father?"

"Aye, love, he's the one who set her up in business. He's been very good to her."

"Then why would she help us?"

"Because she has a kind heart and she knows how very much I love you." He said it so simply that she marveled at all the strange new knowledge that had entered her life. In a mere twenty-four hours everything had changed irrevocably. She had chosen to be a woman, not a girl any longer. She had handed over her life and security to a man she loved, but barely knew. She had learned a secret of her father's she had never dreamed of, and was on her way to spend her wedding eve in a bordello.

She began to laugh, first softly, then more uproariously.

"I love you, Thomas Dalton," she managed to gasp through the laughter. "I have a feeling our life together will never, ever be as other people's lives are."

They entered Billy's house by the back door, climbing as soundlessly as possible past the boisterous parlors and on to the upper apartment where Billy lived. Tom knocked on her door and ushered Deirdre in quickly when the door was opened.

Tom and Billy exchanged glances, unsure of what to say, and Deirdre stepped forward, offering her small gloved hand to the immense blond beauty whose very stature had taken her breath away when she entered the room.

"Tom has told me that you are a friend of my father's, Miss Billy, so it must be doubly awkward for you to help us in our dilemma. I want you to know how grateful I am to you."

Tom marveled at Deirdre's aplomb in the strange situation, and the pained look in Billy's eyes seemed to soften at the frightened girl's show of courtesy.

"You are just as beautiful and gracious as Tom said you were, ma'am," she answered. "I'm pleased to be able to help two nice people find love in this crummy world."

"God bless you, Billy," said Tom, who sensed how awkward the scene was for the woman, whose own life would never hold the comfort or security of a husband who loved her as he loved Deirdre.

"Billy, I'd like to leave her here with you for the night while I try to work things out. I must find Donaher and Andy and arrange a place to stay and a priest to marry us. Do you think she'll be safe?"

"Man, this is the last place on earth Mulvaney'll look for her. She can stay with me in my room, and on the off chance Jim comes here to talk with me, she can stay in the attic till he's gone." Both women winced at the apparent anxiety in the man's face. "Go along with you now, lad," said the older of the two. "Do what you must. No harm will come to her while she's in my house. You must know that." He nodded, and signaling to Deirdre with his eyes, was gone.

Both women eyed each other with discomfort and immense interest after the door had shut. Billy tried to still her pounding heart as she stared at the girl who was soon to have everything she herself had ever wanted. She fought back tears of sorrow, anger, and frustration. She *would not* ever let this woman know the depth of her pain, or the cause of it.

"You look as though you could use a cup of tea and some rest, Miss Mulvaney." She said it quietly and was astounded by the even tone of her own voice.

"Please. Call me Deirdre, Miss Billy. Tea would be lovely, but I'm so nervous, I don't think I could sleep at all. Would it be a bother to you if we just talked awhile?" Deirdre's pulse was racing with the strangeness of the circumstances. The woman was so beautiful, so perfectly beautiful. Could it be that her beloved Tom had known her as a friend and not been her lover? How could any man not want to touch this exquisite creature? She barely heard the words as Billy replied.

"No bother at all, Miss Deirdre. As a matter of fact, I'd like it a lot if you'd talk to me. It's not much chance I get to speak to a real lady like yourself." Deirdre tried to place the strange tone in the woman's voice; was it awe or envy? She couldn't guess. Perhaps wistfulness was closer to the heart of it; the woman seemed wistful. What was she longing for, then? Was it Tom, or was it something Deirdre couldn't even dream of? Something made her want to unravel the secret of this woman, the mysteries of what she knew that Deirdre didn't.

"How do you know my father?" It was a tentative question, but direct. Deirdre was startled by the sound of her own voice as she asked it.

Billy's honest nature demanded a truthful reply; her sensitivity to Tom's love for this unknown visitor made her tread carefully.

"I've known your father since I was younger than you are. He found me when I was poor and friendless, and helped me get started in my business. I know women like yourself are ashamed of such as me, but Jim's been a right good friend to me, Miss Deirdre, and you should know that. I'm proud to know him."

The daughter blushed a little at the thought of her father as the partner in a whorehouse, but she persevered. "And Tom?" Billy heard the terror in Diedre's voice and was surprised that she felt compassion for the fragile, sheltered young girl, who obviously feared the answer but braved the question anyway. She thought for a moment before replying, and then decided to be her better self.

"Tom's best friend, Donaher, is an old pal of mine, love. Donaher was a shipmate of my oldest brother, who got killed at sea a long, long time ago. He's been my good friend more years than I can remember. Anything I could do to help him out, I would. He asked me to help the two of you." It was a nobler rendition of the truth than might have been.

"Oh, I see!" The relief in the smaller girl's voice was immense. "Thank you for telling me." She said it as an afterthought, and Billy smiled at her innocence, wondering if, had her own life been different, she herself might ever have been as innocent as this woman. She doubted it, somehow.

Billy watched the lovely young girl as if studying a rare object intently. She seemed so fresh and tender, so gently bred, and yet . . . there was a backbone there too. After all, she had run away with Tom; that took some courage, to leave a fortune and a protected life. And she was here in the kind of place that nice girls wouldn't be caught dead in; all for the sake of the man she loved. Maybe Tom wasn't making such a bad choice after all.

"Miss Deirdre, I think you ought to know that Tom Dalton loves you more'n anything." Billy couldn't imagine why she said it, but went on anyway. "He'd give up the world for you, and damned few women ever get lucky enough to have a fine man love them like that!" Deirdre recognized the vehement emotion in the big woman's voice. She wondered if it was that because of her strange profession Billy would never be so loved, and her heart went out to her.

"You are kind to tell me these things, truly you are. I want you to know that I love him more than anything and I'll do everything I can to make him happy." She hesitated, wondering if she dared give voice to what was on her mind. "I just don't know very much about men, Miss Billy, and I wondered, perhaps . . . well, it seems to me you must know so much about them . . ." She blushed at her own audacity and Billy, startled by the realization that the lady was seeking advice from the harlot, was speechless.

"I guess that's the one thing in this whole sorry world I do know about, Miss Deirdre," she said with a rueful smile. "I'm gonna get us some tea and cookies and maybe us girls will find some things to talk about after all."

"Will you have me back, Andrew?" Tom stood in the doorway of the Longshoremen's Rest and addressed his words quietly to the burly labor organizer seated before the dwindling fire.

Furuseth rose from his bench with a startled look, hesitated only an instant; then grasped Tom's hand in both his own immense ones; the big Norseman's craggy face twisted itself into the semblance of a grin as he pumped Tom's arm up and down with joy.

"I knew you'd be back to us, lad! I said it to Donaher. 'He'll be back, you'll see,' I said to him. He's with us in his heart, he is."

"Aye, man, I'm back, but I'm not sure I should be congratulated till you hear my story. I won't fool you, Andrew. I'm back because I've been tossed out on my ear by Mulvaney."

"Run afoul of him, lad?"

"Worse than that, Andrew. I've run away with his daughter."

Furuseth's eye widened significantly, but he said nothing.

"I'm afraid we're in for it, Andy. Deirdre's the apple of the old man's eye. He's beside himself about what we've done."

"Are you married up, lad, or . . ."

"Aye, Andy. That at least we'll do the right way. We'll be married in the morning by Father Mulcahey. It's all arranged. Trouble is, I've got to decide what happens next. We need a place to live, I need a job. And to tell you the truth, I think I need to talk things over with you and Donaher."

"So it seems, boy. So it seems. And where's the missus now, if you don't mind my asking?"

"She's at Billy's, Andrew. There wasn't anyone else I could trust her with, and we had no time to plan better."

"You put your new missus in a whorehouse, Thomas? You must have been desperate for sure. And Diamond Jim's mistress to boot. Well, I'll be damned." He whistled through his teeth at the surprise of it all. "How can I help you, lad? You know I will, if I can."

Tom smiled at the honorable man before him and clapped him on his big shoulder affectionately. "I'll not ask you to help us without knowing what's happened, Andy. Deirdre and I love each other; man, she's the dearest thing in the whole world to me. I tried to court her in the proper way, but Jim would have none of it. He'd have sent her away to a convent school if we hadn't run off as we did. But it's sure as hell not the way I'd planned it to be for us."

"But you've learned a trade with the old boy, haven't you, Tom? Surely you needn't come back to the waterfront for work?"

"Aye, I've learned more than you can imagine, Andrew, but with Jim on my tail I'd best lie low for a while or risk getting clobbered. His connections are powerful. He has less pull on the waterfront than elsewhere, and besides, he may hate us but he'll surely not want Deirdre to starve altogether. He wants us humiliated, but not dead, I'm hoping."

"Don't be too certain of that, son, it wouldn't be the first murder he was party to."

The sobering thought hung in the air before Furuseth continued. "What's done is done. No use worrying it to death. What's your plan now, lad?"

"I thought I'd shape up with the men tomorrow, Andrew, and if you'll have me, I'd like to help you with the organizing. I've learned a great deal about the law that can be of use to you."

"Of course I'll have you, Thomas. And happy to welcome you back. Donaher will be a joyous man when he hears. I'm not pleased at all about your present circumstances, however. Have you any money?"

"A bit, Andrew. And Deirdre's jewels from her mother, if it comes to that. What we need first is a flat. Do you know of any? I don't want to leave her where she is past tonight. She's hidden at Billy's, but it's dangerous for them both if Jim finds out."

"Billy's a fine woman, lad. And a bit sweet on you, too, I'd say. But you don't want her running afoul of Jim—that'd be no way to pay back her kindness."

The huge man unfolded his limbs and stood up in the dim light of the large room.

"I've a friend who may help you. She runs a house that's not so dear that you couldn't afford it if she has a room, and you'd not have to be ashamed to bring your lady there. At least for a while till you get on your feet. I'll take you to her, if you want me to."

They left the warmth of the firelit room and raised their collars against the assault of the cold drizzle outside.

"It seems you've given up a good deal, lad, for this girl. Do you think you'll live to regret it?"

Tom looked up before answering deliberately. "She's worth everything to me."

The big man sighed, remembering how vast a thing love could be for a young man, and they both walked on without speaking.

Mulvaney stormed around the office like a maddened bull. His round face red to the point of explosion, he paced back and forth, pounding the desk with reverberative force whenever he stopped long enough to do so.

Deirdre had been gone nearly a day, the ungrateful little idiot. After all he'd done for her—all the love, all the gifts, all the gentle convent training—she had actually defied her own father for that son of a bitch of a Dalton. Well, the young bastard wouldn't live long enough to enjoy his victory, Jim would see to that.

"Duffy!" He thundered the name with a vehemence that shook the bric-a-brac on the mantel and set the chandelier in motion.

The homely Irishman was in the room before the word was finished.

"I want him dead. Do you hear me? Dead as Kelsey's nuts! And don't trouble yourself to make it painless."

"Aye, sir. Who do you want dead?"

"That bastard Dalton, you dolt! He's run off with my daughter and I want him dead and her back in my house by sunup."

Duffy never blinked. The same expressionless look that had fascinated Tom since their first meeting, now made his face seem like a homely pancake.

"I'd be delighted to do whatever you say, sir. Cut off his fingers one at a time, if you'd like me to, Mr. Mulvaney. But there's only one thing about it worries me."

Mulvaney's blood pressure had turned his pudgy face crimson. He would brook no opposition from this idiot employee, presuming on his own kindness over the years to defy him now.

"And what might that be, Duffy?" he said in a quiet, mocking voice, a dangerous nastiness in the tone.

"Well, sir. I beg your pardon for saying it, sir, but what if he's had his way with the girl, Mr. Mulvaney? She might be in the family way, sir, and if that was so, you might not want to kill her husband."

"Family way?" screamed the overwrought father. "The scoundrel's only had her out of my house less than twenty-four hours. She couldn't possibly be pregnant in that time."

"They're married, sir." Duffy's voice was toneless.

"And just how do you know that?" he snapped.

"That priest on the waterfront married them the very first morning, sir. I made it me business to find out."

"A great pity you didn't make it your business to stop them," the old man hissed, but the impassive eyes of the young man never wavered.

"Why not just keep him from work, sir? He can't get a job if you put out the word that he's on your list. She'll have to come back to you then, sir."

Mulvaney heard the words through a dull haze of pain, for if Duffy's information was correct as usual, he was already beaten. If they were married, the deed had been done, the thing consummated. No Boston Brahmin would have his daughter now. Pregnant or not, she was a spoiled piece of goods. Wasted on a man he himself had saved from the life of a day laborer, the life he'd been born to. He lowered his rotund form with defeat into a chair that groaned under the assault. Well, let them go back to that life. Let her find out what it's like to live hand to mouth in a slum, with not enough bread for her children and no better prospects than impoverished old age to look forward to. Let her find out firsthand what her father had struggled so hard to keep her from ever experiencing.

He waved his hand to motion Duffy wordlessly from the room. The boyish man nodded and left, his stealthy step, as always, soundless. He closed the door behind him, and an odd crooked grin suffused his pockmarked face. He smiled to himself for a moment, and then the smile disappeared and the mask was back. He had done a good deal of thinking about where his loyalty lay in this, and had finally decided that for once, Mr. Mulvaney did not know what was best. Tom was a fine man, he'd make Deirdre a good husband and Mulvaney a sensible son-in-law.

Satisfied that he'd handled the problem correctly, Duffy took a piece of wood and a large-bladed knife from the drawer and hummed a random tune as he whittled it into a recognizable shape for a wedding present.

48

Thomas Dalton closed the door of the shabby little bedroom and watched the beautiful shy girl who was now his wife as she stood in nervous silence near the tiny window. He could not believe that she was his, this delicate, gray-eyed girl; too young to be called quite a woman, too womanly to be thought of as anything else. He must treat her with great tenderness and caution, he reminded himself, for much as she loved him, he knew she would be terrified about whatever was to happen. Sex was described to well-bred girls as a fearful thing, and the whole day and night leading up to this had been filled with uncertainty and terror, so her nerves could not be anywhere near equilibrium. He wondered if she was looking forward to their wedding night with a very different emotion from his own.

Tom walked with a quiet deliberate step toward the bed and sat down. He had been puzzling out the proper way to handle both his own urgent desire for his bride, and the repressive training he was certain she had had from her convent teachers. He knew that what went on between husband and wife in the privacy of their marital bed was spoken of in whispered loathing by women to their young female charges. He had heard the stories, and knew that girls of good families were told nothing at all of the mechanics of the act, only that it was an unsavory duty to which they must submit because their husband's baser nature demanded it.

"Deirdre." He whispered the name; the room seemed too still for ordinary speech. "Come here to me, my love." She walked slowly to the bed where he sat, and stood there looking down into his upturned face.

"Are you frightened of me, Deirdre?"

"No, my love, not of you."

"Then you're frightened of coming to my bed, are you, wife?"

She smiled at the word *wife* and touched his thick wavy hair with her graceful hand.

"I've heard awful stories about what it is to be a wife, love, and I'm a little fearful, it's true. But at the same time, I cannot think that lying in your arms could be other than perfect bliss."

"Would you be too fearful to take off your clothes for me, my beauty? I long to see you and to hold you without those stays and laces between us."

Without replying, Deirdre Mulvaney Dalton unfastened the twenty-five tiny cloth buttons that reached from neck to waist, untied the blue silk sash that seemed to her to be the exact shade of Tom's eyes, pulled her heavy-skirted dress over her head, somewhat tentatively shaking it out and laying it carefully on the chair beneath the window. She took just a little too long undoing the corset that encased her fragile young waist, betraying her nervousness in freeing her generous breasts, and stood frightened but resolute before her quiet young husband, wearing only a dimity shift that, while it covered her, didn't quite hide her from the eyes of the man who loved her so very much.

"You are more beautiful than I could ever have imagined, Deirdre. I can't think what it would be to hold you." He stood up so that his great height dwarfed the barefoot girl. "Will you be fearful if I take off my clothes?"

"I shall probably die if you do not" was the surprising reply.

Tom, stripped to his woolen underpants, stood staring at the loving but frightened girl, now his wife, who was pulling down the covers of the bed; after a moment's hesitation he very deliberately took his underpants off too as Deirdre turned to look at him. Her eyes widened in disbelief at the hard shaft that had risen at the sight of her nearly naked body. He smiled despite himself at the incredulous expression on her face.

"I won't hurt you, Deirdre. Believe me, girl, I'll never hurt you."

Tom crept into the bed beside his trembling love and lay for a moment staring at the ceiling, feeling for the right words, struggling with his own urgent desire to hold, to love, to lose himself in her sweet soft body.

I mustn't go too fast, he counseled himself silently. She's had enough fears to deal with these past two days. He thought he could hear her heart beating wildly beside him, despite her quite still form, and, failing words, he turned to take her in his arms. To his amazement, she returned his embrace with enormous fervor and clung to him, saying his name again and again.

"Deirdre, my wife, my love," he whispered into her soft fragrant hair. "Listen to me, for I've been desperate to find the words I need for us. There are such glorious joys I would share with you, but you seem so fragile I fear you'll break. Deirdre, men and women can bring each other such pleasures in their love, that the angels themselves must envy them. I don't want to force myself on you, girl, I want to teach you to want me as I want you. To want me with your body as well as your mind. I can teach you to feel things that you cannot imagine, wife, if you'll let me. Will you try to forget what you've been told by everyone in the world and listen only to me and to your own sweet body and your own heart?"

"Would you have me be a wanton, Tom? Is that what you want for a wife?"

"Aye, girl, I would have you lust for me with every part of yourself. I would have you want my mouth and my hands and my manhood with the same ache I feel when I think of you."

"Is it right, love, for a woman to feel such things?"

He didn't reply but took her in his arms and began to stroke her soft, smooth skin. He pushed the flimsy shift she was wearing up over the tips of her full breasts, and she surprised him by pulling it the rest of the way off, until she was naked and free in his arms.

Her mouth was soft and yielding. He stroked her breasts and took her firm young nipples in his mouth. He played with the long, lean lines of her body until he could feel her respond with an intensity that startled him, and made his heart sing. He took her hands and brought them to his own hot hard shaft. At first she seemed afraid to touch it. How could it be that something so big might ever fit inside her?

The pounding of her own heart deafened her, and yet she thought she heard her name called from far, far away. Tom's mouth was touching, licking, kissing her most private parts, her tender hidden places, and she wanted his mouth with a desperation beyond imagining. "Tom, Tom, Tom." She heard her own voice say his name, but she couldn't imagine that she had had the strength to call him. She was feeling, feeling such things. Her body had taken over her mind, her soul. She was pulling him toward her, his great strong male body on her, in her, entering her wet hot self deep between her legs, deep in her central being. She felt him enter her cautiously at first, then harder and faster and deeper as she began to sense his rhythm and her own nature responded instinctively to the ancient ritual.

How could he be so hard and so strong and so penetrating and yet so tender, so careful of her body? Surely such pleasure as this couldn't be meant for mortals. Deirdre clung to Tom in the almost-dark—exhausted, thrilled, frightened, by the ferocity of it, exalted by the sensuous beauty of what she had just experienced. Tom's huge form was still on top of her but lying lightly now, quiet and spent, holding her so close, whispering love words into her hair, holding her, holding her as if he would never, ever let her go.

I love you, she wanted to tell him, but even those words seemed pale and inadequate, so she said nothing, but held him close and ran her fingers instinctively over his broad back and shoulders, patting him as if he were a child to be soothed; stunned by the wonder of his body, newly hers.

Tom raised himself from where he lay so inextricably tangled with her softer limbs, and looked deep into her eyes before he spoke.

"You are a miracle, girl, and I love you more than everything."

She smiled at the simplicity of the statement and at the shaggy mane of hair that fell forward over his serious young face in the last flicker of the candle they had forgotten to extinguish.

"Can it be, love," she whispered, "that this is what a woman is to feel with her man? It's too beautiful and too fierce." She seemed genuinely confused. "Could it be that I have the heart of a wanton after all, and I'm not the good woman you thought me to be?"

Tom lay back on the bed beside her and laughed at her questioning face.

"Indeed, Deirdre, I think you may have the desires of a wanton and the heart of a woman and the body of an angel and the passions of all three, and I'm the luckiest man in the world tonight to have you for my own wife.'' He touched her flushed face tenderly as he spoke.

"Oh, lass, don't you see, we mortals have been given so little in this life; we toil and strive and suffer and die, but this one gift we have. This gift of the love between a man and a woman that makes us able to bear with all the rest of it. Don't fear it, Deirdre, for it is surely the only gift we've been given, and 'tis paid for by the price of all the other sufferings combined.''

This sobering thought seemed to comfort the Catholic girl, for somehow happiness could be sanctioned if it was sufficiently counter-balanced by sorrow, and something in her told her that for happiness as great as this, a great price would surely be exacted. And she was, of course, quite right.

The newly married couple settled into the railroad flat that Furuseth had secured in Desbrosses Street, glad of the safe haven despite its inadequacies. Donaher and the big Norseman took it upon them-selves to provide furnishings, and even Billy lent a hand in provision-ing the flat with hand-me-downs. An opal brooch of Deirdre's was sold to buy a Franklin stove, and Tom husbanded his savings carefully to buy the necessities of life from the passing pushcart parade, and returned to the docks to resume his laboring.

Deirdre cooked and cleaned and sewed, her love for her husband more than adequate to the task of surviving the rigors of her new environment. Eventually she even conquered her fear of the seedy neighborhood they lived in and began to venture out by herself while Tom was at the docks, always conferring beforehand with Mrs. O'Connor, her landlady, for directions and admonitions.

"Now don't yer never go down near River Street and them nasty places, young missus," the kindly old woman would tell her. "There's elements out there that would snatch a pretty young thing like yerself in a minute. They'd have their way wit yer and sell yer to a house of prostitution, they would." The rheumy old eyes had glittered with anxiety at the thought, and Deirdre had taken the horrifying possibil-ity to heart. She had always wondered how women got into a life of sin, but never had it occurred to her that it might be against her will. She wondered about the generous-spirited Miss Billy, who had gone so far out of her way to help them despite being a woman of the night. This whole new world was so strange to her that no matter how implausible a story Mrs. O'Connor told, she would have believed it.

Deirdre lived for the moment her young husband would walk through the door each night. The sight of his wind- and sun-leathered face and his broad body filled her with a sense of security she had never known before.

They had very little money. After the wealth and cushioned comfort of her father's home, the realities of daily life—the cooking, the cleaning, the mending of a tattered sock instead of sending a servant to fetch a new one—were all curiosities to be coped with. Yet they gave her a sense of permanency and of being needed that she had never remotely felt her in her home full of ease and hired help. Make-do became an intellectual exercise; learning to cook and mend, an intensely womanly education. Even finding out how to shop from the passing pushcarts with scrupulous care became an intellectual enterprise in diplomacy and clever bargaining. With canny Mrs. O'Connor to teach her, Deirdre thought she was becoming almost competent at the haggling that was a necessary part of any purchase.

Often enough Tom brought the men of the burgeoning brotherhood to their tiny flat. Donaher and Furuseth seemed always to be there, and others, too, as their little group began to gain support among the laborers. She strove to have some sort of refreshment for the men at their meetings. Tea, the baking powder biscuits she could now create with some assurance of success, a drop or two of whiskey, which she considered no longer a nicety of the drawing room but rather a necessity of life in the deadly cold that caused her husband to come home often enough with his hands frozen and his feet nearly blue. Sometimes there was not enough for themselves, never mind their guests, but they somehow managed, and despite the hardships the first year of their marriage was the happiest time Deirdre had ever known.

Mrs. O'Connor recognized Deirdre's pregnancy before the young woman did herself. At first Deirdre had thought her morning nausea was the result of her own sometimes unsuccessful efforts at cooking unfamiliar food. Then, when her monthly flow had stopped, she went to the older woman for advice. Never having had a mother to instruct her in the mysteries of womanhood, Deirdre was awestruck at the thought of what lay before her. Wildly happy at the idea of having her baby, she was appalled by her own ignorance of how to go about doing so.

"I want to go to see your friend Billy about my pregnancy," she said very solemnly to Tom the night she told him of her condition. She was shocked to feel her husband stiffen strangely in her arms, as if she had somehow wounded him. "Do you not want the baby, lass?" he asked hoarsely after a long silence, his voice a pained whisper. "Of course I want our baby!" she said, not comprehending his sudden fear. "That's why I've decided to ask Billy for help . . . if it's all right with you, of course. You see, I know nothing about these woman things. I had no mama to teach me, and there's no young woman friend now to help me learn. I know it distresses you to think of my going to a woman of Billy's occupation, but she seemed kind enough when she helped us before, and I would think that with all those women in her house, she must know a great deal about these things." She stopped, out of breath. "Besides, I need a *young* woman who could be my friend, and I don't think I care at all, love, about her profession, if she'll just tell me some of what I need to know."

Tom laughed uproariously in relief, and hugged his wife to his body with such immense strength, she cried out in the darkness.

"I love you, lass, God in heaven, how I love you." He buried his face in her hair and stroked her happy body softly until she forgot his strange outburst of merriment at what seemed to her a perfectly sensible suggestion, and began to moan softly in pleasure at his knowledgeable touch.

"I've come to see Miss Billy, please." Deirdre said it clearly to the blowzy young woman who opened the door, but the girl didn't seem to understand. "I'm Mrs. Dalton; she knows me, you see." Deirdre tried to explain. "I'm sure she'll see me if you'll just tell her I'm here." She wished the girl would invite her in; she felt immensely awkward standing on the street in front of the bordello, worrying about who might see her on this strange errand.

"Sure, honey," said the girl at last. "Billy's upstairs, but I'll get her down. Come on in," she said as an afterthought, and Deirdre entered with relief.

She sat down in the red plush parlor, her eyes wide with fascination, for the night she had spent in this house had not allowed her the opportunity to see the details of the place.

Deirdre felt a certain nervous excitement; being in this "disorderly house," as she knew they were called, was probably the most daring thing she had ever done in her life. Other than marrying Tom, of course, but in that she'd had him to lean on; in taking this action she was entirely on her own. She felt brazen and suddenly very grown up. Just the realization that now she, too, like the women in this house, knew the mysteries of men was a heady notion. She was smiling to herself at her own audacity when Billy entered the parlor.

Deirdre thought she had never seen a more magnificent creature. Without her makeup and with her silver-blond hair flowing over the shoulders of a silken robe, Billy was so mighty a female presence, she took Deirdre's breath away. Suddenly all her bravado was gone; she felt embarrassed.

"Mrs. Dalton. Does your husband know you're here?" Billy's voice was full of concern.

"He doesn't exactly know I'm here this minute," she hesitated, trying to think of how to explain her errand. "But I did tell him I needed to talk to you, and he said he understood."

Billy tilted her head to the side, an odd, quizzical gesture Deirdre had noted when she'd first met her. It made the woman look somehow like a statue in a museum.

"I've brought you a present," Deirdre said tentatively. "It isn't really a present, just some biscuits that I've made." She laughed a little, to cover her embarrassment. "They're really the only thing I've learned to cook well, since getting married." She handed the small parcel wrapped in brown paper and string, shyly, to the puzzled madam, who was beginning to realize that this well-bred lady, Tom Dalton's wife, was trying to be her friend.

"Nobody ever made biscuits especially for me before." Billy said it softly, taking the package from the much smaller woman. "It was real nice of you to bring me a present. No lady ever gave me a present in my whole life." She smiled an almost childlike smile at Deirdre, and sat down beside her on the sofa, undoing the string with the pleasure of a child with a Christmas gift. "We'll have them with some tea," she said, suddenly the hostess; she rang a little bell, and a small black boy came scurrying from the kitchen.

"You have Belle fix some nice tea for Mrs. Dalton, Josiah. Tell her to make it real pretty." The little boy scrambled off, and the two women sat facing each other.

"Billy, I'm very nervous about being here, because I want to ask you a favor." Billy nodded.

"I'm in the family way and I need your help." Deirdre saw a look of distress come into Billy's pretty blue eyes, without knowing why. "I don't exactly know how to say this, but you see, the fact is

I don't know very much about woman things. I don't know any of what I should about being pregnant, and the doctor seemed more embarrassed than I was when I asked him questions. To tell you the truth, I don't even know what questions to ask.'' She looked pleadingly at Billy, hoping she would understand. ''I just thought . . . you were so kind to me the night we ran away . . . and you must know so many things that I don't . . .'' She let the thought trail off unfinished, and looked down at her own hands in her lap.

When she glanced up, she saw Billy smiling gently, her long dark lashes for some reason damp with glistening moisture when she answered.

''I'll tell you what, honey. If you'll be kind enough to teach me what I'd like to know about being a lady, I'll teach you all I know about being a woman.''

When Tom got home that night, he was amazed to find that his wife had spent four hours that afternoon at a whorehouse, in the company of a friend.

49

''They're talkin' lockout, lad,'' said Donaher as he and Furuseth entered the Dalton flat, slamming the door against the cold hall air with a thud. Tom had been waiting news of the union negotiations at home with Deirdre.

''Come in and sit down, will you,'' said Tom, taking the heavy woolen coats from his friends. ''We've been waiting for news.''

''Aye, lad. And no good news it is for all that.'' He glanced at Deirdre before continuing. ''Good evening to you, lass. It's sorry I am to be bringin' bad tidings into your home.''

Deirdre reached up on tiptoe to kiss the big Irishman and the bigger Norwegian on the cheek. ''You're welcome in our home, whatever the news, my friends, and well you both know it.'' She started off in the direction of the little kitchen. ''Would a cup of tea warm you?'' she called over her shoulder to the men.

''If it had a drop of whiskey in it, 'twould put the breath of life back in me old bones,'' Donaher called after her, and Furuseth, who seemed too preoccupied for conversation, smiled at her as she passed him on her way to the kitchen.

"Well, isn't it lucky then that we just happen to have a drop we've been saving for you," she called back to them from the doorway, and both men knew she was trying hard to keep her spirits up in the face of more bad news.

"She's looking a bit wan, laddie, it seems to me. Is it the baby two months off, or the worries about the union, do you suppose?"

"You've the eye of a midwife, Donaher," said Tom with a wry smile. "It's a bit of both, I'd say, that's got her on edge. If I tell her the truth, she worries; if I try to hide it from her, it's worse. Billy's keeping an eye on her these days, and she tells me things are coming along all right with the baby. But Deirdre worries just the same."

"Ya," interrupted Furuseth for the first time, "there's enough to worry about to be sure." Tom looked closely at his friend.

"What's the story, then?" he asked as he watched Furuseth rubbing his hands vigorously together, trying to bring the circulation of warmer blood into cold fingers.

"There's nearly as much fighting among the leaders of the five locals as there is between us and the owners, I trow." Andy's Norwegian accent always became more pronounced when he was agitated, the *j*'s changing to *y*'s and a sprinkling of Norse words moving in with the English ones.

"This one wants to strike, that one wants to bargain, this one wants his name in the bloody newspaper, that one wants to call in the Black Hand to fight the Pinks."

Tom poured a drink into a shot glass for the big Norwegian, who still looked chilled and angry.

"You've been through all this before, Andy. What's the best thing to happen now?"

"The best thing would be if we could negotiate with them, Thomas. Get them to listen to our requests and maybe get enough concessions to last us till the warmer weather. Those bastards even have the winter on their side now, so any delaying tactics we come up with would be useful."

"Delaying tactics my fine Irish arse!" said Donaher. "They know the winter is comin' just as well as we do, Andy! They're sure to use it as a bludgeon to beat some more blood out of our bones."

"What do you mean, Donaher?" Tom asked the question earnestly.

"My bet is they know we can't hold out through the winter, so's they'll cut us back in pay one of these days, on the chance we can't strike back till spring."

Tom looked at Andy for confirmation and saw the truth of it in his sad eyes. A fine christening present for my son, thought Tom, but he said nothing.

There was no point wasting words on futile anger, it was all unjust, all sadistic. The only question was what could be done about it.

"There's a meeting of the five locals a week from Thursday, Thomas. I been thinking, we might use the time to try to palaver with the owners. Just us, without the others, to see what kind of response they make to what we say. Maybe we find out what they planning, maybe not. But we at least get to have our say. I think it would be worth a try."

"What makes you think they'd see us?"

"I been thinking on it, Thomas; you know how to talk like a lawyer. Maybe you could write to Mr. Morgan himself."

Donaher let a whistle escape his lips at that. "Maybe they be curious about what a smart lawyer be doing on the longshore," Furuseth persisted. "Maybe the curiosity be enough to get us in there, ya?"

Tom and Donaher exchanged glances. It would never have occurred to either of them to go to Morgan himself. Maybe that was what made Andy different from all the others. He'd go to God Almighty if he thought it would help the union.

50

The room into which the labor negotiators were led was excessively extravagant. Tom counted seven men at the immense conference table; somber, dark-suited, rich men with disdainful expressions on their well-fed faces. The obvious opulence of these men seemed in appalling contrast to the condition of the little delegation. Tom felt himself bristle as he noted the smug robber baron seated at the end of the conference table, surrounded by his coterie of well-dressed henchmen. In truth, he was shocked that his letter to Morgan had provoked an invitation to this meeting.

Donaher nudged Tom with his elbow and nodded toward Morgan. "He looks like a man who'd peel a potato in his pocket rather than share it," he whispered and Tom knew he was right.

The man at J. P Morgan's right was his in-house counsel. He

spoke first, his nasal voice reverberating in the cavernous room with its thirty-foot-high gilded ceiling and its polished ebony walls. Tom inadvertently thought of the seedy Longshoremen's Rest, where the laborers planned their strategies, and felt anger tighten his gut at the contrast.

"What precisely is it that you workers want?" Contemptuous emphasis was placed on the word *workers* by the man, and the question was pointedly disdainful, as if the very idea of such rabble wanting anything at all was unthinkable.

"We want to be treated with respect, as a beginning, sir," Tom replied with quiet dignity; the educated quality of his speech caught the men at the table by surprise. This was not the voice of a common laborer like the others, they seemed to say to each other with eloquent looks.

"And who might you be?" The question this time came from Morgan himself, a wizened, ugly little man; it occurred to Tom, seeing him in person for the first time, that God had seen fit to give the industrialist the face he deserved.

"My name is Thomas Dalton, sir. I'm the one who wrote you to ask for this meeting to discuss our problems. As I have some small training in the law, I'm acting as the spokesman in these proceedings for the men of the combined maritime professions."

Morgan moved his mouth as if he were chewing something, an old man's gesture, but said nothing.

"I repeat my question," said the lawyer. "What do you men of the 'maritime professions' want?" The sneer in his voice nearly caused Donaher to rise from his chair, but Tom, sensing the movement at his side, put his hand on his friend's arm.

"Our needs are simple ones. We men of the longshore need a hiring hall. A place where jobs can be meted out in an orderly fashion so that the demeaning practice of shape-up, of making a man stand in the rain or snow, hoping to be arbitrarily chosen, can be abolished.

"We need a living wage so that we may feed our families, and the right to bargain with owners in a civilized fashion about what that wage should be.

"We need protection on the job, from unscrupulous overseers who work a short crew and pocket the extra salary, while we suffer injuries because of exhaustion.

"We need to be able to unionize without fear of harassment or lockout.

"We need to be able to air our grievances and have them responded to in an orderly fashion, for the good of all concerned; including the owners, I might add.

"We need to be treated as men, not slaves, or animals.

"We need to be respected for our conscientious contribution to the success of the business of men like you, and we need to be compensated fairly for that contribution." He paused for a moment, looking from man to man around the table.

"Our immediate need is the rehiring of the union sympathizers and the right to arbitrate a raise in pay."

When he ceased speaking, the henchmen looked first at each other and then at Mr. Morgan, curious to see how he would handle such absurdity.

The old man was watching Dalton, his head tilted a bit to the side. When he spoke, the tension in that room was palpable.

"Tell me more, young man." It sounded not unkindly.

So Tom told him more of the conditions under which they worked and the simple need for human dignity they sought. Furuseth and Donaher marveled at his extemporaneous eloquence. When it came their turns to speak, they tried hard not to let their friend down by being less articulate than he.

When they were finished speaking, all three were asked to leave the room while Morgan and his men deliberated about what had been said.

Furuseth relentlessly optimistic, was hopeful. Donaher, with considerable personal knowledge of shipowners, had few illusions; Tom, having seen the cold, soulless eye of J. P. Morgan, knew their hopes were doomed.

"Mr. Morgan wishes to see you, Mr. Dalton." The lawyer's nasal voice broke through their individual reveries, and Tom, curious as to what the next step in the charade would be, stood up and followed the man into the boardroom once again. This time only the elderly Croesus was at the table. Tom couldn't help but see the irony in how the splendor of the room dwarfed the ruthless little man who had built it to increase his own small stature.

"You interest me, Mr. Dalton." The voice was old and hoarse and jaded, but firm and confident as well. "You have done your cause a considerable disservice by your articulation today, for you have made me warier than I have been. I must confess I felt a complacency about this worker business, because it did not occur to me that there was among them a man of your obvious gifts. Now that I know of your potential, you may rest assured I will do all in my considerable power to silence you."

Tom started to speak, but Morgan stayed him with an imperious gesture of the hand.

"On the other hand, as I said a moment ago, you interest me; so I have decided to make you an offer of employment. A bright young man like you with proper legal training could go far in my organization. If you refuse my offer, I shall have no choice but to crush you and your pathetic union, as I have no interest whatsoever in laborers. They are no more to me than pharaoh's army of laborers were to him. Workers build my pyramids, Mr. Dalton, they do not *demand* nor *deserve* concessions. If they fail to build my pyramids, they will be replaced by other workers who will do so. Do I make myself perfectly clear?"

Tom didn't answer, as he sensed the soliloquy was not quite at an end.

"Join me, Dalton, and your future is assured. Oppose me, and when you leave this room, I shall order a lockout of any man even *suspected* of union sympathies. I needn't tell you how far your eloquence will go toward providing sustenance for your laborers when winter comes. Your union is doomed whether you remain with them or not, young man. Why not leave the sinking ship before you drown with it?"

"Do you never wonder about what you will say of yourself to God, Mr. Morgan, at the Day of Judgment?" Tom asked it as only an Irish Catholic might, with a hint of an avenging angel in his voice; he was surprised to see the ugly face wrinkle into a travesty of a smile.

"Have you never noticed, Mr. Dalton, that God seems to be on *my* side and not on yours?" said the wicked old man with considerable malice. The thought remained between them for a moment before Tom spoke, his voice husky with emotion.

"I do not accept your offer of employment, Mr. Morgan. I value the worth of my services too highly to offer them to the Philistines." He smiled. "As to God's position on the question. He has not yet made His views clear to me, as He seems to have done with you. Although I feel certain He will see to it that a day of reckoning comes for men like you.

"It may not be now, Mr. Morgan, not in time to help the men I represent, but you mark my words, the day will come when men like you will no longer be able to exploit the worker. Remember that in the final accounting the Lord helped the pyramid builders and sent the ten plagues to pharaoh.''

"I doubt that He will do the same for you, Mr. Dalton."

Tom stood in the quiet of the boardroom and wished for power; power to smite this cruel, arrogant despot, power to help the army of poverty-stricken men he represented. Rage, frustration, and sorrow, he thought, are the only portion left for the poor by men like Morgan.

He left the building in the company of a grim-faced Furuseth and an angry Donaher. "There'll be many a dry eye at that one's funeral!" growled the burly Irishman with disgust. "He'd skin a louse and send the hide and fat to market."

They walked down the stone steps to the street, but neither of his friends had the heart to reply.

Diamond Jim lay on Billy's big bed with a scowl on his round face.

"You look like a thundercloud tonight, my friend," said the beautiful woman as she seated herself on the side of the bed. She was wearing a revealing black nightgown that on other occasions had driven the man to extravagant protestations of passion. Tonight he was oblivious of everything but what was on his mind.

"You miss them both, don't you, love?" She said it softly, knowing precisely what troubled him. As she spoke she trailed her hand lazily across his bare thighs, but elicited no response.

"No, I do not miss them! They can go to the devil for all I care."

"Diamond Jim Mulvaney, you are full of shit."

He raised one puckish pepper-and-salt eyebrow up as high as it would go, a fierce look that tended to unnerve jurors.

"You are, as always, quite right," he said, and reached out to pull her into the bed beside him, chuckling to himself. He had never really intimidated the women in his life, it seemed.

"Without Deirdre there's no sunshine in my home, Billy. No soft, pretty presence to bring me my brandy at night and tell me I'm wonderful." He smiled at the simple selfishness of his needs. "And the lad, God blast his soul. He was the best I ever had work for me, and if the truth be known, I liked having him around the house to talk to, nights. I expect that's what some men have in a son. It's the reason I didn't send him packing when first I knew they were wanting to play patty-fingers behind my back."

"And part of the reason you were so hard on him when he asked to court her, too," she said sagely. "You always fear your own attachments to people, Jim. That's why, I think, you surround yourself with associates and not with friends."

He scowled again at her perceptiveness. "I've never mistrusted my 'attachment' to you, have I?"

"Only because you think you own me. As long as you think I hang around because you're my benefactor, you don't need to fear that I'll have an emotional hold on you." She smiled at him benevolently, which irritated him enormously. He hated ever to be transparent.

"And I suppose you love me for myself alone, Adonis that I am," he said nastily.

"I'm not denying that gratitude for all you've done for me is part of our relationship, Jim. But you're a damned fool if you think that's all there is to it. We trust each other and we like each other and we fill a lot of each other's needs, and we make very few demands doing it. You're a fine man, Jim, for all your pain-in-the-ass moods and such. But I'll tell you one thing no one else will: You're a good judge of character and a lousy judge of women and love. Where love's concerned, you haven't the sense of a schoolboy, and if you throw away your daughter and her husband because of your stupid pride, then by God, Jim Mulvaney, you deserve to lose them!"

Her bosom rose and fell with the vehemence of her anger.

"You're only mad at him because he outwitted you, anyway. You should be goddamned glad that your daughter's married to a man who's smart enough to do it, and not to some lily-livered, overbred Boston Brahmin with a limp dick and a brain to match!"

Astonished by the whole scene, Diamond Jim hoisted himself up in the bed until his huge belly ballooned over the covers, and watched the woman flounce huffily out of the room, leaving him alone in the bed.

"Well, I'll be damned," he said aloud. "What's got into her, do you suppose?" It was damned ridiculous to be lying in a bed in a whorehouse you happened to own, with no one in your bed. He began to laugh uproariously at the absurdity of the situation, and hearing the laughter, Billy peered back into the room to see his round belly bouncing up and down on the creaking bed.

51

Deirdre pushed the errant strands of hair back from her face and made a valiant effort to straighten up. Her pregnancy was far advanced, and the other wives had been clucking their tongues at her for several weeks now about continuing to work in the strikers' soup kitchen, despite being so far along in her pregnancy. Her husband, too, was gravely concerned for her safety; that the owners might send in thugs to rough up the place that provided sustenance to the families of the striking men, was a distinct, and frightening, possibility.

Deirdre Dalton continued to work despite these sensible warnings, because having something useful to occupy her time was helping her stay sane in the face of what was happening to Tom and the union. At least at the kitchen she felt she was contributing some measure of relief to the destitute families. At least she was sharing in some small way the emotional burden her husband carried.

At first the strikers had been inspired with the early evangelism of a just cause. They'd been so certain that the Italians and the other scabs who'd been brought in couldn't possibly handle their skilled jobs, that they had told themselves it would be over in a week. When the coal handlers had gone out in sympathy, the joy of the union men had been unbounded. Other laboring unions had followed the coal handlers and the leadership—Furuseth from Tom's local, Gilligan, Hardy, O'Connel, and Flynn from the other locals—had been certain that for the first time victory was a distinct possibility.

But the Italians had learned the trade quicker and better than might have been expected. And if these small Mediterranean men could not hoist a two hundred and eighty-pound sack of sugar as an Irishman could, it hardly mattered. At the low wage they received, the foreman could afford two Italians to do the job of one. At last report the loading was behind schedule—but not as much as everyone had hoped.

And, of course, there was winter to contend with, and a particularly cold winter at that. With the food and fuel money growing scarcer in the union treasury, Deirdre knew the soup kitchen was one of the only means of eating available to some of the families. She could tell by the increasing terror on the faces of the women who came to them for soup and bread.

Having tidied up the little kitchen, Deirdre sat down heavily in the rocker one of the older wives had kindly brought for her. The pain in her back was becoming a persistent dull ache. She hoped it wouldn't grow to be enough of a problem so that she'd be forced to mention it to Tom. "God knows he has more than enough burdens to cope with these days, without any additions from me." She said it aloud, and then smiled at the vehement sound of the statement in the silent room.

The strike was six weeks old, and the first flush of righteous indignation and hopefulness of victory had given way to the colder reality of hardship. A longshoremen's pay might be meager, but it was honorable and kept the wolf from the door nonetheless. Strike pay was less, and it felt like charity; worse, a man never knew past the first few weeks how long the union would be able to keep up the payment, so each week the recipients had to try to save as much of it as possible against the weeks when there would be none at all.

The men tended to congregate almost nightly at the Rest now and at the Pythagoras Hall, mulling over the problems, sharing new bits of information, listening to the leaders bolster their courage for another day. But after six weeks without a hint of good news, the leaders themselves were beginning to feel fear and uncertainty dragging at their confidence.

And then there was the disagreement between factions in the labor leadership itself to contend with; each local, it seemed, felt the negotiations should be handled differently—to say nothing of the scab-enforced stone wall the owners had constructed around themselves, which showed no signs whatsoever of crumbling.

The three men reached the picket line feeling as bleak as the weather. Furuseth was somewhat revered by the rank and file; among the men, his immense stature and relentless common sense and dignity made him popular with nearly all the dissenting groups. The men already on the picket line greeted him and his two companions with good-humored handshakes.

"Cold work, this striking, eh lads?" Donaher called out in his deep, mellifluous brogue as he picked up a sign and took his place in line. "Any sign of the Pinks, lads?"

"Haven't seen a one of them this morning." John Reilly, a short burly man with a tough, leathered face and pugnacious bearing, answered. "Too cold for the little bastards, I'd say." His breath delivered the words in small puffs of steam.

"I can't see that we're causing the owners enough trouble yet to call in the Pinkertons. What do ya think, Andrew? Are they hurting enough to be fearful of us yet?"

"Nay, lad," replied Furuseth. "The question is are *we* hurting enough for them to be fearful of *us*." Reilly snorted an affirmative response and fell into step beside the much larger man.

"Any good news from the leaders for us, Andrew?"

"Neither good news nor bad as yet, John. There's a meeting set with their negotiators for Wednesday afternoon, to see if they have any notion of cooperating, or if we're barking up a bare tree. Like as not we'll find out who's hurting who most, when we meet with them."

The men stamped their feet and tried to stay in motion, to keep the cold at bay. Ordinarily they would have taken shifts, allowing the men to duck into the neighborhood saloon for a quick whiskey to stave off the cold; but the owners had pressured the breweries to threaten the saloons that catered to the striking maritime men. No whiskey for strikers, they'd been warned, or there'd be no beer deliveries. Not that it mattered much, as there was precious little money these days for whiskey anyway.

Andrew Furuseth took his place at the negotiating table with the leaders of the five maritime locals and the representatives of the combined steamship lines. His clothes were shabby and his hands those of a laborer, but his stern visage, his immense size, and his personal dignity made him seem formidable to all who gathered in the richly furnished room. Tom and Donaher sat with him, but Furuseth was unquestionably the senior negotiator.

The Old Dominion Line spokesman called the meeting to order in a brisk nervous intonation. "We are here, gentlemen, to arbitrate the current difficulties being experienced by the, er, maritime professions and the owners of the great steamship lines." He cleared his throat nervously and shuffled a sheaf of papers that he clutched in his little pink hands.

"The owners, preferring to deal with this problem collectively, had empowered us, their representatives, to make a rather generous offer on their behalf to the, er, strikers, in the hopes that we may be able to put an end to all this contentiousness." He smiled blandly, and the labor group exchanged glances and said nothing.

The man from Old Dominion, whose name was Harrow, continued pushing his spectacles back to their place on the bridge of his thin nose. "As you gentlemen know, we currently have a plethora of laborers working docks at twelve dollars per week."

"Scabs is what they're called, yer honor," said Donaher. "Not laborers."

Andrew lifted a hand to silence his friend, and the man from Old Dominion continued his speech with a hostile look at the big Irishman, who sat with his wool cap squeezed in his meaty hands.

"As I was saying—despite the fact that the steamship companies have no difficulty in finding men to work the longshore for twelve dollars per week. I have been authorized to offer you thirteen dollars per week in order to end this trouble." He said it as if the generosity of the offer were astounding.

The five labor leaders exchanged glances, and Furuseth spoke.

"Your generous offer is exactly half of what we were already making!" The voice was angry and authoritative.

"You lawbreakers are lucky we're making you any offer!" a nasal voice from another of the owners' men broke in hotly. He was the representative of the White Star Line.

"Surely we are here to behave as gentlemen, sir," Andrew responded with equanimity, "and to arbitrate an honorable disagreement in everyone's best interest. Surely it will do no good to incite each other to riot with hostile words."

Tom smiled at the quiet dignity of the man, which so demeaned his opponent. The White Star man sat down, scowling, and the Old Dominion man spoke again.

"I caution you men not to reject this generous offer. Thirteen guaranteed dollars a week means no daily shape-up, food on the table, and fuel in the grate. Thirteen dollars a week means back to steady work and a chance for a merry Christmas."

Furuseth's face was impassive as he answered.

"I have no doubt you are a well-meaning man, Mr. Harrow, and that you believe that what you say is truth. But it is not. Thirteen dollars a week means *not* enough money to feed your children or your wife. *Not* enough to buy shoes or coats for them you love, *not* enough to hold your head up in the neighborhood because you were able to put a penny in the collection plate, or to help a neighbor in his time of trouble." He paused a moment and looked around the table at the men, smiling wearily. "Thirteen dollars a week is what the men were offered twenty years ago, and they struck because of it!''

"So you see this is why we must continue our 'troubles,' as you call them, until we win a fairer justice.''

"And just what would constitute a fairer justice, might I ask?'' Another of the shipping company men, a lawyer, posed the question.

"That our wages be raised to be the same as those of other God-fearing, hardworking, laboring men; with better pay for the hardest, most dangerous jobs, and with appropriate working conditions.'' He paused again. "We ask no more than that—a fair wage for a fair day's labor.'' He eyed the owners' men with a glint of weary amusement in his eyes. "As we would not be cheated, so would we not wish to cheat you either!''

"He's put them all to shame,'' Tom whispered to Donaher.

"Ach, what'd shame that crowd would turn back a funeral!'' replied his friend disgustedly.

There was quiet in the room for a moment, as if everyone were digesting what the craggy Norseman had said; then all spoke at once, and for the following five hours they argued. By the time the meeting ended, one thing was clear in the minds of the owners' men. The young one who talked like a lawyer was too smart to be bamboozled, and the feisty Irishman was too shrewd. But Furuseth was the real power; if he could be stopped, the others could be brought into line.

52

Christmas came and went, Deirdre and Tom and Donaher trudging to midnight Mass together and heading home for eggnog and plum pudding. The sadness of knowing what hardships the strike was bringing to their friends' Christmases kept their spirits low, despite the fact that it was the married couple's first holiday together.

"It must be hard on you, love, away from the kind of Christmases you had in your father's house,'' Tom said with regret to his wife as they huddled together in their bed in the cold little flat after Donaher had departed.

Christmas at the Mulvaney residence had been a rare spectacle, replete with a tree that touched the twenty-foot living room ceiling, ablaze with candles and red and green velvet ribbons, ornaments and cookies, overflowing with the elaborate largesse that a rich man's home provides. Images of servants, and glittering guests driving up to the door in gala carriages, of overflowing wassail bowls, and Christmas goose to feed an army, welled up in Tom when he thought of Christmas at Mulvaney's. He knew that Deirdre had loved the Christmases in her father's home. They had been her special time to play the hostess and the grown woman.

The young wife looked up into her husband's troubled face with love, and touched his turned-down lips with the tips of her soft fingers.

"I regret nothing of our life together, my dear husband; surely you must know that well enough by now. What do you suppose Christmas would be for me in my father's house without you? And next year at this time the strike will be ancient history, and we'll have our little son to help us celebrate," she said with conviction. Tom held his wife close to his body and buried his face in her sweet-smelling hair; he whispered to her that he loved her, and she wondered if he could possibly comprehend how much it meant to her that she was his wife.

Andrew left the hall long after the others had gone their way. He had no one to go home to.

He had tidied up the chairs and tables after the meeting had ended and the hall had cleared, grateful for the quiet and the space. He needed space to think about their plight; things weren't looking good for the strikers. He sighed at the thought of the angry voices and the hardships the men had described at the meeting. This wasn't his first strike; he'd heard such sad stories often enough before, but they always moved him.

He knew Dalton was deeply disturbed by the tales of privation that were growing daily more intense. Donaher believed so firmly that the union was the only hope, that no pain or problem could dissuade him from the actions they were taking; but Thomas was a man who ached over what he heard and saw, a man who agonized over the part he'd had to play in other men's suffering.

He himself knew Donaher's view of it was the right one. There was no hope at all of bettering conditions without the union. He'd been through all this so many times—other locals, other places, other owners, other strikes. Sometimes they won concessions, sometimes they lost them, but every time they went out, *something* was always accomplished.

He turned out the lights and, checking to see that the windows were fastened, pulled on his coat and muffler, stepped outside, and locked the door behind him.

Standing on the top step, fastening his buttons and tugging on his worn woolen gloves, the man looked up briefly at the cold dark sky. Thousands of tiny white stars stared back at him in the crystal-clear night. The moon was in its dark quarter, but the stars were brilliant, and the old sailor for the thousandth time mused on the beauty of God's great universe and the bounty of the stars that could guide a man safely around the globe if he but knew how to read their map. He pulled his woolen cap down low on his wide forehead and walked briskly down the steps, feeling strangely at peace with himself.

As he reached the pavement Andrew saw the five thugs waiting for him. Ah well, he sighed to himself with a curious resignation before the adrenaline began to flow into his veins, it wasn't the first time they'd come after him. He wondered, as he saw the ugly, sneering faces, if it would be the last.

It was sometime later when awareness began to seep painfully into Furuseth's consciousness. He tried to cry out, but there was something terribly wrong with his throat. He tried to get up, but a swirling blackness overwhelmed him as he did so. His eyes began to clear gradually through the haze of pain, and he saw that he was covered with a thin blanket of snow and that large, sticky puddles of blood surrounded him on the frozen ground. Vaguely he seemed to recall hearing of a man whose throat had been cut but whose life had been saved by the cold that slowed his heartbeat and stayed the flow of blood from the wound to a trickle. He wondered absently if something like that had happened to his own body, for his neck and shoulders were thick with gore, and he felt he daren't touch the wound he knew was there, for fear of the hopelessness it might engender.

He would have to get help or he would die; something told him not to go to sleep, not to let the blackness come again. He began to pull himself painfully toward a distant streetlamp that was casting a puddle of yellow light on the snow of the deserted street, somewhere ahead of him. He began to crawl toward the light. One leg, now, Andrew, he told himself painfully. You can move one leg at a time, man. Now the arm. That's it, man, keep it up now. One more leg,

Andrew, one more leg . . . Laboriously, inch by inch, foot by foot, Andrew Furuseth dragged himself toward the light.

He didn't remember, later, the gang of Plug Uglies who rolled him before they went for help. Didn't remember anything at all until he saw, blearily, Donaher's worried face above his own . . . saw the tears in the man's sparkly little eyes and heard his shout of glee when he moved his head and tried unsuccessfully to speak. He didn't know when that happened that it was a full week later, and that everyone but Donaher had long since given up hope.

53

Dalton, Donaher, and Furuseth, three massive men in a small boat, rowed their way out into the bleak North River, paddling toward where the crowd of men were gathered sullenly, to hear the speech that would tell them how the strike was faring with the owners. Cold, hungry, sad-eyed men in ragged cloth coats and knitted caps, with the inevitably gnarled hands of the longshoreman or seaman, stamped their feet and hugged themselves in a futile effort to stay warm in the damp wintry dusk.

The men in the skiff were painfully aware how near to the breaking point the rest of the men were. Several of the locals were actually talking of going back to work at a considerably lower wage than the one they had left; others were lagging behind in the supply of pickets they were sending out to man the lines—bad signs of weakness in the strikers and not without good reason.

The three men dropped anchor close enough to the old pier to be heard across the lapping water, far enough out for a fast getaway if the police or Pinkertons appeared, as had been happening lately at the Rest and at the Pythagoras Hall. Tom pulled his coat collar up against the cold, wet river wind and rose carefully to avoid unsettling the small craft as he addressed the waiting men, in place of Furuseth, whose injury prevented him from speaking to them.

Diamond Jim Mulvaney sat in his carriage just behind the backs of the men on the pier; snug in a cocoon of fur and wool, he listened as his unwanted son-in-law tried to bring order to the group of unwilling martyrs to the cause of unionism. He was not at all sure why he had come.

He'd had Duffy keep an eye on Tom and Deirdre since their unceremonious departure, of course. He knew where they lived and in what austere circumstances. He knew when Tom worked and when he didn't, and had even ransomed the elegant opal brooch and the emerald earclips they'd been forced to pawn in moments of desperation. That had been around the time he'd learned for certain of his daughter's pregnancy, and had begun fantasizing about what it would be like to have a grandson.

At any rate, it was a curious quirk of fate that Tom was to speak instead of Furuseth at this particular gathering. He'd come to hear the Norwegian; to find out precisely how it was that the union man held these vagabond workers in the palm of his huge hand; but it would be all the more educational to see how Tom handled himself with the cranky crowd of laborers he had chosen for his compatriots. He pulled the fur-lined carriage robe up about him and strained to hear what was being said.

And then it began. Tom's voice, soft at first and then more passionate, talking of justice and honor and freedom. Compassionate, honest words about the sorrow of poverty, the heartbreak of seeing your pregnant wife without a warm coat to protect her, or your children without a pair of shoes for their feet. Angry, forceful words about life before the mast or on the docks, life with no future, no protection under the law, no dignity and no hope.

"I leave you with this thought," he said, after holding their attention for nearly half an hour. "It is a quote from our esteemed State Senator Strathmore on the subject of our union." He held up a newspaper clipping and began to read:

" 'It is ludicrous to imagine that these wastrels could govern themselves, much less a union,' said the senator. 'Were it not for the bounty of the ship's owners, they would spend their lives in stinking brothels, gambling, drinking, and sinning away their wages. They are not men, but ignorant children who must be governed sternly, lest in their ignorance they injure themselves and others.' That, men, is what our Senator Strathmore is telling the New York State Legislature and the government in Washington about us. Gamblers, drinkers, sinners! I ask you, would you be remembered thus, men of the maritime trades? Would you be remembered thus?"

There was a hush on the pier before the first tentative sound of clapping, then the applause began and heightened, finally there was a cheer.

"By God, you've got them, lad!" whispered Mulvaney under his

breath, his Irish sentimentality touched by the emotion of the moment.
"You've got these starvelings willing to starve a little longer for
your dream." He motioned to the driver to get out of the way of the
crowd, now breaking apart and heading in several directions, more
animated than before, once more imbued, if only for the moment,
with belief in their own dignity.

"Will it be home, Mr. Mulvaney?" asked the small, spry driver.

"No," said Mulvaney, as if lost in contentious thought. "Can
you find Desbrosses Street?"

"I can, sir."

"Then do so, man. Number 112 Desbrosses Street."

"That's a rough neighborhood, Mr. Mulvaney. It's getting dark."

"Quite the contrary, my good fellow," said Mulvaney with a
mischievous grin. "It's getting lighter every minute." The driver
shook his head in puzzlement, and turned the horses toward
Desbrosses.

Well, I'll have them back I will, thought the sly old man as the
matched pair of gelded bays clip-clopped over the cobblestones. I've
been a damned fool to castigate my own daughter and the finest
young man I ever had work for me. Damned near didn't have my
grandson to dangle on my knee, either. He chuckled to himself with
the excitement of having made the decision to relent. It always
pleased him to think himself charitable. A grand gesture of forgiveness,
that's what it would be. Back into the fold in time for a fine festive
christening.

Tom and Mulvaney faced each other across the kitchen table in
the tiny waterfront flat, while Deirdre tiptoed back and forth making
tea and trying to be unobtrusive—a difficult task at eight and a half
months of pregnancy.

"God damn it, Dalton, are you daft? Do you not see the condition
of your wife and look around you at the place you live in? What is
wrong with you, man; don't you want to give her a decent home for
the wee babe to be born in?"

"I'd put my wife and children in a palace if I had the means,
Mulvaney, but I'll not put us back in your fine house that you forced
us to leave but a year ago!"

Mulvaney's voice softened; he knew how to move an audience,
and he was not about to be bested in this important contest. "You
must surely have it in your heart to forgive a father for wanting the
best for his only daughter."

"You wanted to own her, Jim. Just as you'd want to own us if we came back. For good or ill, my wife has thrown in her lot with mine. I don't mean to have her on the waterfront very much longer. We're making plans to leave New York when the strike is settled. 'Tis a large country with opportunities outside your sphere of influence, for a man who means to prosper." Mulvaney's small intent eyes looked alert at the unappealing idea of their leaving New York. That would not do at all.

"I want you in the business."

"You threw me out of the business. You'll do it again the next time we quarrel."

"I'll make you a partner. Damn it, man, this isn't a business offer, it's an old man who wants his family back!"

"I can't leave Furuseth and Donaher until we see this thing through." Mulvaney noted that it was not a permanent refusal.

"And what of your wife, do you care naught for her comfort?"

Tom's eyes flashed a fierce hostility Deirdre had seldom seen there. She stepped between the men.

"Father," she said softly. "Tom. You must stop talking of me as if I weren't here. And you must hear me out. Both of you stubborn men must hear how I stand on this, for it's my life too, and I love you both."

Each of the two antagonists turned their attention to the pregnant woman.

"Father, I've been as good a daughter as I knew how to be, all my life. When I had to leave you to marry Tom, I thought my heart would break for the pain I caused you. But after a while I felt immense anger toward you that you kept Tom from any work above the level of laborer, and I thought I'd never recover from your viciousness and cruelty to my dear husband." She stopped for breath, then seeing that she had their attention, plunged on with what she needed to say.

"But now I see that you wish to make amends and, in truth, so do I. There's nothing that would please me more than to have my child know his grandfather. But you must understand, Father, that I will not ask Tom to leave his friends or his cause, for it means too much to him. And besides that, I feel an enormous pride in what he strives to do, against the odds of—you must forgive me for saying it— powerful, ruthless men like you.

"Our home may not be grand as yours, but I'll not have you demean it. Our home is filled with our love for each other and for our unborn child; it's crowded to the rafters with riches of the spirit that you cannot see.

"So I must ask you both, for my sake, to let bygones be bygones. We cannot come home to you, Father, for this is now our home— here on the waterfront, with the people we care for. But we can be a family once again, and we can think kindly of each other for the sake of the child that's coming . . . and because of all the love I bear you two rash, headstrong men.''

54

Tom and Donaher were hunched over the small table in the living room, while Deirdre tried to settle the butterflies in her stomach enough for sleep. She had to pretend, for her husband's sake, that she didn't hear. But she knew, just as all the wives knew, the terror of what their husbands tried to keep from them.

She knew that a handful of men had rousted the Italian scabs at the Old Dominion Line and that the owners had threatened to bring in the dreaded Pinkertons in retaliation. Pinkertons, whose only job it was to put down unions, to maim and to kill. She forced herself to brush her nearly waist-length hair just to stay busy, gripping it near the scalp and brushing it in long strokes over her shoulder and breast, then plaiting it painstakingly into a long plump braid as thick as her wrist.

Tom loved her long loose hair, so she seldom braided it at night as most other women did, but tonight she had an inordinate need for orderliness, as if the very ritual act of tidying could somehow help to hold the pieces of her world together.

She strained to hear the hoarse whispering voices in the living room, striving to quiet the noisy pounding of her heart and the movements of her baby, so she could listen.

"Yer not to go tomorrow, Tom. Not to Old Dominion!" Donaher's voice was adamant.

"I wish I could get away with it, Donaher; believe me, man, I'm torn apart by this thing, what with Deirdre the way she is. But I can't take the coward's way out in this. She wouldn't want me to."

"Bullshit she wouldn't! She'd rather have you alive than dead, lad, and God bless her for wanting it so."

"I'm not going to leave you and Andy to face this thing alone."

"Andy won't be there tomorrow, Tom; he'll be at the White Star."

"Goddammit, Donaher, then I'll not leave you to face this alone! Either our cause is just and we should be willing to fight for it, or we've led a lot of good men down the garden path for our own stupid whims. Now which is it, man? I'll not sit home while you go out to face the Pinks, and that's all there is to that!"

"Yer a goddamned fool, Tom Dalton, but I love yer like yer was me own flesh and blood. If anything happens to yer tomorrow because I got yer into the union thing, I'll never forgive myself!" His voice was gruff and ragged.

Deirdre heard the click of the lock and knew that Donaher had left their flat, but it was a very long time before her husband came to their bed. She pretended sleep, lest her voice betray what she had overheard. She felt Tom lower his large body carefully into the bed beside her; heard him sigh, a long sorrowful sound. She felt him touch her tentatively, tenderly as she lay there longing to speak but knowing that if she did speak, she would beg him not to go. That burden she would not place on his shoulders; it was the only thing she could do to help.

After a while his deep, exhausted breathing let her know that he slept and that she was free to loose the tears that had been welling all the long lonely night.

"Yer love him a powerful lot, don't yer?" Donaher, craggy and good-natured as ever, sat in the corner of Billy's private parlor, a huge mug of beer in his equally large hands. He had headed there straight from the Dalton flat, too agitated by his conversation with Tom to be able to sleep.

"I do, that," she said emphatically. "And a fat lot of good it'll do me, don't you think, mate?" She smiled at the old seaman, and he thought once again that she was the most beautiful woman he would ever see.

"Aye, lass," said the big man fondly. "I know it must be hard on yer, seeing them together like yer do."

She looked up quickly, as if that thought hadn't occurred to her.

"No, it isn't that," she said deliberately. "I can't let it be that, man, for I love her, too. It's the weirdest thing, Donaher, but she means as much to me as he does. I must be daft to have gotten into such a ridiculous situation, but the truth is I wouldn't trade either of them for anything in this world!''

"Not even for respectability, lass?'' His bushy eyebrows went up inquiringly.

"Well, maybe for that!'' she said, and laughed at the fact that he knew her so well.

"How long have we known each other, Donaher?''

"Let's see now, me proud beauty. I shipped out with yer brother, Will, God rest him, when you were just about born. How long ago would that make it?''

"Too long for a lady to let on. my friend,'' she laughed musically. "We've both been through some heavy seas since then, wouldn't you say?''

"Aye, lassie. But we've weathered it fairly, haven't we?''

"That we have, old friend. And we've always been honest with each other, too. Which is why I'm glad you came here tonight—so we can talk about what's on both our minds.''

He looked up from the drink in his hands and nodded.

"We could both be killed tomorrow, Billy. I guess it's as simple as that. The Pinks are a rough lot, and the scabs aren't known for their gentleness, either. It's not that I'm worried about my old hide, lass. I think you know I've more to connect me to the world to come than to this one, since Marie and Dan are gone.''

Donaher's husky voice was serious. Billy reached over and folded one of his huge, callused hands in both her own, and squeezed hard.

"You're worried for Tom, then?'' she asked, knowing the answer.

"It's me got him into this, Billy. Me that introduced him to Furuseth. Me that got him all riled up about injustice and being poor and such.''

"And it's you that he loves, and you that got him a job when he was down and out, and you that's been the best friend to him a man ever had!'' She said it with a firm conviction.

"Aye. And it's me that might get him killed tomorrow morning.''

Donaher tipped back the mug and drained the last of the beer in it. He hoisted himself from the chair and picked up from the table the woolen cap he always wore.

"Whatever happens tomorrow is Tom's choice and God's, Donaher, not yours.''

He nodded, unconvinced. The tall blond woman put her arms around the kindly giant she'd known all her life and hugged him.

His body was like the trunk of a great tree that had weathered the elements and the years. She could feel the weight of his unhappiness as he hugged her back.

"Go with God, my friend," she said, tears at the edges of her eyelids. "I love you, Donaher, you old bear. You take care of yourself for me tomorrow, you hear? You're all I have left of the old days."

He nodded and kissed her on the cheek, feeling the salty wetness there; then he pulled his woolen cap down on his grizzled head and was gone.

The small, taciturn army of pickets were strung out along the gates of piers 48 and 49 of the old Dominion Line. Word had circulated that the truckloads of scabs were to be brought in at six A.M. and that Pinkertons would be on hand to see that they broke through the line. The small, solid force of pickets looked long-suffering and dangerous to Tom as he took his place with Donaher in the line.

As the first small cattle truck crawled into view, the men joined hands wordlessly in front of the gate, laying down their picket signs as they did so; most had armed themselves with a club or weapon of some sort, each had his longshore hook in its accustomed place at his belt. This morning the potential of the hooks took on new meaning.

As the truck rounded the corner of Twelfth Avenue, a row of Pinkertons, incongruously dressed in suits and derbies, rounded the corner with it. There were no weapons in evidence, but every man on the picket line knew that Pinkertons carried guns, and that the police, who were nowhere in evidence, had been paid off to stay out of whatever was to happen, until the damage was done. Allan Pinkerton had perfected his trade of strikebreaking under Andrew Carnegie and others like him, so that his mercenaries had become the scourge of unionism all across the country.

"You, Donaher!" shouted a voice from the truck. "Get the men out of the way!" The pickets recognized it as Jimmy Cahan's, a foreman who had not struck with the workers. He was a decent enough man but had eleven children to feed, and his family's need had overpowered his convictions.

"Yer know I can't do that, Jimmy!" Donaher shouted back, a little sadly. Before this all happened, he had liked Jimmy Cahan, whose love for his growing family was almost legendary on the docks.

"They've orders to drive this truck right through you if they need to, man. For God's sake, get out of the way!" There was a note of desperation in the man's voice, and every man on the line felt the cold nausea of fear in his gut.

"If yer try to do it, Jim, we'll fight yer. You know some of us will get some of youse, before it's over!" Donaher shouted back, his voice hollow.

The Pinkertons lined themselves beside the truck—ominous and expressionless. The procession of men and mechanical conveyance began to inch forward.

Tom stood beside Donaher in the line, the memory of Deirdre's terrified face when he kissed her good-bye an hour before in sharp focus. The insanity and unfairness of what was happening was almost impossible to comprehend.

But what if he died here, beside Donaher? What would it prove, whom would it help, what purpose would it serve? Who would even know it had happened, except his beloved wife and the baby that would never know its father.

Thinking of principle in the dead of night is different from facing men with guns and clubs in the cold, clear light of day, and wondering if any part of your sacrifice means anything at all at the end of it.

He shook his head to clear the nagging thoughts away as he felt Donaher's strong hand on his arm and heard the big man curse in Gaelic as the madness began.

What happened at the gate that morning was so rapid that Tom was never able to put it all into the correct sequence, although the series of individual images frozen in his mind would remain with him until death.

As the vehicle began to pick up speed and it was apparent that they intended to run it straight through the line of armlocked men, a shout arose from a hundred voices as from one.

The longshoremen swarmed the truck as the Pinkertons attacked; arms and legs flailing, men being tossed in midair, the sickening thud of sticks against skulls, the tearing of flesh, the obscene sounds of men hurting and maiming other men—all these images flashed around Tom as he grappled with a black-suited man with a gun in his hand. He heard the man's wrist snap like kindling as he forced the gun from it, and a sick feeling congealed his stomach.

"Tom, watch out behind yer . . ." Donaher's booming voice carried even over the shouts and curses of the melee. Tom ducked and turned; a billy club, missing his head by a fraction, landed stunningly on his shoulder, unbalancing him. As Tom picked himself up off the pavement, he realized that his big friend was trying to keep a weather eye on him as well as battling the Pinkertons and the scabs, an absurdly dangerous task. Tom edged his way toward Donaher, struggling to keep on his feet while breasting the wave of bodies intent on killing each other. At least if they were together in the murderous mass of humanity, Donaher could concentrate on keeping himself safe instead of on protecting Tom Dalton. For the first time it occurred to Tom that he might have done his friend a worse disservice by being with him than by having stayed away. He pushed the thought from his mind and concentrated on the battle at hand.

Back to back, the two large Irishmen fought for several minutes that seemed like years, the line of thugs and scabs seemingly backing off, or at least not making any appreciable progress. "We'll show them sons of bitches a thing or two about Irishers!" Tom heard Donaher shout to him, at precisely the moment he felt a shot whiz past his body. He sensed more than saw the bullet bury itself in Donaher's huge muscular back. As he felt the big man slump against him and heard a weird gurgling sound in his throat, another slug hit his friend from the right, and he suddenly knew they had not been accidental. A row of Pinkerton marksmen were lined strategically on either side of the knot of battling men, their guns trained on Donaher and Tom. They had been told to kill the leaders, and that's what they would do. In a frenzy of horrified realization that he would be the next to go, Tom dropped to his knees beside his fallen friend.

The glazed, wandering look he had seen in Seamus's eyes on his deathbed, he saw in Donaher's. The clear gaze he had grown to love in the aging man was dazed and bleary, and there were tears of pain spilling over onto his leathery cheeks.

Oblivious of the madness of the grunting, screaming throng around them, Tom bent his head to Donaher's; the man was gasping for breath, trying to speak, but the noise of the crowd made hearing nearly impossible. Mindless of what was happening around them or to the danger from the marksmen, Tom pressed his face close to his friend's, an agony of sorrow washing through him as he did so. "Don't die for it, Tom," rasped Donaher. "Take yer missus and yer baby and get out of it. Don't die for it, lad. Don't die . . ." Blood spilled from his mouth in a hideous billow. He stiffened spasmodically; another gush of blood, a look of anger on his face, and he was still.

Tom held the lifeless body in his arms and wept and cursed. The futility, the needless, horrible waste of it! It was a long while before he realized that the sounds around him had ceased and the battle had ended. Only vaguely was he aware of the rumble of the trucks as they passed through the opened gates of Pier 48, unhampered by pickets who were too busy tending their dead and wounded to care who worked the cargo that morning. Not till later did he know that the entire battle had taken only nine minutes.

"I'm going to the West Coast, Tom," Furuseth said at the cemetery after Donaher's funeral. It had been an elaborate affair, paid for by the union men, the services held at Billy's, the pallbearers, Tom, Andrew, and the leaders from the other four locals.

Although he had left no will, Tom had found among his friend's effects, in the room they had once shared, a slip of paper addressed to him requesting that Donaher be buried with his wife and son in potter's field.

"There's a stretch of harbor in San Francisco called the Embarcadero, where I think I'll try again, lad." Furuseth spoke quietly, his voice edged with emotion. "No use to pursue things here now. Tempers too high, spirits too low—and to tell the truth, I got no heart for it since Donaher's gone. God rest him. We've lost the strike, Thomas, but we lost far more than that. He was a brave and good-hearted man, lad." He cleared his throat as if the tears behind his voice made speech nearly impossible. "There are few like Donaher, Thomas. He was the best we can be, we humans."

"Aye, Andy, you're right about the last of it."

"Have you decided your own course, Thomas?" Furuseth took out a large handkerchief and blew his nose loudly.

"I've a mind to go back to Mulvaney, Andy. For a while at least. 'Twould please my wife. And besides, if there's one thing I've learned from this mess, it's never to be poor again if I can help it. If there's a chance at a better life than this for me and my family, Andy, I've a mind to take it."

"You're not wrong in that, son, to my way of thinking. For the likes of me it's a lifetime battle. We win here, we lose there. Eventually we win everywhere, I'm thinking, but it will take a very long time for that to happen. You should not waste yourself on it.

Donaher and me, we're different. We got no one to share with, no one to take care of. You got other responsibilities.''

Tom nodded, heartsick and emptied of the energy to think about it anymore. He had made up his mind at the graveside, as he'd seen the lonely pine box lowered into the ugly hole in the ground, that Donaher's legacy to him would be that he would not "die for it."

He said his farewells to Andrew Furuseth, as he had to his friend now gone, wondering if anyone, anywhere, would ever understand the courage of such men as these. Having embraced the older man in warmth and sorrow, he left him standing at the cemetery gate.

He helped Deirdre into the waiting carriage. Billy, her face veiled in mourning black, was already seated within, her beautiful blond head leaned forward on crossed arms that rested dispiritedly on the sill of the cab; silent sobbing wracked her body, and small drops of salt water made minuscule puddles on the black moiré of her dress.

55

"I've been giving some thought to what to do with you now that you're back in the fold, laddie." When Mulvaney spoke pontifically, his corpulence always added dimension to what he had to say.

"I've been giving it a little thought of my own." Tom said the words evenly, and Mulvaney raised an eyebrow in appreciation of the fact that his son-in-law was a boy no longer.

"You've learned what you needed to know from Tierney and O'Reilly, Tom, and you've acquitted yourself well enough with both. But I never intended you to be an accountant or a lawyer, just to know what they know so's you can watch 'em and know what you're watching."

"What is it you have in mind for me, Jim?"

"Politics, lad . . . and travel. You must see the country to know what makes it tick. See what people need in order to be able to sell it to them. And you need politics because you can't accomplish a frigging thing without it." He looked closely at Tom to see if he looked pleased.

"I've had much the same idea myself, Jim," the younger man replied in answer to the unspoken question. "And I'd like to take Deirdre with me when I go cross-country." Jim noted it wasn't a request, as it would have been a year earlier, but a statement. It amused him to see how Tom had matured during the hardships of the time he'd been with the union.

"Aye, lad. That should be no problem with your own railroad car."

Tom looked up, startled. "Railroad car?"

"My newest acquisition," beamed Mulvaney importantly. "Decided we should start to look as rich as we are, laddie buck. It'll impress the bejesus out of them hicks in the boondocks, wouldn't you say?"

"It will, indeed," said Tom with amusement. "It impresses the bejesus out of me."

Diamond Jim laughed aloud, the tension of the conversation broken. He had noted the subtle changes in his son-in-law since the lad's return and since the birth of his son. Marriage and fatherhood changes a man, he'd told himself; makes him understand the continuity of life, the need for dynasty. Then, too, the lad seemed uncommonly close to his wife. Took her into his confidence and wanted to be with her more than most men would. Well, it was Tom's own business if he wanted to take the girl with him cross-country, although why a young buck who looked like this one would tie himself to one woman on such a trip was beyond him, when there were plenty of willing ladies between here and California, and a bit of sport-fucking never hurt any man or any marriage as far as he could see.

"I need to know more about how the political machine operates before I can be of help with it." Tom knew there was no man living who understood the ins and outs of Tammany like Jim did. It would be a priceless education, if he could get the man to provide access to the sanctum of the Tammany sachems. Not that Tom had any aspirations toward holding office, but rather that his year in the world of laborers had taught him about the importance of power, the importance of knowing how to have it and how to use it. One year with the powerless had seared into his gut the need never to be without power again.

The sphere of Diamond Jim's influence was a continuing revelation to his son-in-law. Although the Mulvaney empire had begun thirty-five years before with lumber in the Northwest, Jim's fortune had astutely expanded, as the country had grown, to include railroads, building, oil, and mining. He also owned two banks in Pennsylvania and had interests in a new growth industry called "insurance."

The lumber company, the foundation of his fortune, continued to flourish in a seemingly endless escalation because of the country's building fever, an agitation that showed no signs of abating when Tom rejoined his father-in-law's enterprises, this time as a partner. The signs and the stationery now read Mulvaney and Dalton, although "M & D" was what everyone had taken to calling the corporation since its rechristening.

"We've diversified, Mr. Dalton," said the taciturn O'Reilly, with his usual relish for safety of capital. "But the lumber business is much like having a money tree. Will be for the next ten to twenty years. Can't build a country if there's no timber to build with. Can't export your goods if there's no ships to dispatch them in. Truth is, *all* new business currently depends on the availability of lumber. We're planning to take as much as we can from the forests while the other businesses of ours are still seedlings. Then in another twenty years or so you'll begin to see some of these other saplings crowding out the lumber in importance to us. But not for a good long while yet." He said it with immense satisfaction.

Tom's education about politics was as rigorous as his education about law and finance. This time Mulvaney himself was the tutor, explaining, showing, taking Tom with him to speeches, to political clubs, to the powerful, and to the people.

"There's nobody with the gift for blather of an Irishman," said Diamond Jim, who was feeling expansive this morning, as Tom fell into step with him in the city hall corridor on his way to the mayor's office. "We've a style that leaves the others at the gate," he chuckled broadly, "because we've got the heart for it, as well as the brains. You might say we supplement the government with the party, and we do it for one purpose, to keep the poor alive."

"Where do we get the money?"

"From a sort of tax, you might say, on certain enterprises. The gambling establishments, the whorehouses, the saloons, and the contractors, mostly. They contribute their share and the party spreads it through like a regular Robin Hood. When the party's in, we build things. Courthouses, schools, bridges. We pave streets and dig more subways."

"And we feather our own nests?" The disdainful note in the question wasn't lost on the astute Mulvaney.

"Yes, indeedy, lad! We collect bribes from the contractors and the man who sells the land to the city. And maybe somebody's cousin writes the insurance on it and somebody else's owns the sand and gravel company. And it puts people to work; ask the plumbers and plasterers and carpenters and painters, and all those others who hold the jobs the immigrants are allowed to have, whether or not they think it's a good system.''

"So you're telling me it's honest graft, is that it?''

"I'm telling you that when the party's in, the people eat! When the party's in, there's a lawyer to help a kid in trouble, there's a man to help you write home to the old country, there's torchlight parades and kids' picnics and excursions to the beach and a thousand other things that make a poor man's life bearable. And when the party's out and the reformers is in, all that's blown away like the fuzz from a dandelion. Now before you make any high falutin judgments about the right and wrong of things, you go ask the man in the street how he feels about the 'corrupt machine,' and he'll tell you how the party got his brother a job and got his widowed mother her pension. Like as not, he'll also tell you that padded building projects are better than no building projects at all.''

"So where's the truth in it all, Jim?''

"Truth?'' Jim laughed explosively at the idea. "Is it truth you're looking for? Well, now, laddie, that's a tall order and one that depends on whose truth you're after finding.''

"There can only be one truth, Jim.''

"In a pig's arse, there can! Talkin' to you today is like waving at a blind horse,. to be sure, if you think there's but one truth to anything in this whole fucking world! The truth is what *works*, lad, and don't you forget it! *My* truth is that I know it all, *your* truth is that you know things I ain't even imagined yet. But what I've got is *experience*. So whose truth would you like to trust to if your life depended on it? Go get yourself some experience, laddie, and then come back and talk to me of the truth.'' He chuckled happily at the consternation of his pupil and turned the handle to the mayor's office door.

"For example,'' he said under his breath, "one truth is that we have a horse's arse in the mayor's chair at the moment, but another truth is that it can be dealt with to be sure.''

"Ah, good day to you, Mrs. O'Shaugnessy!'' Mulvaney swooped off his hat with an elaborate flourish and beamed his most benevolent smile at the mayor's secretary. "And is the great man in as yet, and he with the most beautiful girl ever to get off the boat from County Limerick, secretarying here in his own office?''

Mrs. O'Shaugnessy, a plump middle-aged woman with tightly curled gray hair and rosy cheeks, smiled back at the obvious flattery.

"Now it wouldn't be me you'd be talking of, would it, Mr. Mulvaney, for I'm not as young as I used to be."

"Sure, and what do the young know of anything at all that's worthwhile, would you be telling me that, Mrs. O'Shaugnessy?" He winked at the cheery little woman as he proceeded into the mayor's office at a wave of her hand. "As a matter of fact, I was just after telling my son-in-law here about the value of experience."

Tom laughed good-naturedly at the chiding; he had a lot to learn and the intention of doing so as quickly as humanly possible.

Jim, for his part, recognized in Tom something more than a finely tuned business brain; he saw the kind of visionary instincts that would carry his considerable business success, his name, and his progeny into the future. Tom had the "feel" for the fruits of this new century that he himself had had for those of the old one. Such vision to an Irishman was as tangible a gift as one of more mundane substance would have been to a man of another race. Like the ability of gypsies to tell fortunes, Jim firmly believed that where business was concerned, certain of the Irish had a gift of vision denied to other men. He was a well-contented man in his choice of partner and son-in-law, and he sometimes mused on the exigencies of a fate that had nearly robbed him of both.

The sight of her father holding her little son made Deirdre smile. He was like a man transformed, since Rory's birth. She had never seen him so taken with anything as with his grandchild.

"This one's turned out so well, Tom says we should have a dozen more, Father. What do you think?" Deirdre asked with a smile in her young voice.

Mulvaney leaned back in the rocker till it creaked, holding the baby up over his shoulder with an expertise his daughter couldn't explain, and chuckled.

"Now, that question reminds me of my friend Mr. O'Brien with the eighteen children. Did I ever tell you about him, child?"

Deirdre looked at Tom, who winked at his wife. They had both gotten used to the constant flow of stories, apocryphal and otherwise, that were her father's stock-in-trade with his constituents and also with his family.

"I think I may have missed the story of O'Brien, Father," she said with a laugh.

"Well, now, wasn't he found one morning out riding a bicycle in Central Park with naught on him but his nightshirt. So the policeman on the beat hauled him before the judge for indecent exposure.

"Now the judge says to him, 'Mr. O'Brien, are you married?' And O'Brien says, 'I am, sir.'

" 'And have you any children?' says his honor. 'Indeed, sir,' says O'Brien, 'I have eighteen of them.'

" 'Case dismissed,' says the judge. 'Sure and the man was only wearing his work clothes!' "

All three laughed. Life seemed safer now to Deirdre. She adored her little dark-haired son, Riordan, whom they had already nick-named Rory. He filled her days with the chores of motherhood and a thousand fulfillments she couldn't even name. And she adored her husband, who filled her nights with more love than she had ever imagined possible.

It was lovely to see her father and Tom getting along so well with each other; and the simple safety of no more strikes and no more union organizing made all life seem blissfully worry-free.

Tom was doing well in the business, too. Her father had told her that he had a knack for it, and she was sure that was true. Curiously, the only thing he didn't seem to have a knack for was playing with his son.

He loved the child, watching him carefully as if fearful some harm would come to him; bragging about each new thing he learned, wanting to provide him with security. But somehow he didn't seem to know how to play with him. She felt sure it was tied up somehow in his own childhood, about which she knew so little, but she hadn't a clue as to what had happened to him. She made a mental note to talk to her father or Billy about Tom's behavior, and went back to paying attention to her little family.

56

"Billy, dear," said Deirdre, who was nearly nine months pregnant and confined to the house by doctor's orders. "Do you think we'll have a girl this time?" Her friend had come to spend the day with her.

Billy's practiced eye swept the round belly in appraisal, and she shook her head finally with a frown. "You're carrying too high for a girl, love. It's another son for you this time."

Deirdre put the sweater she was knitting down on her swollen abdomen and laughed merrily.

"What would I do without you to tell me everything, do you suppose?"

Billy laughed too. "You've taught me more than I've taught you, my dear, but I do know about babies. My mother showed me the signs to look for, and I've always had a knack for it."

"Do you think Tom wants another son?"

"I'd wager most men want as many sons as they can produce, but it seems to me he'd be happy either way."

"Do you think he'd be as distant with a daughter, Billy? He doesn't seem to quite know how to be a father to Rory. He loves him a great deal, I know, but there's some subtle kind of distance between them. I don't know what to make of it, do you?"

Billy smiled at her worried friend. "Another thing my mother taught me is that pregnant women get strange bees in their bonnets sometimes, Deirdre. You're seeing worries where there are none, and it's because of your condition. Men just don't devote themselves to children like women do, that's all. Tom's so crazy about you and Rory he's working night and day to give you the things he wants you to have. You just can't expect him to dote on the baby like you and I do."

She smiled her beautiful smile at Deirdre reassuringly. "You watch and see, love, the second this baby's born the whole world will look brighter to you again."

Deirdre sighed and then nodded. "You're right, of course. God just made pregnancy a month too long, and I'm getting twitchy over not being able to move around." She resumed her knitting, and Billy knew her friend felt reassured. The trouble was that, reassured or not, Deirdre was quite right about Tom and his son; he loved the boy, but fathering didn't come instinctively to him. Of course, Rory was only his first; maybe a little practice would do the trick. Billy thought she'd ask Mulvaney about it when she had the chance.

Billy plaited her long yellow hair into a thick braid and wound it around the top of her head, just as she'd seen it done in the *Ladies' Home Companion* magazine. She tucked the last hairpin securely under the golden halo and looked carefully at her reflection in the mirror. She wanted to look beautiful tonight; she hoped she didn't look like a whore.

She'd been thinking about the name a lot lately, ever since Deirdre had been giving her lessons in how to be a lady. She sometimes wondered if the ugly word, which seemed to mean so much, had any meaning after all. It meant, of course, that she sold her body for money. But it seemed to her that most of the women she'd ever known were forced to do the same, one way or another.

Why, then, should only the women of her profession be anathema? She sometimes let herself ponder the question, although she knew the answer. For it was to women like her that other women's husbands came to be unfaithful. To women like her that they flocked for forbidden pleasures and secret dreams. Her whole life was a process of learning and teaching things that no "lady" was ever to know or even wonder about.

She knew, of course, that Deirdre wondered about the things she knew; she'd felt that questioning in her friend's mind for a long time. She knew the young wife wondered if there might be some exquisite knowledge Billy possessed that could provide Tom with a new happiness. But of course Deirdre would never ask the question, and Billy would never volunteer the information. Indeed, she would never do anything to jeopardize their friendship, for it was more important to her than almost anything she could name.

Billy tugged the heavy cloak about her shoulders and pulled on her long gloves, for the snow outside her window had been piling up since afternoon. She smiled ruefully at herself as she did so, for she also knew well enough that Tom needed no new sexual tricks to grapple him to Deirdre's bosom. He loved the ground the woman walked on. Deirdre was his solid earth, his anchor, his lodestone. She was the safe harbor he had always dreamed of reaching, and having reached it, he would search no farther.

Billy sighed a little, a terrible longing for such loving safety sweeping through her uncontrollably, unexpectedly. What must it be like to be a wife? To be loved and cherished . . . to be the mother of a man's children? What might it be like to be respected by a man?

"Well," she said aloud to herself as she opened the door of her room, "I guess that's one more thing I'll never know in this life." Then, feeling angry with herself for the maudlin thoughts, she swept regally down the stairs. If there was one emotion she had learned long ago not to waste time on, it was self-pity.

As she walked down the long stairs a conversation she'd had with

Deirdre a few days before replayed itself in her head. They had been in the midst of her lessons in becoming a lady when it had happened spontaneously; things that had been on her mind had somehow spilled out.

"Do you think one day I'll be able to go out in company and no one at all will be able to tell that I'm a whore?" she'd asked Deirdre earnestly when her lesson for the day was through.

"You are not a whore!" her friend replied emphatically, angry that anything offensive could be attributed to her pupil and friend.

"Ah, but I am, love," Billy had replied softly.

"But it sounds so . . . awful!" said Deirdre slowly and unhappily, at a loss for words to refute the unwanted knowledge.

"It does, doesn't it?" Billy had said. "I've been thinking on all of that now for a while, since you've been teaching me manners and all. Had my life been different than it was, and if I'd had a chance to be a good woman—"

"But you are a good woman!"

"Aye, I am to the best of my ability, Deirdre, but in the eyes of the world it's different! What I mean to ask is this, I guess: Is what we do, my girls and me, so very terrible as everybody says?"

Deirdre looked up questioningly, wondering where the curious conversation was going, and Billy, seeing her expression, continued. "At my house, men are treated kindly, and what they get from my girls is a good time in bed and one that they'd mostly never see at home. Is that such a god-awful thing for us to do, I ask myself? So how do you judge the right and the wrong of it, love? I mean, is a legal wife who treats her husband mean and won't give him the loving that he needs a better person than one of my girls? I doubt it, to tell you the honest truth!"

"What are you saying to me, Billy?"

"That God made me what I am and maybe there's a reason for it somewhere. But sometimes, when I imagine what people think of me, I'd like to pass for something else." The wistful look in Billy's eyes made Deirdre want to cry. "I like it when we go out together and no one knows anything shameful about me. Do you understand? You've made that possible for me, and I want you to know I'm damned grateful."

"A lady doesn't say 'damned,' Billy," Deirdre replied absent-mindedly, the teacher again to give herself time to compose an adequate reply. Finally she said, "I've been thinking about all this too, since I've known you, Billy. I can't judge the right and wrong of your profession, but I do know you're about the best-hearted person I've ever known . . . now don't interrupt me," she commanded as Billy started to speak.

"You're kind and loving and intelligent and fair-minded and you have all sorts of good character traits. If fate had treated you differently, you could have been a great lady to be sure, but perhaps then you wouldn't have made so many people happy as you do now," Deirdre blurted out, looking somewhat embarrassed by her statement.

Billy looked at Deirdre, moved by her love and loyalty. "Sometimes I wonder how God sees it all, don't you, love?" she said softly. "I don't have any religion to speak of, but I sometimes do wonder what He'll have to say to me on Judgment Day. Maybe He'll just take the time to explain the whole thing to us, do you suppose?"

"I just hope He asks me my opinion where you're concerned, Billy, before He makes any decisions!" Deirdre said it with such conviction that Billy laughed aloud. It was very good to have such a friend.

Reaching the bottom of the stair, the young madam heard the sounds of Christmas carols coming from the girls gathered in her living room. Christmas Eve was the one night of the year that her house was closed. There was a tree in the parlor, and a group of her girls were gathered around it in their dressing gowns, singing carols. She knew that any who had boyfriends or family would be going home to them soon; she also knew that the vast majority had no one to go to, no family but the women of this house.

She smiled to see them singing so earnestly and picked up the stack of gaily wrapped gifts she had bought for Tom, Deirdre, Rory, and the new little boy, Seamus.

"We'll all open our presents, girls, and a bottle of champagne, too, when I get back," she called with forced cheerfulness to the gathered singers as they finished their song. "We'll Merry Christmas ourselves to a fare-thee-well!" They waved back at her and called out Christmas wishes as she left.

Billy closed the door behind her and stepped out into the crisp clear December night. Her footsteps on the new-fallen snow made crunching sounds. The singing within had resumed, and the sweet notes rang out clearly in the icy air.

Billy sighed audibly before walking the few steps to the curb, and then squared her shoulders and forced herself to her full dignified stature. She knew better than anyone that Christmas Eve in a whorehouse was a very lonely night indeed.

57

Diamond Jim's railroad car was a symphony of red plush, gilt, and mahogany that was the envy of most of Jim's rivals; Tom had to admit the railroad car was a splendid way to see the country.

Tom lay in the gilded bed of the car and watched his wife with pleasure. She was sleeping so peacefully, away from the two babies who, it seemed, kept her constantly on the move now. He hadn't realized that two small children could be so all-consuming, or that life could be so different because of their arrival.

He was determined that this trip would be perfect. There was business to be done in several cities along the way, and more in Denver, the final destination. But the long stretches of travel in between were to be theirs. Husband and wife again, as it had been before Rory and Seamus had arrived in their lives and made privacy a thing of the past. Much as he hated himself for feeling such twinges of jealousy about the time she spent with the boys and not with him, it was hard to have to share her when it was *she* who meant everything in the world to him. He loved his sons without question, but it was Deirdre who was his life's blood.

Unlike most other men he knew, he never relished being away from his wife, for she was the unquestioned hub of his universe. With her he felt a secure sense of wholeness, an aura of peace and contentment that he had never before experienced. For even in childhood he had been heir to the terrible insecurity of his illegitimacy and the sorrows that had plagued his beloved parents. There was a quiet strength about Deirdre. And more than all of it, she was the most loving person he had ever known.

Deirdre moved contentedly in the bed and stretched in her sleep. He knew she was tired now much of the time, although she never admitted the fact. He touched the brown-gold hair where it had fallen across her forehead, and realized that he wanted her very much. Wanted her entirely to himself; wanted private, perfect time to be his wife's lover, husband, friend. In fact, he wanted her more now than when they'd married; she was his bulwark against a loveless world.

And for this one trip it would be just the two of them again, as it had been in the beginning. He thought it and moved closer to the sleeping woman. She responded to his nearness by curling herself in against his sheltering body. "I love you," she murmured contentedly as she awoke to his touch. "I love you. I love you. I love you."

58

Tom loved coming home to the new house Mulvaney had given them when Seamus was born. He and Deirdre had deliberated for a long while over naming their second son, intending to call him James for his grandfather throughout the pregnancy, and finally settling on the Gaelic version of the name, in remembrance of Tom's first friend, as well. They had wondered if Diamond Jim would be miffed at the change, but he'd seemed elated at the prospects of a namesake, in any language.

"Seamus, James . . . what's the difference if you call him James in the old tongue or the new; he's James all the same," Mulvaney had intoned happily when he'd heard the news, and the deed to the house had been his christening present.

Tom took the mail from the little silver salver on the hall sideboard as he entered the house each evening. It was a ritual they had established; each night as Deirdre took his coat and the children clambered about his long legs, tangling themselves into his stride, he would sort through the pile of letters, tossing them lightly onto the living room table for later perusal, and then settle down to pay some attention to his sons.

This night one letter stood out from the rest; it was written in Abigail Marshall's firm New England hand. Never once had Abby written him at home, and a peculiar apprehension seized Tom as he recognized the letterhead.

"Run along and play with your toys, lads," he said to the two little wild Indians who were clinging to him. Deirdre frowned, both at the concern in her husband's face and at the disappointment in the children's.

"Your daddy has an important letter, Rory, Seamus," she pacified them. "Run along to the nursery for a minute, my loves, and Daddy will play with you when he's through."

Oblivious to the conversation, Tom was already reading the letter, a look of consternation on his face.

"Bad news?" she asked finally.

Tom took an audible breath, as if struggling with what to say.

"Old news, I'm afraid," he finally responded. "My mother is trying to find me. She went to see Abby Marshall to see what she could find out about us."

"Your mother?" Deirdre sounded fully as astonished as she felt. She sensed her stomach tighten. "I don't understand, love. If you knew she was alive, why have you never told me about her?" She refused to believe that Tom had kept something this important from her—or, worse than that, that he had lied. He was not an orphan as he had let her believe. He had a *mother* who was trying to find him. If he had lied about this, what else that she believed of him might be untrue?

Tom looked helplessly at his wife's obvious concern and bit his lower lip before he spoke.

"I've wanted to tell you about her since the beginning . . . so very long, my love." He began, and there was sorrow in his voice. "It's such an ancient wound for me, I just never knew how to talk of it." He reached out his hand to her and she took it, for the first time hesitatingly.

"You see, she was a housemaid in my father's family home. They fell in love, I was born, with everyone against them. They must have loved each other very much to have risked what they did." The sadness in her husband's voice broke through her own hurt; she wondered what more there might be to this story that was so agonizing he had it kept from her.

Deirdre sat down quietly on the floor in front of her husband. She felt as if the security of their whole lives had somehow been breached by this simple omission of the story she was about to hear. Tom took a deep breath before continuing.

"My father somehow got my grandfather to agree to let my mother and me stay in a little cottage on the land. I spent the first light years of my life living at the edge of my father's world. He was a great giant of a man; big and ruddy-haired, free with his laughter."

He looked at Deirdre, as if to make sure she would try to understand what he had to say. "He taught me to ride—God but he loved the horses, like his father before him. He used to take me to the great stables of the manor house and teach me. 'When your mama and I are married,' he would say, 'we'll have fine horses of our own in New South Wales or America, and we'll ride out every morning to survey our domain.' " Tom waved his hand expansively, as his father must have done, and Deirdre could see there were tears in his blue eyes.

"It was a horse that killed him, lass. I was eight years old. I saw it happen." His knees were wide apart; his hands clasped between them, elbows on knees. He bent his head as he continued to talk, so she couldn't see his face.

"The morning after my father died, they threw us off the land. The local priest had some money that my father had put away for us in case of emergency. My dad had left us each a letter, my mother and me. I've never known if he had some kind of premonition of death that prompted him, or if he was just a cautious man who knew the precariousness of our position."

She closed both her hands over his much larger ones and held on. He looked up at her and tried to smile.

"At any rate, my mother went to America and I stayed in Ireland to get my education and 'beat them at their own game' as my father's letter had admonished me."

"But why have you never mentioned your mother before?" she asked tentatively, as if afraid of the answer.

"She remarried and didn't tell her new husband she had a son." He laughed disgustedly. "I saw them once on a trip to Boston years ago. She passed me off as her nephew." The anger and bitterness underlying the simple statement was immense.

"Oh, my dear love," breathed Deirdre, her voice choked with concern. "How awful for you!"

He shook his head affirmatively. "I've meant to tell you, lass. I'm just so messed up where the whole story's concerned, I've never known what to say or how to say it. Intellectually I know she had very few choices as a poor immigrant servant girl who was desperate to make her way. But emotionally? Emotionally, I want no part of her."

He handed her the letter, as if in acknowledgment of the fact that neither of them knew what to say next. It read:

Dear Tom,
I trust that the news I bear will not have too unsettling an effect on you.

Henry and I have had a visitor who purports to be your mother. But there I go in my blunt Yankee way, blurting out the end of the tale before the beginning. This is what has happened:

Yesterday as I was closing the office, a most elegant woman entered, having left a grand carriage outside the door. She was beautifully coiffed and dressed and seemed quite agitated and overwrought.

She announced herself as Mrs. Thaddeus Martin (a name, I might add, that is beginning to be recognized in Boston) and asked for me by name.

She said she was aware that Thomas Dalton had had business dealings with me sometime before and she hoped, indeed desperately hoped, that I might have his address in New York.

Tom, I feel I must impress you with the degree of agitation the woman expressed to me. Her whole demeanor was that of someone in desperate straits. I tell you this not to alarm you, but simply to attempt to render the strange scene accurately.

I, of course, said I was not at liberty to disclose such personal information but that if she would give me a note for you, I would see that it was forwarded.

"No, no!" she cried. "It will be too late by then. My child will be dead." Having said this, she began to sob, and Henry, who was even more unnerved than I by it all, helped her to a chair and began to talk with her.

Well, as you know, Henry has a way that could charm the birds from the bushes, and after a few minutes he had persuaded Mrs. Martin to have a cup of tea and to explain herself.

The story she told us is this: that you are her son, estranged from her because she denied your existence in order to start a new life. This act, I might add, seems to have caused her an excess of guilt (which if I may say so without offending, I have observed to be a typical problem among those of the Irish Catholic faith). At any rate, here's the rub: It seems she has a young child who has been taken ill and is in grave danger of death. She's convinced herself that God is punishing her for having abandoned you. She believes she can save the child only by making a clean breast of it to her husband and accepting the consequences as some sort of penance.

My dear Tom, I would never under other circumstances wish to intrude upon your most private life. However, as this curious situation has been thrust upon me in as uncalled-for a manner as it has upon you, perhaps you will forgive my offering to help if I can.

Henry has convinced the woman not to do anything for twenty-four hours while we contact you. He is entrusting this letter to a friend who is traveling to New York, so I know it will be received forthwith. We have taken the liberty of assuring poor Mrs. Martin that her message will get to you.

If indeed any of this story rings true, I would urge you to try to help this poor soul. She is quite distracted by grief and guilt, and I don't think she is altogether in her right mind.

We cannot know what sorrows exist between you and Mrs. Martin, so we cannot offer advice. We do, of course, send our love and prayers.

Your friend,
Abigail Marshall

Deirdre put down the letter. "You must go, of course," she said simply

"Must I?"

"Your half brother's life and your mother's sanity seem to be at stake, my love. Surely you couldn't live with knowing you had abandoned them when they were in need."

"She abandoned me."

"And it is unworthy of you to do the same." Her voice when she said it was quiet and unequivocal.

Tom nodded, accepting what his wife had said, and took her into his arms, not with passion but for mutual comforting. He held her for a moment, striving to get a grip on his own emotions. Then he walked up the stairs to their bedroom and tossed a few clothes into a bag, wondering at what time the next train would leave for Boston.

Tom rang the Marshalls' bell well after midnight. Henry answered in his plaid bathrobe and carpet slippers, and Abigail was already in the kitchen making a pot of coffee by the time he'd shed his overcoat and galoshes.

Outside the kitchen window the wind whipped sleet and icy rain against the trees and houses with an eerie *rat-a-tat-ta-too*.

"So she *is* your mother," said Abigail as she turned from the stove, her woolen bathrobe tied tightly around a long flannel nightdress.

"Yes."

"I thought as much."

"Now, Abby, dear, Tom is soaked to the bone and dog-tired from the train. Wouldn't it be good if we gave him a moment to get out of these wet clothes? While you make the coffee, I can get out that bottle of brandy you use for medicinal purposes, and then we can attempt to put our heads together by the library fire."

"Provided you'd be wanting the use of our heads," added Abigail laconically as she removed a coffee cake from the bread box, and looking appraisingly at Tom, as if to judge the condition of his appetite, she cut a large slice and slid it onto a willowware plate.

"I'd welcome any help you can give me," Tom said over his shoulder as he followed Henry obediently from the room.

Henry stoked the fire into a crackling blaze of comfort as the mantel clock struck one.

"I'm sorry to be keeping you from your beds—" Tom began.

"Nonsense," Abigail cut him off. "Friendship doesn't watch clocks."

"We'd like you to know that we don't wish to intrude. If you'd rather not discuss this—" her brother began.

"Henry Marshall, this is no time for social amenities! People's lives and consciences are at stake, and I'll wager Tom would welcome the chance to talk it out. It appears to me from what poor Mrs. Martin says, everyone has kept too much under his hat for entirely too long as it is!" She set her jaw as only women of New England stock know how to do, and clasping her hands into a competent position, she leaned toward Tom.

"Out with it, now. What's this all about?"

By four in the morning Tom had unburdened himself of a lifetime of painful debris, he had been given good advice, and he had decided what he must do.

Mary sat at the bedside of her dying child. Twelve years old, the last of her children and the dearest. She had not wanted to send Sean to boarding school with the others of her brood. "He's too young and he's doing so well here in Boston," she had pleaded with Thaddeus repeatedly, but the inevitable had happened in September, and he had, like his brothers before him, been shipped to St. Paul's.

She had never told anyone at all that the child bore an uncanny resemblance to her firstborn, for how could she? Nor had she told anyone that she secretly believed him to be her second chance.

Now he was dying as a punishment to her for her great deception.

"Mama." The boy looked shrunken somehow by the fever that had come on so suddenly. An epidemic on the train, they'd been told. Influenza. Now her baby lay choking his life away just so that she could be punished. "I can't breathe, Mama." The voice was barely audible and sounded exhausted and terrified from the great effort at staying alive. An effort that the doctor had assured them could not continue past tonight.

"It's all right, sweetheart," she crooned, patting back the sweat-soaked auburn hair from his burning forehead. "Mama knows the way to cure you. Mama knows." She lay over the child, her body across his, clinging to him as if to keep life in his small body. She must keep him alive until Tom got there. It didn't matter that the doctor had said the child was dying; when Tom arrived, it would be all right. She would confess her great sin to Thaddeus and to her children, surely her own humiliation and fall from grace would weigh as a worthy sacrifice before God's Throne of Judgment. Surely when she set the record straight, God would give her boy another chance. He couldn't be so cruel as to take this beautiful perfect child just because he looked like Tom and because his mother loved him best. Why, oh why had she ever believed she could live a lie for a lifetime and not be punished? Why had the doctor said that there was no cure for influenza and that now it was in God's hands?

Tom rang the doorbell at seven A.M. The same maid who let him in on his last visit ushered him into the house with the quarantine sign on the door.

He'd felt a momentary faltering on seeing the sign, for he had little children and Deirdre at home to think of and the ghastly disease had no cure.

"I must see Mrs. Martin," he said firmly, and the little maid's eyes grew large.

"She's with the young master, sir, and sick as he is she cannot see no one."

"She'll see me, girl. You must tell her I'm here."

"And why exactly are you so certain she will see you?" Thaddeus Martin's voice was still as death in the quiet house.

"Because I'm—of the family and she has sent me a message" was the reply.

"Your aunt is not in her right mind with the strain of this. She doesn't even want me with her." The man's voice betrayed the terrible fear he lived with. He stood directly in front of Tom to block his way; then, after another moment, he seemed to crumble somehow and Tom could see clearly the desperation in the man's face. Thaddeus waved his arm to the maid in a gesture that meant Tom should be taken upstairs. The maid took him to the top of the stairs and pointed toward a room she was obviously fearful of entering.

The scene in the bedroom was heartbreaking. The fever-flushed child lay still as death on the bed, his breath an ugly rattling sound. The mother lay spent across the covers; her hair had not been combed and hung loose about her shoulders, like a young girl's. Her face, by comparison, looked old and ravaged.

"Mother," Tom said tentatively. "I've come."

The woman who looked up at him from the bed was a different person from the self-possessed lady he had visited years before. Her clothes were disheveled, and her eyes were wild and terrified, ringed by dark brown circles that betrayed the fact that she hadn't slept since her son had taken ill.

"My son is dying," she said in a hoarse voice with no hint of softness in it to overshadow the fear. She stood up suddenly and straightened her dress, and he saw that the expression in her eyes was demented, out of control.

"It's because of my life that God has done this thing, Thomas. And because I loved him best because he looks like you." She pointed to the dying child, as if the very sight of him would explain everything.

"I needed you here so that I can confess to Thaddeus and to my children. If I tell them the truth, maybe God will let him live." Her voice sounded mad to Tom, and he was unsure what to do.

"What does the doctor say, Mother?"

"Doctors!" She spat out the word in a fury. "What do the doctors know of sin! 'Tis a priest we need!"

"Mother, the boy has caught this disease because there's an epidemic. Abby Marshall told me that a whole trainload of boys were taken down with it. Surely all their mothers are not sinners! This has nothing to do with you." He emphasized the last words, speaking them slowly, carefully, so that she might understand.

She turned on him wild-eyed.

"It has to do with me! Every day of my life with them I've lived a lie. I lied to my husband in his bed, to my children at my breast. I lied even to myself and to God! But He has found out. It's just as Father McKuen said it would be. He has found me out!'' Her voice had risen to a shout, and Tom was certain Mr. Martin could not be far away. He tried to stop her by taking her in his arms, but she struggled free of his grip.

"It is the will of God, Tom. He's taking the one I love best to show me the end of my great arrogance.''

"It isn't arrogance to try to live!'' He was shouting now, too. "You had a right to try to live.''

"And what of *his* right to live!'' Her voice was now a cross between a shriek and a wail. "I've killed him with my selfishness. I've killed him with my lies. I've killed him with my terrible sin!''

"Mother, you must try to be quiet.'' He glanced quickly at the boy on the bed and whispered, "Dear God, I don't think he's breathing.'' He put his big hand to the boy's chest, but there was no movement at all. He ran to the door.

"Mr. Martin, Mr. Martin!'' he shouted from the stair landing. "You must bring help, sir. The child can't breathe!''

He ran back to the room and stood transfixed in the doorway at what he saw there. On the bed his mother sat; she had opened the front of her dress and laid the twelve-year-old boy to her naked breast as if he were an infant. She was softly singing an Irish lullaby, and there was a smile on her lips. Her eyes were vacant, as if she no longer lived behind them. And the child, his brother, lay there, his eyes fixed in the unseeing stare of death.

With tears running down his cheeks, Tom pulled the sheet up to cover his mother's body, and that of his lifeless brother. He touched the boy compassionately, and she smiled at him as he did so.

" 'Twill all be all right now, Michael,'' she said in a lilting singsong voice. "The lad's asleep and we can sit by the fire.''

Stunned beyond movement, Tom sat down on the edge of the bed and stared at the impossible scene before him as Thaddeus Martin reached the room in which his wife and the two sons she loved kept vigil.

Thaddeus took in the agonized scene in an instant. He closed his eyes for a moment and swayed slightly, as if he had been hit physically, then he entered the room and walked to the bed.

He tried to extricate the dead boy from his mother's arms, recoiling slightly at the sight of her naked shoulder and breast, then hastily he covered her and turned on Tom with rage in his face.

"Get out!" he hissed. "Get out and have the decency to leave us with our sorrows."

Tom felt heartsick for the man. "They are my sorrows, too," he said quietly.

Thaddeus Martin sank to the bed beside his wife and son, and placing his long, lanky arms awkwardly around them, he began to cry.

59

Mary sat in the rocking chair on the wide veranda of the Cambridge Sanatorium with a doll in her lap, singing and rocking. Tom and Dr. Peabody walked down the gravel path that ran across the wide lawns, and talked. Thaddeus Martin had earlier left for home to attend the funeral of his son.

"We don't honestly know a great deal, young man, about mental illness," said the doctor. "We do know that a severe shock like the one your mother has received, coupled with years of carrying a guilty secret, can temporarily unhinge a person.

"Your mother appears to have retreated to a less painful time in her life. A time when her burdens were lighter and her life safer. How long she will remain there, we cannot say." He looked with a practiced eye at the pain and concern in the young man's face, then continued.

"It is somewhat analogous to a wounded animal retreating to its lair to sleep and heal. Once there, nature takes its course—either the animal dies of its wounds or it heals itself."

"Dr. Peabody, I feel so responsible somehow. As if I should have handled it better over the years, and yet I'm not sure what I should have done."

"Now, now, Mr. Dalton. It will do no one any good for you to take on the same corrosive guilt that your mother carries."

The old gentleman was tall and dignified; what he had of hair was snow-white, and his cheeks were rosy as a child's.

"What can I do to help her?"

"The fact that you wish to help her is a step forward in itself, Mr. Dalton. Come to see your mother every few weeks while this healing takes place. When she's a bit better, your presence and that of her husband will be the key ingredients in her recovery.''

"How is Mr. Martin faring in this, Doctor?"

The stately old man shook his head sadly. "I'm afraid he is understandably devastated by the turn his peaceful life has taken. He, too, is wounded in his way, Mr. Dalton. But he's an honorable man and will, I'm sure, when the time comes, support his wife's recovery." Tom noted that the doctor hadn't answered his question directly.

Dr. Peabody's eyes were bright and alert when he turned them on Tom. "You can help that man, if you choose to, I believe."

"How so?"

"By helping him to understand your mother so that he may continue to love her. She will need love greatly when she begins to heal. Mr. Martin feels abandoned by what he considers her perfidy, just as you once felt abandoned by her lie. You and he have a good deal in common in this, Mr. Dalton, if you choose to see it that way.

"You both must come to terms with the fact that your mother did the only thing she could—she survived. It's a powerful human instinct and not so great a crime after all."

Tom stopped walking and stared at the doctor, not wanting the responsibility of his mother's husband on his own conscience.

"I'm not sure he'll see me," he said.

"Ah, but you'll never be sure of that unless you try, will you, Mr. Dalton?" was the wise old man's reply.

"Mr. Martin, it's apparent to me that we have something to say to each other." Tom cleared his throat and walked from the doorway of Thaddeus Martin's study into the tidy book-lined room. Thaddeus looked up at him with loathing but said nothing. It was the day after the funeral, which Mary had been too ill to attend.

"Mr. Martin, you have every right to an explanation of what has happened here, but I must ask you to bear with me when I say that I don't in conscience know if the story is mine to tell. That's why I've hesitated, you see. It's your wife's place to explain—"

Thaddeus cut in harshly. "My wife, Mr. Dalton, is in no condition to tell me anything at all! For the love of God, man, if you know something that can explain all this and help us, you *must* tell me." The man was trying desperately to keep control of himself, but the strain of the past days had obviously shaken his self-control. Far from the self-possessed businessman Tom had first met, this one seemed badly frayed and somewhat disconnected.

"I only hope you can understand and forgive what I'm about to tell you, Mr. Martin." Even Thaddeus in his grief heard the compassion in the younger man's voice.

"Mr. Dalton, you see before you a man who has just lost his youngest son . . . whose life is in danger of spending the rest of her life in an insane asylum, and whose orderly, happy world has disintegrated in the course of a few days to the shambles you see before you. What can you possibly tell me that could injure me further?"

Thaddeus stood at the window of his library, a tall, angular study in despair. Tom wondered if what he was about to say would not damage this sorrowful man even more; but he knew there was nothing to do but begin.

Thaddeus stood listening wordlessly, his head bent angularly on his chest and his hands clasping and unclasping behind his back as the story unfolded. Tom was surprised to hear himself defend his mother stoutly, trying to mitigate her sin in view of her suffering; surprised to hear his own appraisal of the depth of grief she'd lived with and the horrors of guilt that an Irish Catholic girl must have felt over her carnal sin and her ancient secret. When he had finished, both men stood in silence for a full minute.

"Your father must have looked much as you do, then?" asked Thaddeus finally, and Tom was stunned to hear the depth of jealousy in his voice.

"Yes," he answered, wondering at the love that must have prompted the agonized query.

"She doesn't even know me. . . ." Infinite sorrow edged the man's voice in terrible pain.

"She knows none of us, sir," Tom replied in as kindly a manner as he could, for Thaddeus's suffering had touched him deeply and the sadness of the past days had seeped into his very bones.

"But she speaks to you—"

"Only because she thinks that I'm my father." Tom saw the man wince at the reference to Michael, but he pressed on.

"She knows only her own pain and grief and guilt, Mr. Martin. She blames her sin for my brother's death, you see."

The man looked up quickly at the word *brother* and then looked away again, his expression enigmatic and his eyes veiled.

"She seems to have retreated back to a time before her guilt began . . . to a place of safety where there is no sorrow. I believe, sir, that only your forgiveness can save her life and her sanity.''

"Yes,'' said the older man after a moment, still staring out the rain-dappled window. ''You are most likely right about that.'' He paused for a moment before continuing, then said, ''How bitter is the irony that should make it so.''

"He's a good man, Abby. I wanted to hate him, but I couldn't. He's been wracked by what's happened, but he's a good, fair-minded man at the end of it; I believe he'll stick by her, at least till she's well.''

Abigail Marshall ''humpffed,'' a New England sound, and handed Tom a slice of homemade bread and butter.

"You're to eat that and no complaints about it. You've touched no food in days and you've been exposed to that god-awful influenza, so you must keep your strength up.''

Obediently, but without enthusiasm, he consumed the portion.

"Where's your mother now, Tom?''

"She's been taken to a private sanatorium in Cambridge. The only other place available was run by the nuns, and Thaddeus said the Church had harmed her enough without adding any more damage.''

"What will you do?''

"Come to visit as often as I can, write to her, try to help her husband understand, I suppose. Whatever I can. Why?''

"Because this has been a terrible time for you; I doubt if you realize the toll it's taken. Deirdre's worried sick about you, by the sound of her telegram, and with good reason, I might say.'' Tom nodded absently.

"The boy, Abby, he did look the way I must have looked at that age. I think I'll carry the vision of that dead child in her arms to my deathbed. And my poor tormented mother. You know when I heard the guilt she was taking on herself, I knew for the first time how she must have suffered all those years. To actually imagine that God would punish her by taking the life of her child—it's so grotesque.''

"And quite understandable, I'd say, bred to the idea of sin and punishment as she was.'' Abby seated herself beside Tom at the wooden kitchen table. ''How do you feel about all that's happened? I don't want you heir to the same guilts that are destroying your mother.''

Tom rested his chin on his hands, his elbows on the table; it was impossible to banish the picture of his mother from his mind.

"I feel heartsick for her . . . for him, too, and for the other children who are so bewildered by what has happened. Thank God they're all grown, at least. I'd like to help if I could." He paused as if to make sure that he'd dredged up all that he needed to say. "In a curious way that I don't in the least understand, I feel freer of the past than I ever have."

"Does that you mean you forgive her?"

"Aye, Abby. I forgive her and I wish her well. She's suffered too much already. I've been wrong to make her life harder."

Abby placed her weatherbeaten bony hand over his and patted it as if he were a child.

"You're a lovely lad, Tom Dalton. Any mother'd be proud to have you."

He smiled at her. "I'm to see the doctor at the clinic before I leave this morning, then back to New York, I'm afraid. You've been a good friend to me, Abby. It's grateful I am to you."

"When you come back to see her, stay with us. You may need some moral support in this for a while, and we've broad backs, Henry and I."

Packing for his trip, Tom thought about his conversation with Dr. Peabody. The man had said there was no way of telling how long it would take Mary to recover, if indeed she ever would. The thought of his mother incarcerated in the sanatorium, perhaps for years, chilled him to the bone. He felt a sudden terrible need to see his own wife, to make sure that she was safe. How tenuous was life and happiness, after all; how hideously vulnerable to fate.

He shook off the dreary thoughts and dressed for the Boston weather before bidding good-bye to the Marshalls and heading out into the cold afternoon.

60

Deirdre was growing more beautiful with maturity. At least Tom thought so as he watched her with their two sons: Riordan, tall for six years of age and darkly handsome; Seamus, fair-complected, boisterous, and powerfully built, although only four years old.

She had grown more accomplished, thought her husband, and her grace was that of a woman, not a girl any longer. Her light brown hair was still waist-length when she loosed it, and he loved to watch her sitting at her dressing table in the evening, freeing it from the hairpins that held it into a dignified coif for the day, brushing the loose, girlish cascades of hair that glimmered in the halo of light around the little mirrored table.

Deirdre was aware of Tom watching her playing with the boys this night. She reveled in the fact that he loved her after seven years of marriage, more, she thought, than the love he had felt for her in their early days. His home was his anchor, and maybe that was why she always sensed in him the sorrow and the fear that it might all somehow be taken away.

Perhaps that was why he had a hard time really knowing his sons. Not that he didn't adore them and shower them with gifts and fatherly protection. But there was that curious distance she'd sensed for so long, as if he didn't really know how to be a father. The same instincts that came so easily to her, the nurturing and closeness, came harder to Tom. Perhaps because he hadn't had a real father of his own to be an example; perhaps because he feared losing them too much, unconsciously distancing himself from them lest they be somehow taken away, as had so many people he had cherished in life.

She saw her husband's wonderful sad eyes follow her as she took the pajama-clad boys to their beds. She felt the relief that all mothers feel when their brood is finally tucked in safely for another night. Kissing the two sleepy children and tucking them sweetly under the covers, she had a sudden realization of how much she wanted Tom tonight. The sweet warmth between her legs reminded her that they, too, would soon be in their big feather bed, alone together in their most private world. She was grateful at the thought.

She wondered if other women felt about their husbands as she did. She'd never heard another speak rapturously of sexual love, but perhaps it was just propriety that stilled them. Or perhaps they didn't have husbands like Tom. He was so extraordinary in bed. Not that she had any means of comparison, but it was so impossible to imagine that anyone could be more wonderful. Strong and powerful, and infinitely gentle. A patient teacher, a passionate friend. Free finally of the restraints that seemed to bind him in the day, he was wild and abandoned alone with her in their marital bed. She smiled to herself at the thought of his inexhaustible capacity for bringing her pleasure. She hoped she provided the same for him. She thought she did; he seemed to be so happy with their love.

She turned down the lamp in the children's room and walked to where her husband sat by the fire with his newspaper.

"Would you consider taking your wife to your bed a bit early this evening, my love? I feel a great need to be in your arms." She asked it as she ran her fingers lovingly through his hair. She knew the smile he would be smiling without seeing it. Amused, pleased, in love with her.

He caught her hand and brought it to his lips.

"Aye, lass," he said with a smile in his voice. "I would consider it."

"It's a girl this time, love." Billy announced her prognostication with suitable solemnity, and Deirdre laughed merrily.

"You were right the last time, dear; I can't imagine how you know these things, but I believe you're right this time, too." She let the piece of quilt she was working on rest for a moment on what was left on her lap after the baby she was carrying had filled up the space where her lap had once been.

"I feel so different this time, Billy. So peaceful and placid . . . as if all's right with the world. And this baby is so much quieter and gentler than the boys were. Why, it's like feeling the flutter of a tiny bird when she moves about inside me." She stopped and placed her hands on her swollen belly, as if listening with them. "Here, Billy, you must feel how gently she moves."

Billy placed her slender hands on her friend's abdomen and felt the small life wriggle under her touch. She smiled up at Deirdre's calm and lovely face.

"I envy you, my dear friend," she said, still touching her belly. "This one beautiful thing I envy you." Something genuine and wistful in her tone made Deirdre reach out and touch her friend's face. How ghastly it must be to be a woman and know that you would never feel a life grow within you . . . a life to love and nurture; a life to be part of you forever.

"We'll share this baby, Billy," Deirdre said suddenly and with conviction. "She'll belong to both of us, and we'll dress her up like a beautiful little doll and we'll play with her and do all the things little girls like to do. And . . ." She pushed the pale gold hair back from Billy's face as she spoke. "We'll teach her to be both a lady and a woman . . . together!" They both laughed at the determination in Deirdre's statement, and Billy gave the baby one last proprietary pat before sitting back down at the other side of the quilt they were embroidering together.

What a generous spirit Deirdre was, Billy thought as she rearranged the colored threads beside her embroidery hoop; she had said they would share this little girl-to-be, and she had no doubt that it would be so.

"You're a wonderful friend, Deirdre," she said on impulse, "and I love you very much."

The smaller, more delicate woman looked at her friend and smiled sweetly, openly. "I love you too, Billy," she said, as if their friendship were the most natural thing in the world, and continued on with her work.

Billy began to work the needle skillfully into the cloth, as Deirdre had taught her to do. You could never know how much your friendship means to me, she thought seriously as she savored the goodwill that Deirdre exuded toward her. You, who never in your life had an unkind thought about anyone, could never know how very much I need you to be my friend.

61

"We've got to come to some conclusions about the waterfront." Mulvaney, red-faced as he always was when angry, laid his pudgy hands emphatically on the conference table.

Tom, O'Reilly, and Tierney sat somberly waiting for the rest of the sentence, and Duffy hovered in the background. Tom had wondered how long it would take Mulvaney to realize the enormity of the danger.

Tom had kept abreast of the changes on the waterfront through Duffy; in part because he had steered Jim into ever increasing commercial interests on the docks, and in part because he still felt a visceral connection with the men who worked the water.

Duffy had become Tom's eyes and ears as much as Mulvaney's. Since his return to the firm, Tom had been amused to find that Duffy had become his fanatic supporter with the same loyalty he had theretofore reserved for Mulvaney.

Duffy walked to the end of the table and sat down. Finance and business were not in his domain, but when it came to danger, Duffy would make his presence known. And the Italians meant danger.

"Each and every one of these Italians is connected to what they call a 'family,' " interjected Duffy, without waiting to be asked. He'd been keeping an eye on the potential power of the Italian familial network for some time. "Each family has a head guy called 'padrone' who's supposed to take care of everybody in the family."

"Very cozy, lad," Mulvaney answered with a snort.

"These families have real 'muscle' on the payroll, too, Mr. Mulvaney. They protect their family members, no matter what it takes; a broken nose, a broken head, a shop fire, a killing. There ain't nothin' they won't do for their *padrone*."

"What you're describing, Duffy, is no different from what every other group of immigrants has been party to, in one way or another, in this fair city. You don't think we Irishers have run the political show these many years because we're such sweethearts, do you?"

"That's true, Mr. Mulvaney," answered Duffy seriously, anxious to be heard, "but the problem is, these guys want the docks. Tom here knows they've been bringing in truckloads of dagos that'll load and unload for half of what our guys get. They bring their own bosses with them who talk their lingo, and they hand money under the table to the crew foremen so they get the work. Nobody can compete with 'em, Mr. Mulvaney, 'cause you'll get your head broke in an alley some dark night if you make any bones about what's goin' on.

"They want the warehousing and the cooperage and any other trade on the water they can get their mitts on. And not just so's they can bring in olive oil, either, although that's what they tell you. They're into illegal drugs and a lot of other garbage, and the waterfront is a good place to store all the blackmarket goods they take on in Sicily."

"We've run a little contraband ourselves, my fine bucko. No use getting uppity about that; although I don't hold with this drug business. But I do get your drift. The question then becomes one of what we do about it, yes?"

Tom interjected, "I think we should talk about that, Jim. I'm not sure it does make sense to fight them. We've got enough interests in other areas to make us rich as Croesus, if we never set foot on the waterfront again. . . ."

"We can't let go of so much territory without suffering severe financial setbacks,'' said O'Reilly, whose thoughts, as usual, were of debits and credits.

"There's more to it than that, I'm afraid,'' responded Tom thoughtfully. "The political implications are enormous. Jim's constituents need the jobs on the waterfront. They're being pushed out by unskilled labor willing to work at a lower rate than the Irish. It won't be long before their loyalty to Jim falters, if he can't protect their jobs.''

"Not only that, gentlemen,'' offered Tierney, "they're paying off the foremen, the cops, everybody. They're almost as good at it as we were in the old days,'' he said with a malicious chuckle. "They've bought up the old McQueeney warehouses on piers 23 and 24, so they've got a base to operate from.''

"Is there a possible compromise, Jim?'' Tom's voice was disturbed, concerned. He'd been on the docks himself, he knew the terrors of being pushed out of your only means of livelihood. He also knew that the longshoremen's jobs had been only the beginning. What the Italians wanted was control of the water.

"Not with a war coming, laddie. And a war is coming, sure as you're born.''

"I thought Senator Shoreham and Senator Brush assured us both at dinner that there would be no involvement of this government.''

Jim shook his head in mock sorrow, snipped the end off a fat Havana, and lit it up noisily before proceeding with his thought.

"Wars are synonyms for profits, and don't you forget it. People like you and me and those Italian *padrones* make bloody fortunes out of wars. And where there's fortunes to be sniffed out, idiots like Senators Brush and Shoreham will change their tunes right smart enough, when the time comes. If you think for a minute those beady-eyed little wop bastards are going to stick it to Diamond Jim Mulvaney, just in time for him to miss out on the opportunity of a lifetime, you've got another think due you, my boy.'' He puffed contentedly on his cigar and eyed his son-in-law with calculation.

"What's eating you, lad? It's not like you to turn your back on a profitable enterprise.''

"I don't know, Jim. They're a rum lot, these toughs. Duffy's been sniffing them out for a couple of months, and everything I hear is grisly. There's no subtlety about them. We Irish do our dirty deeds, if you will, by manipulating the laws, or even those who make them; but everybody gets his share, Jim, some lavish, some just the crumbs. But we do it with a bit of finesse, if you know what

I mean. Vincenzo and his crowd are like machine guns, they're mindless and they mow down anything in their way. And their loyalty to each other is something to behold. Maybe we should just lie low for a while before we decide how to move.''

"Long sleep makes a bare backside, my sainted mother used to say, lad. It's best to let them know we're on to them and see how they react." Mulvaney puffed on his cigar for emphasis.

"A man called Vincenzo is the head of the take-over scheme for the longshore. Calls him a 'don,' a leader of some kind. I suggest you and I have a chat with him, Thomas, my boy. Take along Duffy for a little firepower."

"You think it'll come to that?"

"Can't say yet, lad. Can't hurt to be prepared for any eventuality. I've set a meeting for three o'clock today at Vincenzo's home."

"Why meet them on their own ground?"

"To give them a false sense of power, my boyo. Never let your enemy know your true strength till you strike, that's my motto." His little black eyes were sparkly. "And to get the lay of the land over there, too. I want to get a feel for what goes on in Vincenzo's own stronghold."

"How strong do you think they are?"

"Strong enough, laddie. As Mr. Duffy was so kind to inform us, these *padrones* like Vincenzo are the head of a sort of glorified family group, where everyone feels he's under the protection of a powerful leader. Someone who'll protect his interests with the help of thugs, if need be. Interesting concept. Keeps them all in line and gives them a power structure they couldn't have otherwise."

"How much bargaining are you willing to do, Jim?" His son-in-law had learned the wisdom of following the older man's instincts in a battle.

"None at all for the moment, laddie. I just want to listen."

Duffy had ferreted out a considerable amount of information about Vincenzo and his family; through Duffy's numerous efforts and his impeccable connections in New York's seamier areas, Tom and Mulvaney learned the story of Angelo Vincenzo's ascent to power.

In a small town near Palermo, Angelo Vincenzo had been born in 1850. In this harsh area of northern Sicily, many minuscule towns such as his existed primarily to supply peasant labor to the nearby estates and to the seaport. It was a hard town, devoid of pleasantries, and it was the home of many large families like the Vincenzos; but few such families ever had the good fortune to produce a son like Angelo.

Angelo did not excel in school, but he had a tough and large exterior and a wily brain that was apparent from his earliest days. His first real opportunity to gain the respect he would need in order to become an important Mafioso came when he was seventeen. Angelo fancied a certain young lady whose lineage was a trifle grander than his own. She, on the other hand, preferred the attentions of another suitor, and when the other young man asked for her hand, Angelo decided that an affront had been given to his own manhood. He therefore gathered a gang of thugs and beat the man to death, afterward announcing that any suitor who sought the young lady's attentions would be similarly dealt with. Although he was jailed for his ardor, the local Mafia, sensing that a young man of extraordinary talent was in their midst, saw to it that he was soon released.

Don Angelo Vincenzo was a solid bourgeois with a face carved out of travertine marble. He had the disconcerting ability to sit so still for so long that people unfamiliar with the lizardlike ability were sometimes tempted to ask if he was listening. He always was. In fact, his capacity for listening was legendary in his town, where, by means of his natural listening gift, his infinite patience, and his ruthlessness, he managed to gain considerable power at a very tender age.

By twenty-two years of age Angelo was already considered a man of respect by locals of his district, because of his cunning and his knowledge. By twenty-three he had attained the title of "Zu"—or Uncle—a lofty achievement for one so young. It was at this point that one of the local dons began to feel threatened by the considerable reputation the young man was building and decided to challenge the young cockerel. Thus, by the time he was twenty-four years of age, Zu Angelo was also renowned for his brutality in wiping out adversaries.

Shortly after consolidating his interests in Sicily, Vincenzo decided to emigrate to America. He had listened to tales about New York and its opportunities from passing seamen since boyhood, and opportunities were always appealing to Angelo. It did not take him long at all, after his arrival in New York, to make a place for himself in the teeming Italian slums of the city. One waterfront was much like another, he found, and many of the unsavory occupations he had excelled at in Italy, he also excelled at in his promising new land. Extortion/protection was one of his finely honed talents, and his efforts at building a reputation were so enthusiastic that he soon came to the attention of those in the New World who watched for talent.

Angelo imported two of his brothers from Palermo at the earliest opportunity (leaving three behind to keep an eye on his Palermo enterprises), and, being a farsighted man who had listened carefully to the ways of business in the New World, Angelo helped them to set up an olive oil importing business with some of his hard-earned money.

When he had been in New York for eighteen months and knew that he intended to remain, he also imported a plumply lovely Sicilian girl named Rosanna, so that he might have sons to share his labors. Rosanna dutifully produced eleven children in thirteen years, eight of whom survived. As five of them were sons, Don Angelo's family, real and extended, began to blossom into a remarkably productive dynasty.

It was just this dynasty that worried Tom Dalton, for even Duffy, cold-blooded as a gun, sensed danger in Vincenzo's "family." And Tom had learned to trust Duffy in all matters of skulduggery, for in such things his instincts were impeccable.

"Don Vincenzo is waiting for you in the garden." A tough-looking dark-complected youth with no neck opened the door to a house that appeared to be fortified as an armory. Tom and Duffy proceeded through the marble-floored hallway to an iron gate that opened into an arbor hung heavily with fertile grapevines. Beyond the green tendrils of this arbor they could see a small middle-aged man seated in a wooden chair at a round stone table; there were two huge lumbering bodyguards lurking behind him. Two young aggressive-looking men, both with dark curly hair and cautious eyes, were seated with Vincenzo, nodding acquiescently as he spoke, seemingly enthralled by what he had to say. As the Mulvaney delegation entered through the gate, the conversation ceased abruptly and the three men turned their attention to the visitors.

Vincenzo motioned to them with a wave of the hand to come to the table and seat themselves, which they did before he spoke. "Welcome to my garden, gentlemen. You like gardens?"

"Indeed," said Mulvaney with a smile and no further effort at communication. Vincenzo and he were watching each other intently, sizing each other quietly, gauging the distance.

"Whata you want talk to me about, Mr. Mulvaney? You are da

one who ask for dis meeting, no?'' Vincenzo's face was round and lined; his eyes were slightly hooded by heavy lids, and his mouth was thin-lipped and hard. His heavy Sicilian accent seemed somehow unnecessary in a man who had spent thirty-seven years in New York, and the three newcomers wondered if perhaps it was an affectation performed for their benefit.

''It seemed to me we should know each other better, Don Angelo. Many of the people in my world look to you as the head of their family, and to me as the conduit of their government.'' Mulvaney's voice was companionable.

''My people don't needa you government, Mr. Mulvaney. We have our own government, eh?''

The two young men smirked, and the two lieutenants stepped closer, assuming Tom to be the bodyguard because of his size. They ignored Duffy. Tom watched the two adversaries with fascination. Strong, tough old men, both used to the exercise of power; they would be interesting adversaries. The thick Sicilian accent made Vincenzo sound ignorant and staccato, but it was apparent from everything they'd learned of him that his fierce and wily brain was not hampered by his imperfect English. He exuded power.

''You people are interfering with the jobs of many of my constituents on the waterfront, Don Angelo,'' said Mulvaney casually. ''On their behalf I am here to ask you just what it is you want from the longshore.''

''We gonna take over da whole t'ing, Mr. Mulvaney. In two years, we gonna own da waterfront.'' Vincenzo said it simply, and his people smiled at the surly and confident reply.

''That hardly seems sporting of you, Mr. Vincenzo,'' said Mulvaney with an amused glint in his eye that Tom had seen there occasionally before. ''And what if we don't wish to give it up?''

''I didn't say nothing about you *giving*, Mr. Mulvaney, I said we gonna take.''

''Am I to consider that a threat, then?''

''You could consida dat a promise.'' The thin slash of a mouth turned up at the corners in a smile.

''Then there seems little to discuss.'' Mulvaney raised his bulk from the chair, nearly popping his vest buttons as he did so; Tom, having said not a word, rose too, and Duffy moved from his place behind the chair. Duffy watched the two bodyguards in a casual calculation; the fact that they were each twice his size did not seem to disturb him overly. The garden seemed deadly quiet, and Tom realized that the two dangerous men were staring each other down, the same malevolent confidence in both their faces. After a moment Mulvaney led the way to the gate. They had nearly reached it when he turned. "Don Angelo!" he called to the seated Mafioso. The still smiling man looked up. "Do you know your Bible?" Vincenzo looked puzzled but nodded affirmatively. "Consider, then, if you will, the wisdom of Proverbs 16:18, sir." The gate opened and they left the house without further speech.

"What's in Proverbs 16:18?" asked Tom as they reached the street.

" 'Pride goeth before destruction,' my boy," said Mulvaney with a cherubic smile. " 'And a haughty spirit before a fall.' "

62

Vincenzo's *consigliere* had left him the papers to study. The profit and loss statements on the businesses, the cash-flow charts, and the balance sheets. He pushed the stack of papers away from him with an eloquent gesture. He hadn't gotten to be head of the family by examining pieces of paper. That was work for an accountant, not for a *padrone*.

He had been brooding for two days over his meeting with Mulvaney. An interesting character, that one. Strong, tough, confident, not the kind to be easily intimidated. He must be subtler than that in dealing with Mulvaney, for the old pol was a powerful man in this city. The days of Irish political power might be waning in New York, but Mulvaney still controlled a lot of cops and congressmen, and he was rich enough to hire an army if he chose to.

No. This problem demanded Sicilian subtlety and the instincts of a *capo*. He must find the man's Achilles' heel and deliver a blow calculated to defeat him from within. The usual tactics—the fires, the beatings, the threats—if Don Angelo was correct in his assessment of Mulvaney's character, such as that would merely serve to incense the old man into action.

Vincenzo chuckled as he swiveled back in his leather desk chair. It was good to have a worthy opponent. It made the game more enjoyable.

*   *   *

"I believe we can settle the hash of this Black Hand of yours, once and for all, laddie." Mulvaney seemed elated, and Tom marveled once again at the sheer pleasurable life-force Mulvaney derived from business.

"And would you care to tell me how?"

"You know, the old McQueeney warehouses they've bought, lad? The ones they intend as their base of operations on the waterfront?"

"Yes, what of them?"

"A little judiciously well-placed money will have those properties tied up in litigation so long, Vincenzo will be dead and buried before he can use his warehouses."

Tom looked questioningly at his father-in-law.

"I thought they'd paid off at least as many congressmen as we have, Jim."

"Aye, that they have, laddie-buck. But not the right ones, not the right ones. The ones I've got on the payroll will see to it information is brought forth about that McQueeney real estate that'll stand their little black curly hairs on end. It's Tierney that gave me the idea in the first place, God bless his dishonest soul. He remembered that old man McQueeney was never a stickler for protocol, so he went back over the deeds to the property at the town hall, and it seems that old s.o.b. never bought the land fair and square at all! He just appropriated it from a man who got killed in a brawl in a saloon about thirty-five years ago.

"Well, sir, didn't that man just happen to have a little old avaricious widow in Denver who was willing to bring suit against McQueeney's right to sell the land at all. And furthermore, my young friend, a certain senator friend of mine has the notion that the death of Joe Petrosino, the cop who went to Sicily to chase the Black Hand and got his head blown off in Palermo, may have been set up by some of Vincenzo's boys." The story of Petrosino's demise had been a scandal in all the papers the winter before.

Mulvaney waited for an enthusiastic response that never came, so he continued. "And on top of that I've convinced my old pal, Police Captain Peter O'Donnelly, that Vincenzo's olive oil books need looking at on account of reports of black-market merchandise that's mysteriously turning up in New York in Sicilian crates."

"Hold it, hold it, Jim! Why would O'Donnelly risk getting himself killed to expose Vincenzo?"

"Because, lad, he's got only six months or so to live anyway, according to his doctor, and he'd like to leave his wife and kids well taken care of by yours truly when he cashes in.'' Tom shook his head disbelievingly.

His father-in-law had a never-ending supply of cards up his sleeve when it came to getting the drop on an opponent. But it seemed to Tom that there was a basic flaw in his plan this time: he was sure Jim was underestimating his adversary.

''So what does it all mean, Jim? At the end of it, you know Vincenzo will find a way to reach the right people, or he'll just find some other suitable waterfront business to infiltrate. You won't have accomplished anything.''

Mulvaney frowned in disappointment at his son-in-law's lack of enthusiasm for his coup.

''It buys time, lad! Time to fight him, time to consolidate our own interests on the water. And it kicks him in the balls, the insufferable, pompous little bastard who said 'he's a gonna take da whole t'ing away from Diamond Jim Mulvaney.' That's what it does!'' The old man's face was red and his eyes shiny when he finished the statement. He's a formidable old schemer, thought the son-in-law, unconvinced for once that his partner and father-in-law was on the right track, but this time he's wrong.

''They don't give up easy, Jim; this may just be the end of round one.''

''It's a while since I've had the chance for a good donnybrook, lad. I might just have the time of my life if that son of a bitch comes back for round two.''

Tom left his father-in-law's house filled with disquieting apprehension. Jim was a brilliant in-fighter, but he was getting old. This time he was biting off more than he could chew, Tom was certain of it. He was equally certain that there was no turning the old man from anything he had decided to do.

Duffy tucked his newly cleaned and polished gun into the shoulder holster he always wore under his jacket. He had work to do. Mary Louise, his longtime girl friend at the whorehouse on Thirty-ninth Street, had sent him an urgent message, and he had gone to her directly.

''My pal Josie was boffing this dago she's been real tight with for a while, sweetie,'' Mary Lou had told him less than an hour before, a terrified look on her face and a tremor in her voice. ''He was real excited about something having to do with Mr. Mulvaney.''

''What'd he say, luv?''

"He said the *padrone*, you know, Mr. Vincenzo, was gonna teach the old Mick a lesson he'd never forget."

"Did he say how or when?"

"Soon, baby! Soon. Josie said this guy always gets a hard-on just before he pulls a job. You know, it's like it excites him or something to think of killing people. He's a button man for the mob, if you know what I mean. It's his job to kill people for the family."

Duffy's canny mind had been calculating the possibilities ever since he'd left her half an hour before to check back at the office for a suitable weapon. If Mulvaney was the target, when would they strike? They would know his custom of always being surrounded by others, they would know that Duffy was his constant shadow. Mulvaney would be pretty hard to get to, unless they resorted to a bomb or an armed surprise attack, but that was unlike them; they were stealthier than that.

If Tom was the target, it would be easier for them. He tended to disregard Duffy's admonitions and had no compunction about walking unguarded through the streets. "They won't come after me, Frank," he said more than once to Duffy's exasperated warnings. "I'm too big for them, I have the psychological advantage," and he would laugh good-humoredly about it. Yes, Tom would be an easier target, no doubt about it. Of course, he was fairly young and strong and could take care of himself pretty well, if the odds were even. But these little bastards hunted in packs; three or four of them handy with knives, and it wouldn't matter what size you were.

Something about what Mary Lou had told him was bothering Duffy. He couldn't put his finger on it, but something was off kilter, and if Mary Lou was right and the attack was imminent, he'd better find out exactly what was about to happen before he advised Mr. Mulvaney and Tom about the nature of the threats. They trusted him to get the straight story for them, and he wouldn't disappoint them. He'd go back to the whorehouse and see what else he could get out of the girl. He'd already called her to say he was returning.

Duffy eased himself into the woman's room and wordlessly laid the money on her bedstand. There were times when they were together during the day or on her night off, when money didn't change hands, but if he saw her at the house, rules had to be obeyed.

Mary Louise looked frightened, even more agitated than she had been an hour ago, and she looked as if she might have been crying; he thought she must be worried for his safety. She threw her arms around the little carrot-topped Irishman and squeezed him hard for a moment before speaking. "I know you're not here to love me, Frank," she said. "I can tell by your face, you're as worried about your Mr. Mulvaney as I am. I been all twitchy since you left, it's real scary me knowing about it and all."

He nodded. "Did you get any more out of your friend like I told you?"

"I tried to pump Josie, but she's scared, darlin'. She says that bozo'd kill her if he knew she'd ever mentioned what he told her. They'd kill me, too, she said, or maybe throw acid in my face." She said the last with a slight whimper.

"Don't you worry none, Mary Louise, I ain't gonna let nobody throw acid in your sweet little face." He patted the pretty girl as if she were a child. "Did the guy say anything at all you can think of that might give me a clue about whether it's Mr. Mulvaney or Mr. Dalton they're gonna hit?"

Mary Louise moved her face away from Duffy's chest and looked at him with a startled, uncomprehending stare.

"I thought you understood, luv! It isn't just a kill they're after. They want to do something *awful* as an example to other people. I don't know what it would be exactly. Maybe kill the whole family or something. He said they sent one of those letters with the Black Hand on it to Mr. Mulvaney, just this afternoon."

Duffy stared at the girl, his strange unblinking stare. If what she said was true, there mightn't be much time to do anything about it. He wondered why his employer had made no mention of the threatening letter. If Mulvaney was the target, he'd have to find the old man at the Democratic Club, where he'd left him earlier, and escort him to a safer place than home.

Duffy had started for the door when another thought struck him. What if Mulvaney was *not* the target? What if the Black Hand note had been a ruse to throw them all off the track? If Mary Louise was right about Vincenzo's wanting to set an example to people not to fight the mob, maybe they'd do something much *worse* than simply putting out a hit on Mulvaney.

Suddenly, just as if he'd seen it written in a Bible, Duffy knew where they would strike. Those rotten, cowardly bastards could destroy both men at once if they went after Deirdre and the kids.

"Mary Lou," he said finally, his voice strangled by the awful thought that changed everything. "I think I know what they're up to. . . . I think they're after Mr. Dalton's family."

He hurriedly scrawled two numbers on a piece of paper and

pushed it into her hand. "You have to help me, Mary Lou." He said the words urgently. "You have to get to the telephone and call Mr. Mulvaney at the Democratic Club and tell him what I said, and call Mr. Dalton, too. Tell him to lock all the doors and windows and not to let anybody in but me. Understand, Mary Lou! Tell him I'm coming right over. Tell him it's real important!"

She nodded quickly and took the numbers in her hand. He saw that there were tears in her eyes as she kissed him good-bye.

The man stepped out of the closet after Duffy had left the room.

"You did real good, Mary Louise," he said to the distraught girl, who cowered away from his voice. "Now we know exactly where to get him." He smiled maliciously as he opened the door to the next room and gave hasty instructions to another man. She heard him tell his accomplice where Duffy was headed, and she knew with sickening clarity that she had heard her friend's death sentence.

The man returned to her side and spoke again. "You did real good, kid. Now maybe we won't have to mess you up no more." She sobbed by way of an answer and sat down helplessly on the bed. "You did just like I wanted you to. The little Mick'll go straight to Dalton's and we'll nail him before he figures out he's been fingered." He seemed to enjoy the girl's misery.

"You said you'll let my brother go now," she said defiantly through her tears. "You said you won't hurt him."

"Yeah, yeah," said the man with the gun in his belt, "but right now I think I'll have me a little fun with his big sister before I go." His hand was on his belt and he was undoing his pants. Mary Louise looked at him with intense loathing. She'd do anything she had to do to get little Jimmy back safe. The thought of the little boy in the clutches of men like these sent another wave of nausea through her. She thought of poor Frank Duffy as she lay back on the bed. He'd been so good to her, and she'd set him up to be murdered; she couldn't believe this was all happening. Hot, salty tears ran down her cheeks as the man climbed on top of her. She prayed that she wouldn't be sick, God only knew what he'd do to her then.

Duffy left the bordello at a run, jumped into a cab and gave the driver Tom's address, his mind working feverishly about what to do when he'd get there. It was nearly two o'clock in the morning. The killers would probably wait till first light to strike, and he'd be ready for them; thank God for little Mary Louise. Once he'd warned Mr. Dalton and called Mr. Mulvaney, they'd be right as rain. There were plenty of policemen on Diamond Jim's payroll, more than enough to protect the family, if it came to that. The important thing was to get there before the Mafioso did. Tom Dalton didn't carry a gun; Duffy wasn't even sure if he owned one, other than that kept at the office.

Nobody'd ever outfoxed Mr. Mulvaney before; Duffy mused uncomfortably on the implications of such a thing having happened, as the cab raced up Fifth Avenue. Maybe the man was getting on in years; it wasn't like him to underestimate an enemy. Maybe it was getting time for Tom to take over the reins.

The cab ground to a halt in front of the Dalton's limestone house. Duffy alighted from the car, paid the driver, and walked uneasily to the door, looking to the right and left carefully as he did so. As he lifted his hand to the knocker a shape emerged from the bushes in the little garden that flanked the door. Duffy knew Mrs. Dalton tended her flowers with infinite patience; weirdly, he almost told the shape not to damage the roses.

"Drop yer piece on the ground, Duffy, and back away from the door. There's a gun pointed at yer brain, what there is of it." The voice was ugly, deep, and sadistic.

Duffy's impassive stare turned on the gun with its ugly silencer, the feeling of entrapment suddenly encompassing more than just his current predicament. He'd been set up! The realization dawned on him with a dulling finality. Mary Louise had mentioned the Mulvaney family, *knowing* he would head here or to the Mulvaney mansion; doubtless there were men staked out farther up the avenue at the other address as well as here. Mulvaney wasn't the only one who'd been outfoxed; not the only one who had underestimated the enemy. But, by Christ, why Mary Lou? He knew she liked him, maybe even loved him. How had they reached her? The threat of acid in the face? Threats to the little brother she supported? He felt sick to his stomach and mortally afraid. What difference did it make how the betrayal had come. The only question now was how to warn the sleeping family. He was a dead man anyway. One way or the other, they'd never leave him alive to tell the tale.

Duffy said the first line of the Act of Contrition in his head. Then, reaching for his gun in a lightning gesture, he lunged for the shadowy figure in front of him. At least he'd make a racket in his going. He'd warn Tom and save Deirdre and the kids no matter what it cost him; the thought was desperately clear in Duffy's mind when he felt the explosion in the back of his head. The man behind him didn't make a sound behind the huge rhododendron bush, and the silenced bullet contributed only a sickening thud as it shattered bone and tissue, bringing with it permanent oblivion. Somewhere in Duffy's last consciousness was an image of his mother, strangely clear and young.

On the third floor, Thomas Dalton stirred in his sleep and opened his eyes. There had been a sound outside, or had there been? He rose from the bed, trying not to wake Deirdre, who was, as always, sleeping tangled in his arms. He smiled at the slender woman and the little mountain that her belly made in the bed. Only one more month until their third child would be born; he thought his wife had never been as beautiful as during this pregnancy, nor as happy or fulfilled. This was the first pregnancy she'd had in their own comfortable house, without fear or want, and the bloom in her cheeks had pleased him every time he looked at her. He tucked the covers in around Deirdre's sleeping form and tiptoed to the window.

There were men in the street at the far corner, seemingly helping a drunken friend into a car. That must have been what he'd heard. Odd that there should be a drunk on this street at two in the morning; there were no nearby taverns. Perhaps there'd been a party at someone's home.

The car moved slowly off in the other direction, leaving Tom staring down into an empty street. He couldn't shake the feeling of uneasiness that had been with him for the past few days. This Vincenzo business was really beginning to get on his nerves. It was the first time he and Mulvaney had violently disagreed about a course of action.

Maybe it was just sour grapes that were making him feel so agitated. His father-in-law had every right to outvote him when it came down to the wire. He just couldn't believe the Italians would be so easily beaten. The victory had been too simple, it just didn't feel right that they'd accept such a frontal attack on their authority without reprisal. He'd have to remember to get Duffy to do some nosing around in the morning.

He moved away from the window and let himself back in under the covers, debating about waking his wife. She looked so sweet and tender lying there under the thick down comforter, and he suddenly wanted her with a strange urgency. He felt himself harden against the warmth of her body and had to restrain the desire to insinuate himself between her soft, slender thighs. But at more than eight months of pregnancy, he knew it was probably not a wise thing to do. The doctor had told him that sexual relations in the last month of pregnancy could pose a danger to both mother and baby, so with a resolute sigh he turned over on his stomach and attempted to go back to sleep.

63

Tom's uneasiness about the threats for Mulvaney's safety plagued him. He had tried to talk to Jim about it first thing in the morning, but the old man had brushed the notion of danger aside contemptuously.

"They haven't got the balls to lay a glove on us, lad. There's not a man jack among them that would confront either one of us, mark my words. Besides, we have the bodyguards and Duffy. Can't spend your life worrying like an adolescent girl about being molested on the street."

The hairs on the back of Tom's neck were prickly. Something was wrong. Ever since he'd awakened in the middle of last night, he'd felt agitated. And he hadn't been able to find Duffy this morning. Stranger still, he had tried to call his own home a dozen times by telephone, but there had been no answer. Deirdre and the children might be out, but surely the servants would be there. Of course, the new phone exchange often didn't work and the whole telephone system was unreliable, but a growing sense of foreboding was making him tense with anxiety. He'd have to set his mind at ease or he'd never get any work done.

He swung his long legs off the leather desk chair and strode silently to the paneled door of his office. Barely glancing at the ledgers and briefs that cluttered the place, which generally held his undivided attention from eight A.M. till six P.M. or beyond, he turned his key in the lock and walked determinedly into the outer office.

"Delaney." He spoke softly to the freckle-faced young clerk nearest the door. "I'm going home for lunch. Don't let anyone into my office while I'm gone. Use a gun if you must, to keep visitors out. I have a bad feeling about today. And see if you can find Duffy for me, will you? Have him call me at my home."

The young Irish face looked startled by the seriousness of Tom's demeanor, but he nodded intelligently and opened the drawer of his writing desk to show his employer the pistol he kept there.

"Good man," Tom murmured absentmindedly, and hurried from the old building, apprehension growing with each long stride. In all the time he had been married, in nearly eight years, he had never once been home at noon, but there was no question that he must go there today. He signaled to the driver waiting at the curb, leaped into the shiny brougham, and shouted that he was to be taken home and no time to spare.

"Whatever you say, Mr. Dalton, sir. These horses won't lose no time for you if I can help it," said the driver, and they clattered over the cobblestones in the direction of the Dalton home on Fifth Avenue.

Tom's mind was racing. The pieces were beginning to fall into place. Why in God's name hadn't it occurred to him that Jim was right as usual in his calculation, but this time wrong in his conclusion? Of course they wouldn't strike at Tom or Diamond Jim! They'd strike at Deirdre and the children. Through them they could destroy both men in one swift gesture. Suddenly there was not the slightest doubt in his pounding heart that it had already happened. Please God, don't let them get hurt; over and over he prayed the same prayer silently, teeth clenched, fist gripping the side of the carriage with the strength of intense anxiety.

Barely waiting for the horse and carriage to rattle to a stop at his own door, he jumped to the street as the driver slowed the horses; he raced into the silent house.

Mary O'Toole, their round little housekeeper, lay in a dark-stained puddle on the living room floor. Her head was oddly askew. There was a scarlet gash on the side of her throat. Four-and-a-half-year-old Seamus was pulling at her cheek, trying vainly to awaken her, crying at the top of his lungs. Six-and-a-half-year-old Riordan, always the self-possessed, was sitting tear-stained and dazed on the floor at her feet. His little face was bruised and his arm was scratched. He had been part of a struggle.

Tom stood for a stricken moment in the doorway, worst fears clutching with painful fingers at his stomach. "Where's your mother, son?" he rasped hoarsely as he gathered the two little boys into his huge arms. "What has happened to you, tell me everything, lads, so I can find your mother."

The youngest child began sobbing anew, gasping against his father's shirt noisily. The older one struggled to speak.

"Some men came, Father. They were big and ugly and they struck Nana when she tried to keep them out. She called out to Mama to run away and they hurt her with a knife and she fell down." Tom tried to listen to the tortured sound of his son's little voice, desperate to hear the details, terrified of what might come next, wanting to scream out for his Deirdre.

"Hurry, son, tell me everything you can remember. What did they do with your mommy?"

The boy's face was drained of all color, his eyes wide with terrifying remembrance. "They took her, Da. They pushed her and made her cry when she tried to come to us, and then they hit her on the head and she fell down. I tried to help her, Da, I hit the big man and I kicked him a lot, but they were too strong and I couldn't save her." Tears ran down the child's sorrowful face. Tom clutched the little dark head to his own chest and kissed his son's soft hair.

"It's all right, Rory, you did all you could. That's all anyone can ever ask of a man. I know it was awful for you, son, but you must gather all your courage now, if we are to find your mother. Can you help me, Rory? Can you listen very carefully and do just as I say?"

The youngster sobbed into Tom's shirt, and nodded his head.

"Run next door and find Mrs. Devlin or her maid, and get her in here to take care of Nana and Seamus. We'll send my coachman for your grandfather. Can you do that, Rory? So I can go and find your mother?"

"Yes, Da. I can do it."

"You're a brave boy, son, your mother will be proud of you." Tom set his son down on the floor and raced from the house. He shouted to the astonished driver, "Bring Mr. Mulvaney here in ten minutes, if you must kill the horses to do it, man! Tell him they've taken Mrs. Dalton."

There was no doubt in his mind where they would have taken her. She would be in one of the old abandoned warehouses, as a sign of reprisal. They were like that. They forgot nothing.

Sweet Jesus, don't let them kill her; the thought raced again and again through his brain. It was all suddenly so clear to him. Why had he not seen it before? They mean to force us to give in, and they can't do that with a dead hostage; he tried to calm himself with the logic of it. He told himself repeatedly that they wouldn't harm her, but the shrieking in his ears wouldn't be quieted. The shrill, weird premonition of disaster was growing stronger. What he would do when he got to the Vincenzo warehouses he didn't know, but where he would find his abducted wife, and who had taken her, was unquestionable.

Deirdre Dalton was tied hand and foot, and she was gagged painfully. Her hugely swollen belly ballooned out over her hobbled knees as she huddled quietly on the floor in a corner of the icy, barren warehouse room. She was trying very hard to keep her self-control.

The shock of the abduction, the terror for her children's safety, the grim reality of her husband's plight in trying to find her—even these grave horrors were secondary now in her woman's mind, for with growing clarity she knew that the baby was coming.

"Sweet Mother of God," she had prayed desperately, "don't let the baby come yet, it's a month early and will surely die here." But it had become apparent that her prayer would not be answered, and so in a primal ritual known only to all women, through all ages, she began to gather her strength for the ordeal ahead. Knowing that she must not scatter her resources at such a moment, she strove to blot out the terror of her situation and the improbability of rescue. She would not let herself think of the rat she saw sitting under the table staring at her with beady black eyes and licking his whiskers over yellow teeth. She would think only of the impatient child she carried beneath her heart, trying to thrust itself so inopportunely into the world. My baby's strong and determined, she told herself grimly, in an effort to convince herself of her child's ability to survive.

The men had torn her clothing when they carried her to the waiting delivery wagon, and again when she had been so unceremoniously dragged into the cold gray warehouse, with its squealing vermin and smell of aging must. One of them had pinched her swollen breasts repeatedly, spewing lewd suggestions at her helpless form, and had actually thrust his filthy hand up beneath her skirts before the other one had pushed him roughly away. "We don't fuck with no pregnant women, ya hear me?" He had sounded determined, she remembered gratefully. "They shoulda told us she was gonna have a baby. I don't hold with hurting no woman what's in the family way." And the other man had simply grunted like the animal he was and lumbered over to the cot in the corner, where he lay staring licentiously at the helpless woman on the floor.

She had stopped thinking about him, of course, when her water had broken—a trickle at first and then the telltale gush of warm fluid, soaking her petticoats and making life even more miserable than it had been before. She was concentrating on timing the pains, still far apart, thank God, and not yet severe. Soon she would have to tell her captors what was happening, but instinct kept her silent, for with their obviously limited intelligence she could not imagine how they would respond. They might kill her outright, she reasoned, to avoid the problem of having to cope with her plight. She strug-

gled to quiet her own terror, as if by slowing her racing heartbeat
she could slow her labor, too. The time wore on as an endless
struggle against the inevitable.

"Hey, Richie, there's something wrong with the woman," said
the animal after a while. "I been watching her, and she's all covered
with sweat." He looked puzzled.

The other jailer looked alert for the first time. "Oh my God,
Vince. What if she's having the baby? What'll the boss say? I don't
know nothing about women having babies."

"Listen, lady, you can't have no baby here, ya hear me?" The
man called Richie sounded almost kindly, and she tried to smile at
him, for he had removed her gag a while before, but a pain was
tugging at her back and belly, and her fear was getting harder to
hold at bay.

"I think you had better untie me, sir," she ventured when the
pain had passed. "I will help myself, if you can get me some water
and blankets."

"We don't have no water or blankets, lady. We're just supposed
to keep you here till your husband comes, then the boss'll tell us
what to do wit yer both. He didn't tell us nothing about you having
no baby." He sounded plaintive, pitiful, as if he were pleading for
her to understand. "Don't untie her," the man named Vince called
in a harsh, cruel voice. "She's probably only faking anyways."

"She can't do nothin' to us, Vince," said the other. "She can't
run away or nothing, and having a baby hurts a woman."

"You idiot, what's the difference. They'll both be dead by nightfall anyways. You want the boss to come in here and find her
untied? And what happens if her husband comes and she helps him.
He's a big galoot, ya know. He ain't gonna be easy to handle."

Deirdre's heart was pounding in her throat again. They planned to
kill her and Tom. This could not be happening to them.

"I'm gonna untie her, Vince. I ain't havin' no pregnant woman
and little baby on my conscience," and the larger lumbering man
walked toward the suffering woman, a longshoreman's knife in his
big hands, a look of determined compassion in his huge, ugly face.
The other body hurtled at him across the floor. Deirdre watched in
horror as they fell to the concrete a few feet from her body, slashing
at each other with their fists and knives, tearing at each other with an
animal ferocity.

"No, no, please," she screamed over and over as they tumbled
and rolled and rose and tumbled again, but her voice was drowned

by the sounds of fighting, the grunted curses, and the awful thudding and tearing. And then suddenly they were still. Vince astride Richie. He had slashed the prone man's throat. Blood was everywhere, but the sobbing, writhing girl was long past caring.

The man rose from his dead partner's body and stood over her.

"Untie my legs, sir, I beg of you." She rasped out the words between lips bitten raw with fear and pain. "My baby is coming, have pity on us."

"You weren't so keen on having me touch yer precious body a while ago, were you, lady? You can wait for that fine husband of yours to untie you, since you like his attentions so much better than mine. I'm getting the hell outa this place, before the boss gets here. If you live long enough, tell him I didn't much like the partner he picked for me." His cruel laugh rattled against the stone walls in an ugly echo, and he walked quickly from the room. She heard his footsteps resounding on the stone of the warehouse floor, and he was gone.

Desperate beyond endurance, all the tormented woman could think of was getting her legs untied. She edged her pain-racked body to the dead man's, for she had seen the glint of his knife beneath him when he fell. Pushing at his leaden body with her small feet, every motion an unbearable agony, she managed to move the dead weight of the man enough to free the knife blade, fortunately wedged beneath him, blade out. She turned her own form and sawed through the rope that ringed her ankles. The pain of the blood rushing back into her numbed feet was matched by the crescendo of another contraction that swept through and over her. When it had passed, she inched her way up toward the knife, thanking God silently they had tied her hands in front of her and not behind, and laboriously sawed through the bonds around her chafed and discolored wrists.

Deirdre lay back on the cold, hard concrete floor and allowed the flood of relief at being freed to sweep sweetly over her mind and body. She could cope with the pains now. If only the boss, whoever he might be, didn't come, she would survive this horror. Clutching the table for support, she tried to raise her imbalanced body upright. Unable to do so, she crept toward the cot against the wall, every inch an agony, for the child was very close to coming.

"Holy Mary Mother of God, pray for us sinners," she shouted childlike, over and over in her head, mother calling to mother, when the pains swept her. "Tom, my dearest. Tom, my husband, come to me. I need you so much.'' The words formed themselves sound-lessly in her brain. She was afraid to scream for fear someone of the gang of hoodlums might be near at hand in this loathsome place, and when she finally did cry out, the sound bounced noisily off the stone walls and echoed and reechoed in a wailing ricochet of pain.

On the cot at last, she laboriously cut through the fabric of her skirt with the knife she had wrested from the corpse once her hands were free. She would need it to cut the cord. Make me strong, Mary, she prayed silently over and over. Don't let me faint or my baby will die.

The tiny, beet-red infant pushed its way into the world, unmindful of the squalid surroundings or the dead man. Deirdre tied the slippery cord near the baby's body and tried to do the same on her own body's side, but the blood gushing through it made her fingers slip, and the pain that gripped her belly when she bent to the task was too terrible. Despairing, she tied a piece of ribbon from her dress around it, and wrapping the tiny girl child in a scrap of wool and petticoat, she cradled her daughter to her breast and ceased to try. Tom would come soon and make everything all right. He would find the little girl, and he would save her.

The hot, wet puddle between Deirdre's young legs began to widen, but it mattered very little to her now, lost as she was in the sweet baby in her arms, there in the safety of her own mind. She was quietly adrift on a wide, soft river that seemed strangely familiar. She didn't hurt so much anymore, and she was warmer, too. "Tom, my dearest husband, I love you. Remember me.'' She said it, or she thought it, at the end, and the image of the infinite tenderness of his arms around her made her smile.

The warehouse was cold, dank, and forbidding. He had been through eight of the dockside warehouses belonging to Vincenzo before he found the one where Deirdre and the frail little life that was his daughter lay.

The immense damp interior space chilled him to the bone, and he knew in his heart he had come to the end of his quest. If only he had brought help, it wouldn't have taken so long to find her, he cursed himself. If only he had gone home when the apprehension had begun this morning, he might have stopped them; if only he had thought to have his house guarded; if only it had occurred to him that Deirdre was the weak link in the protective chain he and Mulvaney had so carefully constructed.

The tiniest sound broke the silence of the empty warehouse. The squeaky cry of a newborn filled his mind with unbearable anguish, for there could be no reason for an infant to be in this godforsaken place, but one. Tom ran toward the eerie, misplaced sound, all thought of care or stealth gone from his mind.

Deirdre Mulvaney Dalton lay on the small dirty cot in the corner of the gray, windowless room, her body as gray as the stone around her. The movement on the cot was not hers, but that of the tiny whimpering red mite that lay at her breast. Tom stood transfixed in the doorway. The dead man on the floor, the overturned furniture, the trail of blood and fluid on the stone, the sliced ropes; all of what had happened was clear in one overwhelming instant. It was beyond believing.

Rushing to the blood-soaked body of his wife, he gathered her and the tiny child into his arms and crushed the dead girl and the frail infant to his own broad body with an anguished sound, as if by force of will to breathe life back into the pale gray rag doll that just a few hours ago had been his loving, laughing, living wife. Rocking her back and forth, murmuring into her deafened ear, kissing her face and hands, covering her sunken naked belly with his own body, he held them to him in an ancient ritual of anguished farewell. The infant ceased its squeaking as the warmth of his huge body and the motion of the rocking made her world seem safe. It was thus that Diamond Jim Mulvaney found them, after a time . . . the body of his daughter, the sleeping infant grandchild, and the son-in-law he had come to love so well.

"Get back! Stay away!" he shouted hoarsely to the men who were crowding into the doorway behind him, for he, like Tom, had taken in the grisly reality of the scene in an instant. He laid his hand on the young man's bowed shoulders and, in a tear-choked voice, said quietly, "It's time to take them home, son. They shouldn't be in this terrible place any longer."

Tom looked up at him unseeing, and after a moment nodded his assent. As Jim watched with tear-filled eyes, the younger man laid the body of his wife tenderly on the bed and kissed her. He placed the fragile infant in its grandfather's hefty arms, and started wordlessly for the door.

"Where are you going, lad?" Jim asked the question, although he knew the answer.

"To kill the bastards." The reply hung in the air, but Tom was gone. Much later, when Diamond Jim forced himself to remember the scene, it occurred to him that Tom Dalton had also died that day, in the Vincenzo warehouse. For the lad he and his daughter both had loved did not survive the events of that fearful day and night. The man who returned to him the following morning had been gravely changed.

Thomas Dalton killed three men that night, Vincenzo and both his bodyguards, he later learned. The police, having looked at the body of the lovely Mrs. Dalton, whom they had often seen before, they being largely on Diamond Jim's payroll, never questioned the acts of revenge. But Tom, tender and poetic, loving and strong, whose measure Jim had once taken in his living room on a long-ago night, no longer existed.

64

Tom sat in the armchair every night as if he, too, were dead. The funeral had passed him by. It was impossible that Deirdre was gone. If he sat there long enough, he would hear her gentle footfall on the stair outside his study; her voice would ring again through the house, calling to the children; he would feel the touch of her warm, soft breasts as she leaned over his chair to kiss him. The hideous stillness of the house would be banished with her musical laughter.

Diamond Jim, despite his own sorrows, had handled everything— the ghastly wake where Deirdre's beautiful body had lain as if sleeping in an ice-cold coffin in the living room of their home for three unbearable days and nights. Tom had slept near the coffin through each of the nights in a lonely vigil, like one remembered from his far-distant past.

Each night, when the well-wishers had dwindled and left, when Diamond Jim himself had gone to the coffin to kiss his daughter good night and knelt beside it to say a prayer before going home to his own house where he had, in a magnanimous gesture, decided to wake the body of Frank Duffy—each night, Tom would sit beside the body of his wife and talk to her.

How could anyone ever understand how much there was that had been left unsaid? How much of plans unfinished, questions unasked, love unspoken. A lifetime of loving conversations, and only three desperate nights in which to hold them.

"Daddy," Riordan had begged him the first day of the wake, "don't let them take me away from Mama." But in his own oblivion, Tom had barely heard his son's request. It was best that someone take the children away till the funeral was over, he said. He had no time to speak with them now; no time for anything but grief.

Besides, it was excruciating even to look at his children. They were so like their mother; they looked like Deirdre, sounded like her, mirrored her graceful mannerisms in a tiny duplication. He found himself somehow shredded by their very being, found their comapny an almost unbearable agony.

Later, he told himself . . . later he would be able to cope with them. Now he needed to be with his wife. Needed to engrave every memory in stone; to remember every detail of her, of their life together; every nuance of her face and body must become part of him. It was an all-consuming task.

Fifteen days after Deirdre's and Duffy's funerals, an expensive-looking automobile pulled up unexpectedly outside the Dalton house. An armed guard answered the doorbell's insistent ring, along with the maid, for neither Mulvaney nor Dalton intended any more harm to come to their beleaguered family. Tom had killed a Mafia *padrone*, it was only reasonable to assume that there would be an attempt to exact retribution. M & D had hired a formidable army of guards to watch the children.

A small, muscular gray-haired man, flanked by two hefty bodyguards, stood quietly in the doorway and asked to speak with Mr. Dalton. It was an urgent matter, he said. His name was Mr. Enzio Narducci, and he represented the Five Families. The armed guard closed and locked the heavy door, not inviting the visitors in, and ran to the library to alert his employer. He called to the man who patrolled the second floor, where the children slept, as he went. Tom had been seated in the library as usual, holding a book in his lap without reading it.

The announcement of Don Enzio startled him from his reverie. Narducci was Vincenzo's successor. Mulvaney's friends on the police force had tipped him off that a new leader had moved into the vacant chieftainship; they had also told him to beware. The new man was cut of considerably different cloth than Vincenzo. Articulate, educated, and far more Americanized than his predecessor, Narducci was more polished than Vincenzo, but no less ruthless. Tom picked up the phone deliberately, thankful that it worked on first try; he called his father-in-law, and told him to alert the police. Then he instructed the guard to ask the man in.

Narducci had a powerful presence, although he was not tall; a bull-like body, and the stern face of one who brooks no assault on his authority, made the man appear larger than he was. The Mafioso entered the small paneled study, letting his glance wander over the book-lined walls before it came to rest on Tom, standing immobile and exuding hostility. Then he offered his hand to Tom, who refused it. Narducci accepted the rebuke without acknowledging it.

"I am Enzio Narducci, Mr. Dalton," he said in a sonorous voice. "I am here on family business."

"I know who you are, Don Enzio," replied Tom, as calmly as he could. "And whatever your business, I must warn you that my father-in-law and the police will be here shortly."

"They will not be necessary to us, Mr. Dalton," said the visitor. "Our business is with each other—man to man. I am here on a matter of honor." There was a strong Sicilian inflection to the man's intonation, but he was articulate. Tom eyed the older man with distaste.

"I will waste no words with you," said Narducci with confidence. "There has been a quarrel between my family and yours, Mr. Dalton. Deaths have resulted; debts have been incurred. They must be dealt with." He paused for a moment, looking Tom steadily in the eye. "You do not know our ways, Mr. Dalton. But I must tell you that my predecessor broke a rule of my family, although he did not set out to do so. He caused a woman, who was with child, to be harmed. This is not our way. Never should such a thing have happened! Our honor is washed away by the blood of this woman, your wife. It must be restored." Enzio seemed genuinely agitated by the statement; Tom looked at the man without understanding. He had been certain they had come to exact payment.

"You have avenged yourself upon the man who wronged you, Mr. Dalton; this is as it should be. We have seen to it that the man who was in the warehouse with your wife has paid the full price for his disobedience to orders. You see, he was not to have harmed your wife, Mr. Dalton. She was merely to have been the bait to lure you into a trap." Narducci's voice was firm. "In our world, Mr. Dalton, men do not avenge themselves on women and children. Men deal with men. *Omertà*—it is our law. If you have feared for your children, do not do so."

The older man watched the younger carefully as he spoke, as if anxious to make sure that he understood.

"I have come to you tonight to say that a debt has been incurred. And to tell you that you may rest assured it will be paid." His voice was deadly. "By us, Mr. Dalton . . . one day when you least expect it to be paid . . . we will clean the slate. We may be enemies in business now, as we were before, but until the moment comes when we can recover our honor, the debt remains." The man stood a moment, looking pointedly into Tom's eyes as if to be certain that he had understood. Then he turned to leave, and Tom was aware of the immense dignity Narducci exuded as he walked toward the door.

"Whatever you choose to do in the interest of your honor, Don Enzio," Tom called after him bitterly, and with the infinite sorrow of the past two weeks in his voice, "you cannot give me back my wife."

The man turned and looked at the younger one, with what seemed to be sadness in his strong, dark face. "No," he said, almost gently. "That we cannot do." He turned and walked from the study, flanked by his huge bodyguards, who seemed somehow dwarfed by him.

Tom, bewildered by the conversation, followed them. As they reached the door Mulvaney and six burly uniformed policemen burst into the foyer. Tom raised his hand, as if to stay them. "It's all right, Jim. Don Enzio is just leaving." He signaled to his father-in-law with his eyes to wait for an explanation, and then, motioning the angry-looking policemen to the side, let the Mafioso out of his house.

Part Six

RIORDAN

SEAMUS

MAEVE

When a man marries a wife,
he marries his children.
                    —*Old Irish Proverb*

65

"It's the strangest thing in the world to watch, Billy, but the lad hasn't an iota of talent where fathering is concerned." Mulvaney sat in Billy's parlor with a glass in one hand and a cigar in the other.

"What does he do wrong?" Billy asked the question with genuine concern. Her heart ached for Tom and for his children, but now that Deirdre was gone, she felt it improper to visit them. Deirdre's death had left a huge gap in her own life as well as in theirs, for she had lost both her friend and her adopted family.

"It's what he *doesn't* do that's worse, Billy. He barely gives them the time of day. Leaves every bit of their lives to the housekeeper. She's kindly enough, but she's not family."

Billy looked thoughtful for a moment, then said, "I think they remind him too much of her, Jim. Too much of the past that he can't bear to think on."

"Um," grunted Mulvaney begrudgingly. "There's more to it than that, I'd wager. Deirdre used to tell me he didn't get close to the children because he was afraid of losing them or some such folderol. Seems he lost everyone he loved when he was a boy and never got over it." He snorted again. "As if anybody in this world had a happy childhood!" he said derisively.

"You seem down on him tonight, Jim. What's really troubling you?" Billy walked to his chair and perched herself on the arm.

"I'm growing old, Billy. Tom runs most everything now—with a little help from the three old geezers, I might say, but the truth is, he can handle most of it without Tierney, O'Reilly, or me."

"And he's good at it. Doesn't have my flair for the improbable gesture, or Tierney's finagling or O'Reilly's gift for numbers, but somehow he's got enough of everything to make it all work out just fine. And God knows he thinks about nothing else since Deirdre's death."

"Then why the long face?"

"Because the children are sprouting without a mother or a father. Seamus hasn't a thought in his head I can discern, Maeve's as fragile and fey as a fairy, and Riordan nurses a grudge against his father that's a monument for one so young."

"Have you tried to talk to Tom about it?"

"I have, and with as much success as you could engrave on the head of a pin!"

"Should I try, then?"

He cocked his eyebrow at the smiling face close to his own.

"You wouldn't be having designs on the lad, now, would you, lass?"

She laughed her low throaty laugh, and moved from the arm of the chair to his lap.

"Now *there's* a good sign that you're not as old as you pretend to be, Jim Mulvaney. You're jealous!"

He chuckled, too, and wrapped his arms around the beautiful woman who was his friend.

"What say we go to bed and find out how I'm faring for my age?"

They both stood up and hugged. Billy was considerably taller than her mentor. They were a good combination, after all was said and done, she thought as she loosened her satin dressing gown on the way to bed. Tom Dalton was an idle dream, but Jim Mulvaney was a good and faithful friend.

Mary Martin sat in the rocking chair on the wide veranda of the nursing home and tried to concentrate. It was so very hard to keep her thoughts in order. The doctor had told her that she must be in touch with reality before she could ever leave this place. But there were so *many* realities in her head. For a very long time, of course, there had been nothing, then the tiny pinpoints of the truth *they* had in mind for her had begun to break through. The truth she didn't want; the reality that meant her life was over.

She would concentrate very hard on getting her thoughts straight before she saw the doctor again. She was beginning to feel restless behind the numbness. Besides, if it got too painful, she could retreat again behind the blessed curtain of forgetfulness. She still remembered how to go there.

Mulvaney poured the last of the brandy into the crystal snifter and leaned back into the leather comfort of his favorite wing chair. Hoisting his gouty leg painfully onto the footrest, he stared thoughtfully at his son-in-law, who sat reading quietly on the other side of the fireplace.

Mulvaney, who had been suffering increasingly from a variety of the ailments that plague the aging, had allowed Tom to talk him into staying at the Dalton household during his recovery from his latest illness. At first he had said no unequivocally, on the assumption that no young man needs an older one to interfere with his comings and goings. But he had finally relented when Billy had added her urging to Tom's.

Now he was glad he had done so, for his residence in the Dalton household provided him a chance to study the lad at close quarters, as he hadn't been able to do since Deirdre's death. He'd had an opportunity to see just how lonely a man his son-in-law had grown to be.

Tom had nobody. He was not even close to his children, that was easy to see. Jim doubted that a man like his son-in-law could be celibate, and yet it was apparent that womanizing would never be one of Tom Dalton's vices. He worked and read prodigiously, but both were fairly solitary enterprises.

Tom looked up to find himself under scrutiny, and he chuckled as he put down the book he'd been reading, to acknowledge Jim's interest. "You've been watching me on and off now for three solid hours, Jim. Is there something on your mind, or did I spill soup on my shirt at dinner?"

Jim laughed aloud. "Not at all, my boy. Your table manners were a model of decorum. If you must know, I've been contemplating making you a special gift."

"And why would that be, might I ask?"

"Because I'm right fond of you, lad, and because I'm growing old."

Tom frowned at his father-in-law's reference to age; he knew the doctor's prognosis hadn't been good, for when Jim had been told he must stop smoking and drinking in order to be healthy, he'd replied that such health as that wasn't worth going out of your way for.

"Are you feeling ill again, Jim?"

"Far from it, lad. I'm feeling grand, for I've decided to make a magnanimous gesture and it always pleases me to see evidence of what a fine fellow I am." He chuckled again merrily, and Tom smiled.

He liked having Jim in the house with him. He liked the comfort and the continuity of it.

Jim hoisted himself with some difficulty out of his chair. "I'm off to Miss Billy's, my boy. Don't expect me home before the wee small hours."

"It's a good thing the children are in bed, then," Tom said with amusement. "Or you'd be a bad example to them."

Tom was increasingly intrigued by Mulvaney's lust for life; he suspected there was little of sexuality in the old man's relationship with Billy these days, although with a man like Mulvaney you could never be sure.

Diamond Jim took the little elevator up to Billy's apartment on the house's third floor. He was grateful that she'd had it recently installed; he suspected she'd done so because he could no longer navigate the stairs, but of course neither of them would ever acknowledge such a courtesy to infirmity.

Billy greeted him at the door in a peach-colored satin dressing gown that shimmered sensuously in the fireglow from the marble-manteled hearth. She had been his finest investment, without a doubt.

"What brings you here so late, my friend?" She greeted him with a kiss and a warm smile.

"A mighty and magnanimous thought occurred to me this evening, my girl, and I'm here to share it with you." She hadn't heard him sound so expansive and so pleased with himself in months.

"Can't wait to hear," she responded interestedly, helping him remove his coat and jacket, and helping him ease his round arms into the velvet smoking jacket she'd bought for him in Europe.

Billy settled Jim down into his favorite armchair, handed him a Havana cigar, and waited for the story to be told.

"I've been watching the lad, Billy. He's the goddamnedest loneliest man I've ever encountered.

"He works, he thinks, and he reads. I guess he goes with a woman from time to time, I really don't know what he does about his needs. He thinks about Deirdre still, I do know that. I've found him standing staring at her picture in the library on more than one occasion. So . . ." He fixed his most convincing gaze on her and announced, "I've decided that what he needs is *you*."

Billy looked up, startled, and then she laughed.

"So you think you own me so completely you can bequeath me in your will like a silver teapot or a piece of M & D?" Her voice was intended to sound miffed, but she knew he meant to give her what he thought she wanted most.

"I do not!" he replied emphatically. "Indeed I do not. But two things occurred to me tonight, Billy, and I decided to tell you both of them forthwith. One, is that you've been more important to me all my life than I ever let on to you. Now, I know in my heart, I suppose, that you know all this . . . in fact, that you know most everything . . . but nonetheless it bears saying, so I'm saying it.

"The second thing is, I've always known you had a warm spot in your heart for the lad. God knows you'd have to be made of stone not to cotton to a man that looks like that, and I've seen no evidence that you're made of stone." He raised his furry eyebrow at her for emphasis.

"But I've always gone out of my way to make it clear to you that I was jealous of him, and that you were to have no part of him." He paused, as if trying to assemble his thoughts.

"What I'm trying to say is this, Billy. I'm not going to last much longer. No, no, now, I want no protestations! Tonight I just want you to listen to me and indulge an old man's fancy. When I'm gone, if the lad hasn't the good sense God gave him, and if he doesn't come to you of his own volition, I'd like to suggest to you that you go to him!"

Billy looked at Jim in wonder. Could he really be feeling so ill that he felt impelled to make this strange bequest?

"I know I don't own you, Billy, my girl. If you promise not to repeat it to a soul, I'll tell you I've always known it. Much as it amused me to play our little game.

"But here's the long and short of it: He needs you, because he's adrift and you'll be his anchor. And you'll need him because when I'm gone you'll be alone in the world for the first time since you were sixteen years of age. You'll need a protector, Billy, and he'll be the best there could be . . . ." Diamond Jim stopped speaking, and the only sound in the room was the crackling of the logs in the fireplace.

Billy felt a medley of emotions—a vague annoyance at being thought of as a piece of property to be bequeathed in however gentle a fashion, a genuine pleasure at the generosity that had prompted the bequest, and a warm, soft glow at the recognition of the love that Jim obviously felt for both of them.

She reached up and wiped the wetness from her cheeks before replying. "We shall see, my old friend, we shall see about all of that when the time comes." But he knew she understood his gesture. And they smiled at each other, the smile of those who know each other's secrets and love each other still.

66

Mary steadied herself against the brass bedstand and lowered herself gingerly onto the crisp cotton hospital sheets.

The little whitewashed room was pleasant enough, far enough away from her burdens so that she could try to heal. It was important to her now, that she heal.

She looked around her in the sunny room with its meager allotment of furniture; it was not so very different, it occurred to her, from the room she had fled in Tuxedo Park, so very long ago. The thought made her smile ruefully; in that little room she had made the decision to keep her secret . . . in this room she had learned how to be free of that secret's legacy.

Four years it had taken her to learn to be free. Four years of coming back, of climbing the sheer sides of the abyss, toward sanity. And she was sane again; sane and strong enough to go home. Or if not home, strong enough to go *somewhere*.

Mary walked to the window and looked out on the parklike setting of the hospital. She felt peaceful in the safety of its isolation, but lately she had also been feeling that it was no longer a large enough world for her. The doctor said that was a hopeful sign.

She wanted to return to the real world, to the world where people loved and hated, lived, worked, died. She wanted to feel again, to love again, to be part of a family.

Mary sighed at the thought of her family. They would all be grown now; all her children would be adults when she rejoined their world. She wondered if they would want to take her back.

Thaddeus Martin was a lonely man. His children were grown and beginning to forge lives of their own, the store was an all-consuming task for as many hours as he could manage to stay there—but he was a lonely man.

He let himself into the quiet house and shrugged off his heavy coat. The servants were asleep now, and he didn't relish the idea of waking them. So he hung the coat carefully in the hall closet, and turning on the lights as he went, he headed for the kitchen and a comforting cup of tea. For the first few lonely nights—they seemed so long ago now, thank the Lord—he had come home from the store at eleven and had drunk himself into a fitful sleep. After three such lonely drinking bouts and their ensuing headaches and morning incompetency, he had deliberately turned away from the chemical crutch and each evening since, on returning home, he had made himself a pot of tea for comfort.

Thaddeus took the little pitcher of milk from the icebox, the sugar bowl from the cabinet, placed them beside the china teapot, cup, and saucer on a small tray the cook had left out for him, and carried them up to his bedroom. He wondered, as he had every night for years, if his house would ever be a home again.

The doctors said Mary was getting better; her memory had almost completely returned now, and that was a promising sign. But somehow he begrudged her the memories of the time before him; begrudged her remembrance of the shadow-man who had been so rich and handsome and beloved. In truth, he begrudged her the memory of anything that had pertained to the guilty secret that had robbed him of his lovely wife.

And she had been so lovely, his Mary. In the beginning he had hated her for the ruin of his dreams, for her deceit, for the love she had withheld from him. Worst of all, his anger had obliterated all the happy memories they'd shared; remembrances of building a life together, of loving children, of sharing a dream that had begun to come true.

But eventually his memories, like hers, had begun to seep back. He could sometimes now, in his mind's eye, see her as she used to sit on the edge of the bed at night, demurely brushing her beautiful long hair and plaiting it for sleep. He could see her lovely white body, tall and firm and supple even in middle age—and feel the comfort of her warmth in their bed.

Thaddeus drank his tea quietly and wished that Mary would come home so they could try again, and yet even as he wished it he also wanted to tell her of his own suffering. There could be no starting over unless she knew how badly he had been hurt, how dreadfully he had suffered in his effort to forgive her.

The doctor's words rang ominously in his ears: "She may not wish to return to you, Mr. Martin. She has been through torments you could barely imagine, and having survived them, she may not wish to be with anyone who reminds her of her suffering. Your wife may simply wish to begin her life again without you and to take what joy she can from her remaining years."

Ah well, tomorrow he would know her decision.

*   *   *

Thaddeus Martin arrived at the nursing home at seven A.M. He had made it clear to the doctor in charge of Mary's treatment that he must be back in the store by nine. In truth, he was desperately afraid of the encounter and needed the assurance of escape.

In the beginning of his wife's illness, nearly four years before, he had visited the sanatorium often, more out of responsibility than love; it had been very hard to think of love in the wake of what she had done to him. He would come and dutifully sit beside her in her room, knowing that she did not know him as other than a kindly stranger, anger welling in him that she had escaped the resultant chaos of her lies, escaped John's death, escaped his own anger. But of course he knew she had escaped nothing, she had merely postponed her agonies. Finally her doctor had told him that there was no need for these visits until such time as Mary would begin to respond to her surroundings; if indeed she ever would.

So he had dutifully reorganized his household and his life. He had explained to his sons and daughter, who were mostly old enough to understand by the time it had happened, that their mother's mind had become unhinged by their brother's death and that they must continue to be patient and loving and pray for her swift return. He had also buried his youngest son and with him a great many of his dreams.

Thad wrestled with himself whenever he wasn't at the store; when he was there, he threw himself into his business with an increased intensity, an almost impossible feat since it had always consumed him. His fear of the internal wrestling match made him try to prolong his working day as far into the night as was possible, and with the children away at school or college, he had been able to do so, and the years had passed.

Now the time was at hand for decision. He could no longer protect himself from the facts of it by saying, "I'll wait to decide what to do until Mary is rational enough to accept my decision." The doctor had said she was not only rational but nearly ready to go home. With that in mind, just last evening he had decided that if she appeared able to understand him, he must tell her his feelings, all his feelings; he must let her know how her deception had destroyed him as well as her, and how he wasn't at all sure that there could be a future for them together, although he would like to try again.

Mary saw her husband standing with his back to her, at the foot of the veranda steps, looking as if he wished he were anywhere but there. His long hands clutched his hat, and there was agitation and uncertainty in every aspect of his being. She smiled to herself to think how introspective and observant she had become. Four years of nothing but time to think; four years free of the constant demands of children; four years of blood payment for enlightenment.

"You have a right to hate me, Thad." Mary shuddered inadvertently as she said it—the same words she had spoken once before to someone from her past. Her voice behind his shoulder was familiar but changed; lower, frailer, but Mary's all the same.

"Yes." He could think of nothing else to say that would be honest. The sight of his wife as he'd turned to her had totally unnerved him, and all the speeches he had composed fled at her apparition. She was tall and straight as she had been as a young girl, but she was so thin that she seemed to him almost translucent. Her copper hair was almost entirely white, and it was cut short and curled fluffily around her thin face, giving her an ethereal quality like a frail angel.

Mary looked calm, and she seemed nunlike in her composure, despite the animation in her eyes. He felt that if he did not speak, she would probably stand there watching him for the rest of her life, motionless.

"How are you, Mary?" he asked finally, his deep voice hoarse with confusion.

"I'm much better, thank you." She said it as if intent on answering correctly. "It's as if I've been on a very long journey and I'm weary from the hardships of my travels . . . but I'm back now." She motioned him gently to a small bench, and they sat down.

"Do you remember what happened?" he asked tentatively.

"If you mean do I remember our son's death . . . the answer is yes. Most of what followed is still lost inside me somewhere. The doctor says I may never remember it."

"That would be a great blessing."

Thaddeus shifted his tall awkward body uneasily and Mary put her hand on his arm. It had no more substance than a butterfly's landing.

"I want you to know, Thad, how very sorry I am about the deception. How *grievously* sorry." She stopped, as if to say no word could be adequate. "I never really wanted to deceive you, but I became trapped in it somehow and never could find my way out."

"Did you ever love me, Mary?" The evident pain behind the question made Mary search her husband's eyes for understanding. She knew she must tell him only the truth.

"Not in the beginning. Then, I must confess to you, you were simply a way out of my dilemma . . . a means to escape the life of a servant and to start again with some hope for the future."

He winced as she said it; he had known it to be true, but hearing the words somehow made the truth irrevocable.

"But later, as we lived together, had children, built a life, I grew to care deeply for you, Thaddeus. I feel I must say this to you now, because there must not be the slightest shadow of deceit between us when we part."

He looked up quickly as she said it, searching her bright green eyes that now seemed too large, too intense for her fragile face. So she didn't want to return to him at all. She wanted them to part. Of course, he should have known it would be so. It was probably for the best, he had almost come to the same conclusion himself at times. But if that were so, why did he feel like weeping?

Mary waited to see if her husband would refute her offer to leave. Hoping against hope that he would beg her not to go. Ask her to start again. Say that he forgave. Seeing sadly that he did not, she continued.

"I feel that I must say it all, Thad, so that there is nothing left unsaid between us." He nodded, a lump in his throat.

"I grew to love you because you are a good man, honorable and trustworthy. And the more I cared for you, the worse my guilty secret seemed to me. More than once I tried to tell you, but your righteousness always stayed me." He started to interrupt, but she held up her hand.

"Our children always seemed to be more yours than mine. Proper, well-behaved, perfect little people they were—so very like you, Thad. In the beginning I was so frail from sorrow that I had little to give them. Then, later, they seemed somehow not to need me as Tom had. You know they always loved you better than they did me. I suppose I can't blame them for that, but nonetheless it hurt me that it was so." Seeing the pain in his face, she touched his hands, now clasped in his lap, and realized they were shaking.

"But then our last child came, and from the moment he was born, I knew that he was mine. Playful, laughing, adventurous John—I always thought of him as Sean, you know, despite your protests. He was the one who seemed to drain the bitterness from my soul, who made me believe that God had forgiven me my great sin. He looked like Tom, you see. He looked like me, too." She stopped, biting her lip as if to hold in the next words. Finally she said quietly, "When he died, I knew I had been wrong. That God had simply sent him to me so that he could be snatched away—a just punishment for what I had done to Tom and to you.''

"You Catholics have a cruel God, Mary, if you can imagine Him capable of such an act.''

"I couldn't bear it, Thad! The agony, the guilt, the sorrow—the knowledge that I had been the cause of everything . . . it was too hideous to bear. So I went away for a while, I guess. It's very hard to explain. . . .'' She shrugged her shoulders helplessly. "You see, I have been to a place that few people ever return from.''

"And now you must go away again.'' He said it evenly, and she couldn't tell if it was a question or a statement.

"I must make an honest life for myself.''

"I see. And what of our children?''

"They are more yours than mine, Thad, and they're grown now. They'll be all right without me.''

"Is there anything you'll need?''

"My clothes are all too large now. I'll have to have them mended. . . .''

"Money?''

"Tom has said he'll see that I'm taken care of.''

"Then there isn't anything more to say, is there, Mary?''

The middle-aged woman looked at the man to whom she had been married for twenty-seven years and saw him clearly. Bald head with a fringe of pepper-and-salt hair, long, angular body grown more awkward with age, homely hawk-nosed face and such honest eyes. She thought him very beautiful as she said good-bye. She would do him no more harm. That at least was in her power to accomplish. Never, ever would she reproach him, even in thought, for not wanting her back.

Thad kissed her embarrassedly on the cheek, and he could feel the trembling of her body as he touched her in farewell. He stood for a moment, wanting desperately to say something, but it had all been said. She didn't want him anymore, and he would abide by her decision. Never again would he add his own reproach to her burdens.

Clutching his beaver hat, he began the long walk down the winding path to his waiting carriage. It was for the best, of course, that she didn't want to come home. After all, that is what he had decided, too, sometimes, when he'd thought it through; how could there ever be a means of finding their way back from such a betrayal.

He took the handkerchief from his coat and blew his nose hard, the act itself an effort at reality.

But she said she loved me, a small voice inside him murmured, through the cacophony of other voices. She was probably only being kind, the voices argued back. No, she said she was being completely honest. Hah! Honesty, what does she know of honesty? Perhaps more than anyone who has never had to suffer so to achieve it . . . the thought echoed and reechoed in his brain, like a voice resounding in an empty hall.

Suddenly, without knowing he intended to do so, Thaddeus turned and started to run. Toward the nursing home, toward his wife, toward Mary. "Mary! Mary! Mary!" he shouted as he ran, stunned by the unseemly sound and the spectacle he must be making of himself running like a madman.

The woman turned just as she had reached the veranda and was about to enter the house. Never in all her life with Thaddeus had she seen him do anything in the least startling. Through her tears she saw his cranelike body running toward her, angular arms and legs flying, hat clutched absurdly in a hand that was waving to her.

Reaching the porch, panting and oblivious of the people around him, Thad threw his arms around his wife and nearly lifted her from the ground by the strength of his embrace.

"I love you, Mary," he gasped. "I've always loved you. I will not let you go! Whatever has happened is paid for now. We're growing old, Mary! We've spent a lifetime together, you and I. Whatever mistakes we've made, you cannot really want to go! I won't let you go, do you hear me? I won't ever let you go!"

He loved her, he wanted her; despite it all, he didn't want her to leave him. Mary, clinging to her husband, felt the long-closed gates of her heart swing open; creaky, rusted, ancient gates, but open at last to the flood of love that was engulfing her.

"I love you, my dear husband, I love you," Mary Dalton Martin told her husband over and over, and for the first time in her quarter century of marriage, she meant it with every fiber of her heart.

67

"Rum weather for it, Miss Billy, eh?" The leathered little driver, whose business it was to transport Billy where she wanted to go, stretched to his limited height to hold the big black umbrella over the head of his employer, who stood a good twelve inches taller than he.

"Makes no never mind to me, Tim," she said quietly as she settled herself into the carriage's interior and shook the rain from the shoulders of her tailored black coat. She laid the bouquet of flowers on the seat beside her and settled back to watch the rain fall in tiny silver spills down the closed windows to the shiny black door beneath.

Somehow rain and snow always seemed to her the most proper times to go to the cemetery; the gravestones stood lonelier then, more forlorn and more in need of company.

Sunny days, summer days, even lush autumn days with their colorful soft blanket of fallen leaves, made the graveyard peaceful and beautiful, a tranquil garden untroubled by life's passing vicissitudes. But rainy days, snowy days . . . they were the times when those you had loved in life needed company.

There were so many of them now, she thought as the bumpy rattle of the carriage over wet cobblestones, and the isolation of the rain, lulled her into reverie. Her mother and father, all her brothers, Donaher, Deirdre . . . of all her loved and lost, only one had a grave at which tribute could be paid. The rest reposed in potter's field or in the stormy deep. But Deirdre . . . Deirdre had a final resting place to come to. A memorial for them all, it seemed to her.

The carriage clattered to a stop, and Timothy in his soaking slicker held wide the door, struggling again with the unruly umbrella. She smiled softly at his hopeless effort at holding it over her head. Years before, she had scooped him up off the Bowery—the father of one of her girls—and given him a job as a coachman, provided he could stay sober long enough to keep it, she had told him; he had done so, to the best of her knowledge, through all the years. She felt certain he would lie down on the railroad track for her if necessity ever demanded such a sacrifice.

She tied her coat tightly around her, pulled her hood up over her pale blond head, and picking up the bounty of flowers, walked carefully down the narrow path to the double headstone that read:

DEIRDRE MULVANEY DALTON

1883–1911

As a feeble tribute to the value of
all that has been lost in the Wife,
the Beloved, and the Friend, this stone
is reared in devoted memory for
Deirdre, spouse of Thomas Dalton, by him
who knew her worth and loves her still.
Departed this life on the twenty-ninth
day of November 1911. May a more
merciful God grant that we meet again
on the Farther Shore.

That was it, of course; She and Tom both believed in that Farther Shore. The place where those they'd loved who'd gone before would welcome them home.

She stood for a while in silent thought or prayer, just as she had every Friday since Deirdre's death. She'd never told Jim or Tom about her weekly pilgrimage, for this was a private time. Alone with those she loved for quiet conversation and remembrance.

Sometimes, if she was feeling blue, she wondered if anyone would ever lay a flower on her grave when the time came. That was one of the sadnesses of being alone in life, of course; no husband, no child, no family to mourn your passing. The thought of Mulvaney's "magnanimous gesture" came to her, and she wondered what Deirdre would say at the thought of Billy offering herself to Tom. Somehow she thought it would probably be all right.

Billy laid the flowers on the grassy place, wiped away the stinging, silent tears she felt mingling with the cooler raindrops, and said her farewells for another week before returning to Timothy's waiting protection.

68

"Father? Will you come out to watch me play ball on Sunday? I'm pitching." Nine-year-old Seamus stood in his tweed knickers and argyle sweater at the door of Tom's study.

"I'm busy now, son," said the father absently. "Can we talk about it later?"

"But I'm pitching, Father, and I'm really getting to be good. All the guys say so." The child's voice was plaintive.

"And are you getting good at your schoolwork, too?" Tom's temper was short because of the news from Europe about the war. "Your last report card was a disaster."

Seamus's happy, hopeful expression faded, and he looked down at his brown oxfords to ward off his father's gaze.

"I'm better at sports, sir, than I am at school. If you'd come to see me play, you'd understand."

Tom looked at the handsome, ruddy-complected boy, a full head taller for his age than his contemporaries, and wondered what would become of a boy who had no mind for serious things and thought playing baseball well was a good credential for life. When he himself was eight years old, he had watched his father die and had become his own man.

"With the United States getting into the war any day now, I expect I'll be spending the weekend in Washington with your grandfather, Seamus."

"Grandfather is coming to watch me play." The answer sounded accusatory and vaguely defiant.

"Then you'll have no need of my being there, I expect. I'll come to the next game, lad."

The boy started to go, dismissed, then turned for one last word.

"I'm really good at sports, Father. You'd be proud of me if you could see me play."

But Tom was already back at his paperwork. "Yes, I'm sure that's so," he said absently and without looking up.

Seamus stood for a moment and then walked slowly from the room. He hadn't really expected his father to go to the game, but it would have been good if he'd said yes. The other boys' fathers were there to root for them, and he would have been proud to show off his own.

Seamus wished he could be more like his father. He looked like him, but he just didn't seem to have his brain for studies. Rory, on the other hand, who didn't look in the least like his father, was as smart as they came.

Seamus picked up his tweed cap and his bat and ball from the umbrella stand in the hall where he had stashed them. The season would be over in another couple of weeks, and as soon as the weather got a little colder it would be time for football. He was even better at football than at baseball.

Maybe next year, if he went away with Rory to prep school as he was supposed to, he'd get a chance to show off his prowess.

"I've finished first in my form again, Father." Riordan's voice on the telephone was serious and prim.

"That's wonderful, son, we'll have those little Prods on the run yet, won't we, lad?" Tom's voice sounded enthusiastic.

"I'd prefer it if you wouldn't call them that, sir," said Rory. "They're all from very fine old families."

Good God, thought Tom, deflated as always by a conversation with his firstborn. What a bloody little prig he is.

"As you will, Rory," he said, suddenly anxious to end the phone call. "Good luck in your exams."

"Thank you, sir," said the boy, "but I'm sure to do well in them."

Tom put down the receiver after saying good-bye. Never would he have the least understanding of the boy.

Diamond Jim purported to fathom the lad. He was bitter, said the grandfather. He'd been old enough to be injured by Deirdre's death. "You were his idol, lad," Jim had said to him recently. "You never comforted him when you had the chance. He thinks you stopped loving him after Deirdre's death."

"That's ridiculous!" Tom had replied, angry at the interpretation.

"Bullshit!" Jim had exploded at him. "You failed him when he needed you. He lost a mother *and* a father that day, Tom, and if you don't do something about what's smoldering there, he'll pay you back one day. Mark my words."

Tom sat in his study, brooding over the phone call and the remembered conversation.

Maybe Jim was right. He'd try to do something about it when the boy got home from prep school for the summer.

Maeve Dalton wished she knew how to talk to her daddy better. She always knew how to do it in her mind . . . like at night when she lay in her big bed and thought about him. About how handsome he was and how smart to be running all those businesses. She would ask him questions and he would tell her things and he would take her to the circus and the museums and all the places Nanny took her and they would be together.

But somehow it never worked quite that way. It wasn't her father's fault, of course, that he was so busy. And it wasn't his fault she got all tongue-tied and didn't say any of the things she'd planned to.

The sisters in school said God had afflicted her with shyness as a test of courage. And because He probably wanted her to join their order and become a nun when she was old enough.

She looked at herself in the dressing table mirror, pulling her long brown hair back tightly from her face to see how she'd look in the coif of a nun's habit. She stared carefully at the reflection, trying to feel holy, but all she felt was plain. Eyes too big, nose too upturned, lips too pouty, and, ugh, disgusting freckles on her too white skin.

Maybe she'd better join the convent, she thought. No man would ever marry anyone who looked as plain as she did. She wrinkled her little nose at the reflection and let go of her hair, sighing at the hopelessness of it all.

69

"There's a long, long trail a-windin'," the noisy, cheery strains of the song that was on everybody's lips echoed in Tom's head. The maid had been singing it as she dusted his study, and its lingering sentiment hung in the air as he pushed the newspapers to the corner of his desk.

The war that Diamond Jim had been predicting was finally happening in Europe; Antwerp had fallen and the papers were filled with news of a bloody battle at Ypres.

All over the country zealous young men were singing songs and signing up for the war in Europe. George M. Cohan and his family, The Four Cohans, seemed to be inspiring an epidemic of patriotism with their songs and performances at the New Amsterdam Theatre.

Thank God my sons are still boys, Tom said to himself as he read the accounts of the slaughter at Lille and Ypres.

M & D was making a bloody fortune from the war, just as Jim had said it would. The government needed ships to transport cargoes of supplies to Europe, and they needed nearly every other commodity M & D could supply them with. Once again, Jim's acumen and foresight to say nothing of his political cronies in Albany and Washington, had made them richer men.

But Jim was slowing down, or maybe phasing out was a better word for it. Since the fight for the docks and Deirdre's death, the excitement of business, the lure of the one-upmanship he had loved, no longer thrilled the old man as it had. Perhaps, had he not one-upped Vincenzo, he once said to Tom, Deirdre wouldn't have been gone these many years. The thought had occurred to both men.

Whatever the reason, Jim was easing Tom into the driver's seat on everything. Lumber, shipping, politics, real estate; bit by skillful bit he was relinquishing the power and gently withdrawing from the throne room. The palace guard, of course, remained. Tierney and O'Reilly still held sway in their respective domains, and the organization had grown with the years to include a far larger number of employees than it had when Tom had first joined the business. Curiously, Mulvaney had never attempted to replace Duffy. "He was one of a kind," Jim had said when Tom brought up the subject. "I'll have no second-stringer to follow the lad." He hadn't raised the question again.

Tom felt there was more than a simple turning over of the keys to the kingdom going on between himself and Jim. It was an effort at dynasty, a solemn cementing of a bond that promised that the empire would be protected through one more lifetime, at least—with the hope that perhaps another like themselves would appear in the family to carry on what had been built.

Tom knew it troubled Jim that his own relationship with his sons was so tenuous. He knew it would have been a comfort to the old man to look ahead to see a grandson who promised to be a worthy successor. But it was hard to see any small trace of either of them in the boys.

Tom made a note to invite Billy and Jim out for an evening on the town and to spend more time with them both. Bily still seemed to have the ability to bring out the old ebullience in Jim. She had started taking him to movies, the new entertainment.

Mack Sennett comedies and Charlie Chaplin seemed to lift his spirits, or maybe W. C. Fields or Fanny Brice were playing on stage somewhere in town. Tom knew that part of Mulvaney's delight in the theater was the stir he always caused walking in with Billy on his arm. The statuesque beauty in the fashionable new ankle-length skirts and high-buttoned shoes was sure to cause a ripple in any theater, where most people assumed her to be a movie star.

Yes, an evening out on the town was a splendid idea; he'd use it as the moment to tell Jim the good news about the government shipping contract he'd just brought back from Washington; and maybe Rory's birthday party would be a good tonic for Jim, too. He'd make sure that both Jim and Billy had a chance to enjoy seeing the whole family together.

Billy dressed herself carefully for the occasion, if with trepidation.

Tom had insisted she come to Rory's birthday celebration. The children would be there, Jim would be there, and a large group of Rory's friends would be there. She had been less than enthusiastic about the invitation.

"You came to the house all the time when the children were small," he had argued.

"Deirdre was alive then; she invited me."

"Why should her invitation be acceptable and mine not, will you tell me?"

"But what if they find out who I am, Tom. The boys are getting big and Rory is smart as a whip. It isn't wise for the children to know about me."

"They don't know about you! They only know you're my friend and Jim's and that you were their mother's friend when she was alive. Besides, they'll all be off in the garden and we'll have the house to ourselves. I want you to come."

So she had accepted reluctantly.

"Nice house, Ror, old man," said the short blond boy with the glasses as he munched on an hors d'oeuvre.

"My father says yours is really loaded with loot, even if he is a Catholic." The comment came from a taller boy with dark slicked-down hair as they lounged in the library. The music of the band playing and voices in the garden drifted in the opened window, filling the library with party sounds. "Scott, give me a swig, will you?" The blond boy reached into his pocket and handed a flask to his friend, Whit.

"Not bad booze, either," said the darker boy appreciatively, then he thrust the flask behind the cushion of the couch at the sound of approaching adult voices.

Tom, Jim, and Billy, passing by the hallway, noticed the three boys and stopped for introductions.

Riordan shot up from his chair, a stony expression on his face as they entered.

"Why not introduce us to your friends, son," Tom suggested in a jovial tone. The sounds of the party had put him in a good mood, and he was glad that Billy had consented to come.

Rory, calling on his reserve of impeccable manners, performed the introductions flawlessly.

"It's a swell party, Mr. Dalton," volunteered Scott, whose manners weren't bad either.

"Yes, sir," said Whitney, also standing at attention. "Thank you for inviting us."

"Delighted to see you all having a good time," said Tom magnanimously, thinking that maybe Rory's new friends weren't so bad after all. They passed the time of day for a few minutes and then proceeded on their way, Tom having noted Rory's sullenness and the other boys' unabashed appraisal of Billy.

The three adults had reached the hall when they heard Whit whisper to Rory, "Who's the gorgeous blonde?"

"She's my grandfather's whore" was the arch reply.

Mulvaney and Billy stood still as death, but Tom was back into the room so quickly, Rory didn't have time to sidestep the slap that, connecting with his face, sent him sprawling over a small cocktail table to the floor.

Without waiting for the boy with the bleeding lip to stand up, Tom turned his back on his son, the look on his face so fierce that the other two boys scrambled for safety. But Tom walked by them and back into the hallway where Billy was standing white-faced and immobile, as if she'd been turned to stone.

Diamond Jim's powerful voice from the doorway startled them all. His great eyebrows were drawn together in a mighty scowl of abject disapproval and disgust. His voice was black thunder, under stern control.

"It appears that you need to learn some respect for your elders, young man." Jim's portly body seemed to take on stature with his voice as he spoke to his grandson. "Since you think so little of me as to insult me and my guest in your own home, I feel certain you'll understand why there's no reason at all for me to treat you with any respect in return. You'll see no penny from me when I leave this world, you may count on that."

By now Rory was again on his feet, a look of defiance making his handsome face ugly.

"Mark my words, Rory," said the grandfather with exquisite malice. "What I would have left to you, I shall leave to the lady you've insulted—as a reminder that not all the men in our family are arrogant, insensitive, ill-bred dolts like yourself.

"There's an old Irish proverb my sainted mother used to recite to me . . . you'd do well to learn it, lad. 'Don't let your tongue cut your throat,' she used to say. You'll find it sound advice."

With that, Jim Mulvaney walked deliberately back to the hall and offered his arm with a dignified flourish to the shaken Billy. She stood looking into Jim's eyes for a long moment; then, drawing herself up to her full and stately height, she walked quietly from the house on his arm.

Mrs. Thaddeus Martin

April 25, 1915

My dearest Tom,

I can't begin to tell you how much better I have begun to feel, since leaving the hospital. Thad has been so kind to me since my return home that I am actually beginning to believe that it may be possible for me to go beyond the bitterness and sorrow of these past years and to start life anew.

My memory (with very few exceptions, most of which I am grateful for) has returned.

I am able to face my husband and my children (now no longer children, of course) for the first time in my life with a clear conscience. I wonder if you can imagine how enormous is the relief this provides me.

Poor dear Thad, I'm afraid he got more than he bargained for when he married me. Ah well, so do we all get more than we bargained for from this life, I have lived to learn.

At any rate, I wanted you to know how well I am and, of

course, to thank you for all that you have done—in thought, word, and deed—for me, my beloved son. You, who have gotten least from me of all my children, have given most in return. Surely there are no adequate words to express my gratitude or the love I bear you.

In my effort to begin anew, I have decided to send you the last vestige I possess of my past. You will find herewith a copy of your father's will. Needless to say, it has no legal validity, but perhaps the love it contains will sustain you, as it did me for many years.

And so, dear Tom, I am off to my new beginning! Thaddeus and I sail for Ireland next week; from there we will take a month to travel through Europe, as the doctor says I must recuperate in a new place without memories. Thad, in a remarkable gesture, has said he will take a month's holiday from the store so we may be together, and I am looking forward to that as if I were a new bride.

I hope you will wish me well in my new adventure. I sometimes feel myself to be a frail skiff in which to brave the storm, but perhaps with God's help there'll be clear sailing for a change and when we meet on my return you will be pleased to see me both healthy and happy.

With all the love and gratitude that's in my heart, I remain,

Your loving mother,
Mary

Mary sat at the table in the Grand Salon of the lavish ship and relaxed. She couldn't believe it possible to feel so good. They lived well enough in Boston, but the superb luxury of this ship was somehow overblown just enough to be festive. There was a semicarnival atmosphere everywhere aboard, despite the war news that kept filtering to the upper-class passengers from the radio room.

The first-class staterooms were grander than she had imagined they would be. Paneled in ebony and mahogany, each with a sitting room, dining room, pantry, and two baths, they were far grander than the Plaza Hotel, where they had stayed before sailing.

And the salon where she was seated, waiting for Thad to return to her from a momentary visit to a friend at another table, who purportedly had received a news flash from the radio operator, was gilded and furbished with golden sconces the size of fountains. A great golden-banistered stairway was the focal point of the room, and it wound its elegant way up along the mirrored walls made dazzling by the interplay of candles and electric lights reflected in its glittering surface.

"You are the most beautiful woman here," said Thad as he walked up behind her and leaned down to whisper the words, through her elaborate evening coif, into her ear.

Mary smiled up at her husband, greatly comforted by the feeling of love that welled up in her toward the man. "A very pretty compliment, my dear, considering the many beauties in this room." She laughed as she said it, the champagne beginning to make her feel merry.

"There's no woman in this room or in the world I'd rather be with than you, Mary." Her husband said it so earnestly that she knew it was truth.

"Nor any man I'd rather be with," she said, knowing that finally, after all the years, that, too, was true.

Thaddeus Martin beamed at his fifty-nine-year-old wife, thinking her the best of prizes. All the horror of the past few years had left in its wake this one astonishing blessing: that Mary loved him unreservedly. She loved him, and he would prove to her that whatever it was she had longed to have with the other man who had so shadowed their life, she would have with him. The very knowledge had transformed him.

"Shall we go to our state room, my dear?" he said gently, hopefully, and she knew he wanted to go there to make love to her.

Even that aspect of their life had changed since her return from the sanatorium. The physical act of love, which had been a begrudging burden to her through their years together, was now changed into something beautiful and filled with tenderness.

Could it be, she had wondered, that the lack of prowess in lovemaking that she had attributed to Thad through the years had really been occasioned by her own relentless unresponsiveness. As long as she'd clung to the memory of Michael, of being in his arms, not Thad's, their intimate life had been an inept nightmare. Now it was beautiful. Beautiful and exciting.

She smiled at her husband flirtatiously and put her arm through his to walk back to the stateroom, the exquisite white silk Poiret dress she wore swaying sensuously in the glow of lamplight as she moved.

Two young men at a nearby table noted the couple as they walked by.

"Must have been a beauty in her day, don't you think?" said the handsomer of the two.

"I'd say she doesn't look a bit bad even now," replied his companion.

"You know, her husband owns some giant department store in Boston."

"You don't say?" drawled the good-looking blond with a languid interest. "You know it's rather charming to see an old pair like that so much in love. They must have had a great life together."

"You're probably right, old chap, but to tell you the truth, I'm more interested in finding some companionship for myself tonight, while I'm still young enough to enjoy it."

His friend laughed heartily, and they both moved off into the crowd of merrymakers.

The sound that startled Mary and Thad from their afternoon nap was a cross between a roar, a crash, and a rattle. The whole ship seemed battered by violent shock waves, and suddenly alarms, clanging bells, and screams rent the air that had a moment before been still.

Mary sat up in bed and saw that Thad was already on his feet, pulling on his trousers. The clock said two twenty P.M., and husband and wife, eyes meeting in the dim light of the stateroom, knew that whatever had happened, should not have.

"You wait here, Mary." Thad's voice was urgent. "I'll find out what's going on. Whatever happens, I'll be back for you. Put on your warmest clothes as fast as you can, my dear."

"Wait!" Mary's voice was firm and imperative. "You must know something before you go, my love. If this is like the *Titanic* and they can't save us all, Thad, I'm staying with you."

"Don't be insane, Mary. There's probably plenty of room for everyone; but if not, you will be in one of the boats!"

Mary reached out to touch her husband in the gloom of the cabin.

"Thaddeus, my dear friend, this is no time for an argument. I've just found you after all these years; you must know I'll not leave you now!"

His face softened in the eerie glow of the lurching cabin, seeing the love and determination on his wife's serious face. He reached over gratefully and took her in his arms, pressing her to his body for one perfect moment, then he pushed her gently away.

"Put on your coat, Mary, my love. Whatever happens, we'll face it together."

Mary threw a woolen dress rapidly over her head, tugged on her fur coat, and took her husband's hand firmly in her own as they made their way above deck.

Western Union

MR. THOMAS DALTON
M & D LUMBER & SHIPPING
15 JOHN STREET
NEW YORK, NEW YORK
MOTHER AND FATHER ON LUSITANIA. STOP. TORPEDOED BY
GERMAN SUBMARINE MAY 7. STOP. ALL FEARED LOST. STOP.
NEED POLITICAL ASSISTANCE TO GET BODIES HOME IMMED-
IATELY. STOP. PLEASE WIRE IF YOU CAN HELP. STOP.

                                        ROBERT MARTIN

Tom sat near Billy on the couch in Jim Mulvaney's library, as if he'd been turned to ice. His large body slumped, and he held his head in his big dispirited hands.

Billy sat near him, cross-legged on the floor. She felt almost as stunned as he by the awful news in the telegram. The papers were filled with it, of course. The *Lusitania,* a huge ocean liner, had been sunk by the Germans off the Irish coast. There'd be war now for sure for America, but at the moment that fact was irrelevant.

"You're absolutely certain there's no hope?"

"She went down in less than ten minutes, Billy. There wasn't even time to man the boats. It's god-awful cold in the Irish Sea at this time of year. They couldn't have lasted more than a few minutes even if they weren't pulled under with the ship when she went." His voice was hoarse and agonized.

Billy wrapped her arms around his shoulders and squeezed hard, although there was no response. He could hear the tears in her voice when she spoke.

"You'd better say it all out loud, Tom. You'll die if you try to hold in grief this size. I know how you cared for her."

"It's more than that!" He shook off Billy's arms and turned to face her, his face fierce and angry. "It's the fucking unfairness of it!

She fought so hard to get back after the boy died. She fought so hard all her life, Billy, just to survive with scarcely enough happiness to mention.

"But finally, Billy, finally she was happy! Her voice on the phone, her letters—they were filled with it. She'd come to terms with everything. She'd even come to love Thad Martin because he'd stayed with her. And then this stinking unfairness got her anyway! It's as if you just can't get away from it no matter how hard you try!" Billy pulled away from the voice and looked carefully at him. Was he talking about Mary's fate or his own? There was no way to be sure.

"She said this was going to be the beginning of a new life for them, Billy. A new life indeed! Her life was doomed from the day she was born!" He laughed an ugly sound, and she stood up suddenly.

"Now you just listen to me, Tom Dalton!" The words had a sting to them that bit through the haze of his anger and frustration. "Nobody ever said this life was fair or even close to it! Truth is, it's a big stinking mess and all we've got to keep us going is each other and a few good things that happen to us along the way. Well, your mother had a lot more good in her life than some do. She lived to see her kids raised and her life a success. She loved two men who loved her back. She lived long enough for her guilty secret to get out so at least she didn't die with it on her conscience. And most of all, she died with someone she loved in her arms, more'n likely . . . with someone who loved her despite everything she was and everything she'd done.

"Now I'm not saying it's good that it happened, mind you. It's a stinking, rotten, dirty shame and that's a fact! But I want you to know that it's not as if her life was a waste of time! And it's wrong of you to think so!"

She sat back down on the sofa, and Tom reached out for her and pressed himself to her bosom. She felt great sobs begin to rack his body, and she sighed in relief as she looked up to see Jim Mulvaney reenter the room. She signaled to him with her eyes and he nodded, understanding. She'd had enough grief in her own life to know that the worst danger came when you held it in, then it became a great sorrowful sore that none could reach to comfort.

"It's all right, my friend," she crooned to him as she held the large man in her arms as if he were a child, tears running down her own cheeks. "It's all right to cry for her . . . she's your mama."

Oh, Thomas, Thomas, my Thomas, she thought as she held him in her arms. Could any man, even you, ever know the empathy I feel for your mother? Could any of you ever in your wildest dreams know what it is like for a woman who must sell her body in order to own her own soul?

70

The sound of running footsteps jarred Tom from his reverie. A young boy's body hurtled past, and feeling a dragging at his side, he realized with astonishment that his pocket watch had been snatched, the pocket watch Diamond Jim had insisted he purchase with his first paycheck after returning to his employ. "It's the mark of a prosperous man, lad. Can't have it said my protégé is not a prosperous man." And he had chuckled as at some unknown jest.

Tom was in Boston for a meeting with the Marshalls. It always pleased him to think that his long-ago solution to the Gordian knot of Marshall Shipping should have proved so lucrative for all concerned. Particularly during the war, the little shipping business had quadrupled in value.

The boy with flying feet was halfway down the block when Tom recovered his equilibrium enough to give chase. "Stop. Thief!" He called it once and then saved his breath for the running. The boy glanced over his shoulder, his black unkempt hair flopping about his face as he did so, and bounded into an angular alley. Tom's long legs had the advantage over the boy's shorter ones, and he caught the runaway halfway up a fence at the alley's back, scrambling to make it over the top and out of reach of his pursuer. Tom yanked the boy from the fence top unceremoniously and flattened him on the ground, the scrawny arms and legs flailing helplessly under the assault of the large, agile man. He was ragged, threadbare, and dirty.

"I'll have my watch back, lad, if you don't mind." The boy begrudgingly handed up the golden treasure dangling from its broken chain.

"I'm sorry, sir," said the captive in a thick brogue. "I haven't had naught to eat in a long while, sir, and the madness of it took me."

Tom laughed at the sheer Irish audacity of the story and started to get off the boy, but the sudden movement of his prisoner toward escape stayed him.

"What's your name, lad, and how do you live? Is this your only means of eating? Where's your family?"

"Me name's Jack Cavanaugh," said the boy defiantly. "And *I'm* me own family. And I'll be thanking you to get your large self off me leg, sir, or you'll be breaking it into several pieces."

Tom shifted his weight and let the boy up, warily. The scrawny child dusted himself off from the alley's debris and, to Tom's amusement, stuck out his hand pugnaciously for Tom to shake.

"I'll be takin' me leave of you now, sir, if you don't mind. I'm a mite hungry and I'll have to be finding a gentleman with a watch like yours, but shorter legs, if I'm to have me supper."

"Do you not have a home at all, lad?" Tom asked as he appraised the boy's condition with a practiced eye. This one was obviously intelligent and articulate, but destitute, as were so many of Diamond Jim's constituents that he visited weekly.

"Not since I was a wee lad, sir" was the reply. "There's little work for a man of me age, and so I makes me way as best I can."

"And what age might that be?"

"Thirteen, sir. Almost."

"I see. Well, I'll not lecture you about stealing watches and there's precious little I can do to change things for you, but"—Tom reached into his pocket for a coin—"I can buy you a decent meal and give you my card in case you should ever find yourself in New York. If you come to see me there, I might be able to help scare up work for a man like yourself." His eyes twinkled as he said it, but the boy's defiant look was back.

"Jack Cavanaugh takes no charity," he said, and recoiled from the proferred coin. "I'm a proud man, sir, though I may be a bit down on me luck."

Tom pressed the coin and the card into the boy's grimy hands, moved by the gallant effort at pride and by the hunger in the child's eyes.

" 'Tis not charity for one man to treat another to a meal, Jack Cavanaugh. When you get to New York, you can repay the courtesy."

The boy's blue eyes glistened in the dirt-smudged face, and Tom realized he was holding back tears of relief at the prospect of food.

"God bless you, sir," said the boy softly, and then he was gone, darting out of the alley, leaving Tom with memories of another poor boy, in another time and place.

He shook his head to clear away the dark thoughts and hurried to his appointment.

"How goes the Marshall end of the M & D shipping empire?" Tom laughed the question as he hugged Abby soundly and shook Henry's hand.

"As you very well know, we're positively filthy with lucre," laughed back Abigail, trying to regain her balance and look dignified simultaneously. "Hate to think it took a war to make us all rich."

"And you and Mr. Mulvaney are richer still, eh?" added Henry with a benevolent twinkle.

"If Abby has any of her famous blackberry brandy hidden away, I'll tell you just how rich, by the latest tally. As a matter of fact, that's what I'm here for."

They all walked amiably into the little book-rich library, Tom noting, as always, the Spartan, well-scrubbed splendor of everything in the Marshall household. They each sat in a favorite chair as Abby poured her blackberry brandy with a New England economy of movement that always amused Tom.

"As you both well know," he said expansively, "the U.S. government commissioned fourteen million dollars' worth of new shipping for the war effort. . . ."

"A goodly portion of which rolled down the ways in our own little shipyard due to some questionable political hocus-pocus on the part of your Mr. Diamond Jim Mulvaney," added Abigail, handing out the three glasses of dark blue liquor.

"*Our* Mr. Mulvaney, Abby dear," corrected her brother in a kindly voice.

"Yes, of course, Henry. Ours indeed."

Tom smiled at the exchange and continued.

"And as you also know, the war ended before most of those boats were ever seaworthy, although they were paid for fully."

"And a rare pity, too," mused Henry, who couldn't bear the idea of a Marshall-built boat in drydock.

"Well, my friends, what you don't know is that *our* Diamond Jim Mulvaney has just pulled off the coup of a lifetime." He said it with such youthful exuberance shining on his nearly middle-aged face that both Marshalls leaned forward in their chairs in unwitting unison.

"Well, young man, out with it, before you burst with the news." Abby's voice too seemed youthful with the excitement.

Tom leaned back in his wing chair and savored a sip of brandy, as if to prolong the pleasure of delivering the good news.

"You know what a consummate embarrassment it was to everyone in Washington that they'd overbought themselves into a fourteen million dollar mistake? Well, would you be willing to believe that they've decided to recoup what they can of their losses by selling the drydocked vessels for ten cents on the dollar?" He took in the look of astonishment on the two plain faces and chuckled as he delivered the final bit of news. "And our Diamond Jim Mulvaney has gotten them to give M & D first dibs on the lot of them!"

The expression on both Marshall faces was a mixture of wonder, jubilation, and consummate disapproval, thought Tom, amazed that all three emotions could mesh so clearly.

Abigail turned to her brother, whose face was a mirror of her own. "I don't know whether to be elated that we're about to become one of the biggest shipping companies in Boston, or to be horrified that we're doing it at the expense of our own government!"

"There must be heads rolling in Washington over this fiasco," said practical Henry, as if unable to believe what he'd heard.

"I expect there'll be as many people paid off as laid off over it, Henry. I'm as disgusted by the bureaucratic idiocy that allows something like this to happen as you are. But I'm also a damned sight happier that if somebody profits from it, it's M & D that will."

"I'm afraid you'll have to forgive our righteous indignation, Tom," said Abby, who had recovered her voice. "We Yankees have an inbred intolerance for incompetence, second only to our horror of waste. I'm afraid this whole story reeks of both."

Tom turned down the corners of his mouth in mock disapproval. "Well, I must say, I expected a little more enthusiasm from you both over what could amount to millions. Just think how proud your father would be to imagine such a coup for Marshall Shipping."

"Our dear father, who spent the first part of his life as little better than a buccaneer in the China seas, would doubtless be ecstatic," said Abby. "Our mother, who spent her entire life as a Congregationalist, is doubtless this moment spinning in her grave as a direct result of this conversation!"

"Abby, dear," said Henry with uncharacteristic firmness in his voice. "If there was one thing you could say without fear of contradiction about both Father and Mother, it would be that a more practical pair of Yankees were never born in Boston. At the moment I'd say that if they were both here this minute, they'd propose a toast. To practicality!'' said Henry with a twinkle in his eye.

Both Tom and Abigail were so surprised by the unaccustomed stand from Henry that they burst into laughter.

"Henry was always able to get to the heart of things,'' his sister managed through her laughter, "even when he was a child. Father used to tell the story that when Henry was very small and it came his turn to say grace at table, he would say, 'Dear God, please make us graceful.' ''

Henry beamed at his sister's approval, and Tom thought once again of the mysterious fate that supplied him with fine and honorable friends, just as inexorably as it removed from him those he loved the best.

71

A man of larger than life-sized ambitions and enterprises, James Mulvaney, called Diamond Jim by friends and enemies alike, died, as he had lived, flamboyantly.

So said the impressive obituary in *The New York Times*.

What they were referring to somewhat obliquely was that Diamond Jim had had a heart attack in the midst of a meal, while entertaining twelve powerful New York titans at a lavish dinner party at the whorehouse he owned in partnership with Billy Henderson, the most successful and glamorous madam in New York.

Billy's house was no longer a waterfront establishment but had grown to a quite prosperous uptown business on East Seventy-second Street, under Diamond Jim's canny aegis. Politicos, lawyers, judges, business tycoons, movie types passing through New York, all sought the pleasures of her well-run establishment. She was beginning to be a very famous lady at the time Jim left her the share of his net assets he had once intended for Rory, just as he'd told her he would. She was then a handsome forty-three years of age.

The funeral had been attended by everyone of any consequence in New York, and by a delegation from Washington that would have done Jim's heart good had he been alive to participate. It was not

attended by his eldest grandson, Riordan, who, having avoided his
grandfather assiduously since his confrontation with Billy, saw no
reason to attend his obsequies. Rory had expected a battle royal with
his father over his decision about the funeral, and was both relieved
and disturbed by the fact that Tom greeted the news with disdainful
equanimity.

"Small loss you'll be to him, to be sure," he had responded
deadpan to his son's announcement, and had returned to his perusal
of certain papers that Jim had entrusted to him just before his death.
"None of it was as I expected, lad," the old man had said to Tom
on his deathbed. "Not from the day I was born to now," and Tom
had agreed with him heartily.

"Will you miss him, Billy?" Tom asked the question when they
were seated in her parlor, glad to have left the throng of mourners
behind, thinking how very much he himself would miss the remarkable old man who had changed him, enlightened him, badgered him,
and loved him into both business and personal maturity.

"Yes, I'll miss him." Billy smiled sadly. "Not as a lover, Tom;
that wasn't his strong point these past few years, I'm afraid. But as a
trusted friend, a confidant, a mentor, a pal—there could be none like
him."

"A nice epitaph, lass. He'd have liked that one more than the
eulogy by that pompous prelate or the obituary in the *Times*." He
watched her move about the huge sitting room, her rustling black
satin mourning dress showing off her still sensuous body to perfection.
He felt an old stirring in the loins and smiled at the catlike grace of
her movements.

"You were born to be a courtesan, Billy, my girl. You make a
man remember he's a man, with such unselfconscious effort." She
could hear the smile in his voice as he said it.

Billy put down the silver tea tray she was carrying and looked at
Tom inquiringly. She had been around men too long not to sense the
need in one who wanted her. Could it be that his own sense of
honor, or respect for hers, had kept him silent all these years? It had
been eleven years since Deirdre's death, and he'd never made a
move in her direction in other than simple friendship. She smiled at
the courtliness of the gesture.

"I've never quite forgotten you, lass." He said it with great
seriousness, as if in answer to the unspoken question.

"And what of Deirdre? Have you forgotten her?" She asked it not as a rebuke, but with a gentleness that surprised him.

He leaned far back into the chair before answering, as if settling himself for a long reply.

"For years after she died I never went near a woman," he answered her carefully. "She was in my heart and on my mind. I went to bed with her memory each night. I carried her with me in the day. There isn't a way to describe to you the love we bore each other, Billy. I wouldn't even try. At any rate, I was dying inside from the loss of her when Diamond Jim came to me one night and he said to me, 'Son, you must lay my daughter in her grave and leave her there. You cannot end your life because she was so cruelly taken from us. You cannot live any longer as a eunuch and you must let her rest in peace. Cherish her memory. Rest beside her when you die. But live first. Live for both of you. She would not have had you die of grief for her.'

"For a long, long while I thought about what he'd said, and then I did a very strange thing. I walked out into the garden, among the ramblers and the peonies and the wild flowers she loved so much. And I began to talk to her just as if she were alive. I told her how very much I missed her and how much I loved her. I told her all the things I wished I'd said while she lived. I asked her to understand that I wanted to live . . . needed to live. I know it sounds mad, Billy, but I made my peace with my wife that night, and I've been able to deal with it all since then."

"Other women?"

"A few. Good sex, bad sex, whatever seemed necessary at the moment. But that isn't what I want from you exactly, lass. Despite the fact that I well recall your remarkable body and your particular gifts and skills."

She smiled at the compliment. "What, then?"

"I would like a lover who is a friend. Donaher, Mulvaney, Deirdre, the waterfront, the old days. It's all tied up in you, as it is in me.

"I don't mean to make love to you now, Billy. Not with Jim not yet in the ground, nor maybe even anytime soon. But another time. If you were to ask me to come to you, I'd be grateful."

Billy sat down on the edge of the cocktail table she had been standing next to. She looked at Tom carefully, a strange incomprehensible look that he had never seen in her eyes before and that he didn't understand. Finally she said, "You're a remarkable man,

Tom Dalton. I knew it the first night I ever laid eyes on you. What say we have a drink and talk of Jim; it'd do us both a world of good.''

She poured two whiskies and handed one to Tom; raising the glass in a toast, she said, ''To Diamond Jim Mulvaney. May God rest him when he isn't after him for advice!'' They drained the glasses in memory of a man they both had loved, and spent the better part of the night in reminiscence.

72

Seamus Dalton sat on the edge of his bed in the dormitory at Groton, looking sullen. God, but he hated being Irish; it was bad enough that his rusty hair and freckles betrayed his odious heritage, but his disgusting *name* . . . that was an impossible-to-escape giveaway.

He'd been in the new school for less than a week, and already he'd had three fistfights over his Irish name. And now someone had tacked a page clipped from a Boston newspaper onto his door. It was an ad for a local department store looking for part-time help. NO IRISH NEED APPLY was printed in bold black letters across the page. Someone had underlined the words in red crayon.

Fortunately he was big for his age and capable of defending himself. In fact he was a good head taller than most of his contemporaries, so he wasn't much the worse for wear from the battles.

But the truth remained. He was Irish and ''No Irish Need Apply'' had to do with more than just department store clerks.

The first thing he'd do would be to purge the name. From this day on he would be Shay, not Seamus. It was a stupid name anyway; he'd only been burdened with it because of some old friend of his father's who'd died years ago.

His roommate, blessed with the glorious Protestant perfection of nomenclature James Sheridan, had given him the idea. The boy had misunderstood the mumbled rendition of Seamus he had offered on meeting him, and responded instantly, ''Shay, did you say? What a funny coincidence. My father's mother was a Shay. Wonder if we might be related, distantly.''

At that moment the plan had been born. Shay was acceptable; Seamus was not. He would be Shay for the rest of his life.

So must he learn to be all the things that he was not. Learn to be Protestant, learn to be "old money," learn to say things like "old chap" and "let's chat about that." And while he was learning, he'd show them a thing or two about Irish self-preservation. A few broken noses might discourage some of the name-calling and sly innuendo.

His roommate seemed like a good enough sort, if a little bookish. Well, it wouldn't hurt to have a friend who knew his way around a textbook.

So far the only class Seamus had understood was phys. ed.

Dear Father,

I would like you to know that the fifty dollars you send me per month has been carefully invested and is beginning to show a profit.

I have discovered that many of the boys here are short on their allowances toward the end of the month and are willing to borrow at interest rates that are almost usurious. Since I tend to live rather frugally, as most of my time is spent in studying, I have been able to almost quadruple my capital via this kind of speculation.

I have been studying *The Wall Street Journal* and all the business publications I can secure from the library, with the hope of soon having enough money to invest in the stock market.

Lest you think me in any way reckless where money is concerned, I feel I should assure you that I will never gamble with anything I cannot personally afford to lose. When next I am at home, I would appreciate having the opportunity to discuss with you the stocks I've been keeping my eye on, to see if you feel I've made sensible selections.

With best regards and hoping you are well,

Your son,
Rory

Tom put down the letter with a frown on his face. Why the hell was it that Rory did everything right and it left a sour taste in his mouth anyway?

The boy worked hard, got astoundingly good grades, was praised universally by his teachers; odds were he'd even pick the right goddamn stocks! How in hell did they always rub each other the wrong way? It was certainly obvious that Rory had all the components that Seamus lacked. Seamus, who excelled only at contact sports, good looks, and winsome personality. Seamus, who, he had been informed by his daughter, Maeve, was now known as Shay.

Tom folded up the letter with a sigh and made a mental note to send the boy some extra money next month for his "speculation."

73

Billy smiled at Tom over the heads of the crowd of elegantly dressed revelers, and he winked back at her. Billy's friendship had had a salutary effect on Tom's life in more ways than one since they had become lovers. She lifted his spirits and flattered his ego; her history was his history, and she was not a woman to make demands on a man.

The new house was ablaze with lights; the electric abundance was rivaled only by the candlelit beauty of the fabulous crystal chandelier that Tom had taken from Mulvaney's railroad car for Billy, after Jim's death.

The double brownstone had the stature of an embassy, the glowing mahogany staircase designed by Stanford White rose in an elegant spiral to the floor above, from a black- and white-tiled entrance foyer big enough for a ballroom.

The house had been a gift from Tom to Billy, and he knew she cherished it as if it were a living thing. Together they had gone from room to room on the day he'd signed the deed over to her, Billy skimming her finger proprietarily over the splendid wainscoting and intricate paneling; running like a child through the long hallway, listening to the echo of her own laughter in the empty quiet. He had watched her with increasing joy at the happiness he had given her. He had told her he'd bought the house as an investment, but they both knew it was a gift to make her happy, as she made him happy.

He often pondered their odd relationship; there was no question but that his protection and patronage was making her the most sought-after and talked-about madam in New York. Just as there was no question but that she had brought him the most happiness he had experienced since Deirdre's death. Funny how the Lord had always sent him friends in his hours of desperation, salvation for him after the losses that seemed perpetually to overtake his happiness.

Billy looked no less beautiful to him now than she had twenty years before. Her hair was still a golden halo, her body proud of its own splendor, her warmth and womanliness only enhanced by the years. A rare creature indeed.

The thought of the old days unsettled him, bringing as it did so many sorrows. He tried to push it from his consciousness and took a sip from the Tiffany crystal champagne glass he held in his hand. To you, old friend! he thought, raising the glass in a toast to her as he saw her glance his way across the glittering room. Returning the salute with her own glass, Billy smiled dazzlingly at him, and he began to think how nice it would be when all the guests had gone home.

"How are the boys doing at school, Tom?" Billy asked in the car, returning from an afternoon of shopping with her lover and benefactor. It had been great fun for both of them; zipping through the streets of the city in the glamorous yellow Stutz Bearcat, chauffeur-driven; being fawned over by saleswomen who knew a good customer when they spied one.

His face darkened at the mention of his children, as if the sun had suddenly ducked behind a cloud.

"They're well as usual," he replied laconically.

"You should see more of them; drive up on a weekend to see the boys, Tom. They must miss seeing their father."

"I never know how to behave with them, Billy. Rory is cold as a witch's tit; disdainful of a heritage that causes him problems with his rich little Prod friends. And Seamus, he's a likeable enough kid, but no convictions of his own that I can see. He talks sports, sports, and more sports and then politely excuses himself to go play whatever's in season."

Billy considered the wisdom of reading him the riot act about his lack of parental understanding, but thought better of it. The sad thing was he really didn't know how to do it. The easy parenting that came to other men simply didn't come to him. She'd often enough heard Jim describe how appalled he was at the stilted way in which father and sons spoke to each other. Proper, well-bred, disconnected conversations that had puzzled and chilled him, were what he had described to her.

She changed the subject.

"And what of Maeve? How's your daughter faring, then?"

"She seems to be doing all right with the sisters. She's such a frail little thing, the point of a rush could draw blood from her cheek. I suppose the Convent of the Sacred Heart seems the best place for her. At least there she won't have to cope with what the boys face, being rejected for their Irish Catholicism. I swear I've never seen a more fearful, fragile human than Maeve." He smiled ruefully at Billy. "I don't know, lassie, maybe all little girls are as frail as butterfly wings."

"They are not, Tom Dalton, and well you know it!" Billy snapped at him, surprisingly. "Enough diamonds and dresses for today. We're going to find the finest toy store in this city and we're going to pick out a splendid present for you to give your daughter. She needs more of your love; more of your strength to strengthen her." She said it with such conviction that he looked at her, startled by the vehemence.

"And exactly how do you come to know so much about eleven-year-old girls, might I inquire?"

"Because I was exactly your daughter's age when my childhood came to an abrupt end, and because I remember everything about the little girl I was then, as if it were yesterday." Billy paused to remove a lace handkerchief from her bag and turned her head away from him to look out the window as she said it. "I know all there is to know about sad and lonely eleven-year-old girls, if you must know."

Wonderingly, Tom told the driver to find a toy store and then settled back into the leather womb of the backseat, thinking, as he had on numerous occasions before, that women were far more complicated creatures than men.

74

Maeve Dalton was terminally shy. She peered out at life through the frightened eyes of a fawn; skittish, easily unsettled, overly sensitive to what went on around her.

It was as if her senses had been too highly developed, so that there were raw nerve-endings where simple senses should have been. She feared authority from the first breath she drew; motherless, she acquiesced to her nanny's wishes without thought of rebellion. Fatherless for all intents and purposes, she sought to please the somber stranger who reentered her life when his own grief had passed. She adored her father as the kind, strong man who always seemed somehow pained by the time he spent with her; and she feared him as the ultimate authority.

From the time he began to think of Maeve as a daughter rather than as the instrument of his wife's death, Tom recognized in Maeve a frailty that unnerved him. "There are those too gentle to live among the wolves, Jim," he'd told her grandfather, and Jim had nodded sad assent, knowing precisely what Tom referred to.

"You should spend more time with the little lass," he had replied. "She adores you, and she needs to learn to be less timid. Perhaps you could help her feel more insulated from the world."

"I've never seen a child so skittish, Jim. Nor so shy, for that matter. I'll talk to Mrs. McKay about it, perhaps she'll know what to do."

"It isn't a governess she needs, Tom. She needs the security of a family. Not that I'm a great one to give advice about families, but nonetheless I'm sure that a little more of you in her life would make the difference."

The father had listened and agreed, but somehow, beyond being kind to the little girl and showering her with pretty presents, he didn't really know how to do what Jim was suggesting.

When her best school friend decided to join the convent after high school, Maeve had almost followed suit, but her immensely guilt-controlled conscience had fought back. She did not have a real vocation, just a lack of knowing what to do with her life, and that was an unworthy reason to enter the convent. Cecilia, her convent-bound friend, was holy; she was not.

It wasn't that she'd had an unhappy childhood, really. She'd loved the big handsome house they lived in—there was security in having a rich, powerful father and servants and a well-upholstered life-style. It was just that she didn't quite know how to belong with the other children of the rich, who seemed able to grasp life with both hands and to be comfortable in any situation. Often she wanted to run away to her wonderful safe room, with its crisscross windows and its comforting wallpaper with the tiny rosebuds that matched the comforter on her four-poster and the cushions on her rocking chair.

Her father had let her decorate her own room herself when she was eleven, she had constructed it to be perfect, and it had become her safe haven of tranquillity. It was a feminine fortress, fortified with the books she loved, which seemed so much more real to her at times than her real life did. The books transported her to magical kingdoms where handsome princes overlooked her shyness and threw themselves at her feet, asking for her hand with undying devotion.

She always had a hard time talking to boys in real life. Even though she practiced conversations with them in her head beforehand, when the moment came to be spontaneous, the words always stuck in her throat and all the pretty, confident speeches she had imagined never quite happened. She suspected that boys thought her dull and uninteresting, which was really unfair because on the inside she knew she was such an inventive person.

Riordan Dalton graduated with every honor his school could bestow, and Seamus made no pretense at scholarship during his long tenure at prep school. Indeed, his very lack of ambition in that direction had a certain charm about it. He was very good at athletics; if something demanded strength or speed or agility, Seamus could be relied upon to supply it. He was a "sporting man," he told his father early on, and although Tom considered his younger son's pursuits frivolous and inconsequential, he still preferred the boy to Riordan.

Tom suspected that he'd done too many things wrong where both his sons were concerned. But none of it had been intentional. After Deirdre's death he had simply been emptied of anything to give, anything to share. And then the pain of being with them had been too great, too fraught with agonizing memories. To see his children, to hear them, to touch them, had nearly broken his heart; they had seemed to him so very much like Deirdre. Not that he hadn't tried to be close to them, after a time. But he just hadn't had the knack for it that she'd had. When he'd finally reached out for them, they'd been quiet little strangers and it had been too late to start again.

But when it came to business, he suffered from no such ineptitude. He ran M & D with style and talent, and M & D shipping was only the tip of the iceberg. It had spread into construction, transportation, and a lot of other businesses under Jim's canny aegis and had burgeoned under Tom's adept management into a solid, lucrative conglomerate.

Tom had eased himself out of most of the city politics he'd been involved in during Jim's rule. Tammany was now a bad word in the city of New York, and the days of the bosses seemed numbered. Besides, the M & D businesses were now very substantial enterprises, with a life of their own despite political vicissitudes.

Not that Tom thought politics was to be disdained; as a matter of fact, he was taking even more of an interest in state and federal government now that he was less tangled up with the city pols. State and federal governments were becoming the real seats of power, the places where you needed friends who could be useful to the kinds of multipronged businesses he now ran.

Tom sometimes marveled at his own ability to keep all the interests healthy. Jim had, of course, been a gifted teacher, but his own connection to business went deeper than that. Business provided Tom with precisely what his emotional life lacked, the ability to control the odds. The opportunity to use his brain and his guts to make things work his way. No acts of God to reach out and destroy him, no vicious twists of fate. If he played the game by the rules, he won. His money made more money, his armor plating of protective wealth grew more solid with the years, safe from the lightning bolts that plagued him in every other area of life. The Lord giveth and the Lord taketh away. So the Lord had taken away the ones he'd loved best and the Lord had given business. He would take very special pains not to let anything interfere with what was left.

He might not be a terrific father—everyone seemed to agree on that, even Billy; it was a fact that caused him more pain than any of them guessed—but good father or not, he would provide for his own. God alone knew what kind of progeny he had fathered, but whoever, whatever they turned out to be, they would be safe from the world's abuses. Safe from powerlessness, safe from poverty. Then maybe some day when they had children of their own and knew how hard it is to do it all right, they'd understand how much he had loved them and tried to protect them from the worst.

75

"I'd like to come to work in the family business, Father." Riordan Dalton, as always, precise and direct, looking every inch the Phi Beta Kappa that he was, stood in front of Tom's desk. He had made the appointment through Tom's secretary, just as if he were any other young Harvard Law School graduate with a few years' experience under his belt, looking for employment.

"I've brought along a resumé of my academic transcript and the records of the small enterprise I've been running since graduate school. As you know, I haven't any corporate experience, but I believe I would be able to contribute to the business if you'll give me an opportunity to learn."

Tom frowned at his eldest son. It was unnatural for a son to speak so formally to his father. Why the hell couldn't the boy ever behave like a human being?

"When did you decide you wanted into the business, Rory?" It had never really occurred to Tom that Riordan would want to participate in anything that was so directly under his father's aegis. The possibility of their working together unsettled him. Why was he not delighted at the idea of carrying on the family tradition? he wondered. Mulvaney to Dalton to Dalton made all the sense in the world. But it made him uneasy just the same.

"I've always intended to join you in the business, Father. I'm sorry you didn't know it until now." Tom raised his eyebrows at the reproach in the boy's voice, then decided the lad had good reason to reproach him. There was much he didn't know about his son.

"What do you fancy doing in the company, Rory?"

"I've a law degree and a small gift for finance, I believe. I would like to begin where any other man with similar credentials would. I would expect no special treatment, sir."

"You always speak to me as if I were a perfect stranger, lad. Do you suppose if we were to work together, we might get to know each other on a somewhat more intimate level?"

"I really couldn't say, sir." Rory's gray eyes were self-assured. Tom's were uncertain.

"Report to me on Monday morning, then. I'll give some thought to a training program."

"Thank you, sir. I'd appreciate that."

Tom sighed at the boy's relentless politeness. "A charming defect or two," he said later that night to Billy, who listened quietly to the tale of the interview. "I kept longing for him to have just one little charming defect."

"I'm afraid your other son has enough of those charming defects for both of them. He was picked up again by the police last night, I hear by the grapevine. Drunken driving and a high-priced floozie in the car, equally inebriated, I'm told."

"Is that the lad Diamond Jim once told me most fathers would be proud to own, Billy?" Tom smiled at remembrance of a conversation he had once held about the boy.

"Perhaps he spoke only of his sportsmanship, not of his prodigious appetites," Billy replied with a chuckle. "At any rate, he's out on bail, and small harm done. They seem to be becoming fond of him at the police station. I think the captain is a football fan."

"You know," Tom said, leaning back thoughtfully into the large bed they shared in her apartment. "It's almost as if the Lord divided the goods right down the middle, all the brains to one, all the blarney to the other."

"And what do you suppose Maeve got, then?"

"I fear she got only the heart, Billy. A soft and vulnerable heart."

Shay Dalton was having a fine time at the elegant whorehouse with his teammates.

He'd been told by his chums that this was the ne plus ultra of bordellos, outrageously expensive and worth every penny. He figured this was the kind of place his father would go to if the old guy still had anything to do with sex, which he doubted.

The place was run by the old whore his grandfather had hung around with—he couldn't remember her name. Come to think of it, he couldn't remember much of anything after finishing a fifth of vodka and about as much Scotch. He'd have to remember not to mix his drinks anymore. Mixing two kinds of booze could give you a monument of a headache.

He looked at the pretty blond girl lying at his side. Great piece of ass, that one. At least he thought he'd fucked her, but he couldn't really be sure. Sometimes it was hard to get it up if he'd had a lot to drink. Well, what the fuck difference did it make? He was having a swell time anyway, or so he thought as he drifted off to sleep.

"Easiest money I ever made," said the blonde to Billy when she slipped from the huge bed and left the large drunken body to its stupefied slumber.

"The big lummox was too snockered to even give it the old college try."

Billy nodded to the girl and wondered if she should mention his son's condition to Tom. The kid had all the symptoms of an alcoholic. She'd seen it far too many times to be unsure of the signs. Twenty-four years old and this was the third time in a week he'd been unable to make use of the girl he'd purchased. What a damned shame for a son of Tom Dalton to be a drunk at twenty-four. She'd have to think twice before mentioning the story to Tom. He had enough trouble with the other boy. The one she called "the bad seed."

"I really shouldn't let you kiss me like that, Teddy." Maeve Dalton pushed the handsome young man away from her and wriggled self-consciously out of his embrace. Her heart was pounding so hard she feared he might see it through her organdy dress.

"I didn't mean to let you do that. . . ."

"Look, Maeve. All this virginal diffidence may be considered very attractive by those nuns who taught you God knows what at that convent school you spent your life at, but a man doesn't find it so amusing to be led on and then rebuffed like this."

She turned a stricken look back at the blond Ivy Leaguer. "Oh, I didn't mean anything like that, Ted. It's just that I've never really been alone like this with a man and I'm not sure of anything."

Certain of his ground again, he brushed her dark hair back from her pale white skin with a deliberate sensuality and said soothingly: "Don't you worry, darling. Just let old Teddy take care of your precious honor and everything else. You know I wouldn't hurt you for anything in this world." He began to nuzzle at the girl's long slender neck and let his lips graze the side of her face in a maddening tease.

"Oh, Teddy. You make me feel so special. I love it when you

hold me like this . . ." and the rest of the thought was muffled by the experienced mouth that closed over hers and stilled any possible protests.

"What the hell are you doing spending so much time with that Dalton mouse. Mousey Maeve, you know that's what they call her at school, don't you?" The question was asked by Edward Schuyler Moncure III of his roommate, Theodore Brewster Talbot, while lounging gracefully in the Harvard library between classes.

"Mouse she may be, my boy, but her father owns a large portion of the Eastern seaboard, a condition that adds mightily to her attractiveness, in my opinion."

"Boring, boring, boring, old man. Why not pick a rich one with a little more style, a bit of verve, a great ass, perhaps? It's just as easy to love a sexy rich one as an unsexy rich one, I always say."

"Easy to love, perhaps, but not so easy to snare. If you get my drift."

Sky Moncure cocked an eyebrow in his friend's direction and shifted his position on the bench. "Are you seriously planning to snare, then?"

"Listen, Sky, as you well know, my family is filthy with credentials, but where money is concerned, we are borderline genteel poverty cases. A little fresh capitalization could do me a world of good."

"So you'd actually marry the mouse to feather the nest?"

"An ungainly metaphor, but in a word, yes. Or maybe even something better than that."

"Like what?"

"Like I have an interesting plan about to hatch that might get me the money, minus the mouse, but I'm not really sure I can pull it off."

Edward Schuyler Moncure looked at his friend with a new admiration.

"Let me know when the plot hatches, will you, old chap?"

"You'll be the first godfather to the egg," said Teddy Talbot with a self-satisfied chuckle. "The very first."

"Teddy, please don't make me do this. I'm really frightened." Maeve sat up straight in the front seat of Ted's car and struggled to readjust the buttons of her blouse. There was such misery in her face that Theodore Talbot felt a small twinge of guilt.

"I know how you feel, baby. It's just that I'm so crazy about you

I can't keep my hands off you. It's driving me nuts to be so close to you and not able to make love to you."

Maeve's dark eyes brightened at the thought of being loved. She hated to deny him anything, this gilded young man who seemed so smitten with her. She could hardly believe her good luck in having so handsome a suitor, from so prominent a family, fall in love with her. She knew that men were baser creatures than women, of course; the nuns in school had explained all the sordid necessities of sex to the girls. She knew men had a need that women didn't, which impelled them to lure girls into bed and into trouble. The funny part was that ever since Teddy, *she* felt the stirrings of needs, too. Unquiet yearnings that gripped her and made her feel curiously twitchy when he wasn't near, and strangely voluptuous when he was.

"Do you really love me, Teddy?" she asked tentatively, as if afraid of the answer.

The young man watched her face, calculating the emotions he read there. She was nearly ready for the final part of his plan to be put into action.

"Not only do I love you, beautiful Maeve, but I think I want to marry you."

The startled expression on her innocent face almost made him laugh aloud. She had an old/young face, like that of a baby who was weighed down by unbearable burdens. Soft dark curls ringed her pretty face. Her blue eyes were fawnlike, and her pointed little chin, which might have looked defiant in a stronger face, seemed merely fragile in hers.

"Do you really mean it, Ted?" She looked so doleful and pathetic when she asked the question, it almost made it easier for his conscience—after all, he couldn't abide stupidity.

"Of course, I mean it, goose. All I have to do is square it with my family, what with your being Catholic and all. You know none of that kind of thing means a hill of beans to me, but my family is pretty social and all, and you know how awful families can be." He thought he'd done that just right; put her down just enough, put her on the defensive so she'd remember just how good a catch he was. It was a good thing so few people realized just how empty the family coffers were getting to be. Thank God his mother was such a fanatic about keeping up appearances.

Maeve said nothing, and Ted insinuated his hand tenderly inside the collar of her dress and began again to undo the buttons. It was taking him longer than he'd thought to get her into bed, but it would be worth the effort. If he could just get her worked up sexually, he felt sure her own pent-up passions would finish the job. But, God damn, it was taking a long time to get her worked up. Some poor bastard was going to get stuck with servicing her for a lifetime as a husband. He was devoutly grateful it wouldn't be he.

Maeve knelt in the darkened, empty church and prayed for guidance. The heave quiet and the soft aura of light from the votive candles provided a comforting ethereal glow that made the vaulted interior of the old church seem magical and dreamlike.

The bench beneath her knees was cold and not well padded, but the discomfort simply added to her feeling of holiness. The nuns had always told her that pain could be offered up as a sacrifice to God, for the holy souls suffering in Purgatory, so she had dutifully endured what she could over the years in an effort to feel good and filled with holiness.

Right now she felt great need of holiness. This thing with Teddy was getting to be such a dilemma. She couldn't live without him, that was a certainty. When he wasn't near, she pined for him and moped and daydreamed and waited for weekends when he would return from Boston.

The problem was that when he got home, she had to contend with his powerful urges—and her own, for that matter. She hadn't been to confession or Communion for over a month now because of what they were doing. Even in church her body felt quivery at the remembrance of his hands and mouth and body. It was no wonder sex was such a great sin, she thought miserably; it could even make you forget yourself in church. Here she sat begging God and the Blessed Mother for guidance and thinking wild, filthy things. She shuddered at her own unworthiness.

And what of her father? She felt almost as guilty about betraying his trust, as God's. He would be back from the business trip in another week or so, and he would surely find out about the late hours and the constant long-distance telephone calls.

She was startled by a sound in the eerie quiet, and then realized that a young cassock-clad priest had just walked in, genuflected before the altar, and was walking toward the confessional. She felt her heart begin to pound audibly in her chest. This was the third time she'd decided to go to confession and relieve herself of her guilty secret. But each time, she got just this far and lost the courage. How could she tell a priest—a man—what went on between her and Teddy in motels and in the backseats of cars? How could she say how she had deceived her father?

She bowed her head onto quivering hands, enveloped in indecision and unhappiness. Then she slid silently out of the pew, genuflected hastily, and moved swiftly toward the rear of the church and escape.

"Mother, may I present Maeve Dalton, the friend I've told you about. Maeve, this is my mother, Mrs. Talbot."

The elegant middle-aged woman extended her diamond-clad hand to the young girl with an expression of frozen hauteur.

"It's nice to meet you, Miss Dalton. My son has mentioned you to me." The tone was overbred and chilly.

"I'm very pleased to meet you, Mrs. Talbot, I've been looking forward to getting to know you."

The woman, who seemed to have more than the requisite number of cheekbones, looked at her son with affection and at the girl with disdain.

"I don't know that I'm familiar with your family, my dear. Do we know your parents?"

Teddy quickly interjected, "Maeve's father is Thomas Dalton, Mother. He owns M & D shipping, and a number of other very successful enterprises. I believe you know of her grandfather, James Mulvaney."

"James Mulvaney? You don't mean Diamond Jim Mulvaney, the Irish politician. Was he really your grandfather? How very quaint, my dear."

Maeve wanted to melt into the parquet flooring. Teddy should have known that his old New York Four-Hundred family would never accept her. No matter how much money you had, if you were Irish Catholic, one generation off the boat, you'd best stay with your own kind. Maeve knew she could find easy acceptance with the Murrays and Cuddihys and Kennedys and Cushings, but that wasn't what she longed for. The confident noblesse oblige of the first families, the ones who owed their status to having been on Mrs. Astor's guest list of four hundred names—all that could fit comfortably into her ballroom—in the splendid old days when society was really society . . . that was the Everest she dreamed of climbing.

She had envied the children of such families since getting to Vassar, with an insecure, vague longing that she couldn't put a name to. It was just that they seemed so very *secure*, so permanent, so established. The thought of *belonging* so thoroughly that everyone else wanted to belong with you was vastly comforting to the girl who never seemed quite to belong anywhere.

Teddy eyed his mother with thorough appreciation. Had he coached her ahead of time as to how to set Maeve up for the taking, she couldn't have succeeded any better. Just the right measure of disdain, just the right reminder of her anathema, Catholicism. He was pretty sure this visit to Mama would add just the right dollop of desire for the forbidden to the carefully plotted courtship he was inventing as he went along. When he kissed his mother on the cheek and thanked her for the visit, he meant every word of it.

76

Maeve dressed carefully, a feeling of consummate entrapment strangling her breathing. This was the fourth morning in a row she had awakened to a retching nausea. She stood tentatively examining her own reflection in the bathroom mirror, as if afraid of what she might see. Her eyes were puffy, but that was from crying, something she'd been doing a great deal of lately.

There had been times in her life when she'd thought it would be good to have a mother . . . this was one of them. Not that girls usually told their mothers if they thought they were pregnant, of course, but there was comfort, somehow, in the very sound of the word. Never having had one, Maeve had fantasized for a lifetime about what having a mother would be like. As a child, she had stood for hours on end in front of the huge portrait of Deirdre that hung in her father's bedroom, sometimes holding long conversations with the beautiful young girl she had never known, who was nonetheless so powerfully connected to her past and future.

My God, she thought, looking at her distrait image in the mirror—hair tousled, eyes red and swollen, face slightly bloated—my mother was only a little younger than I am now when Grampa had her sit for that portrait.

She thought of the clear, sinless eyes and the silken aura of golden-brown hair that tumbled down over the shoulders of the girl in the picture. What would *she* think of me now? "My God," she whispered to the frightened girl in the mirror. "I don't even really know what Teddy thinks of me.'' Teddy wasn't turning out to be anything at all like what she had expected. Not that he wasn't fun to be with; if it weren't for the sex he always insisted on, he would have been lots of fun. No one before had taken her to such glittering parties and social gatherings. It was a secret pleasure to walk into parties and know that every female eye there was enviously on your escort. Maeve had never felt envied before, it was a powerful aphrodisiac. But there was something missing that she couldn't put her finger on. Men were supposed to be stronger, somehow, than Teddy seemed to be; more like her father. She groaned inwardly at the thought of her father's face if he ever found out.

Maeve pulled the stretching waistband tighter around her middle with fretful fingers. She splashed cool water on her face, in an effort to make the swelling there subside, and the effort of bending to do so caused another wave of nausea to surge through her. There was no help for it, she supposed. She'd have to find a doctor and see what could be done.

"Teddy, the doctor says I'm pregnant." The terror in Maeve's voice made the young man wince.

"Take it easy now, Maeve. Are you absolutely sure there's been no mistake?"

"Mistake? No. The doctor said there's no mistake! Oh Teddy, what are we going to do? You said that thing you wore would keep this from happening. My father will kill us both."

"This just means we'll have to get some money together and have it taken care of."

"Taken care of? What do you mean by that?"

"Don't be stupid, Maeve. We'll have to find a doctor who handles these problems."

"Problems!" Her voice was shrill with distaste and terror. "This isn't a problem, it's our baby I'm talking about; don't you even care?"

"Of course I care, Maeve, but think what our families would say if they found out. It's going to be bad enough when I tell them I want to marry a Catholic. Jesus Christ, baby, you can't expect me to tell them you're pregnant, too."

"But Teddy, I don't believe in abortion! I'm scared. Don't you understand how scared I am? I could die."

"For God's sake, Maeve, don't go melodramatic on me. You're not going to die. I know someone who does this for all the society girls.''

The distraught young woman looked at her lover in disbelief.

"How do you know such a person?"

"I just do, that's all. The problem is getting the money. It'll cost about three thousand dollars."

"Three thousand dollars? I haven't got anything near that in my bank account. Have you? I mean, even if I'd do it, where would we get the money?"

"Well, it's obvious we can't get it from my family. If they get wind of this, they'll never let us get married."

Maeve sat on the edge of the hotel bed with her head in her hands, despair emanating from every part of her body. She was silent for a long while, and he wasn't sure if he should press the girl or not; she seemed pretty high-strung. Finally she spoke.

"Go ahead and make the appointment, Ted. I can't face my father with this." Her head came up, and he could see that her expression had become defiant. "But *you'll* have to get the money. It's the least you can do under the circumstances. If you want me to do this, you'll have to pay for it."

She rose from the bed, tugged on her woolen coat, and walked doggedly from the room without looking back.

The apartment in the Village had no name on the door. Three other young women, each dressed in a hospital gown, were already seated on the shabby sofa, looking pale, dazed, and nervous.

Maeve stepped through the door, wondering if her legs would actually carry her all the way across the room to where a woman in a nurse's uniform was standing talking to a man who seemed to be waiting agitatedly for someone. She guessed that his girl friend must be the one who was with the doctor.

Teddy propelled her forward and took the envelope full of cash from his pocket. Maeve saw the nurse nod sagely toward the envelope; she motioned them to be seated.

"I don't like this place," she whispered urgently, fighting back nausea and a desire to bolt. "Those women look awful. Do you think they're befores or afters?"

"Look, Maeve, I've told you this guy knows what he's doing. You've got to take it easy or you'll make everybody crazy. We're lucky we could even get in to see this guy."

A muffled moan emanated from the inner room; one of the women on the couch started to retch. Another moan, the sound of strangled sobbing, and a muffled male voice, obviously trying to calm the person sobbing, sounded more audibly. The nurse looked agitated and smiled an automatic smile at the waiting women, as if to reassure them.

"You really should put on one of these gowns and get yourself ready, Mrs. Smith," she said to Maeve, who wondered absently who Mrs. Smith might be, until the faces turned in her direction made it clear that she was Mrs. Smith. She gulped back her panic and started toward the gown automatically, when the door opened and a man appeared, propping up a young woman about her own age who was sagging against him, obviously in pain. The girl's eyes, red and swollen, looked up and caught her own. The intensity of the pain in those eyes made her nearly stagger. Not just physical pain, although her sweat-matted hair suggested that; it was an agony of the soul that seemed to stare out of those eyes. They were the eyes of the damned, thought the Irish Catholic girl in her own anguish as she dropped the hospital gown onto the floor. Head pounding, heart beating as if it would tear her chest asunder, she ran. Out the door, down the rickety stairs, not waiting for the elevator, out onto the street, and on and on and on until she reached St. Joseph's Church. Plunging through the double doors, she dipped her fingers gratefully into the damp comfort of the holy-water font, blessed herself, fumbled in her handbag for her rosary beads. Placing her handkerchief on her head, as she had no hat, she stumbled down the aisle toward the confessionals that flanked the altar, praying for strength.

"Bless me, Father, for I have sinned. I confess to Almighty God and to you, Father, that I tried to kill my baby. No, no, it wasn't even born yet! Oh, my God, I tried to kill my baby and it wasn't even born yet! No, Father, I didn't do it, I just planned it. Isn't that almost as bad? I planned it in my mind. I sinned in my heart. No. No. I'm not married. Yes, I'm sorry. Oh, my God, I'm so sorry. I'm so sorry. I'm so sorry . . ."

After a while she was calm enough for the old priest to help her hail a cab and go home.

"Don't panic. This just means we'll have to get married sooner than we thought." Ted was relieved to find out she was alive. After that insane performance at the abortionist's, he was afraid she'd jumped off a bridge or thrown herself under a subway train.

"But they'll find out, now." Her small voice was large with fear.

"It'll be too late by the time they find out. We'll just have to drive to Maryland over the weekend."

"But what'll we do then? Where will we live? You don't have a job. We're both still in school."

"I thought you said you had money from your mother's estate and from your grandfather."

Maeve's eyes widened. "I do, but I never tried to use it. I have a trustee—he invests it for me and gives me my allowance."

"Well, we're going to need a hell of a lot more than an allowance, with a baby coming. And I can't get any from my family. They'll be fit to be tied over my marrying a Catholic to begin with, never mind a pregnant Catholic."

"Teddy, that's cruel. You don't even seem to care about what I'm feeling."

"Look, Maeve, this is no time to be sentimental. This is a time to be practical. We can't live on love alone, you know, and neither can a baby. We need to tap into that trust fund and we need to get married. Not necessarily in that order. We can use the abortion money to get started, but how long do you think that's going to last us?"

Maeve Dalton raised her tear-streaked, heart-shaped face and looked into the eyes of her lover. She didn't see concern or sorrow, she didn't see compassion or love. She saw calculation and cunning. She wondered why she had never seen them before.

"How goes it in Mouseland?" Sky Moncure laughed easily over his schooner of beer and let his eyes wander past his friend Ted to the panoply of reveling collegiate faces in the pub.

Ted chuckled in response and took a gulp from his glass.

"Not bad, my friend. Not bad at all. She's nicely wrapped up in me at the moment, it would seem."

"As well she might be, old boy. You are a formidable catch, as my adorable sister once told me."

"Well, I'm happy to say she's caught me—and I expect I'll be going home to meet Father any day now."

"That serious?" Sky raised his well-bred eyebrows.

"What could be more serious than a premature pregnancy, may I ask you?"

Sky's eyebrows went a little higher, and a small whistle escaped his lips. "That does put a new complexion on things, doesn't it? What are you going to do?"

"Well, it seems I don't have much choice but to marry her. I had hoped I might be able to get her to have an abortion and then blackmail her or her father, but it turns out her trust is tied in knots and she can't get her hands on any money without dear old dad knowing. And he's a tougher old coot than I'd expected. Powerful, too, according to my mother, who has warned me not to mess with him, crass Catholic though he be.''

Schuyler Moncure eyed his friend with a certain amount of distaste. ''So you're going to marry her and try to get hold of the money that way? Sounds painful.''

''Not really. I'll just live like a potentate and fuck around like any normal husband with a rich, dull wife.''

Ted's companion shook his head, as if to preclude having to make comment.

''You don't really approve of my doing this, do you?'' Ted Talbot looked his friend in the eye.

''As a matter of fact, no,'' he replied. ''But then, I've never found myself in need of money. If that happened, I might not be so sensitive to morality. Who knows?''

''What morality? She gets a husband who's a good catch— something that would never happen otherwise. I get the life-style I need. Everybody wins.''

Sky tilted his head to one side and looked curiously at his friend.

''Everyone but the kid, no?'' he said, raising his hand in the direction of the waiter, signaling for the check. He suddenly felt he needed a little fresh air.

77

Thomas Dalton had taken the news of his daughter's pregnancy and marriage with amazing outward equanimity, considering how unnerved he felt about it. They had eloped to Maryland and then had come to him to report on the deed; his new son-in-law, smug and self-righteous, Maeve pitiable in her filial sorrow and guilt.

He had sat and watched and listened as they'd explained the situation, his heart pained by the lack of character that was apparent in the pampered boy and the lack of worldliness that was apparent in his daughter. How in God's name could he have let her grow up so defenseless? How could he have let his own child fall prey to a bounty hunter? For that, without question, was what Talbot was.

He could discern no semblance of love or passion or devotion toward his daughter in this feckless boy. He himself had loved deeply enough to recognize the symptoms in a man. There were no such indications in Ted Talbot.

And Maeve? She surely was in love with the boy, but there was a desperation in it that unnerved him. Could it possibly be that she was so starved for love that she clung to this unsteady spar in a temptestuous sea out of sheer need? Or was it simply the desperate embarrassment about the pregnancy that he was misreading?

He offered to let them live with him, at least until Ted finished his senior year at Harvard, arguing the economic common sense of it and the safety of having servants and family near at hand through the pregnancy. He had expected them to give him an argument about the separation and the weekend commute to and from Boston, but they had acquiesced easily enough, and Tom, listening to the boy assure Maeve that it was the only sensible thing to do, had loathed his son-in-law, remembering that nothing in this world could have induced him to be separated from his Deirdre when she carried his child.

Maeve didn't prosper in pregnancy as her mother had. No blooming cheeks and robust happiness could be discerned in his daughter as the months passed, and no one could have mistaken the grief in her aspect, as more and more weekends passed without Ted's arrival home. The press of schoolwork was what he usually excused himself with; the travails of senior year and exams and job hunting and whatever else seemed plausible. Tom didn't know which was worse, the weekends the boy stayed in Boston or the ones when he returned home and they locked themselves in their room to argue, Maeve's plaintive voice and Ted's petulant one often spilling out into the quiet hallway.

Often enough during the five months they lived with him, Tom wondered where it all might end. Never once did he expect his daughter to die at the age of nineteen.

Complications of childbirth, they had told the waiting press in a prepared statement, but her father knew that she was dead of a broken heart, to say nothing of the bottle of sleeping pills she had consumed on her first night away from the hospital.

Tom had stood, unbelieving, at the funeral mass, listening heedlessly to the heavy drone of the archbishop's bombastic voice. He contributed heavily to the Catholic Church these days; there was political advantage to being on the right side of the clergy, old Jim had taught him that.

"He only wanted your money, Daddy," she had said wanly to him the night the baby girl was born. "He didn't want us at all." It was a poignant, small voice, and he had tried to comfort her. It didn't matter, he said. She would get well and he would help her with the baby and they'd hire a governess and everything would be fine. But she had looked at him with the same despairing expression he remembered from her childhood; it was as if she said, "Why do you never understand?" and he had felt the reproach of it to the bottom of his agonized Celtic soul.

78

The sobbing girl sat on the side of Billy's bed and tried to stay in control enough to tell her story. Her swollen lip interfered with the intelligibility of the tale, but Billy sat still as stone, listening, a fury growing in her soul that was so intense she didn't trust herself to speak.

"He . . . he tied me up and . . . and he was being real cute, Billy, and I thought he was just a kid trying to do something sophisticated with a hooker, you know how they do sometimes. Trying to show off his tricks and stuff." She looked up at Billy and started to sob afresh, but Billy said nothing.

"Then he started to hit me . . . real hard and I said, 'Hey, stop that . . . if you want S and M you'll have to go someplace else, that's not our style,' and then he hit me in the mouth and told me to shut up." She touched the swollen lip for emphasis.

"Go on," prompted Billy in a hard voice. "What happened then?"

"That's when he started talkin' about Mr. Dalton's daughter, only he didn't know I knew who she was or anything. And I just tried to keep him talking, 'cause I was afraid of what he was gonna do to me, so I kept acting real interested so he'd keep talking." She sniffled and reached for another tissue from the bedside table and blew her nose, a childlike sound.

"I know you're hurting, Charlene," said Billy in a kinder tone, "the doctor will be here in a few minutes to take care of you. But this is really important—can you tell me what else our Mr. Talbot said, before Dr. Sands gets here?''

Charlene shook her blond curly head vigorously, so that the Shirley Temple ringlets bounced and bobbed. ''I can tell you everything, Billy, 'cause I know what a nice man your Mr. Dalton is, and I listened real good to what that little bastard had to say 'cause I knew you'd need to know.'' She was proud that she had salvaged some shred of dignity out of this sordid business, and Billy patted the girl's leg approvingly, inwardly seething over the fact that Theodore Brewster Talbot had spent the night of his wife's death in a whorehouse celebrating his good fortune.

''He just kept on talking about how he'd hit the jackpot . . . how his wife just had a kid and then killed herself and how he was really in the money. He said, 'That silly bitch just ate a bottle of pills, just like that'—he said, 'After all my scheming and planning to get her money, she just handed it all over to me on a plate.' I asked him why his wife's dying would make him rich and he said she had a real rich daddy.'' She sobbed again at the memory of the conversation.

''He said the old man asked him if he could have the baby . . . you know, adopt it? And he said, 'Maybe yes, maybe no!' Then he said the old guy practically begged him to let him have the kid to raise and he told him, 'Why should I do that when all I have to do is keep her around to get anything I want out of you?' I said I thought that was real crummy, Billy, and that's when he started to work me over, and I started to scream for Jocko and he just stuffed something in my mouth and punched me real good.

'' 'Who the hell do you think you are, you stupid whore,' he yelled at me. 'You're just another silly bitch like she was.' Then he fucked me for all he was worth—which wasn't much—and then Joanne heard him shouting and me moaning and she got Jocko, and he tossed the little bastard out on his ear.'' The girl was breathless from telling the story.

Billy patted the girl on the shoulder and comforted her. Her mind was on that insufferable little son of a bitch who had killed Deirdre's daughter. Just as sure as if he'd put a gun to her head, he'd killed that fragile child. And he was going to get away with it!

Billy hadn't been this infuriated since Deirdre's death. She prowled like a great cat up and down the carpeted floor of her bedroom, straining to think of a way to fight back. She felt physically ill about the unfairness of what had happened. Maeve dead and that little prick who'd been the cause of it about to walk off with everything.

Dear God, when would it end? This unconscionable loss of people Tom Dalton loved. Maeve dead. Nineteen years old. It seemed impossible to imagine. Deirdre's little girl . . . the one they had hoped for together; the child she and Deirdre had planned to dress and coddle and spoil and love.

And now, she was gone. The victim of her own frailty and of that son of a bitch who had seduced her. Billy thought she would explode with the wrath she felt toward Theodore Brewster Talbot.

The thought of Tom's ravaged face floated into her mind; she had seen him only for a few minutes the day before, when he'd told her the news about Maeve, but that anguished face would be with her always. He had said that he would try to adopt the baby, and she had seen by the desperation on his face that in his mind it was the only way to make reparation; by protecting the new little girl from harm, he would try to make amends for not having saved his daughter.

She had seen him live through so many trials over the years, and yet, this one had been different, somehow. With the others there had always been anger to help mitigate his agony; a fierce, almost animal ability to strike back at those who had struck . . . to wrest some small vengeance from the gods.

But not this time. This time his face had seemed bereft of everything; drained and broken. She had expected him to wring the neck of the little bastard who had killed Deirdre's daughter, but instead he had taken the blame on himself.

"I should have protected her, Billy," he'd said in a strange dull voice. "She was mine and I should have made her strong enough to be safe from the likes of him. 'Tis my fault she's dead." And then he had left her.

"It isn't your fault!" she had wanted to scream after him. "You didn't know how to do better for the child and it wasn't your fault she was so vulnerable!" But instead, she had simply vowed that this one time she, not he, would have the strength to fight back. For Tom . . . for Deirdre . . . for all the frail and vulnerable little girls who had ever been harmed by a bastard. She would fight back.

Billy paused a moment in her pacing prowl, like a tigress who stops still in its tracks for the briefest of deadly moments before it springs. Then she picked up the telephone.

The long black Cadillac limo pulled up in front of the elegant double brownstone that housed Miss Billy's, and a large, thick-necked man got out of the car and walked to the door to ring the bell.

Billy answered the summons and slipped out of the house—looking to neither the left nor right, she walked to the enormous car, and as the rear door swung open automatically, she entered the automobile's darkened plush interior.

The man who faced her exuded power. He watched her entrance with a studied calculation; she could see her beauty register in his eyes, but his face remained outwardly impassive.

She had dressed carefully for this meeting, for this was a dangerous man and she wanted to secure something from him . . . a dangerous enterprise.

"You are a famous lady. . . ." he said. His voice was deep, and there was the confidence of vast power in his tone.

"And you are a famous man, Don Enzio," she replied noncommittally.

"So you have come to ask a favor of me, I imagine. And you are wondering what I will ask of you in return." He smiled enigmatically, and she watched him closely, taking his measure, trying to judge his age. She thought he was in his late sixties, but it was difficult to tell, for the bull-like body was firmly muscled and well cared for.

Finally she smiled; a dazzling smile, for this was a formidable man, but a man nonetheless, and men were the species she knew best.

"Long ago," she said, her throaty, sensuous voice provocative in the confines of the lavish car, "you incurred a debt to a man whom I hold dear. His name is Thomas Dalton." She saw him respond with a quizzical expression; she had his interest.

"I have come to place in your hands the means of cleaning the slate."

"It was a very long time ago, this thing that you speak of," he said slowly, deliberately. "What makes you believe I care any longer?"

She eyed him for a moment in unabashed appraisal, a gesture calculated to make him know that he was being challenged.

"I have been told that you have a long memory."

He nodded.

"And what makes you feel that I will choose to remember this time?" His tone was one of appraisal as well.

Billy sat back against the cushioned seat of the limousine before she answered quietly, but with immense firmness. "Because you are *men,* you and he.'' There was a gleam in her beautiful eyes as she said it. ''A rare breed, Don Enzio Narducci. And men repay their debts.''

He chuckled softly at her reply. ''And what will you give me in return for this favor?'' he asked with amused calculation.

''I will give you back your honor,'' she said without hesitancy.

''You are his woman, eh?''

''I am his woman.''

''Then he is a lucky *man,*'' he said, giving the word the same emphasis she had.

''You will tell me your story and we will see what I shall choose to remember. . . .''

She knew she should feel conscience-stricken about dealing with the likes of Narducci, but she had a fierce conviction that Talbot must pay with something *precious* for what he had done. An eye for an eye and a tooth for a tooth, the Bible had said. Well, this revenge wouldn't be exactly that, but if Narducci kept his word, at least it would let Talbot know that *someone* was watching. Someone who would hold him accountable for Deirdre's daughter and for Charlene and all the helpless little girls of the world. Maybe then Theodore Brewster Talbot would think twice before he ever harmed another.

There was only one thing in the world Tom Dalton wanted now. One thing that could help assuage the sorrow and the guilt. Well, she had done her best to get it for him, even though it had meant trafficking with a man like Narducci. As she reached the doorway Billy glanced down at her slender fingers on the gilded knob. She realized she'd been seized with a sudden desire to wash her hands.

79

The sound of the doorbell rang jarringly in the still, dark house . . . it clanged rudely five or six times, enough to wake both servants and master, and then was silent.

Tom threw a robe around his naked body and moved from the bed. He hadn't been able to sleep very well since having begun his negotiations with his son-in-law immediately after the funeral. God, but he wanted his granddaughter. Megan, she'd been baptized, just as Maeve had wished her to be. At least he'd been able to accomplish that much. Megan Dalton would be her name if he could pull this adoption plan off. It was proving to be a lot harder to accomplish than he'd expected. Not that Talbot wanted the child, the boy had made that clear from the start. But he did want an unconscionable sum of money for her. At first the demand had been a million dollars, but so far, each time Tom had agreed, the price had been upped. The last ante was five million, an unbelievable sum, and one he'd be hard pressed to better if the greedy little bastard kept on asking for more.

He intended to pay the ransom, of course, whatever he had to sell to do it; but the thought of the tiny child remaining for the moment in the hands of the cold-blooded young man to whom she was nothing more than a bargaining point, had unsettled him to the point of sleeplessness. Turning on the bedroom light as he went, Tom hurried to the banister of the second-floor balcony that overlooked the wide entrance foyer.

The old butler padded to the door in his bathrobe and looked out into the empty darkness. No one was there; only a brown paper—wrapped package lay on the ground directly outside the doorjamb.

"What is it, James?" Tom's voice echoed in the marble stillness of the foyer.

"I don't know, sir," replied the servant. "Seems to be a package of some kind."

"Bring it here, James. I'll open it."

The old servant padded up the stairs dutifully and handed the box to his master, who stood for a moment holding the package in his hand, as if weighing the wisdom of opening it.

"Will that be all, sir?"

"What? Oh, yes, James, thank you. That will be all." He turned and walked back to his bedroom. His name was on the wrapper, no return address. He picked up a scissors from the desk, and, sitting on the edge of the bed, opened the parcel.

Inside the wrapper was a plain cardboard box. Inside the box were a folded piece of paper and a legal-size envelope. The paper had nothing on it but the single print of a Black Hand, and the words "We repay our debts" printed in small, neat letters. The envelope contained the adoption papers Tom had been fighting to wrest from Talbot.

Tom sat staring at the portentous papers, his heart pounding, memories flooding him in painful nauseating waves. Deirdre and

Maeve. Maeve and Deirdre. Agonies separated from each other by twenty years. Agonies unforgotten. Evidently someone, other than he, remembered too.

How in God's name could Narducci have known that Talbot was the instrument of his daughter's death? He'd paid a fortune to keep the whole thing quiet and out of the newspapers. So few people knew the truth . . . Tom could not get the agitation in his blood to quiet. He saw clearly in his mind's eye the powerful little Mafioso standing in his library all those long years before. "We repay our debts—" he had said.

So young Talbot had been forced to sanction the adoption in reparation. The papers appeared to be entirely in order. Neatly signed and witnessed. He wondered what coercion had been used to make his son-in-law acquiesce. He was amazed at himself that he felt no pang of conscience at the idea that Narducci had become his benefactor. Rather, he felt immense relief that Megan was now his forever. By God, he would take good care of her.

He felt, too, a mixture of old emotions running through him. Bizarre revenge it was. A twenty-year vendetta at an end. How grotesque to think his life should have presented Don Enzio with a second tragedy staggering enough to repay the debt of the first. He wiped the tears from his eyes and, sighing, folded his robe resignedly across the foot of his bed. He felt old and weary.

"All fires burn out at last. . . ." He had read the line in a book somewhere. The profundity of it had stayed with him.

He placed the note into a small porcelain dish from the bathroom and set it alight; watching the corners curl and blacken and dissolve seemed, somehow, a satisfying ritual of passage. "All fires burn out at last. . . ." He placed the precious adoption papers on the table beside his bed and lay down wearily. He tried to see the faces of his wife and daughter clearly in his mind, but all that he could see with clarity was the vision of a cold gray stone-walled room where a terrible tragedy had begun.

Billy watched Tom's devotion to his baby granddaughter with affectionate fascination. There was something rare and beautiful in his astonishing devotion to the tiny child, Megan. It was as if the baby made it possible for him to continue, possible for him to wrest something dear and perfect from implacable fate.

People wondered, of course, at the oddity of a grandfather so obsessively connected to his grandchild. Only Billy understood that the baby was Tom's link to the past and to the future. Only she knew that Megan was his last chance to redeem himself. He would not make the same mistakes a second time; he would love and care for and raise this little girl himself. "Don't you see, lass," he told Billy. "I've a second chance. I couldn't save my own daughter, but I can give her child all the love I've had stored inside me these many years." Thomas Dalton was fifty-six years of age at the time of his daughter's death.

Tom lifted the tiny child from her nurse's hands and stood a moment settling her onto his great shoulder. The small head rising from the cocoon of blanket looked disproportionately finite resting on so large a body, as if a tiny ladybug had settled on a pumpkin.

The baby seemed to recognize her grandfather's touch and began to make happy gurgling sounds as the man spoke crooningly to her in a voice so low and gentle that the nurse wondered, as she had often in the past, at the man's unique connection to this child. She had seen many doting grandfathers in her years of nannying—they were thrilled to hold the baby, however ineptly, for a moment or two, and equally thrilled to hand it back to the nurse.

Not so Mr. Dalton, who seemed to begrudge the child when she tried to relieve him of his little burden. Nor had he any disdain for changing diapers or cleaning up after the baby in any way. And always, always he talked to her in that strange, gentle voice.

Not that she could make out most of what he said to the baby, although it seemed to be not baby talk but rather stories of some unfamiliar kind. Endless stories and poems and songs and conversations.

Well, if this little one didn't grow up to talk the Devil off a hayrick, it would be a miracle. Here she was, only an infant, and already being taught to expect constant conversation and attention. The nurse had warned him that little Megan would be spoiled, and he had replied with a twinkle in his eye.

"Indeed she will, Nurse. I intend her to have more attention than any child who was ever born." It certainly appeared he was going to keep his word about that.

80

"There's a young man outside to see you, sir." Tom's secretary, the man called Delaney who had been with him for more years than either man liked to count, looked uncertain about the visitor. "He hasn't an appointment, sir." It made Delaney nervous when things were not done according to accepted protocol.

Tom looked up distractedly from the contract he was studying. His hair was sprinkled with gray and there were lines at the corners of his eyes, but the years behind a desk had not diminished the graceful way he moved or the energy in his gaze.

"Did he state his business, Delaney?"

"He said he was here to talk about a dinner you once bought him when he was hungry. He doesn't look hungry now, sir, if I may say so."

"Well, we'd best show him in, Delaney. How else am I to find out what this mystery is all about?"

The thin, nervous man turned for the door and then stopped, as if remembering something.

"Oh sir. I forgot. He said his name is Jack Cavanaugh."

Jack Cavanaugh. It had an oddly familiar ring, thought Tom as he waited expectantly for his visitor. The young man had a powerful build, and his black hair contrasted with his fair skin. His eyes were a brilliant blue, with a merry expression. He was a handsome fellow, whoever he was, thought Tom as he pushed back his chair and stood up to greet the man. He noted the visitor was wearing a slate-colored worsted suit, expensively tailored, with an elegant gold watch fob. He walked with an air of quiet authority.

"Do I have the pleasure of knowing you, sir?" Tom inquired.

"You have the pleasure of once having kept me from starving to death in a Boston slum, sir," was the curious reply.

"You have me at a disadvantage," Tom began, then stopped. Surely this could not be the scrawny ragamuffin in the Boston alley years ago. This man was prosperous and educated. His handshake was strong and enthusiastic.

"Yes, Mr. Dalton, I am indeed the lad in the alley," as if in response to the unspoken query. "Or rather, I was. Life has taken many remarkable turns for me since then, and of late they've been kindly ones.''

"Judging from the prosperous look of you, I'd say a bloody miracle has happened." Tom pointed amiably to the chair opposite his desk. "Please. Sit down. I'd like to hear the history of this curious metamorphosis, if you'd care to tell it. Oddly enough, I've thought of you often over the years and wondered what might have become of you after that day." He stopped for a moment as if remembering. "I confess, I'd forgotten the name you gave me." He waved his large hand expansively as the visitor seated himself in the leather armchair opposite the desk.

"Mr. Dalton, I've come a very long way to tell you my story. If you'll do me the honor of dining with me tonight at the Waldorf-Astoria, where I'm staying, I'll not only tell you my story, but I'll present you with a proposition that I hope you'll find attractive."

Tom's eyebrows raised quizzically. He had intended to go home directly on leaving the office, but his curiosity about this strange visitor was extreme.

"Mr. Cavanaugh," he replied with good humor, "as soon as I've sent word to my housekeeper that we'll return after dinner for coffee and perhaps a bit of port, I'll be delighted to be your guest. Although, I expect it will cost you a mite more to feed me at the Waldorf than it did for me to feed you in Boston, all those years ago." They both smiled at that, and folding the unfinished contract and placing it back on his desk, Tom accompanied the dark young stranger from his office.

They sat in the blue velvet booth at the center of the gilded dining room, delicate porcelain service pieces before them on the jacquard damask.

"So many things have happened to me, Mr. Dalton since that day in Boston," Jack said. "I hardly know how to tell you the story." He paused for a moment, pushing at the gilt-edged dish absent-mindedly, and Tom smiled at the younger man's nervousness.

"We've a whole evening ahead of us, Mr. Cavanaugh, and to tell you the truth, if the cause of your prosperity doesn't turn out to be a lengthy tale, I believe I'll be disappointed." He smiled reassuringly, and Jack laughed softly.

"In that case, I'll begin near the beginning. As you know, I was an orphan. I stayed in Boston till I was sixteen and then struck out to find my fortune; assuming, of course, that somewhere such a thing awaited me. You see, I'd heard of the Yukon and the riches to be made there if you could stomach the cold and the loneliness, so I decided to head that way to try my hand at it." He glanced over at Tom to see if he was listening.

"I arrived at Dawson at the beginning of winter, Mr. Dalton, thrilled by the very sound of the name; by the rough-and-tumble men I saw on the streets, by the idea of fast women. . . ." He chuckled softly, and Tom had no doubt at all that beguiling women might be one of Jack's talents.

"I met a man, in the Dawson Trading Post. An old man he was, but cheerful as a baby. He found me attempting to read a book on prospecting. You know, at that time I'd had no education to speak of, and reading was a laborious and painstaking task. It's embarrassing to remember now, but when he tried to help and befriend me, I thought he must be a con man on the prowl. Although what in God's name I thought he might hope to steal from me, I'll never know.

"At any rate, I ended up living with the man, prospecting an old worn-out claim and learning how not to be a Cheechako." Tom looked up questioningly.

"That's Klondike for a tenderfoot. 'Green as grass and just about as likely to survive the winter,' that's what Ned said of me—Ned Fortnum was his name—and he was right, too. I doubt I would have made it through the first winter without him." He sat quietly for a moment, as if moved by some memory.

"He was as good a man as I'll ever meet, Ned was, Mr. Dalton. Came from New England, from a good family—Harvard educated, too. But he'd chosen to roam because of an unhappy love affair—his brother married the girl he loved, it seemed—so he headed north and landed in the Yukon, many, many years before I did."

Tiny demitasse cups of coffee had appeared on the white damask, and Jack idly played with the spoon as Tom interrupted.

"Sounds as if you learned to care for the old man, Mr. Cavanaugh. Am I right?"

"I owe him everything, Mr. Dalton. He taught me to read and to write like a man; opened the world of books to me. You wouldn't believe it, but in that little cabin he had lined every shelf with books. It was his one concession to the civilized world he'd left behind, I suppose. He would ask me to read to him at night, and in the beginning I resented the effort—now I realize he did it for me so I could hear aloud the words of the great thinkers, so I could understand that there was in me a thirst for a world of intellect beyond what I had ever known.

"There was only one problem we had. Ned and I. You see, Mr. Dalton, I've always loved the ladies, and that got me into a bit of trouble." Tom smiled.

"One Saturday night I went to Dawson. I'd been seeing a saloon girl named Lola and I was pretty well liquored up by the time I went looking to share her bed for the night. Well, I found her with another man, a gambler he was, and I found them cozied up together at the poker table. I picked a fight with the man, and while we were brawling the son of a bitch pulled a gun and shot at me. The bullet missed me by some fluke—but it hit a dance-hall girl in the crowd. Hit her in the stomach and she not more than sixteen or seventeen years old. . . . I knelt on the floor beside her and watched her die about as painfully as you can do it, Mr. Dalton, and it dawned on me pretty clearly what Ned had been trying so hard to save me from." The man's voice sounded pained but steady.

"Did you go to jail?"

"For a week. Then I was let out into Ned's keeping. You see, there's little enough justice in the Yukon, Mr. Dalton. Unless there's a family to clamor for revenge, nobody pays all that much attention to death, and that poor little girl had nobody.

"I guess I needn't tell you that things changed some after that for me. Not that it helps my conscience much to say it. Ned's health began to fail and I took care of him and he took care of me. Taught me history, geography, mathematics; taught me to want to find out more. He was a gentle soul, Mr. Dalton, and strong, too, and you see, I'd never had a family, so I guess we just adopted one another."

"None of this explains your sudden metamorphosis, Mr. Cavanaugh—"

"Ah, but it does, indeed, if you'll just bear with me a moment longer.

"You see, Ned was dying. Day by day he got more frail and less able to care for himself. I used to wrap him in an old wool army blanket and carry him outside on the good days so he could sit and watch the countryside he loved so well—why he loved the Klondike, hard land that it is, I'll never know, but he did love it." He paused again and sipped at his coffee. "My only fear was that his claim would run out and I'd have to leave him to go find work, to feed us. I knew I could never leave Ned to fend for himself, Mr. Dalton, so I shelved my dream of riches for a while and and spent my time with

Ned at my studies—it seemed so important to him, toward the end, that I learn everything he had to pass along—that I worked pretty hard at it. I guess it was my way of paying back his many kindnesses.''

"One morning he was just too weak to go to his chair, and I knew it was only a matter of time for him. 'You're a good man, Jack,' he said to me when he was dying. 'A better one than you know—when I'm gone, take what you want of mine, but don't forget to take the Dickens, it's my legacy to you.' Well, Mr. Dalton, he knew I loved Mr. Dickens's *Tale of Two Cities*, so I assumed he wanted me to have the book as a keepsake.

"He died that night, and I confess to you I sat by the corpse till morning, crying like a woman. He was the only real friend or family I'd ever had in my life, and I felt as if the heart had gone clean out of me when he died." His voice had become soft and sad, and Tom marveled at the story told with such articulate, but sober, emotion.

"After I'd buried him in his fur parka to keep him from the terrible cold"—Jack smiled embarrassedly at his own sentimentality—"I went in to pack up my things, not knowing where I was going but not wanting to stay there without Ned." Jack reached into his breast pocket and took out an envelope, which he held tenderly for a moment before handing it to Tom.

"This letter was in the Dickens, Mr. Dalton. . . ."

The letter was penned in an elegant old-fashioned hand, the letters shaky, as an old man's tend to be. Tom read it wonderingly.

My dear Jack Cavanaugh,

By now I shall be in the bosom of that same Divine Providence that placed you on my doorstep, these few years ago, in my hour of extreme need.

In the time since then, I have learned much about you, my providential companion, and if the truth be known, I have come to care deeply for you, my orphan, my student, my friend, and, perhaps, the child of my spirit.

You have the seeds of fine manhood in you; great strengths and, of course, a fault or two, as have we all. Because of the love I bear you, and the gratitude I feel for your patient kindness in my dwindling days, I intend to bequeath you two precious gifts. I trust you will understand the one to be as important as the other.

My first legacy is an honest appraisal of yourself. You have a remarkable mind. Alert and analytical. Sound. Your heart is no less lovely than your mind, Jack. Often in these months you could have simply left the old invalid to his infirmities. Instead, you nursed and befriended, kindlier and gentler as the time wore on, and the illness worsened. It takes a loving heart and a good man to do the most, when he could easily get by with the least.

On the debit side, my young friend, I see two failings: a hot temper and an inordinate passion for the fairer sex. And since ladies and money are the two most explosive temptations known to man, I caution you about the former.

Which, of course, brings me to the latter. About money I have not been quite honest with you, I confess. At first it was because I wished to test your mettle, then because I didn't choose to complicate our arrangement, and finally, because it was unnecessary between us.

I am a rich man, Jack. Or perhaps, I should now say, "I was"—for you will not be reading this unless Ned Fortnum is in the past tense. I did not work this wilderness all these years without striking it rich. I simply found I had no great use for the riches, once I had amassed them. Now, I find I do.

Take the money that you will retrieve from a safety deposit box in Dawson, and whatever of mine you choose as a remembrance, and go about the business of living. I needn't add that my love and prayers go with you, for these things I'm sure you already know.

> Your loving friend,
> Ned

Tom looked up at Jack questioningly, and the young man shook his head.

"Beyond that letter," he said, "there was only a key and the number of a safety deposit box, in the Wells, Fargo bank. Not until after I had opened the box did I realize just how rich a man Ned Fortnum had been.

"So you see, Mr. Dalton," said Jack as he finished his circuitous tale, "through no fault of my own I'm a rich man. Not as rich as you, but richer than the boy you met in the alley ever dreamed a man could be."

"Well, I'll be damned!" said Tom when he had heard Jack's implausible story. Then he laughed aloud to realize he had intoned the words exactly as Diamond Jim would have done had he been there.

"But why Cambridge? Why was your first instinct to go to a university rather than invest in a business or take a trip around the world or some other such amusement? Why school?"

"For Ned, I think. It was his dream for me to have a real education. So I could fulfill my destiny, he always said." Jack chuckled and then turned serious. "And for myself, of course."

Tom nodded.

"And what now, Mr. Cavanaugh? What will you do with your riches and your proper education, now that you have them?"

"Well, you see, Mr. Dalton, that's the other half of why I've come to see you. The proposition I spoke of earlier today. I would like to offer myself to you as an apprentice, of sorts. I've made it my business to learn a bit about your enterprises. I've a hunch I'd be good at a few of your endeavors. After all, I know the lumber business, from the trees up, you might say. I know a modicum about the gold market and am the owner of a particularly prosperous claim in the Klondike; the one that Ned willed to me, of course, not the meager one we panned together. But more than that, I'm a willing worker and a fair hand at numbers." He paused for a moment and Tom, nonplussed, started to speak.

"Don't answer me just yet, Mr. Dalton; not until you've heard my offer. I told you once I was a proud man, and I don't come presuming on the providence of a chance meeting or a dinner, to ask a favor. I don't wish to come empty-handed, but rather to suggest this:

"If you will let me work as your assistant—apprentice, if you will—learning your business as I go, I'll ask no salary for my services. Further, at the end of this apprenticeship, the duration of which shall be entirely at your discretion, I'll invest a sum of money in a business of your choosing, which I shall run, under your aegis, and in which we shall share equally of the profits."

Tom stirred his coffee softly with the dainty silver spoon before answering.

"That, Mr. Cavanaugh," he said with intense concentration, "is the goddamnedest proposition I ever heard of."

"Is that a yes or a no, Mr. Dalton?" Jack smiled.

"It's a no, Mr. Cavanaugh. But a no that carries with it a counterproposal. I'll accept you as my apprentice for the period of one year from tonight. During that time I'll pay you wages commen-

surate with the work you're able to do for me, as I would with any
other man. At the end of that time, if all goes well, we'll discuss the
possibility of a partnership, at terms that seem agreeable to us both;
if all goes badly, we'll part company. Now, do you accept my
counterproposal, Mr. Cavanaugh?''

"On the proviso that you call me Jack, I do indeed." The two
men, thirty-five years separate in age, shook hands that night on a
deal that was to become a friendship.

"May I ask you why, Jack, after all the years, and on the basis of
an acquaintanceship of perhaps ten minutes' time, you've made me
such an irresistible offer?''

Jack Cavanaugh's handsome face was transformed by an inscruta-
ble Irish smile.

"As Ned Fortnum, God rest his soul, once said to me, Mr.
Dalton, 'I've been alone too long.' ''

Thomas Dalton lay awake in bed that night, flooded with memories of another willing apprentice, long ago. He wondered what
Diamond Jim would have said had he been there; he wondered what
strange twists of fate should have brought him a possible protégé in
the business, just at the time when he had come to realize that no
matter how bright or talented Rory might be in business, they would
never have a relationship.

81

Riordan Dalton was good at business; he had his grandfather's
ruthlessness and his father's luck when it came to speculation. He
also had an ego that Jack found distasteful to deal with. He was not
by nature intended to be an employee for long.

It troubled but didn't surprise Jack that Rory had few friends and
many acquaintances. He belonged to the best clubs, limited, of
course, to those that accepted Catholics, he moved in the best circles
in a very visible way. He had married the prize debutante of the
decade. Cynthia Braithwaite had a mother who was a Harkness and
a family tree that sprouted both Vanderbilts and Astors in profusion.
Although many of the New York Old Guard had raised eyebrows
about Cynthia's choice of a man whose antecedents had been potato

farmers, no one at all disdained the immense wealth that Rory brought to the match.

Jack had made it his business to stay out of Rory's way as much as possible.

"A son is a son, after all, Tom," Jack had said to his employer after his year of apprenticeship was up. "I'll not be having you think I'm after anything that should belong to Rory. Let's just do as we said that night at the Waldorf and let me sink my teeth into an enterprise or two of my own, so you can keep an eye on how I'm doing, and that'll keep Rory from thinking I'm after the job of heir apparent."

"I've a mind to let you keep your finger in the M & D pie as well as letting you try your hand at a show of your own," Tom had replied. "I've had a chance to watch you plenty over the past year, and I've no intention of wasting any of your considerable talents, Rory or no."

So they'd settled down to a way of working that suited both well enough; Jack had enough freedom to test his own mettle, while Tom eased him into nearly every aspect of the M & D business. Tom liked Jack. More than he liked Rory, flesh and blood or not. Why, even the boy's marriage and children had been somehow alien acts.

Riordan and Cynthia Dalton had produced three children at discreet intervals—two boys who were enrolled at Choate by their maternal grandparents at birth, and one girl destined for Emma Willard and Vassar. Tom thought his daughter-in-law and her children curiously bloodless. He devoted his attention to Megan, the child of his heart—and in the business, he followed his own instincts and gave Jack his head.

Jack and Megan. They were the blessed comfort and the means of passing on what he had learned and created. There was a sort of immortality in that, he suspected. Perhaps, when all was said and done, when the wheat was separated from the chaff of life, the only thing left to a man was his hope of immortality. His hope that the struggles and the sorrows hadn't all been in vain.

"We should be buying land in Alaska—*now*, before it becomes a state," Jack finished his impressive presentation with an emphatic statement.

"Alaska's too far away, and it's impossible to exploit its potential because of the cold. And it will *never* be a state!" Rory's voice refuted immediately what had been said, just as Jack had expected him to.

This presentation meant a lot to Jack. It was his way of showing Tom all he had to offer. "With transportation improving daily and new technologies developing, the climate can and will be overcome—and soon. The oil and minerals will make it worth the gamble, and we can get there ahead of the crowd."

"We're just beginning to pull out of the Depression, Jack, there are pressures enough at home to deal with. It would be too much of a gamble for us to speculate in Alaska now. I vote no." Rory's voice was cold.

"We're pulling out of a Depression, Rory," he countered quickly, "but we're pulling into a war, and a war is a synonym for profits!"

Tom, who had been listening thoughtfully to the exchange between the two impressive young men, was startled to hear Jim Mulvaney's words in Jack's mouth. "Wars are synonyms for profits," the old man had said before the last one, and he'd been right. He decided to end the debate before they started throwing punches at each other. Whenever these two got together, the temperature in the room seemed to rise.

"Gentlemen, it's my considered opinion that you are both right," Tom interjected. "I've lived a very long time and a few things have become clear to me in the process." He noted that Rory looked annoyed and Jack looked interested.

"Times change," Rory said acidly.

"Human nature does not!" His father's emphatic reply was like lightning; Rory bristled but subsided. "Europe's being handed over to Hitler on a plate; he's insatiable and won't stop with Europe. Furthermore, our economy is in desperate need of a boost, and war is the biggest boost you can get. Boom times for factories, new wartime industries, everybody back on the assembly line. There'll be war all right, and before too long.

"Therefore"—he took a breath and looked pointedly at Jack—"I'm afraid I shall have to throw my vote with Rory for the moment. There'll be fortunes to be made right here at home and in transport of government goods to Europe." Tom saw the hurt in Jack's eyes, but continued.

"Rory, you're getting cozy with half of Washington. I'd suggest you see how good you are at swinging a few government shipping and building contracts our way, just to be ready for when the war happens."

Jack began to gather his papers together, to keep from having to look at Tom; Rory's dark gray eyes flashed victory.

Both young men closed their briefcases.

"Jack," Tom's voice was neutral. "I'd like a word with you, if you have a minute."

The young man looked up, and Tom saw the deflated look in his handsome face. "Certainly, sir," he said. Waiting for Rory to leave, he seated himself back down.

"That one . . ." he said heatedly when Rory'd closed the door behind him. "He'd torpedo the Ark if he had the chance!" Jack exploded, and Tom tried not to laugh aloud.

"You're right of course about Alaska," he said quietly.

Jack was suddenly angry. "Then why the fuck did you make me look like a fool in front of your son, might I inquire?"

Tom raised an eyebrow, a formidable gesture he'd learned from Mulvaney, and replied deliberately, "Because you have a considerable amount to learn about subtlety, Jack, and this seemed as good a time as any to teach it to you. So if the wind is out of your bagpipe enough so you can pay attention . . ."

Still seething, Jack struggled to control his temper. Tom was right, of course. As usual. His lack of subtlety was his Achilles' heel. He tended to approach Rory with all the subtlety of an armored tank.

"Okay," he said, calmer. "I'm listening."

"There's a war coming and there's money to be made here at home. Easy money. A conservative nonrisk decision on my part, just the kind Rory can live with. It gives him a chance to shine in Washington, a chance to prove his ability and to make new friends that can further his own political ambitions. If we all make money in the process, who's to care whose idea it was.

"Diamond Jim used to tell me, 'Son, the bulls make money and the bears make money, but the pigs never make money,' and there's a power of truth in that, Jack. So, I made the conservative decision— one that also keeps Rory busy and earns us some money while we look good and patriotic gearing up for our war effort, if a war does come, as you and I believe it will."

Jack looked puzzled, but intrigued.

"Now, as to Alaska; Rory's dead wrong about it not getting to be a state. It's too Goddamned close to Russia for us to leave a piece of our own continent within walking distance of a foreign government. Someday Alaska'll be a state—and one day there'll be the technology to farm its minerals and siphon its oil and everything else you laid out in your visionary presentation just now.

"So"—the old amused twinkle was back in Tom's eye as he finished—"if you're over your temper tantrum, I'd suggest that you and I personally buy all the land we can lay our hands on up there, and all the mineral rights. The return on this may not come in my lifetime, but it'll come in yours, so I intend to put my investment in Megan's name with both of us as trustees, for the moment. How does that sound to you, my hotheaded young friend?"

"It sounds like I've got a lot to learn about subtlety."

" 'You can't put an old head on young shoulders,' " Tom said. "That's another of Diamond Jim's choice tidbits. Will you have a whiskey, lad?" Tom chuckled softly as he walked to the cherry sideboard that housed his liquor cabinet and poured a stiff drink into a glass and handed it to his young friend, who took a healthy swallow.

"My God, man," Jack said when he could speak, "that stuff'd make a rabbit spit at a wolf!"

Tom laughed aloud as he poured one for himself and sipped at it. "It's sipping whiskey, lad; not meant for gulping." He sat down in the leather chair again with the glass in his hand, feeling pleased with the way things generally worked between him and Jack. "When can you work out the details of a land deal like the one you've outlined?"

"One trip to Alaska and about a month's time. I know the area pretty well that I have in mind."

"Good." Tom sounded satisfied. "There's another project I'd like you to tackle for me when you get back. It's been growing on my mind lately."

"What's that, sir?"

"When you've worked this deal out, lad, I'll tell you about it. Not before." Jack had seen that expression on occasion; no more information would be forthcoming until Tom was ready.

Jack got up to leave. "I'd best be about it, then."

"Aye."

Jack walked to the door and then turned. "Thank you," he said simply, and Tom smiled at him. He had grown very fond of the lad. Very fond indeed.

Tom Dalton thought about his protégé Jack Cavanaugh with immense affection; it amused him to wonder if Jim Mulvaney had observed him in the old days with the same critical affection he practiced on Jack.

The young man was a real charmer. Men took to him easily, and women . . . well, that was a tale in itself.

If the truth were known, Jack's womanizing and his explosive temper were the only real flaws in his character. That and the fact that probity was not a word anyone would ever choose to describe Jack Cavanaugh.

But he was smart as they came; a natural business brain, streetwise, and accurate in his decision making. There had been much for Jack to learn about running a conglomerate when he had appeared on Tom's doorstep, but he'd learned it, all right. Fast and incisive, he was, and with Mulvaney's flair for the dramatic gesture. Jack could mesmerize a boardroom full of tough-minded businessmen with his style and showmanship. And he could make people believe almost anything.

Tom looked at the Alaskan memo on his desk and chuckled. Jack's memos were a tale in themselves; funny, irreverent, occasionally laced with expletives. The first one of them O'Reilly had seen had practically rushed the old man into cardiac arrest. It had also occasioned his resignation at the age of eighty-one; he had lived through the training of one protégé, he had said, he'd never make it through another.

Tom picked up the intercom on his desk and buzzed his secretary.

"Get me Mr. Cavanaugh, please," he said, and waited patiently for the younger man's voice on the line.

"Are you doing anything tonight, Jack?" Something surprising in the tone of voice made Jack answer, "No, sir, nothing I couldn't live without."

"Good. Then pick me up at my house at eight o'clock. I've a very special somebody I want you to meet."

Tom put down the phone and chuckled again. Billy had been dying to meet Jack for the three years they'd been working together, but something had kept him from introducing them. His personal life was his own, no need to let strangers in on anything that could be dangerous in the wrong hands.

Yes, that was it exactly. This morning he had suddenly known, reading that memo, that Jack was not a stranger anymore.

It was high time he met Billy. He picked up the phone and this time dialed the number himself. He was going to get a big kick out of tonight.

                              *   *   *

The driver stopped the car in front of 12 East Seventy-second Street and held the door open for the two men. Tom had been very mysterious about their destination, although his mood seemed jovial.

Suddenly Jack realized which house they were headed toward. It was the most expensive whorehouse in New York. He'd been there only once, but it had been quite an evening.

"Miss Billy's?" he asked incredulously.

"Miss Billy's," answered Tom with amusement. "She's an old friend of mine, and I'd like you to meet her."

"I'm told the price is pretty steep here."

"Not if you own the place. I'm the lady's partner."

"Jesus H. Christ!" The expostulation sounded so sincere that Tom laughed aloud.

"Surprised, eh?"

"I'm fucking flabbergasted!" said Jack, looking at Tom with a new admiration. "How in God's name did you get to be a partner in a whorehouse?"

"It's a long tale, lad. I think I'll let Billy tell it to you. She's about as special a woman as it'll ever be your privilege to meet, Jack, so mind your manners. She's also about as good a friend as ever a man could have. If she likes you, you can consider yourself one of the select of the earth."

The woman who rose to greet them took Jack's breath away. She was of an indeterminate age, somewhere between forty and eternity, draped in a black evening dress that hung provocatively from one shoulder, where it was clasped with a huge diamond pin.

"I've looked forward to meeting you, Jack," said the woman in a deep, throaty voice, as sensual as anything Jack had ever heard. This woman radiated sexuality; for all the beauty and the dignity of her bearing, the sexuality was what you saw and felt the moment you laid eyes on her. It was a force that somehow had a life of its own.

"Had I known you existed, ma'am, you may be sure I would have looked forward to it too!" He said it with such vehement sincerity that they all laughed.

Tom took off his jacket and tossed it onto the couch, a proprietary gesture, thought Billy, calculated to say "this is my territory." It amused her to think that Tom might still, after all the years, feel a trifle jealous. Men were such amazing creatures.

The evening was one Jack would always remember; he adored Billy from the moment he saw her.

Almost more astonishing than Billy herself was the transformation in Tom Dalton when he was with her. He laughed and joked and talked more openly than Jack had thought possible. He seemed curiously young with Billy. It was obvious that Billy was his oasis. Somehow, Jack had been deemed worthy of sharing in the knowledge of this curious sanctum sanctorum.

Who the hell would ever have guessed that this serious late-middle-aged man who fairly reeked of probity and dignity should have the most fabled madam in New York as his mistress?

Jack went home that night with a new admiration for Tom Dalton and a great desire to see Billy Henderson again.

Part Seven

MEGAN DALTON

She could have called over the rim of the world
Whatever woman's lover had hit her fancy,
And yet had been great-bodied and great-limbed,
Fashioned to be the mother of strong children;
And she'd had lucky eyes and a high heart,
And wisdom that caught fire like the dried flax,
At need, and made her beautiful and fierce,
Sudden and laughing.

—W.B. Yeats

82

Megan Dalton was the closest thing to perfection her grandfather had ever seen. She was beautiful and fair, with translucent Irish skin and pale blond hair. She was quick-witted, and her laughter was like tiny silver bells echoing through the long corridors of the large house. Tom had everything painted pretty pastel colors, so there would be extra sunshine in her life. "No little lass should grow up in darkness," he told the astonished decorator, and consigned priceless burnished wood paneling to a coat of enamel wherever it touched his granddaughter's life.

He talked with her endlessly, teaching poetry and history, practicing Latin and Greek as if they were parlor games. She was as robust and happy as her mother had been frail and wan. She sat on his massive lap for hours at a time, absorbing his stories of Ireland, Boston, and New York. It was as if she were absorbing him into her very being, Jack thought as he watched them—curious alter egos separated in age by nearly sixty years.

Tom had taken to spending half days at the business, more and more of the responsibility passing to Jack and to Rory. Tom's aversion to his son was constant, but his respect for him had grown to the point where he now felt comfortable delegating more responsibility in the business to the taciturn young man. Tom often talked of his son to Jack, interested in his progress, eager for some story that might prove his instincts wrong where the boy was concerned, for he was never certain of his own emotions where they touched his son.

"He's a fine mind and an indefatigable worker," Jack replied, "but he bears you ill will, Tom. It's always unspoken, but it's there, sure as God made little green apples."

"I'm told it's a typical trait of sons in their father's business," Tom had replied sadly. "Rivalry, Jack; the young bull anxious to oust the old one from the herd. To tell the truth, I've no discomfort with the gradual ousting. That's as it should be, in a way. I've built this house of rock for my children, after all. Every man wants a son to carry on his business."

"Aye, Tom. But this one is an odd duck. He bears watching

carefully, to my way of thinking. He's jealous of the wee lass, too, I'd wager."

"Of Megan? But she's only a child."

"Mark my words, she's no favorite of his. He feels you neglect his children for Maeve's."

Tom chuckled softly. "That I do, Jack. Riordan's children are Riordan's children, and those of that bloodless blue-blooded bitch that he married. But Megan is mine."

"Do you understand why you must be an honorable person, Megan?" Tom asked the question as they rested under a tree behind the little stream that ran through the property to the lake.

"Yes, Grandfather."

"Why, child?"

"Because you want me to be."

Tom smiled at the ingenuousness of his granddaughter.

"Well now, I thank you for that, Megan. But there's more to it than that, even."

She looked at him with interest; he always had such fascinating things to say to her, and unlike her nanny and the other adults, he always treated her like a grown-up. He was unquestionably the best grandfather in the whole world.

"You must be an honorable person so that others can trust you and so that you can trust yourself."

"Yes, Grandfather."

"You see, Megan, as you get older, many times it will seem to you that being dishonorable is better. You may think it easier to tell a lie than the truth, or perhaps you may want to take something that isn't yours. And it may seem to you that you've gotten away with it because no one has found you out."

"I know I shouldn't ever tell a lie, but sometimes I want to fib to Nanny."

"Yes, indeed, child, it can be very tempting not to own up to the truth. But just imagine what would happen if I did that, too. How would it be if *you* knew that *I* told lies? What would happen when you wanted to ask me something really important?"

"I wouldn't be able to believe you, like I do now."

Tom smiled at the child with pride and love.

"That's it precisely, lass! Liars can't be trusted. Honorable people can. You must remember that when you get to be grown-up and you're trying to judge the good and the bad in people."

"I always remember everything you tell me, Grandfather," said the little blond beauty with great seriousness. And her grandfather knew that she was telling the truth.

Billy heard the urgent knock on her door as she sat at her dressing table undoing her long hair. She was proud of her blond tresses that no one ever believed were natural. She smiled at the thought of how startled men always seemed to be when they realized all the hair of her body was the same curious flaxen hue. Some ancient Nordic ancestor had probably ravaged the Irish coast and left his genetic gift behind him.

It was late for one of the girls to be coming to her door, she thought with a slight apprehension as she turned the ornate gilded door handle.

"Billy." The word had a frightened sound. "It's Joanne. She's got trouble. The guy she's with is drunk and disorderly."

The madam was annoyed by the disturbance. Such things happened from time to time in any house, but the bouncers could handle it.

"Call Jocko, let him straighten the gentleman out."

The girl hesitated.

"It isn't just any gentleman, Billy. It's Mr. Dalton's son, the big one with the drinking problem. I thought you'd want to know."

"Of course, Alice. Thank you. I'll take care of it." The girl nodded.

"Where are they?"

"The green room. Should I have Jocko meet you there?"

"Yes, indeed." Billy wrapped the fur-trimmed candlelight-colored peignoir around her body tightly, and sailed down the hall.

She could hear the noise in the room from thirty feet away. What a goddamned shame for a man like Tom Dalton to have an idiot for a son. She rapped sharply at the door.

"Get the fuck out of here," a surly male voice greeted the knock, followed by the sound of furniture falling and a frightened female cry.

"Open this door instantly, Mr. Dalton, or I shall have it broken down." Billy's voice reverberated with angry anthority. She had a passkey in her pocket, but she thought she'd give him the opportunity to acquiesce.

The lock slipped back, and after a count of ten she walked into the room. The girl, Joanne, was crouched in a corner, obviously frightened. The sullen young man, naked except for a sheet hastily wrapped around his loins, stood arrogantly near the bed.

For an instant she was stopped by the family resemblance. But this Dalton face was dissipated and surly. This was most assuredly not Tom's sensitive face, just a poor imitation. The very fact of the resemblance made her angrier.

"How dare you abuse my house in this outrageous manner! Men come here for pleasure, not for violence." Her voice was powerful. The young man appraised the mighty form, only barely hidden by the elegant satin negligee, with a practiced eye.

"You're a damned fine-looking woman, Billy," he said with the aplomb of the handsome and rich. "My grandfather had good taste in women, I'll say that for the old boy. Now why don't you just get the hell out of my room and mind your own business. I've paid a lot for this young lady's services, and I intend to get my money's worth." His speech was muddled.

"Put your clothes on, Mr. Dalton, and leave this house. Your money will be used to repair the furniture you've manhandled. You are no longer welcome here."

"Well, I'll be damned," slurred the man, with a nasty smirk. "You're a bit uppity for a whore, aren't you?"

Billy was at his side with such speed he barely saw the movement. She was nearly his own height, and when she struck his face, it was a powerful blow. He was tempted to return the slap, but the sight of the lumbering mountain of Jocko behind her gave him second thoughts about the wisdom of such an action.

"You owe your father better than this!" She said it with such immense dignity that a stab of guilt went through him.

"What do you know about my father? Or are you fucking him, too?"

"I know him well enough to know that you're not fit to blacken his boots." The icy contempt in her voice remained in the air after she had gone. Shay looked around the battered room, then at his naked reflection in the mirror. For a moment he almost felt ashamed. Perhaps she was right. The old man did his best, put up with a lot. Maybe it didn't make sense to live like this anymore.

Then he spotted the half-finished bottle of Scotch on the night table, and pouring some into a tumbler, he let the anesthetic haze fold in over him once again. Jocko watched the man's stumbling efforts to dress and deposited him in a taxi bound for home, wife, and children.

Seamus's marriage had been less successful than his brother's. His wife had been the Homecoming Queen the year he'd graduated from college. The conquering football hero and the bouncy blond cheerleader had settled into marriage and child-rearing with the same enthusiasm they'd brought to sports—and precisely the same intelligence.

Their children were all-American types—a great shock to Tom, who could see no small trace of himself in any of them. The marriage, which had started off happily enough, soon foundered from Seamus's heavy drinking, carousing, and gambling; the traits that Francine had found exciting in a college football hero, she found less so in a husband.

The Seamus Daltons found few occasions other than holidays to connect with the patriarch of their clan, and Tom had long ago grown used to Seamus's frequent requests for money from his trust to pay for gambling debts and women; when the calls came now, he would respond as kindly as he could without any real connection to his second-born son.

Billy poured herself a whiskey and stood at the window on the top floor and watched Jocko helping the large, stumbling man into a taxi.

Tom hadn't had much luck in his children, that was a certainty. Some of it was his own fault, of course; he'd never paid the kind of attention to them that they'd needed. But by God, they'd certainly paid him back for his sins of omission in spades.

She lifted the shot glass to her lips and downed it with a quick toss of the head. She'd always had a hollow leg for booze; she could drink most any man she'd ever known under the table if she cared to. Not that she drank much anymore. But there was something so sordid about seeing that big naked body, so very much like Tom's, but tainted and unwholesome. It was a Goddamned shame, but looking at him, she'd known for sure that Tom's troubles with his children weren't over yet.

The grandfather lifted the beautiful fair-haired child into the saddle effortlessly. She rode with a dignity and style that reminded him of his father. Strange, but a great many things seemed to remind him of his father lately. He wondered if that was just part of growing old.

He hoisted his own large frame gracefully onto a horse at her side, and took the reins from the groom.

"Do you think you can manage so large a brute, Megan?" he asked with seriousness.

"I can do it, Grandfather, just like your father showed you." She smiled a dazzling little-girl smile at him, and he handed her the reins approvingly.

"She looks fine astride, sir," ventured the groom. "I believe she can handle him."

The stableman watched the two ride out over the rolling green hills, one giant form, one tiny one. It was odd to see a grandfather so enthralled with a child that he spent most all his time with her. They were great pals, two of a kind, it seemed. And fine horsemen, both. It was something born in you, the groom suspected, that ability to be one with a horse from the earliest age. Other people could learn to ride well. But a born horseman or horsewoman, that was something else again.

He walked back to the stable, wondering what a man in his sixties could find to talk to a little child about all day long.

This was the second summer the Daltons had spent at the house in Peapack. Megan was fond of the country, and she knew her grandfather had bought the estate so she could ride every weekend and all summer long. It was superb horse country, of course, and her grandfather had bought her a horse of her own to love. The only thing she missed at all when they were in the country was Mr. Cavanaugh, her grandfather's friend. When they were at home in the town house, he was there so often and was such fun to play with. Laughing and always willing to listen. She had decided to marry him when she grew up . . . her grandfather would have been her first choice, but when she'd announced that she would marry him, Jack had laughed and said girls couldn't marry their grandfathers, so she'd just have to settle for him. She had solemnly accepted the proposal.

83

"All right, now, mavourneen, and what do you know of Irish songs would you be telling me?"

Megan beamed at Jack, who sat on the edge of her bed.

Having the measles was a terrible bore; she wasn't even allowed

to read because measles did something awful to your eyes sometimes
and the blinds had to be kept closed all day. Now that she was
feeling a bit better, she'd been restless since early morning.

"I know 'The Minstrel Boy' and 'O'Donnell Abou' and 'Who
Fears to Speak of '98' and 'Kevin Barry' and . . ."

"Well now, that's a mighty repertoire for a wee lass like yourself.
But they all seem to be about rebellions."

"I thought that was the only kind of songs they had in Ireland."

Jack leaned back against the foot of the four-poster and laughed
aloud; the little girl laughed, too, it was such a merry sound.

"I can see I'll have to have a word with your grandfather about your
education, Megan, my girl. For while we Irish excel at rebel songs,
we also happen to have written the best love songs in the world."

"We did?"

"Indeed! And would you like to know why that is, lassie?"

"Oh, yes, I would."

"Why, it's because we Irish are such a passionate race, child!
Wars and loves and deaths and any number of other fine things
always inspire us to poetry of one sort or another."

"My grandfather reads lots of poetry to me."

"Well then, it's going to fall to my lot to sing you a love song. If
you promise to get well really quickly, I'll sing you lots of them."
He smiled at Megan, and she put her arms around his neck and
hugged him.

"I love you, Jack," she said contentedly as he hugged her back.
"I'm so glad you're my friend."

She lay back on the pillow, her pale blond hair fanned out behind
her, big gray-blue eyes watching him, taking in every movement. She
snuggled deeper into the covers and waited for the song to begin.

Jack shrugged off his jacket; he pulled off his tie and opened the
top buttons of his shirt and rolled up his sleeves. It was quite warm
in the house, and he had no idea how long it might take a little girl
to be sung to sleep. He knew considerably more about big girls, but
he thought amusedly that little ones probably weren't all that different.
He brushed the soft downy hairs back from Megan's forehead and
began to sing in a deep rich baritone that thrilled the child strangely.

> Kathleen Mavourneen! the gray
>   dawn is breaking,
> The horn of the hunter is heard
>   on the hill . . .

Mavourneen. That's what he called her sometimes. She thought it meant "sweetheart" in Gaelic. It had a nice sound.

> It may be for years and it
>   may be forever
> Kathleen Mavourneen,
>   I'll come to you still.

"Sing me another song, Jack," she said when all the verses were finished. "That was so pretty."

"With such an appreciative audience, lass, I may stay here singing all night." She heard the nice chuckle in his voice and felt comforted by it as the sounds of the second love song began to fill the air.

> I know a valley fair, Eileen Aroon.
> I know a cottage there, Eileen Aroon,
> Far in the valley shade,
> I know a tender maid,
> Flower of the hazel glade,
> Eileen Aroon.
>
> Were she no longer true, Eileen Aroon.
> What would her lover do, Eileen Aroon?
> Fly with a broken chain,
> Far o'er the sounding main,
> Never to love again,
> Eileen Aroon.
>
> Youth will in time decay, Eileen Aroon,
> Beauty must fade away, Eileen Aroon,
> Castles are sacked in war,
> Chieftains are scattered far,
> Truth is a fixed star,
> Eileen Aroon.

Meagan listened to the beautiful verses as she drifted off to sleep, Jack was right about love songs, they were the best ones of all.

"Have you thought about adding a gambling casino to Billy's place, Tom?" Jack had just returned from London, and the glittering private gambling clubs there were still vivid in his mind. "There's no real reason why the gangsters have to be the only ones making money on gambling since Prohibition."

Megan had gone to bed; Jack and Tom were in the library.

"Why don't you speak to her about it, lad. Billy's always a good listener when it comes to a business proposition." Tom, standing at the fireplace, the long brass poker in his hand, moved the new logs into place among the half-burned remnants of the fire.

"Speaking of business propositions, Tom, there's something I've been meaning to tell you about. Rory's been doing a lot of politicking lately. Trips to Washington and such. I'm not sure how it all ties in with the business."

Tom looked at Jack over the top of his reading glasses, which he tended to wear halfway down his nose when he condescended to wear them at all. "And?"

"And I think it might be worth a trip to Washington to see what it's all about. You've got plenty of friends down there."

"I appreciate the warning, lad, but I've been keeping an eye on his political shenanigans myself. It looks harmless enough to me. Just an ego massage; I think Rory needs to do something well, that I don't do. Politics might be just the thing. Maybe he inherited the instinct from his grandfather."

Jack looked unconvinced. "Let's hope he's after an appointive office. I can't see him having quite the charming personality for an elective one."

Tom smiled at the veiled derision in Jack's voice; it was only natural for him to be jealous of Rory. Besides, he was right about the boy's personality, it wouldn't win any awards for winsomeness.

"You're not worried he'll leave the business?" Tom's eye had a glint of mischief in it as he looked at his protégé, who had the good grace to laugh at the joke.

"I'd buy him a one-way ticket to the moon if I thought it'd get him out of my hair a day sooner!"

But it was Megan who was on Tom's mind. She'd been talking nonstop about Jack of late, and he wanted the man to know he'd made a conquest.

"You're very good with the wee lass, Jack," he said when he'd again seated himself in a chair by the fire. "Have you noticed that she's become your great admirer?"

Jack looked surprised by the shift in the conversation, although he knew Tom felt uncomfortable talking about his son.

"She's not like any child I've ever known, Tom," Jack answered thoughtfully. "She's only a little girl, but she's as old as the hill in Archaim. Old and full of wisdom. I get a big kick out of making her laugh and sing."

"So you think I've made her life too serious? I confess it's not easy for a sixty-year-old to know what's right for a little girl. Sometimes I wonder if I've made the right choices for her."

Jack took a long sip of Scotch and paused a minute before responding, as if thinking. "She seems to me the happiest child I've ever known," he finally said. "I don't mean silly. I just mean happy, content. God knows she must feel so loved, Tom, that nothing on earth could harm her."

"Aye," said the older man hesitantly, "that's what I had in mind for her, Jack; but sometimes I wonder if an old man's love is enough. That's part of the reason I'm so glad you've taken to her. There's a different life-force about a young man, lad—a power and an energy that I haven't got anymore. You have it, and she responds to it."

"She thinks the sun rises and sets on you, Tom Dalton, as well she should."

Tom smiled at Jack's earnestness. "True enough, lad, and it's grateful I am for her love and laughter. The child means more to me than all the rest of life combined. But one day she must grow beyond her love for me; the fact that she knows you will be a help to her when the time comes."

Jack nodded, wondering if Tom was feeling old. Tom Dalton always seemed to him permanent, like a great oak or a monument that has stood the test of time. There was an aura of permanency that made the question of age, as it applied to other men, seem inappropriate where Tom was concerned.

He'd spent a good deal of time over the past few years trying to fathom his mentor, but only after knowing Megan and Billy had the puzzle pieces fallen into place for him.

Megan, Billy, Jack, and the business—these were the items on Tom's agenda; the only items. His sons spent as little time as possible with their father. The other grandchildren were polite little strangers. Jack understood now how it all worked for Tom. Megan, Billy, and he himself sustained the man, and Tom sustained the business as a means of protecting the others.

84

Billy ran her hand over Tom's bare chest tenderly. He'd been preoccupied all evening, and she'd decided to leave him to his thoughts for a while, uninterrupted. She'd taken advantage of the quiet moments to watch him.

The hair on his broad chest, like that of the rest of his body, was varying shades of white and silver. His body was still strong and his muscles taut from exercise, but the skin was beginning to betray his age. The freshness of youth was gone.

God, but she loved him. Loved the strong, lined craggy face with its stubborn jaw and fine straight nose that had grown more prominent and more patrician with age. Loved those eyes of the strangest bluest-blue she had ever seen, and the mouth that could be stern and hard enough to endure sorrow, or soft and wild enough for the most perfect joys.

Could it be that they were growing old? In some ways, most particularly in bed, it hardly seemed possible. They still loved as passionately, still laughed as uproariously, still teased and played and held as fast as they had more than thirty-five years before when they'd first met. How could they be old?

And yet . . . so much had come and gone for them that to count it all must make them older than Methuselah.

"All right now, my darling man," she said finally, wanting to exchange the reverie for something livelier, "you've had more than enough time to brood over whatever it is. Now you can either share it with me, or get out of my bed!" She laughed as she said it, and startled him out of his melancholia.

He reached over playfully and covered her breast with his hand, which was rougher now than it had been in the old days.

"So you'll throw me out of your bed, will you, lass?" He moved his leg in between both of hers and turned himself to lie half on top of her. Looking down into her laughing eyes, he thought once again how miraculously she was able to change his mood and give him joy.

"Without a moment's hesitation!" she replied, laughing softly, "unless you tell me what's on your mind."

"In a minute," he said, as always, in control. He suddenly dropped his head to hers and caught her playful mouth, half-open and off guard, with his own. Startled, she responded by moving her body deftly under his and wrapping one arm around his back; she buried the other hand in his thick silver hair. Wanting him, she felt his own wanting; their lovemaking was so confident, so sure, so knowledgeable of each other's needs.

"I love you, Billy," he said as he entered her, the hard hot strength of him filling her utterly. It was the same for her with him now as it had been the first strange, wondrous night so very long ago. Magic, it was; powerful, wild, intimate magic.

"I love you, too," she whispered as she sensed his rhythm and arched herself in perfect harmony with his thrusting. She felt herself lifted out of the everyday and into that special incredible place that only they could share; that only they had ever had or ever would. I love you, hold me, touch me, yes . . . her body somehow knew the words as well as her mind. I love you, your eyes, your heart, your manhood, yes. I love you. Oh so very much, yes, love, yes, yes, yes . . .

Reveling in the lovely strength and confidence of the man whose life encircled her own, Billy lay beneath his large form when their lovemaking was over, and felt his heart beating wildly in concert with her own. She smiled to herself, nestling her face into the sinewy curve of his neck and shoulder. Some things never change, thank the Lord. Some things never change.

Tom lay naked on the bed, his long legs untangled from the sheet that was tossed lightly over them both. His hands were folded behind his head on the pillow and Billy thought he looked as contented now as he had looked preoccupied just a half hour before. She smiled to herself to think that their lovemaking still gave them both such pleasure. She knew he'd decided to tell her what had been troubling him.

"It's Jack that's been on my mind, lass," he said finally. "I care for the lad, Billy. And I think he's adrift. For all his good nature and his brains and the fact that he beds anything that stands still long enough, he hasn't anything firm to hold on to.

"I've watched him closely, Billy. He's as good to Megan as he is to me or you. He'll play with the child, talk with her, sing to her—did you know he's currently teaching her his repertoire of bawdy sea chanties he claims to have learned at a house of ill repute in Boston?"

Billy laughed at the thought, and raised herself on one elbow so that her breasts exposed themselves unselfconsciously to view.

"Did you know your titties jiggle when you laugh?" asked Tom admiringly.

"Don't change the subject," she chided with good humor. "I'm interested in what you're saying. I like him too, you know."

"It doesn't make sense to me that he doesn't have someone. It's unnatural for a man of his age not to want a family."

"You and Megan are his family."

"That's true, but it's not enough. He's not a shallow man to settle for a lifetime of one-night stands with vapid socialites and movie starlets with big tits and tiny hearts and brains."

Billy smiled at the picture he'd painted.

"If you want my opinion, love, I think he's afraid of loving anyone. Afraid of commitment, afraid of mistakes, afraid of loss. I also think he doesn't trust himself to stay committed. It's just a hunch I have, but I'll bet he's afraid he might not be up to a permanent commitment."

Tom reached over to touch Billy's hair, still long and blond and silken as it fell over her naked shoulder.

"You're most likely right, lassie. I can't say that I've ever known you to be wrong about any man's character. I just wish I knew what to do about it."

"He's young, love. You and I sometimes tend to think everyone has lived as long as we have and knows what we know. He's got time to work it out and find someone to love.

"Besides," she said mischievously, "he's got us to keep an eye on him, so he's going to have to give us both the slip if he wants to go astray, and that's not so easy to do!" She laughed, and the fine lines at the corners of her eyes and mouth were accentuated. Tom thought the small imperfections of aging were endearing in Billy and wondered if she felt the same about him.

He'd been blessed in his choice of women, without question. Two so different, so very different. What might life have been like if Deirdre had lived? He'd wondered it a thousand times. When she'd gone, the abyss had been so total he'd thought the lack and loneliness of it would consume him. It had taken years even to be willing to feel again.

Then Billy had been there. Stalwart Billy. Past illusion, but not past love or lust.

What she gave him had been so very different from Deirdre's gifts

to him; as if she knew just where not to trespass. No demands, no
obtrusive boundaries, no proprietary interests. Just love, and kindness.
And common sense. Years and years of it, until it was obvious that
the unobtrusive boundaries enclosed them both.

"Have I told you lately that you're wonderful?" he said with a
small secret smile playing at the corners of his mouth.

"Not for a day or two."

"I'll be more attentive in the future."

"If you're any more attentive, I'll never get any sleep." She said
it knowing it would please him, and he knew that she knew.

Tom reached out of bed and turned off the light, and they both
went to sleep content.

85

Thomas Dalton was well into middle age. He had instituted a
custom, when Jack first came to work with him, of walking with the
younger man, late in the afternoon by the familiar waterfront. Through
rain or fair weather, between four and five o'clock they would leave
the office, be driven to the piers, and walk for an hour or so, close
to the bustling waterfront that held so many memories for the older
man.

Tom said it cleared his brain to be near the water and away from
the demanding claustrophobia of the office, but Jack had always
believed there was considerably more to it than that for his friend.
The ghosts of the past were thick and lively on the docks—Deirdre,
Donaher, Furuseth, the long-gone companions and loves of his early
manhood. Jack guessed he simply felt more at home there with the
shades, than in other places with the living.

They were walking slowly near Pier 14 one early autumn afternoon;
the cool, crisp wind from the river was rustling the dock dust into
eddies; Tom had been quieter than usual all day and seemed
preoccupied. Jack had tried unsuccessfully to raise two or three
pressing questions, but finally he had subsided into silence, walking
at Tom's side, waiting for him to articulate what was on his mind.
Jack had learned that his partner always kept his own counsel until
he had worked a problem through; then, if he wished a second

opinion, he would throw the question open to discussion, but not before.

"Did you ever have a desire to go home, Jack?" Tom finally asked in an oddly wistful voice.

Jack laughed aloud at the curious thought. "I suppose I would, if I'd ever had one, Tom. But you know what Boston held for me; no more than poverty and a recurrent boot in the pants."

"I don't mean Boston, lad. Ireland is what I had in mind. Green fields, fine soft mornings, the smell of hearth smoke in the air. That kind of home."

Jack looked at his friend sharply. He had never once heard him speak nostalgically of Ireland in all the years they'd known each other.

"I have so little recollection of the place that it's more the memory of what my mother told me about Kerry than what I remember myself," he replied. "Why do you ask?"

"Because I have a need to go home. Unfinished business, you might call it. I want to own my father's house and lands."

Jack whistled softly. He knew the rudiments of the story of Tom's birth, but no more. "Will it be for sale, do you suppose?"

"It is not for sale. I've already made some discreet inquiries about that, but nonetheless I believe it can be had." He paused for a moment, then turned his eyes toward Jack, who was surprised to see them full of pain and sadness. "I mean to have it," he said.

"All right then. You obviously have a plan for acquiring the property. Let me hear it, and off I'll go. I assume you want me to act as your agent."

Tom nodded. "Aye, lad. But to do that you must know a very long and sorrowful story. And you must see a document I've never shown to any living soul but my wife. Let's go to my house and I'll give you what you need to find a way to get Drumgillan back from my father's family. It won't be easy, Jack, but it's so wild a need in me just now, that I must have it done."

They sat long into the night in the library of Tom's gracious Fifth Avenue home, a fire crackling in the carved oak fireplace, leather-bound volumes stalwartly lining the well-polished shelves. Thomas Dalton, with tears in his eyes and a catch in his voice, told the more than fifty-year-old story to his friend, his father's letter held tenderly in his big, age-lined hand.

86

Jack left the Security Analysts' breakfast feeling superb. What a life, after all! What incredible good fortune that he'd met the two extraordinary men who'd opened the door to such a gilded future. He laughed at his own self-satisfaction as he bounded into the courtyard of the Downtown Athletic Club and headed for Wall Street.

Wall Street. What a magical sound that still had for him, the little kid from the slums of Boston, the kid from the Irish orphanage whose first job was as errand boy at a whorehouse. Not bad training for Wall Street, come to think of it. He laughed again and headed toward The Bank of New York. He always got the biggest kick out of meetings with the straitlaced patricians there, each of whom had probably been born in a bank vault at The New York or the Morgan Guaranty.

He had a habit of whistling when he walked, hands in pockets, looking like he had the world on a string, or so *Time* magazine had described him. Jack's rise in the world of business and finance had generated a lot of press. He was excellent copy, the Great American Horatio Alger story: Boy from slums wins fortune, goes to Cambridge, becomes the partner of one of America's great entrepreneurs, squires beautiful ladies to all the best places. Tom knew Jack got a big kick out of the stories, and it didn't really do any harm to keep the name of the corporations in front of the public.

Jack was anxious to get back to the office today, for the final piece of a very elaborate puzzle had just fallen into place and he was excited about setting the wheels in motion. He had finally found the way to get back Drumgillan. He owed Tom Dalton a very great deal. If he pulled it off, this would be a down payment on repaying the debt.

Jack closed the folder on his desk with weary satisfaction. From the moment he had left Tom Dalton's house the night he had learned the old man's life story, he had been caught up in it. What an incredible tale it was; what a tribute to man's ability to prevail.

He had listened with incredulity and sorrow that evening, and finally with a profound admiration for this man who had become his

friend. It was not hard to be moved by Tom Dalton. He was a man
who generated loyalty. He inspired a man to do great things. And
the strange devotion he showed for the little girl . . . that was
something to behold.

Jack pushed the folders across the desk and congratulated himself
on a job well done.

It hadn't been a simple task to find the Achilles' heel. Those
Goddamned aristocrats really knew how to close ranks around their
own, and an estate that had been a royal land grant from the king of
England was protected six ways from Sunday, under the law. Well,
thank God for Randolph's character, or lack thereof, he thought with
a self-satisfied chuckle, that had at least given him a starting point.
Once the detective firm he'd hired had really begun to dig in earnest,
there had been a plethora of unsavory details to encourage him.
They had gone delving after homosexual liaisons, which were not
unusual in the proper English boys' schools Randolph had attended;
but what they had found instead was far more startling. Unexpected
hints at first; and then, after much conscientious digging on two
continents, confirmation of an incestuous liaison between Randolph
and his cousin Elizabeth. It had taken a year and a half to trace the
circuitous story to its roots, to pursue the curious odyssey of the
child he'd sired by his cousin into the family of a distant relative
posted in India, where it had conveniently died of cholera. There
was more than enough in all that to provoke la grande scandale in
the exalted circles in which Randolph and his family moved.

On the other hand, Jack was fairly sure Tom couldn't let him use
the tale of his uncle's sexual excesses alone to undo him. It was just
the frosting on the cake, the final insurance policy against failure; so
he had tucked it all away and attacked the proposition from the
standpoint of finance, feeling on safer ground there. He was certain
there was no ceiling on the budget for his curious enterprise, so he
had plotted carefully and prodigiously. It had taken two years of
painstaking calculation and assiduous buying on two continents in
order to get Randolph by the short hairs. But, by God he had done it
in spades. He did not intend to fail in this particular mission.

Jack Cavanaugh looked at himself in the mirror, adjusting the
black silk bow tie with a practiced carelessness. He fastened the
diamond studs into his dress shirt and slipped his custom-tailored
Sulka tuxedo jacket on over the pleated silk shirt.

The nine-room apartment on Park Avenue that he called home

was really absurdly lavish for his simple needs, but he found that the grandeur went a long way toward impressing business associates, and looking prosperous had never hurt him in his dealings with women, either. He also liked the security of comfort.

"Not bad for an orphan kid," he said aloud to his reflection in the glass, and then laughed good-naturedly at the realization that his valet was standing in the doorway, listening.

"Not bad, eh, Henry?" he asked the man, who managed to smile back thinly. Smiling was something Jack had noticed valets and butlers found difficult to do.

The man helped his employer into his Chesterfield evening coat and white silk scarf, then held the door for him as he passed into the elevator that served his apartment, the only apartment on the twenty-seventh floor of the elegant old building.

"I expect I'll be bringing Miss Delwood home with me, Henry. If you'll leave some chilled champagne for us and lay a fire in the grate, there's no need for you to wait up."

"Yes, sir," was the reply. "Of course, sir."

A fairly constant stream of women passed through the Cavanaugh residences—the apartment or the house in Pound Ridge—although none was ever a serious threat to his bachelorhood.

Jack entered his Mercedes and found his thoughts straying to the Drumgillan file. What must it have been like to love so profoundly, he wondered? To have loved someone as Michael Hartington had loved his Mary, or Thomas Dalton, his Deirdre. He himself had never found a woman who inspired such a passionate connection. He wondered if he was incapable of such intensity. In some strange way he envied them all their passionate devotions. It must be a mighty thing indeed to love enough to risk all for it.

He shook his head as if to clear it. What somber thoughts to be having on his way to pick up one of the richest, prettiest young women in New York. Pretty and rich, he thought, but of no great substance for all of that. Perhaps that was the difference in women who are to be loved profoundly, he thought somewhat ruefully . . . they are women of substance.

And Adela Delwood was most assuredly not the one to inspire an undying love, he thought. Then, annoyed with himself for spoiling a perfectly fine evening before it began, he slammed the car into third and zoomed away from the red light fast enough to leave the other rapidly moving cars in his wake.

87

Jack Cavanaugh walked past the elegantly mahogany-paneled door of the office on the manicured periphery of St. Stephen's Green. The glimmering brass nameplate read ATCHESON, CAREW & MEREDITH, SOLICITORS, and the hushed grandeur of the house's interior made him smile. Old money, superb taste, quiet perfection of detail. He could understand why Randolph Hartington had chosen this Dublin law firm to handle his financial and legal obligations.

When he was ushered into Derek Carew's office, an elderly gentleman with an air of fragile breeding shook his hand. The old man was seated behind an exquisite rosewood desk, with polished brass appointments that shone in the tasteful splendor of the high-ceilinged room.

Mr. Carew began politely. "I'm afraid I shall have to disappoint you in your errand, Mr. Cavanaugh. My client has asked me to inform you that he hasn't the slightest intention of selling Drumgillan. It was, as you perhaps know, a land grant from the king of England and has been in the Hartington family since the 1600s." The words were intoned rather than spoken, in a manner that Jack was certain must have cowed generations of young lawyers. Cavanaugh smiled to himself, warming to his task, for he loved a good fight and none better than taking the pompous Establishment down a peg or two. He had promised himself the night that Tom had entrusted him with his strange life story and his urgent errand that he would secure Drumgillan for his friend, by whatever means were needed. It had taken him two and a half years of effort to amass what he required for the fray; now he allowed himself the full appreciation of just how much he was going to enjoy it.

"I believe he will reconsider," he said simply to Carew.

"What would lead you to believe so?"

"The contents of this envelope." Jack handed a manila envelope to the stiffly elegant man behind the desk. It contained two sealed folders. Carew opened the first, read through it quickly, a frown distorting his smooth pink features.

"Surely you do not expect to *blackmail* my client into selling his birthplace, with the contents of this folder," he said disdainfully.

"That folder contains very accurate and rather unsavory accounts of your client's deplorable sexual habits over a number of decades, Mr. Carew. If it is necessary, I shall, of course, make them public. However, if you will read the contents of the next folder, I believe you will agree with me that it seems unlikely that such a move will become necessary."

Carew eyed the much younger man appraisingly and laid the first folder on his desk with a gesture of distaste. Jack smiled to himself at the effete arrogance of the older man.

The elderly solicitor looked up several times during the reading of the second document, and finally laid it neatly on top of its mate.

"You have gone to considerable trouble and expense to secure Drumgillan for your client, Mr. Cavanaugh. This folder suggests that you have purchased large blocks of shares in every one of Sir Randolph's key holdings. Enough to cause a good deal of discomfiture, I would say, in his financial future, and that of his heirs, should you choose to use them to his detriment.

"Might I ask *why* your client should have gone to such extraordinary lengths to secure this particular property? Surely you have informed him that the hereditary title cannot be purchased?"

"My client has no interest in titles, Mr. Carew. He considers the disposition of Drumgillan a simple matter of justice."

"I see," said Mr. Carew, mildly curious. "I shall have these documents brought to my client's attention immediately, of course. May I tell him the name of the gentleman you represent?"

"You may tell him that Thomas Dalton Hartington chooses to own his father's final resting place."

Mr. Carew's eyebrows shot up. "Your client is the illegitimate son of Michael Hartington?"

"My client is a rich and powerful man who holds your client's future in the palm of his hands, sir. I would tread lightly on the question of his legitimacy, if I were you."

Mr. Carew nodded, as if to acknowledge the point. He leaned far back in his chair, as if considering carefully his next question.

"And what does your esteemed client intend to do with the material in these folders if my client should acquiesce to his wishes?"

"He intends to put them into his vault and leave them there until Sir Randolph's death."

"Very well, then. May I know where you are staying, so that I can get back to you with an answer?"

"I'm staying at the Shelbourne, across the road from the park.

My client has asked me to have you inform Sir Randolph that he will arrive here within forty-eight hours to inspect his purchase.''

Jack rose to go.

"Oh, Mr. Cavanaugh." The old man said it just as Jack reached the door. "I know something of young Michael Hartington, you know." Jack waited for the rest of the thought; Carew seemed to be struggling with something he wished to say.

"It isn't often in our profession that we are party to an act of *justice* being done, is it, young man?" He placed special emphasis on the word.

"Not often," replied Jack, curious about what would come next.

"Tell your client for me, if you will, that through an odd quirk of fate, I have a message for him.''

Jack looked searchingly at the tall, spare solicitor.

"And what would that be, sir?''

"I was with Sir Jeffrey, your client's paternal grandfather, when he died, you see. Our firm has handled Hartington business for generations. At any rate, when His Lordship was dying, and his son Randolph came to speak with him, the old boy was wandering, you know, not quite right in the head, and he thought Randolph was his long-deceased son, Michael.

" 'Where's the lad?' he asked, and Randolph said, 'What lad?' 'The little boy with the red hair; the one who looks so splendid astride a horse,' said His Lordship. Now Randolph, you see, had only one son, as dark as his father, he was.

" 'Tell him he mustn't go away,' said the old man. 'Tell him this is his home, too, and I want to know him better.'

" 'Rubbish, Father,' said Randolph rather nastily. " 'There's no little boy with red hair in this family.' Sir Jeffrey rose up from his pillow in a strange, almost desperate gesture, and he said very clearly, 'Tell him . . . I remember him . . .' and those were the very last words he ever spoke. Everyone in the room, of course, knew who Sir Jeffrey was referring to, so it was all rather embarrassing. But I believe His Lordship regretted deeply that he'd never really known Michael's son, illegitimate or not. He was very fond of his younger son, as I understand it, despite the young man's precipitous behavior.

"So you see, Mr. Cavanaugh, perhaps this is all as it should be.''

"To justice," said Jack in a quiet salute.

The old man's face crinkled up in a winsome smile. "To Justice!" he replied.

*   *   *

Thomas Dalton in his sixties was a handsome, somber man. His large body seemed somehow almost as virile as it had been in his youth, and his arresting blue eyes even sharper with the accumulation of years.

The old wooden jaunting car that carried him to the place where he had lived for the first eight years of his life seemed too small for him, and he had to fold his long legs awkwardly to fit aboard the rickety vehicle.

"You haven't said two words to me since we left Dublin," Jack said irritably. Pleased with himself for having accomplished what he'd come to do, he felt miffed that his friend, for whom he had done the difficult deed so expeditiously, seemed so little pleased by it.

Tom smiled absently at Jack's obvious displeasure and tried to shake himself back into the present.

"I've been thinking what a strange long road I've traveled since I left this lovely place, Jack. 'Twould be hard for anyone to understand what I'm feeling, now that I've come home. It's all so much smaller than I remembered. I've seen it all in my mind's eye so many thousands of times, that to return is like walking into the fabric of a dream."

They climbed down from the ancient horse-drawn cart, and Tom stood for a moment, still and contemplative, before the huge Georgian manse. Then he walked briskly to the beautifully arched and paneled door and knocked for admittance.

"Fifty-five years ago Randolph Hartington tossed me out of my cottage," he said with amusement in his voice. "Today, I shall reciprocate."

A homely young woman with a pockmarked face, dressed in a gray and white maid's costume, answered their knock and led them into the paneled library. Tom felt his father's presence in the room, as well as the ghost of his own childhood, and shook himself to maintain his composure.

A tall, silver-haired man, seemingly somewhat arthritic but looking considerably less than his eighty-five years of age entered the library with the studied grace that Tom remembered.

"So, Mr. Dalton," he said in a languidly well-bred tone. "We meet once more. I cannot say I am any more charmed by this visit with you than I was by the last." The contempt in his voice was virulent.

"You will be as delighted as I, then, that this will be the *last* time we ever need meet," Tom answered evenly.

The old aristocrat smiled thinly and walked to the lavish Queen Anne desk that had been his father's.

"I see no reason for us to waste time on pleasantries; I'm sure you find them as distasteful as I, under the circumstances." He lifted the ivory quill pen from its gilded socket. "I loathed your father, you know—" He spat the words. "He was always my father's favorite. The old boy gave me short shrift, but Michael was the apple of his eye despite the fact that he disgraced the family. I wish to tell you that you are as tasteless and ill-bred as he was . . . robbing an old man of his home." To punctuate the thought, he scrawled his name rapidly across the bottom of the deed.

Jack glanced at Tom and was surprised to see him smiling broadly. It was the first lightening of spirit he had witnessed since morning.

"Indeed," Thomas Dalton replied to his dour relative. "Then it must be a family failing, Uncle. As you once robbed a young woman and her child of theirs."

With a deliberate flourish of the quill, he, too, signed his name to the document and, looking up, winked at Jack, who smiled back, amused by the interchange.

"You've no objection to my inspecting the property I've purchased?" Tom said to Randolph as Jack rolled up the deed and put it into his briefcase.

"I've no objection if you go to the Devil," said the old man bitterly; he turned on his heel and walked from the library.

Jack and Tom watched him go down the long corridor toward the west wing, his silver-handled cane tapping an accumulating echo into the marble stillness.

"If you're having any compunction at all about what we've just done," said Jack with a wry smile, "I should tell you I had the misfortune to meet the old boy's son and heir yesterday. He's as much a scoundrel as his father, I'd say, from my small acquaintance with him. Just as well, I think, to call a halt to this depressing little dynasty." Tom smiled at his protégé. It was somehow important for Jack to have shared his homecoming.

"Well, now," said Jack, the lilt back in his voice. "What say we look about the place. Ever since the night you told me the story, I've pictured it in my imagination. I'd like to see how close I've come to the truth."

Tom put his arm around the much smaller man's shoulders and

propelled him toward the immense French doors. "It all began for me in a little cottage on the edge of the property," he said, himself again. "Yonder, past the bog, was my mother's cottage. . . ."

They walked from one end of the estate to the other, throughout the cool damp September afternoon. They visited the tumbledown mud-walled cottage with its thatch worn through and only a family of field mice nesting in the old stone fireplace standing in the doorway, Tom tried to see himself, a small child, playing in front of the old hearth. They went to the village and inquired after the family of Christopher Dalton, meeting a loutish saloon keeper who, it seemed, was Tom's cousin. He told him the countryside was rife with Daltons of one sort or another. They went through Drumgillan room by room, for, of the entire house, Tom had seen only the kitchen, the morning room, and the place in which his father's body had lain on the night that had changed his destiny, those many years before. It was all so much as his father had described it to him, that he found himself expounding knowledgeably to Jack about details of rooms he had never before seen. He avoided the stable, saying he would save that tour for another time.

At dusk they found themselves in the Hartington family cemetery, and looking for Tom's father's marker, they found one that read:

MICHAEL HARCOURT HARTINGTON

(1855–1882)

The simple statement was cut in the granite headstone, and the verdant Irish grass had encroached upon the territory of the grave, set apart as it was from the larger ones of Sir Jeffrey and Lady Geraldine.

Tom stood for a long moment, his deep, even breathing audible in the tranquil quiet of the purpling dusk; so long, in fact, that when he spoke, Jack was startled by the broken silence.

"Well, Da," he said at length, an eerie sound amid the lengthening shadows, his voice hoarse with emotion and touched with a thickness of brogue that Jack had never heard there before. "I followed your advice as best I could and we beat them at their own game!" In a curious gesture, he patted the gravestone proprietarily. He passed his pocket handkerchief over his brimming eyes, and without looking at Jack, said to him huskily, "I miss him still, lad.

More than half a century he's been in the sod and I miss him still. A fine man he was in those days.''

"Much like his son, I expect, sir," said Jack with a catch in his voice. It had been an extraordinarily emotional afternoon for the Boston orphan. Never in his life had he seen a place that thrilled him as did Drumgillan. The landscape with its rolling emerald fields and tidy stone fences, the house with its graceful architecture and pervasive sense of noblesse oblige thrilled the man. He had never before found a place where he wished he could stay.

"What will you do with the estate, Tom?" he asked on the way to the hotel.

"You know, on the way over I thought to do a mad thing for spite. I thought to make it a home for unwed mothers where girls in trouble like my own mother could go for help. But now that I've seen it, I think I'll keep the old place. At least for a while. Perhaps I'll save it for Megan.

" 'Tis a hard thing to explain, lad, but I love that land. The brown bog, the green fields, the little cottages and the Big House. My father loved the place from lintel to beam; he knew which generation had done what to it; which had added a wing, which had imported a new craftsman to restore the plaster or to perfect the parquet. Now that I think back, it must have been a terrible resentment he carried at having to give it all up. In his heart he wanted it for us, I think. For my mother and me." He shook his head wonderingly. "Lord, he must have loved my mother to give up so much for her. It seems only fair to reclaim what might have been his."

Jack nodded, relieved that Tom had no plan to raze the breathtaking old house. He wouldn't have blamed him, of course, if he'd wanted to tear it down brick by brick. But he would have regretted it.

88

Megan Dalton knew a great deal more than the other children in her class because of her grandfather, so school was something of a disappointment to her most days. Her grandfather had taught her a great love for learning and a respect for books. He had made the

acquisition of knowledge such a joyful game that the dull monotony
of teachers and schoolrooms was a dreadful intellectual and emotional comedown, but it was important to him that she do well at
school, so Megan dutifully excelled.

When the teacher told her how to find Africa on the globe, she
refrained from telling him that she already knew the route Mr.
Stanley had taken to find Dr. Livingstone. When the teacher told her
how to make words rhyme, she didn't tell him that her grandfather
had given her a complete set of the great English poets for her sixth
birthday. When the teacher told her that in second grade she would
learn about history, she never mentioned that her grandfather had
given her a doll from Madame Alexander's when she'd memorized
the line of succession to the English throne from the Battle of
Hastings on without error.

Evenings were perfect. Just he and she and sometimes Mr.
Cavanaugh. Reading and talking and playing chess and going places
together.

She pondered, on occasion, the fact that most children had a
mother and a father, instead of just a grandfather. She thought
sometimes that it would be nice to have a mommy and a daddy, but
on the other hand, it was hard to want for anything with Grandfather
around. He was so very perfect; so big and strong and protective, it
was impossible to fear anything when he was near. He even smelled
heavenly; leathery and tweedy and so very male. And he could do
anything, too. Why, he could ride horses better than the grooms.
And he could speak lots of other languages, even ancient ones, and
he could sing like an angel. And he was never too busy to stop what
he was doing and answer a question or play a game or think up a
riddle or something nice. And when he tucked her in at night, he
would tell her stories of kings and princes, or sing Irish songs to
her—songs of uprisings and rebellions, songs of minstrels, songs of
heroes, that stirred her blood.

She was sort of glad he wasn't married or anything, so he didn't
have anybody else to love—nobody else could ever love him as
much as she did. Nobody could ever understand him the way she
could. It was really a lucky thing that they had each other; she didn't
know anybody else who was loved as much as she, or who loved as
much in return.

Jack and Billy sat in the elaborate parlor of her brownstone,
drinking cognac. From the first moment he had laid eyes on the

woman, he had adored her. The very fact that he couldn't have her made the easy friendship between them work to perfection. She was also a confidante, as no man, even Tom, could be. He often visited her when the opportunity permitted.

"Now, my young friend, suppose you tell me what is so evidently on your mind," Billy said, settling into the oyster-white raw silk couch in front of the fireplace in her apartment. The firelight caught in the pailletted curves of her glistening gown as if a thousand minuscule fires danced on her body. Jack had to control his impulse to touch the incandescence and the woman beneath it. But that wouldn't do.

"So I'm that transparent, am I?"

She smiled by way of reply, and waited. Listening to men was an old art form for Billy.

"I'm restless, Billy, my girl. Itchy feet. Can't decide why I should be less than content with my lot in life—I've got more than any man in his right mind could dream of . . ."

"And less," she said simply.

"Why less?"

"You have no one to love, Jack. No one to hold you in the dark nights—oh, please, spare me the stories of your very social one-night stands; you are talking to one who wrote the book on transient sex. You've no chick nor child, as my mother would have said. You're too old to be a transient."

"It's good to know you don't feel the need to hold back with me!" he said, smarting at her forthright appraisal, but she wasn't deterred by the tone.

"You need to love someone, to be committed to something other than making money and getting your name in the gossip columns. You need a home run by someone other than a butler." Her voice softened. "Don't think I'm not sympathetic, Jack, I've seen the fear of it all before in men. It's hard to overcome."

"What do you mean by fear?"

"I mean a certain visceral terror at the prospect of committing yourself body and soul to one woman and having the courage to have a family. Maybe even the courage to live through losing them, as Tom has."

He looked up sharply at that, and then grinned.

"You are a perspicacious piece of work, aren't you, Miss Billy?"

"That's Barnacle Billy, if you don't mind."

"You're joking!"

"Not in the least; that was my name when I first met Tom Dalton. Most of my clientele in the early days were sailors, not senators."

Jack shook his head with its lustrous black thatch of hair and pugnacious jaw, and took a long swallow of his brandy before speaking.

"There's something else on my mind, Billy. It's Riordan; the little bastard is up to no good with his sniffing up the political bigwigs and kissing ass all over Washington and Wall Street. I've got a bad feeling in my gut about him, and I'm so goddamned frustrated that I can't cut the little bugger's cajones off, I feel I'd like to escape from the whole scene before the holocaust!"

"What exactly do you mean by that?"

"He's only biding his time till he's strong enough to attack, in my opinion. He's out for Tom's blood, and Tom is blind to it. He ought to kill off the insufferable little creep now, before he gains more strength; but instead he helps him gain power."

"Did it ever occur to you that perhaps he's only blind to it because he's helpless to oppose it?" Billy held up her hand to silence him when he started to refute the statement. "He doesn't know how to change things where Riordan is concerned, Jack. He's never known how to reach his children, from the minute Deirdre died. Not because he doesn't want to, but because he doesn't have a clue how to do it.

"Don't you know that people love their children even when their children turn on them? Especially when they feel guilt about not having taught them differently. He's overwhelmed with his own guilt where those kids are concerned. Why didn't he pay more attention to them after Deirdre died? Why didn't he teach them how to have happy lives? Why didn't he save Maeve from disaster? Those are the questions he goes to sleep with nights, Jack. Very few men have to bury their nineteen-year-old daughter and wonder for a lifetime how they could have saved her. And in Tom's case, Maeve was like a sacred trust to him from Deirdre." She paused for breath. "Rory's got his father by the short hairs because Tom cares and Rory doesn't. It's some ass-backwards sense of revenge that Jim Mulvaney used to tell me about; Rory wants to hurt his father the way he was hurt. You see, he thinks his father turned from him when his mother died because he'd failed to save her. You know, just a little kid's distortion of the truth, but it has shaped his whole life."

Jack sat on the edge of the couch, legs apart, elbows on knees, hands between them—a posture of intense concentration.

"How does he have the courage to keep on loving, then?"

"Perhaps he wouldn't if it weren't for Megan. She's repaid him for the other sorrows—refilled the reservoir. You know it's the weirdest thing, Jack, but she's like Tom and Deirdre combined by some magic formula in one little soul. Tom's brain and drive, Deirdre's heart and instinct . . . she's a gorgeous little thing. I've never seen a child like her. And she's his second chance to do things better . . . which of course he has done." She watched the silent watching man. "Would you pour me another brandy, Jack? It seems I need to talk tonight as much as you."

He rose, slipped off his dinner jacket as he did so, and refilled her snifter.

"I've had a strange life, Jack; as strange as Tom's, I sometimes think. Born poor, I'll die rich, but in between, ah, in between . . ." She took a sip from the bubble of crystal, held it in her mouth expertly for a moment, and then swallowed.

"As Tom may have told you, my family were sailors—gorgeous strong men they were—eight strapping brothers, every one different from the last. Three died with my parents in the last great cholera epidemic, and after I'd nursed and lost them, I started out on my own—I was eleven years old—and by the grace of God in having given me a face and body that men fancied, I lived until Diamond Jim Mulvaney found me in a waterfront brothel and gave me the beginnings of all this." She waved her hand gracefully at the lavish room and smiled, a bit wistfully, Jack thought, wondering where the strange train of thought was going, fascinated by the tale.

"Then came Tom Dalton and I loved him from the first night I laid eyes on him, but I knew I couldn't have him for my own—so I did the next best thing and got him a job with Mulvaney and, of course, the rest of it is history.

"You know I loved Tom's wife, too, Jack? It was the weirdest thing how he brought her to me on the night they ran away together. God, I was ready to hate her guts, but instead she became my best friend. She was like that, you know, pure and kindly. No one could have hated her, not even those animals who killed her could have hated her." She smiled again, sadly.

"You know, Jack, she was the only woman in my life who ever treated me like a lady? She used to try to get me to go shopping with her and come to their house and all, just like a regular lady, and I was forever making excuses because I didn't want her to be embarrassed by being seen with Barnacle Billy. Then one day she said to me—you see, she had a gentle way for all her brains and education—'Billy,' she said, 'you are my dear and cherished friend. You've taught me things no one else could, you've eased my mind when I was troubled, you've helped me and my husband when no one else would. You are welcome in my home any day of your life and I don't give a damn about your profession! And if you refuse me one more time, I'll feel you just don't love me like I love you.' Can you imagine that, now? So I went to their house lots of times, even though it broke my heart sometimes to see the kind of life I'd never have—but God Almighty, I still loved to go there, Jack . . . especially at Christmas. It was like a fairy tale come true in that house at Christmas.''

Jack looked closely at the woman, who, it seemed to him, had tears in her eyes.

"Why are you telling me all this, Billy? Why do you sound so sad?''

She looked him closely in the eye, holding his gaze for a moment before replying.

"Because I'm dying, Jack,'' she said finally. "I've got a disease that'll take a couple of years to kill me, but kill me it will.''

He was off the couch in an instant and kneeling beside her and his strong arms were around her and he felt the press of her breasts against his chest through the fabric of his shirt; he cradled her head on his shoulder, expecting her to cry, but she did not.

"I've been waiting for death since I was eleven years old, man, when I sat in that stinking room with my parents' bodies; but he never came for me. The old Grim Reaper just passed me by.'' She laughed hoarsely. "It's all right, Jack, I guess I'm readier than most for him; no relatives but a nice nephew I see once in a while. It's just that I don't want to tell Tom, and that's why I'm telling you the story . . . so there'll be someone I care for who'll understand. You see, my life now, loving Tom and having him love me, too, in his own way, is the closest thing to heaven I've ever known. The doctor says I've six months to a year before the disease starts to show, and I want those months, Jack. I want those precious months, before I have to tell him.''

He nodded to her, moved beyond speech. She sniffled a bit and straightened herself, but still she didn't cry.

"There's two more things I want to say to you while I'm in this mood and I'm still able. One is this: No matter what Tom does about his son, you mustn't get hurt by it or take it personally. He'll do the best he can, and it's my personal opinion that he'll protect both you and Megan, no matter what happens with Rory. It's his Gaesa,* as they say in Ireland, Jack. My mother was Irish, you know, and she used to tell me about such things. It's a doom he can't outrun. He is who he is, and he can do no other thing than be true to that.''

She paused for a moment, as if to be very sure of what she would say; then she spoke.

"The second thing to remember is this: Find someone to love before it's too late. I've had a lifetime of one-night stands and I've had one love—and you can take my word for it, Jack, the loving is all there is in this life that counts.

"It takes courage to love and to commit yourself, but it's worth the price a thousand times over, and you're too good and loving a man not to share your life with a woman who's worthy of you.'' Unexpectedly she leaned down and kissed him on the mouth, a soft kiss, and then she laughed, her old earthy laugh.

"There now, I feel better! I've done all the meddling with fate I can do. But mind you, pay attention to what I've said, laddie. There's truth in the words of the dying, you know.'' And with those words she stood up and walked gracefully from the room.

Jack Cavanaugh sat on the floor near the seat she had been in for a long while, wondering if she understood that this was precisely the reason he would never take a wife. It hurt too goddamned much to lose the people you love. Too goddamned much to ever take the chance.

Billy stood before the mirror in her bedroom and unzipped the glistening, beaded gown and let it slip to the floor.

She was comfortable with her own nakedness, her own body. It had been both her salvation and her destiny. Now it would be her undoing as well. It was hard to believe, looking at the warm soft flesh in the mirror, that there was some terrible force within her that would mean the end of everything. She didn't look any different. Oh, maybe a little more tired, a little less vital. But wasn't that to be expected in a woman her age?

Time had been good to her, of course. Much better than to most. She could tell by the look in Jack's eyes tonight that she was still

*A fate decreed by the Druids at a hero's birth that could not be changed

beautiful, still desirable. It was a gift of sorts, this attraction that men felt for her, although it had been a long time now since she had wanted to attract anyone but Tom.

She ran her hands over her body, touching her breasts, her belly, her buttocks, her thighs—as if to prove to herself that they were still hers. This illness, this horrid news from the doctor, had for the first time in her life detached her from her own body, making it seem an alien thing.

She wondered for a moment if her death would be as painful as her parents' and her brothers' had been—if perhaps this were some latent retribution because she hadn't saved them. But that was just foolishness, of course. Well, no matter what was to come, she guessed she was up to it. She'd been able to handle all the other things over the years; she guessed she'd somehow handle this last great trial too.

She sighed, picked the gown off the floor, and let herself into bed without even taking off her makeup. She was glad to have talked to Jack, glad for him and glad for herself. He was a good man; a better one, in fact, than he himself knew. She hoped that perhaps something of what she'd said had registered. Perhaps she'd make this her last crusade—perhaps she'd teach Jack how to find someone to love before she died.

She thought of her love for Tom, a lifetime passion, really. She'd been only twenty-three when she met him, and now she was soon to die. Another parting for him, she thought, with wonder at why this always seemed to be the way with those he loved. Another parting. Ah well. At their ages, it wasn't such a surprise.

She turned in the big bed, feeling warm salty tears spill onto the pillow. She hadn't cried much in her life—it was as if the tears she'd cried while nursing her family had drained her of her lifetime share. But tonight . . . tonight was a time for tears.

89

Jack entered the Dalton house with the familiarity of a family member. He nodded to the butler, shook himself out of his coat and handed it to the elderly servant, hanging on to the copy of *The New York Times* as he did so.

"Where's Mr. Dalton, James?"

"In the morning room, sir; he's just finished breakfast. Would you care for something to eat, Mr. Cavanaugh?"

"Just coffee thanks, James," Jack replied, already on his way toward the beautiful conservatory that Tom called the "morning room."

Tom was standing at the window, hands folded behind his back, staring out. Breakfast, untouched, and *The New York Times* lay on the table where he'd left them. The paper was open to the obituaries.

"I take it you've already seen the story," said Jack.

"Aye, lad." Tom's voice was soft and sad. "He's to lie in state in the Department of Labor. Did you ever hear the like of it, Jack?" Tom's voice seemed incredulous and triumphant at the same time.

"Andrew Furuseth. The man they tried to murder. The man they ridiculed and browbeat and defiled is to lie in state in the capital. By God, I wish Donaher had lived to see this day." Tom walked to the chair and sat down, motioning to Jack to take a cup of coffee from the tray.

"He must have been some man," said Jack, moved by Tom's obvious pride in his old friend. He knew they had kept in touch over the years and that Tom had contributed money to the old seaman's cause yearly. "It says here he never accepted a salary greater than the wages an able-bodied seaman could earn in a day. Even when he'd been head of the union for decades."

Tom shook his head affirmatively. "He was a corker, Jack. Strong, fierce, tough as nails in a clinch. Not even J. P. Morgan himself could cow him. But he was soft, too. Curiously gentle and sensitive to the needs of others." He stopped for a moment, as if remembering, and Jack thought that what his partner had just said could as easily have described Tom.

"It was he who caused the Seamen's Act to be passed in 1915, Jack. He and no other. It was a bill of rights for seamen. The first time in history they were granted the rights of ordinary citizens on the land. The first time they had *any* rights other than those a sea captain chose to grant them.

"He taught himself the law and acted as attorney for seamen who needed help with their grievances." He laughed softly. "I once saw him build a whole model of a seaman's bunk with his bare hands and drag it into a courtroom to impress the jury with the unconscionable conditions the men lived in."

"We'll go to the funeral then?"

"Aye, lad. It's good of you to want to come . . . I'll take the wee lass, too, I think." Jack looked at him questioningly. "Furuseth was a great man, Jack. I never met a great man before him." He chuckled ruefully. "And damned few after him, come to think of it. Megan should see what happens when a great man passes."

Had it been any other child, Jack would have questioned the wisdom of the idea. But Megan was the oldest little girl in the world. And she was some kind of kindred soul to her grandfather, knowing what he knew, feeling what he felt. She probably already knew more about Andrew Furuseth than the reporter from the *Times* knew. Tom seemed capable of passing everything to the child by some spiritual osmosis.

She would make an astounding woman one day; formidable, of course. But she was a unique creature, and growing very pretty, too. He wondered what would become of her when the old man died, they were so connected.

"I'll make the arrangements," Jack said as they left the house together. "Do you know where he'll be buried?"

"No idea. He had no family, no close ties. He used to talk of being buried at sea; I can't imagine that he would have wanted it any other way."

"I'll see what I can find out."

They drove into the city in silence, and Jack knew his friend was remembering what life had been like a half century before.

Jack Cavanaugh loved Tom Dalton. He was generous to a fault, lavishing his loved ones with tokens of largesse; he was charitable to others, too. He had a relentless affinity for the poor and an Irish sentimentality that had set up both a charitable foundation and a network of charities that he quietly supported without any fanfare.

He also had a habit of remembering the people who had been loyal to him over the years—servants, employees, the families of friends. He'd put a dozen deserving kids through college, Jack knew; he'd never seen Tom pass a beggar on the street without dropping money in his cup.

And Tom's relationship with his granddaughter filled Jack with admiration and wonder. He'd raise a worthy successor in that one. Her aunts and uncles bore the little lass no love, as far as Jack could see. She was the grandfather's favorite, and she would most likely get his stock when he died. He could imagine the number of conversations with lawyers that had already gone into thinking how to contest that particular will.

If the girl had been a boy, he'd have been a real contender, but as it was, there was little enough likelihood of a girl choosing business instead of marriage. Of course, it was difficult to imagine the kind of man who'd ever be able to compete with her grandfather's memory, but then it might be a grand thing for some young buck to try. Oh well, all such things were far in the future, he mused; no need to trouble about them now.

Jack Cavanaugh watched, greatly moved, as Tom and Megan Dalton stood side by side at attention on the deck of the steamship S.S. *Shoharie*.

The funeral services on land had been impressive, homage having been paid at the bier of the old seaman by Supreme Court justices, senators, congressmen, union officials, and notable people from many walks of life. In accordance with Furuseth's wishes, his body had then been cremated and the ashes taken to Savannah, where the urn had been placed in the care of Thomas F. Webb, master of the steamship *Shoharie*.

Tom had had to pull strings to be allowed to participate in the final tribute to his old friend.

It was twelve forty-five P.M. in latitude 47° 03′N., longitude 37° 12′W; the ship was hove to and half-masted; the entire crew stood on deck. Tom, Megan, and Jack were the only nonseamen on board.

The ship's master cleared his throat and spoke in a fine deep voice that carried curiously well over the sound of the sea.

"Fellow shipmates, we are assembled here to execute the last wish of Andrew Furuseth—a venerable man, an unselfish worker for the betterment of seamen, who through legal means has done more to secure the improved conditions under which you work than any other man who ever lived. It is my honor and privilege to carry out his request and to scatter his ashes into the sea that he loved and served so well. I shall read first from the Book of Prayer, the Committal Service of a Sailor to the Sea."

He opened the old leather-bound, well-thumbed copy and struggled to keep the pages from flapping in the wind.

"Unto Almighty God we commend the soul of our brother departed, and we commit his ashes unto the deep, in sure and certain hope of the Resurrection unto eternal life, through our Lord Jesus Christ; at whose coming in glorious majesty to judge the world, the sea shall give up her dead, and the incorruptible bodies of those who sleep in Him shall be changed, and made like unto His glorious body;

according to the mighty working whereby He is able to bring all things unto Himself.''

Jack saw the tears run down Tom's cheeks, and he motioned Megan to come to his side. ''We'd best leave your grandfather to his memories for the moment, Megan, love. Furuseth was part of a turbulent time for him.''

The tall blond child nodded assent, watching with concern as her grandfather stood at the boat rail, looking out over the billowing waves that were carrying his friend's ashes on their final journey home.

90

Megan examined herself in the mirror critically . . . excellent teeth, pretty hair, a little too tall and thin, but very nice legs. Not too bad overall, and boys were beginning to notice . . . if only there was any evidence of the possibility of breasts, everything could turn out nicely. She frowned and turned sideways to see if any protrusions were apparent yet; seeing none, she sighed resolutely and pulled her slip on over her bare chest.

Melissa Hodgekiss had breasts. As a matter of fact, she had more than her share. Life just wasn't entirely fair, that's all. Oh, well, she said to herself as she tugged on her sweater and skirt, maybe Mr. Cavanaugh would wait for her until she grew all the requisite parts. He didn't seem in any hurry to get married, according to her grandfather.

She sat on the bed to pull on her knee socks, and she thought of her grandfather's handsome young friend. So strong and so nice. With a look as if he'd really been around and seen the world.

And to hear him speak was like listening to music, what with that lilting touch of brogue in his deep masculine voice, and always just the hint of a smile in his tone, as if he knew some secret amusement that no one else knew about. ''Oh, he is just gorgeous!'' she said aloud, and then giggled at herself for having done so.

She'd known him all her life, of course. He was the man she knew best besides her grandfather. He was at their house so often, usually with a present, little or big. And when he went on trips, he always sent some special something to her from exotic places; she had keepsakes from him from all over the world.

There were other women in his life, of course. Even at twelve years of age you couldn't help but see his name in magazines; always the eligible bachelor, always with gorgeous socialites or showgirls. But Grandfather always said Jack wasn't serious about any of them. And besides, if he didn't like her at least a little, he wouldn't always take her places!

She finished dressing, gave one more appraising look into the beautiful antique oval mirror beside her four-poster, and glanced at the clock on the mantel. It was eleven forty-nine. Mr. Cavanaugh had said he'd pick her up for lunch at twelve thirty, and she didn't want to be late. She picked up a copy of *A Tale of Two Cities*, and settled into the chintz-covered wing chair by the window to wait.

Jack closed the door to the boardroom deliberately and slipped into his accustomed tufted leather chair on the left-hand side of the massive polished rosewood table. Generally he was more genial in demeanor on arrival at board meetings, but today he had no great interest in being noticed. He wanted to watch the heated discussion at the head of the table.

Rory's calm, calculating manner belied the tension Jack sensed beneath the surface. His intention was always to dominate the assemblage in the same way his father did when present. Calm, dignified, powerful—those were the words used to describe his father's chairmanship, those were the characteristics for Rory to emulate. But they didn't come naturally to him in the same way they did to Tom Dalton. Rory's calm was like an oil slick on a sea storm—transparent and tenuous. His bearing was dignified, but somehow too old and studied to be deemed natural. And the power, thought Jack, that surely is his Achilles' heel. The power is what he longs for; but those around him give it begrudgingly, for they sense that, unlike his father, Rory is not a man to be trusted with power.

Jack watched the group assemble. He wondered why Tom had chosen to absent himself today. To give Rory gradually more and more control, perhaps? Jack knew that Tom did nothing carelessly, when it came to the ordering of his business. It was too visceral a part of him, of his own past and Megan's future. But he was, after all, a father who hoped that his son had the capacity to follow him in the family enterprise. And Jack had to admit to himself grudgingly that Rory was competent enough. If only he were trustworthy, too, he thought, and smiled to himself as the meeting was called to order.

He listened attentively as the numbers were read sonorously through by the wiry little comptroller who had been long ago trained by Dermot O'Reilly, the accountant who, according to legend, had called for an M & D balance sheet on his deathbed.

Abandoning his usual tactic at these meetings, where he found it useful to maintain a high profile, today Jack just listened. He wasn't even sure why his instincts were so on edge, except that Rory had been very friendly toward him over the past weeks; friendly, too, toward others on the board to whom he seldom gave the time of day. There had to be a reason for the congeniality. "When a snake cuddles up to you, lad," Tom had once said to him, "don't be foolish enough to think it's because you're irresistible."

Jack glanced at his watch; it was nearly twelve twenty. The meeting would be over in ten minutes, and nothing untoward had happened. The usual skirmishes, the usual reports, but nothing singular. He pushed his yellow lined pad out of the way and returned his fountain pen to his breast pocket.

"By the way, gentlemen." Rory sounded unusually affable. "I believe it would be in everyone's best interest if we were to initiate a little research project—nothing spectacular, mind you. Just a bit of enlightenment about the competition." He smiled benevolently at the assembly, who, feeling that the meeting was already over, were now concentrating on getting to their luncheon appointments on time.

"What kind of research did you have in mind?" Jack asked. His senses were suddenly alert.

"Just a new notion a Harvard classmate of mine has suggested for us, Jack. The man's something of a statistical genius, you know. His name's Howard Berthold and he's pioneering a new type of research for corporations like ours.

"What it consists of is an in-depth psychological study of the competition. Not just their business strengths and weaknesses—more of a psychological portrait of the management. It's all quite new and, I think, rather exciting. It might take a couple of years to accomplish, of course."

"I would have thought we knew all we needed to about the competition—"

"Yes, indeed," replied Rory smoothly. "I'm sure a great many would agree with you, Jack, and you may be right. But I'm sure you'll agree that such information can't hurt, and it may just provide some useful tidbit that can strengthen our bargaining position. . . ."

"Are we expecting to be doing some bargaining with the competition, then, that we're unaware of?"

Rory remained calm, but Jack could see that he was annoyed; he had obviously expected to slip the research through without opposition.

"I was simply using that as an example, Jack," he said, as if to a slow child. "Obviously, as a member of the board, you would always be made aware of any negotiations of consequence. I simply didn't want to take everyone's time by going into detail about the usefulness of such intimate information." Rory raised his eyebrows meaningfully. "I should have thought the benefits would be obvious to anyone."

Jack smiled a little. "I see no need for such an arch tone of voice, Rory. *I* would think it obvious to *anyone*, that questionable expenditures of money are worthy of discussion. I assume your friend Mr. Berthold is not planning to do this research of yours out of the goodness of his heart." Several smiles around the table made it apparent that the sally had not gone unheard.

The man on Rory's right, a longtime board member, cleared his throat and then spoke cordially.

"Why don't we table this discussion for the moment in the interest of lunch, gentlemen. Perhaps Mr. Dalton will be kind enough to send us all some information on this research and some costs, so we're in a better position to discuss it next time we meet."

Rory smiled and nodded assent. Everyone gathered his papers into waiting briefcases, and the room cleared. Jack sat at the table after everyone had left, thinking, Now what do you suppose that was all about? Looks benign enough on the surface, but there's something fishy about the request. Now what could it be?

He picked up the sheaf of financial statements thoughtfully, and, folding them in half vertically, slipped them into his inside breast pocket and walked to the huge bank of windows that enveloped the large conference room.

The city spread out brilliantly in all directions, viewed from such a high floor. Tiny antlike people and toy-sized cars bustled beneath him, too far away for sound or connection. The sun beating in on him felt warming and secure. Maybe there's nothing to it, after all, he told himself placatingly. Nothing sinister in a little research project. Maybe I just hate the guy so much, I see danger in everything he touches. He turned from the window and walked briskly toward the door.

Maybe, he mused as he let himself out of the room. But I con't think so.

Rory looked over the shining surface of his huge desk. He prided himself on always having a pristine desk top. One of his professors at the Harvard Business School had maintained that the true test of the complete executive was a litter-free desk, since it suggested that all necessary labor was being done, as it should be, by underlings.

He intended to have the research project done, because he needed the information. Somewhere out there was someone or something that would further his plans. When Howard had come to see him about the research, it had all clicked into place for him.

He'd known for a long time that he'd have to find a way to make his own mark in the world. His father was a bloody legend; even Cavanaugh had the Devil's own gift for being recognized. Just taking over for his father would never be enough. He'd always be a son, a maintenance man in a long line of entrepreneurs. But somewhere out there was the opportunity he sought. Why not let someone else do the legwork for him? It made sense to pay people to do your bidding, after all.

Meanwhile, he'd keep after the political possibilities. Rory liked politics, and he was good at it. He had all the right qualities; he was handsome, young, rich, and ruthless. Diamond Jim Mulvaney had been a crude old character, but there was no denying that he had the Irish gift for political genius; perhaps he'd inherited some of it. And the aura of the old man's legend wouldn't hurt, either, with the pols.

Rory had no doubt whatsoever that he could prosper in politics. But the need to excel in business sprang from far different substance. He knew he was good at it; knew he could run rings about most men his age in any corporate arena. But the need was to outdo his father; to hurt him as he deserved to be hurt. To beat him at his own game.

This research project might give him just the fodder he needed to do what was germinating in his mind. If not, something else would come along. After all, he was young, he had time. It was his father whose time was running out.

91

"Grandfather?" Thirteen-year-old Megan, dressed primly in her school uniform, sat in Central Park with the man she loved best in the world. He was getting old, the deep russet of his hair long ago turned to silver, his huge shoulders gently stooped, but not enough to interfere significantly with the stature that had awed men and intrigued women in his youth.

"Why do you seem so sad today?" Something in the way she asked it reminded him of his Deirdre, once long ago in a garden, before she had been his wife. He smiled at the lovely child and patted her knee just above the place where her proper blue and gray argyle socks met her pleated wool skirt.

"I was thinking about your Uncle Rory, child. I suspect he's up to no good, but I can't quite put my finger on what he's got up his sleeve."

She wrinkled her nose in distaste. "He is distinctly not a kindred soul of mine, Grandfather."

He smiled benevolently at the precocious child. She was a rare one, this intellectual pixie he'd helped invent. No, that wasn't quite right. He had nurtured her gifts for a certainty, but he hadn't invented her. She was her own strangely eclectic combination: serious, gifted, headstrong, and unbelievably lovable. He wondered what man would ever be man enough to satisfy all the different parts of her. He wondered if he had done her a disservice in teaching her so much, but she had been like an eager sponge.

"One would think you had sprung from a different seed altogether, lass, from your uncle and his brood."

"Was he always such an alien, Grandfather?"

"I don't know, Megan. I just don't know. 'Tis impossible to remember for sure, but I think he was a different little soul when your grandmother was alive. Something happened inside the lad when she died; 'twas as if he hardened, somehow." He faded into memory for a moment and then returned. "There was such a magic to your grandmother, child. She knew how to nurture the softness in a man . . . how to encourage everyone to be the best he could be.

After she went, nothing was ever the same for me . . . or for Rory, I'm afraid."

"You still miss her, don't you, Grandfather?"

"Aye, lass. That I do."

"Will it cheer you up if I tell you I've decided not to go to boarding school next fall?" She smiled mischievously, and Tom thought he saw a flash of his father in her eyes; the same ebullient spirit.

"Have you, now? And would you care to tell me what that's all about?"

"Simple. I can't live without you."

She reached up spontaneously and kissed him on the cheek. "It's you and me against the world, Grandfather. Always was, always will be, world without end. Amen."

The old man looked at the fresh young girl with unabashed pride and love.

"You, child, are the one real treasure of my life. But I'm afraid it won't always be you and me, world without end. I'm nearly seventy years of age, lassie. Just how much longer do you suppose I'll be hanging around, now?"

"All the more reason why I shouldn't go to boarding school, Grandfather. I intend to have you all to myself, for a very long while yet." She cocked her head to the side and looked at him conspiratorially. "Do you know, I sometimes think that in some weird way, you and I are the same person."

"And exactly what do you mean by that, Megan?"

"I don't know *exactly*. It's just that I know everything about you. From the minute you were born until now, just like you know me. And you know we aren't like any of the other people in our family. They don't even like us, mostly."

"You have a point there, child," he said, chuckling at her perspicacity.

"But we're really special, you and me, Grandfather. It's like, even if you weren't here, you still would be, as long as I'm around. Do you know what I mean?"

"I know exactly what you mean, child, and it's an almighty comfort. You're the only one in this world who knows the whole story from the beginning. It's important, Megan, that continuity. Perhaps someday you'll pass it on to one of your own."

"Well, I'm not ever going to get married, unless I can find somebody like you, and I don't think that's going to be too easy."

The old man laughed aloud, and hugged the child as he stood up from the bench and said, "What say we go feed the squirrels before we get too old and serious for such a frivolous enterprise."

The blond girl, just shy of beginning the assent into womanhood, laughingly took his hand, as she had done ten thousand times before, and skipped down the leaf-strewn path toward the peanut vendor, secure in the knowledge that she was very much loved by a very special man.

The inevitability of the clash between Jack and Riordan was something Tom had taken for granted from the beginning. He kept the two men separate for as long as possible; the fact that once the first year of Jack's internship had passed, he had quite comfortably taken his place running several of his own enterprises—his and Tom's—with very little interference from his senior partner, had made the separation easier.

Nonetheless, Jack was Tom's friend and protégé, and had it not been for the fact of Riordan in the business, he would have been the obvious heir to follow in his mentor's considerable footsteps. But Riordan was the *son*. Uncomfortable as the knowledge was, Tom had to admit that blood was, at the end, thicker than water, and that a place would have to be made in the future of M & D for the latest scion of the "D" line.

It would have been wonderful and fitting, of course, for Jack to be the one to follow Tom in the driver's seat of the prosperous conglomerate; it would have been convenient if Riordan had proved himself incapable of inheriting power. But that was simply not the case.

Tom knew it had taken Jack quite a while to come to terms with the young man, if indeed he had ever really done so. Fortunately, with or without M & D, Jack had more money than he would ever use, and the businesses he and Tom owned jointly were big moneymakers in themselves; so the question of accession to M & D's corporate throne was not one of either avarice or need.

What Tom didn't know was that Jack, in a relentless Irish Catholic fashion, had plumbed his own motivations in an effort to be certain of the genesis of his unmitigated dislike of Rory. The boy meant ill toward the father. Underneath the familial pieties and professional courtesy and the dutiful corporate benignity, he meant to do his father harm. But what to do about it? Tom had no idea how much time Jack spent pondering that particular question.

92

"Isn't this the most beautiful place on earth?" Megan's breathless voice sang into the wind as she galloped with Jack over the rolling green hills of Drumgillan toward the rain-misted mountains far ahead.

" 'Tis that indeed, lass," he shouted back at her, pushing his own horse to keep pace. He loved to ride but hadn't the natural horsemanship of the Daltons, who seemed to ride as if they were part of the beast they were mounted on.

At the top of the next rise he saw that she had stopped and was holding up her hand as if to signal him to silence. She appeared to be listening intently, and reined up beside her as an eerie moaning cry reached his ears over the sound of the wind.

"What in God's name is that sound?" she asked earnestly, looking agitated and concerned.

"I can't be sure from this distance, lass, but I think it's the sound of women keening for the dead."

She looked at him incredulously. "You've heard it before?"

"Aye, I have that." He looked unsettled by the memory, and the horse, sensing his uneasiness, began to fidget. "On the boat coming over from Ireland, Megan; we were in steerage, my parents and me. We were packed in tighter than sardines, and a storm came up at sea and some of the poor devils tried to get up on deck to escape the fearful pitching of the boat, down below. Well, the trouble was, lass, they'd locked the gates from the steerage to the decks above." He paused for a moment, frowning in remembrance, and then continued. "It seems they had only so many life jackets and boats, and they didn't want the poor bastards from steerage getting saved at the cost of the high-paying customers . . . so, they just locked us in."

"What would have happened if the ship had gone down?" asked the pretty fifteen-year-old girl, with horror in her voice.

"There would have been Irish stew for the fishes, I suppose," Jack replied, trying to shake free of the disquieting memory.

"At any rate, there was a terrible panic when the people realized they were trapped and helpless, and in the panic one old man had a heart attack and died. That's when I heard the keening, you see, Megan. For one whole night they kept it up. The sobbing and keening and the howl of the storm about us. 'Tis not a sound you'd be likely to forget.''

She nodded, finding the right words didn't come. Finally she said, "There's something so familiar in that sound, Jack. I know I've never heard it before and yet I have . . . do you know what I mean? They say it's like the sound of the banshee.''

"Aye. So they say."

"Do you know anything about banshees, Jack? I mean, did your parents ever tell you about them?"

"Megan, lass. My parents died when I was so young, 'tis hard to remember what they told me about. All I know of the banshee is that she's charged with announcing death. Why do you ask, sweetheart?"

She smiled at the word, knowing it was not a word between lovers but rather the universal endearment of Irish men for girl children.

"I've been reading up on her," she said very seriously.

"You have, now."

"Yes, I have. It seems that banshees belong to only a few of the old families, and if you've got one, she announces to you when someone in your family is going to die. It seems she comes to your window in the night and cries in an unearthly voice, so you'll know someone is to go."

"She does that, does she?" he said gently, because it seemed obvious that the subject was of some consequence to her.

"They say the keening that Irish women do for their dead is just an imitation of the banshee's lament."

"It's just a fable, child. You mustn't be so disturbed by it."

Megan looked searchingly at the man at her side, her soft gray-blue eyes with the dark fringe of lashes seemingly intent on looking into him.

"My grandfather hears the banshee, Jack," she said quietly.

"Why do you say that, Megan? Surely you're remembering some child's tale he told you when you were a little girl."

"No, Jack. I mean it. He told me he heard the banshee come for his father, the night before he was killed by the horse. You know the story. He told me that was the first time he'd ever heard her, but there have been other times, too. He didn't say when." She paused for a moment. "He would never lie to me, Jack."

"No, lass. That indeed he would not," he said thoughtfully.

Well, stranger things than that have happened, I suppose, he said to himself, somehow unsettled by the whole conversation.

"Your grandfather's an unusual man, Megan, and very Celtic in his heart. I'm not superstitious myself, but neither am I prepared to say there's nothing in those old legends. I just have no experience of that kind of thing myself, lass."

"They say she only comes to one person in each generation, Jack, and then only if there's one who understands. I think my grandfather's banshee will pass to me when he goes. I'm sure that's what she'll sound like—just like that eerie crying in the wind."

She stayed poised, astride the large horse, listening again, then shook her head as if to purge it of the strange sound; she smiled enigmatically at Jack as if there were more she wished to say, then she turned the horse without a word and rode on down the hill.

He stayed on the rise for a moment after she rode off, watching the agile form move away, long blond hair flying, her slight angular body graceful on the chestnut horse.

It was probably only a young girl's fanciful imagination he knew, but it was unsettling.

93

Tom Dalton stood at the foot of Billy's bed at the Harkness Pavilion for a long lonely while, staring at the lifeless body of his dear old friend.

She had been the last remnant of his past; with her passing the final act of the old drama seemed to him to have been played out at last. It was so strange to see her lying there, frail and lifeless; she who had been the most radiantly alive person, man or woman, that he had ever known. It was heartbreaking to see her so still and cold and fragile.

Her hair against the pillow was thin and nearly white; he wondered that he had never noticed it changing color over the last year, the pale yellow blending with the silver in such a subtle way. He wondered, too, that he had never noticed her growing old.

Always, she had been for him, the Barnacle Billy of their first meeting. The peasant courtesan, the earthy, laughing girl who knew more about men than they could ever know about themselves.

"Beware of Rory, my dear friend," she had said to him when she was dying. "What's bred in the marrow comes out in the bone. He's a bad seed." Even at the end, she had wanted to take care of him. He, the mighty entrepreneur, the rich and the powerful Thomas Dalton, whom others envied and feared . . . Billy had simply loved.

She had said a great deal to him in these last days as he sat with her, holding her frail hand in his own strong one; they had remembered everything together. The docks, Donaher, Deirdre, Mulvaney; their mutual destinies, their shared joys and sorrows. He hadn't loved her as he had loved Deirdre and she had known that, accepting it. But he had loved her greatly, and she had known that, too.

He sat again on the side of the bed and brushed the warm tears from his cheeks with his handkerchief. "We have known the days, haven't we, love?" he whispered to her. "We have known the days." He leaned down to the face he knew so well and kissed the colorless lips with infinite tenderness.

"Fare thee well, Billy, my friend," he said softly. "Tell all those we've loved together that I'll be there soon."

He touched her thin cheek tenderly, marveling at how cold it felt already. Then he tucked her away forever in his mind and heart and left the still, sad room behind him.

"Where does he go off to every Friday afternoon, Hank?" Jack asked the question of Tom's chauffeur as the man returned the car to the garage, having dropped off its owner from his weekly errand.

"I don't know as I'm supposed to say, Mr. Cavanaugh, but seeing as it's you, I guess it's okay. He goes out to the cemetery to put flowers on their graves—Miss Deirdre and Miss Billy. Seems as though Miss Billy did it every week till she died for Mr. Dalton's wife, real secret like, and he never let on he knowed about it. But ever since Miss Billy died, it's out to the graveyard every Friday, like clockwork, he goes. Stands for a while by each grave, leaves the flowers, and comes back home."

Jack nodded his head at the story as if such was to be expected, and walked back to his Mercedes.

"I thought you just got here, Mr. Cavanaugh—ain't you gonna stay?" asked the chauffeur, seeing him prepare for departure.

"I was going to talk to Mr. Dalton about some business, Hank, but I think perhaps he'd rather be alone for now. Thanks for telling me the story."

"Sure thing, Mr. Cavanaugh. It's a real nice story, ain't it?"

Jack smiled as he put the car in reverse and waved to the uniformed man.

A real nice story it was indeed.

Megan said good night to the young man who had taken her to the formal dance, at the door. He had kissed her wildly in the car before letting her out, and she'd thought for a moment or two that she was going to have trouble escaping from the tangle of arms and legs that had suddenly enmeshed her. Not that she didn't like the kissing and touching and all the strange physical symptoms they provoked. She did like it all, very much.

It was *boys* she seemed to have difficulty with. There seemed suddenly to be swarms of lusty boys around her, but it wasn't boys that she wanted. They were simply too young; somehow, there was a different presence to a man than to a boy. A different substance, a different rhythm.

She wanted sex, wanted all the strange and hidden knowledge that the boys all seemed so determined to share with her. But she didn't want it with them. They were too young, too self-centered, too callous, too overwhelmed by their own needs.

She wanted someone who would understand *her*; her body, her mind, her heart. Someone who would share those mysteries with her, not just take her virginity as another triumphal feather in his cap. Somebody who would care that she'd shared herself with him. And that somebody wouldn't be a boy, she was certain. That somebody would have to be a man.

94

Rory studied the sheaf of papers Howard Berthold had left in his office; four years of research and psychological portraiture had finally paid off. It could have been done sooner, if Cavanaugh hadn't pursued him so relentlessly about the cost.

He flipped through the lengthy document, smiling occasionally at the psychological jargon, underlining certain phrases on pages of particular consequence. There was a photograph of Senator Harvey Goodhue tucked into a clear plastic pocket at the end of the report. Rory studied the self-indulgent face with a combination of elation and disdain. He put down the large sheaf of papers and picked up a single notepad on which he'd written salient facts:

—Harvey Goodhue
—61 years old
—U.S. senator, fourth term
—loves women and bourbon
—owner of country's third largest lumber company
—dishonest, bombastic, avaricious
—uses son-in-law as a front for clandestine deals
—open to acquisitions and mergers
—ruthless

Rory tapped his pen absentmindedly on the desk blotter. Goodhue sounded like a man he should get to know.

Riordan Dalton sat in a wing chair at the Union League and contemplated the two men with whom he was planning to lunch.

Senator Goodhue was a crafty old bird who cherished such a lusty belief in the American free-enterprise system that he had turned a faltering old family sawmill into one of the largest lumber businesses in North America. His cherubic countenance belied the heart of steel that beat beneath.

Elwood Grady, the third man sipping Chivas in the wood-paneled comfort of the club's library, was Goodhue's son-in-law, a man whose function was simply to front for his wife's father wherever it behooved the senator not to be visible in his dealings. Elwood was a perfect choice for such a job, Riordan mused as he watched the two studiously, for although he was apparently smart and ruthless, he seemed to be not a person in his own right but rather an appendage of his father-in-law.

"You tell me you've decided to sell out your old man, Rory," said the senator. The two younger men looked shocked by the blatancy of phraseology. "But I'm afraid I can't accept the gift without a bit of an explanation."

"Most sons dislike their fathers," volunteered Elwood pointedly, and the senator frowned him into silence.

"Be that as it may, Elwood, damned few of them go so far as to cut their father's nuts off in public."

Rory properly winced at the senator's down-home eloquence, before replying.

"My father raised me to be a businessman, Senator. As it happens, business is the *only* thing he ever took the time to teach me, but he did a splendid job of it. Once, in his youth, he, too, found it necessary to prove himself an equal—in his case it was to my grandfather, Diamond Jim Mulvaney. I now find it necessary to do the same. You might call it a Dalton family tradition."

Goodhue raised his Mephistophelian eyebrow at the glib answer. Then, lifting his glass in a theatrical gesture, he said, "You're as full of shit as a Christmas turkey, son, but that never stopped a man from helping me get richer. We'd like to hear more about what you've got in mind. Wouldn't we, Elwood?"

Elwood grunted his assent, as always, and the three men proceeded to the ornate dining room, their appetites whetted on more than one level.

Shay Dalton, his tall athletic body still handsome but beginning to show the inexorable signs of overindulgence, looked uncomprehendingly at his brother.

"That's a pretty crummy thing to do to the old man, Rory," he said noncommittally. "He's always done okay by us."

Riordan watched his brother with distaste, struggling to keep his antipathy from being apparent. Both siblings and their wives sat in the drawing room of Riordan's town house, striving to maintain an air of cordiality.

Cynthia called a servant to replenish their drinks and ceased her effort at convincing small talk with Francine, who sat uncomfortably on the Fortuny-covered sofa, wishing Rory would soon get to the point of what he was asking of them.

"Father is indeed an old man, Shay. It really is time he passed over the reins. You know very well he'll never do it as long as he controls M & D. It's my position that unless we take steps to protect ourselves and our children, he's quite capable of leaving everything of consequence to Maeve's daughter and that born-again guttersnipe, Cavanaugh."

Shay looked searchingly at his brother; Rory really was a creep. But there was a germ of truth in what he was saying. Father did play favorites where Megan was concerned, and he did seem to give all the prize plums to Cavanaugh. He downed two thirds of what was in his glass before asking the obvious question.

"What exactly is it you want from us, Rory? You know business is your game, not mine, so make it simple." He smiled ruefully at

Francine, who smiled sadly back. She knew her husband, like herself, always felt demeaned in this house.

"I want you to support me in helping Senator Harvey Goodhue to make a successful tender offer for M & D." He said it simply, and waited for the questions he knew would follow, before elaborating.

"Why Goodhue?"

"Because he wants M & D and can pay handsomely for it. And, to be honest, because he's underhanded enough to do it quietly."

"What do we get out of it that we don't have now?"

"A great deal of money, Shay. Millions and millions of dollars, to be exact."

"What happens to the old man?"

"He gets a bit embarrassed, but he'll get over that. He also shares in the money, of course—and he's got a number of other enterprises to play with, if he still wants to keep his hand in; although why he would at his age, I can't imagine."

"You really hate him, don't you, Rory?" Seamus said it wonderingly; there was little about his older brother that he understood.

"My feelings about Father are irrelevant to this discussion, Shay. It's simply a matter of business and self-protection. I don't want what should be ours to go to a spoiled child and an outsider. I've paid my dues and I want my fair share. That's all. We'll never get it while Father remains in control."

Shay downed the last of his drink and walked to the bar to pour another. He'd have to think about the whole thing. It seemed a lousy way to treat the old man, but on the other hand, Rory was right; it wasn't as though he'd be left without anything. Rory seemed to know what he was doing when it came to business, even Father admitted that. But he would have to think about it. Having a few million dollars tucked away didn't sound like something to pass up.

"Let's say I help you. What exactly would that entail?"

Rory looked quickly at Cynthia and saw that she was smiling pleasantly. She had never doubted Seamus's acquiescence.

"It would mean we must round up all the stockholders and get to them surreptitiously. We've got to make them see the financial gain in going along with us. It may not be easy, you know. Some of these things take years to accomplish."

Shay Dalton nodded his head sagely. The last drink had done the trick for him, he was beginning to feel expansive again. It was a funny thing, but a lack of alcohol seemed to diminish him, somehow. But he was beginning to feel better about everything.

*   *   *

Jack studied the chessboard with amusement as Megan concentrated on her next move. She had grown to be a very good opponent. She hadn't as devious a mind as his, that was really her only flaw; but she had a phenomenal memory and a fine working knowledge of other people's strategies.

Megan finally moved her bishop and laughed prettily as she did so, as if she had finally found the long-sought answer to a mysterious question and was pleased with herself.

"I'll fix us a cup of tea," she said, getting out of her chair, which, like his, flanked the fireplace. "While you're working your way out of that pickle!" She laughed again and glided toward the kitchen.

She really is growing up, he thought as he watched her graceful departure. Despite a certain coltishness in her movements, there was a lovely dignity to her, a great rarity in one so young.

She was seventeen or eighteen now, he thought, unsure of which it was. Already she was on the dean's list, despite being two years younger than most of her peers. Tom had said she'd be finished with college at nineteen or twenty at the rate she was going.

"Have you decided yet what you're going to do with yourself when you finish school, mavourneen?" he asked as she returned with the tea tray and cast an appraising eye over the board to see what move he'd made in her absence.

"Why, I'm going to marry you, Jack," she replied with amusement in her voice. "Don't tell me you've forgotten?"

He laughed good-naturedly. "Ah, but with all your knowledge and the fancy book learning they're stuffing into you at college, you'll need another career besides that, surely."

She chuckled warmly as she settled back into her chair. "Well, let's see now, it's a toss-up between writing and anthropology this term. But then, last term it was a toss-up between philosophy and economics. In short, I haven't decided."

"Can you tell me what's in the running, at least?"

She smiled at him mischievously. "It's a terrible problem being born rich, you know. There's absolutely no need for me to work or to struggle or to have ambition. And now isn't *that* a terrible indictment, man? I could spend the rest of my life flitting from New York to London to Paris, buying clothes and taking lovers and accomplishing nothing of value."

"You could marry—" Jack said.

"Indeed. And I want to . . . very much more than you know. And I want children, and order in my life, and so much more. But I also want to do something worthwhile. Not to lie fallow. Not to be just a rich young woman whose only claim to fame is her good sense in choosing her forebears." He smiled at her vehemence.

"Don't you see, Jack, mine are formidable forebears; the men, the women . . . all strong and tough and useful. I want to be useful too!"

"I haven't a doubt that you'll be that, lass."

"I think I'd like to write—I know I have stories to tell—and I'd like to learn something of our business."

He looked pleased by the word *our*. "I'll teach you anything you'd like to know," he said, meaning it.

She looked at him for a long moment, strangely. Then said, "Ah, Jack, if you but knew how much I'd like you to teach me."

He cocked his head to the side and looked at her questioningly, but the moment had passed and she moved her hand deftly over the board and shifted her knight from one square to another.

"It appears to me that I have you in check, my dear Mr. Cavanaugh," she said with a mischievous satisfaction.

He frowned at the realization and turned his attention to extricating himself from the situation. Finally he saw what he must do and moved.

Megan bent her head to focus on the board, and he sat back in his chair, watching her. Her long blond hair fell over her shoulders as she bent forward; it was held in a clasp at the side of her face, so he could see her features clearly as she concentrated on the move.

She was wearing a soft pink cashmere sweater that clung to the young curves of her body as if born there. Although slender, she was full-breasted, and the rounded softness of her body was obvious as she leaned forward over the chessboard. She was very beautiful, he noted, as he had done often before. There was a pleasurable softness about the girl, and no frailty whatsoever. It was an appealing combination.

It was hard for him to think of her as growing up. She'd been so much a part of all his years with Tom Dalton. Hard to imagine that in another year or two she'd be finishing college, and going her own way. Getting married, maybe—although it was almost impossible to imagine a boy anywhere near her age being able to cope with her.

Well, God knows, with that body to spur them on, there'd probably be plenty who'd be willing to try. He chuckled at the thought and she looked up, startled from her concentration. Her face in the dancing light from the fire looked suddenly very Celtic to him.

"You look perfectly lovely tonight, my beauty," he said to her by way of explanation.

"You look decent enough yourself, sir," she said, and returned to her serious contemplation of the board in front of her.

95

Cynthia Braithwaite Dalton finished briefing the servants on what would be expected of them for the gala dinner party. With the Vice-President of the United States and his wife as guests of honor, it would be immensely important to Rory to see that everything was perfectly attended to.

Thank God he had acquiesced to her wish not to invite Seamus and dreadful Francine. The idea that she, Cynthia Braithwaite, had a sister-in-law named Francine was hard enough to bear without having to be in her company more than once or twice a year.

Let's see now, she said to herself calmly, the nameplates have been set, the seating arrangement is perfect. The guest list is star-studded—enough political people, enough theater people. She wondered why senators and congressmen always seemed to have such a weakness for movie stars, especially female ones.

Flowers. It would be good to have something exotic and unusual on the tables; she'd best call Irene Hayes and leave it in their capable hands. They'd know what all the other hostesses in New York had used lately and avoid duplication.

The choice of dress was, for once, no crisis. She'd had Molyneaux do six for just such occasions and Schiaparelli another six, last time she was in Paris. Rory had become so generous about her clothing allowance since his political ambitions had surfaced, she could probably have bought another dozen without any contretemps developing over it. She'd already decided to wear the jewels Daddy had given her at her debut; they were just ostentatious enough to cause a stir, without being the least little bit gauche.

"Will you be putting a note into the children's packages, Mum?" The diffident voice interrupted her reverie. It took a moment to comprehend the servant's question. Children's packages? Oh, of course, it's the second Tuesday, isn't it? Every second Tuesday she had Cook do a box of cookies for each of the little darlings at school. God, it was so hard to remember *everything!*

"Yes, yes, Maggy, I'll jot down something for them; just let me know when the boxes are ready."

It was so hard to know what to write to children at these ages, so hard to think of something different each time. But then, her mother had managed it while she was at Emma Willard, and she must do the same.

Cynthia Braithwaite Dalton resolutely picked up her gold fountain pen and Cartier/Paris stationery and fulfilled her duty as a mother.

Riordan Dalton dressed for dinner, knowing that he'd done what he had set out to do. He finally had all the support he needed to make the takeover of M & D a fairly painless fait accompli. He looked in the mirror, feeling powerful, potent. Finally he was in control of his own destiny.

He was pleased that his father had declined the opportunity to dine with the Vice-President this evening. The old boy really was getting to be a bit over the hill, it seemed. A few years ago he would never have passed up such a politically advantageous evening.

Once this M & D business was behind him, he'd be able to concentrate a good deal more on politics. He'd had assurances from quite a number of Goodhue's cronies that he'd be a shoo-in for an appointed office, if that was what he had in mind. Cynthia would do very well as the wife of an ambassador; she handled the details of hostessing with a genuine flair. Perhaps he'd even run for president!

The family had certainly come a long way in three generations; from potato farmer and railroad navvy to potential President of the United States. Rory hummed a self-satisfied little tune as he made his way down the elegant staircase to the floor below, where his guests were beginning to arrive.

There was something going on. Jack felt it in his bones. Rory was up to something and Tom was oblivious. At seventy-four, maybe he had a right to be oblivious, but that didn't change Jack's obligation to find out what the hell was going on.

He picked up the telephone intercom and rattled off a series of names to his secretary. There must be someone in his wide network of friends and associates who had an inkling of what Rory was up to. If he had to call everyone in his secretary's telephone file he'd find somebody who could give him a clue. And he'd do it before another twenty-four hours had passed.

96

"Son of a bitch!" The words escaped Jack almost inadvertently as he laid down the phone, and the remembrance of the transatlantic voice, scratchy with static, reverberated in his brain. So *that* was what the little bastard was up to—what all the surreptitious meetings and strained silences when he'd walk into the room had been about—Riordan was planning to sell M & D Lumber & Shipping right out from under his own father. M & D, the beginning of the empire; the first Mulvaney triumph. The most emotionally important of all the holdings and by far the richest. And he could probably do it, too. The stock was scattered, far more so than in the other companies. Diamond Jim had left shares to Billy, Tom, Maeve, Seamus, and a handful of others. Over the years more had been sold when political expediency demanded it. Maeve's had gone to Megan, Billy's to her nephew, Seamus would probably sell his to Rory in a minute, if his older brother promised to pay off his gambling bills in perpetuity; Tom had handed over a substantial amount of his own stock to Rory in order to give him more voting clout on the board, after the boy had begun to rise in the business. Jack doubted that Tom and Megan between them had more than twenty-five percent left. According to his transatlantic informant, Rory already had promise of enough proxies to make a tender offer lethal. But to what possible end? Jack punched the desk in fury, kicked the tortoiseshell wastebasket into fragments, and then settled down to think.

The little son of a bitch was obviously doing it out of some distorted sense of revenge; but what else? Rory never did anything that was not to his own personal advantage. He didn't need money, that was clear. What was it he did need? Power, of course, and to kick his father in the crotch publicly, it seemed; but what else?

Politics! Of course, he was dabbling in politics. Toadying up to the power brokers, reviving long-dormant vestiges of Diamond Jim's political machine. Entertaining cabinet members. Everything but kissing babies. He was doing it all to establish himself as a possible political contender. Okay. But how could that possibly fit in with this dirty deed? How could politics and lumber mesh in his devious little brain? Politics and lumber. He wrote the words on a yellow lined pad, as if to help himself conjure a connection. Politics and Lumber. Lumber and Politics.

"Sweet Jesus!" Jack said aloud to the empty room, and the sound echoed as it bounced off each of the paneled walls in turn. "He's selling out to Harvey Goodhue, the lumber senator. That canny old bastard has probably promised him the whole fucking Republican ball of wax if he delivers these timber rights." He slammed the pen down on the pad, *knowing* he was right! Shit! What in God's name would the news do to Tom? He'd have to be told today. If Jack's information was right, the offer for shares would go out officially tomorrow.

How the wheel comes round, he thought sadly as he picked up the phone to dial. There isn't one single thing you can do wrong, or neglect or leave uncared for, in this whole frigging world, without having it come back to haunt you!

Strictly speaking, they didn't need the lumber company. There was plenty without it. But they didn't need to be made to look like fools in front of the whole business community, either, at this point in time. He wondered if Tom had the stomach to fight his son for the company. If this had been in the old days, it would have been different. But now? He had the awful feeling the old man might just hand it all over to the little bastard on a plate.

Thomas Dalton had sat in his leather armchair for a very long while after listening to Jack's tirade on the phone about his son. Now he sat quietly behind his desk, near the window, his big gnarled longshoreman's hands folded on top of his head, his gaze turned out over the tops of the buildings, past the old North River, long ago rechristened the Hudson, toward the distant setting sun that was rapidly turning the waterfront crimson.

His thoughts were farther away than what could be seen from his window. Back, back, back in time they had flown all afternoon. Back to his tiny cottage on Drumgillan where it had all begun . . . back to the stable, holding his father's lifeless head in his hands . . . back staring wordlessly at the abbot with the cat-o'-nine-tails in his hand at St. Ignatius . . . back to his Dublin garret . . . back to the docks with his dear, lost Donaher . . . back with his Deirdre lying sweetly in his arms . . . back to his daughter's passing . . . back to Central Park with Megan's hand in his own . . . back to Rory standing in front of his desk, asking to be part of the business.

He smiled sadly at the thought of Billy's words to him on the day she'd died. "Watch out for Rory, old friend," she had said with her wry, old smile. "He may be yours, but he's a bad seed, sure as you're born." He had never known her to mistake a man's character.

This was indeed a puzzlement that was laid before him. If he let Rory get away with it, he'd look like an old idiot, a happenstance that would damage the prestige of all the rest of his holdings, and Jack's to boot. If he fought the lad, he might not live long enough to see the end of the litigation—he had been feeling very old of late and strangely close to his father. He had no intention of seeing Megan's money tied up in endless legal snarls while his sons scrambled to cheat her out of it; he'd been meaning to make some provision to keep that from happening. Well, perhaps today would be the day. M & D Lumber, where it all began, would perhaps be the instrument of it all coming to an end. But, by God, he'd see to it that Megan was secure before that happened.

It was such a curious fate he seemed to be burdened with. He thought of a line from Megan's favorite poem by Yeats: "The dooms of men are in God's hidden place . . ." Indeed they were.

He had intended to leave his stock in M & D to his sons. Rory had earned his share, and Seamus would let his brother vote his stock in return for being kept solvent. He'd failed with both his sons, but they were his nonetheless, and he'd provide for them. Perhaps if he'd been a better father, they'd be better men.

He'd decided long ago not to leave any part of M & D to Megan. It was too large a tangle and she'd be too unprotected, too vulnerable to the attack that Rory would be more than capable of hurling at her. No. He would provide for Megan with softer, surer fare. Secure and permanent possessions and investments would be hers. Investments that would *give* instead of demanding lifeblood in return. She was fit for a special life; he'd provide her with the money to spend her time doing something useful and happy. And, of course, if she chose business, Jack would be there to help her. Jack had promised that to him long ago. Besides, Jack loved the child; in some curious way he seemed as attached to her as she was to him, despite their more than twenty-year age difference. Tom had watched him over the years with the girl. It was strange, but Megan always brought out the best in Jack.

Finally, gratefully, he stood up and stretched, as if to expunge the lively ghosts. It had been Mulvaney's own that had shown him what he must do about this latest danger. Not that there was any fear in it for himself, but those he loved must be protected. And—he smiled at the Catholicism of the thought—at the end of it, the good must prevail. Just as surely as if the tough-minded, lovely old man had been there in the room with him, James Mulvaney had told Tom what to do.

He picked up the intercom, wondering if his secretary would still be at her desk; he'd lost track of time since the call had come from Jack at noon, and it was probably after five.

"Yes sir?" said the middle-aged female voice that had supplanted Delaney's several years before.

"Call my children, Dorothy, please. And Jack Cavanaugh and Megan. Invite them to dinner tonight at my home and tell them it is a command performance, will you? And Dorothy . . ."

"Yes, Mr. Dalton?"

"Get my lawyer and my accountant in here on the double and see that they bring two witnesses with them . . . and my will."

There was a small intake of breath on the other end of the phone, then a tentative question. "Mr. Dalton. Are you all right, sir? I mean, you're not feeling ill or anything?"

"No, Dorothy. I'm not ill. A bit heartsick, perhaps, but not ill."

A slight pause followed on the other end, then, "Very well, Mr. Dalton. Don't worry, sir, I'll track everybody down for you."

"Thank you, Dorothy. I appreciate it. And not a word to anybody but the ones I've mentioned."

"No, sir. Not a word, sir." He heard the trustworthiness in her voice, and smiled.

Part Eight

FINAL PARTINGS

Lord behold our family here assembled.
Give us peace, gaiety and the quiet mind.
Give us strength to encounter that which is to come,
That we may brave in peril,
Constant in all changes of fortune,
And that down to the gates of death, we may be loyal
and love one another.

—R. L. Stevenson

97

Megan knocked on the door of her grandfather's bedroom with a confidence born of love.

"Grandfather. It's me; may I come in?"

"Your Uncle Riordan would have said 'It is I' . . . and yes, indeed, you may."

"He is a pretentious old poop, isn't he?" said the tall blond girl with a merry lilt in her throaty voice, which sometimes reminded him of Billy's.

On another day he might have chided her for the irreverence; today he just continued putting on his black tuxedo shoes, a fact not lost on his sagacious granddaughter. She sat down on the bed next to him, admiring the size and strength of him, even at seventy-four.

"Something brewing, eh?" she queried.

"The game is afoot, my darling girl. The game is afoot."

She nodded, intrigued, satisfied that he would tell her in his own good time; not wishing to be more inquisitive than she should. As always, she was perfectly in tune with him.

"This game, Grandfather. Are we going to win?" As always, she automatically included herself with him.

"Let's just say we're going to give them a pretty good run for their money."

She nodded, and he marveled at her self-restraint; he knew she must be bursting at the seams with curiosity.

She saw that when he stood up to finish dressing, he seemed to be in pain and straightened his back only with effort.

"Are you feeling all right, Grandfather? You look a little wan to me."

He smiled benevolently at the mother-hen tone in the girl's voice and answered lightly, "For a fellow my age, I'd say I'm about as well as can be expected, lassie. Although as usual, you are quite right in suggesting that I'm a little under the weather."

"Grandfather," she said as she helped him on with his jacket and patted it into place in a proprietary way. "You do know that no matter what, I love you more than everything, don't you?"

Thomas Dalton took his granddaughter's hand in his and then took her unexpectedly in his arms and held her tall, straight form to his own, marveling at the splendid strength in the beautiful young girl. He squeezed her so hard he took her breath away.

"That one thing, Megan, I do know. And it means more to me than all the rest of it put together." He said it with such a vehement conviction that it made her uneasy. She thought she could feel the sorrow that consumed him.

He let her go gently and in a courtly gesture offered her his arm.

"May I escort you in to dinner, young lady?"

"Indeed you may, sir," she said, smiling. "I'll be the envy of every lady there."

"You will be the *only* lady there," he said, winking at her, and they both laughed all the way down the stairs to the drawing room, where the clan had gathered.

Jack surveyed the group with unmitigated fascination. Tom had seated Megan on his own right, much to the annoyance of his daughter-in-law Cynthia, who was a prissy stickler for protocol. Rory, his wife and children, were on one side; Seamus, his wife and children, on the other.

Jack watched the very well-bred Daltons on the right, the rough-and-tumble Daltons on the left, as they all struggled to maintain their apparent good humor despite the weight of their guilty consciences.

"Now, my dear family," said Tom when dessert had been cleared away and only coffee remained. "You must all be wondering why I've asked you to join me here this evening. Or perhaps you have some inkling as to what it might be about." He paused to watch the various adult eyes meet each other cautiously around the table.

"As you all know, I am seventy-four years of age, and although I've been blessed with a robust constitution, it seems to me that an age as advanced as seventy-four carries with it some obligations to one's heirs and assigns. So just today I decided to organize my legal affairs in anticipation of my eventual demise, and—let's call it an old man's whim—I decided to tell you all just how I have parceled out what has been mine for a considerable length of time."

Every eye at the quiet table was on the old man's face. He felt sorrowful to think that these avaricious faces were his progeny. Inadvertently, one of Donaher's Irish proverbs came into his mind: "Unlucky the man whose betrayer sits at his own table." He shook off the thought and continued.

"I have left a generous stipend to my housekeeper, my driver, my secretary, and the family of my previous secretary, Mr. Delaney. Each will be well cared for by my estate until their deaths.

"This house and Drumgillan—the manor house, the estates and their incomes—I have already put in the name of my beloved granddaughter, Megan Dalton. As of today, they are hers"—he smiled benevolently at her startled look—"and as such cannot be considered part of my estate. I trust this will preclude whatever notion any of you might have harbored about contesting my desires, after my death."

He paused to observe the growing hostility on both sides of the table.

"To my trusted and very dear friend, Jack Cavanaugh, and to my granddaughter, Megan, I have also turned over, as of this afternoon, my fifty percent share of each company previously jointly held by myself and Mr. Cavanaugh. I trust this too will be beyond probate. I am certain you will all understand the common sense of this action, as it is only right to expect that Megan be given what would have been her mother's, had she lived."

There was an audible intake of breath at the news, and Riordan started to speak but was silenced by an imperial gesture of his father's hand. "To each of my other dear grandchildren I have left the sum of one million dollars, to be held in trust for them until their thirty-fifth birthdays, a date by which I must assume they will be fully capable of handling and enjoying such a sum and, I might add, they will most likely no longer be subject to the coercion of their parents."

The looks being passed around the table were frighteningly eloquent, and Jack looked up with delight and admiration at his mentor, who, catching the younger man's eye across the table, smiled at him.

"To my two remaining children, my sons, Riordan and Seamus, I intend to bequeath the entirety of my stock in M & D Lumber and Shipping. This is a decision which should, I expect, cause you to reconsider the current clandestine negotiations you have initiated with our esteemed Senator Goodhue. You see, my sons, after tonight M & D will be your only patrimony. Keep it, and the empire re-creates itself for one more generation at least. Sell it, and it will be up to you to show if you can create, as well as destroy. You might be quite unnerved to learn how much harder it is to establish an empire than simply to maintain one.

"Sell M & D, and you are rich men—but rich men with far less power than you had before. Don't mistake it, Rory; the power which you so much enjoy, and which you seem to wield so dishonorably, springs as much from the aura of Diamond Jim's legend and my own strength as it does from the money M & D controls.

"Sell M & D, and your power dissipates, make no mistake about it. Senator Goodhue gets what he wants, but will you? Will he deliver what he has promised, once he's gotten you to sell your birthright? The good senator is not known for his integrity." He smiled a little sadly at his firstborn son. "Could it be that for all your arrogant education, Rory, it has escaped your notice that there is little honor among thieves?"

Tom turned to look at his second son, whose eyes were averted from the confrontation; he couldn't decide if embarrassment or cowardice was more apparent in his aspect.

"And what will become of you, Seamus, if M & D is sold? How long will the money last, do you suppose? How many women, how much gambling, how much liquor will it buy before it's gone forever? Or do you imagine that your brother will support you out of the kindness of his heart, when you are penniless? I think you'd be barking up a bare tree there, lad." The hangdog expression in Seamus's eyes when he raised them to his father filled Tom with sadness. From where, in God's name, had such pitiable weakness come? He could think of no one in his heritage who hadn't had the strength to be a man.

"So you see, my sons," he said quietly but with intense clarity. "At the end, your decision must have nothing to do with me at all. I've run my course, proven my mettle, suffered my defeats, savored my victories. But you, my sons . . . what will *you* become? That is tonight's question, is it not?"

Tom looked at Seamus, not with malice, thought Jack, but with infinite sorrow. Then he looked questioningly at Rory, as if to see if there was any hint of remorse, and seeing only anger, he continued.

"M & D, as you know, is now and always has been the hub of our family's corporate universe—a remarkably productive and potentially important property that we all at this table owe to the canniness and perspicacity of Diamond Jim Mulvaney, whose portrait graces this very dining room . . . and a most remarkable man he was."

Very elegantly and deliberately Tom picked up the glass of champagne that had been poured for him, and tipping the brilliant Waterford flute in the direction of the painting, he said very clearly, a hint of weary amusement in his voice:

"To Diamond Jim Mulvaney, God rest his rambunctious soul. . . .

Who once said to me, 'Laddie, I'm too old a cat to be fucked by a kitten.' "

The old man heard his blue-blooded daughter-in-law gasp "Oh, shit" with the shock of it, he heard his son's ferocious outburst, and he heard Jack Cavanaugh roar with laughter as Megan looked around with startled incredulity at the open hostility that had erupted around the huge table. She was the only one to see her grandfather's ashen pallor as he left the dining room, his broad back straight and determined. She was the only one whose one thought as she hastily left the table was for his safety.

98

There was no question that the old man was dying. The doctors knew it, the hangers-on knew it, but most of all his granddaughter, Megan, knew it. He was still immense despite his age and illness, and lying in the massive bed, in the huge room, he did not seem to have shrunk by comparison.

"Megan." The once resonant voice was a whisper. The coltish twenty-year-old girl, who had just entered the room, confidently moved to his side. She had been with him almost constantly since his collapse nearly a year before. Although he had regained strength for a while after the initial seizure, which she was certain had been precipitated by the awful shock of Rory's betrayal, she had never believed that he would again be well.

"I'm here, Grandfather. I won't leave you." It was a code, of course, between them. She, the only one he trusted with the knowledge that he hadn't left his father at the end.

"Is it finally over, lass?" The once powerful voice sounded tired and small. He had been waiting patiently for her to enter the room; he had something of importance to say to her.

"Don't ask me that, Grandfather. I won't be the instrument of your going." Tears hovered at the edge of her lashes, and she struggled against them.

"You did hear her last night, child, didn't you?" His voice sounded anxious, as if in need of reassurance. When she couldn't bring herself to reply, Tom smiled tenderly at her, as if she were the one to be comforted. "I've a right to know if you heard the banshee come for me, Megan, lass. I've many old friends waiting for me and I don't want to keep them waiting too long now.'' He tried to make his voice sound lighthearted, but she heard the strain clearly bene :th the words. "I long to be with your grandmother, lass . . . and with them all.''

Megan blinked back the tears and spoke as resolutely as she was able. "Yes, Grandfather, she came last night. To the window, the way she does.''

The dying man chuckled quietly to himself. He seemed greatly satisfied by the finality of knowing he'd been called in such an Irish way.

"Then the time has come, Megan mine, for me to make my last bequest to you. Come close to me, child . . . the vultures are all around us; I can feel them waiting to divide the spoils. They're the same fine breed as cast lots for Christ's coat, our family, Megan. You're the only one of them worth a tinker's damn, and you, lass, you're worth an empire ten times over.''

"I love you, Grandfather, don't fear for me.'' He could hear the tears in her voice as she said it. "I'm stronger than all of them put together. I'll do what we promised. No one will ever take our cottage again.''

Once more, the code. The secret past. Strength sprung from a legend.

"Megan, my dearest girl, I'm leaving you my treasures. The money, you may have to fight for, but there's enough of it in Drumgillan to keep you safe, and Jack will help you when I'm gone. But I'm leaving you my 'luck,' Megan. Guard it well, child!'' He, who had been so strong and dexterous, fumbled awkwardly for something tucked into his pajama pocket, and finally, with a difficulty that made her want to cry, he extracted a small key.

"There's a box this key opens, Megan, Jack knows where to find it. Your heritage is there. The letter from my da. God rest his soul . . . I'll soon be with him again.'' His voice was suddenly soft and conspiratorial. "Do you know, lass, I'm seventy-five years of age and I still long for his strong arms around me, and the sound of his fine male laughter in the wind.'' He lay back, as if exhausted by the effort of speaking. "I've never said that to a living soul. Ah well, Megan, now's the time for the saying of it all. I'm grateful there's one of my blood who understands.''

He closed his deep-set eyes, the periwinkle color now faded and blurred. Megan looked about the room, taking silent inventory of the mourners. Seamus was sitting in the corner, drunk despite the early hour, sobbing and maudlin. Rory, cold and deadly, spoke quietly to the family lawyer, not a hint of sorrow in his demeanor. Jack Cavanaugh stood at the window, a quiet dignity in his bearing. Sorrow almost as deep as her own emanated from the man like an aura.

After a long while, Tom spoke again. He motioned her close to his face so she alone might hear.

"When you're low, Megan, read the letter. All my life, when the sadness tried to overwhelm me, I'd read the letter and be proud of who I was, and where I'd sprung from. Remember, child, learn all there is to learn. It will be your escape, as it was mine. Know more than they do, and beat them at their own game . . . just as my father told me to do."

Tom seemed to drift away for a moment, and Megan held his hand tightly, as if to keep him from going.

"I heard her, too, Megan. I'd always wondered if I'd hear the banshee at my own passing." He lay quietly for a long while after that, barely breathing but holding tightly to her hand that lay at his side on the covers. She looked at his pale face; two white lines seemed to have appeared at the edges of his nose, and his mouth seemed pinched and drawn. She somehow knew that it was a sign that he was sinking inexorably toward the sleep of death. His eyes had fallen shut and his face was in repose. Then, suddenly, the shadow of a young smile flickered in his ancient face. He started up from the bed, as if straining to reach someone he alone could see. Tom pulled his hand from Megan's grasp and clutched wildly at the air, as if at an unseen hand. He whispered something she couldn't understand; then he was gone. There was no need for the doctor to tell her that her grandfather was dead, for she had seen him go.

Megan placed the old man's lifeless hand back into her own, touching it to her lips, wet with tears, in a gesture of infinite tenderness. She knelt beside the bed and covered his body with her own. The family gathered in a whispering gaggle, nearer the bed than they had been, but somehow fearful of coming too close. The powerful force that had been her grandfather had vanished. Only an old body lay on the huge bed, and the mind that had kept them all at bay had been extinguished. Megan thought fleetingly how deplorable it was to be so rich that the only emotion people felt at your passing was one of avarice. She had no doubt they'd pick clean the bones if they could, and had a desperate urge to protect him whom she loved.

"Leave him alone!" The girl's voice was loud enough to be heard over the others in the room. "Leave him with me, he's mine."

"Don't be absurd, Megan." Her uncle's precise articulation was emotionless. "The old man's dead. You have no choice but to leave him to the undertaker. He's being waked here in the house. You can have him to yourself after they're through with him. God knows no one else wants the old reprobate."

Jack walked to the bed behind the girl and laid his hand proprietarily on her shoulder, as if to put Rory on notice that she was not alone.

"I'll go, Uncle Riordan," she threw the words at him defiantly, the old ritual repeated. "But I'll be back to say good-bye."

She could hear her grandfather's voice whispering the tale of the first anguish. "I'll be back to bid him good-bye," he had said, and so had she. The circle closed at last.

The elegant high-ceilinged room that housed the coffin was dim and cold when the tall, blond figure quietly settled herself beside the bier and reached into the ornate box to smooth the wild, white hair from her grandfather's handsome forehead.

"Shame to them, Grandfather. Shame to them to leave you alone and you just dead."

How had he managed to pass it all on to her so viscerally, she wondered? Had she been there with him through all his long, tempestuous life, she couldn't have known the emotions of it any better. Like the children of famine or pogrom who share their parents' pain and terror a generation after the danger has passed, she had somehow mystically taken on her grandfather's anguish at his father's passing . . . his anger at the injustice of his father's family . . . his hatred of the Church . . . his despair at his beloved wife's murder, his daughter's death, his son's betrayal—all of it lived somehow within her strong lean frame; every cell of her body shared his secrets.

Megan Dalton settled her lithe form against the enormous mahogany box and began to sing a strange, haunting lullaby to the cold dead body of the man who had shaped her mind and heart. The servants passing by shivered at the eerie keening sound that blended with the freezing wind that howled around the Georgian chimney pots.

*   *   *

Hours had passed. Megan, dozing finally against the cool hardness of the coffin, felt a strong hand laid gently on her shoulder.

She looked up, startled by the intrusion, and saw the intense blue of Jack's eyes, sorrowful and concerned above her.

"I'd like to stay with him too," he said softly.

She looked up at the man gratefully, moved by the fact that he, too, understood.

Jack looked searchingly at the beautiful girl as she rose from her cramped position of sentinel—he had come to take her back to her room to rest. The next day, he knew, would be filled with the endless drain of mourning friends and curiosity seekers; she would need her strength to face it. He had waited after the interminable family dinner, giving her a time for private mourning; now, seeing the sorrowful conviction in Megan's strong young face and form, he knew there would be no leaving her grandfather as yet.

So, with a resolute sigh, Jack patted the girl's soft cheek gently and settled in beside her. Soon she leaned against him and he folded his arms about her lean frame to support her. He marveled at the ease of her lying up against him, of her lying in his arms, and eventually they both slept until the bustle of the dawning day awakened them.

99

The tall, doe-eyed girl rang the bell on the twenty-seventh floor of the expensive apartment building on Park Avenue, with only a slight quiver of the hand to betray her nervousness.

Sweet Jesus, what an Irish face, thought Jack to himself when he opened the door to Tom Dalton's granddaughter the night after the huge funeral that had left him feeling empty and alone.

"Ask me in, Jack," she said in a voice so serious that it made him smile.

"Of course, Megan, come in with you. Are you lonely, lass?" he asked with genuine concern. "Is that why you're here in the middle of the night?"

His speech had the lilting, mellifluous touch of brogue that neither the Yukon nor Cambridge had been able to banish, and she smiled inwardly at the familiar sound, wondering what would become of them both after this night.

"I've been thinking that you and I are family now, Jack; two orphans who've adopted each other." She said it as she walked into the apartment and he closed the door behind her. She took a deep breath as if gathering courage, and said, "I've come to ask you a favor, Jack. For me and Tom."

"Well, now, that sounds important indeed, Megan. Come in and I'll make us some tea, like in the old days, when you were a wee lass that used to be more serious than any I ever saw." He felt curious and uneasy about the earnestness of her demeanor.

"I want you to make love to me tonight, Jack." She said it very quietly and clearly. "I need to learn, and I want you to teach me."

The handsome, middle-aged man stood stock still, on his way to the kitchen, and turned with a look of quiet incredulity in his deep-set eyes. He regarded the girl with absolute attention; there was no point at all in asking if she was serious. She was always serious. Her urgency was apparent; he could only wonder at the reason. Perhaps the strain of the past few days had been more damaging than he'd realized. He spoke softly when he replied. "Megan, child. I can't do that. I'm twice your age, and I love you to boot. You cannot trifle with a grown man in this fashion, lass."

Megan was beside him in an instant, reaching out her hand to him in the oddest gesture of supplication he had ever seen, outside of a painting of Mary Magdalene he'd once come upon in a museum in Brussels.

"Listen to me, Jack. I know this sounds bold and mad, but I know what I'm asking. I'm a woman, Jack, whether you've noticed it or not. I'm twenty years old and still a virgin; not because I haven't wanted to know, or because I haven't had the chance to learn, but because there was never the right one and it wasn't time yet. But there simply isn't time for waiting anymore.

"Don't you see, Jack, with my grandfather gone, I'm all alone. I've got to grow up, got to learn all there is to know. You remember what he always told us both, 'the knowledge is all we have to protect us.' I've been reading and rereading his father's letter all day long. I simply cannot be a child past tonight!" She didn't mention to him that she loved him and always had; nor that he was all that she had left now that her grandfather was gone. She didn't tell him that she had never in her life felt as desperately alone as she had since Tom's death. She paused, breathless, and he realized how close to tears she was. This was not a joke or a spontaneous lark. The girl was in deadly earnest.

"If you won't teach me, someone else will." Megan's voice suddenly jolted him from thought. "But I'd like it to be you."

Until that moment, Jack Cavanaugh had thought that, within reason, he had seen and heard it all. Slums, lumber camps, politics, Wall Street, all of it. But this passionate girl begging him to take her virginity, what in God's name could prepare a man for that?

"Megan, Megan! You're asking too much of me, lass. I care far too much for you to do this thing and then walk away from it. Don't you see, we'll both be changed by it. Things will never be the same between us. Never again, the same as they were." As he said the words he realized how very special their relationship was and how much he would hate to lose it.

Megan stood before the troubled sturdy-looking man she had chosen with such deliberation, and hesitatingly began to unbutton the white satin blouse she was wearing, as if the very physicality of the gesture would make the whole thing real. Over all the months since her grandfather's seizure, when he'd taken it on himself to instruct her about the business and the affairs of Drumgillan, she'd shown amply enough how capable she was; why had he persisted in thinking her a child, when he knew she was a woman?

Do I dare take her at her word? Jack asked himself with immense consternation as the blood in his own body began to answer his question for him. He was not one to be manipulated by a woman, or lured into anything he disdained to do. But Megan was more special to him than he cared to admit, and if she was really serious about what she intended, perhaps it was best after all that it be he. She looked so vulnerable standing in his hallway, half undressed; part uncertain girl, part woman. At least he could see to it that she wasn't manhandled by some lout who'd have no thought for her afterward. Jack shook his head at the absurdity of the situation, and sighed resolutely.

"All right, Megan, if this is how it is to be, let me at least take you to my bed. The learning's better, I think, in a proper bed." He reached out and touched the soft skin of her cheek, marveling at the tenderness of her expression.

Megan nodded, as if she had never really doubted his acquiescence; she wondered if he had any inkling of what she felt toward him. She turned and walked into the bedroom, the man close behind her.

She removed her shirt and skirt and folded them carefully on the bedside chair without looking at him. It seemed that she moved in a kind of fluid slow motion until she was naked, her young firm body seeming vulnerable in the pale yellow puddle of light from a bedside lamp. She looked around quickly for something to cover herself with, and finding nothing, slipped quietly, deliberately, under the covers at the edge of the great island of a bed that filled the center of his bedroom. A bit unselfconscious for one inexperienced, he had thought at first, and then realized that the control was hard won.

He took off his own clothes slowly, standing by the bed beside her, watching her watch him as his strong, stocky body disentangled itself from sweater, pants, and shorts. He thought he had never in his life felt less certain or more concerned over something he was about to do.

He felt himself harden at the sight of her nakedness, but he was careful not to touch the frightened and determined girl as he lay down beside her on the familiar bed. He smiled softly to himself as he felt the warmth of her body next to his own; he felt oddly better now that they were both in bed. Bizarre as the circumstances were, he was a man in bed with a woman . . . a curiously profound thing, that had always seemed to him, no matter how many there had been. Strange indeed it would be if he couldn't stir her blood and make her happy with his skill. It was a gift he had.

Jack turned on his side to face Megan. He reached out his hand to touch her body tentatively, tenderly, and he saw that she was trembling. "You're scared to death by all that's happened, aren't you, lass?" he asked gently. She nodded, but said nothing. He, too, lay silently for a while, deciding how to go about his curious task. Not that it would be hard to make love to such a one as this, he thought. The long, lean frame, the tender belly and the full round breasts with their virgin nipples, the pale shimmery hair between her legs, the vibrant youth of her—all were beautiful perfections to be savored. She was a rare one, and he must handle her with great care.

Jack moved quietly closer and began to talk to her. He spoke softly, his big voice gentle, huskier than she had ever heard it. A voice used only for lovemaking, perhaps; a voice no man had ever heard. He spoke tenderly of many things . . . to quiet her fears, to remind her she was safe with him. He touched her as he spoke, intuitive fingers playing softly in her long hair, stroking her skin with an implausible delicacy. A time or two he let his hand brush softly over the pale silken triangle below her belly, and she was shocked by the strength of her own body's response.

It was blissful to lie there, out of control, she thought, freed finally from the fears she had felt overwhelmed by since her grandfather's death; from the fears that he wouldn't want her. She wished so desperately to be overpowered, not to have to make decisions, not to have to wend her way. To be in his power, utterly. She had wanted to be his for so very, very long. She thought vaguely that she should be giving something back, but he seemed to sense what was in her mind and whispered, "Just lie still, beauty. Take from me tonight. Learn to take softly from a man, what he has to give, lass. 'Tis what a man wants mostly from a woman."

He kissed her skillfully and long, and some deep part of her realized that when the kissing was done, she somehow knew far more than she had known before it had begun. He kissed her lips and long golden hair. He brought his mouth to her firm full breasts with the sweet pink nipples that seemed more experienced than she, and waited, not so very long, until her response to this silent urging was unbounded.

He was talking to her, whispering sweet, lovely things. There was poetry in his voice and power in his hands. She moaned and strained against his mouth as it suckled and licked and kissed and teased her breasts, her belly, her thighs in turn, and he smiled a knowing smile.

"Show me how to love you, too, Jack," she whispered as she twisted herself away from his lips after a while of simply drinking in the pleasure of his hands and mouth; she wanted to give back, to share. After a while he moved her head reluctantly aside, and taking her in his arms, he laid her gently back onto the bed and parted her thighs with infinite tenderness. She moaned and cried his name, and her wetness made him want her all the more as he raised his body over the strong and beautiful girl he had made so anxious for his love.

"Love me, Jack, please love me all you can just for tonight." Megan thought she said the words aloud, but she was never certain. It mattered not at all, for he knew what she wanted, almost before she knew. How many times that night they played the magical game, learning each other's secrets, touching, knowing, loving, feeling, he couldn't remember ever afterward.

Megan lay quietly in his powerful arms, nestled as close as she could insinuate herself against his body. He turned a little to hold her so that the curves of her form fit perfectly into the angles of his own. He kissed her hair at the temples and brushed it back from her face tenderly.

"You look sated, Megan, love. Do you feel so?" He asked the question, knowing the answer. He was skilled at lovemaking and knew what pleasure he had given her, but he wanted her to speak her feelings aloud, for she was a deep one. He wouldn't have her leave him if she were unsatisfied in body or spirit. In truth, he wasn't sure that he wanted her to leave at all. He held her closer to him at the unfamiliar thought, and wondered at his own strange connection to this beautiful young girl. He felt curiously protective and oddly peaceful with her lying in his arms.

Megan looked into his face almost shyly. "I feel filled to the brim with you," she smiled the reply, looking into his laughing eyes. "Wherever did you learn to make love like that, Jack?" The question startled him . . . but then she had always asked him directly, precisely what she wished to know. He found himself wishing fleetingly that she were older, or he younger.

"I learned from a whore in Boston, if you must know the truth of it, Megan. A glorious, generous, simple-spirited lady, who happened to be a whore." He smiled in remembrance.

"Tell me," prompted the girl at his side, and he knew she simply craved the intimacy of sharing history with him. She is so lovely, he thought, so very lovely.

" 'Tis a long-ago tale, lass. It seems another life to me now. You see, I was a Boston Irish orphan, one of the poorest creatures known to God or man. My parents, as you know, had died as they'd lived, penniless in a cold, windowless basement of a tenement in an Irish slum. My father had been injured on the docks by a falling bale, and with a twisted spine and an arm that hung limp at his side, there was no hope of work at all. I was, of course, just a little lad when they died. They'd been feeding me what little they had, you see, and they starved to death of it.

"Well, my beauty, I was sent to an orphan asylum after they found me, and a bleaker place than that God never made; so by the time I was twelve or so, I was out and on my own. Picking up garbage in the streets, running from the police, sleeping in abandoned buildings and such as that, was the way it was for me. As you know, that's how I met your grandfather.

"Well, one night fate must have decided to take me into her own hands, for I parked myself outside a red-brick building where there seemed to be a lot of light and laughter going on inside. I thought they were having a party, you see, and I reasoned that by morning there'd be a feast of garbage for me to stave off my hunger. So I curled up in a ball, in a little hollowed-out place by a cellar window and I fell asleep.

"When I woke up—'twas still night—I saw a woman, perhaps of forty-five or fifty years or so, leaning out the window above me, staring down at my own self.

"How would you like a job, lad?" she called to me, and of course I said I thought a job would be grand—and that, my proud beauty, is where my education of women began . . . for, you see, 'twas what the police used to call a 'disorderly house,' a whorehouse it was, a bit down at heel, perhaps, but a grand place to my un-schooled eye.

"The lady who ran the place took a liking to me, gave me a job as errand boy, bouncer—I was never big, but I was strong, you see—and general all-around helper. Along with my wages, she took it upon herself to teach me about women, and a teacher like Lou few men are ever privileged to have." He paused and looked gently at the girl beside him. She looked so very far removed from the kind of life he was describing, yet she was but a bit older than he had been in those days.

"She took me to her bed whenever time permitted, lass. I had bounced about a bit by then, and I'd poked my cock into a few warm places and fancied myself a capable fellow. But the first time she took me to her bed and I fucked her for all I was worth, she waited the full minute or so it took me, and said, 'Now that you've finished fucking like an alley cat, I'll show you how a man pleasures a lady, if you'd care to learn.' She showed me how to go slowly and touch gently. 'Men always make the mistake of being fast and rough,' she would say with her legs spread wide and me between them, trying to figure out the science of it all. 'Tis the softest, tenderest touches drive a woman mad, Jack,' she would say to me, and she'd take her own hand on mine and show me the way to touch and to love. I thought her body a magical place, lass, for I learned so many marvels there. You know, she was old by most men's reckoning, but to me it seemed she had the body of an angel. She taught me to make it all a grand, manly game, to please a woman—and, to be fair, I suppose I had a bit of a natural knack for it."

He leaned to her smiling face and kissed her mouth tenderly, wondering what she was thinking, feeling . . . and what would happen to her now. He'd been right when he told her they'd both be changed by what had just happened, that nothing between them would ever be the same. "Never again the same as we were—" he had said. But perhaps they would be something better. Seeing the love in her eyes, he felt warmed by it. Glad to have loved her, not just because she was beautiful, but because she was Megan.

That she was an extraordinary girl he had never doubted. That she and he might mean something to each other as man and woman was a more startling revelation. That she had pleased him more in bed than he would have dreamed possible astounded him, utterly.

Where that talent had come from, he couldn't but guess. Although perhaps it made the story of the housemaid and the young aristocrat a trifle more understandable than it had ever been for him before.

100

Jack sat alone in the apartment long after Megan had left, his mind a jumble of confusing thoughts and disturbing emotions.

What in God's name had he done? he wondered. She was barely twenty years old, less than half his age. If anyone else had told him of a more than forty-year-old man involved thus with the twenty-year-old granddaughter of his best friend, he would have been repelled by the unseemliness of it.

A grown man fantasizing about a child; a glorious, womanly child, to be sure, but a child nonetheless. Life might be all right for them for a while of course, but what would happen after that? In ten years he'd be middle-aged and she'd be thirty. In twenty, he'd be old and she'd be young; a desirable woman who deserved better than an antique husband. Yet nothing about what happened over the last twelve hours felt unseemly.

The thought upset him strangely; it had been so unexpected to find the idea of marriage creeping unbidden into his brain. I wouldn't be thinking of marriage so swiftly, he said to himself perplexedly, if I didn't feel something more powerful for Megan than simple lust . . . although, by God, no one could fault me for feeling that for her! The quick remembrance of their lovemaking flash-flooded him, warming him, making him shake his head in wonder at his own confusions.

It would make some things very simple, of course, if they did marry. He could more easily protect Megan's interests, and his own. It would knock Riordan and Seamus and their entire unsavory crew for a loop, without question—and it would provide both Megan and he with a formidable fortune. Sweet Jesus, he thought angrily, now I'm reduced to thinking about her money! But that, of course, wasn't so.

Young or not, she would make an incredible wife, he had no doubt whatsoever about that. He had never known her to do anything in a halfhearted fashion. She showed the same passionate commitment to her loves that her grandfather had. Single-minded, purposeful, full of integrity.

If only Billy were alive. She would know how to sort the tangled threads; she had known everything there was to know about men and women, their lives and loves. Jack smiled to himself at the remembrance of his last conversation with the ailing woman he had so much admired.

"Love someone, Jack . . ." she had admonished him. "Love someone real and passionate and permanent. Someone who'll build a life with you, give you children, make you forget the fears. Trust yourself, man! Trust your own ability to love deeply . . . wildly . . . committedly . . ." She had smiled at his discomfort, and her face had taken on a little of the old animation when she whispered, "It takes courage to be a man and not a tomcat, my friend. Love yourself enough to let someone get inside you to the man I've glimpsed in you. Trust me, Jack! I know men to their marrow . . . my only gift." She had drifted off to sleep then, and he had wondered if she'd meant that the knowledge was her gift to him, or that the intuition was the only gift she herself had been given. It hadn't mattered, really. It had stayed with him.

That was the crux of it all, of course, just as Billy'd known it to be: he wasn't at all sure he was *capable* of loving permanently. Of loving someone through better or worse, in sickness and in health. At least he wouldn't have to worry about richer or poorer, he thought, and grimaced inwardly at his own cowardice. That kind of permanent devotion and spiritual commitment—the kind he wasn't sure he was capable of—was the only kind that Megan deserved.

God, but she was special. The biggest shock of all to him had been the realization of how much he wanted to take what she could give; how much he wanted to absorb the fresh young ardor and the ageless womanly warmth of her.

Tired of indecision, he picked up the phone and dialed Megan's number. He didn't know until she didn't answer, how very much he wanted to say to her.

*   *   *

Megan had given herself the afternoon to try to collect her thoughts. It had taken every iota of strength she could muster to leave Jack's apartment, yet she had known beyond question, lying there in his arms, that she must get away from him in order to sort it all through.

She thought of the incredible perfection of lying with him, loving and feeling loved. She had been prepared to love him—she had even prepared to be rejected by him—but nothing could have prepared her for the power she'd felt in him when they were one; nor for the *powerlessness* she herself had felt—and reveled in—when she was in his arms.

Just the remembrance of it made her uncertain of everything.

"What's wrong with me that I want to lose myself in someone else again?" she chided herself, feeling some kind of reprimand in order and not knowing which kind was called for. Everything was happening so fast—it still seemed impossible that her grandfather was gone. Her protector, her mentor, her roots, her beloved friend—her connection to the past and to the future—was no more. Never before had she been an orphan, in her own mind. Always *he* had stood between her and the world. Could he be gone and she still remain? His loss made life seem too terrifying and open-ended.

And then there was Jack. Stalwart Jack. The man whom she had grown to love in the shadow of her grandfather's love for him. She had known with absolute certainty that she must go to him last night in her loneliness. She had wanted him, so desperately, wanted to make him want her with a fiercely single-minded passion. She had known everything . . . until she'd felt the power of *what could be* between them. A power too overwhelming to be blundered into—too important to be toyed with except with absolute honesty.

Lying in his arms, sated and happy, she had sighed with the relief of safety. No more frightening world to be faced, no more forays into unknown terrain. Oh, God! It was at that precise awful moment she had realized that she must *not* allow that to be the way of it.

She had looked carefully at the sleeping man, so content at her side, and had known beyond doubt that she must find her own identity before she could give herself to him or to anyone. The pain of the realization, even now, brought sharp, stinging tears to her eyes.

Megan laid the last of her sweaters into the suitcase and wiped the moisture from her eyes with a hankie she had tucked into her sleeve. She was determined not to cry anymore . . . she'd cried more than enough after leaving Jack. Tears of joy for what she'd felt with him;

tears of sorrow for the separation that must follow. She dabbed at her eyes with annoyance. "Sure, your bladder's ever near your eye, lass," Jack had told her that more than once in his lilting brogue, when she was a child who cried too freely at the sad Irish poems and songs he taught her. And she would respond to him with G. K. Chesterton's couplet:

> For the great Gaels of Ireland
> Are the men that God made mad,
> For all their wars are merry
> And all their songs are sad!

And they would laugh together over it. She smiled at the thought of how many dear memories she had of him that he probably had no knowledge of.

She heard the doorbell ring, heard James's voice as he responded. She knew the visitor was Jack before she heard him taking the stairs two at a time, her heart beating faster at the sound of his hurried approach. She opened the door to her sitting room to greet him, thinking she had never seen anything as dear as the anxiety on his face as he reached her.

"James told me you were packing—?" He felt the question hanging searchingly . . . terribly unsure.

"I'm going to Drumgillan—taking my grandfather home, Jack. I'm making arrangements to have him buried with his father, and he shouldn't go home alone."

"You would have left without seeing me?" His voice seemed incredulous, terribly hurt.

"No, I wouldn't have done that." She smiled softly at him and reached up to touch the worry lines beside his eyes tenderly. "No, my dear friend, I intended to come to you first to explain."

Jack put his arms around her suddenly, so forcefully he took her breath away. His face looked so sad and confused that she hugged him back as hard as he'd hugged her, in reassurance. Then she disengaged herself from the powerful embrace and led him to the pretty chintz sofa by the fireplace and motioned him to sit beside her, hoping she'd have the courage to make him understand.

"I love you, Jack," she said so simply that he started to reply, but she put her fingers to his lips to silence him.

"For a long time, and so much, that I have to go away for a little because of it. I don't know if it's the right thing to do, but I think it is." She sighed, as if gathering the strength to say what she must. "You see, it's like this for me: All my life, I've lived in my grandfather's shadow. More than his shadow, really. I've lived in my grandfather's soul. Only you in all the world could understand what I mean by that." She smiled at the man, and he could see the unmistakable love in her eyes. "Lying in your arms last night, I found myself wanting nothing in this world but to spend the rest of my life living in *your soul*, Jack, and suddenly it came to me that if I did that—at least if I did it right now—I would forfeit my own soul, my own *self* in the process. Not that I didn't want to do it, mind you—I want to more than I've ever wanted anything! But if I don't find out who I am first . . . now . . . I may never find out.

"It's bizarre, really." She smiled at her own confusion. "I'm so very smart about other things. I know so much . . . and yet I know so little about Megan. Do you know how terrible it is to realize that all my life I've thought of myself as an independent person, when the truth is I've never in my whole life done anything outside the protective circle of my grandfather's love and money and power.

"Don't you see, Jack? I must find out who *I* am, without any man to lean on, before I can give myself to anyone. At least I think that's how it should work. Otherwise, I'm not at all sure that the gift I'd be giving you would be worth very much."

Seeing the sorrow and determination in Megan, sensing the immense effort it had taken for her to make such a wrenching decision, he shook his head softly, then he took her gently into his arms, holding her close as he tried to answer her. When he did speak, his voice was husky and low with emotion.

"I love you, Megan, and it's the most terrible, wonderful thing I've ever felt. I've spent all the hours since you left me telling myself that it's an insanity to think we could ever be together, but wanting you despite everything, more than I've ever wanted anything in my life." He stroked her long soft hair as he spoke, and she knew she mustn't interrupt or move.

"I loved your grandfather, child; God knows how dear he was to me; but I sometimes watched how he was raising you and said to myself, 'What is he doing to that child? She'll be so full of knowledge and wisdom and seriousness, no man will ever be able to cope with her, perhaps no man will ever want to.' And then I held you in my arms last night and I knew that I wanted you more than life itself. I won't lose you now, Megan! I'm not so noble-spirited as to say, 'Do what's best for you, lass, and forget me.' Oh, no, I want what's best for you to be me!

"I'm more than forty years of age, Megan. You can't know at twenty what that means. You can't know the knowledge of mortality that comes with middle age, the understanding of the preciousness of time. If there's to be a time for us, Megan, it must be now, when I'm still young enough to be the things you want me to be."

Gently, Megan pulled back from his embrace so that she could see his troubled, earnest face, for there was no mistaking the honesty in it, or the pain. She prayed for the courage to be honest in return, and took a deep breath before replying. "There's another reason, Jack, why I must do this . . . for both our sakes. I've known you a long time, child and woman. I've watched you . . . watched all the women in your life be passing fancies. All were fine for a time and then discarded. If I stayed now—without knowing for certain who I am, and what I have to offer you . . . and without your having had a chance to think it through—it wouldn't last for us, either. I know in my heart it wouldn't last." She hesitated to find the words she needed. "If you sensed that you had absolute power over me, or that I was unsure of my own worth, sooner or later you'd want to discard me as you've done with so many others. I feel it in my bones, Jack. I don't say this to be hurtful, only to protect us both. I must be a whole person, my love, or we'd be doomed."

He leaned back, startled and a little hurt by what she had said. He looked into the eyes of this strange woman who was old and young at the same time. He wanted her so very much. Could it really be that she understood his own fatal flaw as well as that and still chose to try to overcome it?

"I could tell you that you're wrong, lass," he said quietly, "but I fear you know me better than I do myself." His voice was heavy with emotion. "There have been so many women in my life, Megan. Hundreds, I suppose. I'll not lie to you; we are surely beyond lies now. I had a pride in the bounty of them, old and young. 'Twas as if I sought to find myself in their countless beds. They gave me comfort and pleasure, and for the time I was with them I knew with certainty who I was meant to be.

"But love . . . marriage . . . they never played a part in any of it. Too much responsibility for another person's life, too much commitment, too much fear of my own inadequacy over the long haul."

Megan moved her graceful, slender hand to the side of his troubled face and gently brushed the dark tangle of hair back from it.

"Then there was you, Megan. Last night, in my arms . . . in my mind and heart. You must have been there for so long without my knowing it. I've spent the entire day telling myself all the reasons why it couldn't work for us, and I've only managed to convince myself that I need you desperately." He stopped deliberately, and then, looking straight into her eyes, he said, "I'll let you go for now, if I must, Megan. If only to give us a better chance at later."

She smiled sadly and nodded; the tears shimmered in the corners of her gray eyes, making them seem silver.

He touched both hands to the side of her soft cheeks and tipped her face to his with infinite tenderness. He brought his mouth to hers, gently touching her lips with his own; then, as her lips parted, opening vulnerably, he crushed her body to his with a hard strength that overwhelmed her.

Finally, after what seemed a long while, she pulled herself from his embrace.

"You'll go to Drumgillan with Tom, then?" he asked, trying to regain his own composure. He had known she'd been dickering with Riordan since Tom's death about having him interred in Ireland.

She nodded. "That's where it all began . . . that's where I'll find me, I think."

"Will you spend the night with me before you go, beauty?"

"If I were to lie with you one more time, my love, I might not have the strength to go at all."

He nodded, wondering at the wisdom of the girl, who obviously knew his flaws as he did, and a great deal more as well. If he were to have her, he must win her—despite the love she bore him. Nothing gained too easily would ever hold him long. She was very wise indeed.

"Wild swan ne'er laid tame egg," he said softly.

She looked at him questioningly.

"An old Irish proverb, lass. I was just thinking that you do your grandfather proud."

There was more to say before they parted. When he was gone, Megan sat on the bed beside her suitcases and tried to understand herself as well as she understood the man she loved.

101

Megan Dalton stood with her head resting on her hands, which in turn were resting on the fence rail of the dressage ring behind the stable at Drumgillan.

The soft wind blew the strands of her long blond hair across her face, but she made no move to interfere with them. She was concentrating . . . imagining what it must have been like for her grandfather on the day his father died there. Feeling memories that might have been her own wash through her.

She stared intently at the hard brown ground and shuddered at the thought of soft, warm, loving human flesh being trampled into its unrelenting surface by the hooves of a maddened horse.

She touched the splintered wood of the rail and imagined the little boy her grandfather had been, perched there proudly, full of admiration for his splendid father . . . thrilled with the sight and sound of the glorious morning, until that awful moment when everything beautiful had been irrevocably sullied.

It wasn't hard to see, in her mind's eye, the frenzied stable hands and the tall patrician figure of Sir Jeffrey, rifle to shoulder, tears running down his leathered cheeks.

She felt somehow disembodied by the act of remembering. For days she had gone methodically from place to place on the estate, letting the old stories run through her as if she were a porous vessel.

She had gone to the tiny cottage, now tidy and rethatched but still uninhabited, and tried to sense its presence as it must have been that fateful afternoon seventy-six years before when Mary and Michael had passionately set so many destinies in motion. She had walked the bog and the rose garden, climbed the hill from the lough, and wandered the meandering corridors of the old house in a painstaking pilgrimage of the heart.

Letting the emotions crash over and under and through her without mitigation was the only way to separate herself out from them; she had the odd conviction that if just once she could bear to live all the sorrows through, to let them buffet her and do their worst, at the end of it only Megan should remain.

And she needed to remain, needed to untangle the threads of her own life gently from those of her grandfather. Not in rejection, but in infinite love and remembrance.

It had started for her the soft gray-green day she had seen her grandfather laid to rest beside his father in the Hartington family plot.

She had requested that a temporary marker be placed above the grave until the great Connemara marble cross she had ordered could be completed. She had felt content to think that so Irish a monument would mark his resting place through the centuries, as did the similar crosses at Clonmacnoise mark the remains of monks who had departed this life six hundred years ago.

She had chosen a quotation from Eoghan Ruough O'Suilleabhain, the eighteenth-century Celtic bard, for his epitaph. The marker would read:

THOMAS MICHAEL DALTON

Beloved Son of Mary Dalton and
Michael Harcourt Hartington

1874–1950

What can I do for him I've loved so well
but pray with wistful mind
that Saints and Angels
shepherd him forever . . .

She missed her grandfather; the quicksilver wisdom, the erudition, the deep sonorous voice with the hint of brogue, the pervasive male presence of the man. Yet she knew, standing there at his grave, that she did not begrudge him his rest. Who better than she knew the tempestuous rigors of his life; the loneliness, the sorrows. She was sure he was now with those he loved, whom he had lost for a time. And in a way, she felt only gladness for him.

She had left the little cemetery that day and begun her odyssey . . . her farewell to Tom . . . her search for Megan. She knew as it began that it was what Tom would have wished her to do.

She shook her head willfully to clear it of the lively shades, and looked out over the dazzling green meadow that stretched from horizon to horizon. She looked in each direction for a moment, as if sensing the atmosphere, trying to feel where next she must go.

She wore an old mauve cotton skirt of midcalf length that swayed when she walked, like the petals of a giant flower, and a blouse of sheer white linen beneath a fisherman's sweater. The gentle autumn breezes played on her arms and neck, and she was grateful for being alive.

The decision to return to Drumgillan had been the right one, the only one. "Know thyself," her grandfather had quoted Socrates to her often enough, and she had never had a single doubt that she was following the sage advice until Jack.

Suddenly, uncertainties had crowded in. Was it possible that what she felt for Jack was not love at all, but some obsessive need to be cared for, protected, permitted not to have to know herself? If she was to love Jack and he to love her, first she must follow Socrates's advice.

Megan smiled a little at how hard a task "knowing thyself" had turned out to be. She was learning, of course. She'd already learned that she had courage—it had taken that to leave Jack and New York behind, to start this painful quest for knowledge. She was also well-intentioned. She didn't mean to love any man on the strength of a sexual connection, or without the intention of being able to be true to him. But at least now she was learning to recognize all the things that made up Megan. That was surely the first step out of the abyss.

Megan turned her eyes to the elegant old Palladian house on the hill, standing dignified and unscathed by all the living and dying it had been party to. That's what I must become, she thought, feeling one with the structure. I must be able to contain the living and the dying of them all within me and still be Megan. Richer for the in-dwelling spirits, but nonetheless myself.

She laughed aloud at the lovely insight. If the dear old house could do it—weather the generations, the triumphs, the sorrows and the partings—she could do it too. Her laughter carried across the crystal, silent meadow air and startled a rabbit nibbling a leaf in the rose garden as she passed his way.

Megan stood at the foot of the rolling green hill leading from the silvery-blue lough to the majesty of the house. She loved to look at the benign eighteenth-century mansion, stately against the moody Irish sky. She had been at Drumgillan for half a year, and it seemed in some ways half a lifetime. She'd heard a man in the village say that Ireland carries memories in her mouth like an old hunting bitch, and standing there, feeling the aura of the old house, she understood why it should be so.

The legends buried in the beautiful old sod, interred side by next with the moldered bones of saints and sinners, lovers and warriors, heroes and villains, were simply too powerful to die. Perhaps that was why it was said of the Irish that they were thick-skinned; perhaps they needed to protect themselves from their own legends.

It was not possible, thought Megan, to stand amid the emerald hills, the bottomless bogs, the mist-enshrouded mountains, and not *feel* one with them . . . one with an eternity of others of your race.

She began the winding walk up the hill, as she had done a thousand times, it seemed, since she'd returned to Drumgillan. She forced herself to walk slowly; to savor the rich fragrance of dampness in the air—dampness that made everything smell fertile and about to begin.

She pulled the ecru bawneen wooliness of her fisherman's sweater close around her lean body, feeling the warmth and fullness of her own breasts as she did so. The land stirred something primal in her, just as it must have stirred generations of poets and minstrels, and willful, lusty ladies who took their men to their beds despite the admonitions of priests and the probability of damnation.

"I'm like Ireland," she had written to Jack with conviction the week before. "I'm like the land with its ill-buried legends—enduring, filled with mysteries older than Druid magic. That's why I had to come back here to know who I am and whether I'd survive. I'm filled with other people's lives—not just my grandfather's, not just yours, love—but all the generations of the Irish that have gone before me. That's what I could only find out here."

Perhaps the knowledge was why she wasn't afraid anymore. Not afraid of loving Jack, nor of losing him. Perhaps that's why she had finally asked him to come.

This time it was going to be her love story played out against the permanency of Drumgillan. Not Michael's and Mary's, not Tom's and Deirdre's—only hers. She felt suddenly freed of the ghosts of them all. Willing to let them have their place in her past, not begrudging them the lessons that were their legacy . . . knowing that to be Irish is to share your soul with the lively ghosts of your forebears, to be one with their magic and with their dreams.

She saw Jack standing against the doorway, watching her come toward him. He looked uncertain, as if unsure if he should feel joy or worry at her summons. She waved to him with unencumbered love in her heart, and saw him start down the hill to meet her.

Partial Bibliography

IRELAND AND THE IRISH

Castles of Ireland
Brian de Breffny
Thames & Hudson, 1977

Celtic Myth and Legend, Poetry and Romance
Charles Squire
Bell Books, 1979

The Churches and Abbeys of Ireland
Brian de Breffny and George Mott
Thames & Hudson, 1976

The Course of Irish History
Edited by T. W. Moody and F. X. Martin
The Mercier Press, 1981

The Damnable Question
George Dangerfield
Little, Brown/Atlantic Monthly Press, 1976

Early Christian Ireland
Maire and Liam de Paor
Thames & Hudson, 1958

Facts about Ireland
Department of Foreign Affairs
Dublin

Famine
Liam O'Flaherty
David R. Godine, 1982

The Great Hunger
Cecil Woodham-Smith
Harper & Row, 1962

Heritage of Ireland
Brian de Breffny
Crown, Bounty Books

Illustrated History of the Irish People
Kenneth Neill
Mayflower Books, 1979

The Irish Americans
Andrew M. Greeley
Harper & Row, 1981

Irish Folk Tales
Jeremiah Curtin
The Talbot Press, 1956

Irish Houses and Castles
Desmond Guinness and William Ryan
The Viking Press, 1971

My Jewel and Darlin' Dublin
Eamonn MacThomas
The O'Brien Press, 1974

Old Celtic Romances
P. W. Joyce
Devin-Adair, 1964

Our Like Will Not Be There Again
Lawrence Milman
Little, Brown, 1977

Portrait of Dublin
Desmond Guinness
The Viking Press, 1967

The Reason Why
Cecil Woodham-Smith
McGraw-Hill, 1953

Twenty Years A-Growing
Maurice O'Sullivan
The Viking Press, 1933

LIFE AT THE TURN OF THE CENTURY

American Immigration
Maldwyn Allen Jones
University of Chicago Press, 1960

The American Irish
William V. Shannon
Collier, 1974

Beyond the Melting Pot
Nathan Glazer and Daniel P. Moynihan
The M.I.T. Press, 1970

Boss Tweed's New York
Seymour J. Mandelbaum
John Wiley & Sons, 1964

Boston's Immigrants
Oscar Handlin
Atheneum, 1977

The Bowery
Michael Zettler
Drake Publisher, 1955

Fifth Avenue
Kate Simon
Harcourt Brace Jovanovich, 1979

Hell's Kitchen
Benjamin Appel
Pantheon Press, 1977

Those Were the Good Old Days
Edgar R. Jones
Simon & Schuster, 1971

Time and Again
Jack Finney
Warren H. Green, Fireside Books, 1978

LABOR AND UNIONISM

Bread and Roses
Milton Meltzer
Simon & Schuster, 1977

The Immigrant Experience
Edited by Thomas C. Wheeler
Penguin Books, 1972

The Longshoreman
Charles B. Barnes
Russell Sage Foundation, 1915

Men Along the Shore
Maud Russell
Russell & Russell, 1966

Men Who Lead Labor
Bruce Minton and John Stuart
Modern Age Books

Modern Seamanship
Austin M. Knight
D. Van Nostrand Co., 1937

The Rise of Irish Trade Unions, 1729–1970
Andrew Boyd
Anvil Books, 1972

The Rise of the New York Port
Robert Green and Ralph Albion
Scribners, 1970

A Sailor's Log
Adm. Robley D. Evans
P. Appleton & Co., 1901

Shape-up and Hiring Hall
Charles Larrowe
University of California Press, 1955

The Teamsters
Steven Brill
Pocket Books, 1978

The Waterfront Labor Problem
Edward Swanstrom
Fordham University Press, 1938